KT-381-181

SNOW ANGELS

Also by Elizabeth Gill

THE SINGING WINDS

FAR FROM MY FATHER'S HOUSE

UNDER A CLOUD-SOFT SKY

THE ROAD TO BERRY EDGE

SNOW ANGELS

Elizabeth Gill

Hodder & Stoughton

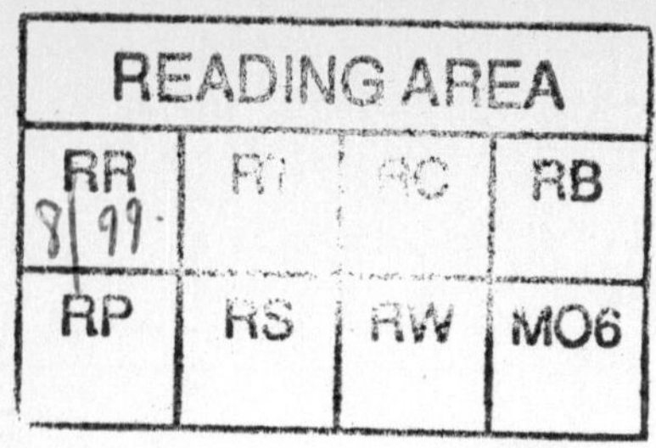

First published in Great Britain in 1999
by Hodder and Stoughton
A division of Hodder Headline PLC

10 9 8 7 6 5 4 3 2 1

British Library Cataloguing in Publication Data
A CIP catalogue record for this title
is available from the British Library.

ISBN 0 340 75089 8

Typeset by Hewer Text Ltd, Edinburgh
Printed and bound in Great Britain by
Caledonian International Book Manufacturing Ltd

Hodder and Stoughton
A division of Hodder Headline PLC
338 Euston Road
London NW1 3BH

For Doug – brother-in-law, drinking partner and friend

PROLOGUE

1890

Newcastle upon Tyne

It was a cold wet November afternoon when Abby Reed's mother died. The doctor had said she would probably go quietly in the night, but Bella Reed had never done anything quietly. She clutched the lapels of the doctor's jacket, her thin hands like chicken claws, and begged him not to let her leave this world and, though he had looked shocked, fifteen-year-old Abby could only agree with her mother. It was all very well for those who were convinced of paradise, but her mother knew that there was nothing beyond a box in the ground of the local cemetery and it was hardly a prospect to be faced with equanimity.

'My dear lady,' he said, 'you must prepare to meet your maker. There is nothing more that I can do.'

'Idiot!' she said, falling back onto her pillows. 'Get him out of here, Abby, I don't want him at my damned deathbed!'

The doctor, shocked even further at the dying mother's foul mouth, almost ran. Abby could have told him it was nothing special. Her father proudly said of her mother that she swore better than any docker. Abby didn't see him out; she stood in the gloom at the top of the staircase which dominated their house and Kate, their maid, appeared from the kitchen to deal with the doctor and the door.

Wind and rain bespattered the entrance hall and the doctor stood for a moment before he faced the darkness. It was past four o'clock and the weather had ensured that what light there had been had gone as the afternoon started. Kate struggled to shut the door and Abby went back to her mother. The room was cosy. She had lit the lamps and the fire had been on in there not just all day but for many weeks while Bella's illness progressed. Bella was lying with her eyes closed.

'Abby?'

'I'm here.' She went over to the bed, sat down and clasped her mother's hand.

'I love you.'

Tears rose in Abby's eyes and in her nose and in her mouth and seemingly everywhere. Her mother did what they called in the area 'naming a spade a bloody shovel'; she always said what she meant. Other people might skirt around a subject, but Bella never did. Abby had been astonished as a small child that other mothers did not treat their children with open affection, that they did not spend time with them, that they did not appear to have any joy in them, but she had always known because her mother had always told her and always shown her. They both knew that Abby would never hear the words again on Bella's lips.

'You mean more to me than anything in this world. You've given me more pleasure than you could possibly imagine. I'm not afraid of death, I just don't want to leave you. Come closer.'

Abby kissed her thin cheek and Bella put a hand on her head.

Her mother didn't even ask for her father. Since her illness, he had taken refuge in his work. Abby didn't blame him for that. There was nothing he could do and to stay around his wife's bedroom would have been an admission of her coming death on both their parts. He would be back soon, Abby thought, and there was life in her mother yet. They would have time to say goodbye. She lay for a little while with her head on the pillow beside her mother. She had not slept properly in several days and nights and she was so exhausted that she let herself drift for a while. Suddenly she heard the door. She had not expected to feel relief and, when she did, got up to meet her father. It was only then that she saw his gaze was fixed on her mother.

'She didn't stay for me,' he said.

The weather retreated for the funeral, but the cemetery was slippery with mud. Abby had insisted on going even though the old Northumbrian way was for the men to go; the women would stay behind and prepare the tea. Her father needed her there. She was his only child and, even though people might look disapprovingly, she didn't care. She held up her head and clasped her father's arm.

It was easier when they got back to the house. They lived in Jesmond, one of the more prosperous areas of Newcastle, in a big semi-detached villa not far from the cricket ground. People were packed in to show their respect. Henderson Reed was a shipbuilder, not the biggest on the Tyne, but well known. Abby helped to dispense tea. It stopped her thinking about her mother.

Charlotte Collingwood, wife of William Collingwood, who was the biggest shipbuilder on the Tyne, came to her. Abby had tried to avoid her. Charlotte was a pretty woman of forty who had given her husband two sons, but Abby despised her. She sat at the top of Newcastle society in a way that Abby's mother had once likened to 'a fairy with a Christmas tree stuck up her arse' and Abby had never forgotten it. Charlotte had come from a top family, a branch of the Surtees who owned land and many fine houses, but William Collingwood had made his way up the social ladder. He was nothing more than the son of a boat builder. Charlotte had been well bred but penniless and now enjoyed fine clothes, a huge country house and more money than she could spend. She had never read a book in her life. Abby treasured her mother's books.

'You must come to us for Christmas,' Charlotte said. 'The boys will be home from school and we'll be having a party. I know you won't feel much like parties, but the change would do you good.'

Abby felt guilty then. Charlotte was being generous, and she could imagine lots of things worse than seeing Edward Collingwood again. He was eighteen, fair and handsome. He went to a top public school, he was well spoken, beautifully mannered and rumoured to be very clever. The younger boy, Gil, as far as Abby could judge, was the opposite: dark, stupid and sullen. He was just a bit older than Abby. They had long ignored one another but, thinking of Edward and wanting to distance herself from her mother's death, Abby was inclined to agree at once. The idea of spending Christmas alone here with her father and the servants did not appeal, though perhaps he would think differently.

Charlotte asked Henderson. He seemed agreeable and Abby knew a lightness that she hadn't felt for months. Bella had struggled with her illness, only giving in when she could fight it no more. It had been a long and dreary autumn and Abby thought that her mother would not have wanted her to grieve further. She had known that her mother was dying; her grieving was almost done. It would do her father good to get away from the house and shipyard for a few days.

The days before Christmas were short and wet and empty. Abby missed her mother all the time and wanted to weep but she couldn't; it was as though a door had closed between her tears and her eyes and even when she ached to cry, she couldn't. She did her best to look after her father and cheerfully presided over meals which neither of them ate. She was tired, but when she lay down to sleep at nights, thoughts of her mother flooded her mind and gave her no rest. Everyone else seemed so cheerful because it was Christmas, wishing each other all the best. Carol singers came to the door. It even snowed. Abby thought of her mother lying in the cemetery with a fine white layer of frozen water above her and no future.

It was therefore with relief, just after midday on Christmas Eve, that Abby and her father drove the several miles out of

Newcastle to the mansion which William Collingwood had built a dozen years ago when he became rich. Abby did not think about the Northumberland countryside; she was used to the big farms and wide fields. Castles were commonplace here, the kind of fortifications which had helped to keep out the Picts and Scots and Border Reivers at different times. Some of the farms had half-ruined towers or castles right beside the house, which might have looked strange to foreign eyes but were usual to those who knew the area. It was prosperous: the fences were mended; the walls were straight and safe; the roads were good.

Bamburgh House was a monstrosity, Abby thought as they pulled in at the gates of the long mile drive. It could have been beautiful; the honey-coloured stone had been quarried from right beside it, but the architect had been having some kind of love affair with Greece. Four enormous pillars obscured the front of the house. It managed to look stately in the slight covering of snow, but Abby was not deceived. She had been there before and thought it the most stiff, unfriendly house she had ever seen in her life. In the summer great arrangements of flowers stood to attention in huge vases in all the rooms. Everything was swept clean; no dusty cupboards in Charlotte's house. The maids were uniformed and unsmiling. The food was always lavish and overdone, so that it put you off before you started, and Charlotte was fond of table centres such as iced swans and animals made from chocolate and marzipan. Neither William nor his wife had any taste. The house, though huge, was filled with furniture. There was not a corner that had not its share of paintings and ornaments and dead animals in glass cases or their heads on the wall. There were tiger rugs and elephants' feet and stuffed birds. It was an animals' cemetery, Abby thought with a little shiver, and the furniture was uncomfortable, all gilt and velvet, short-backed sofas and shallow chairs. Sometimes Abby was ashamed to be there considering that she was aware of how badly paid and housed were William's shipyard workers – her father was always saying so.

It could have been no pleasure to work in that house, because none of the servants ever looked happy, not like Kate and Mrs Wilkins at home, sitting by the kitchen fire no doubt and enjoying the cake and sherry and beef which her father's money had bought for them. She had made sure they had generous presents that Christmas because they had been kind to her all that time when her mother was ill. Abby had been glad also that her father had provided a big dinner for all his workers, gifts for their wives and children in the form of foodstuffs and confectionery and a bigger paypacket than usual for all the men. Some of them drank their money, which was why her mother had in previous years insisted that their families should be given gifts directly as well as extra money. Abby had made sure that this year was even better for them. They should not feel the difference because her mother was dead.

In the huge entrance hall of Bamburgh House stood the largest Christmas tree that Abby had ever seen, glowing with candles. Holly festooned every corner and mistletoe peeped out here and there among the red berries and green thorns. The weather did its best to help, freezing neatly so that the snow turned solid and wet trees glittered as though somebody had put them in just the right place to catch the winter sunlight. Huge fires burned in the rooms. Throughout the afternoon, people arrived and everyone was to stay, some of them for several days.

Abby began to enjoy herself, to be pleased at the dress she had brought. An excited hum came from having so many people in the house and there were wonderful smells and sounds between dining-room and kitchen. Maids went to and fro downstairs until the long tables were laden. Musicians arrived and began to make music in the ballroom. Abby glimpsed Edward, but of Gil there was no sign. A little maid came to help Abby dress. She was very young and chattered more than she should have done, but Abby didn't mind, and it was of her that she enquired for the other boy. The girl's face paled.

'His da leathered him,' she said.

'Beat him?'

The girl nodded.

'Two days since.'

'Why?'

The little maid's face darkened.

'Not for summat you'd think. He didn't do nothin' like lads do. Locked him up an' all, like a dog.' And with that, Abby had to be content.

The evening went well. There were good things to eat: jellies and creams and cold chicken and ham. Abby even had champagne. Edward asked her to dance and, although she shouldn't have because of her mother dying, her father insisted. The music and the champagne made Abby pleased with everything. The light from the chandeliers glittered inside and the frost on the snow glittered outside. Gil did not appear.

'Where's your brother?' Abby enquired of Edward as they stood against a pillar in the ballroom, flushed from dancing.

'In his room.'

'It's Christmas Eve,' Abby pointed out.

'He isn't there by choice,' Edward said.

Abby couldn't rest. She tried to. She reasoned with herself. She didn't like Gil Collingwood and as far as she knew he had neither looked at her nor spoken politely. It was strange. She kept thinking about her mother alone in the cemetery and Gil by himself and it all got mixed up. She had refused a second glass of champagne and contented herself with lemonade, but her mind did not unmix. She danced with several boys, she talked to girls she knew and it should have been the happiest evening she had spent for a long time, but there was an emptiness inside her which grew and grew until Abby could bear it no longer. She left the noise and the music, took a candle from the hall, wrapped a huge piece of chocolate cake into a napkin and then made her way up the first of two wide staircases.

From the rooms below there were lights and the sound of laughter. It was a big house but conventionally laid out, with the upstairs rooms around a central hall. The rooms were well set back. The hall was lit and Abby couldn't hear her own footsteps because there was carpet all along the floorboards. She didn't know what she was looking for, but she saw it anyway. There was a key in the lock of a door as far away from the staircase as possible. She listened hard, but could hear nothing.

Abby brought her candle down to the key and very slowly turned it in the lock. It made no noise. The door opened soundlessly. Abby drew in her breath at the blast of cold air that came out of the room. It was freezing; she could feel it through her dress, straight onto her skin as though she wore nothing. At first she thought it was an unused room. There was nothing personal about it and, though she looked as best she could in the gloom, the grate was empty and clean, there was no light of any kind and the bed was stripped. There were no ornaments, no books, no clutter. There was no carpet on the floor; the linoleum was like ice. The curtains were drawn back and from there the moon threw its white light in through the window. It was, Abby thought, shivering, the nearest thing to a grave. Nobody was in here. There was no sound. She turned to go and the candle flickered in the draught. Then she saw him.

Gil was quite tall, that Abby remembered, but he was curled up as small as he could possibly be at the far side of the bed, right against the wall, like a hedgehog. He didn't move or acknowledge her in any way and, as Abby saw him better, she recognised the whiteness of his shirt and the blackness of his hair.

'God Almighty,' she said.

Her first instinct was to run for help, but she stopped herself. She couldn't do that. Adults lived in another world, a powerful world where she had no place and no influence. If she spoke a single word she would get into trouble and get him into even more trouble, if that could possibly be. She mustn't be found out. She left the room with as little movement as she could. From the room next door she pulled thick blankets and two pillows and carried them back and put the blankets over him and the pillows down onto the bed.

'Gil, are you dead?' It was not the time for formality somehow. 'Gil?'

He didn't move. Abby touched him on the shoulder.

'Go away.' With a strength that surprised her, he shoved the blankets back at her. They enveloped her. She had to push them off. Her heart pounded. She really had thought that he was not breathing. It was her nightmare come back: lying beside her mother, tired from trying to come to terms with the idea that she might lose her, that somebody else would go out of this life and she would not be awake or not be there and be unable to do anything. Nightly she haunted herself, thinking that if she had stayed awake, her mother would still be alive. She knew that it was stupid, but she only knew this in the daylight. When she had been a child the night had held no fear, it was a velvet blackness. She had fallen asleep listening to her parents' voices coming up from below the floorboards. Childhood had been when life was for ever, when nothing would hurt her. Now the darkness was full of devils and they tormented her with guilt and inadequacy.

Abby stared at the window, glad of the moon. There were thick frost patterns on the window. She remembered her mother showing her all the different ones. They were coldly beautiful.

'I brought you some cake.' It was rather squashed by its journey. 'Chocolate cake.'

He stirred after a few moments and then very slowly turned over. Abby made herself not react. There was a big mark across one side of his face where somebody had done what her mother would have called 'backhanding him'. His straight black hair hid the expression in his eyes. He didn't touch the cake as she offered it; he just looked at it and then at her and said, 'You'll get into bother.'

'Nobody will know.'

There was a jug of water and a glass on the dressing-table. Abby went across and poured some and gave it to him and he took the cake and ate it very slowly. Abby was more accustomed to the room now and she could hear the faint sounds of music from the ballroom. It seemed strange here in the almost-silence, like another world. She wondered if her mother could still sense some things from the life she had left, whether there was any way in which sounds filtered through.

She began to cry and almost choked in embarrassment attempting not to. After all these weeks, she chose this moment in which to realise that her mother could not hear the music nor feel the cold. She couldn't touch her or speak to her or have the love between them like a shining light any more. It was all gone; it was over.

'Did you want some cake?' he asked as the tears flowed. Abby shook her head wordlessly and wished for a handkerchief, for control, for oblivion. The candle, which was never going to be anything spectacular, guttered and gave up and she was left in the cold, white moonlight with a boy she barely knew, a hot face, cold tears, a blocked nose and a terrible desire to sniff before her nose ran. It got worse, until she was blinded and everything was salt and even sniffing didn't help. She found a tiny stupid scrap of lace and cotton in the only pocket of her dress and blew her nose. It sounded like a train to her ears. She mopped her face on the edge of the nearest blanket and the hairs from it went up her nose. When the crying took over her whole body, she gave herself up to it until it wracked her. When the sobs quietened she found the blankets over her, and his body, which was surprisingly warm, close. Exhausted, comforted, Abby fell asleep.

At some time in the night she kicked off her shoes and settled herself against him and slept again. Then somebody was shaking her gently. When she opened her eyes he was looking down at her and saying, 'You'll have to go or they'll find you here.'

Abby was horrified. She had spent the night with a boy, slept close against him in a bed. She remembered – did she remember it – his arms around her at one point and then his body folded in against the back of hers. 'Spoons' her mother would have called it, as in polite households where the cutlery was carefully put away on its side, not like in her house where her mother thought people had better things to do like painting, reading and going for walks on Tynemouth beach and making sticky toffee cake. The old familiar loneliness punched at Abby's insides again, but it was not quite so bad today because she had cried and somebody had been there to hold her. At least, she thought that he had. The embarrassment ousted the other feelings and her face burned. She fled and it was only when she reached her own room that she remembered it was Christmas morning.

She washed and dressed and went down to the dining-room, where her father and several other people were breakfasting. She kissed him, but felt somehow as though she had betrayed him, as though she had done something wrong. She couldn't eat. People were merry and there were sausages and hot coffee, but the smell of food made Abby feel sick. She had a terrible desire to confess what she had done. Only the thought that William Collingwood would no doubt beat his son all over again stopped her. They would blame him. She wished that she had not left the party. She watched Edward across the table, sitting with his best friend from school, Toby Emory, and she could not equate him with the boy she had left upstairs, his silent tongue and closed expression. Edward and Toby were laughing and talking about horses. Edward's father had bought him a new hunter for Christmas and they had already been down to the stables.

Nobody noticed that Abby didn't eat. She went off to church with her father and the others in the nearby village. In church, she felt dirty and she was cross with Gil. This visit could have been so pleasant. Another girl, Rhoda Carlisle, who came from Allendale Town at the top end of Tynedale where it met Weardale on the felltops, chatted freely to her as they came out of church. She was here with her parents and two small brothers. Rhoda was a tall, pretty, brown-haired girl who liked books and when they got back to the house Abby was happier. She had done nothing wrong. And then the happiness dropped away from her. Gil was there. He stood out, or was it just because of what had happened? He was taller than the other boys and stood away from them. Abby blushed until she couldn't blush any more and ignored him. It wasn't difficult to do. He didn't even acknowledge her. He didn't smile and to her he seemed unapproachable and aloof.

There was a huge meal and so many people that it ceased to matter. She wasn't seated near him, but with Rhoda, Toby and Edward. Edward paid Abby so much attention that she was flattered and pleased.

It had snowed all the way through the meal but afterwards it stopped and they went outside and threw snowballs at each other until it was too dark to see anything. They called by the stables to admire Edward's new horse and Abby found herself asking, 'What did your brother get for Christmas?' Out the words came. She was astonished at herself and not surprised that Edward frowned.

'I have no idea. Whatever he asked for, I suppose. Why?'

'I just wondered.'

'You just wondered? Tell me, Abigail, what is this sudden interest in my brother?' His eyes danced. Abby could have hit herself.

'He doesn't seem very happy.'

'You wouldn't be very happy if your father had taken a horsewhip to you.'

'Why did he do that?'

'My brother is stupid. He came bottom of the class. No, I lie, second to last, except in geometry. Can you imagine?'

'I don't think that's much of a reason to beat somebody and lock them up.'

'My God, you like him!' Edward stood back, watching her from astonished eyes. 'What is it you like best about him? His elegant manners, his erudite conversation, his fine wit?'

Abby would have given a lot to have said, 'I liked the way he put his arms around me', but she couldn't. And that was the moment she realised she felt proprietorial about Gil Collingwood, as though some kind person had wrapped him up in paper and presented him to her on Christmas morning. She shook her head and laughed but the feeling didn't go away, even when Edward had stopped teasing her. She understood something – that touch was the most important thing in the world between people, that because of it she would have defended Gil against anyone who tried to hurt him. It was totally irrational but her mother, Abby couldn't help thinking, would have approved of the idea. No wonder older people kept younger people apart. There was nothing like sleeping close against someone and seeing the old day out and the new one in for bonding you together.

As she came into the house Gil was in the hall. There were shadows, it was growing dusk and the lamps were lit, but he looked straight at her and Abby looked back at him. His eyes were so dark that you couldn't see the iris in them. He didn't say anything and Abby didn't linger. Late in the evening, when she had danced with half a dozen different boys and hated every moment of it because he didn't ask her and she couldn't see him, she went outside just to get away. It was bitterly cold out there; she had put on her coat and boots. She needed the quietness. It was completely still, just like the previous night, with a huge full moon and a complete quota of stars. Abby walked away from the house on the crisp snow; the trees were thick with it. Further over, the snow became too heavy on one branch and dropped with a dull thud to the ground.

She was feeling a little melancholy. Everyone sounded so happy. It made her think of last year and what things had been like then. Her mother had been well and in her impetuous way had decorated the whole house, made two Christmas cakes and bought Abby every single gift she had shown an inclination for. She wondered whether her mother could have known that it was the last Christmas they would ever spend together and consequently had made it the best ever. Why was it, Abby thought, that you could not return to those times? She thought of her mother's sweet laughter. It had snowed then, too, on Christmas Eve and her mother had taken her by the hand and run outside and they had danced in the garden. Abby could remember the small, square snowflakes on her dark hair. And every year they had made the snow angels. Abby couldn't bear to remember it. It seemed to her now that her childhood was completely lost because her mother had given her that childhood. Her father was a kind man, but it was not the same. It was all gone; it was finished; nothing would ever be like that again.

She heard a movement behind her, jumped and turned around quickly. There was Gil. Abby couldn't help feeling irritated. Did he have to be there every time she cried? Except that she was not crying, not quite. He was taller close to, much taller than she was. Slender and in expensive dark clothes and a white shirt, he matched the night, blended as if he wasn't really there, just of her imagination. Abby couldn't help but compare him with his brother and find Edward wanting. Gil really was very nice to look at.

'You could have asked me to dance,' she said.

'Don't know how.'

'I got six boxes of handkerchiefs for Christmas. I didn't realise they would be so useful.' And she scrubbed at her face and looked at him. 'Do you know how to make snow angels?'

'What?'

She didn't explain further. She stood with her feet together and her arms down by her sides and let herself fall straight back into the snow. Then she swept her arms and legs into a semicircle and got up carefully so as not to spoil the impression.

'There,' she said.

He smiled. It was not exactly an earth-shattering event, Abby thought. He contained it as though the effort of anything bigger would have been too much and it went almost as fast as it came, but she saw it.

'Go on then,' she said, and to her surprise he did.

Gil got up and stood back and Abby looked approvingly at the impressions in the snow before they turned and walked back to the house, towards the music and the lights. Her mother would have been pleased, Abby thought, and she felt peaceful as she had not felt since her mother died.

Chapter One

They say that time heals, but it isn't true. If anything, as you get further and further away from the death of the person you loved, so you see them more clearly, remember them more frequently, wish for them with an emptiness which gets bigger and bigger. Her father didn't mention her mother's name after a while, so that in a way Abby wished she could think of her mother as 'Bella' and that she could shout her name out when she went to the cemetery or when she stepped into a roomful of people. Nobody spoke of her. There was nothing left.

Rhoda Carlisle's father died only a month after the Christmas party. Abby wrote, knowing exactly how Rhoda would feel because she had been close to her father. Abby remembered him. He was a botanist, a kind, unworldly man who cared for nothing but flowers and insects and butterflies. Although he came from a family with a great deal of money, he settled in a tiny dales town without society or worldliness and he had loved it there.

Rhoda soon had other problems. Within six months of her father's death her mother had married again, the son of a local farmer, several years younger than she. People sniggered and said that Jos Allsop had married the silly woman for her money and that she had married him to warm her bed. Abby could only be thankful that her father had not been equally foolish, though she knew that he was lonely. He could easily have married again, he was a prosperous, respected man. In the early days Abby had been fearful every time an eligible woman drew near, but it was as though he didn't see them, as though Bella's death had blinded him. And yet, Abby thought ruefully, he saw too much. Once, when they had come home from what had been an enjoyable party, he put his hand on her shoulder and said, 'Don't fret, lass, there'll be no mistress here but thee.'

Abby stammered and disclaimed, said that she would be glad to welcome into the house anyone of his choice. He kissed her cheek.

'Aye, well, some day.'

The day didn't arrive and in the end Abby stopped watching for it, but she could not help shivering in gratitude when she met Rhoda and her mother in Newcastle one day and Rhoda's mother was big with child. Rhoda looked ill, Abby thought, white and skinny. Her mother chattered nervously. Abby went home to a big fire and a pot of tea. When her father came back she kissed him and thought how lucky she was. They had tea together and sat over the fire and it was only then that Abby recognised the feeling in her. It was happiness.

Two or three times a year they went to stay with the Collingwoods. Edward and Toby Emory had gone to Oxford and there, according to Charlotte, Edward had taken everything before him. Toby didn't care for Oxford – Abby had heard him say so a dozen times – but he stayed there to please his father. Abby understood why. She had met Toby's parents, who were kind, intelligent people. They had six daughters; Toby, the youngest child, was their only son and they were proud of him. They had a foundry which made parts for ships and Toby would join his father in the business when he left university.

As for Gil, Abby couldn't help herself about him. She tried to because he got nothing right. There were rumours that he had been asked to leave school, expelled, though Abby was not told why and Charlotte always said it was just that Gil wasn't very bright. So he went to work instead of to Oxford. What he did there Abby had no idea, because nobody told her. When they did meet he barely spoke to her. Other people might call him shy, but she didn't believe that. The parties he was forced to go to did not make him dance or seek her out and pride forbade that she should go to him. Many were the parties when she danced and talked with other boys and missed him. Yet every time she tried to dismiss Gil from her consciousness, he did something to bring himself back to her.

She fell on the ice that first winter. He was there before anyone else and picked her up and carried her inside. The following summer, when somebody tried to kiss her in the garden of a house where there was a birthday and Abby had objected, Gil pushed the other boy into a pond. Somehow, like a reluctant angel of mercy, he would appear during a crisis.

He grew tall and remote and other girls, thinking there was a mystery and conscious of how he looked and who he was, tried flirting and encouraging him. Abby could have told them it wouldn't work. Even Mary Ann Emerson, who was beautiful and clever and whose father owned a Sunderland shipyard and who boasted that she could get Gil to kiss her, was forced to retreat with a red face and downcast mouth. The only way to deal with Gil was to ignore him. Sometimes, therefore, as they grew older Abby would stop talking to find him sitting or standing near, not joining in the conversation, just there, listening. She didn't encourage him; she didn't dare. Her father, more observant than most, said heavily, 'I wouldn't like that lad to get any ideas about you. There's something about him that doesn't please me.'

Abby was half-inclined to say 'what lad?' but she didn't. In fact, she was rather pleased that it was so noticeable that Gil liked her.

'He doesn't have any ideas,' she said.

'Oh no? Still waters run deep, that's what I say.'

Abby stopped herself from defending Gil.

'He's like his father,' Henderson said. 'I knew him when he was young: quiet and devious and, by God, he let nothing stand in his way. He came from a nice family, his father built boats and they were respected, but he shook them off because they weren't grand enough for his schemes. His poor mother broke her heart over it.'

Abby was about to reply briskly that Charlotte was unlikely to do so, but she caught her father's eye and subsided. William Collingwood frightened Abby. Edward was like his mother, slight and fair and talkative. Gil was taller than his father by now, but he was dark like him. William was quiet and brooding and would brook no argument at home or at work. Her father called him ruthless, devious, and she well remembered the night in Gil's bedroom, the mark on his face and the way that he moved so carefully.

Edward and Toby left Oxford and came north again to go into their fathers' businesses. Abby thought that if she had been either one of their fathers, she would have detected a slight lack of enthusiasm. She thought how difficult it must be when you were a young man with ideas of your own and your father assumed that you would follow him into the business. She felt guilty on that count not being a boy, even though she knew that her parents had adored her. Her father had no one to go into the business after him and Abby could not help but be aware that in the way of men in business, he would have given much to have been able to write Reed & Son over the gates of his shipyard. She knew that her father and grandfather had been shrewd men, had bought up the land on either side of their shipyard for when they wanted to expand, but her father had not done so and she thought this could be because he was unsure of what would happen next. Abby had tried hard for some time when she was younger. She liked cricket. She liked to go and see her father in his office and play with the typewriters and give out the wages on a Friday when the men lined up at the open window of the office, but the actual design and building and business was something which held little interest for her. She had inherited her mother's love of books, kitchens, flowers and gardens and inevitably she spent a great deal of time with her mother.

Her father seemed interested in nothing but the business after her mother died. It even occurred to Abby that there was no reason why he should not marry and father a son so that the shipyard would go on and, although she would have hated it all, she could not in honesty deny that it would have been a good idea.

The world of shipbuilding went up and down like a seesaw, Abby knew, from years of listening to her father talk. There would be a depression, then things would begin to improve. Then, just when it seemed that things would be good for ever, everything would go down again. She was proud of her father: he was a just, even a generous, employer and he did everything he could to help those less fortunate. Gil's father and the other shipbuilders paid their men as little as they could get away with, kept them in horrible little cottages beside the docks and did nothing to discourage drinking and immoral behaviour. When work was short they paid them off, to save their wages bills. How people lived in the meanwhile was not their concern.

Her father's greatest pleasure was to discuss business. She thought it was all he had in common with William Collingwood, so they continued to be friends. Charlotte was inclined to favour Abby's company. Sometimes she took her to see her family over at Hexham, a lovely town with an abbey and many fine houses in Tynedale, twenty miles to the west of Newcastle. Her immediate family had a huge house to keep going and no money, but some of her relations were rich and were the cream of county society. The head of the Surtees family in the area was called Robert. He had an estate in Northumberland and a house in London. Charlotte said that she had her eye on him for Abby.

Abby liked Robert Surtees. He talked to her, made her laugh. He was handsome, educated and had inherited everything early in life when his father died. He hunted, shot, fished, looked after his estate and spent the season in London and Paris. Abby noted with some amusement that his family, even the poor ones, considered themselves above people like the Collingwoods and thought the way Charlotte spent money to be vulgar. Luckily Charlotte was oblivious to this. She visited Hexham in her shiny carriage, wearing long furs unless the weather was exceptionally warm, and expensive dresses, dripping with jewels and playing the fine lady. At one such event, Abby overheard a woman say to another, 'She married a workman. My dear, what do you expect?'

It made Abby laugh to hear William Collingwood described as a workman, but it was well known in the area that he had come from the coal port of Amble, where his father had built cobles – small fishing boats. Nothing he did, nothing he had achieved, no matter how much money he made or business ability he had, could make him acceptable to the upper circles of society beyond Newcastle. Abby thought that privately it must have cost Charlotte many tears.

Edward was the saving grace. He had graduated from Oxford with full honours of every kind and gone into business with his father. He kept returning to Oxford, ostensibly to see his friends. Then Abby heard that there was a girl. She was, the rumour said in Newcastle, incredibly wealthy and outstandingly beautiful, with wit, intelligence and a generous father. William and Charlotte were delighted and a betrothal was arranged for the summer.

Abby was in correspondence with Rhoda Carlisle, who wrote that her new brother, the son of her mother's new husband, was ill and they would not be able to come to the betrothal party, so Abby invited Rhoda to stay. The weather was warm; they could sit in the garden and visit the shops and she would be glad of the company. Rhoda arrived, thin but brown-faced from being out in the fresh air. She clearly enjoyed being with Abby, but when Abby tried to talk of her family, Rhoda changed. Her dark brown eyes clouded and her conversation ceased.

After a week of running along the nearest beach, plodging in the sea, eating lunch in the garden, reading books in the quietness of the shady trees, Abby thought her friend looked a lot better. Then she began to talk of having a shop.

'What kind of a shop?' Abby said as they sat in the afternoon shade, drinking lemonade.

'Oh, I don't know. Clothes, perhaps, or hats.'

'It isn't respectable. You're young and unmarried.'

'Lots of women do.'

'Not women like us.'

'I'll have to do something and soon.'

'Why?'

Rhoda looked everywhere but at her friend.

'Why, Rhoda?' Abby insisted.

Rhoda looked fiercely at her.

'You don't know what it's like with two brothers, the baby screaming and – and him! My mother . . . she can't see anything wrong in him. I have no place there. I want to be away.'

'I'll introduce you to a nice young man at the party,' Abby said, trying for lightness.

'There are no nice men. They're all horrible.'

'You didn't used to think that of your father.'

'I was a child then,' Rhoda said sadly, and Abby thought of her own childhood when nothing seemed to change. The days went on for ever and her parents were always there, her mother teaching her at home, joking and laughing with her, buying her pretty things, making the house light and warm as it had not been since. The best time of all was in the late autumn, when darkness fell across the streets and lights appeared beyond the bay windows. The leaves were off the trees so that the branches looked like long fingers in the gathering dusk; the wood fire gave off its bright flame; the kettle sang; the tea was made; one of her mother's rich fruit cakes and the pretty pink and white china were laid out with a cloth. They would sit there together, sure in the knowledge that her father would be coming home to them. There would be dinner and closed curtains against the draughts, and the round globes of the lamps would take the mystery from the corners of the rooms. They would read and talk and her father would relate his day. They would talk of people they knew and of Christmas to come and they would make plans. Later, Abby would curl up in her warm, soft feather bed. From there she would watch the fire die down and, as it did so, she would close her eyes in the knowledge that everything was right with her world and Christmas would mean all the special things that it had always brought. They had been so happy then. Why did it happen like that: to know that everything was all right and then to watch it taken from you? To know such happiness and to lose it was cruel. Her mother was dead and so was Rhoda's father and there was no hope for the future. Childhood was long gone and all the lovely, endless days would never come again.

Chapter Two

That summer changed everything. It was funny, Gil thought, how you kept on believing that things were going to get better. He had had the feeling all his life that there had been some kind of mix-up and he had been born into the wrong family. His father was little and dark and dumpy and blue-eyed; his mother was little and fair and not quite so dumpy, and so was Edward, whereas he grew tall and dark eyed and it was always known in the family that he looked just like his grandfather Collingwood. This was not a good thing to be.

Gil could remember his grandparents, and with affection, from when he was very small. They lived in a dark narrow street in a terraced house in Amble and his grandfather built boats for the local fishermen. His grandmother had no servants. She had a big oven with a fire and there would be bread set to rise on the hearth. She always wore a pinafore. Her house was clean; the brasses sparkled; she made soup and in her kitchen was a big table at which she seemed always busy.

His grandfather had a workshop and a yard some way from the house on the edge of the village towards the estuary, with Warkworth Castle in the distance. The workshop had a floor thick with wood shavings and the smell was sweet. His grandfather built cobles, without plans or any help, two a year at least. And he had his own coble. Gil could remember pushing it off the beach into the waves when they went to see to the lobster pots and sometimes his grandfather took him fishing for cod. Edward didn't go. Was he seasick? Gil liked being there. He remembered the thrill of fishing, of feeling the tug on the line, the excitement and pride in his grandfather's voice when he caught his first fish and took it home for his grandmother to cook for tea.

They had both been dead for many years, but Gil knew that there had been a quarrel after which the visits to Amble stopped. His father had called his grandfather stupid and unambitious and the worse thing that he could be – a bad businessman. William couldn't forgive anybody for that. Gil had seen him reading the morning newspaper and shaking his head over somebody's bankruptcy and saying, 'I knew all along that he was a bad businessman.'

Being good at things began with school. You were sent away to be frozen, starved and beaten and then you had to be good at lessons. There was nobody to help. If you had a brother that made things worse, because he was obliged to ignore you. No one ever spoke to their brothers.

Gil envied Edward. For a start, he looked like he should and then he was a success at school. He had lots of friends and, though he wasn't a swot, he was good at things. His reports did not send his father into terrible rages that made Gil shake with fear and then cry with pain because there was always a beating to follow and days of being locked up with nothing but a jug of water and a mattress. He would, he thought, be very good at being in prison if he should ever do anything that wrong.

At first he had determined to try harder, but the lessons were boring and the teachers were miserable at best. As he grew older nobody noticed that he was quite good at geometry and drawing, though he wasn't allowed to do drawing. Edward was so good at everything else there was no point in trying. Gil could not compete. Luckily his father didn't notice him much. With each report, the horror subsided after the first few days and his father was too busy at work to think about him. His mother was always out, shopping or visiting, and when she was in she was dressing to go out. She wore beautiful dresses and smelled lovely; she wore gloves almost all the time to save her hands.

Edward had many friends at school. Gil hated the idea. He had to sleep in a room with twenty other boys. The idea of putting up with them for more than he had to didn't appeal. They were stupid. They cared about whether they reached the cricket team. Gil had almost got himself onto the cricket team and had to pretend not to be good just in time or he would have had to rely on other people for something very intricate and that was too awful to be considered. The games master, a creepy man who liked watching boys strip off for games but who was intelligent, said to Gil, 'Be careful, Collingwood, or you might have to do something more energetic than getting out of bed in the mornings.'

Gil promptly became very bad at everything and kept out of the way.

Then, long after he had wanted to leave school, when he was sixteen, there had come a day when he had an argument with another boy. Gil rarely got into fights. He was big so people avoided him, but this time they said he had lost his temper and thrown the other boy out of a second-storey window. At first he denied it because he didn't remember. All he could remember was that amazing rush of feeling that nothing could stop or hinder. Beyond it somewhere he could hear voices, but far off and faint and nothing to do with him.

The other boy had been lucky. He had escaped with a broken leg. Gil was sent home for good to face his father and to be told that he could go to work in the shipyard labouring since he was obviously no good for anything else.

It might have been all right, but it wasn't, because the lads who worked at the yard knew he was William's son. The very first day half a dozen of them got him down onto the ground and gave him a good kicking. Nobody wanted to be seen with him. Day after day there was the kind of work that until then Gil had not thought existed: carrying and moving heavy things. His nails broke and his hands roughened. The dirt wouldn't come off them. The other men used indescribable language, most of it obscenities which Gil soon learned to recognise. Some of them drank heavily and spat frequently and eyed him as though they were going to give him a good kicking, too, though they didn't. The fighting that Gil had done at school he came to be glad of, and that he was big, so when he had fought a couple of them they let him alone.

At first he couldn't sleep for all the aching muscles. And it was strange to spend the day in the dust and dirt among uneducated men and then come home to the richness of his father's house, where his mother expected good manners, punctuality and clean hands and the talk was of social events and people.

After six months his father moved him. It became a pattern. He spent time in each part of the works, with the platers, the riveters, the patternmakers, carpenters, plumbers, while, it seemed to Gil, Edward, Toby and their friends had a good time at Oxford. Gil couldn't think of anything to say when he met people. It seemed to him that he came from another world, and that theirs was somewhere entirely separate and rather silly. They did not know what it was like when you had one wage and half a dozen children, when you couldn't read or write, when you drank all your pay the first night so that you and your family starved all week. Some men would vow not to do it the next time, but they always did because it was the only escape. Some of them were moderate people; some had been saved by religion, but that didn't stop hunger and cold and heat and monotony from being their daily enemies, it just meant that they survived in some way. At home, where his mother insisted on there being half a dozen courses at dinner and enough food for three times as many people, Gil found himself staring. Often the men he worked with were the brothers and fathers of the maids at home, so everybody knew that he went back to luxury each night.

When Gil moved into the offices, among the engineers, the designers and the drawing office, everything changed. He found enthusiasm. He had grown to love the noise and clamour of the shipyard, to see the various processes which put the ship together, but he cared even more for the place where the ships were drawn, planned, designed, calculated. It seemed to him then as though this had all been in his mind to begin with and somebody had just drawn back the curtains. It was like having extra sight. He barely needed any of it explaining to him; he understood immediately. He could see the ship built and fitted; he knew how it went together; he knew that it would live and be something very important, that it could give men freedom, riches, adventure and love. It could give them communication. It could wipe for them fear and distrust and ignorance and it could enable them to kill one another. He could smell and taste and feel the ship even when it was only on paper. He knew how mighty and dangerous it would be and that he cared for this as he would never care for anything again in his life.

Mr Philips, who was the head of the drawing office, saw the enthusiasm, told Gil that if he worked hard he might achieve something, began to teach him and to get the other experienced and clever men to teach him all the things that they knew. Gil left home very early and got home very late and quite often he stayed with Mr and Mrs Philips because they lived in Newcastle. They had no children and Gil could see that as much as he was taking from Mr Philips he gave them back, because Mrs Philips made big meals and was always happy to see him. Seven days a week Gil worked. His father didn't seem to notice. He was so busy initiating Edward into the mysteries of managing a shipyard that he had almost forgotten Gil. Also, Edward had met a girl called Helen Harrison while at Oxford. William, Gil knew, expected his sons to marry for the betterment of the shipyard and the family and Helen had beauty, money and social status. Her fortune would be put to good use.

'We'll have to look round for a likely young woman for you in a year or two,' William said.

That summer, Gil thought a great deal about Abby Reed. The truth was that he was afraid of her. His father said that she was exactly like her mother and that Bella Reed did far too much reading and thinking for a respectable woman. Abby was clever; Gil knew she was. She would talk to Edward for hours. After her mother died she ran her father's house so competently that Henderson Reed didn't bother to marry again. She had a disconcerting way of looking at you from frank blue eyes that unnerved Gil. He had even heard her swear. Her father looked sternly at Gil whenever they met, which made Gil think he was doing something wrong even when he wasn't.

The best days of Gil's life were those spent near Abby. That night with her had been the best night of his life and he could not forget about it as they grew older. She had cried until she slept, exhausted, but she was warm and soft and smelled like blackberry pie. He had drawn near to the warmth of her and put his arm around her and she had moved closer in her sleep. He had also been there to pick her up when she fell and he pushed Thomas Smith into a pond when he would have kissed her. More than that, Gil couldn't manage. He couldn't think of anything to say to her and, as time went on, Abby seemed to become more formidable. Like Edward, she had lots of friends and was always talking and laughing and dancing. Everybody liked her and wanted to be with her. Gil thought there was no room for him near her. He didn't think she liked him. Why should she? Other people were clever and they were smaller and neat. He was always falling over things. Dancing would have been torture.

He saw even less of her when he began to work seriously, but he thought of what his father had said and bided his time, thinking that when he was twenty-one William might consider him old enough to marry. That summer, his mother boasted at the dinner table that she thought she had found a brilliant match for poor little Abby. Abby was always poor and little to his mother, even though Abby was the most confident young woman Gil had ever met. His heart plummeted. Robert Surtees. Who on earth could compete with somebody twenty-five who was his own master, fabulously wealthy, from the top drawer of society, who owned houses and ran his own life, and had known exactly what to say probably since he had been in the cradle? She would undoubtedly make a good wife for a man like him. She was pretty enough to flatter expensive clothes and jewellery, wise enough to run a rich man's household. Her father would be delighted at such a match, Gil knew. He looked in the nearest mirror and saw a half-educated, overgrown boy with no graces. He stumbled away from his mother's table and left the house.

It was a perfect summer's evening, the one before Edward and Helen's betrothal party, and it was a relief to get out of the way. His mother had been fussing for days about the food, the flowers, the airing of beds and the making up of rooms. It was her only talent, he thought, organising parties. Perhaps he took after his mother, being no good at things. Then he remembered the look in Mr Philips' eyes over some of the work he had recently done. His drawings and calculations were 'beautiful' Mr Philips had said, 'just beautiful'. Gil had remembered this over and over again. It was the first time in his life that anybody had praised him. Gil wished he could live in the office. He listened hard to every piece of advice he was given from the educated, experienced men who ran his father's shipyard. If he could have gone in any earlier and stayed any later, he would have.

'You've got talent, laddie, real talent,' Mr McGregor in the engineering department had said. Mr McGregor wasn't supposed to call him 'laddie' or anything else that was familiar, Gil being the boss's son, but Mr McGregor didn't notice and Gil didn't care. It was almost a term of endearment. Mr McGregor and Mr Philips kept him close to them and gave him important, detailed work to do and Gil felt like a sponge, taking everything in. It was not like school, where he didn't understand. Everything he was told now became clear and he soaked up the teaching and the information even more as they began to praise him. Gil wanted to hear it. Every day he wanted to hear that he was good and for the two men to smile and shake their heads in admiration. The looks and words of approval would never cease to be a novelty. He had managed to please somebody and that had never happened before. Gil felt like a highwire act at the circus: among the height and the fear but out there in the middle, doing wonderfully clever things. He had an audience who urged him on to do more and more daring, adventurous and creative things and the results were heady and wonderful. Gil would have done anything to bring to their faces that special glow of satisfaction.

Neither of them said anything to his father, but soon some of the best work was coming from Gil. He heard reported that his father was pleased at the new ideas and the accuracy and skill. Gil would spend hours adding deft touches, making sure that things would work and fit. Mr Philips opened the world of numbers to Gil as ten years of schooling had not and he could see it, he could see the patterns. They were like frost on the windows and rings on the inside of trees. He had felt like jumping up and down. There was order in the universe; there was symmetry that you could alter and change. You had power there; everything had a place and a purpose. Levels and seasons and time and music were all to do with numbers. There came a clarity to Gil's mind that nothing could shift. It was like a flowering, an excitement, a sense of being where none had been before. Gil loved Mr Philips' office as he had loved nowhere in his short life. There he was not clumsy and stupid and self-conscious. Mr Philips would shut the door and when the door was shut nobody dared enter. Very often he went out and shut the door after him, leaving Gil alone and it was bliss; the day went by much too quickly. He was always disappointed when it ended and he had to go home. The office was dusty because nobody was allowed to move anything. Gil knew it was a measure of Mr Philips' growing regard for him that he let him stay there away from other people and other eyes and anything that might break his concentration, but Gil felt as if he could have worked in the middle of Grainger Street in Newcastle and it wouldn't have made any difference. That office, filled with rolled-up papers that had been designs for ships God knew how many years back, was a sanctuary, an escape into another, better world. In some ways, Gil knew he would never come out of it. He was at home here; nothing could hurt him. It was clean and assured. Best of all, were his ideas. He soon came to realise that there was no limit to these. Once you had let that extra eye open which was creativity, it could not be closed. If you nurtured it and gave it space and acknowledged it, the work came to you and it was wonderful.

He had thought to go on from there, that he would prove to people he was good enough to marry Abby Reed. Suddenly she would see that he was clever too and she would love him. They would have a house in town and he would spend the rest of his life in Mr Philips' office and that house. He would not have a hideous Greek mansion and a wife like his mother, who wore gloves even in bed. He had thought, after being at boarding school, that he would want to sleep alone for the rest of his life, but a night spent alongside Abby had buried that notion. He would marry Abby and live in town. She would run the house and they would have children and he would be kind to them. He would not ignore them or beat them or send them away to school. He would read stories to them and at night he would sleep in a big bed with Abby, who was warm and soft and would belong to nobody else.

But his mother had been busy finding a husband for Abby. His parents liked her, there was even that about it. He could have pleased them. She was Henderson's only child; there could be no objection. And when Henderson saw that Gil could do these great designs and such good work, he would be glad too. But his mother had taken Abby to Hexham to visit her family and she had met Robert Surtees and there was no help for it.

Robert was coming to the betrothal party. Charlotte had been clever. Gil allowed himself five minutes to think about being in bed with Abby. He gave himself five minutes a day. He lay back in the warm grass and closed his eyes. He would be able to surprise Abby. Maybe it was not too late. He had learned to waltz so that he could ask her to dance. It had been a long trail. Even making the decision to learn and then following it through had been difficult. He had stood on the pavement outside the dancing school in the narrow street of Pink Lane in Newcastle's centre and hesitated. The door was open, but it was the upstairs room; he had to climb the stairs before him. That was the hardest part. Once upstairs, the middle-aged lady was alone but for the gentleman who played the piano and she had been kind and patient.

'I want to learn to waltz,' Gil said.

'Of course you do,' she said, as though it was the easiest thing in the world. So he learned, thinking of himself and Abby.

The betrothal day came, hot and dry, the last day of June. Light streamed in, denying the darkness even a slender hold, and from early day everybody was busy. His mother went back and forwards with lists and all the servants moved faster than usual. Gil had not thought that his brother's betrothal would have any effect on him. Why should it? But he was aware that Robert Surtees was coming here to see Abby. From somewhere he would find the courage to ask her to dance with him.

The afternoon was hot. The flowers which had been brought into the ballroom were watered so that they would not wilt. As many doors and windows were opened as could be to catch the tiny breeze that fluttered a little way among the garden paths. Early guests walked in the shade of the quarry gardens, where it seemed the rhododendrons had burst into special splendour, their flowers as big as his hands.

His mother sat outside on the terrace and dispensed tea and angel cake and smiles. His father accompanied various ladies with parasols into the rose garden. Abby came in the early evening with her father and Rhoda and Robert Surtees at the same time. Robert ignored Gil, but spoke at length to Edward and Toby, who had come some time earlier with his family. Gil decided that it wouldn't take much effort for him to hate Robert, standing there speaking in refined tones, talking about Cambridge and how much better it was than Oxford, teasing the other two, glancing now and then at Abby and smiling at her. Rhoda didn't have much to say, it seemed to Gil, and she was much thinner than the last time he had seen her.

Gil didn't want to be with any of these people, he didn't understand why. Suddenly, anywhere else in the world would have done. It was as though there was an electric charge in the air. Red butterflies clung to nettles in the stableyard as Gil walked down to talk to the horses and rub their velvet noses. In the evening sunshine, fluttering as though they had been caught and pinned, the butterflies were so still that he could see the tiny black spots on their wings.

Throughout the early evening, people arrived. The musicians played. The dancing began, but Helen Harrison did not arrive. Gil saw the anxious look invade his brother's face. Eight o'clock came and went. Half past eight and still they were not there. Then, before nine o'clock, while it was daylight and only the coolness and the long shadows foretold of night, a carriage came up the drive and stopped in front of the house.

His parents were outside at the bottom of the steps and so was Edward. Gil didn't want to go forward but, almost as though the house itself propelled him, he went and stood in the doorway. It was a defence. He felt as if marauders had made their way through the gates and up the drive and were about to storm the house. They could have been sixteenth-century Border Reivers on an October raid, screaming and yelling, the horses' hooves dull in the night as they rode in to steal everything they could carry off.

Two ordinary people stood beside the carriage, but there was nothing ordinary about the young woman who turned towards him. Gil had never seen anybody like her. Her hair was the brightest shade of yellow. Her face was pink and cream and her eyes were a cool, dark-blue liquid. He could already imagine what her mouth would taste like: strawberries and pepper. Her lashes cast shadows on her cheeks. He thought of her hair loose, of how long it was, past her waist, and of her breasts bared for his mouth and hands. Gil tried to back away from the shocking images, but he couldn't. He had never felt like this about any woman in his life. He knew from that very moment that it was not the first time they had met. He recognised her. Helen Harrison was meant to be his; it had been written, ordained. He could smell the softness of her skin; he knew how she turned in her sleep. He could see her belly rounded with their child. He could hear her distant laughter as she ran away from him in game down a path that led to a rose garden. She didn't move or speak, though her eyes held his. Gil felt like somebody who had been struggling endlessly upstream until he was exhausted. His arms and legs were leaden with tiredness and the water was pulling him down. Her gaze didn't flicker, even when Edward came to introduce them and, as she moved towards him Gil gave up the fight. He went down for the last time and the waters closed over his head.

Chapter Three

Rhoda hadn't danced with anybody all evening and Abby felt disloyal as she polkaed and waltzed. Her mother had once told her that dancing was the only respectable way to get close to a man outside marriage and it was certainly easier than staying near Robert Surtees. She regretted, in some ways, having agreed to go to Hexham with Charlotte. She liked him well enough but no more than she liked several other young men, except that he was handsome and rich, and those were not, she kept telling herself, good reasons for liking anybody. Her father had already noticed Robert watching her and had talked about how smitten Robert was. He called her his sly puss. Abby had brushed him off. All she really wanted was to be with Gil, yet well into the middle of the evening they had not spoken, except in greeting. Most of the time she couldn't see him, the crush of people was so great.

The evening was warm and Rhoda was disinclined to dance, so they went walking outside and here, finally, Rhoda talked to her about Jos Allsop.

'He comes into my bedroom in the mornings, he and my mother, and they laugh and joke and he tickles me as though I was seven. Sometimes when my mother oversleeps, because often she's up most of the night with that brat, he comes alone, getting on to my bed and . . . I'm in my nightgown. He tells me how pretty I've become and during the day he spends a great deal of time with me. He touches me whenever he can. I'm afraid of him. I feel as though he's the spider and I'm the fly.'

They walked back through the quarry gardens to the house and were in time to see Helen Harrison arrive. They stood at a distance.

'Isn't she beautiful?' Rhoda said, but it was Gil's reaction that Abby saw. He had not looked at her like that, nor at any girl that she had ever seen. Abby was wearing what she had thought was a pretty dress, but when she saw Helen's she felt shabby and provincial. It was pale yellow spotted muslin with a tiny blue-and-yellow iris pattern. It was fashionable and shrieked to her of Paris, sophistication, society, adventure and involvement. Helen probably knew all the right people. Her life seemed dull to her. She caught a glimpse of herself in a nearby mirror and saw her defects, the too-long nose, the ordinary brown hair, her thin figure, her square, capable hands. Abby could have wept.

Helen and Edward danced but, afterwards, Helen did what no girl Abby knew would have dared. She walked all the way across the room towards Gil Collingwood and quite obviously asked him to dance with her. Nobody did so except in a ladies' excuse me and Gil had always managed to absent himself upon such occasions. To Abby's dismay, Gil took the girl lightly into his arms as the music started and they began to waltz. He had lied. He did dance. Their steps matched perfectly and there were not now so many people, somehow, because Abby could watch them. Some woman beside her said to her friend, 'Don't they make a lovely couple?' And they did, much more so than Edward and Helen. Gil, tall and dark and Helen, slight and fair, waltzed elegantly about the room.

Abby thought of all the times when Gil could have danced with her and hadn't, but he had known Helen Harrison barely an hour before dancing with her and he was talking to her quite comfortably by the look of things. Abby was angry, jealous, resentful, all things which she had not been before. She hated Gil in those moments when he had his arms around Helen Harrison and was moving her so confidently about the floor and she was looking up into his eyes.

'Did you go to Oxford?' Helen said. 'I met you there, surely.'

'No.'

'Then where did we meet?'

'I don't know.'

'Did you go to Cambridge? I have an aunt there—'

'I didn't go to university.'

'My father says that education is the waste of a good childhood.'

'Wasn't he educated?'

'Yes, I think that's why he says it.'

'My father had little education and thinks the opposite.'

They didn't talk any more. They didn't need to. Gil had danced with no one other than his dancing teacher, but it felt as though he had danced with Helen dozens of times. It seemed as if he could almost remember it. She entranced him. Her eyes sparkled and she was soft and light in his arms. And at the back of his mind, he knew the place that they had met before. The walls were white and so was the bed. It was afternoon and they were inside because of the heat. The houses were white and so was the sunlight and outside fruit grew on the trees, oranges and lemons hanging there such as they never could in England. It was quiet. The floor of the room was bare wooden boards and there was not even a breeze to disturb the thin white curtains at the windows.

Abby went outside. Her feelings were all mixed up and tumbled as though she were an egg timer and somebody had turned her upside down. She told herself it didn't matter that Gil had fallen in love with his brother's betrothed, that he had not shown any preference for anybody before. She wondered why apparently nobody but she had noticed. Was it because she knew him so well? Yet she didn't. They had exchanged barely a dozen words in the past six months. She meant nothing to him and now he must mean nothing to her. She gave a little shiver in the warm night. No good could come of his regard for Edward's bride to be. Perhaps it was just a momentary thing, passing.

'Miss Reed?'

She was standing on the lawn in front of the house. She turned around. Robert Surtees, handsome and smiling, was standing behind her.

'I hope nothing's wrong.'

'It was too hot inside.'

'Would you like to take a walk around the garden?' he said and offered his arm. He spoke so kindly that Abby liked to hear him and tried to say the right thing back. He made her feel easier. It was late, but the night was not dark. A star peeped through here and there.

'Helen Harrison is very beautiful,' Abby said, unable to stop thinking about her.

'She's the most beautiful girl I've ever seen,' he agreed. 'We've met on several occasions. I can't think why she's throwing herself away on Edward Collingwood. She could have had a title. She could have married old money and an old name. She took London by storm and now look at her.'

'What's wrong with Edward?'

'Forgive me, the Collingwoods are common.'

'Charlotte married one.'

He smiled just a little.

'There are people who have not forgiven her. The woman is vulgar.'

'She's very kind.'

'She introduced us. I'm thankful for that,' he said.

Gil knew that, having danced with Helen, he should have danced with other young women. He looked for Abby, but couldn't see her and then spotted Rhoda Carlisle standing alone. She refused. Gil was relieved. He had done his duty and could now go off to think about what had happened. He went into an empty room away from the noise of the party. Beyond the window, in the gardens he could see Abby with Robert. The night was finally beginning to steal past the trees, but he could see clearly in the fading light that they were close together as they walked back across the lawns towards the house.

Gil's only hope was that Helen would go home. During the next few days he did everything he could to avoid her. He stayed at work, but for once work had lost its attraction. He could not put Helen from his mind. She remained at the house. Each evening after Edward came home they would read together and walk in the garden. Charlotte took her visiting to all their friends. In the morning at weekends she would go riding with Edward. In church on Sundays, Gil could hear her sweet voice. Gil wished that she would go away. He wanted to be with her so much he was sure it must have looked obvious, but he could tell that nobody noticed anything different.

He thought that she would probably go after a week, but she didn't. She stayed on because she said she could not bear to be parted from Edward. There was much talk about a wedding at Christmas. Charlotte and Helen spent hours making plans and long lists. Edward and Helen travelled to Durham to talk to the vicar of St Oswald's. Helen's parents had bought a house in Durham so that they could be near to their daughter after the marriage.

Gil couldn't eat or sleep and Mr Philips was beginning to complain about his work. Helen floated in and out of his dreams. When he was with her, he was conscious of his hands because he wanted to touch her so much. Worse still, she seemed to like him and often met his gaze over the dinner table or across the room. Desperate to get away, Gil went to see Abby. He suggested they might go for a walk. Abby looked surprised, as well she might, he thought. For a moment it seemed as if she might refuse, but she didn't. They left the house and walked through the dene near her home. It was pretty, with a stream and trees and shrubs, a bridge and little waterfalls. There were lots of people about since it was a hot July day and Sunday.

'How's Helen?' Abby asked stiffly.

'She's going home this week, I think.'

He hoped. She was sleeping in the room next to his. Why did they have to put her there? He could remember being with her, watching her turn in her sleep, her soft sighs, the sunlight breaking across the room, the shadows against the white walls . . . He dragged his mind back. Abby was talking to him.

'What?'

She looked accusingly at him.

'You haven't heard a word I've said. Why did you ask me to go for a walk? You don't want to talk to me. You never do talk to me or dance with me. You told me you couldn't dance.'

The words stuck in Gil's throat like dry biscuit.

'I can't.'

'But you can! You danced with Helen as though you'd done it hundreds of times. Nobody who hadn't waltzed before could have done it like that. You've obviously known for years.'

'I haven't.'

She didn't believe him, Gil could see. And he couldn't possibly tell her about the little dancing teacher in Pink Lane, it would make him look foolish. The angry look on Abby's face silenced Gil. They walked back to the house, Abby almost striding. Henderson greeted him without a smile and it was then that Gil realised her father didn't like him. What had he done?

'Now, young Collingwood, what can we do for you?' He looked grimly at Gil. 'I hear there's to be a wedding at Christmas. Awful things, weddings. Folk standing around looking stupid and trying to find something to say.' And Henderson stamped off.

Gil waited for Abby to offer him tea. When she didn't, he felt obliged to leave and go home.

Abby ordered tea for herself and her father the minute that Gil had gone. Henderson came in, sat down and drank his tea, but his face was dark and she had not long to wait before he said, 'I don't want that lad here, Abby. I've no objection to being friends with them up to a point, but if I thought you were taken with him—'

'I'm not,' Abby said quickly.

'What was he doing here then?'

'I don't know.'

Helen went back to Durham, but each weekend she came to stay or Edward went to her house. The next Saturday that she was at the house, Edward was out of sorts and she wanted to go riding so Gil was obliged to go with her. They went early before the heat should take the day, while the dew was still on the grass, and it was just as good as Gil had known it would be. He was a better horseman than his brother and riding through the wide Northumbrain fields with Helen was as near to perfection as life could manage. She enjoyed it too, shrieking as she jumped a fallen log, laughing when they raced. He felt as though he was giving her up to Edward again when they got back to the stables.

Her pretty brown riding habit suited her, making her eyes look even bluer, and they sparkled from the exercise. Gil thought that she was nothing like Abby. He was determined to make things right with Abby and went into Newcastle the following day. He found Henderson alone and he was uneasy, following him into the study. Henderson obviously worked on Sunday afternoons. To Gil, from somewhere, there was an echo. Was this what people did when they were lonely? The room had the untidiness of concentration. There were papers everywhere.

Henderson's house seemed small to Gil after the mansion that he lived in, yet it was a big town house with gardens and a tennis court, a conservatory and half a dozen big rooms downstairs.

'This is getting to be a regular thing, isn't it, lad?' Henderson said, watching him.

Being called 'lad' was like being at home and Gil resented the intimacy.

'Jack Philips tells me you have talent.'

Gill had had no idea that Abby's father was on such terms with the head of Collingwood's drawing office. The professional in Gil resented that, but he personally resented Mr Philips talking about him, especially to somebody like Henderson, who couldn't have kept his mouth shut during a sandstorm in the desert.

'Your father is lucky to have two sons,' Henderson said gruffly. 'Abby is out. I presume it's her you came to see. She's gone for a walk with Robert Surtees. Aye, you may well look. He haunts us.'

Henderson was watching him, rather, Gil thought, as though he might grab the silver candlesticks and run out of the door.

'I've got nothing against you, lad. I don't even mind that you're a younger son. But I wouldn't want to think that you were getting in the road here. Surtees is a man of property and distinction with a fine name and good breeding. I'll be the happiest man alive if he asks Abby to marry him. The only thing I lack in life is a son and he's a gentleman. He's educated and clever and knows his way about the world. You're just a lad and you haven't exactly distinguished yourself so far.'

The silence which followed was a Sunday afternoon silence. Gil knew it well. The atmosphere that you got when you went pigeon-shooting on those cool, foggy November days just before dusk came down slowly like a thief. The woods were full of pigeons but you could not hear the flapping of their wings, nothing but the thick white silence before they moved, before you put the gun up to your shoulder and pulled the trigger. Never a day off for pigeons, never a peaceful Sunday, always the possibility of death before teatime, blood staining their grey and white breasts.

He left. Henderson showed him the door and Gil went, Henderson telling him flatly that Abby could be hours so there was no point in waiting and that he had work to do.

There was nowhere to hide. The lengthening nights became a torment of sleeplessness and want. His mother complained that he didn't eat and questioned the cooking. His father finally realised that he was making a mess of things at work and moved him so that he could watch him. After that, working beside his father and Edward, Gil was so miserable that he made elementary mistakes. Finally, one afternoon that autumn, his father lost patience and hit him. It was the kind of blow that sent you into the wall and, since the wall had no give in it, you took the pain twice. He had been thinking about leaving all that week, going he didn't know where, and that strengthened his resolution; but his brother, who had never before defended him, sprang up from the far side of the desk, shouting, 'Don't do that to him!'

They were the sweetest words that Gil had ever heard. Edward was in front of him like a shield. He could hear the quiet threat in his brother's voice when he said slowly, 'Don't hit him.'

William laughed.

'How brave you are,' he sneered, 'brave on the back of your lass's fortune? You aren't wed to her yet. I tell you, you aren't much better than he is. We'll do a sight more when you've wedded and bedded her. Then we might get some work out of you!' And his father left the office, slamming the door. Edward turned around, glaring.

'What the hell is the matter with you?'

Gil could taste blood and he had hurt his shoulder and his

arm, but he got out of the office and down the corridor and into the cupboard-sized place his father had assigned his office before the stone in his throat eased.

Helen had arrived when they got home. It was Friday evening. She was particularly bright at dinner. She wore one of her prettiest dresses and afterwards she played the piano. William had barely spoken and went away to his study. Charlotte sat with a book. Edward came to where Gil was standing by the window and said, 'Toby asked me if I would go into town and play billiards. Do you want to come?'

Gil was astonished and rather pleased. He couldn't understand why Edward should seek his company or want to go out since Helen was there.

'Just going out for a while,' Edward said generally to the room and, since nobody raised an objection – his mother and Helen were forever discussing the wedding – they went. There was a full moon and Gil realised when they got out that it was exactly what he had wanted to do. It made him feel powerful, getting away.

The billiard hall was another world, companionable, warm, comforting. Young men drank beer and smoked and the sound of the billiard balls meeting with a snap across the table and clunking down into the pockets was mixed with talk and laughter. Toby greeted them with obvious delight and Edward seemed happier here than Gil had seen him for a long time. He played several games. Gil didn't do much. It wasn't that he couldn't play, he just didn't need to tonight. He cheered his brother on and gave him lots of advice and Edward laughed and made funny remarks at him. He was surprised at how well they got on and was content to watch the evening go by. He wished, in some way, that he could hold the time. Toby and Edward were like a double act at the music hall, they knew one another so well.

'Did I tell you I'm leaving home?' Toby said to Gil as Edward paused, chalking the billiard cue and considering possible play. 'I've taken a house in Jesmond, just a small house, all to myself.'

Gil envied him. At work that afternoon all he could think of was leaving. Now it didn't seem so important. He was happy in Edward's company. His brother had taken his part but would it last?

'I'm going to plan my garden, immerse myself in it.' He looked tenderly at Gil's bruised face. 'Been fighting again, old boy?'

Edward cleared the table.

'How about a game?' Toby said to Gil.

'He doesn't want to play,' Edward said.

Toby laughed. His teeth were white and even and his eyes sparkled.

'Are you sure?'

'He's quite sure.'

'But you'll play, won't you, Ed?' Toby asked him.

'Play if you like,' Gil said to his brother's enquiring eyes. 'I'll watch.'

Chapter Four

As Christmas approached, what Abby had both most hoped and feared happened. She was dreading the anniversary of her mother's death, as she did every year. Her father's house had ceased to be a refuge and became an emptiness, the house where her mother had been and where the ghosts and memories only served to make the present less bearable. Her father spent all his time at work and the optimistic tone which he had held to at first seemed slowly to evaporate like a pale winter sun in mid-afternoon. He hid among his work even more than he had before her mother died and Abby felt as though she could hear every clock in the house ticking.

Robert Surtees rescued her. Abby, being truthful with herself, acknowledged that she would have accepted invitations from someone less entertaining and handsome than he was to get away. She would have suggested to her father that they should move, but she knew he would see it for foolishness. In any case, they could not leave Newcastle because of his work, so it would be pointless. He hated the country, so they could not move there. Robert provided diversions. This year he had suggested going to the cemetery with her, but Abby had other ideas so they drove to his house near Hexham and spent the day there among his family. Abby suggested to Henderson that he should accompany them, but he only said gruffly that he would go to work as usual.

Robert's parents were both dead. Rumour said that his mother had committed suicide after a miscarriage and that his father had taken to drink and followed her, but Abby found his family sane and kind. There was his grandmother, whom Abby could tell liked her, and various uncles, aunts and cousins. Coming from an empty house to a family who made her welcome was so pleasant that Abby could not tell whether it was Robert she liked or his house and family. His life was so easy, filled with pleasure, the opposite of anything she had been brought up to believe in.

In her world, men worked all the time. Robert had people to take care of everything: an agent to manage the estate, a housekeeper, reliable people to see to his possessions and, as far as Abby could judge, it went smoothly enough so that he could spend much of his time with her.

He would have bought her presents, but Abby refused, knowing that expensive gifts meant commitment. Her father did not hide his pleasure at her conquest. The pride in his eyes made Abby pleased with herself in ways she despised, and in her honest moments she knew that her mother would have laughed in scorn. Sometimes she thought that she heard her mother's voice.

'Going up in the world are you, Abby? It gives you further to fall, don't forget.'

If her mother had been alive she would not have seen so much of Robert, but there was nobody at home and she began to spend her days with him. Her father encouraged the friendship and was eager to go to the big house for Christmas. Abby thought of Gil then, making snow angels. She had not made them again since that first year, had no inclination to do things like that with Robert, though she did other pleasurable things. They went skating when the ice was hard that winter and roasted chestnuts and gathered holly. Abby liked going out into the cold air and coming back to see the lamps lit in Robert's house.

It was the kind of house she would have wanted for her own,

so far removed from the pretentious Greek mansion of the Collingwoods' as a house could possibly be. Parts of it were five hundred years old and Robert told her that his family had lived in some kind of dwelling on that same piece of land for eight hundred years. Various members of the family had added on to the house when times were prosperous, so that it had no coherent heart to it. People like William would have hated it. There was no symmetry, no organisation, just a mish-mash of half a dozen eras. Abby loved it because it bespoke the personalities of the Surtees family, the silliness in the folly beyond the house, their fear in the tower which had protected them, their artistic merits in the long gallery which housed paintings by several famous artists of the past. There was a lovely garden where Robert's great grandmother had grown herbs to cure ills, and a rose garden which his mother had designed shortly before she died. This was what houses should be about, Abby thought, the sum total of a family, not an image of one time, erected to impress people. It didn't impress the upper classes, Abby thought, they only laughed at it. Then she was ashamed of herself.

Beyond Hexham it was not too far to visit Rhoda and when Abby went there to stay overnight, she understood why her friend was not happy. Jos Allsop looked Abby over like she was a prize sow, Abby thought. His gaze lingered on her breasts and hips and legs. He came into the bedroom in the early morning when they were still in bed and his hot gaze upset Abby, even though he didn't touch her. Rhoda's mother was pregnant again and the house seemed overfull of noise and people. The small boy who was Jos's son was spoiled, shouting and screaming when he could not have what he wanted immediately, so that Abby's fingers itched to smack him.

There was plenty of money. The house was big, the food was good and there were servants, but Rhoda's mother ignored her daughter and her guest and Jos gave them too much attention. Abby was glad to leave the little town and go for a walk on the moors, even though the day was cold and bitter and up there nothing stirred.

'I used to love it here when my father was alive,' Rhoda said, her brown hair blowing about for she had refused a hat. There was nothing to stop the wind. The stone houses stood as a testament to good buildings and materials. Abby understood how Rhoda felt. When you knew you were loved, you could abide in such an inhospitable place, but when that security was threatened, the bleakness of it seeped into your life just as the wet wind blowing across the heather had soaked her gloves so that her fingers were starting to go numb. There was nothing here for people who were lonely. She thought, it strange that she could be so lonely amidst the elegant buildings of the Newcastle streets and Rhoda felt just the same out here, where the wind and hail blew horizontally across the unfriendly land. She even felt sorry for the sheep, who were huddled in for shelter against the backs of the drystone walls. It gave her a little glow to think that Robert waited for her when she wanted to go back to the more civilised atmosphere of Hexham. Rhoda had no one and it was difficult not to feel sorry for her, though Abby knew pity for an unworthy sentiment. Rhoda seemed to have lost her mother as well as her father and Abby thought that this was true. In a sense, when one parent died you lost both of them for the other one, being no longer part of a pair, was altered in some way. Rhoda's mother now belonged to another man and Henderson belonged to his work, which he had gone to as surely as some men went to whores' beds; but Abby knew that the most important part of Henderson, that which fools would call his heart, was buried alongside Bella Reed in the cemetery and that in some ways Abby would never get him back. He belonged to his dead wife and that was why he had not married again. Abby did not know whether to be angry that he had given up or to be glad that he had not made a bad second marriage. Neither seemed of benefit to anyone.

She walked a long way with Rhoda, beyond where she would

have been glad to turn back, grateful not to face the savage wind which screamed across the felltops. But Rhoda seemed oblivious to the weather; she had so little to go home to that was of any ease or comfort. Jos's family would be there for Christmas and, though Abby had met them only briefly, she could see what kind of people they were. They were like Charlotte in a sense: they cared nothing for books, music or religion; nothing spiritual came near them. The men were crude and the women were vain. They had never seen beyond the dale nor hoped to and were secretly, she thought, afraid of everything outside it. Jos was one of them. She worried that he would be cruel and self-indulgent and that Rhoda would suffer. There was no longer a book in the house nor a piano. He drank and smoked, slept long and, Abby suspected, bedded Rhoda's mother like a rutting goat. He did nothing useful because Rhoda's father had left more than enough money for them to get by. Robert must have despised him, she thought. Abby made certain that there was nothing between the two men beyond pleasantries, though when she left she could not bear to look back and see Rhoda standing along with her sheepdog outside the door.

'You will come and stay with us for the wedding?' Abby had begged, and it was not just for Rhoda but for herself. She did not want to go and see Gil's hungry gaze on the girl who was to be his sister-in-law, yet she had no excuse to offer for her absence. Rhoda would provide support and had promised to come unless there was snow and the weather prevented her.

The wedding was fixed for two days before new year and Abby watched anxiously from the windows as the sky darkened and snow began to fall. Rhoda was to come to her the day before and to stay for more than a week afterwards. Abby's plan was that it would snow then so that Rhoda would be obliged to spend several weeks with her in Newcastle during January and February. That way, neither of them would be lonely.

Robert took Abby to several parties during December. Everywhere she went, Abby was accepted by Northumberland society because of the man beside her. He asked her if she would visit his London house in the spring and here he would show her the city and take her to see the sights. Abby had not been to London and was excited at the idea. She had grown comfortable with him and had ceased to hanker after a boy who had proved stupid enough to fall in love with a woman he could not have. Abby felt the armour of Robert's love and was content.

It had not at first seemed to Gil as though his brother had changed. All their lives, Edward had taken little notice of him and the day in the office when William hit his younger son would not make the difference. Gil assumed that Edward's sympathy would pass, so he stored squirrel-like in his mind the way that his brother had defended him and the evening spent in the billiard hall. But, as each day went by and Edward did not revert to the superior scathing person whom Gil could not like, Gil stopped thinking about that day.

Because he could not have Helen, it seemed somehow that at least he had gained his brother and, more and more, it felt traitorous to him that he should want her. He tried to put the feelings from him and it also seemed, and this was strange, that in some ways they changed places. Edward's work became less and less competent so that Gil began helping him, covering for him, making sure that William's wrath did not come down on Edward. Edward was restless. It did not please him to stay at home by the fire – and the weather was foul. He would go into town and play billiards and drink and, to Gil's surprise, his brother drank a great deal. He always asked Gil to go with him, which was an even bigger and much more pleasant surprise. Sometimes, Edward would not have reached home without him.

At first Gil was flattered by the invitations, that his brother would introduce him to his friends, but it also occurred to him that if Helen had been waiting for him he would not have wanted to leave her. Sometimes she came to stay and Edward took her to the theatre or to see friends, but he did not often go to her parents' house in Durham. Night after night, Edward played billiards. He would drink and laugh and call on Gil to admire the best shots. Often, he drank so much that he was not sober by morning.

Sometimes they went to Toby's house. He lived not far from Abby, though it was a much smaller house. Gil thought it strange inside, unlike any house he had seen before. The walls were painted white and there were no carpets, just polished wooden floorboards. There were no ornaments; everything was simple and uncluttered. There was a big garden at the back, but not much to see, all black and brown and bare-treed in the winter weather.

'What do you think?' Toby asked Gil on his first visit.

'It's like a monk's cell.'

Edward laughed so much that he choked. Toby grinned.

'It's so . . . sparse,' Gil said.

Toby went to the window and looked longingly down the garden.

'In the summer I'm going to sit out there under the trees and drink wine.'

Edward was leaning against the wooden shutter on one side of the window and Gil could see that he was also imagining himself there.

Edward was silent on the way home. Everyone had gone to bed by then, but he would linger, not because he wanted to keep the day, Gil thought, but because he wanted to steal as much of the night as he could, as if the morning held some kind of terror. The wedding was a week away.

'Come in by the fire and have some brandy with me,' he said, and Gil went.

In the small sitting-room, which was truly the only comfortable room in the house and everybody tended to go in there, the fire was kept burning brightly and the brandy decanter shone in the reflected fire, the housekeeper having discovered that they would often finish their evening here. Edward poured the brandy and they sat down by the fire. Gil considered the dark liquid in his glass.

'Do you mind if I ask you something?'

'What?' Edward stretched out his legs. He looked happier now than he had looked all day, as though brandy and the fire were his only pleasures.

'Are you frightened of marrying Helen?'

Edward looked at him.

'Of bedding a woman? I have bedded women before.'

'No, that's not what I meant.'

'What then?'

'Of being different, the responsibility, the – the commitment. Does it weigh you down, only you seem so—'

Edward didn't answer straight away and then slowly.

'Yes, it's frightening and strange. What made you think that?'

'You go out so much and you drink such a lot and . . . you take me with you like you had no company. You have Toby and your friends.'

'I wanted to get something back. No, that's not true. I wanted something I never had: to be close to my brother.'

'Toby's more like a brother to you than I am.'

It was a secret smile and an unhappy one that Edward gave. His face almost hid it and he shook his head.

'I wanted . . . what was it . . . I wanted memories, but when I searched for them in my head they weren't there. All I could see was this space and my father shouting at us and the smell of my mother's clothes, the smell of her powder. And she was always coming and going like something that's never still. I feel like I'm losing something, yet when I search my mind there's nothing to hold on to. And that day in the office . . . I wished I had been kinder to you.' It was only drink, Gil told himself when his brother, embarrassed by the words, had gone to bed; but when Edward left the room all the magic went with him. Gil had not known until then that his brother held the magic. He had thought that it was the night or the brandy or the firelight. He realised then for the first time that the magic is only within people. The room was cool without his brother, and silent, and had nothing to do with him. Something was over and something new was just beginning and there was nothing left to do but go to bed.

Chapter Five

Helen and Edward's wedding day was as white as the icing on their three-tiered cake, but didn't prevent anyone from getting there since the snow was decorative only and quite soft. The service was held in St Oswald's in Church Street in the middle of the small city. From outside, you could see the cathedral in the background. Gil felt that his father would have been better pleased if the service had been held there, but Helen's parents seemed determined that William should not be allowed to ask everybody of importance in the entire northeast.

Edward had been drunk every night for a week and on two occasions, nights when he had not asked Gil to go with him, had not come home. His mother would have protested but his father said, 'Let the lad alone. He'll be leg-shackled soon enough.'

Durham couldn't help looking pretty in the snow, with its narrow streets, grey river and magnificent cathedral and castle, but when Helen walked up the aisle of the church she looked to Gil like some kind of sacrifice, as though the vicar was about to slay her on the altar. Gil had to make himself not stand in front of her to protect her from what looked to him like ancient rituals up to no good. For the rest of her life she would be Edward's, belong to him in the most basic way possible, sleep in his bed, bear his children, obey him, be there for him to come home to. It was like a cattle market, Gil thought. Edward didn't smile and

Toby, who was his best man, looked so pale throughout the ceremony that Gil was convinced he would faint. But Helen shone. She wore a long veil and a cream dress and nobody in the history of the whole world had ever been as beautiful. If he had doubted that she loved his brother, he doubted it no longer. She looked as though she had waited all her life for this moment. Her responses were clear and precise, whereas Edward's were low and mumbled. Edward was better after the ceremony, laughing and throwing pennies for the local children who gathered in the street. Since the day was now bright and fine and the snow had retreated to lawns and rooftops, he insisted on walking with his bride on his arm the short distance to her parents' home down New Elvet and across Elvet Bridge to the towpath where her parents had a gate to their house on the riverside.

It was a big townhouse. They went in by the gate and up the winding path through bare trees to where the house stood with its front to lawns and the river and its back to Claypath, up the bank from the marketplace. The older people went by carriage but the younger ones walked, laughing and chatting as the sun made the snow glisten.

Abby had said nothing but hello to Gil and he didn't speak to Robert, for whom he had developed hatred. Rhoda Carlisle looked pretty in yellow and when Gil ventured to tell her so, since he was beside her and had to say something, she smiled and said, 'Actually, it belongs to Abby. I haven't a decent dress to my name. Who needs dresses when you live in the wilderness?'

'I thought you liked it there.'

'I did. Things like dresses only matter when you have little else, don't you think? I used to love Allendale Common. Now, I would give almost anything to get away.' She stopped and let the others troop past and it seemed only polite to stay with her.

She stood looking out across the River Wear, taking great breaths of fresh air as though she needed to store them. When the others had gone up the semicircle of stone and in by the French windows at the front of the house, the quietness was pleasant, only the birds in the trees. Later they danced together at the ball that was held that evening in a huge hall at a nearby college. Gil danced with Helen, but she was so happy she couldn't speak. He asked Abby, but she refused.

'I'd rather chop my feet off,' she said. 'Why don't you go and ask your sister-in-law? You seem to like her well enough.'

'I suppose you're going to marry Robert Surtees.'

Gil couldn't believe he had said this, but they were far enough away from the music and other people so he didn't need to be discreet. She turned cold blue eyes on him.

'He hasn't asked, so it would be indelicate of me to say much other than that he's a gentleman and you're a stupid boy!' She turned with a swish of her skirts. Gil was angry. He went after her even when she ventured outside. Snow was starting to fall in big, dangerous flakes.

'That's not fair!' he said and, when she wouldn't stop, he got hold of her bare arm and pulled her around. 'I came to you.'

'To me? Oh yes, I remember. Sunday afternoon in the dene. You bothered to come into Newcastle to see me and then you ignored everything I said.'

'You say too much.'

'You love Helen.'

For months now, ever since the moment he had seen her, Gil had denied to himself that his regard for his sister-in-law was love. He had called it misguided, immature, inexperience, all number of things, but he had not called it love and he did not expect to hear it on anybody's lips, least of all from Abby. He tried to think. He tried to be truthful and the images of the warm country and the white room flooded into his head.

'It's – it's in the past,' he said.

'What past?' Abby laughed and her eyes glinted with fury. 'You haven't got a past, not that kind. I'm not blind. I saw you when you met her. I saw how you looked at her.'

'I recognised her.'

'From where?'

'I don't know.' Desperation got Gil further. 'Please, Abby, I do care about you. I have always—'

'No, you haven't. You've always ignored me.'

'I didn't know what to say, what to do. Give me a chance, please.'

'This is just because you can't have her. Do you think that's what I want? Some other woman's leavings? She could have had you if she had wanted, couldn't she? She didn't have to marry your brother.'

'She loves him.'

'Does she? Well, good luck to her. I'm glad it's not me, marrying a Collingwood.'

Abby remembered later the things that she had said to him and she thought that her mother would have been ashamed of her, but at the time it felt as though Gil deserved everything she threw at him. And she did throw it. Words were such horrible weapons and he was defenceless; he had always been defenceless in that way. She thought he was a product of a cruel upbringing. He had never learned to talk his way out of anything because he had always been physically hurt. He waited for the blows in that kind of situation, he expected them, and whereas if she had been a man he might have defended himself with his fists, he couldn't do it so he had nowhere to go.

'You're common. You're not a gentleman.' Robert and his friends and their company were to blame for this, Abby thought. It was true that Gil's grandfather had been a poor man, that his father had built a monstrosity of a house, that they cared for material things such as people of quality did not, but it wasn't something he could help. She threw insults at him and Gil begged and pleaded with her not to marry Robert. How scornful she was, how unforgiving. The worst part of all was that she loved him. She liked Robert well enough, she saw it all clearly, and she knew that marriage to him would be comfortable and easy because of his money and independence; but the young man in front of her was the person she always looked for when she walked into a room. All those evenings when they hadn't talked and hadn't danced didn't matter as long as he was there. When he wasn't there, every party was boring. He had nothing to recommend him: no breeding, no talents; he didn't even love her. She was to be his escape from a love which he could not have and she thought that she could not bear that he should want Helen more than he wanted her. Yet without him there seemed little point to anything. Her pride brought despair to his face.

'If you ever cared for me at all, don't leave me like this, please.'

Abby thought she would go to her grave hearing him say that and she told him airily, while the snow provided a white carpet, that she would marry Robert and he could go to hell. Which was, she thought later, exactly what he did.

People began to leave as the snow fell heavily, but all the Collingwoods had to do was walk up the hill towards the Harrison house, where they would spend the night. Helen and Edward were not having a holiday. He planned to take her to Paris in the spring.

'Besides, Toby and I are going to the Solway to shoot geese at the end of the month,' Edward had said.

Gil's room had a big fire and huge floor-to-ceiling bay windows which looked out over the darkness of the river where the castle and cathedral were outlined as gigantic shadows against the white sky. They frightened him, those buildings. Anything frightened him which could exist for hundreds of years when most men were dead at sixty. How many suffering souls had looked on those same walls and made no impression? For how many more generations would they stand while people died in a thousand different ways? Gil hated buildings that lasted. They should fall as men fell, it was only decent.

Helen and Edward had gone to bed. In a room across the hall, his brother was enjoying his first taste of a woman who did not belong to him. It was as though Helen committed adultery, except that no one else but him would know the wrong of it. He tortured himself thinking of her in his brother's arms while his memory, or his imagination, or some part of his mind, gave him her laughter and the happiness of them both and the child inside her, his child, the only one she had. He could feel her, taste her, yet his arms were empty and the longing hurt so much that he would have cried to ease it except that he couldn't.

The snow laid a heavy look on the night. The fire died slowly in the grate. He didn't go to bed. He stayed by the window, saw the night through and told himself that it would never be as bad as that again. His brother would have deflowered his bride by now and you couldn't do that twice.

Chapter Six

Abby had not been kissed before and didn't know what to expect, only that the timing was wrong. She was still upset about Gil. It was sweet enough, standing in a shop doorway with Robert, quite alone with him, and having him put his mouth on hers, but she kept thinking back to Gil and wishing she had said different things.

She and Robert had lingered on the walk to where they were staying with friends, dropped back from the others.

'I want to make you mine,' he said. 'Will you marry me, Abby?'

Her first instinct was panic and refusal, but she had known for some time that he had been leading up to a proposal; he would not have spent so much time with her or asked her to go with him to London.

'May I talk to your father about it?' he said.

Henderson, she knew, would be delighted. He had not thought about such things as an advantageous marriage but since it had happened, apparently of its own making, he could enjoy it. He didn't like Gil, Abby thought, but Robert was the son-in-law every man dreamed of. She thought that even her mother would have been pleased. The only criticism Henderson might have made, and he had not voiced it, would be that Robert knew nothing of industry and would be unlikely to want to take on the shipyard as Henderson got older. In a way, Abby could make this up by Robert's prosperity and position in society and also she could ease some of the hardships of her father's life both past and present. With her married and settled, his responsibility would cease and maybe then, she thought, he would consider his own life, feel less guilty about going out except to work, find a social life, even perhaps a wife. More than anything, Abby wished to free her father so that he could have some future. All the important things in his life seemed to be in the past.

The following day, which was Sunday, the Collingwood family travelled back to Newcastle in the evening. Edward had nothing to say. Both he and Helen were pale and Helen fell asleep in the carriage against Gil's shoulder. She was still asleep when they got home. Edward yawned as he got out of the carriage and, glancing back, said to Gil, 'Carry her, will you? I'm so damned tired and she'll fall over the step and break her neck if she has to walk.'

Gil carried her up the steps and over the threshold into the house. Almost awake by then, she thanked him in a small voice and went away to her room. His parents went to bed but Gil wasn't tired; he felt as if he would never want to sleep again. It was almost midnight when Edward, to Gil's surprise, came into the small sitting-room just as he had on so many nights before his marriage and poured brandy for them both. He sat down in the chair across the fire.

'You can come to the Solway with us,' he said.

'What?'

'Goose-shooting. Toby's going and Ralph Charlton. Come with us. It'll be fun. You don't get much fun.'

'I can't if you're not at the shipyard.'

'Father won't miss me. I do so little when I am there.'

'You have no feeling for it.'

Edward finished his brandy and went across and poured another. Gil hadn't touched his drink.

'Oh, I have plenty of feeling for it. I hate it almost as much as I hate him. The two are bound together so closely, how could I feel otherwise?'

'Is there something else you want to do?'

'Yes, I want to go to the Solway and shoot geese.'

'No, I meant—'

'I know what you meant,' Edward said and he sighed. 'When I was a child and did something wrong, he used to thrash me and I could smell the shipyard on him, that particular dirty smell, sweat and work and mud and water and grease.'

'The smell of the Tyne.'

'Docks and those disgusting hovels he keeps people in. Do you imagine he ever thinks about them?'

'No.'

'Do you think about them?'

'Sometimes.'

Edward downed his brandy.

'I knew you did. You're a good man, Gil.' And he yawned and wished his brother goodnight.

Gil managed to avoid the row, though even from his office he could hear his father's voice and then Edward's and at one point they were both equally as loud. Helen's fortune had been put to the company's use and it had been a huge sum of money. Money altered the balance of power, Gil thought. Edward had been given a big office next to his father's. He cared nothing for it and Gil had lingered there, admiring the view and wishing it was his. From it you could see, or imagine you could see, the extent of his father's domain.

There was a steelworks, an engineering works, a huge shipyard. There were blast furnaces, foundries, machine shops and chemical laboratories. The noise was tremendous from thousands of men performing skilled jobs. Enormous chimneys poured out smoke; ships were on the water; ships were being built; men scurried everywhere and Gil knew that beyond it all, his father had had the great gates repainted at the entrance to the shipyard. They proclaimed: 'Wm. Collingwood & Sons'.

They had begun with iron, now it was steel ships, warships, battleships for various navies from China to Spain, and oil tankers. On the wall of his father's office was a portrait of a man called John Rogerson, the owner of the *Mary Rogerson*, the first ship, they believed, to take crude petroleum in barrels from America to London. Anything could be done; anything could be achieved.

The noise suddenly increased as the door was flung open and his father strode down the corridor and came into Gil's tiny office.

'I suppose you're going as well, are you?'

'Don't start on him!' Edward said, following him in.

Gil didn't think he had ever seen his brother so angry.

'Well, are you?' His father, Gil reflected, didn't frighten him any more. He hadn't realised.

'No, I'm not.'

'He doesn't want to shoot the ickle-wickle geese,' Edward teased him.

William threw Edward a black look.

'You're idle, idle and good for nothing!' He slammed the door on his way out. Edward pulled a face.

'Freedom!' he said. 'Nothing but me and the geese.'

Gil had imagined that the weather would be so bad that they wouldn't go anywhere, but Helen wanted to shop and for some reason she asked him to go with her, so he went. It was a perfect day. She wanted to try on various dresses. Gil felt that his mother would have been more use, but he quite enjoyed it, sitting on a chair while she came out wearing each one, asking him what he thought. The truth was that she looked lovely in them all, though he managed to persuade her not to buy a bright pink creation with feathers. It was easy. All he had to say was, 'I don't think Edward would care for that' and her face would fall.

They went out for tea. They spent an hour in an art gallery looking at various portraits of Grace Darling who had, with her father, gone out in a coble to rescue people from the ship foundering on the rocks. Gil could remember his grandfather telling him about it. There were other paintings of Tynemouth and local people and places. It was a cold, dry day and lots of people were about. Musicians played on the street corners and families gathered in cafés to drink tea. Helen ate cake, drank her tea and went home laden with parcels. In the evening she wore one of her new dresses and they stayed up until late. Gil was happier with her than he could be with anyone else.

She was so excited on the day that Edward came home. She couldn't rest and kept going to the window to look for the carriage. He was late and it was dark and cold, but she ran down the steps in greeting, her eyes bright with tears. She didn't leave Edward's side that evening until he asked her to play the piano and then she kept looking across at him and smiling.

'How many new dresses did you let her buy?' he asked.

She went to bed, but Edward lingered for a while and Gil stayed downstairs after that, enjoying the night and the fire. Then a white figure appeared soundlessly from behind him.

'My God!' he said. 'I thought you were a ghost.'

'Is Edward not here?'

'No, he went up ages since.' Gil stood up and he saw that she did not even have a dressing-gown or slippers.

A tear fell and then another and several more followed quickly. Gil stared.

'Helen?'

She backed as he moved towards her.

'Very silly,' she said, 'excuse me.' And she ran away.

* * *

Robert saw Abby's father, but it was a brief interview. Her father came out of the study looking like a short fat sunbeam and Abby was pleased to see that he looked happier than she had seen him look in years.

'I only wish your mother was here,' he said.

Her mother could not have fully approved of Robert, Abby knew, but she smiled and enjoyed her father's pride and pleasure. Her mother liked people to work.

'I don't mind admitting to you,' her father said later, 'that I thought you had a hankering for young Collingwood and in all conscience I couldn't have given you to him.'

Abby had seen Gil that day in town with Helen and they had looked so happy. They looked right together, it was strange. They were laughing and she had hold of his arm. They had stopped to look in the jeweller's on the corner of Pilgrim Street and Abby dodged back into New Bridge Street to keep out of their way. Gil would never care for anybody but Helen and she had been right to agree to marry Robert. They would be happy.

Robert wanted to be married straightaway and she could see no reason why they should not be. There were arrangements to be made but he, having no parents, cared nothing for a big wedding and she, knowing Henderson's hatred of weddings, cared nothing for it either, so they set the date for around Easter and made plans. He would have bought her the whole of Newcastle had she let him, stripped his house and had her refurbish it, turned all the flowers in the gardens to roses since she loved them and toured around the world so that she could see every wonder on God's earth. Abby did not want to go away for too long. It would be hard enough for her father, she knew, to lose her from his house so that he came home to no one but the servants. To leave the country for any length of time would be too much. He disabused her of this idea.

'Abby, I had my youth, I had my marriage and I was lucky, for your mother loved such a fool of a man as I was. This is your turn. Go away for as long as you like. I'm happy for you. I couldn't be more pleased. Have this time and enjoy it. It may not last long if there are to be children.'

'Would you be pleased?'

'Everything about you pleases your old father.'

Robert would take her to Paris, Rome, Florence, Venice and anywhere else that she wanted to go.

'We could spend the whole spring and summer away. We'll start in London and go on from there and you'll see the house and I'll introduce you to all kinds of people and you'll like the shops and the theatres and everything.'

Abby had not thought much about being away from home, but now the idea appealed to her. She couldn't wait to get away.

Rhoda had stayed with her until after Christmas and Abby wrote to ask if she would be a bridesmaid and to tell her about the wedding, to ask if she would help to choose the dresses and the flowers and when could she come and stay again because there was much to plan and do. Rhoda replied immediately that she would be glad to come and stay, for there was now a new baby in the house, a girl. The baby rarely slept; her mother and Jos quarrelled continually; there was no peace. Abby wrote back to say that she could come and stay for as long as she liked; she would be glad of the company. Robert, she told him, ought to find someone of their acquaintance so that they could make up a foursome when they went out.

He looked at her.

'Rhoda Carlisle? I didn't realise that you were so close.'

'She stayed with me at Christmas, Robert.'

'I thought that you were sorry for her.'

'She's a very nice girl.'

'Forgive me, she's a country bumpkin.'

'She is not!'

'She knows nothing and she's strange. She goes walking up on the fells alone. She has a thick dales accent and she's very odd. She even had to borrow a dress from you, as I recall you saying, for Helen and Edward's wedding. No, I don't think so, Abby.'

'Her father left her a great deal of money.'

'Don't be vulgar.'

'I'm not sure I'm the one who's vulgar here.'

It was their first quarrel, Abby realised, watching his face go white while he restrained his temper. Here in her father's house in the sitting-room, where Kate and Mrs Wilkins would hear them, they were fighting, but she was upset to think that not only did he not like Rhoda but he was ungentlemanly enough to say so.

'I have asked her to be my bridesmaid.'

'Then let us hope you have so many that no one will notice her.'

'I wasn't planning to have more than one.'

'Perhaps after we are married you will choose your friends more carefully. Between Rhoda Carlisle and Gillan Collingwood, you have nothing to offer.'

Abby was suddenly furious.

'There's nothing wrong with Gil.'

'Everything is wrong with him,' Robert said roundly. 'Not least that every time he's in a room with you, he doesn't take his eyes off you.'

Abby wanted to faint for the first time in her life. She put one hand on the chair arm.

'He does not!' she said.

'He watches you dance.' Robert laughed. 'It's pathetic,' he said. 'He doesn't have the wit or the manners to ask you to dance, he just stands there. Don't tell me you didn't notice the poor boy was lovesick for you. Haven't you ever noticed him hovering? Can he speak, or is he really as stupid as he appears? You really weren't aware of him?'

Abby's hands shook when she and Robert had tea a few minutes later. She couldn't trust herself to pick up a cup and saucer. The cake which Mrs Wilkins had made so carefully and so lightly stuck in her throat.

* * *

February was a long cold month and March was worse somehow, perhaps, Gil thought, because you looked for it to be better and it was not. He was only happy at work and even then it was difficult. His father and Edward quarrelled frequently and though it was not in front of him, the atmosphere suffered both at home and at work. It was a curious thing to find his father at odds with Edward and in harmony with him and, although Gil didn't like it, somehow it favoured him. He took to his old habit of hiding in Mr Philips' office and his father at long last realised what was going on and called Gil in.

The room was full of light that day. It was late March and the evenings were beginning to lengthen noticeably. His father had big windows in his office, so what light there was always benefited the room. Plans and designs were spread the length and breadth of the huge desk. As Gil walked into the room, his father looked up and then he smiled. Gil could not remember that having happened before and knew that for once he had succeeded in pleasing William.

'I wondered whose hand this was that I could see here. I knew it wasn't mine and I know my men too well to mistake them. They're bright lads, some of them, but not at this level.' He looked hard at Gil. 'Old men make good judges, but young men make good designers. I'm a good businessman, but I was never a good designer. I remember looking through some papers of my father's once and realising that if he had had ambition, he could have held the whole world. How ambitious are you, Gil?'

At last William had called him by his name. Gil hardly dared speak.

'I want to build the best ships the world has ever seen.'

William clenched his fist.

'The best?'

'The biggest, the fastest, the most beautiful.'

William's eyes danced with pleasure.

'All right then,' he said, 'you will and we will find the business, sell the ideas, get the contracts. We will build this company into something the world will never forget.' He came forward and clapped Gil on the back.

It was the happiest day of Gil's life. He worked late and then he went home with his father. The next day his father gave him an office which was so big it was scary. It had in it a huge turkey rug and was all brass and mahogany. He installed Mr Philips and several other people whom Gil had requested in the offices next to it, so that it was as if Gil had his own section of the works, and he had Gil's name put on the door in bold black letters.

'Well, well,' Edward said. 'What's this?'

Gil wanted him to be pleased, but he could tell that Edward wasn't. Edward walked around Gil's new office and said nothing.

Gil was almost sorry that his father had recognised his ability. He had enjoyed the brief time of having Edward's affection. He had liked being part of the magic circle of Edward's friends, the billiard hall, the bars. He had liked the way that he was accepted as Edward's brother. Now Edward was going to put him back out into the cold and Gil felt as though his new-found status at work was a very high price to pay.

'Father admires you,' he said thinly.

'I don't think he does.'

'He told me so. He thinks you have – what is that word – flair. You. When did you ever show any true ability for anything? Now, however, you have blossomed. That's what we must call you from now on – Blossom. Toby will approve. He loves flowers. What kind of a flower do you think you are?'

'Shut up!' Gil said.

'I wish you well. You can have the whole bloody thing as far as I'm concerned. I hate every last stone of it!' Edward strode out of the office. He did not come back to dinner, nor did he return later. Helen had been out buying new clothes again and Gil was called upon to admire her dress. His father said that he thought Helen had enough dresses to wear a different one every day of the month by now.

Helen had started to drink wine with her dinner. Although

William didn't approve of women drinking he said nothing to one glass, but of late she had had two. Tonight she had three and stumbled when she left the table. Gil was standing beside her and hoped that he had obscured his father's view but, left alone with his father and the port, he knew that William, pouring from the decanter, had seen what happened.

'I don't approve of men going out every night like this,' he said now. 'Damn it, the lass is still a bride. Where is he?'

'I don't know.'

'You go with him, don't you? Women, is it?'

'Billiards.'

His father laughed.

'Is that all? Have a drink.'

Gil drank some port, but slowly.

'Women shouldn't drink,' his father said. 'It's bad enough that men do it.'

Gil thought it was ironic that, having lost Edward's company and confidences, he should move on to his father. They dined in the small dining-room unless they had company and he liked it. It had two big fires and was warm and it was close to the kitchen so the food was always as hot as it should be. His mother loved candles and it was all silver and white and, since neither of his parents cared anything for economy, it was lit with a hundred dancing flames which softened the features on older people and enhanced those on younger. He could hear Helen playing the wistful tunes of Mozart on the piano in the room next door and outside was the peace of the Northumberland countryside. He had never before relaxed in his father's presence, but he did so now.

'The lass plays well, even after too much wine. I did see.'

'I know.'

'No, you didn't, you thought to hide her. It's a fine thing is chivalry, even if she doesn't deserve it.'

'I thought she did.'

'Aye, mebbe. Hasn't turned out to be much of a husband, has

he? Still, neither do most men. Do you think you will? I thought you might have had Reed's little lass, but I see she's to wed young Surtees. I wish her joy of it. His father was useless and his mother was worse. What about Rhoda? I like the lass. She's got eyes like fell water – bonny. Her father was a strange one but good company and clever and he left her a deal of money. What do you think?'

'I don't know,' Gil said, taken aback.

'Well, don't leave it too long. She looks ripe to me.' And his father finished his port and went off to the study, doubtless to move on to the brandy, Gil thought.

Helen cried when she went to bed. Gil couldn't hear or see her, but somehow he knew. And why should she not, he thought honestly. After that first night, Edward had had no regard for her, treated her as though she was unimportant to him and all the dresses and all the wine in the world would not make up for that. He no longer went out riding with her; he took her out as little as possible; he took no pleasure in her company that Gil could see and often, as tonight, he did not come home. Gil knew, because he waited up for him.

When he went to bed at one he could not pass her door without opening it. He wanted to make sure that she was well, he told himself. She was asleep and it was not surprising. The room smelled strongly of brandy and there was a decanter a third empty and a glass, well-fingered. She slept heavily; he could hear her breathing. He was tormented with the idea that, being unused to spirit, she would lie on her back and vomit and choke. He told himself that he was stupid, but he couldn't leave her. So as the fire died and the room darkened, he kept alight a candle and stayed there, watching at the window from time to time in case his brother should think fit to come home. He tried to will him there. He tried to go back to where they had been during the short time when he had basked in the sun of his brother's love.

He wanted that again so much. He conjured up the billiard hall, red and gold, and the laughter of the young men and their carelessness. Edward wanted the sunlight for himself alone. He wanted Gil in the shadows behind him and now, in the dark depths of the unforgiving night, Gil wanted that too. I would have stayed there, he thought, to have you like me.

Helen stirred in her sleep. Gil went over and tucked in the blankets around her. The night was cold, but if he fastened the shutters he could see neither the room nor the driveway outside. Her hair was braided but her features were slack with drunkenness and her breathing was all brandy. Gil took the glass her lips had touched, poured a brandy for himself, sat down halfway between the window and the bed and saw the night through. He dozed a little and when he awoke, red was streaking the sky. When he got up, he could see the snowdrops in the front garden which had blossomed within the last few days. Spring was coming to the Tyne valley. It was always late, but he loved it the more for that. The waiting was worthwhile.

Edward did not come home. Gil left Helen's room when the streaks of light showed through the sky. She was not sleeping so heavily then, though he could imagine the headache and the sickness that she would have when she awoke.

He went off to work and was busy there all day, doing what he had always wanted to do, so that he forgot about her. When he got home she was pale and listless, ate little at dinner, drank nothing and afterwards didn't attempt to play the piano. Then Edward came home. He had tickets for the theatre that Saturday evening. She was at once a different person, smiling and lively. She clapped her hands and became excited. Edward offered to play a card game with her and she agreed. They went off to bed together early but later, when his parents had long gone up and Gil was trying to talk himself into making his way up the stairs rather than falling asleep on the sofa by the fire, she came down. The servants had gone to bed and Gil found her clattering about in the kitchen by the poor light of one candle.

'The brandy's in the sitting-room,' he said behind her. She jumped and turned and the candle hovered dangerously.

He lit the nearest lamp and saw by its glow Helen in a long white cotton wrap, wide sleeves lace-edged and pearl buttons from neck to toe. She looked so small in the huge space of the cook's domain.

'I didn't come for brandy.'

'I should think not, after last night. Don't you feel ill?'

'What do you know about it?' she said.

'Why don't you go to bed?'

'I don't want to. It's silent there and the night is so black and—'

'I'll take you up.'

'I'm not a child.'

'Come on.'

He put out the light, lit another candle in the hall and led her up the stairs by the hand. In her room, half a dozen candles burned and the fire was almost out. Gil put some wood onto the fire to make a pyramid and it began to burn. He secured the shutters over the windows and pulled the curtains tightly across.

'Your maid is supposed to do that.'

'I didn't want her to. It makes me feel closed in.'

'It's too cold for anything else,' Gil said. 'Aren't you going to get into bed?'

'With you here? Hardly.'

'Go on, I'll tuck you in.'

He did so, but he knew that tears were close.

'It'll be all right tomorrow,' he said.

Helen shook her head. She looked woodenly at him for a few seconds and then turned away. She began to cry, silently and without moving. The room was changing. Gil couldn't help but notice it and was glad that he had not been drinking heavily, or he would have blamed it on alcohol. It seemed to him that the few candles gave out the light and flame of fifty and that the fire became amazingly hot so that it warmed the whole room. The night was well shut out, but the curtains seemed thin like muslin. From somewhere behind them came the faint breeze of an early summer night with the air gentle such as at the onset of the new season. The walls were coloured golden from all the flickering flames and the shadows were large upon the walls from the fire.

'Don't cry,' Gil said, hoping his voice would bring normality back.

'I'm not crying,' she said and to prove it she turned over towards him. It was as though someone else offered the tears because she gave no indication of them. Her face did not tremble; her nose did not run. The tears, unaided and unacknowledged, poured down her cheeks as though somebody was standing with a bucket behind her eyes and she was just some vessel through which they were going. She didn't sob and her throat didn't work; only her hands gave her away. Her fingers closed on the bedcovers and clenched there.

Gil was sitting on the bed. He took hold of her frozen fingers and rubbed them to put warmth back into them. She sat up and smiled at him and the room was all white, just as he had seen it in his mind a hundred times since they had met. Could you recognise the future like that? He had thought it was the past. Where was it? If things had already been arranged, if fate was there, then her marriage to Edward had been threatened from long before. Perhaps his brother had not stood a chance because time was mixed. The past and the future were more powerful together than the present, which was all Edward had had to offer.

It was just as he had known. His recognition of her had been right. They knew one another well. Gil had never been with a woman, but her body was not new to him and half the delight was in touching her again, in having her back from whatever distance they had come to be together. After the first kiss he could not have left her, even if his life and the lives of half the world had depended upon it. He had been lonely for her for years, waited for her for decades, mourned her loss, dreamed her presence, seen her in the distance a thousand times, wished that other women had her face, her body, her voice, her laughter. She had never been another man's wife. She was his and she came to him confidently, surely. In his mind it was summer in whatever warm country they belonged to. The very stones of the house were bleached by the sun.

She came to him naked, joyful, greedy, as though she, too, had waited from a long way off, as if distance was a prison and she had escaped. Her body was warm and soft and her hair became loose from the tight braids which usually held it. She was not crying, she was not speaking, yet her voice was full of love.

He had wanted her for so long and nothing could stop them from being together. It was like a fight, a struggle to be near and, though all the demons of hell should try to stop it, nothing could. Each kiss was better and each caress brought her body nearer, until near was not sufficient. He thought the light flickered, even the shadows retreated and beyond, he knew for a split second, was the clarity that told him it was a Northumberland winter's night. He felt the hesitation on her, a second's resistance. Her body fought and then yielded. All the devils in hell screamed and Gil knew triumph. She was his. It was meant to be and nothing could alter his possession of her. You could not go back from there; it could not be undone; it was too late. She gave a cry and he knew it for pain. The winter wind howled beyond the window. The room was cool and the dying flames of the fire threw twisted shadows upon the walls. The bed was a tormented mess of sheets and blankets, and Helen lay sobbing, half clinging and half resisting. He didn't let go of her, not until it was over, not until her hands released him and her body drew back and then he stopped and left her.

In the candlelight with the bedclothes thrown back, on the white sheets there was blood, enough for him to recognise what it was, sufficient for him to stare. She was turned away from him as though ashamed and crying softly.

'Helen?' His voice sounded hoarse, as though it didn't get much use. She turned further away and tried to get in among the blankets, to pull them up to cover her body. He hauled them out of her hands and dragged her back to him. She protested and fought and he put her down so that she should look at him. She closed her eyes and turned her head away, but he waited.

'Helen?'

Resigned, she opened her eyes, though she still didn't turn her head or look at him.

'What?' she said with a hint of impatience.

'Tell me that was not the first time.'

She closed her eyes again, but only for a second and then she said, 'What would be the use?' Her voice was tired, almost hoarse, as if she had spent hours shouting and fighting and had no more to offer.

'Why?'

She smiled. She changed in that instant. She was not the person that he had thought, the pretty empty-headed girl. She was not as he had seen her.

'Do you know how I spent my wedding night? Alone. I spend all my nights alone.'

'I don't understand.'

'He doesn't love me.'

'If he hadn't loved you he wouldn't have married you.'

'He's afraid of your father. He married me because your father wanted my money.'

'No.'

She looked at him clearly.

'But you love me, I know you do. You loved me the moment you saw me and I knew you wouldn't hurt me.'

'I just did.'

'Oh, that.' She stretched like a well-fed cat. 'That was divine. If you knew how I've ached for you.'

Gil covered her body in kisses and caresses. She tasted like rich fruit, like peaches and she felt so soft. He hadn't realised that a woman would be quite so soft, all rounded and warm. He found that he could make her body lift for him, that he could make her desire him just as much as he desired her. He could make the tips of her breasts harden under his tongue and have small noises of need make their way past her lips. It was wonderful. Best of all were her eyes. When she opened them it was as if someone had lit a candle there, for they were blue shine. He felt as though he had discovered the perfect secret, the greatest pleasure. Her tongue was so pink and her teeth were so white and he felt as if he could do anything now. He had the whole world there in bed. Nothing else mattered. He thought that he would never be lonely again.

Chapter Seven

Edward came to Gil in his office in the middle of the following morning and said, 'I'm playing billiards with Toby and the others tonight. Do you want to come?'

Gil didn't know what to say. He couldn't look at him. Edward came further into the office and closed the door.

'I didn't mean the things I said to you. I'm not jealous, really I'm not, but I wanted to please the old man too and I can't, no matter what I do, whereas you seem to be able to do it all the time.'

Gil was too ashamed of himself, too guilty and wretched to speak.

'I thought I might taken Helen to Venice in May, try to make up for things. What do you think?'

'I'm sure she'd like that.' Gil was amazed at how calm his voice was. Could he be a natural liar?

'I'll surprise her. So, are we playing billiards tonight?'

Gil couldn't think of an adequate reason to say no.

Every minute hurt that evening, watching Edward walk around the billiard table. It had been a wretched day. Gil couldn't work. His mind replayed his seduction of his brother's chaste wife with himself cast as the villain. The billiard hall had been a haven, now it was just another place. Edward had not changed. He smiled across and asked for advice and Gil tried to be the same. Toby was full of talk about his garden, the containers in which he had planted bulbs which were flowering and the flowers which he was growing from seed on the window ledges of his white house.

'There'll be roses and I'm going to have a lavender hedge at either side of the path so that when people brush against it there will be an exquisite perfume. Do you know you have eyes that change colour?'

Gil looked at him, startled.

'In the evenings they're almost black; during the day they look like sherry. Curious.'

The room felt airless to Gil, even more so than usual. He made an excuse and went outside. After a few minutes Edward followed him. The Newcastle night was full of sounds and the pub opposite threw orange light across the pavement. He heard Edward and moved away. There was a bridge not far and they walked there and listened to the water as it made its way down to Tynemouth and out into the North Sea. Further on were the docks and the shipyard where their father had made his fortune.

'When I left Oxford I swore to myself I wouldn't come back here,' Edward said, leaning over the bridge and scowling into the dark water.

'So why did you?'

'I can't help it. I've tried to leave, but every time the train pulls out of Newcastle station my bloody stupid heart breaks. I don't know how to go. I want to but I can't. If I was born a thousand times, it would always be here, Tynedale, or Tyneside and Bamburgh beach. It belongs to me. When I was at Oxford I used to wake up in the night because I thought I could hear the pipes.'

Gil didn't want to go back inside and either Edward didn't want to or he understood that Gil didn't, because they took the last train home. The stars were bright and Edward sang local songs as they walked from the station.

Gil had half-imagined that Helen would be waiting in his

room and dreaded it, but she was not and everything was silent. He made excuses to himself, said that it had only been once, swore that it would never happen again. Edward would take Helen to Venice and things would get better. He fell asleep thinking of this, so tired that he could think no more.

All that week Helen was smiling and bright, even though Edward went out each night and stayed out on the Saturday. Gil's hopes began to lift. He had made a mistake. Everybody was allowed a mistake. He didn't think of her all the time; he didn't even want her.

On the Saturday night when it was late, therefore, it could not possibly have been that when he passed her room to go to bed he opened the door and went inside and closed and locked it. There were candles and there was a fire and he had not even the excuse that everything changed, because it didn't. And she had not gone to him and she was not crying. Anyone else would have thought she was reading. There was a book open beside her and a glass of wine untouched on the table by the bed. She watched him lock the door and come to her and he knew then that she had been expecting him. Her hair was loose and brushed and shining gold and she wore a nightdress that showed off her arms and shoulders and breasts and it had buttons conveniently placed down the front. Gil sighed and sat down on the bed.

'How did you know?' he said.

'I've waited every night.'

She leaned forward and kissed him, friendly and sweet. That was when Gil realised that the moment you think you have conquered an enemy, all is lost. He had thought he could make his mistake and go back to where he was before and it was not so. He had thought he was strong, that he didn't want her. That was laughable now. He had not thought that he would betray his brother a second time, but then he had not thought that he would betray his brother the first time. He was not the person he had hoped to be. All he wanted, or would ever want, was her. She got out of bed and kissed and kissed him like somebody starving and held him and begged and started to pull his clothes off until Gil helped. He couldn't understand how he had managed to keep away from her all that week. The part of his mind that knew this was wrong was deliciously employed like a parent, telling him what an evil person he was. He was pleased to show it how bad he could be, putting her down and taking her like she was a whore without kisses or caresses, then cradling her in his arms and giving her wine and laughing and telling her all the things that he had not been able to say the first time.

The wind got up outside and they threw back the curtains to watch the stars in the clear night, which seemed bigger and nearer and twinkled on and off as if in entertainment while the candles guttered and the fire died and Gil wished that the morning would never come. She was so wonderful, she was so beautiful and he knew that she loved him, that she had always loved him, was born to love him. She was nothing to do with Edward, or anyone else, so it didn't matter that she had married him. They talked about silly things and when the fire was out and the candles were gone and there was no light from the windows so the last vestiges of respectability were finished, in the complete blackness they made love and Gil knew that she had never belonged to anybody but him and that she never would. The responsibility was strange. Finally she slept and he listened to her breathing and knew then that neither of them would ever die. He acknowledged that it was all stars and folly, but it was all there ever would be and he would have given up the rest of his life for the sake of these few hours with her.

Chapter Eight

Abby's wedding to Robert Surtees was not as she had thought it would be. It was almost as though someone else was marrying him. His family, and especially Charlotte, took over. She had to have half a dozen bridesmaids; there had to be five hundred guests. Robert, as Charlotte pointed out frequently, was the most eligible batchelor in the county and therefore certain standards had to be met. Abby wanted to deny it all, wear an old dress, run away, but for his sake she went through with it. If they had loved one another differently she would have suggested they should elope, but he was important and she was not, so she meekly accepted his cousins and friends to attend her on the day and all the ideas that the women of his family could devise. Later, she swore to herself, it would be different.

It was May, the best time of year to be married, with all the flowers out. Her father was so pleased. The wedding breakfast was to be held at Robert's house since it could accommodate all the guests and the fine bright day meant that people walked in the gardens and sat about, talking. Rhoda was her chief bridesmaid. The Collingwoods were all at the wedding, though Helen looked pale.

Edward had started coming home at night, though nobody knew why, and Helen had become nervous. Gil was already worried and would have kept from her had he known how to. Each day he swore to himself that he would not go to her and each night he went; but on the first night that Edward came home to dinner, Helen drew Gil aside after dinner and without looking at him said, 'It must stop.'

'I can't stop, I don't know how.'

He drew her into a darkened room along the wide main hall of the house and began to kiss her.

'We could leave. We could go away—'

'He came to my bed.'

'What?'

In the darkness Gil could see nothing.

'He came to my bed. He's my husband.'

'When?'

She didn't reply.

'When, Helen?'

'I don't want to talk about this any more.' She wrenched away, tore from the room and when he followed her she was sitting close beside Edward by the fire in the drawing-room.

Gil couldn't eat or sleep or work. As far as he could judge, Edward bedded his wife nightly and she made no objection. William began shouting at Gil in the office. Gil thought of various wild schemes and dismissed them, but he admitted to himself after days and days of denying it that Helen did not, in spite of what she had said to him when they were together, love him. Her eyes lit when she saw her husband in a way in which they had not done for him even at the height of passion. He counted for nothing. When his brother was present, she didn't notice him.

On the day of the wedding she didn't leave her husband's side. They moved around together, talking and laughing with everyone, her hand through his arm. Edward looked so happy. Toby stood and watched them too and he came to Gil.

'How are you, dear boy?' he said.

'How's your garden?' Gil asked him.

'I could fill it with black tulips,' Toby said.

Gil became more and more miserable. Helen didn't look at him; Abby didn't speak to him and later when there was dancing, Rhoda refused. Her mother and stepfather were there and her brothers, including the small one, her stepfather's child, who tugged at her skirts for attention. Gil felt like doing the same.

Abby had once as a child had a pot doll dressed like a bride. It could not be played with because it was in white and would get dirty. It sat in a glass case, untouched and useless. That was how she felt on her wedding day, something to be looked at and not touched.

She had missed Rhoda. There had been no one to whom she could confide her doubts and fears, the way she didn't like certain members of Robert's family. She liked to listen to Rhoda's problems, too, but this time Rhoda had come with her family and would go back with them. She seemed different, less approachable and had nothing to say. Even though Abby's thoughts were caught up in her wedding, she was shocked to see how thin Rhoda had become. Rhoda excused herself by saying that she had not been well, but she was silent. Abby wondered whether she was slightly envious because she wished that she could get away from her mother and stepfather and her life in Allendale Town. Rhoda seemed more unhappy than ever and there was little Abby could do. She resolved to have her stay for a long time when they came home again.

Abby endured the day well enough, speaking to everyone, smiling all the time, finally escaping into the garden when everyone was dancing. She could not bear another silly remark about her marriage. It was still light, though a star peeped through. She walked in the cool silence and it was such a relief, until she came to a big pond in the middle of the garden and found Gil by himself. He, too, had lost weight. He glanced at her and then down.

'You look—'

'Like something off a Christmas tree. I know. I had a doll

who looked like this. She was called Ethel and her underwear was stitched to her dress.'

She waited for Gil to laugh or at least smile.

'We're going away,' she said to fill the gap. She felt a wave of homesickness and she had not set off yet. 'We're going to Paris and Rome and Venice. We might see Helen and Edward.'

In the quietness Abby's mind replayed accurately the way that she had refused Gil and how Robert had told her Gil watched her when she danced. Robert had been right. Gil had no graces, no conversation. He didn't even look at her. He ought to have wished her well, basic manners decreed it. From the ballroom, Abby could hear the musicians strike up a waltz.

'I must get back,' she said and picked up her skirts and ran across the lawn towards the door.

Gil walked around outside for a long while and then back towards the house. At the side of the house in the shadows, he could see Rhoda and a man. She was obvious because of her bridesmaid's dress: they were all alike, pale blue. She was standing against the wall. The man with her had one hand on the wall as though he was somehow holding her there, though he was not. As Gil drew nearer, he saw that it was Jos Allsop. Rhoda looked distressed as far as Gil could judge, her body drawn back against the wall as far as it could be. Jos was speaking to her in low, soft tones. Gil's feet crunched on the gravel and Jos turned around, quickly taking his hand away from the wall. Gil didn't know what made him say it, but when Allsop challenged him with a rude, 'What do you want?' he said, 'Rhoda promised to dance with me.'

'She's changed her mind.'

'I haven't.' Rhoda looked up bravely, though her voice trembled. Allsop cursed and walked away. Gil couldn't understand why he was concerned about her. She didn't matter to him. She was trembling and kept glancing past him fearfully as though her stepfather might come back. She looked like someone who wanted to run far away, a creature who longed for the cold dark moorland and obscurity. The bleakness of her situation struck Gil as much the same as the way he felt. He put her hand through his arm and walked her slowly back inside. They stayed together. Gil needed the support. Rhoda was like a wall between himself and the other people who were there. He was not flattered. If she left him she would have to go back to her mother and stepfather and, he realised, anything was better than that. They danced twice and when he went to get Rhoda a drink, his father came to him and clapped him on the back.

'Her father left a tidy sum, lad, and if she's happy at home then I'm a Dutchman,' he said.

Abby had not worried about her wedding night. Her mother had talked openly to her about such things.

'Men are not gods. If they had been, they wouldn't have such ridiculous bodies which can provide such intense pleasure. Be kind when you marry and generous in bed and with luck you'll enjoy yourself.'

Abby did enjoy herself and was glad that her mother had given her permission to do so. Abby had no one to compare with Robert, but for sheer enthusiasm and joy he was impossible to fault. He quite clearly adored her. She did think he very possibly had been to bed with a number of other women as rich young men were inclined to. He made her laugh, which was a good start. They had champagne and Abby was more certain than ever before that she had made the right choice. He was kind and helpful and didn't embarrass or upset her. She was so pleased at her decision to marry him and could not help thinking of what Gil would have been like – clumsy, most probably, because he would know nothing of women – but her heart thudded that she had even thought of him. Abby wished she could be sure that he was all right because he hadn't looked it that day and she was partly to blame. She wondered what he was doing now and she thought of Venice. They would be there, the four of them, among the wonderful buildings and churches and he would be at work in Newcastle without anybody.

Waking up in bed with another person was a pleasant surprise. They set off for London the next day and Abby tried not to look back, thinking of her father. He had assured and reassured her but, since he had not been without her before, Abby did worry.

The Mayfair house was huge and terrified her, but she had to do nothing so the terror passed. The housekeeper there was used to running everything and, though she was polite and discussed menus and guests with Abby, everything ran smoothly without any assistance from her and she was relieved. All she had to do was be the hostess at her first big party, be advised by her personal maid what to wear, and smile and chat to all Robert's friends. This, Abby conceded, was not difficult.

A life of pleasure was something she had not had before and it was strange. There were parties, at least one every night, and concerts and plays and different people to meet. Being up most of the night, it would be lunchtime when Abby rose. There would be visiting; either people would come to her or she would go to them and after a while she began to recognise everyone.

They went to Paris several weeks later, but in a way it was similar to London because most of the same people were there. She liked the new sights and the warm afternoons. They stayed for so long that Robert said Venice was not the place to go next, it would be too hot and smelly, so they went to Florence and there again were people she knew. Abby would have liked to go off and explore Florence alone, but she was not allowed to do so, other people declaring that it was not safe, so she had to endure their constant chatter all day. If she picked up a book she was almost bound to be interrupted and she discovered it was not the done thing to read.

'Are you bookish?' she was asked more than once.

Robert seemed happy to stay in Italy or in France and when they finally made their way back home he was reluctant to go any further north than London. Abby felt that it would have been churlish to have insisted. They were together constantly, but he didn't always come to her bed and Abby found that she was quite glad of the quietness, since she was now rarely alone. He put her first in everything. He loved to see her in new dresses; he bought her expensive jewellery; they went to parties together. Other men went out without their wives and Abby was pleased when he began to do so occasionally; people had teased her that he loved her so much he couldn't bear to be out of her sight.

Before the winter began, Abby had a dream. She dreamed that Gil was a child again and that his father was turning him out of the house. She dreamed this two nights running. On the third night she thought that she was standing on the beach below the castle at Bamburgh. It was snowing and he was calling her and she couldn't see him through the snow.

Abby dreaded going to sleep and would lie awake during the quiet – at least comparatively quiet – hours of the London night and try not to wish herself in Newcastle. She had nothing to complain about other than that she missed her father and longed to see him. Robert complained that she had nothing to say. She caught a cold, developed a bad cough, became reluctant to see other people and was always tired. All during the first dark days of the winter she thought about her mother and about her father all alone and finally she went to Robert.

'I must go home for Christmas,' she said and he sighed and kissed her and reluctantly agreed.

It was William's idea that Rhoda should stay. At first Gil resented his father's high handedness but, while Edward and Helen were away in Venice, it was pleasant to come home and find somebody there. Rhoda was the least demanding person he knew. She would go walking alone, but he could go with her if he chose. She loved riding and didn't ask for company, though if he suggested they should go out together she seemed glad of the company. She was happy reading in the evenings, but loved the theatre. She was quiet in company, but she would talk to him when they were alone. Helen and Edward were gone three months and during that time Rhoda came to stay twice. Both times she looked so happy to come and so miserable when she had to leave that the second time Charlotte persuaded her to stay longer, so when Edward and Helen finally returned Rhoda was still there.

On that first evening, Helen drew Gil aside in the hall and said, 'What is Rhoda Carlisle doing?'

'What?'

'Do you love her?'

'I don't see what it is to do with you.'

'You belong to me!'

She said it so loudly that Gil look around in alarm, but there was no one near. Recklessly, she put one hand into his hair and began to kiss him. Gil did not remember a kiss having tasted better. He wanted to stop her, but he couldn't. He drew her into the nearest empty room, a sitting-room, and there he said to her, 'I don't belong to you nor you to me.'

'I missed you. Venice is a place for lovers.'

'You love Edward.'

'He doesn't love me.'

'He's your husband,' Gil said flatly, 'and he beds you, isn't that right?'

'He does his duty.' Her words sounded so bitter and she stumbled over the next ones. 'You may as well know now – I'm having a child.'

'A child?'

'Edward's child. For all his . . . lack of interest, he managed that.'

'Well then.'

'I miss you so much. I kept thinking what it would have been like there with you. It would have been heaven. Do you still love me?'

'There's no good in my loving you.'

'But do you?'

'You know I do. I always will.'

'What a foolish thing life is and what tricks God plays on us.' She came closer to him so that her breath was sweet and warm on his face. 'You can't marry Rhoda Carlisle. She's off the moor-tops.'

'I shall have to marry someone. I can't lead the rest of my life like this.'

'Not her. Please. I don't think I can bear it. I'll have to lie there alone at night and you'll be with her.'

'That's what I do.'

'But Edward's hardly with me. You could be with me.'

'You can't treat me like that. I can't spend the rest of my life living just for being in your bed sometimes, watching you with Edward the rest of the time. You do love him, I can see it in your eyes. You can't want that for me, even if you don't love me. It isn't right. If you care for me even just a little, let me go.'

'What am I to do?' Helen said. 'There should be a time for us, I know there should. I'm so lonely and I missed you so very much. I can't live in this house with you married to another woman, not after what you've been to me. You make love to me as though you'll never have the chance again, as though it's always the first and last time. Don't do it, please.'

'Helen, I have to try.'

'No!' She cried and clung and kissed him and pleaded and begged. It reminded Gil somewhat of that day when he had tried to persuade Abby to marry him. He blamed her still for his unhappiness. Living without Abby was like this room, empty and cool; he was moving around, falling over things all the time, clutching at anything which he found, from despair. He somehow had to put Helen from him physically and mentally and it was no good. In the end, she ran out of the room and up the stairs and finished her battle alone. He went along the hall in search of Rhoda.

When it came time for her to leave, Gil panicked. He did not want to be left there with Edward and Helen together and the longest ever nights. Rhoda had kept the edge from the loneliness and he did not want her to go. They walked in the quarry garden along to the ruined castle. From there they could look back across the fields to the house. It was late evening, well after dinner and everything was silent and still.

'You'll come back soon,' Gil said.

'If I'm allowed.'

'Are you afraid of Mr Allsop?'

Rhoda didn't answer.

'Has he done something?'

'No,' she said hastily, 'at least no more than many men. He can't replace my father and my mother prefers him, I can see that she does. I don't think she loved my father half as much as she does this man and he is – he's unworthy. He's . . . uneducated and uncultured, so stupid that he doesn't realise it and he knows I despise him and yet—'

'And yet?'

Rhoda looked at him from narrowed eyes.

'He thinks that young women like him. He's old – at least old compared to men your age but he . . . he actually thinks that I desire him, whereas he disgusts and revolts me. His stomach sticks out and his hair is thinning and he drinks too much and he smokes and his breath and clothes—' Rhoda wrinkled her nose. 'If he was a kind man, none of that would matter but . . . I miss my father. Every day of my life I miss him. But I have liked being here with your family.'

'Enough to come back?'

'Oh yes. I would give anything to come back.'

'You don't have to give anything. You can come back any time.'

'I love your house and I like your father and mother and Edward and Helen and – and everything.'

Gil moved forward, very slightly. He couldn't think afterwards why he did it. Rhoda drew back sharply, fell over a rabbit hole in the grass and landed awkwardly. Gil got down to help. She was trembling and trying not to cry.

'I didn't mean to scare you.'

'You didn't. It was just . . . I don't want to go and leave you. I'll miss you. You're the first man who's been kind to me since my father—'

'Rhoda, look.' Gil sat down beside her in the grass. 'I know it isn't how it should be but . . . we get on very well. If we got married, you wouldn't ever have to go home again.'

She was shocked by the idea, Gil could see. He was shocked himself, but he had to find a way out of his life as it was. A struggle went on behind her eyes, but she agreed. He had not expected, either, that he would be so happy when Rhoda said she would marry him. It made everything so much better straight away. When they went back to the house and announced it, Edward clapped him on the back, his mother cuddled Rhoda, but it was his father's reaction which satisfied Gil most. He said, 'Well done, lad!' and he told Rhoda she was the bonniest lass in the county.

Helen did congratulate them, though stiffly.

The reaction from Rhoda's mother was positive and after that either Gil went to Allendale Town to stay for the weekend or Rhoda came to Bamburgh House. Gil had long since decided that he disliked Jos Allsop and spending time at the square, stone, dales house was not a pleasant experience. He imagined that it could have been if Rhoda's father had been alive.

Allendale Town was very pretty, the countryside around it two dales, the valleys of the Rivers East Allen and West Allen. The rivers went for a short distance before meeting the river South Tyne at Allen Banks, but each made its own way, separated by the moors that surrounded the town, a monument to the lead mining industry which had been its mainstay for a hundred years.

Rhoda had lived there all her life and knew everybody, but life inside her home was bleak. Allsop drank. He made good use of all the pubs in Allendale and there were many of them. When he came home, those who were wise kept their distance. Gil was unlucky enough to meet up with him outside the Rose and Crown in High Street.

'You're a brave one,' Jos said as he staggered into the road, 'marrying that. Her dowry's the warmest thing about Rhoda. You'll get nothing from her. Like the January snow she is, pretty but too cold to touch.'

Gil had to remind himself that he was staying in this man's house and went off without saying anything.

They walked up on the moors and Rhoda was always ahead of him, dashing here and there to show him a special place that she cared for, her favourite view or a stream almost as brown as her eyes. She knew the names of the birds and the flowers. She could pick her way easily as though she knew every inch of the land. He liked to stand and watch her, slender with her brown hair blowing about. She reminded him of a young deer, moving surely, quite at home, and she was happy there, looking back from time to time and smiling or pointing ahead at something she had seen. Sometimes she would let him catch her up, but mostly she preferred to go on ahead so Gil would slacken his pace and let her show him the moors. He came to understand that she felt safe with him and it made him feel good to get something right. He bought a ring for her finger. Its pretty green stone suited her and Rhoda could hide behind that. Nobody could touch her.

That autumn as Helen grew fat, Edward began once again to go out almost every night and William complained with just the three of them in the dining-room after dinner, when Edward tried to excuse himself.

'By God, you're not excused. Where are you going?'

'I'm going for a game of billiards. Do you mind?' Edward spoke softly, but Gil knew that he was most unhappy at being questioned.

'I do mind, yes. It's the third time in four nights. We have a billiard-room here. You can play against Gil.'

'He doesn't play my game,' Edward said, looking at the door.

'And what game is that?'

'You wouldn't understand.' Suddenly he looked at his father and there was anger in his face. 'I've given you an heir for God's sake, what more do you want?' And he left the room.

William was as white as the tablecloth and almost immediately went off to his study. Gil couldn't help feeling rather left out because Edward no longer asked him to go. What William didn't know was that quite often Edward didn't come home.

At weekends when Rhoda was there, he did stay at home or they all went out together. It was a happy time. Gil's father generously gave him a fortnight's holiday towards the end of the summer, Rhoda stayed the full time and they had picnics by the river and sat out in the garden under the trees. Helen had accepted that he would marry Rhoda and chose to make a friend of the other girl. They went shopping and came back with all manner of exciting things. There were parties both at their house and at friends' homes, expeditions to the seaside and even a short break at Warkworth just beside Amble, staying with friends.

'Doesn't your father like Warkworth?' Rhoda ventured when William had told them he didn't understand the foolishness of wanting to go there.

'He was born at Amble. My grandparents were very modest people.'

Rhoda insisted on finding them in the graveyard, which Gil had wanted to do but hadn't liked to mention. Someone, his father probably, he thought, had erected a huge marble angel at the head of their plot.

'Dear me,' Rhoda said, 'it stands out, doesn't it?' And she betrayed herself with a giggle.

'It's typical of him,' Gil fumed. 'He ignored them when they were here and insulted them by this monstrosity when they were dead.'

'He probably didn't mean to.'

'How can you defend him?'

'He's your father. He's very nice to me. I wish my father was still here.'

For the first time in weeks and quite disloyally, he knew, Gil thought of Abby. Abby was probably the only person who understood the relationship that he had with his father. He missed her. He had tried to stop thinking about her after she had married Robert Surtees and gone away, but the memories of her were good and sometimes made him smile. He was glad that she was happy. She deserved to be.

Chapter Nine

The emerald ring on Rhoda's hand glittered. Abby had read or heard that the darker the stone, the more expensive it was and the emerald was so dark that it was almost black with green glints, subtle and as rich as velvet.

'It's nice, isn't it?' Rhoda said shly and Abby hugged her.

'You could have told me!' she said. 'You could have written.'

'I wanted to surprise you.'

'You have. Oh Rhoda, I'm so pleased for you. It's a wonderful ring. Who is the lucky man?'

'Gil Collingwood.'

Abby's heart fell. It really did, she felt it. She was jealous and upset to realise that not only did she not want Gil, she didn't want anybody else to have him. No, that was not quite true. She didn't want anyone she knew anywhere near him, so that she had to hear the details about the relationship and Rhoda was her closest friend. Abby wished she could shout at Gil. In a way it was as though they had both betrayed her, somehow, stolen one another away from her. Her sense of justice rescued her, but it was difficult to sound enthusiastic.

'Gil?'

'Yes, why not?'

They were in the sitting-room of Rhoda's home, Abby had called as soon as she got back. She was pleased to see Rhoda looking so much better but now that she knew the cause of it, pleasure was hard to pretend.

'No reason, it's just . . . I didn't think it. He's . . . well, not your style, I thought.'

'I had to get away. I had to get out.' Rhoda glanced at the door as though someone might come bursting in at any moment, but it remained peaceful.

'You don't love him then?'

'I couldn't love any man.' And Rhoda shuddered. 'Mind you, I do find that I like him. He doesn't try to grab me, though I was convinced that he would, and he is rather fetching, don't you think? So tall and good-looking. He's a gentleman too. I didn't know that. Kind and generous,' Rhoda said, moving her finger so that the emerald glittered.

'Does he love you?'

'No. No, I don't think so. His parents like me and of course they like my money.'

'That's very cynical.'

'I don't mind. He's not boring, either. Men do tend to be boring. I think he's clever.'

'Clever, Gil?'

'I think he is. We're going to America.'

'America?'

'He has been . . . what's the word . . . "negotiating" . . . with a shipping line to build an enormous ship and after we're married we're going to America with the head of the shipping line and his wife and if Gil is clever enough, Collingwood's will get to build the ship. So he will be doing lots of work and seeing important people in New York, but I'm inclined to think it will be glamorous.'

Abby was inclined to think so too and the sting of envy hit her like a train. It was stupid and illogical and she tried to dismiss it, but what she most missed about having a husband who didn't work was the excitement of industry, the problems, the tensions, the possibilities. She had never thought that not working might be dull, but it was. The days were not enlivened by talk that mattered, because nothing mattered except births, deaths and marriages. The rest was gossip.

Why should not Gil and Rhoda be happy?

'Do you remember me saying that I would have a shop? You said it wasn't respectable. This is and I like his family. I like being there.'

'Bamburgh House is hideous.'

'I love it! His parents are kind and Helen and I go shopping. They're a family like we used to be. I want that again.'

Abby was also jealous of the friendship which had apparently sprung up between Rhoda and Helen. She and Helen could never have been friends and Rhoda was inclined to talk about her a lot and about the coming baby. Abby felt left out. She had not found any close friends among Robert's circle. Most of them were from the south and made fun of her northern accent. Abby had tried to modify it, but she could almost hear her mother's scorn. The women talked about one another and the men drank and played field sports. Abby thought that she would not have minded so much if Robert had taken any interest in her father, her friends or her home. He tried to keep her from them and talked of going back to London soon.

'We've just got here,' Abby had objected, 'and there's Rhoda and Gil's wedding.'

'Precisely. You don't really want to go? It's not the event of the year. He's nobody and she's a bucolic fool. They've only asked us because of who we are. Collingwood and I can't stand one another. I'm not going.'

It was the same whenever she wanted to go to Jesmond and spend a little time with her father. Robert always had a good reason not to go. Abby was worried about her father. He had lost weight and seemed distracted about work. Robert complained if she stayed overnight because he had social events planned, people to stay or just that he missed her.

'You could come with me,' Abby pointed out.

'I've no wish to stay in that dark little house in the dingy Newcastle streets when I can remain at home in the country. Your father could come to us.'

'He's working.'

'It's time he gave up working at his age,' Robert said. 'There are other things in life.'

Abby suggested this to her father and he stared at her.

'Sell this business?'

'There's nobody to take it on after you.'

'I'm not dead yet and you'll have children.'

She didn't like to tell him that her children were hardly likely to work in a shipyard and was only glad that Robert was not there, or he would have laughed.

'The yard has been my whole life since your mother died. What else would I do?' he said.

'You could retire and come and live with us.'

'Robert would like that,' her father said sarcastically. 'I suppose you think I can take up hunting and prance around in a bloody daft outfit like he does.'

Her father, Abby had realised lately, had only just given up on the notion that his son-in-law would develop a special interest in the shipyard. They had nothing in common, nothing to talk about. Robert saw her father as a foolish old man and Henderson thought Robert useless and shallow. Trying to keep the peace between the two of them was not easy. She knew that her father was lonely, that though he said nothing he hated her to leave and she felt sick and weepy each time, looking back at him standing by himself on the doorstep. Each time she tried to get away from Robert, he had found something to stop her: friends were to visit, they were to visit friends, or there was a social event which she could not miss. It was some time before Abby admitted to herself that social events and many of their friends bored her. She spent too much time with them doing nothing and it all seemed so empty.

* * *

For a long time now, Gil knew, it had been his father's ambition to build a ship which would cross the Atlantic faster than any other and take the Blue Riband. He was closer to his father than he had ever been and could do little wrong in William's eyes. His forthcoming marriage to a girl his father liked who had money was another joy. Gil worked hard, his father praised him and his ideas and Gil clearly demonstrated his ability for shipbuilding, designing and engineering. He was sometimes quite surprised himself. He had no idea where this ability had come from. Edward had none and, though his father was a shrewd and accomplished businessman, he didn't have it either. Some men would have been jealous, but Gil knew by then that William saw his sons as an extension of himself. This was why he had been so upset with them as children when he saw that they might turn into people beyond his control. He relied on Gil very much at work and it was a huge burden. Sometimes it would have been a relief to be allowed to fail, occasionally to make a mistake, but when he did his father went into terrible rages. Gil's mistakes were fewer and fewer. He had trained himself to think no longer about Helen, and his growing friendship with Rhoda was a big help. His mind returned to his work and he kept it there. To lose his father's new-found regard was too much. Helen would have Edward's child soon and a mother, Gil had discovered, was not nearly as attractive a prospect. If she had been growing fat with his child, he would have adored her and the child, but the fact that each day he was faced with a woman who more obviously than ever belonged to another man discouraged him from wanting her. And there was Rhoda. He was making her happy. Gil had not been able to do that with anyone before, but Rhoda was easily made happy and he liked it. He determined to be faithful, kind and to look after her and he was convinced that once they were married everything would be right.

In the meanwhile, he was happy at work and knew that, happy, he turned out his best. His father came to expect that everything he did he did brilliantly and Gil wanted more and more to bring that proud look to his father's face. He never again wanted to be that dreadful person he had been as a child and a youth. He knew that his father had despised him. Now it was different. William's gaze was soft on him and Gil knew that out of his hearing William was inclined to call his son a genius. Gil knew that he was far from it. He had limited abilities in almost every way, as though God had seen fit to endow him with one gift and take everything else from him. Gil had begun to build a reputation as a designer of fine ships. They had plenty of work. People were beginning to respect him.

For some time his father had cultivated a man called John Marlowe. He was a rich man, the owner of a shipping line. He lived in London but had a house in Newcastle, which had been his family home. William invited John and his wife, Edwina, to dinner at Bamburgh House. Charlotte was worried that they would not be good enough for the Marlowes and was surprised to discover that Edwina cared nothing for fashion and John ate sparingly. Afterwards, John sat by the fire with Gil and talked about his ideas and ambitions. The Germans had lately built very fast liners and the government was not happy that British shipping might be overtaken in this way. If the Germans could build bigger and faster liners, they could build bigger and faster battleships. The government wanted to build two big liners and there had been much discussion for almost two years while they looked for the right shipbuilder, Gil knew. Collingwood's had already submitted a great many designs. The first big problem was the shape of the ship and experiments had to be carried out.

'We could make a model. It's been done before. A big model so that we could do testing to see whether the shape would work.'

'It's performance I'm interested in,' John said. 'The government will provide two and a half million at two point seven five per cent interest and an annual subsidy of one hundred and fifty thousand pounds. The structure and the shape do interest me, but it's the speed I'm counting on. You would have to guarantee it. How long to launch?'

'Eighteen months.'

'It would cost you money. The river isn't wide enough and you would need new machinery and sheds.'

'It's been my father's life's ambition.'

'And yours?'

'It would be interesting.'

John laughed.

'We would interfere a great deal, a committee from the Admiralty and from us. Would you like that?'

'It would be worth it. You'd pay in instalments.'

'Do you have the latest prices?'

'Of course.'

'I'm taking Edwina to America at Christmas. I understand you're getting married. We could do some real talking and there are people in New York I want to introduce you to.'

William had not been taking part in the discussion. Gil understood that. Later he went to his father in the study.

'He wants me to go to New York with him, to talk to people and, I think, so that he and I can talk properly about it and in private.'

'I want to build these two ships like I've never wanted anything in my whole life,' his father said tightly.

'Don't worry,' Gil said, 'we'll get them.'

He called himself rash afterwards. He went to bed and worried, but he would have promised his father the heavens and the earth if William had expressed such a desire for them.

From time to time the shipbuilders of the river met to discuss ships and men and wages. Henderson was always there and Gil went with his father and Edward. After Abby was married and went away to France and Italy, it seemed to Gil that Henderson was different, quieter and less interested in business. At one time at these meetings he argued because he was a better man than most. He paid what other men considered to be high wages and was badly liked for it. Worse still, he would not join the federation that the others belonged to, where wages were kept at what they considered to be an acceptable level so that the men who worked for them could not cause problems by leaving to go to another shipyard which would pay better. Henderson built good houses for his workmen and Gil knew that he had financed schools and places of recreation. Bella had been a wealthy woman when she married Henderson and Gil thought that if Henderson had had a son, he would have expanded his yard, his father having shrewdly bought up much land on either side of the present shipyard. Now, however, it was as if the spirit had gone from the man. Gil admired the things he had done and hoped that when he married Rhoda some of the money would be used to better things for the men, though if their bid was accepted for the first of the two liners a great deal of money would be needed. He had estimated it would cost ten thousand pounds to widen the river and they would need huge covered berths so that they could work in bad weather and new electric machinery for faster production.

Gil admired Henderson from afar because he knew that Henderson disliked him. Quite often after these meetings the men would go drinking together, but Henderson was never asked. He was lonely, Gil knew, at work and at home. He had no friends in the business and no son and Gil thought that Henderson might have started to realise what kind of a man Abby had married.

At one of these meetings in the late autumn, when Abby was still away, Gil refused several invitations to go out afterwards. His father frowned. Henderson had already left. Gil ran along the streets after him as Henderson rounded the corner into Eldon Square, a pretty place right in the middle of

Newcastle where musicians often played and ladies gathered in teashops.

'Mr Reed!'

Henderson didn't hear, or didn't want to. Gil ran, shouting again, only slowing down when Henderson stopped and turned. Gil stood, panting for a few moments.

'I almost lost you,' he said. 'Will you come for a drink with me?'

'No,' Henderson said and walked on.

'I know you don't like me—'

Henderson stopped again and looked squarely at him.

'Your father's a bastard,' he said. 'What does that make you? I'll tell you. You come from a long line of third-rate people. They may call you a genius, but that doesn't make you a gentleman.'

'It doesn't make you one either,' Gil said, losing his temper. 'You're rude! All I asked you was if you would go for a drink. "No, thank you" would have done. I don't need to hear how base I am. I've got nothing to gain, after all. Abby didn't ever want me. You had nothing to be afraid of then and you certainly don't now.'

'What do you want?'

'I just want to talk to somebody who improves houses and conditions and things.'

'I'm amazed you're interested.'

'Why shouldn't I be interested?'

'Because you're a bloody Collingwood and all they ever cared for was money.'

'That's not true. My grandfather was a boat builder and a good one. He built cobles.'

'I know he did, lad.'

'Don't call me "lad". I do have a name.'

'One drink,' Henderson said.

They had gone into the nearest fuggy little pub and played dominoes and been there until it closed. After that, they met at least once a week. Henderson wasn't easy. He tore Gil's ideas to pieces in a way in which Gil would never have survived from his father. He scorned what he called 'misplaced philanthropy' as though it was something he hadn't heard of, but Gil could see enthusiasm in his newly fired eyes. Also, Gil could talk to Henderson about anything and that was new. Henderson didn't accept that he was brilliant or that he was stupid, just that he was a shipbuilder who was doing his best. They had long, complicated discussions. He told Henderson his ideas for the liner, knowing that Henderson would not say anything to anyone. It was such a relief to be able to throw ideas around without having to prove anything and, after the ideas had gone back and forward a dozen times, it was as though the discussing of them fined them down, improved them. Gil became more sure, more confident; he trusted Henderson's judgement and he knew that Henderson enjoyed the discussions. He invited Gil to the house, something Gil was flattered to do. Nobody else knew. They played dominoes by the fire in bad weather.

Gil tried to introduce some of Henderson's ideas at work, but his father objected strongly.

'We're not bloody women, to go interfering in the men's lives. Stick to designing ships, I'll do the managing,' he said.

Gil had also tried to talk to his father about wages for Edward and himself.

'You have an allowance. You can hardly call it mean,' William said, 'and you can run up bills all over town. You go to the best tailor. We have accounts everywhere, jeweller's, shoemakers'. What the hell more do you want? I keep you extravagantly.'

'It's not quite the same thing,' Gil said.

'Is there something you want? Name it.'

'No, there's nothing,' Gil said.

Abby was surprised to walk into her father's house one cold day after Christmas and find Gil and Rhoda there. She had not seen Gil happy before and he was almost like somebody different.

'I thought you didn't like him,' she said to her father afterwards.

'I can talk to him,' Henderson said.

'You mean he talks about work.'

'If you like, and Rhoda's a good lass. I think they make a very nice couple.'

Abby thought they did too and was astonished. Rhoda was well dressed now as she had not been and was wearing sable against the weather. She wore a jaunty little hat and a big smile and she looked at Gil from time to time as though to make sure he was still there. If they were not in love, which Rhoda had assured her they were not, they certainly looked as if they were. Their families both approved, Abby knew, and they knew one another well and were comfortable together.

'You are coming to the wedding?' Rhoda said.

'When is it?'

'In April. Gil's mother wanted it sooner, but the arrangements couldn't be made in time.'

'I'm not certain that we can. We're going away.'

'Do try and come. It won't be the same without you.'

'She's got too grand for us,' Gil teased, looking at his bride to be. That was when Abby thought that he was no longer in love with Helen, which was not surprising. Babies were hardly conducive to romance.

Helen's baby was born in a snowstorm, so she endured several uncomfortable hours before the doctor arrived. They called him Matthew. The christening was delayed until after the bad weather and Helen took a long time to recover from the birth. Edward continued to go out every night. He did not seem interested in the baby or in her. Gil was glad of Rhoda then because she was a big help. She loved the baby, spent hours with him and, when Helen wasn't well, sat with her, cheered her, even encouraged her to go out from time to time to distract her.

Helen did attend the wedding but looked as though she should have been home in bed. It was a mild day, the first week in April, and Rhoda was married from the little stone parish church in Allendale. Her stepfather gave her away and was doing his best to look pleased about it, Gil thought. The wedding breakfast was at their house on the edge of the town and he could not but think of how unhappy she had been there and of how pleased he was to be taking her away for good.

They were to spend the first night at a hotel in Hexham and then to make the journey south to meet the Marlowes in Liverpool to join the ship which would take them to America. They were waved away from the house. It wouldn't take long to reach Hexham, but Rhoda said more than once on the journey that she was tired. She had been so bright until then. Now she was pale. She said little during the journey and even less when they reached the hotel. Shown to their bedroom, Rhoda looked at the big double bed and turned away.

She ate nothing that evening, pushing the food around on her plate, and when it was time to go to bed and Gil asked if she would like to go on ahead, she nodded and escaped.

He stayed downstairs worrying and had a glass of brandy. He could not help thinking of Helen, of being in bed with her, of her beautiful body. Rhoda had not let him touch her; she was afraid. He didn't know why, but he had an idea that Jos Allsop had tried to put his hands on her. Gil had not done so; he had been careful and was prepared to be patient now. He made his way slowly upstairs and opened the door of the room. The bed was empty. She was not there. Gil wandered about upstairs for a few minutes and then went downstairs, trying not to look obvious, but she was nowhere that he could see. Finally he ventured outside, doubting that even Rhoda would have gone outside in such cold windy weather. It was difficult to see anything in the dark, shadowed streets though the abbey stood out against the sky and the houses around the little green in front of the hotel had street lamps. He could see a small figure some way off. He paused for a moment or two. What was she doing out here? Was she so afraid? He hadn't understood. He wondered whether to go back into the hotel and wait, then decided against it and began to walk slowly towards her so that she might see or hear him and would not be shocked. She was not wearing a coat and the wind was whipping down from Hexhamshire Common. Was she imagining herself there, wishing herself beyond his reach? Her folded arms were thin and her hair blew about. He didn't go too close in case she ran.

'Rhoda?' he said softly.

It was several moments before she turned, as though she had been in some other place. He went to her and took off his jacket and tried to put it around her shoulders, but she backed away, shivering.

'I used to stand up on the fell and watch the lights on in our house when I was little, knowing I could go in out of the cold any time.'

Gil searched for the right thing to say. He had heard of animals caught in traps who chewed off their own limbs to be free. Was that what she had done, limping to him, damaged? She drew further away and turned in the direction of the open country as though she might run into it and away from him.

'You don't have to be afraid of me. Come back inside. You'll take cold.'

She didn't say anything. Gil had known that she had not the feeling for him that Helen had had, but he had not thought things as bad as this.

'Have I done something?' he asked.

She shook her head.

'Do you think I'm going to hurt you, because—'

'No. No.' Her head was down. When she looked up Gil was horrified by the bleakness in her face. 'I've deceived you,' she said.

The only thing Gil could think of was that she had given her body to somebody else and, if she had, it was considered a very grave sin, that she should have done so without marriage, that she should have married him regardless. She had a good right to be afraid.

'Tell me,' he said.

'I don't know how to.'

'You must.'

'I'm unchaste.'

Unchaste. What a strange word and what huge significance it carried. He was uncomfortably aware of the double standard: that she was meant to be totally inexperienced but that he would not have been censured for such behaviour, except that he had done something much graver and was in no position to condemn anybody.

'I don't care,' he said recklessly. 'Do you love him? Was it that you couldn't marry him? Was he married? Tell me before we freeze.'

She looked clearly at him.

'It was my stepfather,' she said.

Something in Gil signalled recognition, as though some tiny part of him had known and that was why he had tried to protect her, but most of him was revolted. He couldn't take his eyes off her. Fascinated horror gripped him.

'You went to bed with Allsop?'

Her face filled with anger.

'I didn't!' she said.

Coldness took a hold on Gil inside as well as out.

'He took you against your will?'

'You didn't really think I would have gone with a disgusting, awful person like that.'

'Why didn't you tell somebody?'

'Who was I supposed to tell?'

'Me, for a start.'

'You wouldn't have married me! I had to get out.'

'There are other ways.'

'Nobody would have believed me. You can still send me back! You haven't had me yet!'

She ran. Gil cursed himself and ran after her. When he caught her, she thumped and kicked him. He shook her.

'Stop it! Nobody's going to send you back!'

'I'm second-hand goods, that's what they call it. I'll go. I'll just go.'

'You're not going anywhere. Come inside. I'm bloody well nithered.'

He dragged her back into the hotel and marched her upstairs and into the bedroom. Luckily the fire was blazing nicely and the room was warm. Gil's feelings were so mixed up. He was rather inclined to smack her round the ear for deceiving him, but the idea of Allsop raping a vulnerable person like Rhoda was beyond belief. In any case, he had sworn to himself that he would hit no one except in self-defence. Part of him also wondered whether perhaps she was lying because she didn't want to go to bed with him. Rhoda wouldn't even come to the fire. She sat in the shadows, curled up in a chair.

'Come over here, for goodness sake.'

'You're going to hit me.'

'I am not. I'd have done it before now. Did you really like me so little?'

'I like you very well considering you're a man.'

'Then come to the fire.'

There was brandy and glasses. It seemed a sight more appropriate than the champagne which sat like a reminder of what they might have been doing. He poured brandy, gave her a good measure and she sank down onto the rug by the fire. Gil sat down in an armchair nearby and drank his brandy gratefully.

'Did you tell your mother?'

'I tried to. She called me a whore and took a stick to me, as though it was my fault.'

'But she believed you?'

'Does that mean you don't?'

'I haven't made up my mind.'

'Why would I lie to you?'

'So that you don't have to go to bed with me.'

'All you have to do is force me and then you'd find out anyhow.'

'I'm not in the habit of forcing women.' He thought that sounded arrogant, somehow, but he needed a refuge. This was not how he had envisaged his wedding night. He had imagined it happy, difficult perhaps, but he had liked Rhoda, liked the wild person in her, been confident that they would deal well in bed together. He had desired her, not like he had wanted Helen or loved her as he had loved Abby even, but he had thought that he could have her as his wife. To his shame, there was also a distaste that another man had had her first, either willingly or unwillingly. He had wanted her to be completely his so that he could try and remake himself into entirely hers and it was not possible, he could see that. If she was lying then she cared nothing for him and if she was not, then she wouldn't go to bed with him. Either way, there was no chance that he would be saved or could save himself from the slavery that his love for Helen had turned into. He was too shocked to be tired and too miserable to sleep.

Rhoda sat on the floor beside his feet with her legs tucked under her, making herself very small, both hands clutched around the glass as she stared into the fire.

'I'm sorry,' she said.

'Yes, I imagine you might be.'

She turned her head and looked at him.

'You don't know what it's like! It was vile!' Her voice shook.

'Why don't you go to bed?'

'No!'

'Well at least get up off the floor. You must be in a draught.'

She sat in the chair across the fire for a while and then, without saying a word, got up and undressed without showing her body and got into bed. She lay down with her face turned towards the wall. Gil got up, went and stood by the window and sipped at his brandy and watched the storm throw itself at the little town with its abbey and stone houses and shops, solid black shadows in the night.

Eventually she fell asleep and Gil's mind gave him Helen and the nights that they had spent together. He ached for her, longed for her. The loneliness was intensified because of the girl who slept in the bed. He drank some more brandy. It was strange how you could fill up the loneliness with alcohol. You shouldn't have been able to, but you could. If you hadn't been able to, you would have gone mad.

He thought of the men in the shipyards. They were like Helen, some of them, they had been trapped by sex or circumstances, by disappointment, pain or betrayal. He and Rhoda were like that now, for she had trapped them both. Beer filled the emptiness because there was nothing else, no love, no comfort, no education, no opportunities. They could not even get away. Religion was like beer for some of them. They found God and swallowed Him in great gulps.

The brandy took a good hold on his mind and body and soothed and comforted, but he did not stop thinking about Helen. Edward would be out and she would be lying in bed alone and he was married and could not go to her again. Would it be worse now that he was married, or had it been as bad a sin before? He thought it had. It had always been as bad as it was going to get, a betrayal of his brother and his family and Helen's marriage, whatever that was. It was done and couldn't be made right. Nothing would change it.

It was almost morning and he was sweetly drunk when he went to bed. It was just as well, he thought, it really was all that was left beside the work. He could feel sleep coming at him just beyond, stealing past the brandy, covering him up, cuddling him, holding him. If he tried very hard he could remember Helen's caresses, feel them, taste her mouth and her body. He could remember the warm land with its blue sea and the white villa and the mountains, the garden with its orange trees, the breeze gently disturbing the curtains in the bedroom. She was smiling at him, kissing him. They were together and nothing else mattered.

Chapter Ten

The ship was not nearly as big as the kind of liner that John Marlowe wanted, but it was comfortable; indeed, to most people it would have appeared sumptuous. Gil interpreted how important his presence was to John by the suite of rooms they were given. Just yesterday, Rhoda would have run about exclaiming excitedly at the pretty furniture, the view from the portholes; now, she merely looked at the big double bed and said nothing. Gil had awoken beside a reluctant woman for the first time and he didn't like it. Neither did he like the hangover which sat on his brow. It was not a good start. She lay, silently turned away, so he turned over towards her.

'Rhoda? Rhoda, look at me.'

She turned to him. Her eyes were swollen with crying, though he hadn't heard her.

'Let's make a bargain, shall we? I won't touch you so give me back the Rhoda I knew yesterday morning. We're going to New York.' When this produced no response he said, 'I'm not going to do anything to you.'

'It isn't that! It's just that . . . I shouldn't have married you.'

'What alternative was there?'

'Somebody else, not you.'

'You mean there's somebody you like even less?'

'I do like you. I like you very much.'

'Why don't we leave it at that then and do the best we can?'

'I'm sorry.'

'If I ever meet up with that bastard again, I'll kill him,' Gil promised and got out of bed.

There were plenty of distractions on board ship. He was glad of them and more pleased than he had thought he would be at John Marlowe's presence. He was grateful to Edwina, who kept Rhoda occupied and, after a day or two, Rhoda seemed to relax and begin to enjoy herself. John knew a great deal about shipping but nothing about ships, Gil thought, but he also knew what he wanted. As they went over the ship, Gil explained in great, though not very technical, detail; he kept the problems to himself and they were vast.

For a long time now people had preferred intermediate liners like this one, with lower running costs, but things had changed. Germany and America were becoming powerful and it was time for might and skill to be shown. The British government had its face to keep up and, though the cost was high, it might be even higher if they did not. They could not afford to lose their hold on the claim that they were the greatest shipbuilding nation in the world. Gil knew very well that Germany educated its engineers and designers, that it trained better its skilled men, that it took more quickly to the ideas of new machinery. The British were rightly famed for their lack of schooling, their inability to move around. They clung to one piece of land as though every other part of the earth was foreign territory, like small animals in burrows. As for new ideas . . .

Gil stood by the rail and watched the water and thought of himself, his hatred of school, his love for Newcastle. There was something which mattered here that he could not quite comprehend. It was nothing visible, nothing tangible, he only knew that somehow the ship would be built at Collingwood's, that in spite of wrong ideas and mistakes and sheer pigheadedness, if he was given the word to build this new ship in a year it would be rising like a soft monster, dwarfing the men who had gathered resources, materials and skills. In a year and a half it could be a being such as had never been seen on Tyneside before, the greatest ship the world had ever seen. Part of him was still looking at his reflection and seeing lack of education and experience, but his father had been right. Designers had to be people with uncluttered minds, men with goals, without distractions, fresh, new, exciting. He could feel this ship inside his head and inside his heart and he knew that it would be built.

To win a place on the Admiralty list to build large liners was what most shipbuilders dreamed of and he would have it. Other people might tender for the liner, but it was his and he would promise John Marlowe the whole earth to gain it, recklessly propose dates and times, and finance, skills and feats of magic. He would do anything to gain this ship.

Gil discovered that he liked John Marlowe. He had been prepared to cultivate the man for what he wanted, but during the voyage they became friends and that was more than he had hoped for. John was much older and when they had met Gil had seen disbelief in his face that a young man could produce anything close to what he wanted, but as the ship made its way towards New York they sat up into the night over a drink and talked and Gil could see that John's confidence in him grew with each hour. He was a rich, influential man who knew other rich, influential men. He was shrewd, so that in a way Gil began to see himself as John saw him and he was happy about this.

Less successful was his relationship with Rhoda. She avoided him during the day, but that wasn't obvious because the whole purpose of the trip was business and she had no place there. He knew that she was ashamed of what she had done and he was ashamed of the way that he had reacted, so when they did meet they spoke softly to one another as people might think newly weds did. At night, Gil put a pillow between them that she should feel easier. He let the business matters sweep over him like a tide. It was important that he should not falter because his marriage was a disaster. The one had nothing to do with the other. He put them into different sections of his mind and dismissed the marriage. He treated Rhoda as though they were good friends and, as they drew nearer to New York, he could see the look change in her eyes. The building of the new ship was all his concern. If he could secure this contract, no one, least of all his father, would ever doubt him again.

If Gil had had nothing more important to think about he would have been thrilled with New York, its huge buildings – the skyscrapers – the different communities of people from different lands, the Irish, the Blacks, the Jews, the Italians. It was noisy such as London could never be. The Marlowes had friends there and in some ways, Gil thought with surprise, it was as class-conscious as anywhere at home. Your name and your background were everything. The women were very beautiful and extremely well dressed. Abby, Gil thought, would have hated it.

John introduced Gil to his business acquaintances and to Wall Street and business in the city. Rhoda went to see Central Park, the animals in the zoo, the shops. They stayed on Park Avenue and it seemed to Gil that for somebody off the felltops, Rhoda dealt with this sophisticated, scurrying life as though she had been used to it. John seemed to take great pleasure in showing Gil around. He took him to a German beerhouse on the Upper East Side and, in contrast, to the newly built Waldorf Astoria, but nothing touched Gil, not the glamour, the money, the music, the intricacy, the poverty or the people. Rhoda would come home with wonderful tales to relate of whom she had met and how she had spent her day. She went to the opera and he was obliged to go with her. He hated it and all the time his mind did a tortured dance between the way that she would not let him touch her and the ship he might not be allowed to build. His dreams had in them the frenzy of New York and a hunger which went round and round. He couldn't sleep; he was full before every meal and, on the second to last night of their visit, the worry and frustration were too much. She was inclined to chatter now in the bedroom but he silenced her with his mouth, put her reluctant body down onto the bed and slid his hands inside her evening dress.

If she had fought he didn't know what he would have done, but she did what he imagined she had done with Allsop. She pretended she was not there. He knew very well where she was, up on her beloved moors, probably on some warm August evening, when the bell heather was as rich as rubies and there was nothing but land, sky and the occasional cry of the sheep. Her face was turned away, the blood drained, her eyes distant and her body like marble. Gil saw himself and was revolted. He dropped her and got up off the bed.

'Christ Almighty, I'm sorry.'

It all seemed so incongruous. The room was enormous, and it had gold-coloured curtains. The bed and the other furniture looked like it had come out of some French brothel, he thought savagely, having never been into a French brothel. It was all gold and white and spindly as though it would break from even slight ill-use. It was not often that Gil wished himself back at Bamburgh House; he did not often feel safe there, but he wished it now. He tried to get out of the room but Rhoda, nimble-footed from the fells, reached the door before he did. When he turned, she put herself into his arms and said, 'Don't be sorry. It wasn't your fault.'

'I want to go home,' Gil said.

'We will and you will have the ship. You will, you will. It will be all right.'

'We will. We're fit to build the first express liner. We are.'

'Now let's go down to dinner.'

There were always eminent people there but tonight John had made sure that Gil was seated opposite a railroad millionaire. Soon the talk was of shipping and railways. The little fat man with the clever eyes impressed Gil.

'The idea is that you could buy a ticket in London to pay for your passage to New York and then go on anywhere in America by rail. Does that seem like a good idea to you, Mr Collingwood?'

'It might if I could have some part in the deal,' Gil said.

John laughed.

'Mr Collingwood is my man,' he said. 'He's going to be involved in all my best endeavours from now on.'

'I think we did it,' Rhoda said when they got back to the bedroom at an advanced hour.

'I think we did it too,' Gil said.

When they got home, relations between his father and Edward were worse than ever, but it was his mother who told him.

'Edward has stopped going into the office and he comes home once or twice a week to see Matthew and Helen. I don't understand what's going on,' she said.

Gil went to Toby's house, but when Toby opened the door he was alone.

'Yes, he's here,' Toby said, beckoning Gil inside. They went through the house and out into the garden. It was late spring and the day was soft. Toby offered Gil a wooden seat. 'He's in bed asleep. He was drunk.'

Toby gave him wine that tasted of gooseberries. The garden was filled with herbs, lavender and thyme, rosemary, a dozen different kinds of mint and various tall flowers which Gil did not recognise, pink and violet and white. The garden was like some kind of tapestry woven in Toby's favourite colours.

'Did you get the contract?'

'Nothing's signed yet.'

'But it will be.' Toby stretched out his long legs in front of him. 'You have to admit, Gil, you've turned into Golden Boy.'

Gil squirmed in his chair.

'I wish we could be as we were. I don't seem to be able to have my father and Edward.'

'Having everything is an extremely costly business,' Toby said.

'He spends a great deal of his time here.'

'He has spent a great part of his life away from here,' Toby said, looking at him.

'It's you, isn't it?' Gil said slowly.

'Of course it's me. What did you think it was? You knew. Don't pretend to be so innocent. You went to school. Tell me nobody tried to bed you, you with your sweet face. Didn't you ever?'

'No.'

'How very boring.'

'It's not that, it's just—'

'That you like women. I had noticed.'

'If it was you, then why did he marry Helen?'

'Because. Happiness is a myth. It's something either in the past or in the future. You think you can catch it if you say your prayers and eat your cabbage and please your father, but all you really have is now and pleasure. He did try very hard.'

'Who did try very hard?' Edward said loudly behind him. Gil looked into his brother's bloodshot eyes and knew then that he had always known what could now be spoken of.

'You did,' Toby said, putting back his head. Edward looked straight back at Gil before he kissed Toby on the mouth.

Gil thought of his father. There was no way William would ever believe that his son could love another man. Gil thought that if William found out it might kill him. Yet Gil could understand why his brother had fallen in love with Toby. There was something very special about him. He oozed peace and Edward had not known peace in his life. The small white house with the wooden floors; the books and cosy fires; the smell of bread baking and chocolate cake cooking, and beef with onions bubbling gently on top of the stove; the garden with its tall trees at the end of the paths thick with greenery in summer; herbs for the pot and the small secret places where you could sit and dream

– who would not have wanted to escape to such a place, to a person who demanded nothing, was always on your side, to be loved without criticism, to be accepted without question? Women could not do that. The war between the sexes could never be over. In some ways it was easier to give in. Toby could understand Edward's problems as a woman could not. They had been brought up together, gone to the same schools, knew the same people.

'And how is married life?' his brother asked softly.

Chapter Eleven

When she was in Northumberland Abby very often went to visit her father on Saturday afternoons. He usually finished work at lunchtime when the men did and she would arrive in time to have a meal with him and to stay the night. Sometimes Gil was there, calling in after work or coming on Sunday afternoons, when he would have Rhoda, Helen and Matthew with him. The baby made Abby feel uncomfortable. Henderson seemed taken with the child and, although Abby did not think herself particularly maternal, she knew that it was expected she would provide an heir and at least one other male child. She had not thought about this when she had married Robert, but he seemed to take for granted that they would have children. So far nothing had happened and by the time autumn came, Abby was starting to worry. She also thought that if they had a child, Robert might not care quite so much for the socialising, or at least differently, though Matthew's birth had not encouraged Edward Collingwood to be seen about any more frequently with his wife. Helen was so pale and listless that she was no advertisement for childbearing, Abby thought. Gil was very thin. In fact, Rhoda was the only one of the three who looked at all happy.

Abby wished that Robert had been with her. She loved him and she knew that he loved her, but he would not go with her to see her father, much less anybody else's father. She knew that Gil went to see Henderson because they had business interests in common and Henderson was, surprisingly for him, delighted to see another man's success. Gil had gained the contract to build the biggest ever liner and Henderson was as proud as if Gil had been his son. It made Abby wretched to see them together. All Robert seemed to have in common with his friends was enjoying themselves and, while there should have been nothing wrong in that, Abby was uncomfortable with it. Robert would laugh and call her middle class, but it seemed to her that money and position brought responsibility with it. He had frowned at that.

'Are you telling me that I treat my people badly?' he had said.

It was a source of pride to him that 'his people', as he called them, were well paid, well housed. He looked after them; he did more, Abby thought in honesty, than William Collingwood had ever done for his workforce. Abby tried to tell him firstly that they were not his, and secondly that he could have done much more with his money to help other, poorer, people. He didn't understand what she was talking about, nor would he let her use any of his money for what he called her good causes. People who did not work for him were nothing to do with him. He had no sense of general responsibility.

Abby knew that he did much more than many people in his position – some of them treated their servants and their workmen very badly – but it seemed wrong to her: she thought that not to use power for the general good was another way of misusing it and Robert spent so much on big parties and keeping up his houses and things which she considered unnecessary. She tried to talk to him, but he called her his little do-gooder and tolerated her. Abby knew that she ought to have been grateful for such a generous husband. Gil had no independence. He had nothing, Abby reasoned, yet there was something about him which she found difficult to dislike, the occasional reluctant smile, the way that he was quiet and did not put himself forward like Robert would have. He did not attempt to dominate the conversation. Robert was often loud, shouting across the room to people or manoeuvring the talk for his own ends, towards his own interests, regardless of other people. But then, Gil did not know that conversation was a tool, she thought. He used it sparingly.

Henderson talked to Matthew, took the child up to his shoulder and then into his arms as he had no doubt done with her when she was that small. Abby could tell that he was charmed and wished she could have told him that she was having a child. It seemed to be the one thing she could have done. Robert had people to do everything else. This was all she could do for him. Several of their acquaintances and friends had children, some who had not been married much longer than them. This was her place. Instinct told her that the more concerned she became, the more difficult it would be, so she went on partying and talking to people, buying new clothes which she did not want and putting up with those friends he cared for whom she did not like, as part of her wifely duties.

To his credit, Robert did not mention children. She didn't think he cared particularly, but the women of his family were prone to asking after her health very often and Abby knew it was for one reason. It was not that she and Robert did not go to bed together often, though not every night. Three or four nights a week he did not come to her bed and she was quite happy alone, though a little hurt to think that he would not come just to sleep with her, that there must always be a reason. At first she did not mind, but it soon occurred to her that after she had gone to bed, the house was very still. One night, she ventured into his bedroom to find it empty. The next time he didn't come to her, it was empty again. He was nowhere that she could discover in the house and even in a house that size what could he do at night but sleep, read, smoke or drink by the fire? Abby went back to bed and, if she had been the kind of woman who wept much, she would have done so at the suspicions which thereafter crossed her mind.

Over dinner the following evening she said to him, 'Tell me, Robert, do you go to whores?'

Her husband choked over a mouthful of beef. He took a long drink of wine, coughed until his eyes ran and, when he had wiped his face on his napkin, he said, 'Dear God, woman, what a thing to say!'

'Do you?'

'Of course I damned well don't!'

'Then you have somebody else.'

Robert took another swig of wine.

'Whatever happened to tact?' he said.

'Do you?'

'Abby, my life is mine.'

'You have a mistress, then.'

He looked severely across the table at her.

'Well-bred women do not discuss such subjects,' he said.

'I'm not well bred, so it doesn't count.'

'Do you want me in your bed every night?'

'I certainly don't want you in anybody else's.'

He looked down at his plate for a second.

'How can I say this without sounding nasty? Women like bed. Ladies don't. I respect you and I also expect, as your husband, to come to your bed when I choose. The subject is closed.'

'How can you go to bed with another woman? I'm your wife! Aren't I a good wife to you? Is it because I haven't conceived a child? Is it?'

'It has nothing to do with any of that.'

'What has it to do with then?'

Robert sighed.

'Men have needs. I don't wish to discuss this any more,' he said and got up and walked out.

Anybody would have thought, looking at Rhoda, that she and Gil had the perfect marriage. She seemed happy. This was what she had wanted: freedom. She shopped with Helen, spent time with the baby, chatted with Gil's father and mother, ate chocolate and read by the fire when the weather was bad and spent many hours walking on her beloved moors. Each night she turned the key in the lock of the door between their bedrooms. Gil asked for nothing. Most of the time he stayed at work.

The contract had been signed and work was going ahead. It was going to be a massive task. It would take ten thousand pounds to widen the river and covered berths were to be built, he had insisted on that. His father had argued that they would be draughty and would exclude light, but Gil had promised John Marlowe a launch date eighteen months ahead and he was not about to go back on this. He had also built a self-propelled model of forty-six feet and was doing all kinds of testing in a specially built dock. The results were exciting. If he changed the shape so that it was slightly finer, he would need less power for better speed. The broader beam meant the river must be dredged and widened but many shipbuilders, including his father and Henderson, had been gradually doing this for years and were only pleased at the proposal. They were not quite so pleased at having to contribute financially.

Gil would have stayed overnight often in the office but since Edward came home so rarely, and only then to see Matthew, Gil didn't. He went home to his polite wife and his cold bed. His temper had suffered too. At work sometimes now he could hear William in his voice. Things which seemed obvious to him had to be repeated. People did not work efficiently enough or fast enough to suit him or John or the Admiralty and from time to time they sent their dreaded committee to interfere. It took all Gil's self-control not to shout at them too.

One night that autumn, when Gil had gone to bed late, he awoke with a start in the darkness, knowing even as he opened his eyes that someone was in the room. It was Rhoda. She had a candlestick in her hand and her face was full of distress. The room was chilly because the nights were becoming cold and the fire had gone out long since. She looked ridiculously young, her hair in plaits and her nightdress long and white.

'I had a bad dream,' she said.

It must have been very bad, Gil thought, to get her into his room.

'Sit down,' Gil said. He pulled off the top cover, gave it to her and she wrapped it around her. 'Do you want to tell me about it?'

'It was awful. I was up on the moors and I got lost. I don't get lost because I know them but it was dark and cold, so very cold . . . and I was alone. The wind was doing that sort of low moaning sound it makes when there's heather or bracken. I couldn't see and there was nowhere to go and I stumbled and fell and hurt myself and then—'

'And then?'

'That was all. When I woke up—'

'It's all right. You can stay here.'

'No, I—'

'It's all right,' he said again slowly, trying to reassure her. Rhoda hesitated, but when he drew back the bedclothes for her she got in and after a short while she went to sleep. He awoke briefly some time later to find her cuddled in against his back, sound asleep. She was still there when the maid came in with the early morning tea. Rhoda would have run like a startled hare when she had gone but he said, 'No, stay there and drink the tea. I never have time. I have to get to work.'

'But it's early yet.'

'I always go at this hour.'

He bathed and dressed. When he came back into the room, she had drunk the tea and gone back to sleep.

That evening when he returned home, she didn't say much. She ate nothing at dinner, and as the evening progressed became very pale. Usually she went to bed early, long before he did, but tonight she lingered. Gil knew the courage it took to face the following night after you had had a bad dream.

'Shall I see you upstairs?' he offered in the end.

Rhoda looked like a child caught out in mischief.

'There's no need.'

'I'm going to bed anyway.'

He lit a candle for her and took one for himself, but when they reached her room Rhoda hesitated.

'I can leave the middle door open if you want.'

Still she didn't move.

'Do you want to come and sleep with me?'

She did. After that she slept in his bed every night. By day she rode her horse out on to the moors, took the dogs with her, or took them for long walks. She went shopping in town with Gil's mother and bought pretty clothes and ornaments for her hair. She went visiting with his mother and Helen. She seemed happy. Each night when Gil came home, if it was before bedtime she would run to him and kiss him. After a while, that winter, she grew bolder and would hug him. If they were alone she sat on his knee and snuggled her face in against his neck. She talked to him about her day and she would tease and kiss him and stroke his hair. In fact, apart from the way that she slept in his bed, she treated him very much as she had undoubtedly treated her father when she was a little girl, he thought. She would play games in the woods with him, hiding behind trees and having him call her and popping out unexpectedly. She wrote him silly notes and sat by the fire for hours in the bad weather reading novels. Gil realised by the end of the winter that Rhoda adored him. For her, he was her father come back to life.

He tried to get her to kiss him, but she backed away in horror at anything more than what she had allowed. He tried to get her to talk about Jos Allsop but it seemed that she did not understand; she had wiped from her mind whatever her stepfather had done to her. To onlookers Gil could see that his marriage looked perfect. Men turned envious eyes on him. Rhoda was beautiful now, safe with him, loved by his family, cared for in that great house, looked after. She could not be touched. When they went out, elegant and beautiful she clung to his arm. Other men were of no interest to her. She didn't leave his side and Gil could see their envious glances as they imagined her smooth young body. She put on weight and became rounded. Her skin glowed; her eyes shone; her teeth sparkled. She was completely happy with him, Gil knew.

When they had got back from America and Gil had seen Jos for the first time, the other man looked so much as usual, so ordinary, that Gil was not convinced he had done anything. He was not sure that his wife was stable, so he kept both himself and her away from the man and was civil when he had to be.

She loved presents. Gil quite often took her to the jeweller they frequented in Newcastle and there he would let her choose earrings for her pretty ears, bangles for her slim wrists, chains to put around her neck where he was not allowed to kiss her. He bought emeralds to match her engagement ring and watched the pleasure come into her face. She was like a child at Christmas and she would thank him profusely, cover his face with kisses, rush from the carriage to show everyone what he had bought her. She told him how much she loved him.

Gil bought furs for her exquisite body and she leaped on him in bed and kissed him. She hated the smell of whisky and, before Gil had been aware of this and had drunk some one night before bed, she recoiled in front of him, her eyes wild with fear. He never drank it again. There was more than one triumph in this. Sometimes her mother and stepfather came to the house and Rhoda unwittingly played the devoted wife. She liked to touch Gil, mostly, he knew, to reassure herself that he was still here; but to other people it looked as though she wanted him. Gil could see the puzzled look in Allsop's face and saw himself as other men did. Young and married to her and she hanging onto his arm, wearing beautiful clothes. And she was lovely. Allsop was always at least half drunk when he saw them, so it was difficult to be certain what had happened. He ignored his wife in company and she was pregnant again. Rhoda didn't seem to mind his presence as long as Gil was there, but sometimes he detected a glitter in her eyes and when they had gone she would often disappear up onto the fells alone.

Right from the beginning, Helen believed that Gil and Rhoda's marriage was a success, he could see. She kept out of the way unless there was some outing planned. It was, he thought, the best that she had loved him, leaving him to make his marriage work. He wished that he could have said something instead of having to play out this painful charade for Rhoda's sake. There was no way to better things. Night after night, Helen went to bed early and Gil was sure that she drank herself to sleep. She didn't talk much any more, or pay much attention to her child. Nothing seemed to reach her. She always proclaimed herself willing to go out with them, but sometimes she could be silent all day. He became afraid that life would always be like that, Edward coming back only to see his child, Helen alone and he pretending for Rhoda's sake that life was good. Only the work was any comfort and, as the weeks went by, he saw the ship begin to take shape and there was a kind of happiness in that. He solved each problem as it happened. He had, with Mr McGregor's help, seen the engineering problems, most of them from the beginning, and with the experts from the drawing office and the design team done tests, but even so he was worried. If they had got this wrong it would be the biggest mistake in the history of shipping. On a bad day he was convinced the new ship would be a failure; on a good day he could visualise it on the water. He reported progress to Henderson every week when he saw him to play dominoes and he only wished that they could have been together on this project. He dreamed of joining forces, of amalgamating the two shipyards, of being able to work with Henderson every day. He was an easier man than William.

Henderson's health, however, was another matter. Sometimes he was too unwell to go to work and one evening that summer he collapsed when Gil was there, so that Gil had him put to bed and sent for the doctor. He also sent a message to Abby. The doctor had been and gone before she got there, white-faced. Gil knew that she was remembering her mother's illness and death.

'Doctor Brown says he'll be all right.'

Gil said this half a dozen times in the ten minutes after Abby had been up to see her father. He was sleeping, she said. Abby had never been a fat girl, but she was much thinner than she had been a year since, Gil thought, as she sat down in the garden and he gave her tea.

'Are you sure the doctor said he's going to get better?' she asked again.

'Certain.'

'He's not going to die. I don't think I could bear it. When I leave him he looks so lonely, but perhaps it's a reflection or it's my own loneliness that I see. I hate leaving him. It feels like a betrayal every time. I'm so grateful to you that you spend time with him.'

'It's not a hardship,' Gil said. 'I like him. I wish my own father was like him.'

'He and Robert don't get on. I thought they would. They seemed to like each other so well at first. If anything happens to him . . . Don't worry, I'm not going to cry.' She smiled bravely. 'Every time I see you I do it.'

'Yes, it's not very flattering,' Gil said and turned her smile natural.

Abby wanted to stay at the house with her father but she couldn't. She had her marriage to think about. She had discovered that things could not be mended in the bedroom; even alone with Robert, other women got in the way. It was difficult to be warm towards a man who had told you that you were inadequate. She had discovered that Robert kept a mistress. Not a long-time mistress; he would keep a young girl for a while and then pay her off. At least Abby thought that they were young girls. They seemed to her to be, much younger than she was but old enough for him. In bed he was no longer gentle with her. He kissed her once or twice and then mounted her as though she was a horse, Abby thought. He rode her until he was done and then got off. She wondered if that was how he treated his mistress and had to stop herself from asking. Night and morning he bedded her and Abby did not have to wonder why. The subject of an heir had become important and her husband came to her bed regularly. She was, however, determined not to send him from her into another woman's arms and pretended she was eager to have him with her, though the endurance was hard to bear. Robert was a man experienced with women; he could surely tell the difference between enthusiasm and determination. If he did, he gave no sign of it. There was no child and things were more difficult than ever.

Chapter Twelve

When John Marlowe's ship was ready to be launched it was a great day at Collingwood's shipyard. It would be another year at least before the ship was fitted out, but the hull was finished. Edwina Marlowe, John's wife, was to launch the ship, which would be called the *Northumbria*. For once William had called for a special party for all the workers and their families and inside the shipyard offices themselves a feast had been brought in for the Collingwoods and their family and friends.

It was a cold grey autumn day. The Tyne looked leaden, but the crowds who had gathered to watch the launch were cheerful and so were the men who had built the ship, and who now lined its decks.

Helen was there with Matthew and her parents. Edward had come; Toby was there in the background; Abby and Henderson were there, and even Robert. Rhoda was bright-eyed, cosy in furs, holding Gil's arm and beaming at everyone, her cheeks pink from the cold. She knew that this was his moment of triumph, his first ship, and the biggest ship ever to be built here. He could feel the excitement in her, her pride at his achievement. Edward came to him.

'Well, little brother, what a day.'

Gil looked at him. He was drunk; not the kind of drunk that falls over and sings and shouts, but the slow drunkenness that is never quite sober. Edward smiled at Matthew and took the child from Helen. Gil was glad that he had caught the look that Edward bestowed upon his son. He thought it was the biggest love in his brother's life; nothing flawed about it. Edward loved his child purely. Gil hoped that he would feel the same when Matthew became a little older and was not just his son but a separate person. William had never been able to make that distinction. Even now Gil was 'my son, the genius', whereas he had turned his back on Edward. The only thing Edward had done that his father was pleased with was to provide an heir. It was the sole reason his father let him into the house or, on the odd occasion when he chose, to come to the works. Neither of them would ever be free of William.

Henderson had insisted on coming even though he was not looking very well. Abby was pale with the cold and Robert didn't speak to Gil. He couldn't think how she had persuaded Robert to attend a ship launch.

'Are you thrilled?' Edward said. 'You must be. The biggest ship ever. You did want the biggest, the best, the fastest. It was what you wanted and it's beautiful.'

He was right, Gil thought, it was beautiful. No wonder men called ships 'she'. This mighty being which he had created in his mind, seen so long ago in his head, this ship would make his reputation. He knew with a sureness he rarely felt that it would cross the Atlantic and take the Blue Riband and that his father would fairly burst with pride. Collingwood's would be made for ever and ever. Even now, he knew, the men spoke of him with respect, were glad to work on his ship. Gil wanted to do more and after this he would be able to. William would give them more money, build them better houses, ease their difficult lives. Gil would have more power in the shipyard and be able to do things.

More than anything, Gil wanted Henderson Reed's approval that day. He didn't know why; it was bad enough constantly needing his father to be pleased. He felt like a spaniel, wanting to be continually patted and told how clever he was; but Gil had such respect for Henderson and he knew today that Henderson was there just for him, even though the older man neither looked at him nor spoke to him. He leaned against Abby as Gil had not seen him do before. He was standing next to Robert, but they ignored one another. Henderson's dislike of his son-in-law had grown.

Edwina moved forward in the cold Newcastle day and said the wonderful words.

'I name this ship *Northumbria*. May God bless her and all who sail in her.'

Rhoda clutched Gil's arm even more tightly and, as the bottle of champagne broke over the ship's bows and the contents spilled over its perfection, Gil thought that if he lived for another hundred years he would never be as happy again. The ship began to move very slowly down the slipway towards the cold water of the 'queen of rivers'. The Tyne opened its arms and received the ship into its depths and the water came up on every side. The men on board and the people round about cheered and took off their caps and threw them in the air and were still cheering when the ship came to rest in the middle of the river.

It changed in those seconds, Gil thought. He felt like the parent watching the child become an independent adult. It was a separation, a letting go, a loss, a farewell, a parting. There was still more than a year's work to be done, but he felt that it was not his as it had been. It was plucked from his imagination and was gone. Gil wanted to run from this mighty being that his mind had conceived. He was afraid it would turn into a tyrant.

They went back to the offices through the many hundreds of people who had come to see the launch and it was easier there, drinking champagne and receiving the good wishes of his friends, of all the other shipbuilders who had come to the launch and many other important people of the city. Abby and Robert seemed at home there and went around chatting to their friends.

Edward and Toby left as soon as could be considered decent, though Toby came to Gil and congratulated him warmly.

'My dear boy, I'm so pleased for you,' he said.

Henderson said nothing, but Gil didn't mind. The old man's eyes were light on him, so Gil went over to him.

'Champagne, Henderson?'

'No bloody fear. I'll stick to ale.'

'How are you Abby?' Gil asked her as she reached her father at the same time.

'Very well indeed,' she said and Gil knew that she was lying. He knew her so well. 'We're going away.'

'Anywhere nice?'

'To France, I believe. It's warmer there. I'm trying to persuade my father to come with us.'

'Can't leave the yard,' Henderson said.

'Aren't you ever going to leave it, Father?'

'Not before I drop dead.'

Abby smiled, but it was a forced affair. Henderson watched her go to her husband and then he looked at Gil.

'I want to tell you something.'

'What?'

Henderson's watery eyes turned paler as Gil watched.

'I was wrong about you,' he said.

'Why, Henderson, you couldn't have been.'

'It isn't funny. If we could only look into the future. I can't stand him. He's never done a day's work in his life. He hasn't contributed anything. "By their fruit shall ye know them." That bugger hasn't got any fruits. He hasn't even given her a child. I wish I'd let you marry Abby.'

'It wouldn't have been any good. She didn't like me and she's so bossy,' Gil said lightly.

'Takes after her mother. She was sharp was Bella. I wouldn't care if he made her happy. Runs after other women.'

* * *

That night there was a big party at the house. Everyone danced and the musicians played well into the morning. Helen wouldn't dance with Gil or with anybody else.

'What's the matter?' he asked her.

'I caught my leg on the table edge at home the other day.' She called her parents' house home, Gil noticed.

'Is it all right?'

'It will be, but it hurts just at the moment. Go and dance with Rhoda.'

'Helen—'

'I know. Go and dance with her,' Helen said gently.

Rhoda was unusually happy that night. Gil wondered whether she had been drinking wine but, since she didn't care for that and laughed when he suggested it and said, 'I'm so proud of you,' he didn't worry until they went to bed.

It was late and dark and the house was silent by then; they had been among the last to go to bed. Gil didn't want the day to end because he wasn't sure whether he would ever be able to have another that was as good as this one. She got into bed and sat there with her knees up to her chin and watched him as he lingered by the fire with a last drink.

'Gil—'

'Mmm?'

'Have you ever thought about having children?'

'What?'

'You know, that we might not.'

'Children?'

'Yes.'

'I can't say it bothers me one way or the other.'

'You wouldn't mind then, if we didn't.'

'I don't know yet. I might, yes.'

'I think I might too, in the long run, eventually.'

'We don't have to think about it now. We've got years and years.'

'Aren't you coming to bed?'

'Shortly.'

'Now?'

'I don't want the day to end,' Gil admitted, 'it's been so perfect.'

'Could it be better?'

'No, I don't think so.'

'Maybe it could.' She got out of bed and came over to him and sat down on his knee. This was nothing new, but the way that she kissed him was.

'I thought you didn't want to do this,' Gil said, stopping her for fear he had misinterpreted.

'I didn't, but you're not him. You've proved over and over that you're not and I love you.'

'Rhoda . . . I think the act is . . . always aggressive.'

'I don't think you're very aggressive,' she said, smiling. 'Don't you want me because of him?'

'My God, yes.'

'I would like a child and you're the kindest man I've ever met. You make me feel safe, completely secure. I think I might be able to . . . I don't feel as if I'm your wife. I feel rather as though I'm your child and it's nice and for a while it was . . . You love me. Nobody who didn't love me could have been as good to me as you have been and I love you. I've been lucky with you. I didn't know at the beginning. It was just a gamble and I was desperate to get away from him and . . . not just from him, from all of it, the memories of my father and the way that my mother had become somebody I didn't know and their foul children . . . I feel so lucky. I want to spend all my life with you. Come to bed now.'

But he didn't because she didn't get off his lap and she giggled and kissed him. Gil tried to talk to himself, be very slow and careful because he didn't really believe she was going to give herself to him, not after all this time. It would make the day good beyond all reason and that had not happened to him before. There was always a hitch, always a flaw, always some bastard to spoil it and nobody had yet spoiled this day. He could spoil it now if he was clumsy or if the memories of her stepfather intruded and he was sure that they would. The act was a taking and he was not sure whether she could bear to give any more, whether there was anything left other than the child she had so far offered as herself. He tried to think what Allsop had been like apart from the obvious brutality. It had most likely been her bed, so as she went on kissing him he very carefully eased her down onto the rug in front of the fire and held her to him. It was difficult after so long not to want her too much for caution, but he had spent months building her confidence. One mistake now and it could all be gone. He talked to her, kissed her, remembered what had happened last time he got hold of her like this in New York, but it was quite different. She was warm, willing. She wanted him and it was much easier than he had thought. When she tensed even slightly, he stopped touching her and asked her if she wanted to stop, but she said 'no'. There was a slight reluctance on her, but he thought that she had watched Matthew for so long and decided that she wanted a child. Since she trusted him sufficiently she would put up with this, the cost with him would be worth the eventual result. He realised now that Helen had wanted him almost to the point of madness. This was not the same, pale by comparison, but it was better than nothing unless it should break down the trust again and she should retreat into that wild being of the moors she protected herself with. He felt awkward, as though he might drop her and smash everything, so it was almost a relief to have her. She turned her face away. It was the first time in such an act that Gil had felt dirty and troublesome and ashamed. This must be what it was like when you went to a whore, somebody who didn't want you, who was doing this for a reason and not for pleasure. How could men enjoy somebody who didn't want them? And yet you could, he realised; biology itself said so. Having her even like this was ecstasy after so long. He wished he could have run to Helen. He didn't know why he hadn't gone to her on all those many nights when she slept alone and he slept alone and there was nothing to stop them. Even when Rhoda slept in his bed he could have sneaked out. She would not have known. And Edward was in bed at nights with Toby. Yet in a way he had condemned them all.

When it was over, Gil wanted her more. It was like having one sip of champagne, one chocolate after years of doing without. Helen had always taken him into her arms but Rhoda didn't, as though he was a dress she had tried on and decided didn't suit her. Failing to please was something Gil knew he was good at. He had spent years trying to please Abby, his father, Henderson, Edward. The one person he had not tried to please was Helen. They had started off from the same place and when they went to bed there were no winners and losers, no lovers or beloved. It all balanced and worked and had been right in so many different ways from the beginning, always new but always right, always safe and so dangerous, so deliciously, spectacularly pleasurable. He wanted to crawl away and find her, so that he could not be in this permanent competition with himself where, no matter what he did, how hard he tried, he failed always as though some part of him was standing on a high rock above, saying, 'no, not quite, just a bit more' and he was hanging on to the rock by his fingertips and slipping down. One day he would slip altogether and after that there would be no more trying to succeed.

'Did I hurt you?'

'No.'

'Was it like as if it was him?'

'I don't remember.' She got up.

'You don't remember?'

She looked at him.

'I had pushed it from my mind, a lot of it. I just remembered the brutality and the fear, but there was none of that here. I wish it had been the first time, that's all. I'm your wife. I don't want to be anything else.'

She reached out and Gil put his arms around her. They went

to bed. He couldn't sleep for wanting her, but in the morning she kissed him and encouraged him and this time she didn't turn her face away. She laughed and made rash promises and it was Sunday, so he didn't have to go to work. They stayed in bed for as long as might be considered decent among people who had been married for so long. They got ready and had breakfast and went to church as usual, but all the way through the service Rhoda made eyes at him so that he could concentrate on nothing but her. There were visitors in the afternoon and many people had stayed, so they had no opportunity to be alone or to sneak away. The evening was endless and the talk was of the great new ship. Gil couldn't have been less interested. All he wanted was to take his wife to bed. After dinner, they slipped away to his bedroom, pulled each other's clothes off and made love and it was, he thought, the first time then. And a miracle had occurred. Saturday had been a perfect day. Sunday was even better.

Chapter Thirteen

Helen didn't go back to Durham with her parents when they left that Sunday, even though they tried to persuade her. There was nothing at Bamburgh House for her now except that William and Charlotte loved Matthew and encouraged her to stay. Gil had been thinking too much about Rhoda that day to consider Helen, but the following morning early, when he got up to go to work his mother, to his surprise, was already up. As he came downstairs, she had a worried frown on her face.

'Helen isn't well. I think I ought to send for the doctor.'

'She was complaining about her leg on Saturday, but I didn't think anything of it.'

'Was she? I didn't know there was anything wrong and her mother didn't mention it. She wasn't limping. She has a fever.'

His mother was obviously in need of reassurance so Gil went upstairs with her to Helen's room. It had been a long time since he had been in there and he was not comfortable. He thought of the nights he had spent there in her arms but when he saw her, thoughts like that left him. His mother was right. She didn't seem well. The sweat stood out on her forehead and her cheeks were burning. He touched her forehead with his cool hand and she opened her eyes and smiled at him.

'That's nice,' she said.

'Is it your leg, Helen?'

'My what?'

'Your leg. You said on Saturday—'

'Oh no, it's fine,' she said. 'This is just a chill. I need to sleep, that's all.'

She closed her eyes, and turned her back on them. Gil followed his mother out of the room.

'I hate to bother the doctor,' she said.

William came downstairs as they stood in the hall at the bottom.

'Helen is unwell,' Charlotte said. 'She says it's just a chill.'

'She knows her own mind, surely. Stop fussing, woman. Come along, lad, we're late.' And his father went off along the hall to the dining-room.

Gil was happy at work. He was thinking of how pleasant it would be to go home to Rhoda and, long before the day was done, when the autumn light had gone and the cold evening had begun, he stared from the office window, thinking about his pretty wife and the homecoming she would provide. A single star was twinkling above his office window. He got up and watched it for a while and thought how lucky he was. He had everything. If it hadn't been for the fact that William insisted on them working until six, he would have gone home at half-past four. Since then, he had not been able to concentrate. He had not thought he could feel so much joy. He let his mind wander past the ship launch again and the men throwing their caps into the air as the ship went down the slipway, the noisy crowds shouting and cheering, the party afterwards and how beautiful Rhoda had looked and everybody had been so pleased, then home to the second party. And Rhoda. She had completed everything. His wife loved him and he loved her and nothing could spoil it.

He was standing there when his father came into the office.

'Your mother won't be pleased if we're late for dinner,' he said and they left.

Gil watched that same star from the carriage window as they drove home in the darkness. It was a cold, clear night with barely a cloud and the moon was full, so there was plenty of light. When they reached the house there was a horse and trap by the door. That was when Gil thought of Helen for the first time. The doctor.

He hurried inside, along the hall and into the drawing-room. His mother and Dr Brown were in there and they turned towards him faces that told him nothing good.

'Is Helen ill?'

'She's not well,' his mother said.

'What is it?' He directed his look towards the doctor as his father came into the room.

'She has a badly infected leg,' Dr Brown said.

'Her leg? She said it was better.'

'I would say it has been increasingly bad for at least a week.'

'A week? Why didn't she tell somebody? Shouldn't she be in hospital?'

'I don't want to move her. She's too ill. Nothing could be done there which cannot be done here. I will arrange for nursing and we will do our very best to look after her.'

Gil stared at the doctor's careworn face. He looked tired.

'What does that mean?' he said.

'It means that her condition could deteriorate and quickly. She should have been looked after several days ago.'

'Didn't her parents realise?'

'Presumably not.'

'But she must have known. She . . . she must have,' Gil said and there was a small, sick feeling which began in his stomach and seemed to make its way through his body like a snake.

'Sometimes these things seem unimportant, especially to people like mothers who have the concerns of their children to think about. They don't understand that neglect can lead to serious consequences.'

'Edward must be sent for,' William said from behind Gil.

Gil couldn't believe what they were saying. He left the room, ran through the hall and took the stairs two at a time, along the hall to Helen's room. When he opened the door, Rhoda was sitting on the bed with a cool cloth in her fingers, dabbing Helen's face.

'Helen?' he said and she opened her eyes.

'Why are they fussing? I'm not ill. I'm not ill, am I, Rhoda?'

'No, of course not,' Rhoda said soothingly.

Gil sat down on the bed and took Helen's hand.

'Do you remember the house, Gil?' she said.

'What house?'

She laughed. Her voice sounded hoarse and her laughter was full of disbelief.

'The house in Spain.'

'Was it in Spain?'

'Where did you think it was?'

'I don't know.'

'At the top of the mountain. It was best at the top of the mountain because we got what breezes there were. You do remember it?'

'Yes.'

'And the bedroom? The way that breeze used to catch the white curtains in the bedroom. You said it was as if they were doing a dance. The bedroom in the afternoons.'

Gil glanced at Rhoda to see if she was taking any notice, but she pressed his hand and shook her head to imply that she knew it was nonsense. His heart was beating so hard that it hurt. He and Helen had not talked about this before. He was not aware that she knew any of this and it was nonsense. It was. Before she had arrived at the house as Edward's intended bride he had never seen her, he knew that he hadn't. He had always told himself that it was the way he had justified wanting Helen, taking her. He had pretended to himself that they had had some other life, that they had been lovers before, but they had not talked about it. Yet here she was describing the very scenes that his mind had given him a hundred times. He could almost smell the lemons and oranges in the garden, see the blue of the ocean, feel that soft breeze which had made its way across the mountain, cooled in the high air above the valley wherein lay the little white town. He could see it clearly now, the neat houses and the palm trees, the long evening shadows. People would be sitting outside drinking wine and talking and children played games in the quiet streets. Yet his sensible mind told him that he had not been to Spain. He had been to America. He had memories of New York, but they didn't seem as clear to him as the place where he and Helen had been and not been together.

Helen was watching him and her eyes were so bright that he could hardly meet them.

'You thought I didn't remember,' she said.

'I knew you did,' he said cheerfully.

'We didn't talk about it. I thought you might think it was silly. We were there together. It was wonderful. When I saw you again, do you remember, you were standing at the top of the steps here and I was talking to your parents below. I knew it was you.'

All this while Rhoda was applying cool cloths and looked as though she was taking no notice of the conversation. To her, Gil could see, Helen was a girl in a fever, unaware of what she was saying and he was agreeing with her to keep her as calm as possible.

Later, the doctor sent a nurse, but Rhoda would not leave Helen's side. She stayed there all night. Helen slept fitfully and she talked a great deal. Some of it even Gil couldn't understand. All night and all the next day she burned and sweated. Gil's father insisted on them going to work.

'There's nothing we can do here,' he said harshly. 'The doctor has it in hand. We have money to make and orders to see to.'

'Surely for one day—'

William looked severely at him.

'Is it a service to stay here with her? You'll be better off at work and so will I.'

His father was being practical, Gil knew, and so he went and in some ways it was better. There was nothing they could do and Helen recognised nobody that morning so it was unlikely she would know whether or not he was there. Edward had arrived at the house early that morning so, from his father's way of thinking, there were sufficient people. He and Gil would be in the way. Gil did no work. He sat at his desk and his mind flooded with guilt and responsibility and the heavy notion that she might die and he would not be there. He told himself that she wouldn't know him even if he was there. When, after the longest day of his life, they finally went home, though there were grave faces in the house she was not dead. Gil ran up the stairs and into the room and there he stopped just inside the door. The young woman in the bed was not the girl he had loved. She was shrunken and grey and her hair was like seaweed on the pillow. Her eyes had no life. She looked tiny.

The nurse and the doctor were there. Rhoda was standing by the window. His mother was crying softly in a chair and Edward was sitting in front of the fire, not looking at anyone. Her parents were there, too, and they all looked so distressed that Gil knew she was not going to get better. He had not noticed until then that the room was different from how it had been when he and Helen had shared a bed. In those days there were always flowers and books, writing materials, pretty covers on the chairs and colourful bedclothes. Now it was all white and there was nothing to relieve it as though, he thought scarcely able to form it in his mind, she had attempted to recreate their bedroom in the house at the top of the mountain. There were white curtains at the windows which would not keep out the bitter autumn weather. Where had those come from? Had she so desperately needed somebody that she tried to recreate that time?

She opened her eyes and said his name. She had aged several years since the night before and her face was almost transparent. So was the hand she stretched out to him. He went to her, sat down on the bed beside her and took her hand.

'I was waiting for you to come,' she said.

'I'm here.'

'It's so hot. It's always so hot. Ask for some water.'

Gil put the glass to her lips and she swallowed a little.

Beyond the white curtains he could see the cold winter night, with lots of stars. He could remember lying in bed with her, watching those same stars, the windows flung back wide in spite of the cold because she had said that night was too pretty to be closed out. There was a white sheen upon the lawns; he had seen it coming back in the carriage. He had been so happy the night before. He ought to have known that such things could not last more than a few hours. He wanted to cry. He wanted to tell her that he loved her.

'Everything is so white,' she said. 'Isn't that good? I do love you.'

'I love you too.'

The room was silent. It had been silent before, but the atmosphere changed then. They might think it just a sick woman's rantings, but it was hardly appropriate that, with her husband in the room, she should tell his brother that she loved him. Not that anyone would expect her to say such a thing to the husband Edward had been to her.

'Do you think I did this on purpose?'

She was quite lucid, Gil thought.

'No.'

'Perhaps I want to die.'

'I don't think you do. What about Matthew?'

'Children have a future. What was my future to be?'

Gil didn't know what to say to that. The sick feeling that hadn't left him since the day before was almost enveloping him. He wished that all these people would leave the room. He wanted to say wild things to her.

'You're not crying, are you, Gil?'

'No.'

'You look as though you are. It's the first time you've ever cried over me.'

'You didn't really do this on purpose?'

'What, to punish you? Do you think I would? I will see you again you know. This isn't the finish. Though I have to say that when I saw you here the first time, a great deal of the feeling I had had for you had already gone, but you did love me, more than you loved anyone else?'

'Yes.'

Rhoda turned from the window. Gil could see her from the corner of his eye. Would she go on thinking that he was just responding to a dying woman?

'I want to tell you something, Gil, something very important. I want you to look after Matthew.'

The silence changed again. It was not hostile, but it was as if the other people in the room felt left out, ignored, that they had realised she wanted nobody but him near her when she was dying. Her mother and father moved in their discomfort and Edward was watching him. Her voice was down to a whisper and even that seemed an effort, but everyone in the room could hear her words.

'Of course we will.'

'No, you.' She tried to get up from the pillows and couldn't. 'Matthew is your son. I'm sorry that I deceived you. I had to lie. I thought I was the only one losing by it. Edward isn't fit to look after him and he isn't capable of fathering a child. If he says he is, then he lies. When he's drunk he thinks he's a man and he never was. Matthew is yours.'

The silence seemed to hang in the room for ever. Then Rhoda gave a hoarse cry and broke it. She ran. It was the only way she could ever meet disaster, by running away, Gil thought. If she had managed to pretend that Helen was not in her right mind, then the moment might have passed . . . Edward was on his feet. Charlotte went after Rhoda. Without looking, Gil could see his brother. There was nothing to lose between them; it had been over long since. He had known that his brother had used him as a pawn in some complicated game and that those evenings at the billiard hall were not for him. The few days when Edward had seemed to care for him and even want his company were dispelled on the afternoon Edward had looked at him and then kissed Toby Emory on the mouth. They had not been born to love one another, as perhaps brothers often weren't, though it seemed so wasteful to Gil. People born of the same parents were meant to go together like pieces of the same jigsaw, but he and his brother had been born to destroy one another and there was not even any pity in it. You could not point to a time and say here was where it went wrong. It was broken and lost and there was nothing but the ruins of it now. And Edward blamed him about Helen. He could understand that. He had always blamed himself over it and the shock of the child was cold on him.

Did Edward believe her? If he did, then in those seconds he had lost the only thing which kept him a Collingwood. If the child was not his, then there was nothing to hold him here. In a way it was what he had wanted. His freedom lay just beyond the door, but the pain of losing his son could not be worth it. As for the girl dying in the bed, he had betrayed her before she had betrayed him and her revenge was complete. Edward came across the room towards them.

'Matthew's my son, he's mine. He's mine! You said he was mine.'

Helen smiled faintly.

'I tried to forgive you. You can try to forgive me.'

'Never! I hope you burn in hell, you bitch!'

The confusion was somehow nothing to do with Gil. He took her into his arms.

'Don't worry,' he said, 'I'll look after Matthew.'

Edward was shouting and people were crying, but Helen lay quietly in his arms and smiled at him.

He didn't know what time passed before his mother came back into the room.

'She's gone! I tried to stop her but she wouldn't listen to me and she's gone out into the night and I'm so afraid!' Charlotte went to William.

Gil put Helen's body carefully down and then he swiftly left the room. He sped down the stairs and, pausing only to collect a coat, opened the front door. It was a savage night. Wind blew the rain almost horizontally. He could see by the hall lights, then he was out into the bitter weather and the door was closed behind him. He called her name, moving away, trying to think where she might have gone – not far, surely, in this. Then he thought of how she would be feeling, of what Jos had done and of what he had done. She might go anywhere. It was almost impossible to see, but he knew the countryside around his home so he went to all the places that they had gone together and those that had been her favourites. He shouted her name and the wind took it away a thousand times. He didn't know which direction to go in, so he tried to go everywhere.

It was the longest night of his life and he was soaked through within minutes. He stepped in deep water every so often, banged himself off trees where there was no light. The wind whipped rain across his face, his feet and fingers were numb and his hair provided a way for rain to make its way into his eyes so that it stung and inside his collar and down past his shirt. The rain turned to sleet and, halfway through the night, to snow and though some sensible part of himself said that she would have gone home, he stayed out in case she had not done so. When morning came the snow was worse than ever; it was a blizzard. When darkness fell again, he returned to the lights of the house.

There was an uneasy silence in the hall. He threw off his heavy coat and made his way into the drawing-room. His mother and Helen's mother were there by the fire with Matthew. His mother looked up briefly, her mother not at all.

'She came home?' he said, but he knew the answer before his mother gave it.

'No. Your father and Edward and her father and all the other men are out looking for her.'

He found dry clothes and went back out, but the blizzard was worse than ever and the light began to fail in early afternoon. From time to time he heard her name shouted, but he didn't meet any of the others. He went on and on and felt as though now he could go on until the end of time. It was dark again and he was lost. He was trudging through deep snow and fell over something and knew that God was watching. Even a second or two without the knowledge would have been some consolation, but there was no doubt that he had found her. It reminded him very much of being small and watching farmers take their dead lambs from snow drifts. She was too cold for there to be any life left in her. He knew then that everything that mattered was over, that all the promise of the world was finished and that whatever happened now was the merest detail. But for Matthew, he would have stayed there. Helen's words went round and round in his head. Edward would not take the child. His father and mother would take it and bring it up as they had brought him up. It was not a thought for men who scared easily. William, having only one grandchild, would not let Helen's parents have him to live with them. He would train the child for the business; he would beat him and humiliate him and . . .

He held Rhoda in his arms, much as he had held Helen those few hours ago. How strange, how unkind, how very terrible, to be punished with such sweeping purity so that there was nothing left that could be redeemed. He picked her out of the snowdrift and carried her home, away from the fells that she had loved so much, where she had left her spirit, where she had spent her last hours heartbroken because of what he had done. They would not meet again. He would go straight to hell and his sweet precious wife, whom men had treated so badly, would go to God and nobody would hurt her again. And God had other plans for him, he could sense it; it was not over yet.

He slipped several times. She became heavy and the wind and the snow took his balance from him with the dead weight in his arms. He slid down slopes which had been banksides and fields before the whiteness devoured them. The night went on and on as though the Day of Judgement had arrived, which it had. There would be no daylight again. At last, however, he came within sight of the house. He was inclined to leave her body on the doorstep as the little black-and-white cat he had had as a boy would leave mice as offerings, but he managed to open the front door and make his way into the hall and from there to the drawing-room.

They were all gathered. Rhoda's mother, who looked like her for the first time, burst into a screaming torrent of accusations and tears. Jos Allsop came forward and tried to take Rhoda from him and Gil swung away.

'Give me my daughter.'

'She was never your daughter, you bastard!'

'Give her to me. I'm going to kill you!'

They took her from him.

'She's dead,' Allsop said unnecessarily as he and Edward and William leaned over her, after they had put her onto the sofa and put a blanket around her. 'She's frozen, trying to get back to her mother and me, trying to get away from him and that mucky bitch!'

Gil glanced around. He had not noticed, but Helen's parents were not there. He didn't know what Jos Allsop was talking about. Nobody was dead. In a minute, Rhoda would open her eyes and smile and say how funny that he had been fooled and everything would be all right again. Helen and her parents had gone home. He waited and waited for her to open her eyes.

William looked at him. The soft look was gone. Gil backed away just a little. He was a child again and his father was going to beat him beyond pain and lock him into a room so cold that his body would go numb.

This was not happening. There was an old saying, what was it? Yes, he had it. Something about God only giving people what they could bear. Things like this didn't happen. Nobody could bear this, not even the strongest, ablest person in the world could bear this. Rhoda was asleep; she was cold; it had been a bad night. She was not dead. She could not be dead.

Allsop went for him, but his father and Edward were in the way. Gil was glad. His father knew and everything would be all right. His father cared for him now, because of the things he had done and would tell Jos Allsop that there was no place for anger here and no need and everything would be all right.

'Leave him,' William said.

'I'm going to kill him! Now or later, it doesn't matter to me.'

'Give me the child,' William said to Charlotte and her face changed. She held Matthew close to her and began to cry and protest. Gil couldn't understand why. Her crying was almost a wail.

'It isn't true. Helen was out of her mind with fever. You know she was. You can't do this. I won't let you. He's the only grandchild we've got or will have now. If you can't think of anything else, think of the family. He's your heir. He's the only person to inherit. He's the only one we've got.'

They prised the child from her. Matthew was crying at all the upset. Gil wasn't surprised. His father thrust the child forward, for some reason, at him.

'Take him and get out.'

Charlotte was almost screaming. Gil stared at the small, struggling boy.

'It's too cold for him to go anywhere,' he said sensibly. 'It's a blizzard.'

The men were actually holding Charlotte back and she was fighting with them, his demure and elegant mother.

'Take him.'

Gil took the child if only to shut him up, for he had begun fighting and screaming too, just like his grandmother.

'You will never come back here again, do you understand? You are not my son. You are not welcome here for the rest of your life and neither is your bastard.'

Gil looked at him. There was an explanation somewhere, but

he couldn't think of it and Matthew was not happy with Gil. He kicked and fought and great tears ran down his face.

'You could keep him here just for tonight. I would go and I could send for him when the weather is better.'

'Take him and go.'

'Right,' Gil said, matter-of-factly, and he took the screaming, kicking child and let two of the servants usher him beyond the front door. He stood on the step as they bolted the door behind him. He waited as though the weather was going to improve, when it was obvious that it was not. As the child's screams and kickings subsided because it was so cold, Gil undid his coat and put Matthew inside it. Then he began to walk away from the house, up the drive. Matthew was no longer fighting, though he was still crying.

Gil began to walk and his mind soon turned to practicalities. He had no money on him; he had nothing and it was snowing hard.

It took him most of the night to walk to Newcastle because the snow was so very deep and the wind had blown great drifts into the hedges and the insides of the road and on the road itself where there was no protection. He kept losing his way so although it was not a long way, it seemed it. It was early morning when he reached Jesmond and banged on the door of Henderson Reed's house.

Kate had just got up, by the look of her. She ushered him into the sitting-room and hastily cleaned the grate and emptied the ashes before assembling a new fire. Matthew had long since fallen asleep. Gil put him down on the sofa, carefully not bringing to mind the images of Rhoda. Henderson came down the stairs, fastening his dressing-gown.

'What in hell's name is going on?' he said, looking from Gil to the child and back again.

'I need a favour, Henderson.' To Gil's surprise his voice worked and it sounded clear and steady.

'Name it.'

'Will you keep Matthew here for a few days? It won't be long. It's just for now. It's so cold outside and he's so very little.'

Henderson was giving him a special look, one Gil hadn't seen before, as though Gil was a rather likeable imbecile and had to be humoured.

'I won't ever ask anything of you again as long as I live,' Gil offered. 'I swear it to you before God. Please.'

'Yes, of course,' he said. 'Come and sit by the fire. I was just going to have some breakfast. What would you like?'

Gil felt certain that he would not eat again before death.

'I can't stay,' he said lightly, 'but I will be back for him.'

'Mrs Wilkins has some particularly fine ham to cook. That with an egg or two and some coffee. You prefer coffee, don't you?'

Kate came back into the room bearing the coffee pot and cups and saucers, and milk and sugar on a tray.

'Has it snowed much in the country?' Henderson asked, pouring coffee and handing him a cup. Gil had not heard Henderson talk so much or be so convivial. Usually he was the opposite: grumpy and quiet. Perhaps the entire world had run mad.

Gil swallowed some of the hot liquid. It was tasteless.

'I wouldn't ask you, but I'm afraid for his wellbeing.'

'Small children need looking after,' Henderson agreed.

Gil put down his coffee cup and walked out.

'Wait just a minute—' Henderson began.

Gil got himself out of the house very fast. It was still snowing.

Chapter Fourteen

Robert had insisted on going back to Europe. Abby was tired of it and she was worried about her father. She wanted to stay in Northumberland. It was raining in France, so she could not see the advantage of being there. They had travelled down through the countryside and in some ways it reminded her of Northumberland and made her ache for home. The little villages and farms and the countryside around made her long for her father. She was tired of all the endless moving about that her life had become; she was tired of Robert's friends and of doing nothing useful. She had discovered that where there was nothing but leisure there was no leisure, and though she had tried telling herself over and over again that other people envied her life, her husband, her houses, her dresses, her jewellery and her not having to work, anything which there was too much of could become monotonous.

If she could even have helped poor people; if she could have given money to decent causes, assisted people who needed help, that would have been something; but Robert did not believe in change so she was allowed to alter nothing, not even a set of curtains in any of the houses. She was sure that the feeling he had had for her when they were first married had evaporated almost entirely. He spent most of his time in pleasures which had nothing to do with her, men's pursuits, shooting, fishing, drinking, playing cards, going out to clubs and to various sporting matches. Abby was meant to carry on their social life alone and it was a lonely occupation.

She was still not pregnant, though he came to her bed three or four times a week. He did that out of duty and she let him out of duty. Her mind, having nothing to do, thought long on Newcastle and her father. She tried not to think about Gil. She could see that he was happily married and that his work was going very well. People talked about him with respect. Abby tried to be glad for him, but it was difficult. She knew that when you had regard for people you should wish them well, but it was difficult when he was so happy and she was not. She had homesickness and kept thinking of her father waving her away from the door of his house in Jesmond. Every time she did so the tears rose in her eyes and sometimes fell down her cheeks and she would chide herself and say that it was for lack of anything better to do that she was self-pitying and it was the worst thing anybody could be. She wanted to be home so much that the countryside around her made it worse. Though the weather was wet and cool, the countryside shone, the stones of the houses seemed bright and the fields were so green. Each morning she would walk up to the bakery and buy fresh bread for breakfast and it was the most wonderful smell in the world.

She was so afraid not to be there. She was afraid that her father would die while she was in France. She told herself to be rational; she told herself that it was unfair to Robert. He had wanted to show her this part of France, the countryside to the west of Bordeaux where his friends had a house, Perigueux, and the little villages around it. Robert loved being abroad. He spoke several languages fluently. It was one thing about him which Abby admired. He had spent most of his life going from country to country and knew French, Italian and Spanish.

The people they stayed with there, Veronique and Marcel, spoke little English. Abby found it difficult, stumbling along, not understanding their fast speech and there was no one around her who spoke English. She liked their way of life. They lived for food and wine and Veronique did not have servants as Abby did. She ran her own kitchen and from it every day came wonderful smells of onion, meat and garlic.

The surrounding countryside was peaceful and Abby went for long walks when the weather was not too bad and spent what time she could reading by the windows of her room, which overlooked a huge pond. But she was not left alone long. They could not understand why she wanted to go out alone and either they or one of their friends insisted on going. They had lots of friends and there were visitors every day or invitations to lunch or to dinner.

When she had been there for two weeks, Marcel caught Abby in the dimly lit hall one night and tried to kiss her. When she showed that she was shocked at his behaviour, he only laughed. He was middle-aged and fat and Abby found him unattractive, but it did not stop him from trying to make love to her several times after that. Finally she suggested to Robert that they should leave.

'We've only just got here,' he said.

It was a month, a long, long month.

'How much longer did you think we would stay?'

'I don't know. Over the winter, perhaps. They're glad to have us and I'm enjoying myself.'

'I would like to go home.'

Robert groaned.

'What a provincial little person you are, Abby,' he said.

Abby endured Marcel's advances as best she could during the days that followed. But for that, life was pleasant enough. At least Robert was happy. They had been there another three weeks before Abby caught her husband coming out of Veronique's bedroom during the afternoon. Abby hated the idea of lying down in the daylight, but at least it gave her a chance of being alone to read. How could you possibly be tired when you had done nothing for years and years and it was not summer, it was not hot in the afternoons. She thought that she would go mad if she had to endure much more of this boredom.

She had left her room sooner than usual and then she saw Robert. She stared him out and went back to her room. It was a pretty place with a wooden floor and rugs, pale walls and pretty walnut furniture. He came to her.

'I want to go home,' Abby said.

'Must you be silly about this?'

'Silly?' She glared at him. 'You're the one who's silly, carrying on like that.'

'She gives me what you do not,' he said.

'And what is that?'

'Passion. She has more feeling in her little finger than you have in your whole body. You're as cold as the place you come from. You never loved me.'

'I do love you. I wouldn't live a life like this for somebody I didn't love!'

'I have given you everything!'

'I don't want to be given everything. I am going out of my mind with the tedium of it. I've never been so bored in my life. I'm going home.'

'Go then!' he said and slammed from the room.

Going home was not easy. Abby had to find her own way, but she had plenty of money. She had not travelled alone before and had a great deal of time to worry about the future. She thought that if only there could be a child, it would alter everything. He would be pleased, proud; they would have something in common, something important to share.

Her spirits lifted a little when she reached England, even though it was bitterly cold. As she travelled north, it grew colder. There was the remains of what had been deep snow in the hedgebacks and against the walls, but she was glad to be there and, with each mile that took her north, her spirits lifted. She didn't go off to her home in the country; she went to Jesmond. A bitter wind was blowing in Newcastle. She left the station and hired a carriage to take her with all her luggage to her father's house. She couldn't wait the short journey to get there; she thought her heart would burst. She gazed from the window at the familiar landmarks, the houses, churches and pubs. When the carriage stopped outside the house she got out and ran up the steps to the door. Her only fear was that Henderson would not be at home, though it was Saturday afternoon and by rights he should have been. She opened the door and was about to call out when she entered its warm friendliness, then she noticed that a child was standing at the far end of the hall beside the kitchen door. He was very small, watching her with the concentration that only children have. Even in the dim light of the hall she recognised him immediately. He had Gil's dark Collingwood eyes. It was Matthew.

Even when he had stopped using his own name, they had recognised him. Gil hadn't thought how well known he was in Newcastle and how he stood out, being tall and dark and well dressed. Every shipbuilder in the area belonged to the same federation as his father and they would not employ him. Nobody dared offend William Collingwood. There was also disgust on their faces as the word seeped out about what had happened. He could have gone to Henderson and Henderson might have taken him on, but then again he might not. Gil couldn't bring himself to ask. Even somebody as skilled as he was had no future here. He thought of leaving, then he thought of Matthew. He knew that Henderson would lend him money and he could have gone to Glasgow, to Ireland, even to Germany or America, but there was some stubborn feeling in him that wouldn't go.

He couldn't get taken on even in some lowly position amongst people who knew him so in the end he pawned his clothes, took some which looked as though they should have been thrown out, let the stubble grow on his face, changed his voice and his name and got taken on, after a number of rejections, at his father's shipyard. It was ironical that the only person who would employ him was his father. Down at that level, nobody cared what your name was as long as you kept your head down and worked. Gil's hands were sore for weeks and his body ached from the unaccustomed physical activity, but in a way it was a relief. The other life was gone and he did not want to think. He worked and then he went back to bed. He had found lodgings in one of the houses his father had built down by the docks and it was awful. It didn't matter much. The food was bad, but Gil didn't eat. The beds weren't very clean, but he didn't sleep much. It was noisy because the area was full of pubs and dockers and people coming off ships; different languages were common and so was drunkenness. There were prostitutes on the streets; there were people sleeping in the doorways and the alleys. Gil drank quite a lot, but so did everybody and the men he worked with took him as one of them. You couldn't fake the local accent; a man from another area stood out immediately. The language was unintelligible to anyone else, it was so thick and spoken so fast, it was its own language, but Gil had heard it from birth and had worked among labourers before. Nobody asked questions and the talk was all about work, so he was quite at home.

There was the question of Matthew. Gil didn't feel like a father, whatever that was, and he didn't know what to do. He didn't expect Henderson to pay out anything for the child so he went to the back door of the house from time to time and gave Kate money. The shocked look on her face and the way she didn't ask him in told him what they thought of him, so he said nothing. He didn't even ask after the boy, he just gave her the money and left. What he had after that paid for beer, whatever he bought to eat and his bed at the house. The only way he could sleep was to drink and it had become a habit. You went to work and then you drank and then you went to bed. He knew that a lot of his mates were married and that they drank their pay. Gil no longer cared about anything or anybody. He wanted never to care about anything again. He didn't even care that he was doing the lowliest work beside the most beautiful ship that anyone had ever built. It wasn't his any more. He could look on the majesty of this being he had created and feel nothing. In several months' time it would leave to do its work and he didn't care if he never saw it again as long as he lived.

Abby moved further into the hall and the child ran away into the kitchen to be scolded by Kate's voice, but Matthew said something and Kate came into the hall.

'Why, Mrs Surtees,' she said, 'I didn't know you were back. Come in and keep warm. It's bitter out.'

She ushered Abby into the sitting-room.

'Mrs Surtees is here, Mr Reed.'

Abby had longed to see her father so much but now she didn't understand what she had been fussing about. Henderson looked perfectly well and he got up and hugged her; but he was so glad to see her that she was pleased she had come back. He urged her nearer the fire, Kate took her outdoor things and her father asked after Robert. He showed some concern that she had travelled alone. Abby tried to convince him that there had been no quarrel, it was just that she had badly wanted to come home and he had wished to stay in France. She didn't think her father was fooled. A man and wife should be together and they were not and he knew her too well to think that her jovial attitude was real. Abby was not altogether happy, either. He did not explain Matthew's presence and for some reason Kate kept the child in the kitchen while Abby and Henderson had tea in front of the fire. Abby wasn't hungry. In fact, she felt sick and the feeling increased as she stayed. Her father was not natural with her and although he was well, he looked upset, his eyes were dulled.

After tea, when he had still offered no explanation, she asked him, 'What is Matthew doing here? Is Rhoda in town? Is Gil coming to collect him?' Abby didn't really want to see Rhoda and Gil; her own unhappiness would seem worse against their apparently perfect marriage.

Her father looked down into his empty teacup, positioned it carefully back on the small table beside him and then he looked at her.

'I was deceived in him,' he said.

'What?'

'When he was young and I thought then that he was . . . that he was capable of doing ill, I was right. I was fooled. I thought he had changed. People don't change. I'm old enough to know that. There was a time when I wished that I had let you marry him. You did want to marry him. I'm so relieved now that I didn't allow it. I can't sleep for relief. I thought I didn't like Robert but he's good-hearted and kind and—'

'I don't know what you're talking about,' Abby said.

'I'm talking about that bastard, Gil Collingwood. He left his child here.'

'His child?'

'Yes, his child. Matthew is Gil's. Newcastle is thick with scandal.'

Abby couldn't believe it. Then she did, and coldly. Gil had loved Helen, he had always loved her. Why should it be any surprise that he had fathered a child on her? That was just the kind of thing he would do. But his own brother's wife . . .

'Helen is dead, and Rhoda and he—'

Abby couldn't take this in. She held her father's hands while he explained haltingly the things he had heard. They ended her love for Gil. She knew that she had always had a caring for him but, that teatime over the fire, she stopped loving him. How could anybody love somebody who had done such things and how could he possibly expect her father to keep his child there? Henderson was worried and upset about the child and Abby knew that worry and upset were the very last things he needed.

'Where is he?' she asked.

'I don't know. He's been back to the house with money, but only when I'm at work.'

Abby's heart banged with anger against Gil that he should do such a thing, that he should take advantage of a man like her father, who had been his friend. It played on her mind. When she went to bed she didn't sleep, thinking of Rhoda and Helen and what Gil had done. The shock went round and round in her mind and got louder and louder. She questioned Kate and learned that Gil looked different, that he looked like a workman. She asked her father where he might have been taken on, but Henderson said that nobody would do so. Mrs Wilkins came to Abby and said shamefacedly, 'I know where he is.'

Abby stared.

'How do you know?' she said.

'I just do. Found out. He stands out, even like he is. He's working at Collingwood's.'

Abby was amazed.

'But the men would know.'

'Wouldn't know their own mothers some of them. Don't care neither, labourers.'

'Labourers?'

'He's living in Hope Street.'

Hope Street. The very name was laughable, Abby thought. It was a broken-down place right beside the docks. Nobody respectable would ever go there. All the next night she couldn't rest and on the Monday evening, when her father was lying down, she ordered the carriage and to the driver's consternation insisted on going to the very worst area of the docklands. Abby tried to take comfort that she was not alone, but he was a small, slight figure who had worked for them for several years and never spoken unless he had to. Luckily it was a vile night, bitterly cold and sleeting, so nobody was standing around outside.

She told him to stop and then she knocked on several doors, had no answer from three and did not know what to say to the others since Gil was unlikely to be calling himself by his own name. She persevered. Seven doors later, she enquired of a short, fat woman whether she had a lodger and the woman laughed.

'Half a dozen of them. Anybody in particular?'

'He's tall and dark and about my age.'

'Down the pub, pet.'

'Which pub?'

'Over yonder,' she said and shut the door.

Abby told herself that she could not possibly go into a pub. If he was not there, anything might happen. Even less than respectable women didn't go into pubs. It was predictably called The Ship. Abby walked up to it and went inside. It smelled. It smelled of sweat and dirt and beer and bad breath. The men, in a cloud of smoke from both tobacco and the fire, were indistinguishable from one another in their caps and suits. There was a tremendous noise but, as Abby made her way from the door towards the bar, it began to die down and she could see the man behind the bar, his eyes getting bigger and bigger. By the time she reached him, there was silence. He flipped up part of the bar top and came out from behind.

'Eh, pet, you can't come in here,' he said.

'I'm in,' Abby said.

There were calls and cries.

'I'm looking for somebody.'

'You can take me home with you, petal,' some wit yelled and there was laughter. Abby looked around her for sight of Gil and admiring eyes met hers everywhere.

'Has he got a name?' the barman asked.

'No.'

'Well, that's a fresh one. Howay, out of here.'

He put a hand on her arm. Abby pulled away, knocked into somebody and fingers grabbed her bottom. Fury sent the blood into her face. She turned and there was further laughter. The barman started to drag her towards the door and another man said, 'Don't fret, I'll see the lass home.' He put an arm around her waist. Abby panicked, tried to get away and couldn't. The laughter was louder now and unfriendly, jeering, and he had a good hold on her. The barman, who suddenly seemed a friend, let go and retreated.

From the darkness of the corner to one side of the door a man who had been leaning against the wall straightened in the shadows and Abby recognised something about him even before he levered himself away from the wall and began to come to her across the room. His height declared it to be Gil so she didn't know what she had seen first, just that she knew, because in their lives he had walked across a good many rooms towards her. Some angel of mercy he made, she thought cynically, but her heart knew it for deliverance. The panic which had claimed her almost ceased, but when he got close and she saw him better, she was afraid of him for the first time in her life. His cap was pulled low over his eyes, his face was pale beneath several days' growth of beard and his eyes were narrow slits of black light. He was very thin, wearing the same kind of clothes as the other men, dark. He moved slowly and carefully like a watchful cat and Abby was not surprised when the man let go of her without being asked. All the man said was, 'Yours?'

'Aye.'

Gil walked out of the pub, leaving her to come after him and the men parted and let them through. As the pub door closed behind her the conversation started up again like a full tide. Outside it was snowing. Abby glanced up the street. The carriage was quite a long way from her.

He didn't even turn around. He looked the other way up the street as though something interesting was happening there in the darkness. Even at his worst, Gil had usually had manners. He didn't seem able to manage that now. Abby took a deep breath.

'I want you to take Matthew,' she said.

Gil turned. He looked her up and down and said nothing.

'I want you not to involve my father in your . . . business. You had no right to ask him to take the child and less right to leave him there. Do you want his friends and business associates to think that he has anything to do with you?'

Again his eyes took in the street. Then he looked her straight in the eyes and she wished he hadn't. She stepped backwards.

'I'll come for him in the morning,' he said in a low voice and then he walked away. Abby breathed deeply once or twice, then ran back to the carriage as fast as she could and went home.

To say that her father was not pleased at what she had done would have been an understatement. He had not often lost his temper with her, but he did so then.

'You had no right to go to him. Did you think about the danger in such a place? Did you think about what he could be like? Did you even consider me?'

'I don't know what you mean.'

'I like having the boy here. I don't have much in my life any more. I like him.'

'And when Gil comes to you and asks you for other favours?'

'He won't,' Henderson said quickly.

'How do you know?'

'Because I know him.'

'You like him still,' Abby declared in wonder.

'No! Yes. I don't know. I just . . . I shouldn't say this to you. Having Gil around me was like having a son. I'm horrified at what he has done, but I miss him. I miss him a great deal and having Matthew here was like balm to the wound. Gil has let me down, he's let us all down but the child . . . the child was a link with him and he was something I had not known before.'

This hurt Abby. Firstly because she was a daughter and secondly because she had not produced a grandchild. Thirdly she felt as though she should have been around her father much more, not gone jauntering around the continent for no reason but pleasure. Her father was a lonely man and she had not helped and he had gone to people like Gil to make up for her neglect.

'He can't take the child,' Henderson said.

'He must.'

'And what is he supposed to do with him when he's at work? Leave him with some slut in Hope Street?'

'He said he would come.'

'You had no right to ask him.' Her father regarded the fire for a while and then said, 'How does he look?'

'Thin, poor, his nails are all broken and his hands are ingrained with dirt and—' She stopped. Henderson's body twisted in denial of what she was saying to him. She only hoped that when Gil arrived the next morning her father would either not be up or be at work. She didn't want them to meet. She had deliberately described Gil as he was so that there would be no shock if they did meet. 'He doesn't deserve your sympathy,' she said briskly. 'He doesn't deserve anybody's help. He doesn't have to come into the house and you don't have to see him.'

Henderson was still angry when he went to bed but he said nothing more and Abby knew how disappointed he was. Not only that his judgement had been wrong, but that he felt he had lost Gil and Gil had been a valuable part of his life. Gil had made him happy. All that was finished now. Abby was sorry to deprive him of Matthew's company, but she knew it was for the best. It could do no good for any of them to have Gil connected with the house, coming there. A clean break was best, she thought, but when she lay down to sleep she kept remembering what he had looked like and she couldn't rest.

The following morning Henderson was thankfully still in bed when Gil came to the back door. Kate came through, saying briefly, 'He's here.'

Abby would have thought Matthew would be reluctant. He did not know Gil as his father. Gil didn't look as he had. It was surely all too different for a small child to take in. She thought he might even be afraid, but the child went readily to the door and looked up trustingly into Gil's face. Gil got down beside him just like a workman did, a neat balance for a tall man, and smiled and spoke softly and confidingly to the child.

'Hello, Matt. Are you coming with me?'

Matthew put his fingers onto Gil's face.

'Yes,' he said instantly. Gil stood up and swung the child up into his arms, a long way for him, and Matthew smiled in delight.

Neither Kate nor Abby said anything and Gil didn't acknowledge Abby. He took the child, walked away down the yard, out of the gate and down the back lane without a word. Abby followed him and stood by the gate, watching. There was something that troubled her. She didn't know what it was and it was only a tiny bit of her that was concerned. Most of her was glad to be rid of him once and for all, she thought, and it would have been feckless to have kept the child here. She went back into the house, glad for what she had done. Her father didn't mention it or Matthew's absence. He ate little and went to work and Abby debated what to do. She didn't want to go back to the house in the country where she would be alone and at least if she was here when her father came home to dinner, she would be there for him.

All that day she put Gil and Matthew from her mind. Every time she did so, she saw the image of them walking away down the back lane and something niggled at her. She was ashamed to have done such a thing to a tiny boy and from time to time her cheeks burned with guilt. Her father duly came home at half past five and he had nothing to say. He pushed the food around on his plate at dinner and afterwards went to his room. The house was silent. Abby went to bed and slept, but she awoke in the depths of the night and couldn't get back to sleep. She saw the cold autumn day in and when it was a respectable hour and her father had gone to work she ordered the carriage and once again made the journey into the docklands.

It was a different world from anything she knew and so busy during the day. The carriage jolted seriously on the uneven streets; the roads were filthy and the houses the same. She got out and made her way along the street. She thought of Matthew alone in that house with that woman. Gil would have to leave him there. She thought of the small child in among the dirt and God knew what kind of people. She knew that she couldn't leave him there. She hurried along the street, banged on the door and after a short while it was opened.

'You again? Owes you money, does he? Or are you married?'

'Is the child here?'

'The bairn? Upstairs. Him an' all.'

Abby stopped.

'He's not at work?'

'Nay, he didn't go. I told him, he doesn't pay for the bed during the day, it's needed for others.'

Abby trod straight up the grimy, uncarpeted stairs. The dirt crunched under her feet. At the top of the stairs were two doors. The first door that she opened showed half a dozen people in bed, sleeping. The other room was tiny and had in it a small child standing at the window. She thought Gil had left him there while he slept next door until she noticed the bed in the shadows across the room. She closed the door. It shut out the snoring from the other room, though she could hear other noises from the street below, people walking and shouting and machinery grinding somewhere. Matthew watched her carefully, silently.

Abby couldn't believe that Gil could sleep like that while two people were in the room. He must be exhausted. The covers on the bed made Abby's hands itch to take them off and wash them. They were beyond dirty. He didn't wake up, even when she sat down on the bed. It was bitterly cold in the room. He didn't move when she said his name. He opened his eyes. The light had gone from them; they were dull smudges. She stood up and moved back.

'Abby.' He made as if to sit up and then changed his mind.

'I had second thoughts. Matthew can't stay here.'

The look on Gil's face showed such relief that she was glad she had come.

'My father's got used to him. Would you let me take him back?'

'I wish you would.'

He still didn't move. Abby couldn't understand it. She went across to the little boy but he backed away from her.

'Matt?' Gil called from the bed and the child ran across. 'Go, just for a little while, just for now.'

Matthew began to cry. It made Abby think of how a small animal would have reacted. Children knew things that adults had long since forgotten. She hadn't thought he would go so readily with Gil and she hadn't imagined that he would not want to leave this vile place. Matthew tugged at the bedclothes and Abby caught a glimpse of what had been a good shirt at one time. The light from the rain-spattered window showed what looked to her like blood. She tried to meet Gil's eyes but he was concentrating on the child, talking to him and adjusting the bedclothes. Neither his face nor his eyes told her that there was any kind of problem.

She went to him.

'Go with Abby now,' he was saying.

'Is there something the matter?'

'No, everything's fine.'

She touched Matthew, drew him away a little. Then she pulled at the bedclothes. Blood, all wet and shiny and frothy, a lot of it, so much of it, all over his clothes and all over the bed, sticky, oozing, bright red, more blood than she had ever seen in her life. Abby's experience was cut fingers and knees. Blood was something that stopped almost immediately, but this was not. Her first instinct was to try and stop it, but when she touched him her hands sank in it.

'Oh God. Oh my God, what have you done?' she accused him, starting to cry. 'What on earth have you done?'

Hearing her, Matthew began to cry too.

'It's nothing,' Gil said.

The blood ran down Abby's hands, down her wrists and onto the white cuffs of her blouse.

'I'll be fine. Please take him.'

'Oh yes, fine,' Abby said. 'What are you going to do, lie here and die?'

'I'm not going to die.'

'No? No, of course not.' Why had she had not noticed the grey of his face, the pain in his eyes? 'What happened? What on earth happened? No, never mind. A doctor.'

Gil clasped her wrist in his fingers.

'No!' he said.

'I see,' Abby said, suddenly cold and crafty. 'You think you can just die on me and I will do nothing.'

'You don't have to do anything. You're not owing me. As long as you take him, that was all I was bothered about. Just take him and go.'

'And have you on my conscience for the rest of my life? I will not!' She dragged free, wiped her hands on her skirt, picked up the child and went carefully down the stairs. The woman came out of the kitchen.

'Don't close the door, I'm coming back in a minute,' Abby told her.

She ran down the street with Matthew in her arms and ordered the driver to take the carriage down the narrow road. When they reached the house she told Matthew to stay inside and then urged the driver into the house. He was not keen and when he saw Gil, he was even less so.

'He's a goner,' he declared, 'might as well leave him here.'

'I will not,' Abby said firmly. 'Gil, I want you to get up.'

'I can't.'

He had never seemed as big to Abby as when she tried to move him. The driver eyed the blood with distaste but, seeing her determination, pulled Gil out of the bed. They hurt him, but Abby knew that if she didn't get him out of here he would die anyway and she didn't want him to. She didn't think about this at the time because she would have said that she didn't care any more, but she felt responsible, she wanted nothing to do directly with anybody's death. Somehow they got him out of the room, Gil walked part of the way and he certainly walked down the stairs because they were so narrow and steep that he couldn't have been carried down them, at least not by a small woman and an old man. He was unconscious before they reached the end of the street, but all Abby had to do then was get him home.

Dr Brown was not a happy man. He tut-tutted over his patient.

'Knifed,' the doctor surmised, 'I would say. Nasty wounds. It didn't help moving him.'

'I couldn't leave him there,' Abby said and the doctor looked surprised at her vehemence. She had discovered that guilt came in various forms and, stupidly, all she could think of was Gil begging her to marry him. She kept telling herself that it was a long time ago and of little consequence any more, but it did not make her comfortable. She engaged two nurses so that neither Kate, Mrs Wilkins nor she would have to go into the room where Gil lay half-conscious. She would have nothing to do with this and there was no reason why their servants should have anything to do with it either. She had sent a note to her father and he came back, quietly delighted to see the child, but he came out of the bedroom grave-faced.

'Doctor Brown says he may not last the night,' Abby told her father as they drank coffee in the sitting-room.

'It could be the smallest funeral ever,' her father said. 'Why didn't you leave him there?'

'Would you have wanted me to?'

'You could have taken the child and come home.'

'He asked me to marry him once,' Abby said. 'I told him to go to hell.'

'He seems to have managed it very successfully. I'm so disappointed.'

Gil didn't die during the night. Abby went to bed and told herself she didn't care and was wretched. She knew because she went in, told the nurse to go downstairs for a while and put the kettle on, the fire would be bright all night. She sat down by the bed and watched him. The room was silent. Abby sat down on the bed, afraid that he was quiet.

'Don't die on me. I don't want your death on my conscience, you bastard. How could you? How could you do such a thing? You, of all people. Why couldn't you die before I got there? That would have been easy but oh no, not you.'

Gil opened his eyes, reached for her hand and, when he found it, closed his eyes again and after that was quiet. When the nurse came back, Abby went to bed. She even dozed for a little while but she dreamed about him each time and then woke up, so in the end, when the daylight finally came, she pushed back the curtains. It was snowing. She thought of that Christmas time after her mother had died when she went to Bamburgh House with her father and Gil's father had beaten him for stupidity and she had taught him how to make snow angels. It was such a long time ago.

In the darkness of the corner in the pub there had been deliverance. Amidst the smoke and the talk of the mighty ship they were building he was vaguely happy. Anonymity there. It didn't matter who you were or what your name was. If they couldn't remember, or hadn't heard, they called you 'Geordie'. Everybody was 'Geordie' here. The beer went down like velvet nectar and settled there so soothing inside you. It took the edge off everything, so that you could look back on anything at all and it was bearable. Amidst the sing-song sound of the Newcastle voices he felt safe. He didn't have to say anything; he was accepted here, at home, warm and comforted and he could go back to the night with beer for a blanket and disappear beneath it until the morning came. The morning wasn't to be thought of, but then again there was only that gap between waking and working. Once he was working, the time went by because the men were there. They hid him. He could hide amongst them for a hundred years.

And then the door opened and a woman walked in. He thought it must be the first time a respectable woman had ever walked into such a place and she was more than respectable; she was quality. Such an entrance, such a dress. It was blue and his swift mind told him through the beer who it was, because she nearly always wore blue. Part of him was admiring, but most of him was angry because he knew straight away what she wanted. He drew back slightly into the corner and watched her. She couldn't win here, but she didn't seem to know that or care; she was ready to take on the pub. The landlord wasn't a bad man and Gil didn't worry until Eccles got hold of her. If Eccles got her outside she was done for, so he went over and got in the way. Eccles wouldn't take a chance, not on somebody a lot bigger than him, even for a bonny piece like that and she was trouble, even Eccles would know that. She had always been trouble. He was so proud of her and wanted to smack her face.

He went outside and she followed him. He didn't look at her because he was so angry. All she was thinking about was her father and herself. The boy didn't matter. Her father and her mother and herself had been the only people who had ever come into the magic circle of Abby's mind. He doubted that her marriage was a success. What would she be like in bed? Very bossy, probably. Poor Robert, given instructions. And yes, he had been right. She started up straight away, going on about how ill Henderson was. It was all guilt, because she wasn't in Newcastle most of the time; she went swanning about on the continent, doing God knew what with all Robert's posh friends, idle and wearing clothes like she had on now, which some poor bitch had ruined her eyesight stitching. She didn't know anything and she didn't care about anybody. He listened to her ranting on, gave the answer she wanted and walked away. She stood there in the street looking stupid in her silk dress and her bonnet, or whatever the hell it was, standing there like Lady Muck.

He didn't go far. He couldn't count on Eccles or some other clever bastard not coming out of the pub before she reached the carriage, so he waited and watched from the end of the street until she got there and inside, the door slammed and the carriage moved away before he went any further.

He went home. My God, it was home. Beer and oblivion. He wouldn't care, but the woman had offered him free board and lodgings when he first got there in return for bedding her. When he had refused the offer, she got two lads to try and throw him out. Gil had put them both down the stairs, had listened to the sound of the way that they bounced. After that she didn't say anything and within days he was accepted in the area. Workmen were loyal to one another, at least in certain ways, so he had a tiny room to himself most of the time, though somebody else often slept in his bed during the day. He could not think now how his life had been, how complicated. Now it was simple. He went to work, he got paid, he got drunk and he slept. He let nothing else into his conscious mind except that twice he had gone to the kitchen door of Henderson's house and given Kate money. He had seen the disgust on her face, on so many people's faces. He expected nothing more, it didn't matter. There was the present.

He tried not to think about Abby. She came from another time and it seemed so far away now, like something in another life. He would have to take the boy. He decided on that before he went to sleep. He could feel the way that his mind emptied. The beer did that. It kicked out all those creepy, itchy thoughts that turned your stomach in the darkness.

The following morning he had to go early to Jesmond. It would still make him late for work, but there was no help for it. One of his workmates lived nearby and his wife had a small child, so on the way back he would ask her, if he paid her, whether she would look after Matthew. Also he would have to think about finding somewhere better to live. Matthew could not be kept in a hovel. There was not going to be enough money to pay her, somewhere to live and eat reasonably well, but he pushed that to a space at the back of his mind. First of all, there was Matthew to collect.

The funny thing was that he missed him. Discovering that he had a child had not been a pleasant shock, but he felt sympathy for the little boy because his whole life had been altered. He had lost his mother and his home, his grandparents, prosperity, security and the biggest shipyard the Tyne had ever seen. Almost everything had gone. What Gil hadn't known at the time was that Matthew knew him better than he knew Edward; though Gil had not seen the fascination for someone else's child, Matthew was used to him, to seeing him around the house, to him being part of the everyday furniture of his small existence and, because Gil was the only familiar person when Gil went to the back door and got down and spoke to him, the child came straight to him with gladness in his face. Gil had thought that he was beyond feeling, but when he took the little boy into his arms he knew that he was not and that he would try everything to get back a decent life for him.

He carried him all the way back. He called in at the house where he was hoping to leave Matthew and Jem's wife was agreeable, tried to tell him that she would take no money. People in Newcastle, Gil thought, had to be some of the most generous in the world. She didn't ask questions about where Matthew's mother was. She accepted the child and Gil promised that he would pay her. He even spoke to Jem about it at work and the young man, who was about his own age, tried to say that they would not take money for such a thing, even though they had so little. Gil said again that he couldn't leave Matthew without paying.

Suddenly the world looked better; it looked as though

something might work out. At the end of the day he collected Matthew from Jem's wife and she offered Gil to stay and eat. He tried to refuse but he couldn't because the smell of the stew she had made was like nothing he had ever come across in his whole life, so he and Matthew stayed and Gil was actually hungry. The taste of the vegetables and the small amount of meat was heaven. When he set out down the street he didn't even want beer for the first time. Things had changed that day. It was the best day in so long. He got halfway down the street when he glimpsed somebody in the shadows and put Matthew down but he was not quick enough because he didn't like to let loose of Matthew completely. In those few seconds his attacker came upon him and it was too late. The first cut was almost enough, the second had him on the ground, the third wasn't really necessary, yet all he could think about was the boy.

He couldn't think when it had happened. Was it dark or was it the next day? Could it have been light? Could he have gone home and slept and then come out the next morning? He didn't remember much. He remembered pretending to Matthew that nothing important had happened. He remembered crawling up the stairs and it was like mountaineering. He remembered gaining the bed and after that his full concern had been that he was going to die and there was nobody to take Matthew. He cursed Abby a thousand times for what she had done. If only she had waited two more days, then it wouldn't have been important. He was going to die and leave the child in such circumstances. And then she had come back. What he wanted was for her to walk out with the child and leave him. The world was nothing to do with him, but she had shouted and sworn and called him names and pulled him off the bed. The pain was unbearable, excruciating. She shouted and shouted at him, and the noise had brought other people near, not too close, blood always made them back off. Abby's fishwife act was so annoying that he managed to get down the stairs and into the carriage. After that, everything went black. He was glad to be dead.

When he opened his eyes he was in a very clean bed, in a great deal of pain, his head didn't feel right and the people around him weren't clear and he felt sick. There was nothing beyond the bed and from time to time things came and went at such a rate that his head spun round and he blacked out. There was nothing going on beyond the bed of any consequence. The pain filled his whole life because it wouldn't stop and it made him sick. Only unconsciousness worked, and then not much. He wandered in and out of it and the dreams were all of finding Rhoda up on the moors, frozen. He found her there again and again, a hundred times and then a hundred times after that and each time it hurt more and each time she was dead anew and it was his fault. And he couldn't die. He tried hard, but he didn't seem to be able to. Then it occurred to him that perhaps for people who had done such unforgivably dreadful things, this was what death must be like, continual pain, nothing but pain and finding Rhoda dead for all eternity because he had done it with his stupidity. Helen and Rhoda had gone to heaven but he had killed them and he would stay here in hell, in pain, for ever and ever.

Chapter Fifteen

Robert came home. It was inconvenient. Abby's monthly bleeding had not arrived and she was so excited by the idea that she didn't want anything to interfere. She felt as though his coming home would bring it on. She would not be pregnant and she wanted that more than anything in the world. But Robert was repentant. The moment they were alone in the house in Jesmond, he pulled her to him urgently and apologised.

'I've missed you and I'm sorry. I behaved like a bear . . . and worse. It isn't that I love her or any of the others, it's just that . . . that's how I've always gone on, it's how men do go on. I worried that something might have happened to you and I was angry and—'

Abby kissed him and held him close. She didn't want to tell him that she thought she was pregnant until she was quite sure. The door opened and Matthew came in.

'Who's that?' Robert asked.

'This is Matthew,' Abby said brightly. 'Matthew, this is Robert. Do you remember him?'

'Edward's son? At least—' Abby nipped his arm and he stopped until she had told Matthew to go to the kitchen for a biscuit.

'You heard.'

'I heard all right, even in London. What is the child doing here?'

'We have Gil staying.'

'What?'

'Somebody knifed him.'

'Pity he didn't kill him,' Robert said. 'Why is he staying here?'

'There was nowhere else.'

'He shouldn't be near decent people.'

Abby forebore to point out to her husband that he was in the habit of taking other men's wives to bed, though not his brother's of course. She wondered whether he would have done so.

'You shouldn't stay here where he is. And what about the female servants?'

'We have two nurses. Nobody has to go near him.'

But she did. She didn't tell Robert that either. She didn't tell him about the way that Gil had cried out Rhoda's name over and over when he went out of his senses. He had almost died. The doctor had said he was going to and she was pitiless, but her father had gone into the sitting-room and wept.

'How can you still care?' she demanded.

'I can't help it.'

It was difficult to resist, Abby acknowledged. Gil had lain in that bed looking about seventeen with his hair all over the pillow and his eyes wild, calling out again and again for the wife whose death he had caused. He didn't speak Helen's name. The nurse held his hand and soothed him. Abby slammed out of the room several times, only to come back. She made herself leave the house. The weather was bitterly cold and windy. The rain threw itself all over the bedroom window and often she would stand there by the light of one lamp and the fire looking out over the dark, freezing streets. She wanted to choke his young neck for the way he had murdered her regard for him. She let herself think about Rhoda for the first time. It made her so angry, the waste of it. She walked the streets for hours during those first days; once, she walked all the way to the river and cried. In the shipyard, she knew, Collingwood's were busy with the ship which he had fought for, designed and built. In a few months it would be finished. He had been so proud of it, so glad to please his father, she knew. Henderson reported that Edward was back at work, that his father was grateful, that William had been petty enough to amend the sign on the gate so that it read 'Son' and not 'Sons'. Abby knew that she ought to have gone to see Charlotte, but with Gil in bed at home it hardly seemed right, and people were beginning to realise that he was there. When everyone found out, it would damage her father.

Gil started to get better. Abby didn't go into the room any more after that. She didn't want to speak to him. When they finally did come face to face she said, 'The minute you can walk, I want you out of this house.'

'It isn't your house,' Gil said flatly.

'My father has his reputation to think about.'

'Why don't you go away, you make me tired?'

Abby's temper flared, even though she knew he was right. He was still in bed and so white-faced and dull-eyed that she knew he couldn't cope with this.

'You ungrateful bastard, I brought you here.'

'Nobody asked you to! And stop calling me names. You have a filthy mouth.'

'I could call you a lot worse than that. I could call you things you deserve.'

Gil's eyes wavered.

'You don't have to call me them, I know what I am,' he said.

Abby hadn't meant to go that far. She got herself out of the room and didn't venture there again and, since Gil was too weak to come downstairs, they were both safe for a while. When he finally did get up there was nothing but pleasantries between them. Abby watched Henderson with Matthew and hugged to her the idea that soon she would be able to tell him he would have a grandchild of his own. He loved the little boy and was open with him. When Henderson came in from work, Matthew would go to him straight away, sit on his lap by the fire in the evening and talk all kinds of nonsense. Henderson read him a bedtime story each night and there was often laughter from the kitchen when Matthew was in there. When Gil got better the child rarely left his side and in the afternoons, when Gil would lie on the sofa by the sitting-room fire, Matthew would lie with him and go to sleep.

Henderson rarely spoke to Gil, but Matthew sensed the tension and would go from one to the other if they were both in the room so that very often Henderson stayed in his study and worked during the evening. One evening he was gone only a few minutes before coming back into the sitting-room, thrusting some papers under Gil's nose and saying, 'You've been in there, haven't you?'

'Well, I—'

'You've been into my study. You've altered these plans.' He shook the papers at Gil.

'Just here and there.'

'How dare you?'

'I . . . the – the figures weren't right.'

'They were perfect.'

'No.' Gil finally looked up. 'They weren't.'

'How can you tell? You didn't have the other papers or figures that go with it.'

Gil looked apologetic.

'I just know. I can tell by the design, the shape of it and the – the other things. I didn't mean anything, I just . . . could tell and . . . it doesn't look right, you see, here and here.' He pointed. 'And you could alter it here and—'

Henderson cursed and walked out. Abby said nothing. Gil went to bed. A little later, when she thought he might have calmed down, she opened the study door.

'May I come in?'

'Everybody else has been in. Why not?'

Henderson rubbed his face with his hands in tiredness.

'Has he spoiled it?'

'Spoiled it?' Henderson threw down his pen and laughed shortly. 'It takes other men weeks to work out things like that. He can do it in half a day.'

'But why?'

'I don't know. I don't think he knows himself. I knew something was wrong with it, but I couldn't see what. He only has to look at something. I wish I had a man with half that ability working for me. I could clean up. I could better Collingwood's. He doesn't do calculations like I do; he can see the answer. It's God-given, that kind of ability. It's a pity. I'll lock the study door in future.'

In the bedroom and the sitting-room Abby found scraps of paper with figures and lines and drawings. She kept throwing them away and it was almost as if they came back in or reappeared. He scribbled and drew. Sometimes she thought he wasn't even aware of it. Henderson started picking them up and taking them away into the study with him. Finally Abby took the pencils, pens and any paper she found and locked them away in the bureau. After that, Gil did nothing. He was not well enough to walk far so he couldn't go out and he would sit with a book on his knee and stare out of the window for hours. Matthew had coloured pencils and soon there were little drawings on the daily newspapers and in the margins. Irritated, Abby grabbed a blue pencil out of Gil's hand.

'Will you stop doing that? Look at the mess you're making! My father hasn't read that yet. What are you, a child?'

'I've got nothing to do.'

'You're not well enough to do anything. You can hardly walk.'

'I can draw.'

'You can't. My father doesn't want you to. It upsets him when you interfere with his work.'

'Pictures?'

Abby bought him some drawing paper and some pencils

when she went shopping. His drawings were all ships. They were not calculations or designs, they were just ships, intricate beautiful ships, some of which she suspected were not built yet. Henderson tried not to take an interest but, since the drawings were everywhere, he ended up asking about them. From there, it was a very short space to how they were built, what they had inside, what made them work, what the future of shipbuilding was. Her father could not keep off his favourite subject, especially when he could discuss it with somebody who knew exactly what he was talking about.

And then Robert came home. Abby was torn. She wanted to go back to the country with her husband and repair her marriage and gloat over her possible pregnancy, but she didn't want to leave her father with his apparently increasingly pleasing guest who was not well enough to leave but was well enough to carry on intricate conversations about shipbuilding. She had seen that light in her father's eyes before. It was enthusiasm. Robert did not want to go and leave Gil there either, but when he suggested to Henderson that Gil had been there long enough, Henderson wouldn't listen.

'What do you want me to do?' he demanded, standing before the study fire while they tried to talk to him. 'I can hardly put him on to the street. He can't work.'

'You could give him some money and he could go and stay in a hotel or find a house.'

'Give him some money? He's not getting any of my money.'

'It costs you to keep him here, doesn't it? And that child must be eating you out of house and home.'

Mentioning Matthew was a mistake, Abby thought. Her father doted on him.

'Children are cheap when they're little,' Henderson said with a parent's authority.

'Your father likes him,' Robert told her afterwards.

'Yes, I know. They talked about ships all day on Sunday.'

'How boring.'

It wasn't, that was the funny part, Abby thought. It wasn't boring, not like when Robert and his friends recounted the day's hunting. Perhaps it was just that in her home shipping and shipbuilding and politics and economics had always been discussed. Her mother was a business and political person, somehow, and over meals and over the fire and in the garden in the summer they had talked as Henderson and Gil did now and she found herself joining in and being listened to, having her views seriously considered such as did not happen in her world. She remembered her mother and father's friends, who read and were well informed and came to dinner and talked over the important happenings of their world. That had all stopped when her mother died and she missed it. She kept forgetting who Gil was and what he had done. She wanted to be there because it was exciting. She longed for the evenings when her father would come home and they would sit around the dinner table and eat good food and drink wine and talk. The weather was foul even when spring came, but she was glad of that because there was nothing more satisfying than sitting around talking while rain poured down the windows. She even fantasised a little, ruefully, thinking that if she had accepted Gil's proposal all that time ago, this would be their life now. She left Helen out of the equation of course, that would have spoiled the picture. She imagined Matthew as her child and that she and Gil could have lived here as man and wife with her father. It would have been perfect. She shook herself out of this. If she had married Gil, she would be dead by now. His love for Helen had been his weak point. She didn't know if he loved her still, if he had ever loved or been kind to Rhoda. She kept having to remind herself that he was not really this polite, sophisticated person across the dinner table. He was wicked, evil, he had cost two women their lives. There was no way round that. What kind of man bedded his brother's wife under the same roof as he lived with his own wife? Had he gone from one to another? She dismissed that. He was not capable of it, but then he was not really the person he seemed to be. He was much too clever to let anybody see what he was really like. His survival depended on his ability to fool other people and her father was fooled and she had been close.

Robert didn't stay at the house and she only stayed one more night while she gathered her luggage and her thoughts, but she went to Gil, in his room, when he went upstairs to bed. It was the only place she could be sure of privacy. She knocked on the door and he opened it and she followed him inside.

'I want you to make me a promise,' she said.

Gil didn't look surprised.

'I know,' he said.

'How can you know?'

'You want me to leave.'

'Yes. Will you do it?'

'No.'

'For my father's sake?' When he didn't answer she said, 'Then for me. I saved your life. You owe me that much.'

'I didn't ask you to save it and I didn't want you to. I asked you to take Matthew and I'm grateful for that, but I have scores to settle, I have things to do.'

'I don't know what you mean.'

'You must take some responsibility since you insisted on keeping me alive.'

Gone was the urbane conversationalist. Gil's eyes were like black ice and his voice was soft and deadly.

'Responsibility?'

'Why don't you go back to the country?' Gil said and turned away and eased his jacket off. He was still doing that carefully, she noticed.

'I don't want to go back to the country and leave you here with my father.'

'What on earth do you think I'm going to do to him?'

'I daren't think.'

'Don't be silly, Abby. Have you told Robert that you're expecting a child?'

Abby's heart lurched.

'What?'

'Have you?'

'I haven't told anybody yet. How did you know?'

'I remember what Helen looked like when she was pregnant. So beautiful.'

'She was always beautiful,' Abby said impatiently.

'But that special glow. That's what you look like. Your hair is all shiny and so is your face and your eyes and—'

Abby was offended, not just that he should know without her telling him that she was pregnant, but that he should dare to mention Helen in the same breath.

'You still love her,' she accused him.

'I shall always love her.'

'You're disgusting,' she said and went to her own room.

There was nothing left for her but to go home and when she had done so she was glad. She made a visit to the doctor immediately, who confirmed that she was having a child and she was able to tell Robert on her very first day back. She had not seen him as glad about anything. It made her think that perhaps now her marriage would work. He wanted to tell everybody that she was having his son. Abby warned him.

'It could be a girl.'

'No, it isn't possible.'

He insisted on having a party and Abby could not refuse because she wanted him to be this glad. Her home was pretty with spring flowers around it and the coming summer. She could envisage herself sitting in the garden with her new baby, how proud he would be. Everything would be right now. It was like the beginning of her marriage again. Robert didn't leave her at night; he didn't drink too much; he didn't go out much without her. People came to visit and the party was a great success. Everything she suggested, he agreed with. Abby was happy except when she went back to Jesmond, which she did each Sunday to see her father. The one thing Robert refused to do was be in the same room as Gil, so he wouldn't go. Abby didn't blame him. It looked to her now as though Gil would always be there, he was so comfortably settled. He had been to her father's tailor and wore expensive clothes. When she complained to her father, Henderson said simply, 'He earns his keep,' and this was another thing she worried about.

Gil had started working, designing for Henderson. At first just at home and then at the shipyard. By the time her pregnancy was almost over, Gil was at the shipyard drawing office every day. When she went to the house, he was always working. There was another downstairs room which had been her mother's private room, where she wrote letters, read and sewed. They had turned it into another study and there Gil worked. It meant that she could have more time alone with her father, but it didn't please Abby. Gil was polite to her. She barely spoke to him, but Henderson was happier than she had seen him since before her mother died. It made things worse somehow. He was so enthusiastic about work and she knew that with Gil in his drawing office he could build bigger ships, take on competitors like Collingwood's and she feared that.

William and Charlotte had come to the party. Abby hoped they did not know that she had taken Gil back to her father's house in Jesmond and it was obvious by the way they reacted that they thought Henderson responsible for the whole thing. He was in part, Abby thought now. Henderson would lose his friends because of Gil. People would not endure such things. William did not mention Gil, but Charlotte said to her, 'William is in a dreadful rage and has declared he won't speak to your father ever again, that he will do him out of business. He had no right to take Gil in.'

'Doesn't he matter to you, Charlotte?' Abby said, thinking of what it was like to bear and bring up a child and have everything go wrong.

'Matter to me? How could he?'

'He's your child.'

Charlotte hesitated and then she said, 'You can't imagine what it's like having a child you don't care for. I tried hard to love Gil and now he's broken my heart. I'm so glad to have Edward, so pleased to have one who acts as he should. We didn't know that Helen had betrayed Edward, that that was why he had gone away. How awful it must have been for him to find out that his wife cared only for his brother. What a dreadful woman she was, don't let us talk about her. And as for poor Rhoda . . . We have Edward back now and William is so glad. They go to work together each day and it's my only comfort. Tell me, how is my grandson? Has Gil poisoned him against us?'

Abby didn't know what to say to that since Gil didn't mention his parents and Matthew was too little to realise what was happening. Charlotte was eager for every detail: what Matthew looked like, how much he had grown, what he could do and say now that he couldn't when she had seen him, whether he was being properly looked after. She soaked up each detail; her eyes were hungry. Abby told Gil this, but he said nothing and, when she spoke of Edward marrying again and having other children so that Charlotte would not feel quite so bad, he laughed and said that it was unlikely.

'Why, because he broke his heart over you and his wife? How could you do it?' Abby had long wanted to say this to Gil. 'How could you take your brother's wife? And what about Rhoda? I didn't think you would marry anyone you didn't love, even to change things. I thought you were happy together. I didn't know that you were—'

'It's nothing to do with you,' Gil said.

He wouldn't say anything more and Abby wanted to think well of him, but she couldn't.

On a warm summer's night she went into labour and it seemed like a very long time. In fact, it was thirty hours of extreme pain before the child was born and it was a girl. Abby was only glad that the child was healthy and that she was well soon afterwards, but Robert did not trouble to hide his disappointment. The day after the birth he got very drunk and stayed out all night and Abby knew that it was not in celebration. He did buy her a beautiful diamond bracelet to thank her for his daughter, but it was too late by then. Abby realised that she had committed a *faux pas*. The christening for the little girl was very small, only immediate family, and she had to arrange it herself when she recovered. Nobody mentioned it. Neither did Robert appear to care what the child was called. She was immediately banished, to the upper reaches of the house, surrounded by nannies and nursery maids, so that Abby's vision of sitting in the garden with her child did not become reality. Even Henderson wasn't interested. Only Gil seemed bothered and she couldn't understand that.

'I thought you'd bring her to see us,' he said, looking at Abby's empty arms when she came to Jesmond for the first time after the child was born.

'I didn't realise your passion was for babies, Gil.'

'I can't say it is but . . . she's your daughter. You look tired. How do you feel?'

She was tired. Nobody else had mentioned it and she wished anybody except Gil would be nice to her. She was tired of fighting to spend time with her daughter, tired of Robert not wanting the child around him. It was unfashionable to see your children except for an hour in the evening and babies didn't seem to count. If she went upstairs to the nursery, the nanny made her feel out of place; nobody asked after the baby. It was almost as though she didn't exist and Robert had been astounded when she had suggested taking the child out with them when they went to visit friends. No baby, Abby concluded, could ever have been so unwelcome and all because she was the wrong sex.

That Sunday afternoon she lay in the hammock in the garden at her father's house and swung gently, looking up at the blue sky, while Henderson dozed in a deck chair and Gil played silly games with his son on the lawn. It was so peaceful and she missed Georgina. She had not even been able to choose the child's name. How ironic, she thought, that they didn't particularly want her but she had to be called after her great aunt for some reason. Abby could not help remembering her own happy childhood, all the time spent with her parents, especially her mother. She determined that Georgina should not grow up like this, but when she looked around at other daughters she realised that they were not often with their parents, they weren't allowed to speak until spoken to and there were no careless happy childhood days as she had had. They were packed off to schools or to the upstairs of the house or rarely seen. Abby thought that many of the men cared more for their dogs and horses than they did for their children. Georgina would be brought up in the country, not invited to go away with her parents to London or abroad to visit friends.

'You're making a fool of yourself,' Robert said, 'and of me, wanting to take her with us. She has to be watched all the time. Nobody can have a sensible conversation when a child is there. Really, Abby.'

'I feel as though she hardly knows us.'

'I can't think what you mean. Children need routine. Nanny has it all in hand.'

A month after the child was born her husband walked into her bedroom and to her surprised face he said, 'We have one female child. It won't do.'

Abby wanted to burst into tears. She didn't want him near her. She didn't want anybody near her just then, but he got into bed and there was no way in which Abby could refuse him. It would have been difficult to say who was the colder there. Robert did not waste his time on kisses. He had her as he might have had a street walker, but with less enthusiasm. After that, he had her night and morning except when she was bleeding and she bled with a kind of determined regularity so that his efforts were all in vain. She felt so old, so used up and so useless. She knew that he had to have a son, but nothing happened. Robert began to drink and gamble and sometimes he even stayed away from home that autumn. Abby couldn't help being glad of it. She felt physically sick at the idea of a man in her bed. She didn't want to be pregnant again, but she thought that if she was he might at least leave her alone. It was not to be, and when she went to Jesmond on Sunday she watched Matthew growing up and was envious.

Chapter Sixteen

Gil went to see Toby. It wasn't far. He didn't know what his reception might be. It was early Saturday evening and it was full summer. Gil remembered what Toby's garden was like at this time of the year and how cool and elegant his house was. The young man who opened the door was barely recognisable, bearded, unkempt and so thin that his cheekbones stood out. He smiled brilliantly.

'My dear boy,' he said, 'how are you?'

Gil hesitated.

'Do come in. Do. Do. It's been an age.'

The house was different, and it was not just the atmosphere. It smelled cold, as though no fire had been lit in there a long time, and though the garden was sunny and the day was bright the warmth did not penetrate the house. It was not very clean. Dirty dishes were piled up in the sink. Toby offered to make tea and then called himself silly because there was no fire to heat the kettle. When he would have offered wine, there was none of that either. There was whisky, so Gil accepted that. In the sitting-room there was a bigger muddle, as though nothing had been tidied away for a very long time; books and papers in great piles on the floor and on the seats. They went out into the garden and Gil tried not to stare. It was completely overgrown. The lawn was high; the flowers had gone wild and were choked with weeds, but Toby didn't seem to notice. They sat on wooden chairs and Gil remembered being here with Edward and how he had kissed Toby. He had also thought that Toby might blame him for Edward's leaving him. He hadn't been sure before that Edward and Toby no longer saw one another but he knew it for certain now.

'How are you, Tobe?' he said.

'Extremely well. How are you?'

'About the same.'

'Yes.' Toby smiled.

They sat in the wreck of a garden and drank whisky and it seemed incongruous.

'My parents are wanting me to go back and live at home,' Toby said after a while.

'And will you?'

'I expect I shall. I'm getting married.'

'Married?'

'My father is quite old, you see. I'm the youngest.' Toby looked seriously at Gil. 'Try not to blame Edward.'

'I don't!'

'Your father spent years telling him how he would inherit everything and how important the shipyard was and that he must provide a son. And it is important. One's family is important. If they turn you out, where have you to go? You know that. I have to go home now and pretend, just like he did. I love them, you see.'

'But would you have done so if Edward had stayed with you?'

'I would have given up everything,' Toby said. 'He blames me for what Helen did. He thinks if it hadn't been for me, she would not have gone to you.'

'She loved him,' Gil said.

'He did love her, in a way. I think as much as anything it was this house and the way of life, the simplicity. It wasn't just me. If he had cared so very much, he would have left altogether. I would have gone anywhere with him.'

Gil left Toby sitting in the garden, looking out over what had been perfection.

That night, for no reason, Gil awoke and thought there was someone in the room. There wasn't. He got up and made sure, but when he went back to bed he remembered his attacker and for the first time knew that it was Jos Allsop. He couldn't understand then why he had not known, but from somewhere his mind gave him an extra sight and, as if from a distance, as though he was an independent observer, he saw the man and the action and the knife. He saw the hatred and he could hear in his mind the way that Jos had reacted when Rhoda was found and, to his astonishment, he realised that Jos thought Rhoda loved him. In his twisted mind what he had done to her was what she wanted him to do and he bore no blame for the fact that Rhoda had died, whereas in Gil's better moments, when he was not completely blaming himself, he knew that Jos had played a great part in Rhoda's mind and that he had pushed her towards her death long before anyone else had had any part in it. That was not to say that Gil excused himself in any way. He knew what he had done, that if he had not given Helen a child, if he had been a stronger person and not gone to bed with her, that he could have had Rhoda as his wife. It was always there in some part of his mind that Rhoda's death was his punishment for sleeping with his brother's wife, but that was not the whole of it, that was not all of it. Allsop was a strange, twisted man and he had not done Rhoda any good. Jos Allsop had tried to kill him. Perhaps he would do it again. Gil had no idea of his whereabouts, but he would make enquiries and find out.

Sleep deserted him. The cruel night showed him his dead wife and his father's accusing face and the family that he had lost. The emptiness was such an ache and it didn't go away. Gil watched the night turn into morning. Mornings were never as bad.

And this one wasn't. Matthew came in and threw himself on the bed and laughed and Gil could not be sorry for everything because his son had come out of the liaison with Helen. There was nothing as precious in the world, in the whole of life, as a child and he had been lucky there. He and Matthew had a pillow fight and after that they went downstairs to have breakfast with Henderson. It was a ritual. Matthew would climb up onto Henderson's knee and eat ham and eggs from Henderson's plate. He liked it best when Henderson was having boiled eggs because he would have the top from the eggs, which he liked to scoop out of the shell. Then he would have soldiers, digging his bread and butter into the yolk so hard that it spurted out of the top. Henderson would cut small squares of ham and feed them to him.

After breakfast Gil and Henderson would go to work and here Gil felt safe and increasingly happy. He had thought the men in the drawing office would not accept him because of what he had done and it was true that nobody said much, but they had already known that he was skilled and capable and they respected his work. Each morning he and Henderson would sit in Henderson's office and talk. One morning that winter they sat there watching snow falling softly on the shipyard beyond the window and Henderson said, 'I want to build a big ship.'

Gil smiled.

'What's funny about it?'

'Just that I thought you might. The place isn't big enough.'

'It could be. We have plenty of room.'

'It would cost.'

'If you got me the contract for a big ship, I would make you a partner.'

This was beyond generosity. Henderson got up, coffee cup in his hand, and looked out of the window at his domain.

'You did it before.'

'John Marlowe is a very respected man. He won't have

anything to do with me and a lot of other people would go the same way if you made me a partner. You've given me a job, I'm grateful for that.'

'If I died the shipyard would be sold, there's nobody to take it on. I have this vision of me in a wooden box and Robert Bloody Surtees spending my money on drink and women.'

Gil didn't return the straight look Henderson gave him.

'Yes, he does,' Henderson said, 'dear bloody women. He would spend my money on high class whores and backing horses. Do you think I want that? He gambles too. I don't like a man who gambles. Men are meant to work, not go on like that. I wish Abby had never married him. She isn't happy. He didn't even give her a son. If they'd had a son, everything would have been different and maybe I could have hung on long enough if he was a decent sort and liked ships. Na, that's not true. No son of Robert's could tell port from starboard on a Tuesday afternoon. What do they do, these men who care for nothing? How do they live? You have a son. I can't say I'm overly impressed with how you got him, it was a sorry business, but he's there and he's going to be a good lad.'

'He might want something else.'

'Aye, he might, but in my experience things like business are in the blood and you can't change that. Get me Marlowe's next ship and I'll give you a partnership.'

'It would have to be better and faster than the *Northumbria*.'

'So tell him. You could have total planning control,' he said as Gil hesitated.

'If you made me a partner nobody would bother with you socially ever again.'

'If we built a bigger ship than the *Northumbria* they would have to. Anyway, I don't care about things like that. Tea and gossip, that's all it is. I like my office and my own fireside. To hell with other people.'

* * *

Gil went to Allendale Town that winter to see if Jos Allsop was there but the big stone house was locked up and the curtains were pulled. He went into the nearest pub to make enquiries and found that, after Rhoda's death, Jos had been crazy with grief and left and that Mrs Allsop had taken the children and gone back to her family in London where she had come from.

Gil walked the streets for a while until the next train came, but he hated every minute of it. The little town had not changed. He paused. Rhoda's body was lying in the churchyard not far from the church where she had been married to him. He had not attended the funeral, had not felt the right to do so. People would have been shocked. He walked among the gravestones and picked it out, it was so new. They had put her unmarried name on the stone 'Rhoda Carlisle, beloved daughter of Jos and Mary Allsop'. Beloved daughter of his. Rhoda would have hated that. And she would have wanted her father's name on her grave. Gil wondered if her father had been the only person that Rhoda ever really loved. If there was heaven, then she would be with her father and possibly happier than she had been on earth, but he suspected that Rhoda was not far away, walking on her moors, her hair blowing in the cold wind. People were already saying that her ghost walked the moors. Gil could believe it. He went back to Newcastle in search of John Marlowe.

Marlowe was easier to find. He had offices in Newcastle. Gil had been prepared to make an appointment or even to be told that Mr Marlowe would not see him but after the secretary went through into the big office that belonged to him, the door opened immediately and John came out. He didn't offer his hand, he just looked hard and said, 'Gil. Come in.'

The office was luxurious: thick carpets, oak flooring, wide windows, heavy doors, a huge desk. It was the only office Gil had seen which was bigger than his father's. John leaned back against the desk. He was a big man, heavy. He folded his arms across his massive chest and didn't ask Gil to sit down. Gil stood with his hat in his hands and said nothing.

'You're a long time with your apologies, leaving my ship like that.'

'It didn't need me any more. All the important work had been done, it was just detail and the men were there to see to it. It'll be fine. I have nothing to apologise for. Is she finished?'

'Aye.' John stood up straight. 'The mightiest ship the Tyne has ever seen. I'm so proud of her and very angry with you.'

'I know.'

'Do you? The Admiralty was not pleased to have to deal with other men over this, that you turned out to be the kind of person who created the biggest scandal we've seen for years. This ship did not need any of that and neither did its backers.'

'It'll take the Blue Riband on its first voyage—'

'You don't know that!'

'Yes, I do. You couldn't have built that ship without me and you know it and they know it. You didn't have the expertise. I guaranteed you that ship and all it could do, and it will.'

'You're very confident.'

'I'm the best.'

John smiled grimly.

'You're the worst bastard I ever met but yes, you're the best.'

'So, have you given the second ship to somebody else?'

'Not yet. Do you want her?'

'What do I have to do?'

'You could try living a respectable life, that would be nice.'

'You don't care, not really.'

'The Admiralty cares.'

'Sod the Admiralty.'

'Henderson doesn't have the shipyard to build it; he doesn't have the people.'

'He will have. He has space and money and me and I'll get the people.'

'From your father?'

'If I have to.'

'Business shouldn't be this personal.'

'As far as I'm concerned it's always personal in some way. I'll build you a better ship than the *Northumbria,* faster, cleaner, sleeker and in two years.'

Gil and Henderson walked around the site, the huge space of land around the shipyard. It was a cold blustery day, the wind coming off the Tyne. Gil paused.

'Why did you buy all this land? I mean, it was a clever move but you might never have needed it.'

'My father bought it.'

'Very shrewd.'

'He was a rich man, didn't need to work but, unlike fools like Surtees, he liked to be involved in what mattered. And Bella had money. I would have kept it for Abby but she hardly needs it.'

'She might.'

'When's this? He's rolling.'

'He's gambling heavily so I hear.'

'We'll build a fine ship,' Henderson said in satisfaction.

'You'll need housing. You'll need new berths and sheds and cranes and—'

'What's all this "you"?' Henderson said. 'It'll be us. I'm going to put your name on the gate.'

'I'd rather you didn't, it'll upset Abby.'

Gil had other plans. He went to see Mr McGregor at home that Saturday afternoon. McGregor was a Glaswegian who had come from Scotland especially to work for William Collingwood. He was a top engineer; Gil could not have built the *Northumbria* without McGregor's help. He was also a Methodist, a clean-living man who had been married for twenty years, didn't touch a drink and had probably, Gil reflected standing in the middle of the living-room, never had such a person as himself in his house. Gil knew also that McGregor had admired his mind and it was the only reason he had let him in. Mrs McGregor luckily wasn't there.

There was no fire in the room and the smell of polish hung in the air. Gil could see his breath. Mr McGregor didn't even offer him a cup of tea.

'So,' he said, eyeing Gil coldly, 'what can I do for you?'

'I need you.'

'How?'

'I'm going to build Marlowe another liner.'

'Mr Marlowe cares more for money than for principles.'

'I'm not talking about either of those things, I'm talking about expertise—'

'I've worked for your father for fifteen years and you think you can walk in here and take me on like I was a docker?'

Gil paused.

'May I sit down?'

'You'll not be here that long.'

Gil looked at him. He had spent months working alongside this man, their minds were in harmony.

'I'm young. I made a mistake.'

McGregor glared at him.

'A mistake?'

'Have you not made any mistakes?'

'Not of that calibre. My wife hasn't taken her life because I lay with another woman. Dear God, man, what worse could you have done? Your father is . . . he's . . . he was proud of you. Aye, he's a hard man,' McGregor said before Gil could. 'He brought you up hard and what did you do? You designed the most wonderful ship on God's earth and then you threw it all away over a woman.'

'I'm going to build a better ship.'

'I daresay. And will you throw that away too?'

'I'd do it again for her.'

Mr McGregor shook his head.

'It was the proudest day of my life when we launched the *Northumbria.* If I live to be a hundred I won't feel that again.'

'You would if you came and worked with me. I'll pay you better, build you a new house—'

'I canna be bribed nor bought—'

'The chance to work on another big project. Will you get that at Collingwood's, something to test your mind to its limits? You want that, it's what you live for. You need the challenge.'

That was what persuaded McGregor, the opportunity to use his excellent brain. Mr Philips was easier. He didn't like William Collingwood and when Gil mentioned more money, more freedom and a better house he said, 'You only had to ask.'

Gil was pleased with his work. After that, he and Henderson organised the kind of improvements and expansion they would need and the contract was signed. Henderson didn't put Gil's name on the gate but he did make him a partner, it was all drawn up legally. Nobody was told. Gil took every good experienced man away from Collingwood's, including almost the entire drawing office. He took the best-skilled men. They had been badly treated over the years by Collingwood's so they were eager to leave, pleased with the good conditions and more money and housing he was offering them. Gil began systematically to dismiss every man who did not work to the limit of his abilities so that Reed's would soon become the most efficient shipbuilder on the river.

He also travelled to various parts of the country and abroad to make sure that he lost none of the contacts that he had made during his time at his father's shipyard. Since they knew of the *Northumbria* and he could tell them that he had secured the contract with Marlowe and the Admiralty to build another huge express liner, they had sufficient confidence to promise him work, a great deal of which would have gone to Collingwood's.

The following spring the *Northumbria* left the Tyne and on her maiden voyage she took the Blue Riband for the fastest crossing ever between Liverpool and New York. It was difficult for Gil not to think of her leaving the Tyne and worse when she broke the record as he had predicted. He wished he could have been at his father's shipyard when the news was brought, but he knew that it was as bitter and sweet to his father as it was to him and that because of it his fame spread even further and it did him nothing but good. The orders came in, the shipyard was expanded, he and Henderson even bought another piece of land on the river and began setting up another yard to deal with the rush of work. Gil and Henderson were invited nowhere socially, but he didn't care and he didn't think Henderson cared. The work was so exciting and the light in Henderson's eyes made up for a lot, and when he came home in the evening there was his child and a decent meal and a good bed and a bottle of wine. They sat by the fire in wet weather or in the garden in fine and they talked about the shipyard and about politics. Things could have been a lot worse, Gil decided. They had been and no doubt they would be again, so he took pleasure in the present and his friend and his child and his work.

Chapter Seventeen

Abby became pregnant again that summer and was so thankful that she didn't know what to do.

'This time it will be a boy,' Robert said, satisfied. After that he left her alone in bed and she could only be grateful.

She went to her father's every Sunday and there, to her anger, she was happy. The little boy grew more interesting and attractive every week and there was always beef for dinner and Yorkshire pudding. Her father and Gil sat by the fire and she talked with them and drank her wine. In the afternoons if the weather was good they would take Matthew to the park and sail boats on the pond and she was able to behave like a child, screeching and yelling as the sails on the boats filled with wind and they raced to the other side. She was even happy looking over the bridge at the dene, watching twigs or leaves in at one side and out at the other. She and Matthew would dash to the far side of the bridge to see if they emerged, or whether they had caught on the side or on a rock or a piece of something bigger which was floating past. She always told herself on the way home that she had been very foolish, that Robert would have despised her, but the simple pleasures were stored in her mind. She was as desperate as Robert for a son, not only because he and his family wanted an heir but because she had seen Matthew. Georgina was a difficult child who cried frequently and Abby found herself hoping that she didn't have to see much of her.

One Sunday in September, when her father had declined a walk to the dene because the wind was cool, she was standing with Matthew watching their twigs disappear under the bridge when suddenly a pain wrenched at her insides. Abby gave a cry and clutched her stomach, waiting for it to disappear. It came again, even more sharply. She slid down onto her knees and shouted and Gil came running over the bridge to her. She was fighting for breath amidst the pain.

'My baby.'

'No, it can't be,' Gil said, getting down beside her.

The tears began to run down her face from the pain. When it eased a little, Gil picked her up.

'You can't carry me all that way.'

'Save your breath,' he said, and urged the little boy to stay close.

'It's gone. I can walk. Put me down.'

'Keep quiet.'

The idea of losing this child was more than Abby could stand. She closed her eyes against his shoulder. She was not heavy, he could carry her, but she didn't want him to. She had lost weight during the last few years. Unhappiness did not make you fat, Abby discovered. Gil was big, but he wasn't very fat either. Sheer hard work did that. She was reminded of when she had hurt her ankle and he had carried her into the house. They had been so young then and Gil had been a different person. He didn't seem like a different person. If she could have forgotten about Helen and Rhoda, he seemed to her very much the same, only speaking when he had something to say. He was easier with the child, laughing and playing, throwing Matthew into the air and catching him when he came down, mock-fighting with him on the lawn or on the rug in front of the fire, sitting quietly with him reading stories or playing draughts with an old board and bottle tops. Thinking of Matthew made her feel even worse.

By the time they got back to the house the pain was excruciating and she could feel the warmth seeping between her legs. Gil put her down on the bed and ran to get the doctor. Kate helped her out of her clothes and into her nightdress, but the blood was not reassuring. Some hours later, with Robert and Gil in the same house downstairs, Abby lost her baby, a bloody lump that they wrapped in a cloth and quickly took away. With the physical pain gone and the doctor trying to quieten her, Abby cried and cried.

Robert came to her.

'It doesn't matter,' he said, 'we've got plenty of time for other babies. Don't cry.'

'I don't want another baby, I want that one.'

'What were you doing?'

'Nothing.'

'I didn't realise that you were spending so much time in that man's company.'

'I'm not. We took Matthew for a walk. There's nothing sinister or intimate about that. I don't even like him.'

'Then why go?'

'Because of Matthew. Why else?'

'You go out with a man other women would die rather than be seen with because he has a child? What must people think?'

Abby didn't want to talk about Gil or think about him, she wanted to think about the child that she had lost. She hid in the pillows.

'I think you had better stop coming here on Sundays. It obviously isn't doing you any good.'

Abby wanted to say that she came to see her father, that Matthew was a bonus, but she was so tired that she couldn't. Her father refused to go to the big country house, which was Robert's domain. Abby couldn't understand why men had to be so difficult. All she wanted to do was sleep, wake up, be pregnant like before and not feel that dreadful pain which had brought her to her knees and the horrible sensation of her child's lifeblood running down her legs. She wished also that Robert was the kind of man who would put his arms around her, stroke her hair and tell her that he loved her. There was a time when he would have. She sensed his impatience, his disappointment with her and the failure that belonged to both of them because they had not produced a male child. The idea of him in her bed again pounding at her body was the least appealing of all. Abby didn't look at him. She feigned sleep until she did sleep and by that time, somewhere in her vague unconsciousness, he left the room.

Gil had kept out of the way after Robert had arrived. He was working in his little office when Robert came downstairs and was surprised when the door opened and Robert glared at him.

'Stay away from my wife,' he said.

Gil knew that he was to blame for a great many things, but Abby's miscarriage was not one of them. Robert came into the room and closed the door. Gil wasn't very happy about this. This was his room. He stood back against the edge of the desk.

'Everybody knows what you're like with women and I haven't forgotten the boy that you were, standing for hours at the edge of the ballroom watching her dance. If you go anywhere near her, I'll see to you personally.'

He slammed the door after him. Gil winced. Matthew was in bed. He hoped the noise didn't wake him. Gil went through into the sitting-room shortly afterwards, saying hopefully, 'Has he gone?'

'Aye, thank God. Couldn't stay under the same roof with you and me, not even for her sake, poor lass. I don't think she'll have any more.'

'Why not?'

'The same thing happened to Bella,' Henderson said sadly. 'We wanted a big family. She used to talk about how lovely it would be to have them all gathered around us. A dynasty, a whole family of Reeds, that was what she wanted. She lost two before Abby and another after her and there were no more. If that was what he married Abby for, he's going to be disappointed. He seemed to care for her so much.'

When Gil went upstairs to bed he found Abby on the landing, a thin white figure, vague-eyed. Gil was about to ask her what she was doing up when he realised that she wasn't awake. He led her gently back into her room and put her into bed. She woke up, looked accusingly at him and said, 'What are you doing here?'

'I'm tucking you in.'

'Why?'

'Because I adore women in white nighties. Lie down and go to sleep. It doesn't hurt, does it?'

'Not any more.'

'Good.'

'And I will have lots of other children you see. Lots. That one didn't matter. It's gone. It's gone.'

Gil sat down on the edge of the bed and Abby said, 'I never want to go back to the dene again ever,' and started to cry. 'I want my baby.' She put her arms around his neck. Briefly there was the feel of her face and hair and then she drew back and said, 'What am I doing?'

'Lie down and go to sleep.'

Abby lay down and he tucked in the bedclothes, left the lamp burning for her and went to bed.

When she went home nobody mentioned the baby; it was as though the child had not existed. Christmas came and Abby wasn't well. Robert did not come into her bedroom. She thought the doctor had talked to him so at least she had peace there, but she was tired and her spirits were low. Quite often on Sundays she didn't go to Jesmond. Occasionally she would visit friends in Newcastle and call in to see her father on Saturday evenings. Robert was resentful of her absence, but with Robert saying he wouldn't go to Newcastle and her father refusing to go into the country, Abby grew tired of them both

At Christmas she saw William and Charlotte and even Edward. She tried to talk to Edward about work; she thought that at least might interest him. He looked at her.

'Is it true that you saved my brother's life?'

Abby had no idea that anyone knew, though she also knew how difficult it was to keep a secret in a city like Newcastle where people were so closely involved in business and one another's interests. She managed what was meant to be a smile.

'Me? He stayed at my father's house. He's still there, though I wish things otherwise.'

'I have heard lurid stories, though God knows how they could be worse than the things he had already done.'

'My father has done himself a great deal of harm keeping your brother there.'

'He hasn't done us any good either,' Edward said grimly.

'What do you mean?'

'Don't you know? Gil's trying to destroy us. He's taken all the best men, left us with the rubbish. He's taken all the best work, and he's taken the contract which my father fully expected to get. We built the *Northumbria* but when it came to the same thing again, the Admiralty gave the bloody contract away. To him. The devious bastard. Here we are, the greatest shipyard on the Tyne, scrabbling around for bloody work and him—'

Abby rarely saw Gil. On Saturdays when she went to the house he was usually still at work, or if she went in the evenings he didn't come out of the office. She saw Matthew unless it was late and he was in bed. The visits were unsatisfactory. Henderson, tired after a week at the shipyard, had nothing much to say. Abby could remember a time when she and her father had delighted in one another's company, when she had hated leaving him, had looked back from the carriage until she couldn't see him any more and he stood waving her out of sight. Now he didn't even get up, but wished her goodbye from his armchair, and the house did not feel like her home any longer. Gil seemed to have taken it over. Perhaps that was what he had done with the shipyard, though she couldn't have said. Nothing was altered in the house; it was exactly the same as it had always been, but somehow his presence had made everything different.

She had dismissed from her mind the rumours that Collingwood's were having a bad time. Business was like that; no-one knew better, but Edward talked so bitterly about his brother. There was hatred in his voice. Abby was not surprised at that, but she had thought the cause was Helen's betrayal and therefore Gil's. She had not considered practicalities and she had not thought Gil devious. When she did see him he was usually with Matthew, laughing and playing silly games, and she could not see him now in any other role.

Edward did not look like Gil's brother. He had grown fat and looked older, worn and weighed down by loss and disappointment. William was silent. Charlotte was the only person to discuss Abby's miscarriage and Abby wished she wouldn't.

'You must take better care, stay in bed, rest. A child is vital.' Charlotte gave her advice on what to eat and what to do until Abby itched to be gone from her. Charlotte was not the person to advise anybody on children, Abby thought. Her sons were no credit either to her or to William.

Abby did not see her father before Christmas, but on Christmas Day she grew restless. They had guests who had been there for several days and she was tired of them. She went for a long walk in the early afternoon. The sky was heavy but it hadn't snowed and she decided that she would go into Newcastle and call in on her father. She could stay overnight with friends if she wished. Robert was playing billiards, several of his cronies around him, all rather drunk and laughing, and he paid little attention when she said she was going to Jesmond.

'Tell your father I wish him all the best,' he said, waving a billiard cue at her.

'I just want to make sure he's well,' she said.

She took the carriage, called in on friends not far away, was assured that if she wanted to go and see her father for an hour or two she could come back to them if she liked. It was the middle of the evening when she knocked on the door of Henderson's villa. Nobody answered at first, but after a while the door opened and there stood Gil in his shirtsleeves. Abby was determined to be merry and wished him all the best and Gil ushered her into the house.

It was silent, that was the first thing that caught Abby's attention. There was no Christmas tree, no lights or decorations. There were no revellers; there was no smell of meat or pudding or brandy or any of the trappings which went with this day and the house was cool. At her house there was a huge Christmas tree. Holly and mistletoe hung everywhere and people were laughing and drinking and playing games. Tomorrow there would be hunting; she would go along to drink a stirrup cup with them and everybody would be warmly wrapped to see them away. It was a wonderful sight and traditional. Then they would all troop home to big fires and delicious food and champagne.

Gil led the way into the little office.

'The fire's lit in here,' he said. Abby stared. He was quite obviously working. 'Your father's in bed, I'm afraid. He was tired and so was Matthew. Kate and Mrs Wilkins have gone home.'

'You let your servants go home for Christmas? How very modern and how uncomfortable for you.'

She looked with distaste at the papers on the desk, the small fire in the grate and the way that the curtains were still open, letting in the draught. Snow was falling. Gil looked like a clerk, not an important man. His sleeves were rolled back and his fingers had ink on them.

'My father isn't ill?'

'He's fine. He was tired.'

'He works far too much.'

'Yes, I have tried to talk to him, but he loves it.'

'I was talking to your brother. I saw your parents and Edward, they came to a party at our house.'

Gil tried, she thought, to disguise the hunger in his face, but he didn't quite manage it.

'How is he?'

'He's got very fat. I expect he eats too much.'

'He takes after my mother. She used to have full weeks when she didn't eat for fear of not being able to fit into her dresses.'

'Are you trying to take everything from them?'

'Am I doing what?' Gil said, obviously taken aback at the question.

'He said you have taken their best men and their work and that you have a huge contract to build a liner. I didn't know that. I didn't know that you were involved in such projects.'

'It's just business,' Gil said.

'Is it?'

'Your father wants to build up the shipyard, to make it bigger, to handle bigger ships. I think he's always wanted to do that, but it was too much for him on his own.'

'And now he has you and can.'

'Something like that.'

'You got the big contract yourself.'

'I did build the *Northumbria*.'

'I thought it was Collingwood's who did that.'

Gil looked at her and there was something about the look which silenced Abby and he said softly, 'I am Collingwood's. Edward knows nothing and my father—' He didn't complete the sentence.

'And you have stolen their best men.'

'I haven't stolen anything. I pay them better.'

'It's about money, then.'

'When is business about anything else?'

Abby determined to change the subject.

'Working on Christmas night. I don't know. You could offer me a glass of wine.'

He went off to the kitchen and came back with glasses and a bottle. It was not, Abby thought, tasting it, the kind of thing she was used to. It was very inferior, thin and white.

'So,' she said, waving her glass, 'no parties? Is this what you do every night?'

'Yes.'

'My father often goes to bed early?'

'Quite often.'

Here at the back of the house it was strangely silent. She had forgotten. There was nothing but the darkness of the garden and the softly falling snow. How strange that this was the town and so quiet, whereas in the country where they lived it was so noisy.

Gil's conversation, Abby thought, was almost non-existent. He had no social graces nor needed any because he was asked nowhere, not even on Christmas night. She thought of all the socially adept men she knew who would entertain her, talk to her, make her laugh. They would have done more if she had just said the word. It was no secret that her marriage was difficult and that her husband had frequently bedded other women. It would have been little fault if she had gone to any one of the rich, handsome men she knew and they would have been glad.

Gil was not her social equal. He was nobody. He was, it was allowed, good in his field, but work was not the criterion by which men were judged in her world. Even their tailoring was more important. Their hunting prowess, their shooting ability and their bedroom manners mattered and not one of them would ever have sat here without a jacket, with ink-stained fingers and expected her to sit there with them, silent, drinking a not particularly good wine. He didn't even look up much, but Abby knew him too well to think that this meant he was particularly concerned about any of these matters. The seeming vulnerability and his jacketless, tieless state, the confusion of the room, the quality of the wine, entertaining a lady in a scruffy little room with papers strewn on every surface and books on every chair – he had had to move some so that she could sit down – none of it registered with him. He didn't care about the silence between them or that she was not entertained.

Gil seemed so young, sitting there looking down into his wine, waiting for her to go away so that he could get on with his work. Nothing had touched him; none of the tragedy had brought lines to his face. He seemed years and years younger than Robert and his friends, though he had worked all of his life and they had not.

'Are you worried about him?'

'What?'

'Your father,' Gil said.

'I'm afraid that he will die.'

'I am looking after him. We come home early in the evening and have tea with Matthew and he doesn't work after that.'

'I'm sure you are.'

'You think it's all too much for him.'

'Well, it is.'

Gil came to her and Abby was confused as she wasn't with other men. He was so tall and his hair was black in the lamplight and so were his eyes.

'You always blame me for everything.'

'That's not true!' She looked up at him and wished she hadn't. His eyes were guarded. He moved back slightly, as though he hadn't meant to get that close.

'It's just that—' Abby couldn't get the words out '—having lost my mother I was hoping he would live to be old and . . . I'm afraid that if he goes on working too hard . . . I don't want to talk about it, not even the possibility. This wine isn't very good.'

'I don't know much about wine.'

Abby thought she should go home. He clearly didn't want her there, interrupting his work. 'I should go, you have a lot to do.' She indicated the papers that were overflowing the desk. She was going to put down her half-full glass and managed to tip the contents down the front of her blouse. Luckily the blouse was the same colour as the wine, more or less. She scrubbed at the mess with a handkerchief.

'A wet cloth would help,' Gil said.

'I don't want a wet cloth. It wasn't much. I'd drunk nearly all the wretched stuff.'

And then she looked at him and he was very close. She could see the base of his throat where the top button of his shirt was undone. She reached out and touched his arm.

'Gil—'

It was like the night they had spent together, Abby thought, and all those other times. He was the only person in the world who could reduce her to tears without doing anything. All those men that she knew and flirted with, men she called her friends, couldn't have made her cry if they had broken her arms. And then he did what she had wanted him to do when it would have been all right for him to do it all those years ago. Now, when it was not permissible, when she was married and he was disgraced, when they didn't even like one another, he took hold of her and put her against him and kissed her.

Abby had never before kissed a man she was not supposed to kiss, so she was not sure whether it was the illicit bit of it that she liked best or whether it was that she had waited such a long time. She knew at that moment why she hadn't bothered with other men and presumably the illicit bit would have worked just the same. And all the hundreds of times that Robert had touched her, he had not kissed her like this. His kisses had been ungenerous somehow, impatient perhaps, or was she doing him a disservice with hindsight? Robert was a very experienced man with women; he knew all about kissing. Robert knew a great deal about everything when it came to this, but she saw with a frightening clarity that all the times when he had, did not make her his as even this single kiss made her Gil's. She had always belonged to him, perhaps even before that freezing cold night in the bedroom. That had been Christmas too, almost to the day.

It wasn't that he tried to seduce her; he didn't. Any other man having got that far would have had his hands on her in seconds, but Gil put his arms around her as though she was distressed and it was only then that Abby realised she was. All she had was her father and of late they had not got on. He didn't care for Robert and Robert disliked him and that made it difficult. Gil didn't even kiss her a second time; he held her in against him so that nothing could hurt her, with his arms between her and the rest of the world and she didn't cry. It was as though he was used to her there; she was meant to be there. This was really what women wanted from men, Abby thought, comfort, a little protection, a place to go to be safe from time to time

The last person Gil had kissed like this had been Rhoda and the memories came back, the triumph of the launching when the ship's hull was finished, that weekend which had been the best of his life only to turn into the worst, the way she had run, the looking for her and the greatest misery, finding her cold and still in the snow on the moors. This made him want to deny that she was dead, to pretend to himself that he had her back, that nothing had happened, that she was in his arms. He couldn't do that. Perhaps he could have with another woman, but not with Abby. He cared for her too much to do that, fought with himself and won, remembering what had happened when he gave in to what he wanted. He drew away but she followed him, kissed him. She didn't hold back at all. She got her hands up to his neck and touched his throat. Gil could smell the wine down the front of her blouse, the sweet and lemon scent of it. He could feel the way that her fingers slipped to the first button on his shirt. He was astonished that she should do such a thing. Abby hadn't altered at all. She was still the bold girl who had gone upstairs to find him, turned the key in the lock, covered him in blankets and given him chocolate cake. She looked at him, smiled at him, put her hand into his hair in caress.

'You could at least take off your hat,' Gil said.

'Shall I?' She took out the hat pins as if she were doing tricks. She took the pins out of her hair, too, so that it swung down past her shoulders and she took off the jacket that she wore and started to undo the buttons on her blouse. He grabbed hold of her and she laughed. The smell of wine seemed to fill the whole room. The images of Rhoda faded. All he could remember was that he had wanted her when she was sixteen and all the nights when he had been alone and all the days and the evenings when he had done nothing but work. Months and months of not being able to touch anybody. Now he could. She didn't stop him from unfastening the garments that hid the rest of her body from him and then he could touch her, put his mouth on her, draw her close to feel her skin against his skin.

Abby wondered if her father had ever drawn her mother down on to the rug in front of the fire in this room. It seemed doubly wrong to be doing this here. A man she was not married to, a man who had the kind of reputation which excluded him from society, was making love to her in her mother's sewing room. The papers got in the way from time to time and fluttered about her. Some of them slid off the desk when Gil moved away from it and into her arms and his ink-stained fingers were slow and cool and a little uncertain. Not like Robert. Robert was always certain, but then Robert did not prize her except as the mother of a child as yet unborn. It would be funny, she thought, it would be so funny if she could have a child from this night. After all, Helen had done it. Helen had had his child, but that was not just from one night, that was something that went on for months and months, didn't it? Abby did not believe that he was the kind of man who would bed his wife and another woman in the same house. Gil wasn't made like that. He couldn't have done it, she knew that he couldn't. Yet he had, apparently. Robert would have. He had done it in France and any of his more decadent drunken friends might have done it merely as a pastime, but Gil was not a drunk and he was not an idler. His eyes were clear and his mouth was sweet and he had not spent years swigging whisky and laying women and smoking foul-smelling cigars. He was also, Abby thought a little gleefully, the kind of man who had concentration. You could tell that from his work. He thought about one thing at once and gave it his entire attention and just now he was concentrating on her. She would have bet a thousand pounds that there was nothing going on in Gil's mind which reached beyond the edge of the rug.

The firelight turned his skin to gold and put a halo around his shiny hair. All the times that Robert had made sexual advances to his wife meant nothing more to Abby than the papers that had fluttered to the floor. She felt sorry in several ways, because it all seemed so base and meaningless and so utterly pointless. She was angry with herself, too. It seemed to her that she could have and should have married Gil. She would have wrested him away from Helen and he would not have gone through all the hell that his life had been and she would never have lain under a man like a victim and endured the invasion of her body. Her life with Robert was nothing to do with anything that she had ever wanted, she could see that now.

He was being more and more careful, as though at any minute she was going to deny him. Slower and slower the kisses and caresses became, even though Abby had yielded her body long since. It was ironic, she thought savagely, that Robert did nothing but take her and that she was actually going to have to ask this man to.

'For God's sake!' she said into his hair.

'Are you sure?'

'I'm dying here,' she said with a little choke of laughter. 'Please.'

'I didn't think you would.'

'What the hell else do you think I'm doing here, bare on a bloody rug?'

'You have a foul mouth for a woman.'

Abby got hold of his hair.

'I love you. I love you and I want you. Now.'

He took her at her word. Abby closed her eyes and after that she couldn't think at all or even want to. Her mind fought briefly. It was wrong. She was not married to him, but that only served to make it better. It was exquisite, nothing like the way that Robert came to her, but that was duty and obligation, it was all about contracts and commitments and the carrying on of names. It was not the act which was important it was the result, whereas this was purely pleasure. This was like chocolate and ice cream, chilled wine on a hot day, firelight on a winter's evening. She could feel the fire, not near enough to burn, and the rug which was thick and the draught which came under the door because the fire had begun to die down and the logs gave off a sweet scent in the grate.

Outside she could hear the wind lifting the snow, but the house was silent. Robert was prone to whispering obscenities into her ears, but Gil didn't even tell her that he loved her, as though speech had nothing to do with him. He said not a single word and there was no grunting or labouring. In the silence Abby bit her lip so hard that she could taste blood, as though there had been some kind of agreement that nothing should escape her lips beyond a sigh. There had been times when she had wondered at herself whether she felt any real passion at all. In the early days of her marriage, the intimacy had been sweet but it had not been like this. Robert had called her cold and she had thought the fault lay with her. Other women seemed to like him well enough. She had come to the conclusion that she was the kind of woman who preferred affection, but it was not so. She craved him like food after a long fasting and the more she had of him, the more she wanted. She only hoped that her body might turn out to belong to some other woman so that afterwards she would not have to go under a table and hide somewhere for embarrassment. Robert had not had this response from her; he had not been hers like this; she had not felt like his. She liked Gil better and better.

She felt so triumphant, so powerful, so wonderfully, screamingly alive. She felt as though she would never be alone again; he would belong to her for all time. There was nothing to go back to and no need. Everything was in the present.

Gil was only dimly aware of the room, the silence, but he could feel the forces around him trying to stop him. All the intelligence and all the guilt and responsibility had hounded him to here. He had kept away from women. He had thought he would never hold anybody again and the Puritan in his upbringing told him sternly that he was not entitled to, that he had committed too many grave wrongs. He could not free himself of Helen dying and of Rhoda up on the fells. He found himself entitled to nothing but his work and his child and, since it had been offered him, the friendship of the man he admired above all others. If Henderson knew what he was doing now . . . He was going to lose Henderson. The man was his only friend, he was not well and was gradually getting worse. He didn't tell Abby that. He didn't think he needed to, but he was all Gil had. At work, the men did as he told them. His business reputation meant that not only did they not question him, but neither did they feel themselves to be his equal and it was difficult to be friends with people who weren't. All he had was his work and his child and Henderson and a third of the triangle was about to be lost for ever.

This was just momentary, he knew. She was going to hate him afterwards when the magic had died with the firelight. He was not entitled to her, was taking something he was not meant to have. But she had wanted him and there had been so many nights spent alone. When he hesitated because he knew how wrong this was, he had given her a way out she had told him that she loved him. Gil knew that it was nearly always men who did that. Was she doing it for what she wanted? So he gave her what she wanted and part of him felt so calm, so cool, so detached, whereas the other part of him wanted her so much that he couldn't see beyond it. That part took over until only a vague sorrow and awareness remained and he could not have identified it. He took her past reason, past thought, past the kind of control where she had put her teeth into her lip until she cried out. Helen had taught him a lot about pleasure, about the things that women wanted men to do to them. Somewhere beyond him he had an impression of white curtains fluttering in the breeze. Then they stilled and the Newcastle night threw snow at the window. He didn't care that somebody might hear her cries, or that the tears spilled or what might happen afterwards, just that she would remember, that it would matter, that nothing would ever be the same again.

The fire had darkened in the grate and the lamp was low. The draught under the door made Abby shiver. It was worse than she had feared. There was no easy escape. They were not in bed, so she could not turn away and bury herself in the bedclothes. She was naked on a rug with a man who was not her husband in the room where, as a little girl, she would sit on her mother's knee and learn the clock. Somewhere above them her father slept. The room was full of shadows. Abby was glad of that. At least she could not see herself or him very well. He began to dress. She watched his beautiful, lean body disappearing behind his clothes, ordinary working clothes. She did not understand why he had such an effect on her except that he was so good-looking. He was nobody.

He glanced at her from dark secret eyes and said lightly, 'Regretting it already?'

'I have to go,' she said. 'I'm staying with friends.'

He didn't argue. Robert would have put up a fight, tried to get her to go to bed with him so that he could have her again, so that they could sleep together. There was no question, either, of her walking there by herself. She put on her coat and he found his in the hall and they stepped out into the street together. It wasn't the kind of weather for talking, but even if it had been a summer's night she thought the only sound would have been their footsteps. She directed him briefly as they went and when she reached the front door, he wished her a brief goodnight and left her there.

It was as though nothing had happened. Abby went inside by the fire and sat for a while with her friends, talking about small matters. Then she went to bed. She couldn't believe what she had done. Men did that to high-class whores, walked in, spoke of love, had them and then left, without any kind of affection or relationship. They paid, too. Short of offering Gil money, she had done all that. She couldn't sleep. She watched the long night finally fade into morning and then she went back to the country.

It felt so normal there so that she was easily able to convince herself that nothing had happened. She tried to put Gil from her mind, to excuse what she had done, but she couldn't. She stayed at home, glad of the safety, able to play hostess to their friends and go to various social events. Everything was bearable until the evening almost a fortnight later when Robert wandered into her bedroom rather drunk. It was late and she was almost asleep. Without any ceremony at all he got into her bed and tried to take hold of her and Abby refused for the first time.

'Whatever is wrong with you?' Robert demanded.

'You've had too much to drink.'

'If I'd had too much to drink, I wouldn't be able to do this,' he pointed out.

'You're not going to do it.'

'Goddamn it, you're my wife.'

'No!'

Abby punched him in the eye and he laughed, but it wasn't funny. She did not want Robert to touch her; she felt as though it would wipe out the existence of the lovemaking between Gil and herself. Abby knew that Robert was entitled to her body, that there was no reason he would see that she should refuse him and that he would not expect it, since she had not refused before. He didn't mean to hurt her, but he insisted on having her so she gave in and let him, after which he said he couldn't think what all the fuss was about. For several days afterwards, as his eye went dark red and yellow with bruising, he bragged that Abby had acted like a prize fighter.

He staggered off to his own room to sleep and didn't appear until noon the next day, when Abby was having lunch with friends. By the time she came back, people had arrived for dinner. To her surprise he drank nothing and when she went to bed he followed her there, putting up both hands in surrender.

'I'm sorry,' he said. 'I've wanted to say it all day. I do most sincerely apologise. I was drunk and you were quite right and if I've hurt you—'

Abby began to remember why she had married him.

'I'm not hurt,' she said, but somehow she was now much more so than before. She was hurt for him because she should not have gone to Gil, wished she had not, was glad that she had left him. It did seem, though, as the days went by that Robert was drinking more than ever and there were other nights when he came to her room. She didn't refuse him again, no matter how drunk he was.

Sometimes he stayed out all night and one morning that spring he came home as Abby was breakfasting. He looked tired, unshaven, defeated. He sat down near her in the dining-room and refused everything but coffee. When the maid went, he got up and walked to the window. It was a cold rainy March day and the daffodils in the garden had been knocked over by the weather as they were every year, Abby thought.

'I have a confession to make,' Robert said.

'What's that?' Abby thought it must be a woman or some social thing he had agreed to while drunk, so when he said calmly, 'I've lost the London house,' she was astonished.

She looked up from her toast and marmalade and coffee.

'Lost it? How can you have lost it?'

'At play.'

'You gambled away our house?'

'I had to, Abby. I had to do something. My losses were huge. It was either that or blow my brains out. Perhaps you'd have preferred that?'

'It would still have been a debt of honour, so that wouldn't have helped,' Abby said dryly.

'You know these things so well.'

'How could you have lost so much?'

He turned away from the window, came back to the table and sat down with a sigh.

'I wasn't going to get involved but I keep promising myself that I won't drink and when I don't drink I have to do something, you must see that. When I'm drunk I'm disgusting to you. It's not a road I want to go down. After all, I have no son to leave it to. I'm sorry, I didn't mean that. I don't mean to reproach you. It's my own fault.'

He talked and talked; he paced up and down; he became more and more upset all morning. He began drinking when they had lunch, 'just a glass of wine', a bottle and then another. After two glasses of brandy he fell asleep on the sofa in front of the fire. By teatime he was awake and they had tea and cake and then a carriage arrived. It was late in the day for anyone to come to the house uninvited so Abby's heart beat hard and she was right. It was Kate with a note from Gil. Henderson had collapsed at work.

Robert offered to go with her, but he had no enthusiasm and was still recovering from his lunchtime drinking. Abby had imagined it would be difficult to go back to the house in Jesmond, but she didn't give that a thought now. Her concern was all for her father. She ran into the house, stopped short as Gil came into the hall.

'Where is he?'

'Upstairs.' He caught her arm as she would have gone. 'Easy, easy. Come into the sitting-room a minute.'

'He's dead, isn't he?'

'No. He's asleep. Have some tea.'

'I don't want some bloody tea!' She twisted away from him, though it wasn't necessary, he wasn't holding her.

'The doctor says he should make a complete recovery but he won't be able to go back to work for some time.'

'Who cares anything about that? I've begged him to stop.'

'It's his heart,' Gil said. 'He loves his work, you know that.'

'If it hadn't been for you he would have been content with the way things were. He's too old for all these ambitious schemes. He would probably have given it up long since.'

'That's not true. His work is all he has.'

'He has me and you and Matthew.'

'People aren't enough. All he's really had since your mother died is his work. He isn't the kind of man who does other things. He's even bored on Sundays.'

'He hasn't been well for a long time, it's just that you haven't told me,' Abby guessed.

Gil had not been surprised when Henderson was taken ill. He had seen it coming and for a number of days had suggested to Henderson that he should stay at home, but Henderson wouldn't. He was too involved in what was happening and Gil understood because he had felt the same way when the first express liner was being built. It was wonderful to watch it take shape and to be involved in all the different processes as they went along. He knew that Henderson had had the same ambition as his father, he had just not put it into practice for lack of help and support. He had that now and was enjoying himself, but he was also ill and the illness made him frustrated. He would not stay at home no matter how he felt. Gil didn't feel quite the same about the second ship. It was not lack of novelty, it was what had happened since. He didn't trust anything any more and he was proved right when one of the men ran into his office to tell him that Henderson had collapsed. Finding the older man on the floor made Gil's own heart misgive. He knew then that it would only be a short time before he did not have Henderson either to work with or to go home with. He couldn't imagine what that would be like. He didn't want to. He sent for the doctor and sent a note to Abby. When the doctor said Henderson could go home, he took him.

He and Abby hadn't met since the night they had made love on the rug in the little office, but he could tell when he saw her that that had gone completely from her mind. All she wanted was for her father to be better and they both knew that wasn't going to happen. She stayed the night, sitting up in her father's room while Henderson slept. Gil wished he could reassure her, but the words would mean nothing so he didn't say them. He looked after Matthew, read him a story, went up to make sure that Abby was all right, put Matthew to bed and then did some work. It was only when Abby came downstairs late that he could tell she remembered what had happened between them, because she came into the office to see him.

'He's sleeping peacefully now,' she said to fill the silence.

'You're not going to stay up all night with him, are you?'

'I think I might. If he takes another bad turn I want to be there. You go to bed.' Gil began to protest but she said, 'I'd rather you did.' So he went.

He didn't sleep. Having lost so many people whom he loved in so many different ways, Gil didn't think he could stand Henderson's death. He went through it again and again to try and arm himself for if it should happen, when it would happen, although he knew that you couldn't prepare yourself for something like that. The idea of being completely alone with nobody but a child for company was impossible to face, so it was not just for Henderson's sake that he was upset, it was for himself. Henderson had done so much for him, much more, he knew, than he deserved. He was aware that Henderson would not live to see the big liner built and it seemed cruel that he would not achieve his ambition. William had done that, though it must have been a sour victory when the *Northumbria* left Tyneside and he was not there to see it. He wondered how his father had felt, why there was no pure pleasure, no undamaged triumph.

In the darkest hour of the night he left his bed and went through into Henderson's room. Abby had fallen asleep in the chair but her father was breathing freely and easily and the rest would do him good, Gil thought. He went back to bed for fear of disturbing her. He was glad when daylight came and he could go to work and leave Abby in charge. She stayed almost a week and during that time they did not have a private conversation. Gil stayed at work as much as he could. She sat upstairs with her father in the evenings. At the end of the week she went home and Henderson was strong enough to tell Gil that he was glad she had gone.

'She fusses over me.'

'She worries about you.'

'She can worry about me from the country.'

He stayed at home for the first two days of the following week, but insisted on going in for an hour or two on the days after that, even though Gil tried to dissuade him. He had dragged from Gil every detail of every happening and even when Gil came home in the evenings he questioned him closely, as though he couldn't know enough about what was going on in his shipyards. Gil was happy to tell him as long as Henderson didn't want to go back full time. It was difficult for Gil to manage both shipyards, but when he suggested putting a manager in at the smaller yard Henderson lost his temper and called him names. Gil knew it wasn't good for him to be upset, so he went away to the little office and worked. An hour later Henderson put an apologetic face around the door.

'All right, all right, I'm sorry. I shouldn't have shouted and cursed like that. Yes, we'll have a manager and yes, I'm a silly old fool. Being old means having to give things up and I'm not ready to do that yet.'

'I wasn't asking you to give anything up—'

'Yes, you were. You and Abby both think I shouldn't be there. I want to see that ship finished.'

'The big yard needs all the help it can get. It needs both of us.'

'It's a good thing you didn't go into the diplomatic service, you're totally transparent,' Henderson said. He came into the room and closed the door. 'I've got something to say to you, something I should have said before. It's serious and you aren't going to like it.' Henderson looked down at his feet and then straight into Gil's eyes. 'You're very like your father. I know you don't want to hear that, but it's true and until you got here he was the most successful man on the river. Now he isn't because you've taken it away from him. People can't help their nature. You have one advantage over him: you're cleverer than he is and it's good for us because we are using that for our gain.

'I've talked to my solicitor recently. I've changed my will. I've left you everything.'

Gil went cool with shock.

'You can't do that.'

'I have done it.'

'Henderson—'

'I know the argument, but let me just say this first. I was mistaken in Robert Surtees. I regret it. He hasn't made Abby happy and I don't trust him. I'm not saying you would have made her happy. I think your personal life has been deplorable, but I trust you in other ways. I don't want him to get his hands on anything that belongs to me. I've heard lately that he has gamed away his London house. God knows what more he will do. I wouldn't care if he was a sensible, honourable businessman but he isn't and I'd rather he didn't get his hands on a business which has been my life's work and belonged to my father. You know what you're doing and you have a son.'

Gil didn't say anything immediately. It was such a long, complicated speech. Then he got up from where he had been sitting at the desk working when Henderson walked in.

'Abby would never forgive me,' he said.

'I would never forgive you if that bastard ruined my business. They don't need anything from me and Abby has no legal comeback. She's not my dependent; I can leave my assets as I choose. They're rich. The only thing I ask is that if he were to gamble everything – I'm not saying he will, mind you, but disappointed men do strange things – if she needs help I want you to look after her. Promise me.'

'What do you mean "a disappointed man"?'

Henderson's eyes were red and watery but his look was direct.

'You know what I mean.'

'No.'

'She loved you. I kept her away from you. He loved her in the beginning but I don't think she ever loved him. She married him to ease my mind. I think he realises now that Abby didn't care for him as she cared for you.'

'It might have been the worse then if we had married.'

'Possibly, I'm not saying otherwise.'

'There are other ways. You could give me a share and give her financial control—'

'No.'

'Then half.'

'That would make it worse. I want it all in safe hands.'

'Robert isn't a bad man.'

'No, worse than that, he's a fool. Abby's like Bella was. She would rather do without if she couldn't have everything. Abby would have broken her heart when you were unfaithful to her, but she didn't love Robert sufficiently to break her heart over him. That's about all I have to be thankful for. Now, I've said my piece, I'm going to my bed.'

When he had gone, Gil let himself remember how he and

Abby had been that night in this little room because it was clear to him now that it would not happen again. She had lied to him that night, told him that she loved him. It was not true. It had been once, but it was not any more. His behaviour had altered that but this would finish everything. When he lost Henderson he would lose her too and this time for good. She would think he had put his own interests before her father's or hers. She would not forgive him.

Chapter Eighteen

Gil and Henderson were invited to Toby's wedding and they went, not least because the girl he was marrying was a cousin of John Marlowe's wife, Edwina, and they could not afford to upset John and Edwina. Toby privately told Gil that 'there's no need to worry, old boy, it's a rush job, she's expecting'.

'You got her pregnant?'

'I sincerely hope so. If somebody else did it I'm not going to be very pleased. Don't give me that naive look, it doesn't suit you.'

Toby's parents looked so pleased and would hardly be any less so when they found out that their new daughter-in-law was having a child. It was what they had wanted.

John and Edwina very sportingly, Henderson said later, stuck with Gil and Henderson. Abby came over to say hello. Robert didn't. It was difficult for Gil because all his family were there. To have to sit across the room from Edward and his parents at the reception was one of the hardest things he could think of. It was miserable. John made him laugh and Edwina squeezed his hand and promised to invite him to dinner. After a while, when the food had been eaten, the toasts had been made and the speeches finished, several people drifted across to talk to John and he introduced them. They could not afford to offend him and so stayed talking. Gil would have given almost anything to have his brother speak to him. Edward didn't look at him. Charlotte chatted, seemingly oblivious, to all her friends and William glowered in the corner and said little.

It was a lovely day and the wedding meal was held at Toby's parents' home. The guests walked through the gardens and sat about outside on stone walls with champagne glasses in their hands and chatted. Matthew ran round the garden with the other children. Gil did not miss the way that his mother looked hungrily across at his child and he thought of how she must have missed him. He was her only grandchild and she had been so distressed when everything went wrong. She didn't go to Matthew, so Gil thought she must have been given clear instructions by William, but he could see the longing in her face.

Edward avoided Toby except for what was polite. As the day drew towards evening, when everything had been said and done, Toby came to Gil and said, 'Spare me some time or I shall go mad.'

They walked some way to the river with glasses of wine and sat there out of the way of other people. There was a tiny stone bridge. Toby sat down, let go of his breath and said, 'Tell me it's the right thing to do.'

'How can I after what happened to us?'

'It isn't like that.'

'Don't you love Edward now?'

'I wish it was as simple as that. She is a very nice girl.'

'She seems so.'

'We have a great deal in common. She loves gardens and good food and wine. We've bought a house and I really did enjoy that since she has taste. I think we shall deal very well together. Your brother and I are in the past. He has nothing to offer and I have too much to lose.'

'But you love him?'

'I shall always love him. Other things matter, other kinds of love, I didn't think that I would want a child, but I find that I do, isn't that strange?'

'I don't see why it's strange.'

'You love yours, don't you?'

'More than anything on earth.'

'Anything?' Toby said, looking up as Abby approached.

'The dancing has started,' she announced. Toby excused himself and walked back to the house. 'You're meant to ask me.'

'I don't think that's a very good idea.'

'Why not?'

'You know why not. You shouldn't be seen with me.'

'If my father is, then I can't very well ignore you and I'm determined that one day you will. There is nothing wrong with now.'

So they went back to the house and waltzed twice. People watched closely. Gil was inclined to think that he would fall over his feet or hers, but he didn't, though he couldn't talk to her and dance at the same time and there was little pleasure in it. Gil had thought in years past of what it would be like when they danced together and it was so disappointing, he so potentially clumsy and Abby aware of the watching eyes. Later Gil danced with Edwina and she invited him and Henderson to dinner the following weekend. Gil was astonished at the social success of his day, though when he looked up after that dance his father and mother had left. Edward left soon afterwards and Henderson was looking tired so they went too. Gil put Matthew to bed and, when he came downstairs, they sat in the garden and drank brandy and talked about the wedding and the various people.

'You should try to make it up with your father,' Henderson said.

'No.'

'He'll die one day and your guilt will be all you have left.'

'No, it won't.'

'No? There is too much at stake. A parent gives to a child so much that the debt can never be repaid, even a harsh parent.

People only find that out when they are parents. Hating him is not the way.'

Gil took his brandy and went to bed.

Edwina did her best to admit them to her social circle but Henderson didn't want to go places, he was too tired, and though Gil had thought that he longed for company he found that it was not so. If he took Henderson they had to come back early; if he went alone he missed him and he had always found conversation difficult, especially with women. He realised that the only person he wanted to see was Abby and since, if she was in the area she came every weekend to see her father, he had her company, after a fashion, which was to say that she avoided him as much as possible. Gil was not insensitive. He kept out of her road as much as he could and if that was impossible, was as courteous as he could be.

Henderson began to fail visibly. He no longer went into work for any length of time and Gil was so concerned about him that in some ways it was easier if he didn't; but when he was at work and Henderson was at home, he worried because he was not there for him. The ship was taking shape and Gil was inclined to hurry it because he was determined that Henderson should live to see the launch. All through that long, hot summer and into the cool of autumn Gil worked until he was dizzy. He didn't sleep much; the problems of the two shipyards made him over-alert because they were too much for him without Henderson. He had lots of very good help, but it was not the same. Each day when he came home, no matter how late, Henderson always wanted an account of how the day had been and since there were almost insuperable problems all the time, Gil was obliged to invent a good deal of pap for Henderson's ears so that he would feel there was nothing to worry about. His storytelling abilities seemed to have improved a good deal, until one day when Matthew said to him, 'I want to hear a story like you tell Grandpa Henderson.'

Henderson either didn't notice that Gil had become a fairly accomplished liar or he didn't want to know and he would sit with shining eyes and listen to the tales from the shipyards, but Gil became so exhausted that he couldn't eat or sleep and kept nodding over his desk in the afternoons.

The idea of a social life became a dream. He could not mix freely with people and they did not want him in spite of Edwina's efforts. So Gil worked and watched Henderson lose weight, watched Mrs Wilkins try to tempt his appetite with delicious food and Kate hover over him on Sunday afternoons while he slept; he watched at the way Matthew would approach him cautiously and move quietly about the house.

By November the hull of the ship was nearly finished and Gil was pleased enough to congratulate himself on having managed that. He took half a day off on the Sunday, went home in time for the big meal in the middle of the day. When Henderson slept that afternoon by a big fire in the sitting-room, he took Matthew to the park to sail boats and for once enjoyed being with his noisy child as they raced their boats across the pond and the cold backendish wind filled the sails of the vessels. Gil thought about the launch; he thought of Henderson's face as the big ship slid down the slipway, how proud he would be, how pleased. It would be a punch in the face for all those people who did not acknowledge them; perhaps it would even make up for the hardness of their life. It was a bigger ship than the *Northumbria* had been, yet a sleeker more modern ship because this time he had used the full extent of his creative powers. His father was not there to keep a bridle on him in any way. Henderson would stand admiring and only criticise what he knew and that was not design. This ship looked what it was, entirely his creation. Sometimes Gil would stand back and be surprised that he could have done such a thing; it was not possible that men built such huge and terrible things. Mr Philips was a happy man these days, with the kind of pay which enabled him to buy good suits and take his wife to Blackpool for her holidays and Mr McGregor, though he said little, was ready to build powerful engines for all the work which should have been his at Collingwood's and was his behind the gates of Reed's.

Mr McGregor had a guilty conscience about his father, Gil was aware. They had as much work as they could handle and he knew that he was seriously damaging Collingwood's shipyard because times were hard, orders were lower than they had been and yet his order book was full because his fame had spread abroad. When he went occasionally to Marlowes' for dinner it was not for gossip and pretty women, it was to meet clever, influential men, often from other countries, men who cared nothing about his former life and knew much about his work. Gil felt as though nothing in the world could stop his success now.

He went home for tea in the gathering dusk that afternoon, Matthew dancing ahead of him carrying the boats. It was cold. There was the promise of rain, he thought, sniffing the air. Matthew ran into the sitting-room to be there first to see Henderson, while from the kitchen came the sound of teacups rattling and the smell of an orange cake which he knew Mrs Wilkins had made earlier, Henderson's favourite. Matthew, chattering, left the boats in the hall and ran through into the sitting-room and Gil followed him. Henderson was still asleep in his favourite armchair. Matthew ran off to the kitchen to help bring in the sandwiches and cakes. Gil warmed his hands by the fire and waited for Henderson to wake up. He didn't. When Gil got down beside him, he knew that Henderson was dead. He tried to convince himself that it was not so, but he had seen death too many times not to be sure that it had claimed his friend.

He went to the kitchen and told Mrs Wilkins and she and Kate kept Matthew in the kitchen while Gil went for the doctor. When he confirmed that Henderson was dead, they moved him upstairs into his bedroom. Gil had sent for Abby and when she came he went into the hall to meet her. She was thin and white and looked terrified. He had said little in the note, not wanting her to travel into town knowing for certain that her father had died, but he knew that it was in his face.

'Where is he?' she said in a voice just above a whisper.

'Upstairs.'

Abby looked at the stairs as though they were a mountain.

'Shall I come with you?'

'No.'

'He's dead, Abby.'

She nodded and went on up. Gil went back into the sitting-room, where his small son was making quite a good job of crying and eating orange cake. He sat down and took the child onto his knee. Abby was upstairs such a long time that Gil wanted to go to her, but he didn't. He put Matthew to bed; shock had made him exhausted. He went straight to sleep. Kate had cleared the crumbs and dirty plates and when Abby finally came down she made tea. Abby sat and did not drink the tea and stared into the fire.

They had lost a good many of their friends as well as their London house that year. It was strange, Abby had thought at the time, how the two went together. The house had belonged to Robert's family for so long that nobody spoke of it, but his losing it alienated people, they were so shocked. Charlotte had been vocal in her disappointment, but Abby thought that if she had been the kind of person who criticised, she certainly could have done so with the Collingwoods. Their business was starting to go downhill, the competition from German and American and Irish yards, on top of Scottish and the damage Gil was doing, was too much. They had tried to replace their top men but clever, skilled men were difficult to dislodge from other yards and William would not offer better wages and housing and other schemes such as schools and churches, which many shipyard owners did in other places. He preferred the old ways, relying on his business ability and reputation. It was not enough. Gil had made Reed's the premier shipyard on the Tyne and when people spoke of him now it was not about scandal but with respect because of the mighty ship which would make his name and the kind way in which he treated his men. Unlike other yards, he didn't lay them off when times were hard, but then he seemed to have insured himself against hard times. There was always work and if there wasn't Abby knew that Gil went abroad in search of it, unlike many of his competitors. Men fought to work for him because they knew that they were almost guaranteed security. Her father had loved the business which Gil had built up, he had loved being part of it.

Robert was away when her father died. She did not know whether to be pleased or not. He had gone shooting with some cronies. Strangely, now that they had no London house Abby longed to be there as she had not before and to be reassured that they still had lots of friends, though she did not know what she might miss about those who had deserted her. She told herself that it had just been a house, that it didn't matter, they still had the house in Northumberland and it was so much more spacious. But the loss of prestige was huge and she knew that when Robert was sober, he was disgusted with himself, which was the world's best reason for not staying sober. The comfort was that he did not gamble when he was drunk. Shooting, he was neither drunk nor gambling so Abby tried to be happy that he was not about when her father died. They had not liked one another at all towards the end she thought, Henderson because he considered Robert an idler and Robert because Henderson had been ill on and off for a long time now and he thought that Abby was in Newcastle more often than he wanted her to be.

Abby felt lost as though she had no one. Robert was not to be relied on and she could not ask Gil for any help. She did not need any help with the funeral arrangements, having taken care of everything when her mother died. It was strange how Gil acted the part that her father had then. He went to work and she stayed at the house. The one thing that was different was Matthew and he was a comfort to Abby, diverting her mind, when she would have been sad, to everyday things such as playing games and reading stories. He had started school and could read and write very well and was inclined to read to her when he thought she was more upset. They went shopping together and he entertained her. She took him out to tea in Eldon Square.

Robert came to the funeral, sober, beautifully dressed in an expensive suit, smiling and attentive, saying all the right things. Matthew stayed at home with Kate and Abby got through the entire service and burial without weeping. It was Gil who was no help that day. Wearing a dark suit, speaking to no one, she could not hear his voice when the hymns she had chosen were sung and during the burial she did not see him at all.

Back at the house, people who had barely spoken to Henderson for years gathered to drink tea or sherry or whisky and talk about old times. She heard her mother's name mentioned. Kate had taken Matthew out to tea. Abby was grateful to both her and Mrs Wilkins, who had helped to organise the food and drink and kept going around making certain that nobody was without a glass or a cup and saucer. John and Edwina were there; even Toby had come. Abby was grateful to them. Toby's wife was not there. She had only a few days ago given birth to twin boys and, even though Toby's dark suit and sober expression were correct for a funeral, he could not suppress the triumph in his eyes and the happiness which shone in his face.

'What have you called them?' Abby managed to ask.

'Frederick after my father and Richard after Henrietta's father. Don't you admire the tact?'

'A very good move,' Abby said.

Gil did not come back. Even after everybody had gone and she had read Matthew a story, put him to bed and gone up a little later to make sure that he was asleep, he did not come home and Abby was angry. She was used to this, to men leaving women to do everything. Then they would come back, drunk and useless. It was only when she heard the front door at around ten o'clock when everybody had gone to bed, that Abby got up ready to make stinging remarks. Then she remembered she had no right. He was not her husband. One night could not call him her lover and he was certainly not her friend, but she had needed him that day and he had not been there. He should have been and he was not. She went out into the hall.

'Where have you been?' she said.

Gil was taking off his coat.

'Work.'

'To work?' Abby was shocked. 'Today?'

'Things don't stop, you know.'

He was certainly sober, she thought.

'I would have thought that out of respect you should have given the men the day off, closed the shipyards.'

'Your father wouldn't have wanted that.'

'How do you know?'

'I just do,' he said, and went into the little office and shut the door.

Abby was too angry to do what she knew she should have done and let it rest. She followed him there.

'I've had a houseful of people all afternoon. I didn't see you at the burial.'

'I didn't go.' He was shuffling papers on the desk.

'You weren't there?'

'I have a ship launch next week.'

She stared.

'You can't launch that ship now.'

'It's ready and it will go.'

'It would be a sign of disrespect. Besides—'

'Besides what?'

'Well . . . there will be things to sort out, the will and . . . I have asked Mr Brampton to read the will tomorrow. Perhaps you could find time for that. You – you ought to have closed the shipyards. I presumed you had.'

'Time's money.'

Abby looked down. She didn't want to continue this conversation. She and Gil had been living in the same house for several days and she had not thought about him, but in this room it was impossible not to. She wished fervently that she had not given herself to him, most especially she wished that it had not been here. She left the room and went back to the sitting-room fire, but the room was more empty than it had ever been without her father so she went to bed.

There was always a fire lit in the little office but no doubt Kate, like Abby, presumed that he would not work that day, though what else they thought he was supposed to do Gil couldn't think. He had had to go to work. Everything was going wrong and had been for several days, as though the yard knew that Henderson had died. He had to be there to sort things out and it was just as well: he couldn't bear the house; he certainly couldn't bear the church and the idea of the cemetery was not to be considered. He thought of all those people in Henderson's house. He knew they would come, people who hadn't even visited when he was ill, some who had turned their backs when he took Gil into his house. Where had they been when Henderson was recovering from his last illness? Where had they been when he was lonely? Where had they been after his wife died? They had been at home among their families and now they had the audacity to pretend respect.

Robert had not even spoken to Gil, as though Gil was allowed to feel no loss, yet he knew well that people would count Henderson Robert's loss and would no doubt have offered their condolences, shaken his hand, sympathised.

Gil had said his own farewell to Henderson that afternoon beside the big ship that Henderson had not lived to see launched. He had seen to it that the ship would be ready next week, that she would move cleanly and swiftly down to her baptism in the water of the river that Henderson had loved so well. Henderson was not in that wooden box in the cemetery and he was not in the church; he was in his office at work and walking among the men and standing admiring beside the ship, looking at it with proud eyes and winking at Gil in joy. He would always be there and it was the only place that Gil could bear to be.

They gathered in the sitting-room alongside Kate and Mrs Wilkins for the reading of the will the following afternoon. Abby already hated that room since finding out that her father had died in it, as though the room was somehow responsible for his death. She wasn't much concerned about the will. She had been her father's only child and it would be good to have her independence. She knew that with what her mother had left, the two shipyards and the house, she would walk out of here a rich woman. She had of late been concerned about the loss of their London house through Robert's gambling, though to her knowledge he had lost nothing since. The others were there for small bequests. She only wished that Gil would sit down, but he didn't. He walked about the room until the solicitor was ready to begin and then stood at the window with his back to everyone.

Mr Brampton was all that you imagined a solicitor to be. He coughed a great deal as though he had a permanent cold and he didn't shift around in his chair like other people because he was used to sitting all day. He wore a suit, not as expensive as Robert's but very nice, and he was small and slender and precise.

First of all, Abby discovered that her father had left some money in trust for her daughter. Mr Brampton said, hesitating and coughing, that this could not be touched until Georgina came of age and was for her alone. Abby was rather pleased about this. How far-sighted of her father to have provided so well for his only grandchild. He had not mentioned it nor given any indication that he cared particularly for a child he had rarely seen. Then Mr Brampton went on to the house. She was looking forward to this because this was her home. She had always loved it; it had been a sanctuary, the place she had been happy with her parents. She had never had a house completely her own. She loved every piece of furniture, every room, the paintings, the conservatory, the garden. Her ears deceived her then as she listened to Mr Brampton's politely monotonous voice. Her father had left the house to Gil. She ran the words over in her mind for mistakes. He could not have done such a thing. In stupefaction she listened. Robert was to have her father's watch and she was to have the ring he always wore on his little finger – a wedding gift from her mother – and Mrs Wilkins and Kate were to have five hundred pounds each. They both gasped with pleasure at this. And that was all. It was over. She listened for further words but there were none. Abby couldn't move for shock and disappointment. Mrs Wilkins and Kate went out and Robert went to Mr Brampton and said what she had wanted to say.

'That can't be right.'

Mr Brampton looked severely at him above his spectacles.

'I assure you, sir. I dealt with Mr Reed all his life and it is exactly right.'

'But what about the works? What about the shipyard?'

Mr Brampton glanced across the room towards Gil.

'That has nothing to do with this, sir. The shipyard did not belong to Mr Reed and was therefore not his to leave.'

'It didn't belong to him?' Robert's face was getting redder and redder, like coals with bellows at them. 'The shipyard has been in the Reed family for two generations. How could it not belong to him?'

'It belongs to me,' Gil said.

Mr Brampton coughed again and tried to excuse himself but Robert objected, glaring all the while in Gil's direction.

'How could that be?' He had gone from scarlet to white, whiter than Abby could remember him being.

'I was made a partner almost from the beginning and then gradually, after he knew that he was ill, Henderson made it over to me. It's perfectly legal. Mr Brampton here is a stickler for the law.'

Mr Brampton nodded sagely.

'It can't be right. You came here with nothing.'

'I went into the business with a contract for the biggest express liner ever to be built. Such a project is worth a great deal of money.'

'So you bought your way in.'

'That's what people usually do.'

'I knew nothing of this.'

'Why should you? You haven't shown any interest in the yards. You haven't put any money into it. You've yet to set foot past the gates that I know of, and you know nothing about shipbuilding or industry. It would take a foolish man to leave things so badly.'

'But it's worth a great deal of money.'

'Only as a business.'

'It could be sold.'

'It isn't going to be sold. It's going to go on exactly in the way that Henderson intended.'

'I shall get my solicitors onto this. I don't think he would have done such a thing to his only child.'

'You'd be wasting your money,' Gil said.

Robert was almost sneering.

'I see I've been duped,' he said. 'Everything they say about you is true. You've done a gullible old man out of a fortune. You complete and utter bastard. I'm not going to sit down under this. I'm going to put you on the street. I'm going to make sure that you have to do what you should have done – what any man with any honour would have done after you caused your wife's death and that of your sister-in-law – I'll make sure that you leave the north and can never come back!'

He slammed out of the room. Mr Brampton followed him, coughing and taking his papers. Abby and Gil were left alone. She didn't know what to say. She thought that she had never been as angry with anyone as she was with Gil now. She could barely speak.

'How could you take everything? I trusted you.'

'I haven't taken everything—'

'What more is there? The business, the house with everything in it—'

'You can have anything that you want from it, that was just an oversight—'

'You didn't even tell me. You could have, surely you could have. Why didn't you refuse when my father suggested that—'

'He didn't suggest it,' Gil said, finally looking at her, though with caution. 'He went to Mr Brampton and did it.'

'But you must have been there, when the partnership was set up—'

Gil didn't answer that.

'So legally everything is yours. Morally it belongs to me and if you have an ounce of decency in you you will give me what is mine.' She looked at him and Gil met her eyes.

'No,' he said.

'You have known about this for a long time, haven't you?'

The trouble was, Abby reflected, that Gil never had been any good with words. He couldn't talk his way out of anything. Words were no use to him. Drawings now, he could do that. His genius was for shipbuilding but he was a seriously flawed person and inadequate.

'Everything comes down to numbers with you,' she said. 'It didn't matter that while you were – while you were screwing me on the floor—' he flinched over that, Abby noted '—you were in fact the person who was about to steal my inheritance. You weren't even man enough to tell me!'

Gil wasn't looking at her any more. Abby was reminded unbearably of the boy he had been, silent, unapproachable, not asking her to dance, not talking to her, eyes downcast. She could see his eyelashes. And the anger and the feeling that she would weep if she didn't do something made her go over and hit him. She smacked him hard across the mouth with an open palm. Afterwards she wished a thousand times that she hadn't. The sound echoed around the room like a shot, it was such a clear clean noise. Gil didn't react at all and Abby knew that intimacy with physical violence did that to you. It reminded her of the night that they had spent together so long ago and she had thought he was dead. He had been knocked across rooms and beaten beyond endurance many times. This was nothing. He just stood and waited to see if she was going to do it again.

'You let me give myself to you knowing that you were going to inherit almost everything,' she said through her teeth.

'What did you want your father to do, let your husband waste everything?' Gil's eyes fired.

'He could have left it to me. The law does give women rights.'

'Like shite it does! Nothing is tipped in your favour. A decent lawyer could get it all from under you in days. Then what would happen?'

'I'm not a child!'

'Abby, I would rather it hadn't been left like this—'

'Of course you would. What would you want with a house and two shipyards?'

'Your father was concerned about you. He wanted to secure it.'

'He's certainly done that. Did you talk him into it?'

'That's not worthy of you.'

'So, you screwed me on the floor and all the time you were stealing what was mine. And even after you had me, you didn't tell me.'

'I didn't know. And as for the rest, you wanted me to.'

'Well, it couldn't have been very good because I don't remember wanting you to do it again. In fact I distinctly remember leaving. Do you remember that?'

All he said was, 'Don't.'

'You haven't changed at all. You're devious and cowardly and I wish I hadn't gone to you. Do you know what I discovered? That you think every woman is Helen. I imagine you called Rhoda "Helen" in bed or at least thought of her that way.'

'Do you have to throw that at me? You couldn't run the shipyards without me and that's all that's important. Your father wanted it to be the best and it is. How long do you think it would go on like that without me? Or did you think that I would work with Robert telling me what to do?'

'I thought it would go on as it is.'

'You think I'd do this for a wage? You mistake me for somebody else.'

'I think I have,' Abby said and, with as much dignity as she could, she walked out of the room, out of the house. All she wanted to do was get away, whereas in another sense it was the last thing she wanted. She wanted to be there with her father and even possibly with her mother. She wanted the past, the time when everything had seemed to be in front of her, when nothing had gone wrong. It was hard to think of Gil as an interloper and a thief as well as everything else.

Robert talked. She would have said nothing, but he told everybody that Gil had taken his wife's inheritance so that people were shocked afresh at Gil's behaviour and no doubt, Abby thought with some satisfaction, it would destroy what social life he had carefully managed to build up. After that day she couldn't bear to go past the house so she kept away from that part of the city when she came into Newcastle, but she missed her father more and more.

The following week the ship was launched. Gil provided extra money for the men and a big feast for their families, which was what Henderson had wanted, but it was a subdued affair because of Henderson's death. Local dignitaries stayed away. Edwina was there with John, but she was very quiet, and Gil surmised that he had seen the last of her dinner parties. People who did come complained about the bitter cold of the day, but Gil felt nothing. He watched the big ship slide down into the water and all he could think was that Henderson had been robbed of his triumph and that people thought he had cheated the old man. He went home, had tea with Matthew and put the child to bed. A little later, when he was sitting by the fire, Kate came in and hovered.

'Can I have a word?'

'Certainly.'

'I'm getting married. Jack McArthur.' Jack was a plater at the yard, Gil knew him well.

'We'll have to find a good house for you.'

'We're leaving. Jack has been offered a job on the Clyde.'

Gil gave her his congratulations. Later still, Mrs Wilkins came in. Gil knew, though this lady had said nothing, that once Henderson was dead she would not stay. She thoroughly disapproved of him, though she had not even by a look given him to think she disliked him, but he understood. They would both think Abby should have everything. She was the daughter, he was an outsider and much, much worse.

'I don't want to stay here without Kate and I've worked long enough. I have a sister in Alnwick. I'm going there.'

Gil wished her well. He was about to lock the doors when somebody banged on the front door. When he opened it, John Marlowe stood there.

'Thought you might like to go out,' he said.

The pubs were shut so Gil had no idea what he meant. John didn't drink or gamble to excess and he couldn't take Gil anywhere respectable because nobody would want him there. He went without asking because John had done a great deal for him but when the carriage stopped and they got out and went inside the building, he realised where he was. The hall of the house was brilliantly lit and gaudy. A beautiful woman dressed in a blue satin dress came along the hall towards them, smiling. Her shoulders rose creamily and bare.

'Mr Marlowe, how are you?' she said.

Gil wanted to go home. He would have said so had the man been anybody but John. John introduced them. He was obviously a valued client. Very soon Gil found himself in a bedroom with a blonde-haired girl who was prepared to do anything for him, so she said. Gil couldn't afford to offend John Marlowe, so very reluctantly he went to bed with her. To his surprise nothing devastating happened. The roof didn't fall in, somebody didn't haul him out of there complaining that he was doing wrong, but something went cold in Gil's head, it was the only way he could think to work out what he felt. He didn't care who she was or how she had got to here or what might occur afterwards. She was an object to be enjoyed. He had her and then he drank some wine and then he had her again and then he went home. He didn't even offer to pay; he presumed that John paid. He went home and slept well.

Chapter Nineteen

Abby dreamed about her parents. She dreamed of being a child and of the happy times. When she awoke she was miserable. She could no longer take refuge in her father's house. People were right: Gil had not cared for Henderson; he had played the old man like a fish and taken everything from him. It was proof enough, they said, that he did not come to the churchyard or attend the funeral tea, and that he had gone to work that day and that he had launched the ship just as he intended a few days later. Charlotte wept bitter tears as she stood in front of Abby's drawing-room fire. Gil was never to redeem himself. She had seen Matthew at Toby and Henrietta's wedding that summer and William would not let her acknowledge the child.

'Edward is obviously not going to marry again. Indeed, I don't know what he does. William complains that he is not at work, that he is often absent. Sometimes he doesn't come home at night, so whatever women he does see are not respectable. Was ever a woman so cursed in her children?' Charlotte turned a wet, red face on Abby. 'William says we must sell the house.'

'Sell it?'

'We cannot keep it up. He had that house built for me.'

If Abby had been frank she would have said that Bamburgh House was a small loss, having never liked it, but it was Charlotte and William's monument to their success and she knew how much it meant to them. But how would they sell it? Nobody of any taste or discernment would buy it.

'William says there is a house in Westoe which would do very well.'

'Westoe Village is pretty,' Abby said, thinking of all the elegant Victorian houses in the little village just outside Newcastle. Some of them had big stone walls and behind them big gardens. 'It would be very convenient,' she said.

Charlotte was upset at the loss of prestige as much as the loss of the house, Abby thought. It was a very big house for just the two of them. Perhaps at one time they had expected to found a dynasty; now they had no one. But they would not think of it like that. This was a matter of pride and Charlotte's pride was almost all gone. Abby privately thought that if Charlotte could learn to hate Gil, it might help. William obviously did and so did she. The loss of her father was all caught up with the feelings that she had for Gil. She had not realised, either, that she needed to have the house to go to. It had been somewhere to get away from her life in the country, from the husband who was rarely at home and the child she hardly saw.

Charlotte had grown very fat and when Abby did see William he looked like an old man, tired, disappointed and angry, but she had not thought things in such a way that the big house would have to be sold. She knew how she had felt when Robert had lost the London house. It had changed things, their place in society, their friendships and relations between them. When she looked back, Abby could see that her husband had been proud and confident. Now he stayed away a lot and came home drunk or penniless. Abby felt that she had no one and began to take her child away from the upstairs of the house, where she seemed like a prisoner. There were lessons in the mornings, so Abby insisted that in the afternoons she should see Georgina. This meant leaving the house because if she did not, Nanny would interfere and people would arrive and take up her time. They didn't do much. They went shopping or out to tea, but it was Abby's only pleasure. Going into Newcastle was a mixed pleasure because it had been the city of her childhood, but in a way she saw herself and her mother doing just such things and for the first time she enjoyed her daughter's company. She refused Robert's wanting to go abroad as they had done so often in the past. He went by himself and she was glad of the respite, because he did not allow mourning. When people died, Robert's reaction was to ignore them. Since Henderson's death he had not mentioned her father, nor would he permit the wearing of black. It seemed to Abby that Robert was pretending that nobody ever died, most especially nobody who mattered. Somewhere inside him his parents lived, she thought, because he could not bear that he should lose anyone.

If there had been anything decent about Gil at all, Abby thought, she would have gone back to the house, if only to talk to somebody about her father. She found herself outside in the street across the road several times and she was afraid. She didn't know how she had got there, only that she couldn't leave. She remembered Gil saying that she could have anything she wanted from the house and the truth was that many of her personal possessions were still there. She wanted them; she wanted something to remember her father by, but she could not make herself go there either when he was not there or when he was. She had heard that Kate and Mrs Wilkins had left, so the new servants would not know her sufficiently to let her past the doors. They certainly wouldn't allow her to take anything from the house and Abby wanted not to see Gil again.

Gil had chosen new servants from out of the area, chosen them for their backgrounds and ability. He paid them well and expected high standards. The house was always perfect. Meals were on the table at exactly the right moment; cupboards and drawers were orderly; his clothes were put out daily, washed and starched and ironed. Everything was in its place just, in a way, as it had been before, only more so. He had altered nothing. The house was just as it would have been and daily he expected to find Henderson there. His not being there was, in Gil's mind, a long, long corridor where Henderson was just out of sight, just out of enough distance so that Gil could not wave at him.

He went to work except on Sunday afternoons. He came back at teatime every day so that he could spend some time with Matthew, but when the boy went to bed Gil worked. One day the spring after Henderson had died – it was late March and it should not have been warm but it was – the sun was pouring in through his office windows. Usually he would have ignored it and gone on working, the outside world did not intrude here, but for some reason he couldn't stand it any longer and he left the office and went home.

It was a Saturday afternoon, that would be his excuse. The men weren't there. Some of the office staff were, especially, he thought smiling grimly, those who expected to be noticed. The air beyond the shipyard was soft, springlike, so he went home early. When he opened the front door he could hear laughter and when he opened the sitting-room door, Hannah, the general maid and Matthew were playing some kind of game, hands crossed, spinning round and round in the middle of the room. She didn't see Gil at first, or hear the door.

Gil hadn't seen anything much of this girl except her obedient demeanour and the way that she cleaned and polished the house to a high shine. Gil had kept the new servants in their place; he didn't want intimacy of any kind. He didn't want to regret their leaving when they went as he had regretted and resented Kate and Mrs Wilkins. For several months the house had been like the office, well run, almost military. He blamed the old servants for going, even though he knew there was no reason why they should not have done and they had been right to go; but they had taken from him the last vestiges of his life with Henderson. Day by day he carried with him the stone of Henderson's death and the way that Abby had left him. He had known what she would do and say; he had known that they would quarrel and she would hate him, but the knowing of it before it had happened had made things worse in a way because there was nothing he could do to stop it. Her love had counted for nothing in the end. He didn't care that Robert was going pretty much to the devil; in some ways he was glad. Henderson had foreseen all that and planned carefully. Gil missed him every minute, he missed the old servants and he felt betrayed because they had been part of the family and had left his son just as though he didn't matter. Matthew had cried a lot because things had changed so much and Gil had thought he was the only adult in his child's life, but it was strange how things moved on. His child had obviously developed a close relationship with this girl from Yorkshire.

They spun round faster and faster, giggling and shouting, until they were obliged to let go. Then they collapsed into a heap on the thickly rugged floor, helpless, out of breath, triumphant. In those moments Gil remembered what youth was meant to be like.

Her cap had come off, the pins loosened. It reminded Gil uncomfortably of the girls he paid for on Saturday nights. Hannah was no different, it was just that she had been luckier and he held her fate in his hands just the same. He paid her well to clean his house. His sense of justice would not let him take anyone's labour for less than he thought they deserved. His servants were higher paid than anybody he knew. John Marlowe laughed and called it indulgence, but Gil knew well by now that money meant independence and it was more important than anything. This girl had no independence from him yet. If he chose, he could put her on the street and then she would end up, if she was lucky, pretending to some man that she enjoyed being put down and laid for money.

And then she saw him. She blushed crimson. She had pretty brown hair and deep blue eyes and she was breathing very quickly, partly from the exertion but partly now from shock and fear, he knew. Gil hadn't realised until then that she was afraid of him. He was never rude to his servants, he never made difficult demands, so he thought. It was his power over her that she feared. She retrieved her cap as she got up and stood there in front of him like a condemned prisoner, lowering her eyes and handling her cap nervously.

'So,' Gil said lightly, 'what about some tea?' and he smiled at her.

She looked up, bit her lip and was for a second Abby, biting her lip to bleeding on the rug in the study. Her colour came back to normal. She said, 'Yes, sir,' and scuttled out.

'You frightened her,' Matthew observed.

'What am I, an ogre?'

Out of breath Matthew flung himself onto the sofa.

'Yes,' he said.

It was the following day that Abby went to the house. She made herself. She wanted so much to see the place and to have something belonging to her father and, although she dreaded going, she could not not go any longer. She tried to shield herself against Gil before she got there, to think that probably she would see Matthew, which would make it easier, and that she only had to speak a few words to Gil. She could envisage what it would be like. He would be working because he always worked. She would not remember what they had done in that little room and he would most likely be frigidly polite. He might let her collect her things and take something of her father's and it would be formal, not as bad as she thought it was going to be. She would get through it. She had to.

She knocked hard on the door and was surprised to find it opening immediately as a small boy ran at her.

'Aunty Abby!' he said in obvious delight and hugged her. 'You never come to see us and now I'm going out.' He indicated several small boys on the pavement whom she hadn't noticed, and an adult, presumably somebody's father, armed with a cricket bat and a ball and cricket stumps. 'We're going to the park. Will you still be here later on?'

'I will try.'

'You'll be staying for tea. I'll be back.' And with that he waved and ran off, shouting behind him, 'Daddy's in the sitting-room. Go in. Hannah's half day.'

Abby went into the gloom of the hall, except that it wasn't gloomy because the spring sunshine poured in through the stained glass of the inner door. She stood there expecting any second to hear her father's voice. There was the faint smell of Sunday dinner, roast beef and Yorkshire pudding. She paused by the little office but, since Matthew had said Gil was in the sitting-room, she made her way there. He hadn't lied. Gil was in the sitting-room. He was asleep. He was lying on the sofa. The fire burned softly in the grate and through the windows the garden was full of daffodils and other spring flowers in small cream, blue and red clumps beyond the lawn.

He didn't wake up even when she moved around the room. It was exactly as it had been, her father's chair in its usual place. She thought of the reading of the will, the last time she had been in here, her anger, Gil's stubbornness and the way that she had hit him. She could not reconcile any of it to the young man who was asleep on the sofa. He looked so harmless, lying on his side, obviously very tired. His waistcoat and trousers were dark, his shirt was white and his eyelashes were so . . . He opened his eyes and the impression disappeared. His gaze was cool like tap water. He sat up slowly. Abby glanced at the door.

'Matthew let me in,' she said. 'I know I have no right to come here.' Abby had rehearsed this, but she hadn't counted on her throat being so dry that she couldn't get the words out, '—but—'

He got up. Abby wished he hadn't. He was much bigger than she. She knew very well that he could dominate a room just by his presence. He didn't, but he could if he chose. She had known businessmen all her life and she could imagine him in the boardroom, saying nothing and reducing other people to blancmange.

'You can come here as often as you like, though it hadn't occurred to me that you might want to.'

'You said . . . that I could take something. My things are here and . . . some things which I think my father would have wanted me to have.'

'Help yourself,' Gil said.

Even getting out of the room was difficult. It seemed to Abby to take a long time because he was watching her, or at least she thought he was watching her. She closed the door with a slight bang, not out of temper but because her hands were sweating. How could he manage to be so predatory without doing anything, she thought in irritation. It was because you didn't know what he was thinking or what he would do to further his ambition and she was well aware that he would do anything to get what he wanted while all the time looking so civilised. It was a veneer, nothing more.

She went upstairs to what had been her own room and, to her surprise, it was exactly as she had left it. It was clean; everything was dusted and polished, but the things she had left here were undisturbed. It looked as though she had gone away for a while and would be back. There were books on the bedside table. Some of them had been her mother's. One of them was open and she picked it up. It was open at the very page where she had left it. Her combs and hairbrushes were on the dressing-table. She had not taken those because Robert had insisted on buying her more expensive ones. Her old wooden jewellery box was there and a brooch that her mother had given her as a child, two silver owls with emerald eyes. At least, she had thought at the time that they were emeralds and her mother did not tell her otherwise and spoil the dream. There were various wooden bangles, a silver chain with a cross her parents had given her on her first communion and a silver ring with a pink stone which her parents had brought back from Cornwall. It was like being a child again. There was a jar of cream and in the top drawer, pins and some papers. She closed the drawer. And then a thought occurred to her and she could not resist it. She left the room and stole across the landing towards her father's bedroom. When she opened the door she was so shocked that she couldn't move. Nothing had been touched.

She opened the wardrobe and there were all Henderson's suits, his shirts, his ties, his shoes. She even thought she could smell the cigars he sometimes smoked. The bed was made up and she thought at any moment he would walk in and her heart would piece back together again. The view from the window was of the tennis court. She remembered him picking her up when she was little and standing her on the window ledge to watch her mother playing tennis down below with a friend.

Feeling rather like Goldilocks now, she went into the room next door which was where Gil slept. For some reason, she was not a bit surprised to see that it was empty. She thought at first that he must have moved into another room, it was so bare, and then she thought of his room at home. It was completely cleared of any mess or any sign of possession. There was no book; there was no evidence of anyone's stay; it was like an unoccupied hotel bedroom. Only when she opened the wardrobe were Gil's clothes to be seen and it was so neat that it frightened her. Nothing was an inch out of place. It was symmetrical; everything lined up; it was mathematical in its precision.

'Find anything interesting?' he said from the doorway. Abby spun round and looked at him. He looked so enquiring but friendly. She held his eyes steadily.

'Why do you keep my father's things?'

'You can have them if you want them,' Gil said.

'You've kept the house exactly as it was when he was alive and this is . . . this is—'

'My bedroom,' Gil said. 'I don't remember you having any particular inclination to be in here before.'

'I was just curious.'

'About what? There's nothing to see.'

'So I observed,' Abby said and went past him to stave off any more questions.

In the end Abby took very little, some books which had been her mother's before they were hers, some cufflinks which were not valuable and had been left on her father's dressing-table, the little silver owl brooch. She sat upstairs in her father's room and stayed, dry-eyed, thinking of him there. She hadn't realised how long she was until Matthew burst in.

'You are still here! I hoped you would be. Come downstairs. Daddy says the tea is ready and there is chocolate cake.'

Abby tried to say that she wasn't staying, but the boy's face fell.

'You must stay! I haven't seen you in ever so long.'

Abby went. Her idea of fun was not eating chocolate cake with Gil, but Matthew chattered all the way through tea, eating rapidly and talking at the same time, so that Abby thought nobody had ever told him to do one thing at once. Even though being there was difficult, it was worth it for Matthew's shining face and boyish talk. She thought that he was very advanced for four. The children she knew of that age clung around their mothers and didn't talk. Matthew didn't stop talking and knew a great deal about cricket. He seemed so happy she could not help but think that if Gil had got nothing right in his life but this, he certainly seemed to have got the hang of parenting. Obviously his son had never been beaten or shouted at or made to feel at all unwanted. When he had finished his tea, Matthew went back outside to play with his friends. Abby waited until the door was closed and then she said, 'He's a very nice little boy.'

'You can never tell. Presumably I was a very nice little boy.'

'You hated cricket.'

'Team games,' Gil said scornfully.

'Isn't Reed's Yard a team?'

'No, it's a dictatorship.'

She almost smiled.

'I thought you'd have had the gates repainted.'

'Why?'

'It isn't Reed's any more.'

'Abby—'

'No, don't,' she said quickly.

'You don't know what I was going to say.'

'You were going to plead your case and it's not something you're any good at so you might as well save your breath.' She got up. 'I only stayed because of Matthew.'

'If you want to come back—'

'I don't. You may keep my father's belongings but there's nothing left of him here, I can see that. I shan't come again. Goodbye.'

Abby chose to go back past the gates of the yards, but the first just said 'Reed's' on it as it always had and the newer yard said 'Reed's Yard No 2' as though it was some poor relation and not the biggest shipyard on the Tyne. She could not help being glad that Gil left that at least as it was. Her father would have been pleased about it, his name still there.

John Marlowe had in some ways taken Henderson's place in that he had become a friend. It was a strange kind of friendship. Gil was not invited to his home and John didn't come to his house. Often John was away. He had other houses and he went away on business frequently. Sometimes Gil was away, so there were long periods when they didn't see one another. On Saturday nights, however, if they were both in Newcastle they went out to dinner and for a few drinks. Then they went to the high class brothel to which John had introduced Gil.

Sometimes John called in at Gil's office unannounced. He knew that Gil would go home early, have tea and spend some time with his son, but that invariably he went back to the office. John usually turned up late in the evening and Gil would talk over their work with him as he had done with Henderson. He would call unannounced, timing his visits well when everyone had gone home. Gil imagined that this was deliberate. Although they were business acquaintances, it would have done John no good to have cultivated Gil as a friend. In the office they could talk undisturbed. When they went out, they went to obscure places. It was almost, Gil thought with humour, like having an affair with a married woman. Nobody must know; it was furtive and secretive and had about it an air of intimacy which he liked. John Marlowe's mind was always full of new ideas.

Gil had copied his father's way and had windows which overlooked the river. As the evening drew in, he would sit with his feet up on the desk and drink whisky. John would call in, and in the summer months when the sun stayed late they would watch the shadows fall across the river and they would talk.

On one such September evening, when the shadows were beginning to darken in the corners, they had spent an hour talking about politics when John said suddenly, 'I hear your father's house is up for sale.'

'I gather, yes.'

'And there is a buyer.'

'Is there?' Gil looked across the empty desk at him.

'You know bloody damned fine there is, Gillan, it's you.'

'That's just a guess.'

'Playing cat and mouse with the old man, are you? Does he know it's you?'

'I don't know.'

'You've done it through a third party? Do you want him to find out? You want him to see how badly he needs to sell, is that it? You can't really want it.'

'How do you know?'

'What are you going to do there? Remember your wonderful childhood?'

'I don't intend to live in it.'

'What if there's another buyer?'

Gil laughed.

'Who the hell would want it?'

John considered his whisky glass.

'Are you going to pull it down? It's a nice site.' John swilled the whisky around in his glass as though it was brandy. 'What are you going to do with it?'

'I don't know yet.'

'It was his goal, his main ambition, it was part of his dream. Your father clawed his way up the ladder. He did everything he had to do to get there. He even cast off his parents. Now you're ruining him.' Gil didn't answer that. 'What are you really going to do with it?'

'Nothing. I'm going to do nothing.'

He had bought Bamburgh House not knowing and not caring whether his father knew who the buyer was. That winter, when he had a free day, he went out to the house.

Winter was never the best time for such outings, but he was pleased with it. There were no animals in the fields, the grass was long on the lawns and it had about it a neglected air. The front door had come open; someone had thrown stones at most of the windows so there was glass on the floors; the snow had blown inside. It was a bitterly cold day and Gil stood in the middle of the room which had been his father's study and remembered the harsh words, the blows. He went upstairs to what had been Helen's bedroom and thought of the nights they had spent there together, the only truly happy nights of his life.

He had debated with himself whether to pull the place down but in the end he decided that it would be a fitting monument to the Collingwood family to let it go to ruin slowly so that people would point from a distance, the grass would grow knee high around it and the birds would find a nesting place.

A bird – he couldn't decide what kind, small and brown – flew into him on the stairs and Gil knocked out some more glass so that it would have plenty of room to get out. It found the exit when he had gone downstairs. He watched it fly away in the direction of the quarry garden and a bitter wind moaned through the hall. Glass crunched under his feet. The window ledges were thick with dirt. The windows which had been left intact were streaked with rain and, because there were no curtains, the grey winter light filtered into the hall where the Christmas tree used to stand.

There was one room he didn't go into and that was his bedroom. As a child he could remember the morning sunlight twinkling in there because it faced east. Edward's room had been comfortable; he had rugs and a fire and books, but William decided that Gil behaved so badly at home and at school that there would be no comfort. What might have been a refuge had been nothing better than a dungeon until the night Abby had spent with him. Gil went back to Jesmond, back to the servants who were polite and competent and to his shipyards where everything was done as it should be and he didn't want any of it. All he wanted was his child; it was such a relief to be able to go home to Matthew.

Chapter Twenty

Abby couldn't believe at first that Gil had bought his parents' house. She knew how much he had always hated the place. Charlotte and William did not know about the sale until afterwards but, since they did not have another buyer, they would have been obliged to accept Gil's offer, she thought, even if they had known that he was the purchaser. But she wondered whether William would have been prepared to endure the humiliation of knowing that his son had bought Bamburgh House. They would have waited a long time for another buyer, she thought.

They moved to Westoe and bought a house there. Although much smaller, it was a great deal prettier than Bamburgh House had been, but Charlotte and William hated it from the beginning since it reflected their reduced circumstances. They needed fewer servants and only one gardener and Robert reported that there was no saying how long they would be there. The depression deepened. William put the men on short time and finished many of them so that he would not have to pay them while times were hard. Abby tried to talk to Robert about helping them financially, but he said that he could not afford it. She didn't argue. She privately thought that he considered it none of his concern, but she had heard talk that Gil bought houses and took people off the streets, that he set up facilities so that people at least had hot food, drink and shelter, especially when the weather was cold, wet and windy which it so often was. It did him no good in the eyes of other shipbuilders. They despised philanthropy of any kind, thought that if the men were given that kind of help they would not work.

'He's soft,' William said of his son. 'He was always soft. Does he think he's going to save the whole world?'

Robert laughed.

'There's nothing like a good hard winter to rid the streets of rubbish.'

Gil gave work to as many people as he could afford and helped a great many others. Henderson, Abby thought, would have approved. She could almost see her mother smiling. Abby went into Newcastle to help. She told no one and she didn't see Gil because he was not doing the work personally, he had delegated it, but it was done and she was proud of it. She used what little money she had and what influence she had to get other people to give. She could not understand that they would not give up even one of their many comforts for the plight of those who were without food and shelter.

Abby sometimes passed Bamburgh House on her way to and from Newcastle and she only hoped that Charlotte had not seen the destruction that the winter weather and Gil's neglect had wrought here. It was a deliberate act of destruction. How angry William must be, though he didn't show it, how frustrated that his son could afford and would allow this monument to William's ambition to fall slowly into ruin. Gil could not have thought of anything better to upset his father.

Charlotte rarely came out to the country to visit. She was so envious of the beautiful house which Robert and Abby owned. It had been, Abby admitted to herself, one of the reasons she had married Robert. She loved it in all its seasons, in all the different times of the day. Its mish-mash of styles betrayed the affection in which the family had held their home and there was one big comfort about it: Robert could not gamble it away; it was entailed through the male line. Abby knew therefore how important it was that she should produce another child, but Robert was drunk or absented himself from home so often that this seemed unlikely. When he was there he did not come to her bed and Abby did not want him there.

She knew that they ought to have had other children, that it was not considered wise to bring up an only child and though she had been an only child herself, there had been many times when she had wished for family. When things had gone wrong, a sister or a brother might have been of some help. Especially since her father had died, she had nobody. Gil had always seemed like almost family; she had known him such a long time and he had been closer than anybody else in that respect, but that had gone too since her father had died. Gil had become the enemy. Abby thought she liked that least of all. Since Henderson had died, she had lost them both. There was no one to talk to who understood anything important. Sometimes it was all she could manage not to go to Jesmond and tell Gil she wanted to be friends, she needed him and she would have to remind herself of what he had done. Even now, she could not believe it.

Gradually the paintings, the furnishings, the horses, everything which could be sold, was, as Robert gambled more and more. Abby even tried to get him to stay at home. The day came when she went to her jewellery box to find nothing of value left in it. The presents which he had given her to commemorate their betrothal, their wedding, anniversaries, birthdays – sapphire and diamond earrings, diamond bracelet and necklace, half a dozen beautiful rings and even the emerald set which had belonged to his mother and been in the family for many years – it all went. Abby tried to talk to him, but she could hear her words and she had no new argument to give him. He had not listened to her before and there was no reason why he should do so now except that, she said, 'Soon there'll be nothing left. Then what will we do?'

He gave her a clearer look than he had given her in years.

'I loved you,' he said.

'I loved you too.'

'No.' Robert shook his head. He was rather drunk. It was the middle of the afternoon and the shadows were stealing across the lawn beyond the drawing-room windows. It was Abby's favourite kind of day in winter, cold and wet but if you were inside with a fire and plenty of food, you could rejoice in the cold weather.

'You never loved me,' he said sadly. 'You always loved that bastard, Gillan Collingwood.' And he got up and wandered from the room and closed the door with a tiny click.

He didn't come back. Abby didn't worry at first. She didn't worry until the following day, because although he sometimes stayed out overnight it was rare that he stayed out for longer than that. She worried, too, for how lucid he had appeared, for how bitter he was. Therefore in the middle of the afternoon when a carriage pulled up outside the house, she got up in agitation. Two policemen were shown into the bareness of the drawing room and for once Abby did not think about the lack of good furniture, the marks on the walls where the paintings had been taken down, the silver that was gone, the ornaments. She was watching their faces and she knew before they said anything that the news was not good. They were very sorry – they weren't sorry, it was just that they didn't know what else to say – they were very sorry, there had been an accident. Mr Surtees had been shot. The truth was, Abby thought brutally, that her husband had taken a double-barrelled shotgun to himself, so there couldn't have been much left of him. Still, he must have been recognisable. One of the many Surtees cousins had found him in their barn. Why, Abby thought idiotically, didn't he do it in his own barn? They had concluded that he had fallen over and the gun had gone off. It was a ridiculous notion, but of course a Surtees could not have killed himself. His father had not drunk himself senseless and killed himself. The trouble was that it was the name of intelligent, honourable people and if he had killed himself then he had dirtied the name and there was no room for that. Abby, like everybody else, would have to pretend that there had been an accident.

Abby blamed herself. She tried not to but it was difficult. She thought of all the things she might have done, of the help she could have given him, of the love she had withheld and he was right, at least he had been at the beginning. She did not love him and, although she no longer loved Gil, it had always been too late for her to love Robert, so many things had been in the way. They had been too unalike and yet people said that opposites attracted and they had been that.

She tried to shield Georgina from the knowledge of what had happened, but she had to tell her child that her father was dead. It would have been harder still to say that they were penniless and homeless, because that was what happened.

The family gathered in the house, even Charlotte, full of concern. It was Charlotte who said to her – no doubt there had been a family meeting at one of their houses and she had been nominated because she knew Abby so well – 'You can't stay here.'

Abby stared.

'Not stay?'

'The house is entailed and you have no place here. You have no son. It all belongs to Robert's cousin, Gerard, and his wife and family will want to move in immediately. You'll be able to stay for a few days until you find somewhere else, but no longer, you must realise that.'

'I have nowhere to go.'

She thought that Charlotte might have cared sufficiently to say 'but you must come and stay with us', only she didn't. Abby thought that in a way Charlotte was rather pleased at what had happened. Abby was worse off than she was, whereas of late she had had to watch Abby in the loveliest house in the county while she made do with a polite Victorian stone house in a village. It did not suit Charlotte's ideas of who went where. This was her triumphant moment. Abby had not borne a son and was to be turned out of doors like a stray cat.

Nobody offered her refuge and she had no money. There was nothing left. The stables were empty; the furniture was worthless. Robert, Abby thought grimly, had made sure that he cleaned them out before he shot himself. Had he not, just for a moment or two, considered if not his wife then at least his child? It seemed he had not. She did not recall a single instance when he had spoken to Georgina or asked for her company. The child shed no tears except for her mother's distress and Abby was so angry with her dead husband that she could find no sorrow or any grief.

Abby could not believe that his family or his friends would not offer her some help, but they didn't. They all came to the funeral and she was obliged to find food and drink in the house. The only good part of Abby's day was when she noticed Gil had come to the funeral. That, she thought, was kind of him. People didn't speak to him, but he seemed oblivious to that and although they had no conversation, she was aware of him in the church and afterwards at the house where he stood alone, not clutching a glass as some men might have done if they were left to their own company but standing quietly by the window as though he was waiting to see what would happen. Abby didn't have to wait long. The cousin who was inheriting showed her no mercy.

'You must leave and within the next week or so,' Gerard said. 'Anthea has plans for the house. We have a great deal to do here, so much to alter,' and he looked around the drawing room as though counting the costs. 'The builders are to begin soon.'

Abby stood there in her drawing room, in what had been hers, she reminded herself, and panicked. What was she to do? Suddenly she hated them all. They were eating her food and drinking her whisky and there was practically nothing left. Her own comfort was that when there was no more whisky they would go, but it seemed that Gerard intended to move in that very day. Could he not have given her a little time, a few days to consider? She thought he would have liked her to leave right there and then. As she stood by herself in the middle of the house which she no longer owned, Gil walked across the room to her.

'Considering your options?' he said.

'I don't have any, it seems.' Abby wished that her voice was more steady. 'The stables are empty, the cellar's empty, the bloody coffers are empty, there's nothing left, there's nothing—'

'And the scavengers are here,' Gil said, nodding in Gerard's direction. 'Is there somewhere we could talk?'

'What about?'

Gil didn't answer that, so she led him into the nearest empty room and it was very empty. Even the furniture had gone from here. It had been Jacobean, hideous but worth money and there had been a number of good though also dark and hideous paintings on the walls. The afternoon sun threw its relentless gleam onto the empty walls and the bare floor.

'Did it himself, did he?' Gil asked softly.

'Of course he did. They blame me. I blame me too. Why did he have to do it? I'm not going. They aren't going to turn me out of here.'

'Abby, look . . . you do have somewhere to go. Your father only left me the house on condition that if you ever needed it you should have it.'

Abby looked straight at him.

'How could he have known?'

'He told me that he wished he hadn't talked you into marrying Robert.'

Abby sighed and went to the window. She couldn't believe that she would have to leave this place. It had been one of the main reasons for her marrying Robert and she didn't believe Gil.

'My father didn't talk me into it. I wanted him. He was the catch of the county. I thought—'

'What?'

'I don't know now, I don't remember.' She sighed. 'You can't give me the house.'

'Why not?'

'Because everybody will think I'm your mistress if you do.'

'Straight to the point as always.'

'It's true.' Abby turned from the window and smiled at him. 'They'll say, "what other reason could he possibly have? Nobody is that generous." '

'I loved your father.'

'I know you did.'

'No, you don't. You think I was nice to him for what he could give me.'

'That too, perhaps. I suppose you're going to tell me that he gave you the business for the same reason.'

'He gave me the business because he had nobody else to give it to and he wanted it to go on. There's a great deal of money, Abby. If you won't have the house then you could buy a house—'

'And you think people would be deceived? You know a lot about ships but you don't know much about people. My reputation wouldn't stand it, things are bad enough.'

'And what use will that be when you end up in Hope Street, selling yourself because you don't have any money?'

Abby laughed. She hadn't laughed for a long time and it eased the great boulder inside her.

'I don't think things are quite that bad,' she said. 'I could go and be a barmaid at The Ship. Do you remember The Ship? You came across the room and rescued me. You can't do that this time.'

'I could if you let me. Wouldn't you rather do the dignified thing and leave?'

'What, with you? It would ruin me.'

'Your husband has killed himself. You don't really think you're going to be asked to polite parties? Come with me. We don't have to see each other. I'll move and you can have the house all to yourself. It's waiting for you.'

Abby allowed herself a few seconds of longing for the home that she had loved so much.

'Where would you go, Bamburgh House? It would almost be worth it to see you there, hating it so much. I don't think you ever loved my father or me enough to let yourself go back there.'

'The choices are gone. Where's Georgina? Go and get her and pack a bag.'

'I'm not going with you. Nobody would ever speak to me again.'

Abby left the room, wandered through the hall, striving for breath because there were fifty people in the drawing-room and none of them should see her cry. They would be talking about her, what a bad wife she had been, how she had not provided a son, how they had known all along that she was a silly choice, that she was middle class, beneath him with different ideas, that she was not beautiful and read too much and was too opinionated. They wanted to get rid of her. Abby was wretched. She knew that she had not been a good wife to him, she wished that she could begin again.

She ran away upstairs. She did not want to face Gil, afraid that she should change her mind. She watched from the window until his carriage left and then she went back downstairs to face the mourners. She had been right. Gerard had no intention of leaving. He moved in that very day and, although she questioned the solicitors, apparently he was entitled to do so. After all, her husband was dead. His family swiftly followed and they began immediately moving in their possessions. It improved the look of the house straight away since there was very little left. New servants were employed and they ignored Abby. At the dinner table she was fed and so was Georgina, but they insisted on her moving out of her bedroom, which was the second most important, and no one spoke to her.

She made a trip into Newcastle to find work, but the work

which she could have found in a shop or a factory she was turned down for because, even at her shabbiest, she would not fit into such a place. As for office work, she could not learn to type in a week. There was also the question of Georgina. Where would they live and who would look after her? The winter streets were wet and gloomy, or was it just how she felt? The problem seemed insoluble. After a full day trudging the streets, she found herself getting on a tram that went to Jesmond. She hadn't intended doing that, but it was dark and cold and had rained for most of the afternoon and she could not go back to the comfortless house which had been hers without looking at the house where she had spent a happy childhood, the best time of her life. She got off the tram and walked. She stood in a puddle and her feet were soaked. She stopped across the street. Lamplight was soft in the windows. It was evening now. Gil would be at home. She could not resist crossing the street and banging on the front door. She heard footsteps in the hall and a maid opened the door. Beyond her, Abby could see the hall just as it had always been. The tears which she had not shed for so many days threatened her now, half convinced that her parents sat beyond the sitting-room door. She was ushered in and the door opened. Gil and Matthew were sitting by a big fire, eating cake and drinking tea. The teacups winked in the firelight. Abby thought her heart would burst. Matthew shouted his hello and bounced across to her and Gil pulled a chair close to the fire and gave her tea and cut her cake.

The night closed in around the house. Abby tried half-heartedly to leave but Gil dissuaded her and it was so easy to stay. Georgina was safe at home. It was just one night to remember how things had been, but she could not even do that. When Matthew was safely in bed and they were having a meal, she said to him, 'I need some work. You employ women.'

'Not women like you,' Gil said.

'What do you mean? I can learn.'

'You wouldn't like it.'

'I don't have to like it. I have nowhere to go and nothing to do. Please.'

'You were married to Robert Surtees, you can't just—'

'Then what can I do?'

'I told you, you can come here.'

'I don't want to do that. If you let me work . . . I could work . . . Please, Gil.'

'Stop begging. It doesn't suit you.'

'What are my alternatives? I have to work.'

Gil got up and came across to her and he got hold of her hand.

'Look at that,' he said. 'You've never worked a day in your life.' And he turned her hand over and touched the soft palm. 'Women who work are either considered as little better than prostitutes or they live in reduced circumstances, and what would you do with Georgina?'

'I would manage! Please.' Abby wrenched her hand away and got up. 'You are so—'

'What?' When she didn't answer, he said flatly, 'I'm all you've got left, you can't afford to turn me down. You can have this house and part of the business. You could marry again eventually—'

'Whatever makes you think I want to do that?'

'Abby, if you go out to work you would lose your reputation just as badly as if you came and lived here with me, no matter what the circumstances. Socially you're finished.'

'Well, thank you. Out of the frying pan and into the fire, that's very nice.'

'There are worse things.'

'I shan't ask you to name them.' Abby stood for a few moments and then thought of something. 'Why haven't you changed anything in the house?'

'We could go back and collect Georgina in the morning and you could pack your things and bring with you whatever you want.'

'I don't have much. What are you doing this for, you can't want me here?'

'It was part of the deal. I got everything and when you needed it you got it back.'

'I don't want it all back. I don't want you to leave and I certainly don't want the business.'

'Why not?'

'Because you would leave that too, I know you would. Besides, it isn't the business which was my father's. You built it.'

'There's enough to go round,' Gil said roughly.

The next morning they drove into the country and collected her child. She packed her clothes and her few possessions and left the house which she had gone to so optimistically such a long time ago. She felt nothing but relief. Gerard and his wife and children waved her away from the front door. Abby didn't look back.

Chapter Twenty-one

Living with Gil was not as difficult as she had thought, but then nothing could be. To anyone who was not suffering from her husband's suicide it might have been considered dull. There was no social life, no invitations came and there were few visitors, only the tradesmen. She had nothing to do. The house was run rather, Abby thought, as he probably ran the works; she was just glad she didn't have to work for him. He didn't say anything but the servants minded him, as her mother would have said. It should have got on her nerves that the whole thing moved like an army camp, but it didn't. She was so glad to be back there, it was coming home both literally and in her head. She had not eaten or slept properly for a long time, but she did now and the two children liked one another immediately. Georgina was happy, therefore it was difficult for Abby not to be.

No one came in drunk; nobody gambled anything away. Gil came home promptly at half-past five for tea. At seven o'clock he either went back to work and was there long after she went to bed, or went into the study and was seen no more. He left for work at six in the morning. Sometimes she heard him. Occasionally he went out and came back late, but Abby considered it none of her business, which was quite refreshing and, although he did drink sometimes in the evening, it was never to excess so after the first two or three times of seeing him do so Abby relaxed. Gil did not get drunk; he did not shout and lose his temper and empty the house of everything which was comfortable. He would take a glass of brandy into the office or, if she stayed up late, there was the faint smell of whisky, but it did not affect his speech or his actions so she didn't care.

Nobody talked about marriage. If the local gossips thought she was sleeping in Gil's bed, let them think it. She hadn't lived with a man like this since her father and it was rather comforting. He didn't make demands; he didn't complain; he didn't make her feel as though she ought to be responsible for anything. He insisted that she should open a bank account and he paid money into it each month. That had been a hiccup.

'Why?' she had said to the suggestion.

'Presumably you need to buy things. Think of it as the start of what I owe you.'

That put it on a different footing. It was a handsome sum but, considering he had taken her inheritance, Abby didn't care and spent it freely. She thought that she was a kept woman, but was doing nothing for it. That was not quite true. She had undertaken the caring of the children. Matthew seemed delighted that she and Georgina had come to live with them and treated her straight away as he would a mother. For somebody who couldn't remember his mother, she counted this as a bonus. He had started school. She took him there each morning. Since Georgina was quite desperate to go, watching all the other children, Abby talked to the kind woman who ran the small school and Georgina was soon going in the mornings. Luckily it wasn't far to walk, because she had to collect Georgina at lunchtime and Matthew at teatime. There were only a few pupils and it was really just one room with a yard behind, but the children seemed happy there and quickly learned their letters. She or Gil read to them both in the evening before bed. It was all so civilised, Abby thought, rather like marriage was meant to be and probably never was.

Georgina had fast caught onto the idea of having two

parents and would listen for Gil at the door, run to him and throw herself into his arms. Having had one father who ignored her, she was not about to start calling him 'Daddy' as Abby had feared, but called him by his first name. In vain did Abby point out that this was not considered respectful, but since Gil called her 'Georgie', something else Abby didn't like, she left the whole problem to resolve itself. Georgina adored Gil and Abby thought it was not surprising. Robert had not shown his child attention or affection, but Gil managed both. He would throw her up in his arms and she would scream in delight when he caught her again. He would listen to endless tales that the children told about school, read long stories, sometimes the same one over and over again so that he would lean back against the bedroom wall, eyes shut, and relate word perfect whichever story it was that had been requested. He told her her paintings were brilliant and her numbers and letters were superb. Abby feared that Matthew might feel left out, so she took him to the park to play cricket when it was fine and to sail boats when it was windy and encouraged his interests. She took both the children shopping and out to tea and for various day trips in the fine weather.

That summer when the children were at school Abby would steal time and lie in the hammock in the garden and imagine to herself that she was young again. The garden had not changed, it was just as her mother had planned it and, although they had a gardener, she spent time there, helping and suggesting and generally getting in the way, enjoying the various plants in their seasons. She wasn't unhappy; she didn't mourn Robert and her vague feeling of guilt soon went away.

It took a long time before she felt restless, before the day she went upstairs to her father's room and decided that it was time to clear it out. She was half inclined to do so without saying anything to Gil, but when the children had gone to bed one autumn evening and he had retreated to the office – still the little room which had been her mother's, he rarely ventured into the study which had been Henderson's – she knocked on the door and went in.

'You don't have to knock.'

'I don't want to disturb you.'

Abby no longer thought of this room as the place where they had made love. She had come to terms with that. She went in and stood for a moment and then said, 'I though I might clear out some of my father's things from his bedroom.'

Gil frowned.

'I did mean to do it,' he said.

'People could use all those clothes. Some of them are good, and it's past time – and other things.'

'What other things?'

'The dining-room curtains are dropping apart.'

'I thought your mother had chosen them.'

'It was a long time ago. They're in a terrible state.'

'I don't mind what you do.'

'Right.'

Abby emptied her father's bedroom. When she had finished there was nothing left but the furniture and, much as she had dreaded doing it, she felt better. Then she bought new curtains for the dining-room but once she had done so, the rest of the room looked shabby and out of place. After that, it became a compulsion. The house had been her mother's and then her father's, though it had not been Gil's. Now it seemed that it could be hers and there was something unstoppable in her that wanted to make it so. She had not refurnished a house before. She had been allowed to touch nothing in Robert's houses, things were so old and valuable, whereas here her mother had been sensible, practical. Gil objected to nothing. For one thing he was too busy and for another he either liked what she did or was too cautious to tell her that he disliked it. He paid for it all without complaint, though Abby questioned him more than once as to whether it was costing too much. She was fearful of ending up like Robert, caring more for property than for people.

That winter when the cold weather came, she spent a lot of time at the houses that Gil had set up for homeless people and at soup kitchens, providing hot food and clothes and bedding and she was glad to be useful.

The depression that had been creeping up for years took a hold on the area and many businesses closed down. One of the first to go was Collingwood's shipyard. Abby thought that she could not feel sympathy for Charlotte but, when Gil's parents had to leave what they had thought of as a modest house in Westoe and live in a terraced two-bedroomed property in a street in Jesmond, she did feel sorry. Charlotte had had nothing to do with her since Abby had left Robert's house and gone to live with Gil. One day when the weather was for once less bitter, she took the children to the park. There she spied a little fat figure of a woman watching them from across the way. She left the children playing happily and walked slowly across. The cold wind blew the woman's hair about where it escaped from her hat.

'Hello, Charlotte,' she said.

Charlotte wasn't looking at her. Her eyes were fixed on the small boy who was giggling.

'That is Matthew?'

'It is, yes.'

'How big he is for his age.'

'Doesn't he look just like Gil did at that age?'

'Oh no, Gil was sullen and difficult. He would hide a lot and not come out and he wouldn't learn to read or write.'

'I believe excessive ability often takes people that way,' Abby said stoutly.

'Is Matthew clever?'

'Average.'

'He must take after Helen.'

Abby was amused but careful not to let it show. Just then, Matthew bounded across.

'Come on, Aunty Abby, we have to get back. Hello.' He beamed at Charlotte.

'I'm your grandmother, Matthew, do you remember me?'

'Are you?'

'You have two. Your other grandma lives in Durham.'

Abby tried to move him away but he was intrigued, as well he might be, she thought.

'You have two grandfathers. Don't you know anything about them? And an uncle. Do you remember your Uncle Edward?'

'Is this true?' Matthew said, turning Gil's dark eyes on Abby.

'We have to go. We must get back. It's teatime.'

Abby had to almost drag him away and she was not pleased with herself. When Gil came in shortly after they got home, for once Georgina was not first down the hall and Abby could hear him from the sitting-room. 'I met my grandmother. You didn't tell me about her. Why didn't you tell me?'

'Did you now? Where was this?'

'In the park near the entrance. She was standing there by the railings. Why don't we see them? She told me I had another grandmother and two grandfathers but we never see them.'

'They don't want to see us.'

'But she did.'

'They didn't before now.'

'Why?'

'Because I did something wrong, something they didn't think I should have done and your grandfather, that's my father, he turned us out of the house.'

There was a short silence. Abby wished she could have stopped her ears.

'It must have been something very bad.'

'Yes, it was.'

With a wisdom well beyond his years Matthew said, 'You don't want to talk about it, do you?'

'No.'

'I would like to see them.'

'We'll have to think about that.'

Abby couldn't eat. Gil didn't reproach her; he didn't lose his temper; he didn't say anything. She had not faced anybody with that much restraint and it was just as bad as if he had called her everything he could lay his tongue to. She didn't meet his eyes all the way through tea and was so glad to get up from the table that she hurried. He went to the little office and stayed there. Abby dealt with the children but by the time she had put them to bed, she couldn't bear it any longer. She walked into the office without knocking, slammed the door and said, 'All right, say it, say it! I shouldn't have gone across. I didn't think. She was in the park and it is a public place. They live here. What did you expect? They live ten minutes' walk away. You knew this, you knew what it was like, that Collingwood's had closed, that they have lost almost everything. What did you expect me to do?'

She waited for the onslaught. Robert would have made the house ring.

'Matthew followed me,' she said, starting up again quickly. 'I thought he was playing.'

Gil was staring at the wall.

'I saw her on the street the other day,' he said slowly. 'She looked so little and fat and old.'

'Does this mean you're going to let him see them?'

'No.'

'And when he asks?'

'I'll think of something.'

'Don't you think he's entitled to see them?'

'I think we've discussed this sufficiently.'

'You wrecked the house, you put him out of business, you ruined their lives. Isn't that enough?'

'He did it himself.'

'He'll die some day and then you'll be sorry.'

To her astonishment, Gil laughed.

'Do you know that's exactly what your father said. What on earth makes you think so? I'll dance on his grave. I've bought the property.'

'What property?'

'Collingwood's.'

'Don't you own enough of the riverside?'

'I couldn't resist.'

'He's an old man and he's finished. What pleasure is there in that?'

'I got it cheaply,' Gil said, 'so very cheaply. I'm going to put "Reed's Yard No 3" on the gates. Then I think I'll be satisfied.'

Abby was angry.

'And what are you going to tell your son, that you didn't bed your brother's wife and your own wife at the same time?'

'Hardly, even though it's the truth.'

'Is it?'

He had not spoken about this before, at least not to her, but he was sufficiently upset, she knew, to do so.

'You really thought it of me?'

'Men do.'

'You mean Robert did, bed other women?'

'He did it all the time.'

'I cared about Rhoda and Helen very much and I didn't betray either of them; it was my brother I betrayed. I thought I loved him. I thought he meant more to me than anybody in the world, but I took his wife and his child. Matthew was the only thing that mattered, the only person he really loved ever I think. I destroyed it and Rhoda and Helen both died because of it, but I never played any woman false. I never did.' He got up and was out of the room before she could have stopped him or said anything, though what she would have said or done Abby wasn't sure. It was undoubtedly the longest speech of Gil's life, and she believed him.

She went after him, at the time she wasn't quite sure why. He would have been better let alone but she went, along the hall and he was standing there in the gloom as if not sure where to go or what to do. She decided it for him because he turned around as she approached and drew her to him and tried to hold her and kiss her. For some reason all Abby could remember was the last embraces that her husband had given her and her regard for him surfaced. She did not feel guilt about his death; she felt resentment and anger.

'Take your hands off me!' she said and before Gil could turn back into himself from being Robert she had spoken in rage and he backed off and walked out. He left the front door open. It was a vile night. Wind and rain threw themselves in as he opened the door. Abby hesitated only just before going after him, but it was too late. The street lamps told her that the street was empty, so where he was she had no idea.

'Gil!' she shouted in case he was close enough to hear her, but even if he had been it was doubtful whether it would have turned him back. Abby cursed herself but then she realised that it was true. She didn't want any man near her, not after what Robert had done.

There was nowhere to go, Gil discovered, nowhere except work and that wouldn't do. In the end, after walking the streets for a short while, the weather drove him to make a decision, so he went to the brothel where John had taken him. Mrs Fitzpatrick who owned it welcomed him with a smile. He hadn't been there in the short months since Abby had come back to Jesmond and it was only now he could see how much he had hoped that he could gain her affection again. He and John had done some late-night drinking, but he had refused to go to Mrs Fitzpatrick's. John had laughed.

'Why bother when you have it at home?' he said.

'It isn't like that.'

'It isn't like that for me either. Edwina withdrew her bedroom favours a long time ago,' John said with a sigh. 'Women. If the pretty little Mrs Surtees isn't giving you what you want, why do you keep her? The whole world thinks you're bedding her and the odds at the clubs are that you'll marry her.'

Gil could see now that Abby wouldn't marry him, that she

wouldn't let him near her, even after he had just told her that he had done nothing dishonourable towards women. She wouldn't believe him. Why should she? Men were like that, Robert had proved it and after Robert why should she want anyone else? She had what she needed: a roof, money, comfort and security for her child. He could not turn her onto the street. Gil could see them going on like that for years and years. He had known that she did not love him, but he had not known that she was disgusted with him.

Mrs Fitzpatrick knew that he favoured blondes. When he came here all he thought of was Helen. He didn't have the same girl twice; he didn't want anything to do with them other than bed. They were all blonde, they were all pretty, they were all the same to him. He was directed upstairs and went and knocked on the door. The rooms were all the same, too, as though Mrs Fitzpatrick wanted to encourage anonymity. Men could be anything they wanted here and the girls could be anyone they wanted, which was why he came here. After the first time he had tried to make himself not go, but the memory of being able to have a woman like that stayed with him. It was the only way he could think of Helen.

He opened the door. The rooms were all sumptuous, huge beds and lavish bedhangings. It was a very expensive place. The girl was blonde, of course, and dressed in red underwear which would have looked ridiculous except that it didn't at Mrs Fitzpatrick's.

'Good evening.'

'Hello, stranger,' she said smiling.

'Have we met before?'

'Everybody knows you. The girls have all dyed their hair yellow, hoping you'd come back.'

'Whatever for?'

She stood up. She was very pretty and went in and out in all the right places.

'Because you tip better than everybody else. Lucky old me.

You're the most generous man in Newcastle, my petal. When you've been here, somebody always has new dresses and new scent and oh, all sorts of things. Now it's my turn. Some men are mean, they're mean all over but you . . . you're a star.'

Gil took off his jacket and took her into his arms and held her close and it was such a relief.

'My dad works for you,' she said.

'What does he do?'

'He's a joiner.'

'So what are you doing here?'

'I like it.'

'Nobody likes it.'

'It's my work. It's what I'm good at. Some days are awful and some days are . . . not so bad.'

Gil laughed.

'That sounds like work,' he said.

She was good. He insisted on knowing her name, which was Sylvia, but to him she was Helen. They were all Helen. He didn't drink much when he was there, but he needed a couple of whiskies to complete the illusion and then she was Helen, so beautiful in his arms. He was back there in that house with the narrow cobbled street outside and the smell of breadmaking in the alley in the early morning and the sweet scent of lemon flowers. She was all he would ever need or want there in the soft white sheets. He was making love to her and she was giving herself to him freely such as nobody had done since. It was only there that he acknowledged his life to be a nightmare. There was nothing in it beyond her, there never had been. He had never had his brother's love or his parents' affection; Rhoda had been all need and Abby had married a richer more eligible man than he was, but here Helen would give herself to him completely and it was all he needed.

He stayed the night with her and the illusion was complete. He could even come back into reality as far as to imagine the house that he had let go to ruin way back during those wonderful stolen nights when he had been happy. That brief time had altered everything, finished his life, but now he remembered why he had done it, that it had seemed worth it, that he had wanted nothing but her.

In the morning the magic died. She was just a pretty girl in bed with him and beyond them the Newcastle streets were busy from the early hours and the room seemed tawdry in the harsh morning light. He drew back the curtains and it was still raining.

'Do you have to go?' They always said that. Mrs Fitzpatrick had trained her girls well; they always pretended they were reluctant to see you go, even if they had wished you in hell several times during the night while you made good use of your money and their time.

'I should have been at work an hour ago.' He washed and dressed and she watched him from the bed, her bare shoulders so kissable and inviting. He would pay on the way out, but he always gave the girl some money. This time she recoiled from the wad of notes.

'I can't take all that!'

'It's only money.'

'Missus will think I've robbed you. I'll be on the street.'

'Go back to your old man then.'

'No fear.' She took the money and laughed and kissed him. Her breasts were so soft and her mouth was so warm that Gil wanted to stay. He walked out into the cold of the Newcastle streets and thought how unremittingly cruel life was, how spiteful. People were always going on about what a wonderful world it was, but it wasn't true. It was shite. The deserts burned you, the sea drowned you, the ice froze you, you dragged some kind of existence out of it all, taking the bread from another man's mouth if necessary, and then you died.

He walked to the office in the pouring rain. It was a long way and took most of the morning and he had had several meetings planned. His secretary would be having fifty fits. He reached it and shook the rain off his jacket and she came pale faced to him.

'You have a board meeting and—'

'Yes, yes.'

'Mrs Surtees is here.'

Gil slicked back his shiny wet hair and went into his office. It looked so comfortable against the grey of the morning and the greyer of the river and the thick dark steel of the sky. The fire was burning, the lamps were lit and Abby sat there with her hands in her lap.

'You didn't come back,' she said, just above a whisper. 'I was so afraid when you didn't come back. I didn't mean it, I was just—'

Gil went back to the door and ordered some coffee and then he went to her.

'You thought I was going to shoot myself, yes?'

'No—'

She made him ashamed, sitting there with that anxious look on her white face. He got down beside her as he did with the children and said, 'I'm sorry, I should have understood better than that. It won't happen again.'

'But—'

'Go home. You look as though you haven't slept. We'll have some coffee and everything will be all right.'

She had been hurt too many times. Gil resolved not to do it again, but things changed. After that he quite often stayed out all night, there was nothing to go home for beyond the children. Sometimes he went back and had tea with them and read them a story, but more often he stayed at the office until late and then went either to Mrs Fitzpatrick's or drinking with John Marlowe. John seemed to have time on his hands unless he was working and Gil surmised that his home life was no better. Edwina was, John said, absorbed in the world of culture. He said it in such a funny way, as though Edwina had been caught in a mouse trap. She sat on committees and chaired meetings to do with the local arts and had other ladies to tea in the afternoons. She did not drink and abhorred smoking. She went to bed early and got up early.

'She's pure, blameless,' John said with a laugh.

One evening he persuaded Gil to go to the billiard hall with him. Gil didn't want to go. It was the same place that his brother and Toby had frequented in the old days but, since there was no alternative except the office, the whorehouse or the pub, he went. It hadn't altered. It was just the same with the big baize tables, the low lights focused on them and men standing around drinking beer. He had always liked the atmosphere, the talk. It didn't matter what you did or who you were here, you were accepted. You didn't even have to play, you could just be there. To Gil's surprise, Toby was there with another young man. He seemed pleased to see Gil.

'If we weren't in public I would hug you.'

'I can get by without it,' Gil said.

'This is Everett. He's quite charming, not as handsome as some people but very talented.'

'What about Henrietta?'

'My dear boy, we have the perfect marriage, two lovely little boys and she is expecting another.'

'You amaze me.'

'Why should I? It's the simplest thing in the world, rather like threading a needle. You should try it some time.'

Gil laughed. He couldn't help asking, 'Do you see my brother?'

'Yes, often.'

'You do?'

'We're the best of friends, we always were. He's working for someone else. I think he likes it.'

'Nothing could be harder than working for my father,' Gil said grimly.

'He's not well. You should see him.'

'I don't need any advice.'

'Families,' Toby said with a sigh. 'Would you care to play with Everett?'

'Thank you, I've got John somewhere.'

'It's your loss,' Toby said and went off, smiling happily.

Abby relived that evening again and again. It was funny, she thought, how the smallest things mattered. Nothing had happened and yet Gil was different after that. She had not thought that he came home to her or for her. She had thought that his life carried on as it had before she arrived, but she could see now that that was not true. He had liked coming home to her. Now he didn't. The only reason he came back was for the children. All the charity work and all the time spent with Matthew and Georgina seemed dull because, even though she hadn't known, she had looked forward to him coming back. It was too late. He didn't give her the chance to redeem herself. He stayed at the distance where she had put him. She could smell perfume and whisky and cigars around him and she knew what that meant. Robert had always smelled like that, decadent, indulgent.

Gil went to work every day but Sunday and then he and John would go to the pub and come back at around three, very much the worse for beer, eat a huge dinner and then fall asleep. Many was the Sunday afternoon when the weather was fine and warm and the children were about, but Gil was no longer available to take them out. At first they complained, but it was in vain. He didn't hear them. Then they complained to Abby and she tried to talk to him and, though he listened and agreed, it didn't make any difference. Gil's life had taken on some pattern he imposed upon it and he didn't choose to alter it for anyone else. He would stay out all night on Saturday, go to the pub, have his dinner, sleep and go out with John in the evening. On Mondays and Tuesdays he stayed at the office until late, on Wednesdays he stayed out all night and on Thursdays and Fridays he played billiards. It was as rigid an existence as he had had before, but different. His room was always a complete mess now, though the maids didn't complain, they just cleared up all the clothes from the floor. The office at home was clean and empty because he didn't work there. It was like living with someone else and all for . . . Abby didn't know, for a few moments when he had tried to touch her and she had stopped him?

She had another problem. Matthew had started disappearing on Sunday afternoons. Gil didn't notice. When questioned he said blithely that he had been to the park playing cricket with the other boys. Since it wasn't far it seemed a perfectly plausible explanation, but Abby had the feeling that it wasn't true. It happened the next Sunday, too, so the one after that she left Georgina playing by the fire – it was not a fine day – and followed him. She had suspected what he was doing and so it proved. She had difficulty keeping up, though she thought she knew where he was going. She had to see him go in the front door. She kept back a little way but was close enough to see the short fat woman who embraced him. Abby walked slowly home through the poorer streets, uncertain what to do.

Matthew came back with glib tales of cricket. Gil went out. Abby put Georgina to bed earlier than usual and she stood Matthew by the fire in the sitting-room and said, 'I know where you went.'

She could see his small face deliberating. Was it worth a lie? Might it work?

'You went to see your grandparents.'

Matthew frowned. He looked a lot like Gil when he frowned.

'They are my family,' he said.

'And what about your father?'

'He doesn't care,' Matthew said bitterly. 'He doesn't care about anything except the shipyard. He never comes home and when he does he brings that man with him.' The children, Abby thought, didn't like John Marlowe. They didn't say anything, but they called him 'that man' and blamed him for keeping Gil away from them. Georgina no longer ran along the hall at teatime; she no longer listened for Gil's footsteps. Like most other men Gil had compartmentalised his family but then, she reasoned, they weren't his family. She was a leech and Georgina was her daughter. He kept them separate and mostly ignored them. He provided money and not his time or attention or regard and she had done it.

'What if he finds out?'

'Will you tell him?'

'What if I don't tell him and he finds out?'

'He won't. He doesn't notice anything.'

'If I promise not to tell him will you stop going?'

'I don't see why I should.' Abby didn't see why he should either.

'Because he will be very angry.'

'He's never angry.'

The opposite was true, Abby thought now. Gil was permanently angry, it was just that he didn't shout or lose his temper or give any signs other than obscure ones.

'Matthew, your father doesn't like being crossed. A great many men have regretted it. I know he looks . . . even tempered but you are a very small boy and you must accept that your father would not like you to see your grandparents.'

Matthew became the small boy that she was speaking of and started to cry.

'My grandfather is ill. He stays in bed and they are poor and my father did it. He did it! He did! I hate him!'

He ran upstairs. Abby went after him.

'I hate him! I hate him!' In the room that was his own, Matthew shouted again. 'I know what happened. I know what he did. My grandfather told me. He's a horrible man. He's horrible and when I am older I shall go and live with Grandfather and Grandmother and never speak to him again!'

Abby didn't know what to say.

'What did your grandfather say your father did?'

'He made them poor. He took the house and the business and everything and they have nothing and he – he—'

'What?'

Matthew looked straight at her, his dark eyes spilling tears.

'He killed my mother,' Matthew said.

Chapter Twenty-two

Gil couldn't remember her name. Was it Sylvia? It could have been Desirée – where had she got that name from? – no, no, it was Chloe. He was convinced that Mrs Fitzpatrick named her girls as one would name a new puppy. They were probably all called Ethel and you couldn't possibly call a girl Ethel in bed. Ethel and Agnes and Agatha. He was sweetly drunk. Not so drunk that he couldn't take her, just drunk enough so that her name didn't matter. He listened to her catching at her breath in the silence. It was three o'clock in the morning and the Newcastle streets were deserted. It was his favourite time. You could conquer the night by not asking it for sleep, he had found that. He no longer had to pretend that she was Helen and the vision had gone. He could not, even the worse for half a bottle of whisky, conjure the images of Spain in his mind so that they flooded the room. Helen was dead. Each night he knew it and it was so unforgiving. You couldn't distance yourself from such things, yet he was a long way from her now, so far that he could not remember what she tasted or felt like. The life that they had had was no closer than the way someone would see it in a book, with words and paper between you and it, nothing of substance, nothing there. She was gone from him as though someone had closed every door between them. All he had now was the work and the whisky and this girl whose slender thighs were parted for him. It was all there was and he had been a fool not to know it.

Gil felt nothing when he saw his brother from across the billiard hall. He had not expected that. A thousand times he had pictured them meeting again, what he would say, what he would do. All the years when they had not seen one another and not spoken he had missed Edward more than he missed Rhoda and differently from how he missed Helen. He missed him in a way that said 'it's your own fault'. He wanted to see his brother, but he did not feel as though he deserved to do so. It was hard, too, because Edward was always near, at first either at the works or at Bamburgh House and then a hundred times Gil thought he saw him in the Newcastle streets. He was always mistaken, but each day he looked just in case. Even to catch sight of him would somehow help, but until the night in the billiard hall he had not. They could have met face to face on any of the big streets. People who knew one another met every day; the chance of it happening must be big, but they didn't. He couldn't understand that. At Toby's wedding he had not looked at Edward because of his parents, but in the billiard hall they were not there and it was different. Night after night in the loneliness he had dreamed that they met. The best dreams were where it had all been a mistake and it was the old days and he was at home. In fact, it was not the old days because there had not been a time when they were as happy as he saw them in his mind, when they were both married and their parents had smiled on them. No such time existed except in Gil's subconscious, but he would awaken and feel cheated and then guilty. He could not free himself from what he had done. He knew that he never would, that he must learn to live with the person he was because he had made too many mistakes and could not go back and undo them. Neither could he make reparation. There was nothing to do but go forward and hope to try and do better in the future. He was beyond that, too. He didn't want to do better, he wanted to drown in whisky and women and never sleep again while it was dark. No more of those nightmares which had Rhoda and Edward and Helen in them. Gil had discovered that if you could sleep during the hours of light you didn't have nightmares. It was as if they were not allowed. You could sleep a damned sight more peacefully when there were not deep shadows in the corners pulling faces at you.

His daytime dream was that Edward would come to him, forgive him, that everything would be made right, but when it happened it was not the lovely summer day that his mind built into it, it was late at night in a billiard hall and even though Edward must have been fully aware of Gil, he ignored him just as though he did not exist. Toby was with him, even came across, greeted him.

'My brother?' was all Gil could say.

'I don't think he wants to talk to you.'

'What is he doing here?'

'He comes here a lot, we always did.'

'With you?'

'Who else?'

'But . . . your family.'

'Don't be silly, old boy, they aren't old enough to play billiards,' and Toby departed, smiling.

'Do you want to go?' John asked, seeing his expression.

'Yes.'

'Mrs Fitzpatrick's?' John said when they got outside into the street.

'My God, yes.'

With Chloe in his arms, Gil felt happy.

'He didn't kill your mother, Matthew,' Abby had said. 'How could you think such a thing?'

'Grandfather said so.'

'Your father has looked after you all those years. Who are you going to believe first?'

'Grandfather and Grandmother have wanted to see me but my father wouldn't let me. You know that's true. Grandfather says that my father is a bad man.'

'He has done many good things,' Abby said. 'He helps people who have nothing. He gives them shelter and food and he gives thousands of jobs to men in Newcastle.'

'He doesn't like me.'

'That's not true.'

'Then why do I not see him?'

'He's very busy.'

'He's very busy going out to the pub with that man,' Matthew said.

'This must stop,' Abby said, 'and you must not go and see your grandfather and grandmother again. Do you hear me? If you disobey me I shall smack your bottom until you can't sit down. Do you understand me?'

'You can't do that!'

'Try,' Abby threatened.

She went to see Charlotte and she could see by the look on Charlotte's face that she knew Abby had found out. The house was tiny and gloomy and William upstairs in bed.

'What's the matter with him?' she asked.

'I don't know, he just isn't well.'

Charlotte's furniture, what she had left of it, was far too big for such a house and dwarfed each room. It looked incongruous, towering there. The walls were painted brown; the fire smoked; the windows were tiny and from next door came the sound through the thin walls of somebody having an argument. How had Charlotte come so low and did Gil really want his parents like this? She couldn't believe that he did, that he had brought them to this and would let them survive there as best they could. She took Abby upstairs and Abby had to go even though she didn't want to see William. The man in the bed looked old and grey and smaller but he said, 'What are you doing letting his whore in here?' and closed his eyes.

Abby said nothing until they had gone back down the steep, narrow stairs again.

'Do you think that of me?'

'Everybody does,' Charlotte said.

'It's not true. Just because we're living in the same house . . . You know why I'm here. Matthew is not to come here again. If Gil finds out, I don't know what will happen.'

'What more can he do to us?' Charlotte said simply. 'We love the boy. We have nothing.'

'I have told him that he is not to come back and if he does it will be the worse for him. If he does turn up here, you are to send him home. Are you listening to me, Charlotte?'

'No, why should I?'

'William has poisoned his mind against Gil and Gil doesn't deserve that.'

'It was only the truth. He won't let us see Matthew, has told him stories about us.'

'That's not true. You must send him home.'

The following Sunday Abby tried not to let Matthew out. Unfortunately he went anyway, but she followed him and banged on Charlotte's door. When nobody answered she walked in, searched the lower storey and, finding nothing there, went upstairs and dragged Matthew out of William's bedroom. They couldn't stop her. William couldn't get out of bed and Charlotte wept. Matthew resisted. He twisted and turned, he kicked her and thumped her and when she got him into the street it was worse. It took her a long time to get him home and her patience and temper were worn out by then. She smacked him until he howled.

Unfortunately Gil chose that precise time to come home. Sober as water and neat as a new penny he looked gravely at her as she walloped his child, the first time that anybody had done so, Abby knew. He didn't interfere; he left her to it on the sofa in the sitting-room. She sent Matthew to bed, put him there herself and then she went downstairs, listening to Matthew's sobs beginning to quieten. She went back into the sitting-room, hoping that Georgina's presence would protect her but Gil came in.

'Georgina would you mind going to your room for a little while?' he said.

'Have I done something too?'

'No, I just want to talk to your mother. You can go to the kitchen if you would rather and see Hannah.'

'She isn't there,' Georgina pointed out as she left the room.

Abby wished she could go to her room too.

'I wasn't expecting you,' she said.

'Obviously.'

'It wouldn't have made any difference. He knew what would happen, I had already told him.'

'He's seven,' Gil said.

'He understood perfectly.'

'Are you going to tell me what he did?'

'Why, are you going to unsmack him if you don't agree?'

Gil looked hard at her.

'Tell me.'

Abby gave in.

'He went to see your parents, not once but several times and I told him not to do it again. He lied to me and then he disobeyed me and your father has told him that you killed Helen and he hates you. Is that enough?'

'It's ample,' Gil said.

'I thought it might be. However, if you spent less time screwing women and drinking whisky and playing billiards, I daresay things might not have come to this.'

Abby had to leave the room because she had never smacked a child before in her life and she felt sick and wanted to cry. She was bruised and battered from trying to get Matthew home while he kicked and punched her. Luckily there was nobody in the kitchen, it being Sunday afternoon, so she busied about there, instead of crying. She made some tea and sat quietly at the table, pretending to eat chocolate cake which had been made early that day and was still fresh, and drinking three cups of tea before she could even think of moving anywhere.

After a while Gil came in. She made more tea and cut him a piece of chocolate cake and they sat in the kitchen as they had never done before. He ate his cake. Men were so insensitive; they could eat even if somebody was dying.

'Did you see my father?'

'He called me your whore.'

'How did he look?'

'He looked defeated. He's old and tired and you've beaten him and now I've beaten your child. No wonder we are all so happy.'

'You think I ought to take Matthew to see them?'

'I think you ought to allow him to go. I think you should arrange for Helen's parents to see him if they want to. You could write to them. After all, they can hardly blame Matthew for what happened. He is the only grandchild any of them has. How could they not want to see him?'

'Because he's mine?'

'That's not his fault.'

Gil took a deep breath.

'All right, I'll let him go. Will you take him?'

'There's nobody else,' Abby said.

Gil didn't write. He went to Durham the following day to see whether he could locate Helen's parents, but it was as he had feared. They had moved. The people who were living in their house didn't know where they had gone and neither did anybody else that Gil could find. Determined, he travelled to Oxford but they had not gone back there and he knew that if they were in London he was wasting his time because they could be anywhere. He came home and went back to work. He tried to talk to Matthew but every time he walked into the room, his child got up and walked out. He caught hold of Matthew once and tried to get the child to talk to him but Matthew just looked past him.

'I have said that you can go. What more do you want me to do?'

Matthew continued looking past him, so Gil let him loose.

On the Sunday Georgina stayed at home. Gil made sure he was there to stay with her and Abby took a silent Matthew across the streets of Jesmond to where his grandparents were living. Abby had sent a note to say that he could come and had received nothing in reply, but she assumed that Charlotte would be agreeable. Where else did they have to go on Sundays? She would have left him at the door when Charlotte opened it, but Charlotte's distressed face told her this would not do. She ushered them inside to the fire and then she looked tearfully at Abby.

'William died last night,' she said.

Life could not be so unkind, Abby thought. It could not do this to them. Matthew ran to his grandmother and huddled in against her skirts and she held him there with one pudgy hand.

'Oh Charlotte, I am sorry.' Abby's mind did swirling things. How on earth could she ever tell Gil that his father had died without seeing him and that he had given his permission too late.

'Did Edward see his father before he died?'

'Of course. He lives just around the corner. He's so good. He comes every day. He has a good position, you know, he works for Blade's. They aren't as big a firm as we were, but they turn out solid ships, William always said so.'

'You didn't think that perhaps—'

'Abby, you know William. I did suggest that he ought to see Gil but he wouldn't. They're so alike, so unforgiving. What am I to do?'

'I'll talk to Gil.'

'No. I couldn't. I shall manage.'

'You have a family.'

Charlotte managed a wry smile.

'They're as badly off as I am in that great tomb of a house they have. I never thought to go back there. The house takes everything and it's so uncomfortable and so cold and . . . I don't want to go there.'

Abby gave her some money. Charlotte tried to refuse it, but it was only politeness.

'Leave the boy with me a little while. I'll bring him back. Gil isn't there, is he?'

'He is at the moment but—'

'I'll bring him to the back door and then I don't have to see him.'

Abby walked slowly home, wishing that it was four times as far. She even went round by the dene but she knew that Gil was expecting her just to drop Matthew off and come back, so she could not be too long. Even so, she lingered. Gil was not a happy man, she knew that. Happy men did not behave like he was behaving. Happy men, Abby thought savagely, did not go to bed with whores. She had a sure idea that if a man was bedding a woman at home, a woman he liked and desired, he would not go out to pay for it, not unless there was something seriously wrong with him. And that was her fault. He was a man. If she had gone to bed with him he would have stayed with her. Men were not so complicated. All they needed was warmth and time, like bread. Robert had taken everything from her, at least that was how it felt. She had nothing left for Gil and he had desperately needed somebody. She didn't want to be touched, not in that way. Comfort would have been nice, but men were not much good at comfort alone, not until they were very old presumably. He had gone to his work, like her father had done, but he was much younger than her father and had found time to fit in whisky, billiards and women. What would he do when he found out that his father was dead?

She went reluctantly home and he was hovering in the hall.

'You were a hell of a long time. What were you doing? What did my father say? Were they pleased? How long is Matthew staying?'

'Come into the sitting-room.'

What difference that would make she couldn't think, but somehow it seemed better than the hall. She knew Gil very well, but she didn't know how he was going to react.

'Gil—' She looked up at him and she didn't have to tell him. 'Your father—'

'No. No, not now, not now. No.'

'He died last night.'

'Of what?' Gil said, as though this was important, as though it could not have happened.

'I don't know, he just did.'

'No, he can't have done, not like that. He would fight, he would—'

'He's been ill for some time.'

'Nobody told me. I didn't know. No, I did know. I didn't think . . . Couldn't I have seen him? Would my mother have let me see him?'

Abby lied valiantly.

'I think the end was very quick.'

'No. You said he had been ill for some time. It couldn't have been. Was my brother there?'

Abby cursed Gil's quick mind.

'Was Edward there?' he persisted.

'I really don't know.'

'Yes, you do.' He was watching her closely. 'My brother was there. My father said goodbye to him. My brother was there. He didn't want me there, did he? He didn't want me there. And my mother . . . my mother didn't.'

Abby tried to take him into her arms but he wouldn't let her.

'What about Matthew?'

'Your mother wanted him to stay and it seemed sensible,' Abby said, trying to be normal.

'Are you going for him?'

'In a little while, yes. You were going out with John, weren't you? Why don't you go?'

Gil went. There seemed nothing else to do, she was right. But when they went to the pub he wasn't thirsty and, although John talked to him and especially about his father, Gil couldn't hear. They went to Mrs Fitzpatrick's, but he walked out. All he wanted to do was go home, but when he got there he didn't want to be there either. Abby was still up, she was sitting by the fire.

'Matthew came home?'

'Yes.'

'What about my mother? I was thinking about her. What will she do?'

'Edward will take care of her.'

'Edward?'

'Yes. He has a house you know, not far away.'

'I'm sure he does. I see him sometimes, in the billiard hall. He's got very fat. He takes after my mother.'

Gil went to bed. He stole into Matthew's room and watched his son sleeping. He knew now all the things that were unholy to know, all the things that if God had cared about anybody, he would have told them before they were born instead of letting them go crashing about destroying everything. The trouble was that you had to live a life and lose everything, to suffer and then to die, yet you didn't know that when you set out. You didn't know how to lose everything, so God demonstrated it to you. This was the last thing he had to lose, the very last person, so he made a bargain with God: if Matthew should leave him he would die, he would deliberately die. He would take away the gift that God had given him; he would take it away to punish God for expecting so very much of anybody. He would cut off that life so that he would never again see the tide full on Bamburgh beach.

He went to bed and his mind gave him the good times. It was

laughable. There hadn't been any good times. His mind would not be stopped, it dredged itself. Sick sentiment gave him the light in his father's eyes the day that the *Northumbria* was launched. He remembered how proud his father had been of him the day that John Marlowe had signed the contract for the *Northumbria.* He thought of drinking brandy with his father and how William had given up port because Gil didn't like it, the hand on his shoulder and the way William had bragged to his friends about 'my son, the genius'. He wished again and again it could be that night when his father had said casually to the butler that from now on there would be only brandy after dinner because that was what Gil preferred. And he wished that it could have been different. He wished more than anything that his father had even just once told him that he cared. He never had and he never would. William had gone to his grave without saying it and he wished that he had never been born. William had not loved him. He could have plucked the moon and the stars down from the sky; he could have prevented the sun from rising and the night from falling and William would not have loved him for it. The magic that he had made in ships was admirable and William had admired it and called upon other people to admire it, but it was not love. And yet he had given Gil so much, all the things which his own father had not given him: prosperity, security, education, high position and the chance to succeed in a business which his father had built so very high. Gil had destroyed that business and his father's house and his father.

Chapter Twenty-three

Gil did not go to the funeral. Abby could not help being relieved. She had had the feeling that if he went, there would be trouble of some kind and more trouble was beyond what he could bear. Besides, after all this time it would be an empty gesture and he could afford none of those. He had been unpredictable. She had thought he would go to some whore and stay there maybe for weeks, or that he would get drunk and go on being drunk, which was what Robert would have done, but he didn't. He kept on going to work each day, he came back at teatime and he was silent. It was the silence which irked Abby. Gil had been silent for most of his life and quiet for the rest of it.

The funeral was very small. It seemed sad that a man who had helped to shape Tyneside's future should be ignored now because he had failed. Failure was not allowed in this world of business and being poor was not to be thought of; indeed, people thought it was catching. They stayed away, all the people who had money and influence, they did not come to see Charlotte through her ordeal and, although for years Abby had thought Charlotte silly and trivial, she felt sorry for her that day. Money had meant everything to Charlotte because until she had met William she had so little of it. Now she had little of it again. Abby resolved to ask Charlotte how badly off she really was, or whether Edward would look after her. He was much in evidence that day, putting his arm around her, supporting her in the almost empty church. No more than a dozen people had come to see William laid to rest. Abby was ashamed of the people of Newcastle that they could treat anybody in such a way.

Charlotte cried throughout the service. Abby sang as loudly as she could because Gil was not there and because her father was not there and because William was not there and she felt angry because Charlotte had been let down by other people.

Afterwards they went back to Charlotte's horrid little house, where somebody had provided tea and cake. Abby couldn't swallow a crumb. She thought of Gil at work. She had kept waiting for him to drop to pieces. Nothing had happened, or maybe it was just that people dropped to pieces each in his own way and Gil had done so without anybody noticing. You couldn't watch somebody's heart break. Abby scorned that as silly and she knew that it was not what she meant, it was just that people were silently desperate. That was what Gil was like and she didn't think there was anything to be done about it. He had destroyed William, had wanted to destroy him, had wanted to take some measure of revenge, but William had died and there was no revenge as complete as someone's death. He had seen his father as young, as able to fight him, as able to come back from his corner like the prizefighter he had always been. He had not known, or had not chosen to acknowledge, when his father was beaten. To Gil he was the same man he had been when Gil was a little boy and defenceless. He was mighty and powerful; he was not in a wooden coffin in the earth, finished and done for.

She came back to a silent house. Hannah had taken the children out for the day. The last thing Abby had wanted was for Matthew to demand to be taken to the funeral. Funerals were not the place for children, at least this one was not for him; but after he was told that his grandfather had died, Matthew reacted as Gil would have done and said nothing. He did not cry or ask questions and when she had suggested that Hannah should take them out for the day, he seemed eager to go. Abby didn't blame him. It was what she wanted to do, to pretend that none of it had happened, that they did not have the future to face.

Hannah and the children duly came home and they had something to eat and Abby put them to bed early and read them a story. Georgina fell asleep in the middle of the story, worn out from her day by the sea – Hannah had taken them to Tynemouth and Georgina had spent a considerable amount of time excitedly relating her day to Abby. William's death did not touch her at all; Abby was glad of that. Matthew must not have mentioned William that day and Georgina did not know him. It had been a good day out to her. She had seen the gulls and been on the beach and been bought sweets. It was all she needed to make her happy. Abby wished that adults could be like that, needing so little to produce happiness. Matthew needed more. She sat down on the bed and cuddled him. He drew back slightly. Abby thought he would probably not forgive her for smacking him and she didn't blame him.

'Are you all right?'

'What will happen to Grandmother?'

Abby would have been interested to know.

'I expect she will go and live with your Uncle Edward.'

'Couldn't she come and live with us? I suppose Daddy wouldn't let her.'

Matthew's dislike for Gil over the past weeks was making things worse.

'He would if she wanted to. She is his mother.'

'I don't know much about mothers and you certainly aren't like one. You hit people who are smaller than you.'

'I didn't know what else to do. You were so bad.'

'Was I? I'm like my father then, aren't I?' And Matthew drew away, turned over and pulled up the bedcovers.

Abby went wearily downstairs, the truth ringing in her ears. She asked Hannah for some wine. At least that was one thing that had improved since she came here. There was none of that thin vinegary stuff that Gil thought was wine. It was thick and red and went down wonderfully. She had two glasses before Gil came back for dinner, and felt a lot better.

They ate. At least, he ate. Abby couldn't manage a single mouthful. He didn't ask her about the funeral; he didn't drink any wine. He retreated to the office. Abby sat there, drinking wine until her hands shook. She didn't hear the knocker. The first inclination she had of anybody was when Hannah came through into the sitting-room, saying, 'Mr Edward Collingwood's here.'

Abby stared, sobered immediately, said, 'Bring him in here,' and went across the hall into the office.

Gil didn't look up, he was working.

'Edward's here,' Abby said. He looked up then, stared at her, through her. 'I've had Hannah put him into the sitting-room. Do you want me there?'

'No, it's all right,' he said.

He went out. Abby stood leaning against the desk in the office, shaking.

Gil was used to what his brother looked like, had spent so many hours watching him covertly from across the billiard hall. That place had been a sanctuary at one time and, more than that, it was the place where his brother had shown him friendship. Gil knew very well that the best thing brothers could be to one another was friends. Those first days at the billiard hall he had loved Edward like never before, had been a new person in that he had thought his brother cared for him. In his best hours he could imagine them as old men, sitting around the fire talking about their lives, comparing the good times and the bad and speaking of people they had known, and having their grandchildren around them. He thought that they would grow more like one another as they became older. He had heard of brothers doing that, of them starting the same sentence in the same way, pausing at the same time, laughing together. It would seem a nauseating similarity to the young, but he had for so long wanted something from his family that would show their regard, that he had loved Edward too much. Expectations of that kind were never fulfilled, yet he had believed it so. He knew now that he had been Edward's alibi for the kind of love which was not acceptable. Edward could not go home and tell his parents that he loved another man. What kind of society, what frightened people would deny a love like that? And the struggle against it had been costly.

His stupid heart was hopeful, was ready to begin again, to draw near. He reminded himself that there was no place to go here, nowhere near his brother was there a space for him.

'I thought you might have come to the funeral,' Edward said.

'Don't you think that would have been a little hypocritical?'

'Hypocrisy has its place at these affairs.' He paused for a moment and then said, 'I wanted to see you this once before I go. I'm leaving. Strange how it took my father's death to liberate me. Before, somehow, I couldn't go. Of course there was money. I've been keeping them for a long time.'

Gil's insides suddenly had a pair of iron grips around them, the pain was so bad that he could hardly speak.

'Where are you going?'

'France.' Edward smiled faintly. 'We always did intend to. Toby has found us a house not far from Bordeaux. A few acres, a big garden.'

Gil could not believe this.

'Toby?'

'Are you like everyone else and deceived? How could you be with what you know?'

'But he has children, sons, and a wife.'

'It's no good,' Edward said. 'No matter how hard you try, it doesn't work.'

'He'll lose his family, his parents and . . . everybody.'

'That's what passion does, isn't it? We have tried so hard and now we can't try any longer.'

Gil couldn't think of anything to say.

'Wine, decent bread, a few flowers and Tobe's happy. The rest was just from wanting to please other people and there's never any good in that. I won't be back. I just wanted to see Matthew one last time.'

You could be jealous of a child, Gil discovered, even if that child was your son and you loved him. Somewhere inside he was shouting, 'Me, me!' but no words came out. Words were weapons that he didn't know how to use. He was afraid of them, they could undo you in seconds.

'I haven't forgiven you.' Edward said this with a smile and Gil was only glad that he had no heart left to break, there were so many pieces by now that the damage was limited. Sometimes he thought comfortably that middle age would find him smug because there would be nothing left.

'I didn't expect you to,' he said.

'I know that you'll look after Matthew. Can I see him?'

Gil took him upstairs to where the child was sleeping, but a strange feeling began to gnaw at his insides. It was a familiar, sick feeling as when something was about to go wrong. When it happened you felt as though you should have known, as though you should have looked around you, located it before it got that far. Edward spent a little time upstairs, seeing Matthew at his best. Then they came back down again and stood in the sitting-room. Edward looked at him and the gladness that Gil had felt when Edward had arrived evaporated.

'I did love Helen,' Edward said. 'I know you think I didn't, that I used her like some kind of shield because of Toby, but I didn't. We were just friends then, at least I liked to think so, wanted to. I think he cared for me differently than I cared for him. There are many different kinds of love. I did love her. I didn't really marry her because our parents wanted it, I craved her. And she was pleased enough with me until I brought her to Bamburgh House and she saw you.'

Gil looked into the darkness beyond the windows and

remembered how Helen had looked when he had first seen her.

'After she saw you, my love affair was over,' Edward said.

'No.'

'It was an instant thing, wasn't it? I couldn't have been deceived about what you felt for one another. You loved her from the moment you set eyes on her.'

'Yes, but it wasn't—' Gil said and stopped.

'Wasn't what?'

'I can't explain. It wasn't the first time we'd met, or it seemed not to be.'

'Where had you seen her before?'

'I don't know.' He couldn't tell Edward about the house in Spain, or how he thought of their past that way.

'That's ridiculous, Gil.'

He sounded so normal, so natural, as though they had not been estranged for years and Gil's mind stored up the remark in case his brother should not be civil to him again this side of the grave.

'Are we talking about other lives here?' Edward said sceptically.

'No, of course not.'

'Then what?'

'I don't know. It ruined my life too!'

Edward pondered for a moment or two until Gil regretted the outburst.

'On our wedding night she wouldn't have me and all the nights that followed I wasn't you. I longed to be you.'

'She said you didn't want her, that you wanted to be away from her.'

'I had no choice. I shouldn't have gone through with the marriage, but I thought it was one of those passing fancies that women have and the settlements were all sorted out by then.'

'She loved you!'

'But she went to bed with you. Yes? My wife was a virgin when you had her, was she not?'

'God help me. I was second best.'

'You were never second in anything,' Edward said flatly. 'You don't believe in being second, you've proved that again and again. Don't you see yourself as you are? You're totally without principles. You will do whatever is required to reach what you choose. Your mind is with your – your reckless ambition and your taste for revenge. Even Abby. Look at her. You could have married her.'

'She wouldn't have me.'

'Was this before you seduced my wife or afterwards? Look at yourself, Gil, what success, what achievements and what cost. And as for Father, you took away everything, even his dignity.'

'You hated him too.'

'Not sufficiently to make him watch the house he loved fall into ruin and the gates of his shipyard locked against him. I didn't reduce him to taking handouts from his elder son, or dying in a mean, shabby hovel. How could you hate anybody that much?'

'He turned me out.'

'Oh yes, now we come to it. You bedded your brother's wife, deceived your own wife and each of them in her way killed herself over it—'

'No!'

'Yes, they did. But Helen won. Her child lives. And you think that he's yours.'

The sickness was a headache now and a dizziness but Gil said calmly, 'Are you going to tell me that he isn't?'

'No.' Edward looked clearly at him. 'The plain fact is that my wife had you and me together, if you'll forgive the bluntness. Contrary to what you believe, I do like women, I have enjoyed their bodies and even though my wife chose to give herself to you, she was so beautiful and I wanted her so badly that I took what she offered me. How naive you were. We were both bedding her. I don't think she knew whose child it was. I certainly don't.'

'But you let me think . . . and you let me take him. You let me take the blame. You watched Father put me out because of it. You let me leave with him. If you thought he was yours, why didn't you fight for him?'

Edward's gaze was patient.

'You're the most capable person I've ever met. You had more to offer—'

'I had nothing!'

'I knew that if you believed he was yours, you would move heaven and earth for him. And you have. He's happy and that's all I care about. How happy would he have been if there had been more fighting, if the truth had come out? How could he have been shielded from it all? It was bad enough that he should lose his mother. He needed a solid background. You've provided that very well. I have no intention of upsetting things and I'm about to make the life for myself that I want. I have Toby. In a way it's so much easier to love another man, and he loves me as no one else in my life ever has, completely and to the exclusion of everyone else. All I want is a little peace. I owe you nothing, you took what you could. I have to go. Toby is at my house making a daube, practising his French cooking. The smell of it will be halfway down the street by now. I don't suppose we shall ever meet again. I hope not. Goodbye, Gil.'

When he had gone, Gil went to bed. He pulled a pillow to him and closed his eyes and willed sleep to come to him. At least it was night, at least it was cold, at least it was October. He couldn't have borne that it should be summer and the stones of the house should be baked hard and the white curtains should catch the breeze beyond the bed and billow like sails upon the water.

Chapter Twenty-four

That autumn Gil went out to the country to see Bamburgh House and was ashamed of his handiwork. The house itself looked affronted. Birds flew in and out of the empty windows. Inside, everything was wet and in bad repair. It looked worse in the winter weather. The lawns were knee high; the bare trees were as black as mourning and there was about it an unnatural silence such as he had heard only in graveyards before now. He had to suppress the desire to close the outside doors in some futile form of protection or reparation. He wished that he had not gone there and when he went back to his neat house in Jesmond images of the house haunted him. Even at work he could not put from his mind the sadness which he felt. He no longer remembered with bitterness being thrown out of there or the bad way that his father had treated him. All he could remember was standing in the drawing-room and hearing Helen play the piano. He had had to stop himself running toward the sounds.

He wanted to pull it down so that all evidence of her would be gone, but he couldn't. His inclination was to repair it and go and live there. It was, he knew, the only way in which he would get his mother out of that awful little hovel where his father had died. She insisted on living there as though it was some kind of shrine, rather than a gloomy little street house. Gil gave her money, but she mourned William and insisted that she could not move since Edward would be coming back. There was no point in telling her that he would not do so. She believed that he would and she would not listen to the gossips who said that Edward had run off with Toby. Her son could not have done such a thing and therefore he had not. She told everybody that Edward had endured a dreadful life because of what Gil and Helen had done, that it had been too much for him and he had gone, but he would come back. Many other people did not believe that men could do such things; his mother was not alone in her ideas. They could not have run away together, they had both gone but they had gone differently, separately. The Emorys, anxious to stem the talk, agreed with this and put about a tale that their son had worked too hard and that his mind was affected. Insanity was the easier option.

Charlotte would not see Gil. He did go once, but she would not answer the door and took to shouting at people through the letter-box. After that, when Abby went to see her, the doors would be locked and the house in darkness. Abby knew that Charlotte rarely went out. She thought that people were speaking about her and laughing on the streets. Abby tried to persuade her to come to them, but she would not move.

'There is one thing which would work,' Abby said, confronting him in the little office one November evening when the rain had poured down the windows for two days.

'What's that?'

'You could take her to live at Bamburgh House again.'

He was surprised at her perception.

'She wouldn't.'

'I think she would.'

'It's in very bad repair.'

'You could put it right. You have nothing else to do with your money. I think you owe her that.'

'I owe her nothing!' He got up. He didn't intend to, but he couldn't talk about this calmly.

'What will you do then? Let her stay there and go out of her mind, because that's what she will do.'

'Always straight to the point,' he said savagely.

'Don't you care about her at all, not even a little?'

'No!'

'Then why did you let her see Matthew?'

'That was for his sake.'

'He's not going to think very highly of you if you don't help her.'

'I don't want to go back there.'

'I think you should.'

Gil looked at her. She hadn't changed from being a young girl. Her eyes were so blue and intense and there was that strength, that steeliness, which insisted on doing the right thing.

'I'll do it on one condition,' he said.

'Which is?'

'That you come with me.'

'Me?' Abby's blue eyes rounded. 'I'm not going to live there. I always hated it. Besides, I love this house. Are you trying to tell me that you can't afford to keep two houses?'

'No.'

'Well then, I shall stay here.'

'Then so will I.'

'Gil, this is my home. I was born here. I spent the happiest childhood anyone could have. My mother and father both died in this house. I love it.'

'Then we won't go anywhere,' he said.

Abby couldn't move him. She knew it was wrong. She tried telling herself that it was his fault alone that his mother was behaving as though she should be locked up, but as the days went by and all she could get from Charlotte was crying from the far side of the front door, she lay awake at night worrying about the responsibility. All she knew was that she had been unhappy away from here, that all those supposedly exciting times in London and Venice and France and all the other places Robert had taken her were times when she had longed to be here in Newcastle. She could not give up this house for anybody, much less for a woman she had always despised as weak and stupid.

Even Matthew could not get his grandmother to open the door. All the contact they had was that if they left groceries outside, Charlotte would take them in. She allowed no visitors and she did not leave the house. Abby looked around at the four walls she had chosen instead of Charlotte and despised herself. She despised Gil even more for making such terms and didn't talk to him, but when he did come home, which wasn't often, he had missed tea and had to eat separately. Abby, from politeness' sake, had to endure his company and make conversation and not throw her wine glass at him across the table as she longed to do.

'Couldn't we keep the house on?' she asked eventually.

'What would be the point?'

'It's always better to own property. We could rent it out.'

He looked at her across the table.

'Have you ever considered what you might do if your parents really died?' he said.

Abby went white; she could feel herself.

'I don't know what you mean,' she said.

'Yes, you do. You're keeping them alive by staying here. You still have your mother's books and your father's cufflinks and—'

'Those are keepsakes. I've changed a lot of things in the house and you shouldn't say such a thing!'

'Have you ever loved anybody as much as you loved them?'

'No, I haven't and if you had an ounce of decency you wouldn't hold your mother to ransom over something as stupid as a house! You waited until your father died before you did anything. Are you going to wait until she does?'

'I don't know, am I?'

'You're low!' Abby was on her feet with temper. 'Low and

devious! I don't think you care about anything. You unscrupulous bastard!'

Gil sat there as though somebody was being rude at a dinner party and it was nothing to do with him.

'When I think of what you used to be like,' Abby said breathlessly, 'when I think—'

'Don't think too long,' Gil said and he got up and walked out.

Abby lasted three more days and then she went to Charlotte's house, shouted her name through the letter-box and, when she could hear her breathing from the other side of the door, she said, 'What if I told you that you could go back to Bamburgh House?'

There was no answer.

'Charlotte? Can you hear me?'

There was another short pause and then Charlotte said, 'I can't though, can I?'

'If Gil had it repaired you could. Would you like that?'

'We were happy there when the children were little and we were young. We were happy. We had everything. I had jewellery and furs and beautiful gowns from London. And we had lots of servants and grey horses and . . . William was a good husband to me. I miss him.'

This had not occurred to Abby. Nobody thought of William like that, but his wife obviously did.

'I couldn't live there alone.'

'We would come with you.'

The sentence was out. Abby heard it and knew there was no way in which she could retract it. There was silence from beyond the door. She wished that Charlotte would refuse, prayed that she would. Abby thought all that was keeping her upright was the fact that she was living in the house that she loved so much. She could not give that house up for Charlotte, there was no reason why she should, yet things were not good at home. Gil had given up any pretence at family life and was coming home less and less. Abby was haunted with the way that Gil had behaved as they had grown further apart. She tried to reason with herself. They were not married; she was not responsible for him, but since Edward had left and his father had died, Gil seemed barely to notice anyone or anything beyond work and whatever he did when he was not at work and not at home. And Abby knew very well what he was doing. She had to tell herself not to panic, that Gil was not weak like Robert. He would not ruin them financially no matter what vices he took up and he would not take a gun to himself, he wasn't made like that. William had been strong in some ways and Gil was like him. She was quite certain that, no matter what happened, Gil would be at his desk at work by seven in the morning. She wished sometimes that she could just go over to make sure that he was, because more and more he didn't come back at night.

The day after she had made this announcement to Charlotte she actually tested this theory. Gil hadn't come back that night and she had wanted to talk to him and not wanted to. Wanted to won and so, early the next morning, she got up and made her way across the town to the number two yard. It was the big place and he spent most of his time there. Work was fully started when she reached the office. The clerk in the outside office looked surprised to see her, but ushered her inside without a word. There was Gil looking as though he had gone home early the evening before, had dinner and gone early to bed. He was bright-eyed, immaculately neat and scrupulously polite. Abby did not know how to get past this kind of defence. She wondered where he kept his clean clothes, whether whores were offering a laundry service as well as the other kind these days. Nobody who had drunk brandy half the night and screwed some little bitch into the mattress could look like that, Abby reasoned.

'Coffee?' he said, having greeted her.

She shook her head.

'Tea?'

'No! I didn't come here for—'

He looked at her attentively.

'I want to talk to you,' Abby said. 'When are you coming back?'

'Six o'clock?'

'No, I mean when are you really coming back?'

He didn't look at her. He leaned back against the front of the desk and regarded the rug in front of it with rapt concentration.

Abby sighed.

'I have suggested to your mother that we should go and live at Bamburgh House and she has agreed. If I come with you and give up my father's house, will you come home?'

He stood for a few moments before he said, 'All right.'

Abby only remembered to breathe when she had left the office.

It cost her a good deal to say goodbye to the house she had loved so much. She felt wretched, but there was nothing practical to be done. Gil sold the house quickly, presumably in case she should change her mind and as though he had had buyers waiting in the wings. Once it did not belong to them, Abby was downhearted and wished to be gone before she could bear no more. Charlotte came to live with them and Matthew spent a lot of time with his grandmother. He and Georgina stayed up for dinner, although Georgina was inclined to nod before it was over. One such night, just before they moved, Matthew surprised Abby by saying, 'All my friends are going away to school soon. Do you think I might be able to do that?'

Abby knew that Gil wanted to be friends with his son again, but the colour drained from his face.

'Boarding school?' Abby said, to fill the gap.

'I could be on a proper cricket team and Harry English says they have great larks in the dorm after lights out. If I don't go I shall be left here for weeks and weeks and they'll be coming back telling me all about it, and Harry's brother, Timothy, is going.'

Gil said nothing.

'When is Timothy going?' Abby said.

'Next autumn. Could we go and look at his school?'

Abby glanced across the table at Gil. She knew that Matthew would not appeal directly to Gil.

'Grandma thinks it's a good idea,' Matthew urged.

'Education is very important,' Charlotte said. 'William always thought so. Boarding school is good for boys. It makes them independent and strong.'

Gil let the silence empty and widen. Luckily the meal was over. Everyone left the table. Gil went into the little office and closed the door. Abby deliberately made herself not go after him. She had no place in there and if he had wanted conversation, she reasoned, he would not have gone in. She put the children to bed. She occupied Charlotte until it was late and then she went to bed. It was a thankless thing to do. Sleep did not arrive. She put on a dressing-gown and went back downstairs. Softly she opened the door of the office. He looked up.

'Maybe we could go out and look at the house some time?' she said.

Gil sat back in his chair.

'Is it nearly finished?' Abby said.

He stood up.

'I've got the plans somewhere.'

'You didn't tell me.'

'I didn't think you were interested.'

'Show me.'

He located rolled-up papers, which she had assumed were work, and spread them across the desk. Abby went and peered hard at the different drawings, the front of the house, the sides, the back.

'It doesn't look the same.'

'It isn't meant to.'

'You took the columns away!'

'They weren't actually doing anything important, holding anything up, they were just . . . decorative.'

'That's a matter of opinion.'

He smiled.

'It makes it look entirely different,' Abby said.

'This is the inside. We've moved the kitchen and chopped up the hall here—'

'I rather liked the hall. Has your mother seen these?'

'No.'

'Bathrooms!' Abby said.

'And proper heating. It was never warm.'

'I'd like to see it.'

He rolled up the plans.

'You don't have to humour me,' he said. 'Matthew can go away to school if he wants to.'

'That wasn't why—' Abby began and then stopped.

'Maybe you should go to bed.'

Abby's face went hot with temper but she controlled it.

'I'd like to see the house.'

'You'll see it when it's finished.'

'Did you do all the designing alterations yourself?'

'Of course.'

'Did you pull down the bedroom where we slept the night, or the bedroom where you spent the nights with Helen, or with Rhoda? Do you seriously believe you can go back there and live after that?'

'It's all different,' he said. 'If you'd looked closely at the plans, the upstairs is altered beyond recognition.'

'And you won't remember?'

'I've done all my remembering. I'm going to go back there and have it for mine now.'

'Isn't that what your father did?'

Gil didn't answer that.

'It was your idea,' he said.

* * *

They moved in the middle of the summer which helped, she thought. It was one of the hardest things that Abby had done because the house in Jesmond had been sold. She felt like a deserter. The garden was full of all the flowers that her mother had loved and she was aware that once she left, she would not be able to come back again. It felt so cruel to leave this place that she loved and move to one that she despised. The last few days, while they were packing, she barely looked at Gil or spoke to him but every moment she was aware of what she was losing.

The children were so excited. They knew that they were moving to a big country house, that they could have ponies, that there would be lots of space, that they could choose their bedrooms and they could have big parties, Grandmother had said so. Abby was inclined to think that they would miss their friends, but she didn't say that to them. She didn't want to dampen their enthusiasm. She kept busy, packing, making sure that everything went well. On the moving day she was too miserable to say goodbye to the place. When she reached the first sight of Bamburgh House, it was such a shock that she forgot she had hated it. It did look different; it looked welcoming. The huge pillars were gone and the front of the house was open to the light and the day. The long windows were filled with sunshine and it seemed to Abby that she could see Gil's hand everywhere after that. Inside, where there had not been huge windows there were now, so that the house caught every bit of sunlight. The walls were no longer dark and dingy; the stairs which had been stone had been replaced with wood; the hall which had had huge stone pillars and stone walls had been altered, too. There were fireplaces and wooden floors and it was warm. Upstairs, there were bathrooms between the bedrooms with doors leading in on both sides and there again were more windows, but it was warm from the central heating and there were thick carpets.

It was barely furnished apart from that. Gil had done nothing other than basic alterations and the furniture they had brought with them disappeared into the huge spaces. Charlotte and

William had furnished every inch and nothing much was left but, with the evening light coming in through the drawing-room windows, Abby could imagine what it might look like. Abby thought Charlotte would want to begin at once making it as it had been, but when Abby tactfully suggested that she might like to help she looked horrified.

'I did that once, I don't want to have to do it again.'

Charlotte, Abby thought, had recovered quite remarkably. She looked well, happy, even thinner. She liked being with the children.

Abby began to furnish the house. She did it slowly and could not help being pleased with the results. There wasn't much you could do with a library where the walls were oak panelled, indeed, she rather liked that room; but the dining-room she did in varying shades of yellow and when the morning sun came in and they had breakfast in there she was comfortable with what she had done.

The summer was here and she discovered the gardens and the various flowers that she knew her mother would have liked. She talked to the new gardeners, made plans for next year, read books; she thought that the one disadvantage about her father's house was that you couldn't make progress in the garden, as much had been done as could be, whereas here everything could be altered apart from the way that the quarry garden had its rocks and the various trees. Much of it was a wilderness and she was keen to begin again. She hadn't realised she was talking so much about it until she noticed over dinner one night that Gil was not listening. He was the only one there, the others had all gone from the table when the meal was finished. She shut up and listened to the silence.

'I didn't mean to go on about it,' she apologised.

'No, no, it's nice. Do you still miss the other house?'

'Not much. Not as much as I did, not since I learned to bore you over the dinner table about the garden.'

'It looks fine,' he said, 'so does this room.'

'Do you think it does? I'm worried you won't like things.'

'Why?'

'Because you don't say anything. I can't ask you, either, because you aren't here or you're in the study working. I have to just go ahead and hope you don't hate it.'

'Why worry?'

'Well, because you have taste.'

'God preserve us, do I? Don't tell anybody.'

Early that summer they went to look around various schools for Matthew. He was so enthusiastic. He ran around talking to people and asking about the sports teams and enthusing over the dormitories. It all looked wonderful, Abby thought, the huge and imposing buildings, the great stretches of green playing fields, the hundreds of boys all wearing the same clothes. Gil tried to talk him out of it, saying that there were perfectly good schools in Newcastle. Charlotte took the opposite view and Matthew was more inclined to listen to her these days.

'Why doesn't Dad want me to go?' Matthew said wistfully to Abby one evening when they had come back from looking at a well-known school in Yorkshire.

'Because he hated school,' Abby said, on her knees weeding a border. She liked doing this, it made her feel better and she needed to feel better. Gil was working fourteen hours a day and was silent when he came home. She tried to make herself talk to him or, even better, go to him, but she was convinced that if she went to bed with him, Helen would somehow be there. There was an atmosphere in the house. She was convinced it was of her own making and sometimes she thought she heard the faint sounds of a piano when no one was playing.

'But I'm not him,' Matthew pointed out reasonably.

Abby sat back on her heels and looked at him through the sunlight.

'He knows that and you may go if you wish. He hasn't said that you can't.'

'I know that.' Matthew dug his toe into the soil. 'But he doesn't want me to, does he?'

Abby couldn't say that Gil felt he had lost his child, firstly to his mother and then to his parents' hatred for him and now he was going to lose him physically to the kind of establishment which he despised.

'If you're happy there he won't mind, and if you aren't happy you don't have to stay.'

'Did he have to stay?'

'Yes, he did.'

'Why?'

'Because your grandfather insisted and . . . he wasn't very clever at school.'

'But he is very clever,' Matthew pointed out. Abby rather wished Gil had been there to hear the pride in his son's voice.

'It's a different kind of cleverness.'

'I'm good at cricket,' Matthew said. Abby watched him go racing back up the garden path towards the house and thought that Matthew would probably do very well at boarding school. He would be the sort of boy who wouldn't mind getting up for early morning cricket practice and he had a good memory for all those dreadful lessons. A great many men got through life with little more.

There was a part of Abby that became happy that summer. Georgina loved the country and Gil bought her a pony and taught her to ride. He spent more time with her daughter than he did with her, but Abby let him. She knew that he needed to be with the child. On Sundays when he was at home, he and Georgina went riding in the fine weather and she always declined the invitation. Abby couldn't abide horses. She thought they were the stupidest animals on God's earth, but Georgina adored her pony as only little girls can and Abby had to stop herself from objecting to the time she spent at the stables. She was convinced that the grooms used bad language and said things to Georgina that they shouldn't but the effect was that she turned into a lovely girl that summer and she had something she had never had before, a secure home with a man who came back, even if he was late. Abby could have forgiven Gil a lot for that. He was also a safe man, she thought, remembering Jos Allsop and Rhoda. Georgina could climb all over him, hug and kiss him, know that he would throw her into the air and catch her, tease her and that she would remember him later as the father to her child, when she was grown up. Abby remembered Henderson with such affection and it was important.

She knew also that Gil was taking comfort in the fact that Georgina was not going away. That autumn Matthew went to school. For days and days there had been arrangements to make, clothes to buy, the big trunk open in his bedroom. The maids named socks and packed pyjamas and then they all went by train to Matthew's school in Yorkshire where his best friend was going too. He didn't even mind leaving Gil and Abby; he ran off with Jonathan, not looking back. Abby thought she had never seen a boy so right for boarding school.

That night when they got home Gil prowled the house as though he was going out. He didn't go, but Abby watched carefully. He eventually shut himself into the study and then, when it was very late, he went upstairs. Abby had gone to bed hours since, but she hadn't slept so she got up, tied a dressing-gown tightly around her waist and knocked on the door. She couldn't hear anything and hesitated, but when she opened the door he was standing by the fire as you might at an inn when you had just come in from the cold, fully dressed except for his jacket and holding a whisky glass in his hand. That made her hesitate again. Men and alcohol were such a dangerous combination. She had not forgotten what Robert was like after several drinks, insisting on going to bed with her, the whisky sour on his breath and his actions so uncaring, mechanical, cold.

'At least close the door,' he advised.

She came into the room and shut the door.

'Are you thinking about Matthew?'

'Leaving him there was like being ripped in half.' It was not, Abby concluded, his first drink. She waited for maudlin reminiscences, for long drawn-out sentences, for a tirade on the horrors of public school, but nothing happened. Robert was too much in her mind. Drunk, he had said everything he thought. Drunk or sober, Gil did not, she surmised, say even a tenth of what he was thinking and he sifted it all first. This sentence had slipped past the whisky, but it was the only one.

'He'll like it,' Abby said helpfully. 'He'll be on the cricket team in no time.'

'It's the wrong term,' Gil said.

'Oh. Yes. Rugby?'

Abby made herself cross the room to him but he didn't encourage her, he didn't even look or make conversation. It was rather like opening the door of an ice house and hoping for even a small blaze.

'I thought you might have gone out,' she said. 'I thought to Newcastle to that dreadful Irishwoman's establishment.'

'She's Scottish,' he said.

'I thought you might have.'

He said nothing. Gil might not have the hang of conversation, Abby thought, but he had definitely mastered the pause.

'Gil—'

'No.'

Abby wished very much now that she had stayed in her room, because he turned around and looked at her and it was not the kind of look which you met happily.

'You don't know what I was going to say,' Abby pointed out.

'It doesn't matter. Nothing you can say will make any difference so you might as well go to bed.'

Abby went.

Chapter Twenty-five

Sometimes it's difficult to distinguish between nightmares and life. Sometimes you think you're going to wake up and then you realise that you aren't asleep, that you won't have the relief of waking up and knowing that everything is all right, that your mother is downstairs cooking eggs and your father is walking the dogs in the field and that there will be butter and honey and sunlight and it will be morning. So when Gil found himself on a boat for France, no, let's be clear, he told himself, it's a ship, it's too bloody big to be a boat and the grandson of a boat builder, and the son of a shipbuilder, ought to know the difference to these things; he was on a ship without reason that he could think of, that was when he concluded comfortably that he was asleep and it was just a dream and whatever happened it didn't matter because he would awaken, he just had to get through it.

It wasn't a big ship; it wasn't the kind of ship he built. He saw all the design faults, he saw all the repairs that needed doing. He thought that if he had had any choice, with his knowledge, he wouldn't have got on the damned thing. Worst of all, it didn't balance. Now that was all right as long as the weather was fair, but so often between England and France the weather was bad, but he was reasonably happy about the trip because his brother was there. Edward was actually smiling at him as he hadn't smiled for a long time. Gil couldn't think how long it was. He was happy then. If Edward was smiling, there couldn't be much wrong. Toby was there, too, and they were talking together and laughing and it was like it had been in Toby's garden, at least he thought it was, when the flowers were out and the sun was hot and the wine was cool. They were all going to France, he had known that they were. They were going to build a new life there. The sea was calm like the pond in the park at home, the sunlight turned the water to silk, they sat on deck and drank wine. Toby described the house on the river with its orchard and its garden and its fields, where the hens scratched in the yard and the kittens played in the hay and the unfortunate rabbits sat in their hutch prior to being banged on the back of the neck, cooked and eaten. The dogs slept in the shade during the hot afternoons and friends came to call to take them off to five-course, three-hour lunches in tiny village restaurants. In the evenings the river played its own music and sometimes it rained hard and briefly and refreshed the trees so that the leaves looked polished.

Gil was looking forward to all this, but in a way he didn't want the journey to end. He was tired; he wanted to stay for a little while until he became impatient of the calm sea and the warm air and the way that the ship moved slowly away from England toward the shores of France.

Then it was night time. They were still at sea and, as they sat outside, it seemed impossible, suddenly mist began to steal from the horizon towards them. It wasn't a slow thing. One minute it was clear and the next the mist was coming towards them, silently moving over the surface of the sea until there was nothing in his vision beyond the ship itself. Soon the calm night was gone. The wind got up and, although the mist cleared slightly so that he could see the size of the waves that were beginning to chafe at the bows, it was as though the ship were held and constricted by that fog. It began to rain, which should have cleared the fog away but it didn't and the rain and the waves got all mixed up so that there was water everywhere and the ship began to lurch.

At first he was down below deck. Each time the ship rolled he and everything else in the cabin slid all the way along to the opposite side and he would wait, suspended there on the floor with everything against him, pinned. There would be a few moments when the ship's side was high out of the water and then the ship would roll the other way and he would slide all the way back across the floor to the other side and everything in the cabin would slide with him. Then he was on deck. He could see the water coming over the bows and he could see the size of the waves. They were so big and so wide that he couldn't see anything above them or anything around them and the water swilled across the decks. Toby was there, smiling, so it couldn't be that bad, and he went below and there was Edward.

'What's it like up there?'

'It's quite a storm, old boy,' he said.

'This isn't fair, you know, Tobe, we are the men who make the ships, we shouldn't have to put up with this.'

'I wish there had been another way. I wish that I had been a bird and could have flown. I didn't ever trust these blessed things.'

'I wish we were in France.'

'We will be soon. The storm can't last much longer.'

He went back up on deck again and the ship rolled and rolled and rolled and rolled and the whole world turned into sea. There was nothing but water. There was no ship to be seen. Then it was cold and he was falling and there was a great wall of salt water.

It was just a dream. He was down below. Toby was up on deck and then he wasn't and Gil knew that the house in France was just as much of a dream as this, that it had never existed and never would exist except in their imagination. It was the nightmare that was real, the storm and the fog and the ship rolling over. He was down below and he realised now that they would not get to France. Funny, but because it was a dream he didn't really care. He could indulge himself. He could think to himself that the world was well lost. He could think that their sons meant nothing to them now, that nothing mattered beyond the love between them. It had been everything. It had been the most important thing in both their lives, so if it should end here, it was right. They had given up everything for one another so it was fitting, comfortable. The October night was not cold and he remembered what he had heard about October storms. They should have thought of that before they set out, he acknowledged. Suddenly it was cold, it was frightening, it was that horrible helpless falling beyond the side of the cabin and he was shouting Toby's name and somebody was screaming.

Gil woke up. He was in his bedroom at Bamburgh House, not the bedroom he had had as a child but the best room in the house. The October sunlight was pouring through the big wide windows where his father used to sleep, the bedroom he had claimed as his right. He turned over. The bed was soft and reassuring and the sheets were cool on his hot skin. He had thrown the bedcovers off at some time and only the sheet covered him. The curtains had been drawn back by the maid some time since and the windows were open as he preferred them. When he opened his eyes he saw the tray with the tea which she had left and had grown cold. It was late. It was, in fact, Sunday. Abby would have taken Georgina to church by now, so at least he did not have to meet her steady gaze over breakfast. He dismissed the dream. His brother had gone to France with Toby a year ago and, although he had heard nothing, had expected to hear nothing, he had no doubt that they were happy together, having cast off all their responsibilities. He got up, shaved, bathed, dressed and did all the other tedious morning things, then he went downstairs to meet the day.

Abby came back. Georgina reproached him because he had not got up early to go riding, but the day had clouded into rain so Gil could not even promise her that he would go later. He and

Abby sat by the fire having a drink before the big Sunday meal. Then a carriage pulled up outside and a man got out. They didn't recognise him, but Gil did when he was announced, it was Mr Emory, Toby's father. Gil hadn't seen him since Toby and Henrietta's wedding and he had aged. Gil wasn't surprised.

He hadn't been able to put the dream from his mind and now that he was confronted with somebody who would have mattered to it, Gil was most unhappy. He offered Mr Emory a drink and to sit down close by the fire. The man accepted whisky and a seat, but he didn't look straight at Gil and after a minute or two, clutching his whisky tightly in his hand he said, 'I have some grave news, Mr Collingwood. I have had a letter from France. There has been an accident.'

'A shipping accident?' Gil said, unable to stop himself.

Mr Emory looked keenly at him.

'Only in a manner of speaking. It was a boat.'

A boat. It was just a boat. He had been wrong; it was just a dream. Only a boat.

'My son and your brother . . . the boat capsized on the river near – near to their home. They are both dead.'

Mr Emory looked out of the window as though he could see something, whereas in fact the short autumn day was not offering much light any more even though it was not yet two o'clock. The weather was bad and the days were short.

'All I wanted was a son. Every time we had a child . . . I was so proud of him.'

'You have three grandsons,' Abby said helpfully.

'My son was disgraced before he died. We tried to tell people differently, that he was suffering from some disorder . . . He's better dead.'

Gil was half out of his seat, words were on his lips, but Abby's fingers closed hard around his arm as she said, looking straight at Mr Emory, 'We were both very fond of him and we don't judge.'

'Your generation is extremely lax.'

'I understand that every older generation thinks the same of every younger.'

'In my day a man was a man and a woman was a woman and women did not argue.'

'Insufferable prig!' Abby shouted when he had gone.

She told the cook to give Georgina some dinner and explained to the little girl what had happened. Abby had discovered that if you told children the truth, it was surprising how well they reacted. Georgina remembered Edward only vaguely so she didn't care about that, but she cared that Gil would be upset.

'I thought he might like to go for a walk,' Abby said.

'He won't want his dinner now,' Georgina said, 'and it's a shame when it's Sunday.'

Abby kissed her daughter and went back to the drawing-room. He was sitting as she had left him, staring into the fire. 'Do you want to go out for some air?'

Gil glanced at the window. The day was dark and the mist had come down, rolling off the moortops just as it had in his dream across the water. It was starting to rain, lightly against the windowpane. He shook his head.

'No.'

'Another drink?'

'That would be good.'

She poured him a large scotch. They sat there and drank too much. It didn't take long; neither of them had had anything to eat since breakfast. The servants had enough sense not to come in and build up the fire. The level on the bottles went down steadily as Abby kept the glasses supplied and by the end of the afternoon he had fallen asleep in her arms. She kept him close and stroked his hair and thanked God for alcohol.

Mr Emory tried to insist that Toby's body was brought home for burial in the family plot just as though nothing had happened. Gil managed to frustrate this aim. It wasn't difficult; the authorities didn't want anything to do with it, so he went to France and made sure that the two young men were buried together as they would have wanted to be. He was glad that he had gone and done what he thought was right, if only because it made him feel better. The worst thing was that when he went to see the French lawyer about what was to be done with the house, he found that they had left the house to him.

'No, no,' Gil said, in the lawyer's office, 'Mr Emory has dependents.'

The lawyer frowned and he looked so much like Mr Brampton that Gil wondered if it was the same man in different guise.

'Needy people?'

'No, they're very well off, rich—'

'This has been left, as I understand it, to one or to the other if anything happened and then to you. It was their wish. We ought to respect the wishes of the dead. We are a long way from England, Mr Collingwood, in legal terms. Would Mr Emory's family want the house?'

'I shouldn't think so.'

'It is a very nice house.'

It was a very nice house beside a singing river. The smell of lemons and oranges came from the glass house attached and the curtains in all the bedrooms were white. Down the street in the square during the night there was the smell of baking. Gil knew because he stayed in the house where his brother and his brother's lover had been happy. From the hills came the breeze, from the church the sound of a bell, in the square children played and sometimes just before he fell asleep he thought that he could hear the piano at Bamburgh House and see Helen's slender fingers playing Mozart. He caught the colours of her dresses in the corners of the bedroom against the white walls, those dresses she had bought in Newcastle with him when Edward had gone duck shooting on the Solway and left her there. Sometimes she had just left the room and there was the sound of her laughter down the garden paths and across the river. And in the distance two young men were rowing upstream and singing silly English songs and laughing and all the while the river flowed beyond the windows.

Chapter Twenty-six

Matthew came home for Christmas, full of energy and stories about his new school and with the kind of glowing report that Abby felt sure Gil had never had. He had been top of the class in almost everything and regaled Georgina's reluctant ears with boastful tales of his exploits and doings. Georgina complained to Abby that she wished Matthew would go back to school. Matthew went to Gil in the study one evening and asked if he could go to work with him. Gil was astonished and rather pleased.

'You haven't offered to take me,' Matthew said. 'Other boys' fathers do.'

'I didn't realise you wanted to. I thought you might want to do something else when you get older.'

'What?'

'A doctor or a lawyer or . . . you aren't very old yet.'

'But that's what we do, we're shipbuilders. We're the best shipbuilders on the Tyne.'

So he went to work with Gil, questioning everything, talking to the men, going around the various departments. Only when it was the end of the day and they were back in Gil's office did Matthew say, 'The shipyard gates don't have our name on them like other people's. Why don't they?'

'Because originally two of them belonged to Abby's father, Henderson and he was called Reed, as you know.'

'But the third yard was ours.'

'I didn't want to upset Abby by renaming them.'

'You could call it Reed and Collingwood – or Collingwood and Reed. I don't think she'd mind.'

'I would rather leave it. I don't think it matters what we're called as long as we do the best work and people know it.'

Back at dinner that evening, Matthew said to Abby, 'Don't you think the number three yard should have the Collingwood name on it?'

'Matthew—' Gil said.

'It was my grandfather's, after all. Nothing has our name on it.'

'I don't think people are likely to forget him because of that,' Gil said dryly.

'I agree with Matthew,' Charlotte said.

'You can agree all you like,' Gil said, 'it won't make any difference.'

Edward's death had affected Charlotte greatly, Abby thought, and she blamed Gil, though not in front of him. Abby had expected that. Helen and Gil were to blame for every wrong which hit the family, according to Charlotte, though she had to admit that there could be some truth in it. What man would not have looked for some other kind of solace when his younger brother had stolen and seduced his wife? Abby tried to talk to Gil on several occasions but, not surprisingly, she thought, he had nothing to say. His mother confined her remarks to her friends and to Abby, but he knew what she was saying behind his back, Abby felt certain.

It snowed heavily the first week that Matthew was at home. Abby watched it from the little room she had adopted as hers for writing letters and seeing the cook and making up menus and sorting out the day-to-day matters of the house. She stopped writing her letter on the Saturday afternoon and watched

Georgina outside. She was making snow angels for Gil. Abby thought that her child was the one person he ever really relaxed in front of and only then when he was alone with her. Unobserved now, so he thought, he was making snow angels too and they were laughing. They went on to build a snowman. Abby felt left out. She went and put on her outdoor things and followed them outside. Georgina showed her the snowman and then declared that she was cold and was going inside, her gloves were soggy and her fingers were numb. Gil and Abby walked across the lawns and into the quarry garden. In there it was like a fairytale, the trees laden with snow, the stones brushed with it, the paths white and untrodden until they got there.

He wandered away in front. Abby picked up a handful of snow, squashed it into a snowball and threw it at him. It hit him square in the middle of his back. He turned around and threw one at her just as accurately and then another and then another.

'All right, all right!' Abby said, squealing, and he came to her and brushed the snow from her coat. 'Why do men always do that?'

'What?'

'Compete, mow you down, whatever. You try to get the better of me.'

He moved away again. Abby tried to think what to say. It was the closest they had been since the afternoon when they had received the news of Edward's death and he had fallen asleep with his head in her lap. She threw another snowball at him and he laughed as it missed and went past. Then he came back to her. He looked at her for a moment and then he put one hand firmly into the middle of her back and pulled her to him and kissed her.

Abby had been hoping for conversation, had been trying for weeks to talk to him. She knew that Edward's death had upset him badly and she had wanted to help. His grieving for his brother was something totally private; he couldn't or wouldn't share it and had told her nothing of what had happened in France. That afternoon when they had drunk too much and he had fallen asleep with his head in her lap had been as close as they had got and he had not even acknowledged it, just woken up, got up and left the room. Until now, that had been all. Now he had hold of her in a very definite way and it was not, Abby knew, a precursor to a meaningful conversation. Within seconds she would have had to struggle to get away and he was pressing on her mouth the kind of kisses which she had forgotten and well remembered, sweet and deep and rather less decent than anything that should have taken place outside. She made a tentative attempt to stop him. This was not a good idea. Somebody might see. It was daylight. It was freezing. There were several inches of snow and even Robert had not been this unsubtle. Gil had been around whores too long, Abby thought.

Being in a bedroom with the windows open to crisp frost was the nearest Abby had come to this. He was not content with kisses and got his hands inside her clothes with the kind of swift expertise which Abby had long ceased to admire in men. Women's clothing was about as intricate as it could be, but it didn't seem to make any difference. You could tell how old or experienced a man was in ways like that and Gil's experience betrayed him.

Abby would have talked to him if she had imagined he was going to listen but he was past that. He had been beyond conversation since Matthew had gone to school, so there was no chance of that here. She could not help remembering also the lover that he had been, gentle, kind and warm. That was not the man who drew her down into several inches of snow. The ground was icy, wet and unyielding and it had begun to sleet, not big white flakes of snow, but hard like bullets and the sky was a peculiar dark grey, like steel. She said his name a couple of times in protest, but he didn't hear her. The trees where the snow had not covered them were bare and wet and black and the stones in the quarry garden threw huge jagged shadows across the twisting paths.

Most unhappy now, Abby had to make a decision. Was she

going to stop him? Was she going to tell him that she wanted to talk to him, when this was the first time he had come near her in so very long? It was not even that she trusted him to be kind to her any longer. He was too hurt for that. When your worst fears have all come true, what is there left? She knew that Gil had loved his brother with the kind of desperation that would not be dispelled. He had loved Edward without any love in return and that was the hardest thing in the world. She had not forgotten his face or his silence on the day that Edward had left. Gil didn't know how to shed tears, so there had been no release, not even a word. He had not seen his brother again and now he never would, neither had he gone to anyone for any kind of comfort.

Abby was beginning to get extremely angry with herself. Somehow she should have read this situation and stopped it before it started. He would have understood, listened. He was not Robert, not insensitive and uncaring so that it would have cost her nothing to deny him. He had always tasted and felt wonderful to her. Now he was blind and deaf, only his instincts were working. He had done this dozens of times to women he paid. Abby called herself names. She felt stupid. And her body perversely wanted him, even here. She wished she could kill him.

Soaked, frozen, furious, Abby knew with a sinking heart that he was going to do what they called locally 'giving her a bloody good seeing to'; she could tell from the concentrated way he went about it. Gil was meticulous about everything he did. It wouldn't change anything, things like this didn't. She felt stupid.

His deft hands had discarded her underwear and reached her body. It shouldn't have mattered. Robert had taken her dozens of times when he was drunk, when she didn't want him to. Gil was not drunk and she did want him to, only not like this, not from bitterness and whatever place he had come to in his mind with his father's death on his conscience and his brother's hatred. She let him have her and was immediately sorry. He couldn't even be like Robert, careless and clumsy; he had to be himself, accurate and sure. Was this what William had been like? Had he resented and hated his background and his parents and himself so much in the end that he would use Charlotte this hard? Would Gil have noticed if she had made further feeble attempts to stop him? Perhaps he wouldn't have, she thought. Even now, she wanted him. She wouldn't have wanted Robert like this, would have denied him her consent and he had been a gentler man than Gil in lots of ways. Gil was young, not thirty yet, but all the beds he had been in showed on him here. This was not force; it was experience and he made her want him. There was nothing selfish about it in the end. He brought Abby's body to a sweet height and in her mind she cursed him for that final betrayal. It was unfair.

There was nowhere to go when it was over, no blankets to curl into, no pillows to hide against and even then he didn't talk to her. She imagined that even the girls at Mrs Fitzpatrick's got some form of conversation, but he put his clothes back to rights as though nothing had happened and left her there. Abby sat in the snow and cried and called him every name she could think of. Eventually she was so cold that there was nothing to do except fasten her clothes and go indoors and order a hot bath.

John Marlowe called in at the office that week and they sat by the fire and drank whisky.

'Allsop's been seen around Newcastle these last few days so just be a mite careful. We don't want your pretty little Missus Surtees back on the streets again, do we?'

'I'm not even certain it was him, John.'

'Who else?'

'It could have been anybody. I just had this idea that it was. I didn't see him clearly.'

'And he likes you so much?' John said.

'I assumed he was dead.'

'Why?'

'I don't know. I hadn't heard anything, nobody had.'

Later, when the whisky had been drunk, Gil made his way back to the country. He thought about Jos Allsop and when he got home he called the appropriate male servants and told them that they were to admit no one without evidence of identity and to stop anybody who came into the grounds, no matter how far from the house. He had already arranged security in his shipyards, with men on the gates and night watchmen on the premises. You lost too much if you didn't look after things.

He called Abby into the study after dinner and told her.

'All I'm saying is be careful and for the next few days keep the children close until I can find out what's happening.'

Matthew burst in at that moment.

'Jonathan sent me a letter today and he wants me to go and stay with him!'

'Matthew, have you ever heard of knocking?' Gil said.

Letter in his hand, Matthew was silenced.

'Go and wait outside.'

Matthew went.

'Try and be kind to him,' Abby said.

'What?'

'He's a small boy. You treat him like an adult.'

'He's very precocious.'

'I wonder where he got that from,' Abby said as she walked out.

When she had gone, Gil cursed himself. He didn't know what to say to her, hadn't known since that day in the garden in the snow. He just wished he hadn't done it. It had made things worse, if they could get any worse. He called Matthew inside and read the short letter inviting Matthew to stay.

'You can't go to Jonathan's, not for a few days.'

'Why not?'

'Because I say so.'

'I'm bored here, there's nothing to do. I hate living in the country with nobody but stupid Georgina. I hate this place and I hate you!' Matthew said and banged the door after him. Gil went after him, got hold of him by the back of his collar and marched him back into the room.

'You're going to hate me a lot more if you aren't careful,' he said. 'You'd better brighten your ideas up, because if you bang the door again like that or say rude things to me I'm going to put you over that desk and beat you. Do you understand me?'

Matthew nodded and then ran. He left the door open that time. Gil didn't think any more about it. He had discovered that work meant you could ease things out of your mind and he had a lot to do before he went to bed, so he worked until it was almost midnight. He heard the gentle click of the door and looked up. White-faced, Abby hovered in the doorway.

'Matthew's missing,' she said.

'He's what?'

'He isn't in his room and he isn't in the house—'

Gil was on his feet, the familiar sick feeling gathering momentum all the time inside him. Within seconds he was dizzy.

'He can't be far,' Abby said reassuringly, 'it's a horrible night.'

'He could have been gone hours, ever since . . . No. Oh God.'

Gil sent the men searching and he rode over to the Charlton household, which was the nearest neighbour. Jonathan was the son of Ralph, whom Edward had been friendly with. All the way there he told himself that this was his fault, but he was sure that Matthew would be there. He was not. The house was in darkness, in silence and though he banged on the doors and got them out of bed, he was without hope by then.

Ralph and all the men he could find offered to help and Gil was grateful. They went to all the houses nearby. He could hear voices calling Matthew's name over the hills, the fellside and the banksides and all the time his mind gave him Jos Allsop and Rhoda. Reason deserted him. It was a cold, wet night. Gil could not believe he had to go through this again and he thought somehow that Allsop would appear and hurt Matthew, that he would have been stalking the house, that he could have persuaded Matthew away, that he might have lured him into

Newcastle and kidnapped and killed him. All night he searched and the other men of the district did the same. They found nothing and, just as daylight began, it snowed huge flakes which turned into a storm. He remembered finding Rhoda dead in the snow like some neglected animal and how he had carried her back to the house and how Allsop had reacted. It was all happening again. He didn't want to go back to the house in case someone else had found Matthew dead, or that he had not been found at all and would be discovered cold and still or in some back alley in the city, Allsop having taken out his feelings on Gil's son.

When full day arrived he made his way back to the house, Abby heard him and came into the hall. Her colour was normal and behind her hovered a small figure.

'We found him,' she said, 'just a little while since. I've called off the search. He had hidden to frighten us and fallen asleep.'

It was not relief that Gil felt, it was an overwhelming desire to thrash his child. As he took a step towards her Abby backed with the boy behind her. Gil got her by the arm.

'Come out of the way,' he said.

'I will not!'

Matthew started to cry.

'He's just a little boy. You leave him alone!' She started to fight with him as Gil reached for his son. She was crying, too, but her hands were clenched into fists. Even though she was small and slight, she got in the way quite effectively, but not sufficiently to make the difference in the end. He could have stopped her altogether by knocking her out of the way. It wouldn't even have taken a great effort and Gil could feel the tremendous well of temper surging its way through him. He remembered it. He remembered how he had put the boy out of the second-storey window at school. He remembered throwing men down the stairs at the house in Hope Street. He remembered being in the study with his father and being called stupid and worthless and beaten until he couldn't move. He remembered being thrown into cold rooms and left there for days. And he remembered Helen smiling at him and lying to him and pretending that she cared about him when in fact she had only really cared about his brother. He wanted to break something, to see something bloody and down and destroyed.

Abby had backed as far as the stairs. There was nowhere for her to go now, with the child still behind her. She was fighting with him, but Gil had hold of Matthew and was pulling him out from behind her.

'You won't do it, you won't!' she declared, hanging on. 'I won't let you be William! You're not, you're not.'

He didn't hit her. He released her while she was pushing from him and she fell, the stairs got in the way and he had Matthew to himself, not fighting or crying or protesting in any way. He remembered that too, that horrible resignation, the knowledge that if you cried you would be beaten until you stopped, the awful sick anticipation. The little boy's face was grey-white, the tears had dried and his eyes were all one colour, black with fear, and huge. He was so small, so unable to do anything to stop an adult from punishing him. He was like a terrified rabbit that couldn't move.

The hope for the future if he could learn enough and please sufficiently and contain all the evil feelings. He could be taught that approval and success were all that mattered, that if he was clever enough he could have a house like this and expensive carriages, all the stables full of horses and all the rooms filled with furniture. He could have servants and tables laden with food and a cellar full of wine and his pick of women. He could have the whole world admiring him, he could have everything.

Gil picked the child up and said, 'I think you ought to go to bed, Matthew. You must be worn out,' and he carried him up the stairs.

Abby fussed gently, put the child into bed and talked to him in a soft voice. Gil went back downstairs and into the study. As he opened the door the snow had stopped, the sky had cleared and the sun appeared over the horizon and spilled all over the floor in a mighty surge of dazzling brilliance. There was nothing left to do but go to work, so he went. He wasn't even tired. He spent the day going around the various shops and departments as he sometimes did just to keep everybody lively and all day the sun streamed in at the windows. The snow had gone from the streets and there was a special buzz about everything because it was Christmas Eve and the men would not be at work for the following two days. In the time before Henderson's influence they had only Christmas Day, but Gil was a believer in holidays and gave them time off at Easter and in the summer and he paid them. He was well hated in the shipbuilding federation for his high wages and lenient ideas and good ships, he thought, smiling. They would have New Year's Day, too, because a great many of these people were Scottish and a great many more felt more Scottish than English and would rather have gone to work on Christmas Day than New Year's, so he accommodated everybody and gave them both. There would be a servants' dance that evening at Bamburgh House and many of the servants would go home for a day or two. He and Abby, instead of having big parties as many people did, would have a quiet time, fetching and carrying for themselves. He pictured them eating in the kitchen and making free of the house as they couldn't when other people were there. They could sit in their nightclothes by the fire if they wanted, he thought. He had planned all this. The plans were ruined. He thought of her falling awkwardly on the stairs, her defence of the child and of the fear in Matthew's face.

He didn't go home. He didn't ever want to go home again. Staying at work was so easy by comparison. The problems could be solved, they were not people, unpredictable and complicated. When it was quiet in the evening he helped himself to whisky and grew used to the idea that Jos Allsop had not abducted or murdered his child. He heard John's heavy footsteps outside his office, so by the time the big man had reached him Gil had a glass ready half filled with golden liquid.

'Get wrapped around that,' he said.

'Cheers,' John said. 'Got some good news.'

'I could take some.'

'Allsop. Found dead in the river this afternoon, belly up like a fish.'

'I couldn't be better pleased. Somebody did him in?'

'Don't know,' John said, frowning and taking his favourite seat across the fire. 'Rumour has it he fell in, drunk. Everything all right with you?'

'Aye, everything's fine.'

'Want to go out?

'Why not?'

They went to the pub and then they went to Mrs Fitzpatrick's. Gil was rather drunk when he got there and decided that all he wanted to do was go home. John laughed.

'It's all right for some people, they've got it on tap,' he said.

By the time he reached home the drunkenness had worn off with the cold night air. He had expected the house to be in darkness, but it was lit like a Christmas tree. Then he remembered the servants' dance. The hall was deserted. It was evidently over and quiet. People had gone to bed but Abby was there, wearing a very pretty, low-cut blue dress. She had a mark on her face. People would think he had hit her, Gil thought.

'Just as well I didn't save you the last waltz,' she said.

'I forgot.'

'Of course. What could compete with the delights of the pub and the whorehouse?' She turned away and would have walked away up the stairs, but he stopped her. He led her into the nearest room, which was the library. There had obviously been no fire in there for several hours, or possibly at all that day. Nobody went in there except him and on the day of a party people would be unlikely to need books. Abby stood against the door and didn't look at him. Gil had been going to apologise, but that was before he realised about the dance. He wanted to say to her that he hadn't meant to hurt her, that he hadn't intended to, that he hoped the mark on her face hadn't caused her embarrassment, that he hoped the servants had not heard them fighting. It was a vain hope; they had made a lot of noise. Two people fighting like that would not have been ignored by even the least curious servants. Probably all that day there had been talk. Probably they thought he had knocked her over. Her face, to his mind, didn't give enough evidence, it would have been a much bigger mark, but people didn't care about that, they would believe what they chose to believe. He had fought with her and attempted to beat his child. For these things men were not forgiven. The servants' dance, the way she thought he had deliberately stayed away, the drinking was true, the whore . . . he was starting to wish that he was safe in the arms of Chloe or Desirée or somebody who didn't matter, whose name didn't matter . . . these things had not been important on their own but they were the cap to it, rather like the top of a boiled egg was to some people the dearest part. He wanted to apologise to her but he couldn't remember how.

She stood there and regarded the side of the bookshelf with rapt concentration.

'It's Christmas,' he said.

Abby stared at the wood. Gil looked at her throat. The way that her dress scooped down like that, you couldn't help noticing at close quarters what a pretty neck she had and the way that her shoulders were so soft and white and her breasts just hidden by the top of the dress would be . . . He wished again that he was back in Newcastle where it was simple, where nobody fought and argued and used the kind of language Abby did, where he could do what he wanted to do to her. All those girls had beautiful bodies because they were expensive. They were all, in fact, more beautiful and much younger than Abby was. He thought of the way she had protected his son against him. She would have fought until she couldn't fight any more, not just because of Matthew but because she well knew that he did not forgive himself his iniquities.

He put his hands on her waist and slid them around to the back of her dress. There he found the fastenings quite intricate and hidden so that they would not spoil the line of the expensive dress, but he knew these things, had been around women long enough to know how to undress them. That was one problem you didn't have at Mrs Fitzpatrick's: they were half undressed to begin with and because you paid, you didn't have to undress them at all if you didn't want to. They would slowly remove the clothing that they wore if you liked, but he liked to take their clothes off for them. He began to undo the fastenings now.

She tasted and smelled so wonderful to Gil that he wanted her like he had wanted nobody else. Her neck was long and slender and invited kisses all the way down the column of her throat and in the hollows of her shoulders. He could feel the dress loosening from her body, obligingly slipping so that the palms of his hands found the exquisite warmth of her breasts.

'Will you stop it!'

It was only then that Gil realised she was trying to get away. He was not used to that. Nobody did that. He looked vaguely at her.

'What?'

They were on the sofa. He hadn't realised that either, hadn't known that he had put her there, hadn't felt or heard her protesting.

'I'm not a whore!'

'I know that.' But she felt just as good as the girls at the whorehouse, better in fact, much better and, sitting up with her hair tumbled and the dress down to her waist and the angry fired look in her eyes, he was loathe to release her.

'It didn't stop you though, did it? It didn't stop you before, outside?'

Abby was not crying but her voice was catching as though there was some constriction in her throat. He thought about before, the snow falling and the soft ground and her body so warm against the cold air. He remembered his hands, wet from the snow, finding the heat of her body as it emerged from her clothes and the ecstasy of having her in the stillness. There was no other stillness in the world like that of falling snow. The whole world was stopped and silent and she was his, completely his like they would not be parted for all eternity.

'You treated me like this then!'

'No. No.' Kissing her now, her body brushing against his shirt, his hands unable to prise themselves away from her. 'Don't leave me. Don't. Please.'

She was off the sofa, pulling her dress up to where it was supposed to be. He couldn't move, tried to be seconds back to where they had been when she was letting him kiss her, touch her. He would not acknowledge that there was a space between them and now the cold night was making its way between them. He knew what that was like, the icy, godforsaken hours of nobody and nothing. He had tried to steal beyond them with women, but he could not forget all those nights and weeks and months and years without Helen, all those days without her, knowing that he had not come from her and would not go back to her, all the time, all the people who meant nothing with their kind and unkind faces, all the ships going down the slipway had not eased the emptiness. Nothing eased it except this.

Abby was angry. Her mind was full of what had happened the previous night. She had never before had to fight with anyone and it had appalled her. When had Gil turned into his father and why had she not noticed it until then? William had been bad-tempered, autocratic, impossible and unforgiving, but she was not Charlotte. She would not stand by and let him beat his son. It was true that Gil didn't hit her, but he caused the circumstances which made her fall and hurt herself and she still had to go on trying to stop him from taking Matthew from her. When the fight was over she relived it, shaking, again and again. Even when Matthew was in bed, where Gil had safely put him, when there was no question of brutality, there had been the possibility and that was enough for her. They had put the child to bed in daylight and then he had actually gone to work. She couldn't believe it. No apologies, no concern. He had left the house, left her to manage as best she could without sleep, his upset child, the staff dance, the Christmas arrangements. Then he had quite obviously stayed out, got drunk, had a woman and finally had nothing better to do than come home. And now . . . maybe there had been no woman. Even somebody young like Gil couldn't have gone without sleep, working all day, got drunk, had a whore, come home and . . . put his mouth and hands on her like this. Abby felt nothing, just cold as though she had been left outside for too long. He was insensitive, like all men were. Robert had done this many times, it didn't mean anything to him; but Gil was not like that, she knew he wasn't, she couldn't have cared so much about him if he had been.

She had begun to resist but he didn't take any notice, pulling the dress down to her waist. He picked her up and carried her over to the sofa and there in the softness of the cushions he put her down. The bloody room was anything but warm and the books smelled like damp books did, sort of mouldy and as though they had never been outside in the fresh air. The whole room had an atmosphere that Abby hadn't noticed before and didn't like now. It was neglected, unwanted, turned aside, cold words on cold pages. The winter wind screamed around the house, making its way down the chimney and into the empty grate and the room was filled with bitter air.

She went. She left him. She didn't say anything. She didn't even say goodnight, as though he had done something unforgivable. The room was so cold, the shadows were so thick, the night was God and nobody could alter it. He made himself go upstairs. He could go back to Chloe tomorrow or the next day and he was safe there. She was young and beautiful and obliging. She tasted good and smelled good and had breasts like apples, round and firm, and a bottom that was neat and high and a waist so slender that he could meet his fingertips around it. She had long blonde hair and bright blue eyes.

He walked out of the library and went upstairs. The night was unforgiving and all the ghosts came at you from the corners when the lights were out. It was easier when Chloe was there. Maybe she would marry him and he wouldn't have to go to bed by himself any more. There was brandy in a glass by the bed and he knew that when he had drunk half a bottle, Helen would not be dead any more. She would just be in another room and Edward would be playing billiards and his mother and father would be having a party. He could soon hear the music and the laughter down below and he could have the ship launch and see the *Northumbria* slide down into the Tyne. It had been the best moment of his life and he could have it back any time. He could have it back any time at all. There it went again, hundreds of Newcastle people cheering and the men throwing their caps into the air and his father standing beside him smiling and the proud look in his mother's eyes and Rhoda . . . He wished Chloe was here. He wished that she was here.

Abby worried. She told herself over and over that he was uncaring and not worth her losing sleep. The night was bitterly cold with a heavy frost and a lot of stars so that both ground and sky twinkled. She stood with the heavy curtains pulled back, but it was cold even though she had kept the fire going in her bedroom. Tomorrow it would be Christmas Day. She didn't decide to leave the room or to go into Gil's room, she just went. She opened the heavy oak door of his room and a blast of freezing air hit her. It was in dark shadows because the curtains were pulled well back and the window was wide open. Abby fumbled about in the dark and finally found the lamp, but it wouldn't light. Eventually she found a candle. That didn't help much, but it gave enough light for her to see Gil.

She had seen Robert in that state too many times not to know how drunk he was. He was unconscious, face down on the bed with one arm under his eyes, fully dressed in neat, expensive clothes. He had blotted everything out with brandy, taken himself into oblivion. She went over, closed the window, pulled the curtains and then she went back to bed.

Christmas Day was difficult. She went to church with Charlotte and the children. Gil was downstairs when she got back. He didn't look like somebody who had been drunk the night before, he was just the same and laughed at Georgina's kisses and cuddles. He was too indulgent with her and had bought her far too many Christmas presents, which she unwrapped gleefully. For Matthew a beautiful cricket bat, which he insisted on using, so he and Gil went outside in spite of the weather. One of Abby's presents from Gil was a silver locket containing photographs of her parents. He was good with presents.

They had a big meal and went out for a walk, watching the sun set over the horizon. As the evening drew in she put the children to bed and when she went back downstairs, heard him ordering the carriage.

'Gil!' She went after him into the drawing-room. 'Where are you going?'

He looked at her in slight amusement.

'What?' he said.

'If you go . . . if you go to that place—'

'What will you do about it? Beat me when I come home, withdraw your favours, leave me? Well?'

'Stay here.'

'What for?'

'Those girls only do it because you pay them!'

'Nice and simple,' Gil said.

'You were drunk last night.'

'That wasn't entirely because you wouldn't let me have you on the sofa.'

Abby hoped diligently that nobody was listening.

'You sleep with the windows open.'

'For the stars,' Gil said and left.

Gil had great hopes of Chloe. He hadn't been there in a long time. She greeted him with enthusiasm and she was so pretty, seventeen or eighteen at the most. She didn't mind the windows open or the whisky or anything at all. From her bed you could hear the sounds of the streets outside and when it was late you could throw back the curtains and see those same stars. They hadn't altered, they were Helen's stars, they went on and on.

He knew the girls. At least, he could distinguish some of them though he tried not to because after a couple of drinks, by candlelight, naked in his arms, each of them became Helen. But tonight it didn't work. Chloe wouldn't turn into Helen. She remained a pretty young girl with a Byker accent, dyed blonde hair and an innocent willingness, in spite of her trade, which Helen had never had. Helen had not looked at him like that, desperate to please. Chloe undressed for him and then she seemed almost like a child. Gil turned away, then he turned back and put her into bed and covered her in bedclothes. The room was freezing. Gil stood by the window and watched the stars and drank brandy and the room grew colder and colder. He went on drinking to try and make the magic happen but it didn't. All he could see was Abby standing in front of Matthew, protecting him from somebody twice as big as she was who could kill her. He spent most of the night watching the stars from the window while Chloe finally went to sleep and the brandy took its hold on him.

In the morning when he left to go to the office, he caught an anxious look on Chloe's face. He sat down on the bed.

'What's the matter?'

'Nothing.'

'You're supposed to say "I don't want you to go." '

Chloe's face slipped.

'You weren't happy.'

'I was very happy.'

'No, you weren't. I didn't make you happy.'

'And I'm going to complain to Mrs Fitzpatrick, is that it?'

'Maybe.'

'It had nothing to do with you.' He lifted her chin and looked into her clear blue eyes. Then he kissed her on the cheek and gave her a handful of money. 'Go and buy yourself a new dress,' he said.

Gil went to the office. Only the watchmen were there and the maintenance people, but the fire burned in his office as it did every day. He had given the men an extra day's holiday. The talk in the clubs, John told him, was that they said he would bankrupt himself. It made him laugh. He liked being here when few other people were. He worked in the silence and drank coffee all day and enjoyed the light-headed feeling that came from eating nothing for too long.

Towards evening he sat by the window and watched the river and debated whether to go home. Mid-evening he heard a noise, assumed that it was John, poured whisky and then realised that the steps were much too light. Abby appeared in the doorway. Gil didn't even get up. He looked into the golden liquid so that he wouldn't have to look at her. She was so beautiful, not as angry as she had been, but there was fire in her eyes. He got up and went to the window. All the shapes outside were defined against the clear sky, all strong and tall and looking as though they would last for ever, when none of them would. They were buildings and ships and one day none of it would be left.

She seemed to think she could get his attention when in fact the whisky and the night held him inside its magic circle and nothing could get past. The smell of the whisky was sweet and sharp and the night was doing its special floor show with its stars and all its terrors. He thought that, later, when the golden liquid had completely gone, he would be part of it somehow. The view of his shipyard was beautiful; it was possibly the best view in the world. Gil took another swig of whisky and regarded the night. He was prejudiced about the Tyne. He couldn't look at another river and love it like this. He wished he could hold it in his arms. Whenever he launched a ship, he imagined the Tyne taking the ship into its arms like a lover.

'Aren't you going to speak to me?' she said from the other end of the room over by the desk.

'What is there to say?'

'You haven't talked to me at all since you came back from France. You've screwed the arse off me of course, but that's not quite the same thing.'

Gil turned and looked mildly at her.

'One of these days somebody will leather you for your language,' he said.

Abby came to the window.

'You haven't said a single word about Edward.'

'He's dead,' Gil said flatly. That was the first time that he had acknowledged to himself that Edward had died. He had known it in his head, but he had not believed it in his heart. There was a bit of him that still thought he could go any night of the week to the billiard hall they had frequented in the town and there, among the quiet talk and the slow movements of the players, his brother would be across the room, not speaking to him or looking at him, glancing up at Toby from time to time and smiling his slow smile, his fair hair haloed under the low lights above the tables. Toby would be leaning on his cue and suggesting where the next shot should go.

In Gil's mind it was always a night when Edward would

suggest after dinner that they should go out. Then they would be in the fuggy warmth of the room and Edward was smiling and there would be another day and another time and another chance. But there was not any more and never would be.

'Did you go to Mrs Fitzpatrick's?'

'Yes.'

'Why?'

'Because you wouldn't let me "screw the arse off you",' he said.

Abby stood for a few moments as though in admiration of the view and then she said softly, 'That's not true, is it?'

Gil leaned against the wall so that he didn't have to say anything, so that he couldn't even see her except from the corner of his eyes.

'You were never really like that, not like Robert and his friends who would bed anything that looked vaguely female. Why do you go?'

Gil took a sip of whisky and stared out at the darkness of his shipyard.

'When I've had a few drinks, every woman is Helen.'

Abby considered her hands carefully.

'Is that why you put me down into the snow?'

'I wanted you near.'

'That was fairly near,' Abby said.

'It was you I wanted.'

'Sure?'

'Yes.'

'So I'm not Helen. She is dead, you know.'

'Yes, I know.'

'Then why does everybody have to be her?' He didn't answer. 'You've had a drink or two now. Am I Helen?'

'No, of course not?

'Then what? What?' She thumped him. 'Goddamn you, talk to me!'

The whisky flew everywhere. Gil put down the empty glass.

'Don't do that!' he said.

'What, this?' she said, thumping him again and he got hold of her. 'Come on then. You've had enough whisky to float a ship. Put me down and make me Helen. She didn't even love you!'

'Yes, she did!'

'When? When she waltzed off to Venice with your brother? When she came back pregnant? When she accused you of fathering Matthew? When she killed herself to spite you?'

'She didn't!' He shook her.

'If she loved you, why didn't she give up Edward and marry you? She never loved you and you know it! And no matter how hard you try, it won't make any difference and no matter how many women you put down in the starlight, it won't alter anything.'

Gil released her when she twisted away from him. She didn't go far, just nearer the window, leaned against it, looking out.

'You can't make people love you, not Helen and not your father, not even Edward.'

Gil couldn't answer that and she turned to him again and said, 'That's the worst of all, isn't it, Edward?'

'I betrayed him.'

'He didn't care about you.'

'There were days . . . when he did. There were times when I thought he did, but I wanted him to so very much. He loved Toby.'

'Isn't that slightly different?'

'I don't know. I don't know where love and touch differs, where it begins and ends, but I know what it feels like when you don't have any, when people don't want you near them or even in their company. People who grow up together have special things between them or they should have, don't you think?'

'I loved my parents, I miss them. Why don't you come home?'

'You don't want me.'

Abby sighed.

'That was just because . . . of what happened. I was afraid. I thought you were going to knock me out of the way and beat Matthew.'

'I was.'

'But you didn't.'

'That was because some termagant got in the way.'

'I'm not that bad. You could have done it.'

'I turned into my father.'

'Almost. Gil—' Abby moved nearer. 'If I hadn't loved you very much I wouldn't have let you put me down into the snow like that. I wouldn't have let anyone else in the world do it – I thought you knew that at least.'

'It wasn't like that,' he said. 'I love you.'

Abby took a deep breath and let go of it.

'So, you weren't you just screwing the arse off me.'

He looked disapprovingly at her.

'If you say that once more, I will wallop you.'

Abby grinned.

'That would be a big novelty,' she said. 'I doubt you're capable of it.'

'Just don't.'

'Will you do me a favour then?'

'What?'

'Don't go to Mrs Fitzpatrick's.'

'I didn't do anything when I got there. I haven't been there since before we left Newcastle. The only woman I've been anywhere near is you.'

She went closer and reached up both hands to his shoulders and kissed him very gently on the mouth.

'Come home,' she said. 'I love you and you have the children and even your wretched mother tolerates you.'

He smiled a little.

'She's got better,' he said.

'She's almost bearable,' Abby said. 'please come home.'

* * *

It only occurred to Gil when they got there that since he had come back from France, the piano playing had stopped. Was that why he could no longer conjure Helen's image? Or did it have more to do with the fact that the children, who were supposed to be in bed, heard the carriage and ran down the stairs in greeting? He picked them up and they squealed and giggled and Georgina put her arms around his neck. He took them into the small sitting-room, which was the cosiest room in the house. Abby had placed big squashy sofas at either side of the fire. It was high and bright with logs. Gil sat down with Georgina on his knee and Matthew cuddled up to Abby. Gil's mother came in.

'My children went to bed at seven,' she said. 'I don't approve of all these new-fangled ideas.'

'It's the holidays, Grandma,' Matthew said.

'I love Christmas,' Georgina said from the depths of Gil's shoulder, where she was almost asleep.

'Far too many presents,' Charlotte said. 'Your uncle has died. A little respect would be nice.'

'We could go to France in the summer,' Gil said.

His mother looked sharply at him.

'Whatever for?' she said.

'They left us the house. We could go and stay there.'

'You didn't say.'

'The legalities aren't finalised yet.'

'Is it a nice house?' Matthew said, sitting up.

'It's a lovely house,' Gil said, 'by a river.'

'We could go fishing.'

'I could go as well,' Georgina said.

'I don't know that I want to go to a house where—' Charlotte seemed to remember the children and stopped herself.

'He was happy there,' Gil said.

'You don't know that,' his mother said roughly.

'Charlotte—' Abby said.

Gil's mother looked hard at her.

'You spring very quickly to my son's defence, Abigail. When

people do that it's high time they were married,' she said and stamped out of the room.

Gil watched Abby press her lips together so that she wouldn't laugh. They put the children to bed and sat together on the sofa.

'I think she will come to France,' Abby said.

'Only if we get married.'

'I would do anything to please your mother.'

'And me?'

Abby moved closer.

'I could do things for you that Mrs Fitzpatrick has never heard of.'

He laughed. She pushed him over and leaned on him.

'You doubt me?'

'Not for a second.'

'In bed I think. I don't want to be interrupted.'

Abby couldn't help but pause when they passed the doors of the drawing-room, but the piano was silent and still. She would not have admitted to him that she sometimes heard Mozart when there was nobody in the room. When they reached her room the fire was burning brightly but the thick curtains were open. Abby went across and closed out the night, the cold sky, the stars and the bright icy moon. It was what was going to happen inside the room that mattered, she thought, and nobody and nothing could stop her from making him hers. He would belong to her now and nobody else would ever have him again, she swore. She knew a lot about swearing; her mother had taught her. Her father had always proudly said of her mother that she swore better than any docker. Abby went over to Gil and started to undo the buttons on his shirt.

'Did I ever tell you that you have the world's most exquisite shoulders?' she said and she put her mouth to his warm skin and began to kiss him.

BORN IN EXILE

Gollancz Classics:

PETER SIMPLE
by Captain Marryat
introduced by Oliver Warner

PETER IBBETSON
by George Du Maurier
introduced by Daphne du Maurier

TWO NOVELS:
THE SEMI-ATTACHED COUPLE
THE SEMI-DETACHED HOUSE
by Emily Eden
introduced by Lord Avon

THE MANCHESTER MAN
by Mrs. G. Linnaeus Banks
introduced by W. L. Webb

BORN IN EXILE
by George Gissing
introduced by Walter Allen

MEMOIRS OF AN ENGLISH OFFICER
. . . by Captain Carleton, . . .
MEMOIRS OF MAJOR ALEXANDER RAMKINS, &
THE HISTORY OF THE REMARKABLE LIFE OF JOHN SHEPPARD
by Daniel Defoe
introduced by J. T. Boulton

BORN IN EXILE

GEORGE GISSING

Introduced by Walter Allen

Gollancz Classics

General Editor: Martin Seymour-Smith

LONDON
VICTOR GOLLANCZ LTD
1970

First published 1892
Gollancz Classics Edition 1970

575 00391 x

PRINTED IN GREAT BRITAIN
BY EBENEZER BAYLIS AND SON, LTD.
THE TRINITY PRESS, WORCESTER, AND LONDON

BORN IN EXILE

Introduction by Walter Allen

OF THE HERO of *Born in Exile* Gissing wrote to his German friend Eduard Bertz, "Peak is myself—one phase of myself," and the autobiographical element in the novel is obvious. It can be felt, for one thing, in the intense personal passion with which Godwin Peak is rendered. The novel was written at a time when the autobiographical impulse seems to have been strong in Gissing. It was published in 1892, a year after *New Grub Street*, in which Gissing had portrayed himself in the unsuccessful novelist Reardon and also bestowed some of his own experiences on other characters in the novel. *New Grub Street* has always been the most famous of Gissing's novels, deservedly so, for it is a remarkable work, not only as a record of the calamities of authorship during the last years of the nineteenth century but also as a dramatisation of contemporary theories of the novel and of changes in what today are called communications. It is the best constructed of Gissing's works and was his most successful during his lifetime.

Born in Exile, on the other hand, seemed doomed to failure. It was turned down by Smith, Elder, the publishers of *New Grub Street* and of a number of Gissing's earlier, books, and by several other firms as well before it was accepted by A. & C. Black. The reviews it received were lukewarm; the *Athenaeum*'s man wrote, "The young man"—meaning Peak—"is scarcely a hero over whom one can become very enthusiastic." Yet it seems to me that in the corpus of Gissing's work *Born in Exile* must stand next to *New Grub Street*. It is a novel of great intellectual power and of a fierce intransigence. It reveals Gissing as a man who has profited by and made his own some of the most revolutionary ideas of his time, ideas which, embodied in the character and behaviour of Peak, link the novel with European masterpieces. And it remains, in my view, a disturbing and uncomfortable work. Everything in it is contained in Peak—all the other characters are pale compared with him, which is the main flaw in the book—and Peak is a figure of an intellectual arrogance and fanatical ambition unmatched in English fiction except by Joyce's Stephen Dedalus as we see him in *A Portrait of the Artist as a Young Man.*

To speak of the autobiographical element in *Born in Exile*, however, does not mean that the novel is in any way a transcript of actual experience. Far from it. Peak is a creation of Gissing's imagination, a projection of one side of the author, a side which is explored with extraordinary boldness. One might say that in a sense Gissing in Peak is imagining an ideal manifestation of himself. That in actuality he was capable of nothing like Peak's behaviour all the facts of his life show.

He was born in 1857 in Wakefield, Yorkshire, where his father kept a chemist's shop. A brilliant schoolboy, he won a scholarship at the age of fifteen to Owens College, Manchester, later to become Manchester University but then mainly concerned with preparing students for the intermediate examinations of Oxford, Cambridge and London. At Owens his career was as brilliant as it had been at school. He took first place in Latin and English in the examination for honours following the intermediate B.A. examination and won the Shakespeare prize. It could have been assumed that he would go on to university proper, enjoy a distinguished career there and in the fullness of time become a professional scholar. However, he fell in love with a young prostitute, Nell Harrison, and in order to help her took to thieving from his fellow students. He was caught, expelled from the College, suffered a brief term of imprisonment and then packed off to the United States. That was in 1876. In the States—he got as far as Chicago—he scratched a living teaching and writing, sometimes scarcely above the subsistence level, if *New Grub Street* can be taken literally, and a year later returned to England, where he tracked Nell down and married her.

He supported her and himself by private tutoring in London until she left him to go back to the streets. She died in 1888, the year in which his first novel, *Workers in the Dawn*, was published. Three years later, he married again, with results scarcely less disastrous. According to H. G. Wells, who was a good friend to him in his last years, his second wife was a servant-girl whom he had picked up in Regent's Park. They had nothing in common, and she was to die mad: but before then Gissing had met the French translator of his works, whom he later married. He died at Christmas, 1903, at St. Jean-Pied-de-Port, in the French Pyrenees. Wells was at his deathbed and was later to put the contents of his delirium on the eve of death into the mouth of the dying Uncle Ponderevo, in *Tono-Bungay*, an ironical transference that Gissing would not have appreciated.

"Poor Gissing," Henry James said, "struck me as quite particularly marked out for what is called in his and my profession an unhappy ending." His was a life impossible to contemplate without pity and also, it must be admitted, without some irritation, for if ever a man invited suffering he did. There is throughout his work a repellant streak of masochism. According to his friend Thomas Seecombe, in his later years he used to ask, of a new author, "Has he starved?" and one can't help feeling that it gave him considerable satisfaction that he had. According to Wells, in *An Experiment in Autobiography*, he had "no customary *persona* for miscellaneous use". It is something one feels that Godwin Peak also lacks. Wells goes on: "He felt that to make love to any woman he could regard as a social equal would be too elaborate, restrained and tedious for his urgencies, he could not answer questions he supposed he would be asked about his health and means, and so he flung himself at a social inferior whom he expected to be eager and grateful." In this respect, Godwin Peak's behaviour is the exact converse of Gissing's in life.

But there was something else, which relates him directly to Wells, who was nine years his junior. Both were "new men", among the earliest representatives of those intellectuals from the lower middle class who found expression for themselves in imaginative writing, intellectuals who had made their own way in the world and had come up outside the traditional channels of English Education. Wells, who had the greater handicaps to overcome initially, possessed the more powerful and original mind. There are times, indeed, reading Gissing and the much overrated *Private Papers of Henry Ryecroft* in particular, when one feels that if all had gone well for him and he had become a don, he would have been a very dull don indeed. But things did not go well. There was the disgrace and humiliation in Manchester, which one can only assume was a traumatic experience for him. Its effect, socially, economically, psychologically, was to place him in the limbo of the dispossessed. You might say his constant theme was the displaced person, as the titles of so many of his books suggest—*The Unclassed*, *The Nether World*, *Born in Exile*, *The Odd Women*, *Human Odds and Ends*.

After his return from America, circumstances, forced him into the life of the London slums. What followed was natural enough: for a time he identified himself with the proletariat and became a socialist. But only for a time. As early as his second novel, *The*, *Unclassed*, we find the novelist Waymark, who is plainly the spokesman for Gissing himself, saying: "That zeal on behalf of the suffering masses was nothing more or less than disguised zeal on behalf of my own starved passions. I was poor and desperate . . . I identified myself with the poor and ignorant; I did not make their cause my own, but my own cause theirs." Gissing's disillusionment with the workers was, in fact, rapid, and he was soon an intransigent anti-socialist, motivated, it is difficult not to think, by a mixture of outraged disgust at the poor and of fear of them. This lack of human sympathy is his least attractive trait, and it sometimes becomes ludicrous, as when he writes of young Oliver Peak in *Born in Exile*:

His brother Oliver, now seventeen, was developing into a type of young man as objectionable as it is easily recognisable. The slow, compliant boy had grown more flesh and muscle than once seemed likely, and his wits had begun to display that kind of vivaciousness which is only compatible with a nature moulded in common clay. He saw much company, and all of low intellectual order; he had purchased a bicycle, and regarded it as a source of distinction, a means of displaying himself before shopkeepers' daughters; he believed himself a modest tenor, and sang verses of sentimental imbecility; he took in several weekly papers of unpromising title, for the chief purpose of decyphering cryptograms, in which pursuit he had singular success. Add to these characteristics a penchant for cheap jewellery, and Oliver Peak stands confessed.

Plainly, a more harmless youth never existed.

Nevertheless, this lack of sympathy was part and parcel of Gissing, as it is part and parcel of Godwin Peak. It is the concomitant of Peak's intellectual arrogance, his inordinate ambition and his contempt for everything that seems to him vulgar and commonplace. The form his ambition takes, however, is a very odd one, for it is rooted entirely in class-consciousness. A product of the lower middle class, he sees himself as an aristocrat. He conceives himself as having been born in exile or as being, so to speak, a changeling. His ambition is to be accepted as the man he is in his own right, as a man of natural distinction. But the only way in which he can be thus accepted, as a gentleman, lies in his marrying a lady. And the one hope of his marrying a lady lies in his becoming an Anglican clergyman.

One can trace the stages in the evolution of Peak's ambition easily enough. There is the outburst, while still a schoolboy, to his younger brother:

"I hate low, uneducated people! I hate them worse than the filthiest vermin . . . They ought to be swept off the face of the earth! All the grown-up people who can't speak proper English and don't know how to behave themselves, I'd transport them to the Falkland Islands . . . and let them die off as soon as possible. The children should be sent to school and purified, if possible: if not, they should be got rid of . . . There's nothing I hate like vulgarity. That's why I can't stand Roper. When he beat me in mathematics last midsummer, I felt so ashamed that I could hardly bear myself. I'm working like a nigger at algebra and Euclid this half, just because I think it would almost kill me to be beaten again by a low cad."

There is Peak's relinquishment of his academic career when his uncle opens his restaurant opposite the College gates. This, of course, is the objective correlative of Gissing's own expulsion from Owens, and the passion in the writing is such that we almost believe that Peak's disgrace, had he stayed at College, would have been comparable to Gissing's in life. Then there is the avowal to

Earwaker: "If I ever marry at all, it will be to a woman of far higher birth than my own . . . I have no other ambition in life —no other! Think the confession as ridiculous as you like; my own supreme desire is to marry a perfectly refined woman. Put it in the correct terms: I am a plebeian, and I aim at marrying a lady."

So begin the months of conscious hypocrisy—for "no vulgar profit; his one desire was for human fellowship; he sought nothing but his solace which every code of morals has deemed legitimate." An arrogant rationalist, he has written an anonymous article in a review ridiculing the pretensions of a popular book that seeks to reconcile science and religion. Then, having recognised in Sidwell Warricombe the "perfectly refined woman" of his desire, in order to ingratiate himself with her and her wealthy father, he quite cynically declares his intention of studying for ordination and plans for himself a career in the Church.

Loss of faith and religious doubt were among the most popular subjects of late Victorian fiction; the most famous of the novels dealing with them, Mrs. Humphrey Ward's *Robert Elsmere*, had been published only four years before *Born in Exile*. But Gissing brings to the subject a wholly new kind of treatment. For those who suffered it, loss of faith was a highly serious matter. Rejection of Christian theology did not mean rejection of the Christian ethic. Indeed, as we see both from the life and from the fiction of George Eliot, loss of faith often seemed to carry with it a moral obligation to assert belief in the Christian ethic more intensely than believers themselves always felt it necessary to do. This is not true of Godwin Peak, and herein lies the originality of his conception. Unlike George Eliot and Hardy, with his "hoping it might be so", he is quite without nostalgia for faith. Moreover, he does not believe that it is possible for a truly educated—i.e. scientifically educated—modern man or woman to accept Christianity. As Professor Jacob Korg has written: "The disturbing paradox of *Born in Exile* lies in the fact that Peak's hypocritical deception is due, not to lack of moral responsibility, but to uncompromising intellectual honesty. Man's life, seen from a scientific point of view, seems to him to be trivial and futile"—and to Peak the scientific point of view is everything. He has learned from his geological studies that the one sole incontrovertible truth is that of "inconceivable duration". It is in the light of this that he defends himself to his friend Moxey:

"Honest? Honest? Who is or can be honest? Who truly declares himself? When a man has learnt that truth is indeterminable, how is it more moral to go about crying that you don't believe a certain dogma than to concede that the dogma may possibly be true? This new morality of the agnostics is mere paltry conceit. Why must I make solemn declaration that I don't believe in absolute knowledge? I might as well be called upon to inform all my acquaintances how I stand with regard to the theories of chemical affinity. One's philosophy has nothing to do with the business of life. If I chose to become a Church of England clergyman, what moral objection could be made?"

That passage follows shortly after his first experience of staying with the Warricombes in Exeter:

The murmur of amiable voices softened him to the reception of all that was good in his present surroundings, and justified in the light of sentiment his own dishonour. This English home, was it not surely the best result of civilisation in an age devoted to material progress? Here was peace, here was scope for the kindliest emotions. Upon him—the born rebel, the scorner of average mankind, the consummate egoist—this atmosphere exercised an influence more tranquillising, more beneficent, than even the mood of disinterested study. In the world to which sincerity would condemn him, only the worst elements of his character found nourishment and range; here he was humanised, made receptive of all gentle sympathies. Heroism might point him to an unending struggle with adverse conditions, but how was heroism possible without faith? Absolute faith he had none; he was essentially a negativist, guided by the mere relations of phenomena. Nothing easier than to contemn the mode of life represented by this wealthy middle class; but compare it with other existences conceivable by a thinking man, and it was emphatically good. It aimed at placidity, at benevolence, at supreme cleanliness,—things which more than compensated for the absence of higher spirituality. We can be but what we are; these people accepted themselves, and in doing so became estimable mortals. No imbecile pretensions exposed them to rebuke of a social satirist; no vulgarity tainted their familiar intercourse. Their allegiance to a worn-out creed was felt as an added grace; thus only could their souls aspire, and the imperfect poetry of their natures be developed.

It is on good intellectual grounds that Peak proposes to himself "a life of deliberate baseness", and his intellectual honesty, his intellectual pride, are such as to prevent him from hiding from himself the fact of his baseness. By any standards, it seems to me, Peak is a most striking piece of characterisation, and if we are to look for parallels with him in the novel we must go outside English fiction. In his resolute acceptance of the death of Christianity and in his determination to make his own morality he is a Nietzschean figure, and his true affinity is with Dostoevsky's Raskolnikov and Turgenev's Bazarov. *Crime and Punishment* and *Fathers and Sons* are, it goes without saying, much greater novels than *Born in Exile*. All the same, it is the index of Gissing's achievement in *Born in Exile* that Peak is not extinguished by the comparisons and that in the end they are the only comparisons that can be made.

PART THE FIRST

I

THE SUMMER DAY in 1874 which closed the annual session of Whitelaw College was marked by a special ceremony, preceding the wonted distribution of academic rewards. At eleven in the morning (just as a heavy shower fell from the smoke-canopy above the roaring streets) the municipal authorities, educational dignitaries, and prominent burgesses of Kingsmill assembled on an open space before the college to unveil a statue of Sir Job Whitelaw. The honoured baronet had been six months dead. Living, he opposed the desire of his fellow-citizens to exhibit even on canvas his gnarled features and bald crown; but when his modesty ceased to have a voice in the matter, no time was lost in raising a memorial of the great manufacturer, the self-made millionaire, the borough member in three Parliaments, the enlightened and benevolent founder of an institute which had conferred humane distinction on the money-making Midland town. Beneath such a sky, orations were necessarily curtailed; but Sir Job had always been impatient of much talk. An interval of two or three hours dispersed the rain-clouds and bestowed such grace of sunshine as Kingsmill might at this season temperately desire; then, whilst the marble figure was getting dried,—with soot-stains which already foretold its nigritude of a year hence,—again streamed towards the college a varied multitude, official, parental, pupillary. The students had nothing distinctive in their garb, but here and there flitted the cap and gown of Professor or lecturer, signal for doffing of beavers along the line of its progress.

Among the more deliberate of the throng was a slender, upright, ruddy-cheeked gentleman of middle age, accompanied by his wife and a daughter of sixteen. On alighting from a carriage, they first of all directed their steps towards the statue, conversing together with pleasant animation. The father (Martin Warricombe, Esq. of Thornhaw, a small estate some five miles from Kingsmill,) had a countenance suggestive of engaging qualities—genial humour, mildness, a turn for meditation, perhaps for study. His attire was informal, as if he disliked abandoning the freedom of the country even when summoned to urban ceremonies. He wore a grey felt hat, and a light jacket which displayed the straightness of his shoulders. Mrs. Warricombe and her daughter were more fashionably equipped, with taste which proclaimed their social standing. Save her fresh yet delicate complexion the lady had no particular personal charm. Of the young girl it could only be said that she exhibited a graceful immaturity, with perchance a little more earnestness than is common at her age; her voice, even when she spoke gaily, was seldom audible save by the person addressed.

Coming to a pause before Sir Job, Mr. Warricombe put on a pair of eyeglasses which had dangled against his waistcoat, and began to scrutinise carefully the sculptured lineaments. He was addressing certain critical remarks to his companions when an interruption appeared in the form of a young man whose first words announced his relation to the group.

'I say, you're very late! There'll be no getting a decent seat, if you don't mind. Leave Sir Job till afterwards.'

'The statue somehow disappoints me,' observed his father, placidly.

'Oh, it isn't bad, I think,' returned the youth, in a voice not unlike his father's, save for a note of excessive self-confidence. He looked about eighteen; his comely countenance, with its air of robust health and habitual exhilaration, told of a boyhood passed amid free and joyous circumstances. It was the face of a young English plutocrat, with more of intellect than such visages are wont to betray; the native vigour of his temperament had probably assimilated something of the modern spirit. 'I'm glad,' he continued, 'that they haven't stuck him in a toga, or any humbug of that sort. The old fellow looks baggy, but so he was. They ought to have kept his chimney-pot, though. Better than giving him those scraps of hair, when everyone knows he was as bald as a beetle.'

'Sir Job should have been granted Caesar's privilege,' said Mr. Warricombe, with a pleasant twinkle in his eyes.

'What was that?' came from the son, with abrupt indifference.

'For shame, Buckland!'

'What do I care for Caesar's privileges? We can't burden our minds with that antiquated rubbish nowadays. You would despise it yourself, father, if it hadn't got packed into your head when you were young.'

The parent raised his eyebrows in a bantering smile.

'I have lived to hear classical learning called antiquated rubbish. Well, well!—Ha! there is Professor Gale.'

The Professor of Geology, a tall man, who strode over the pavement as if he were among granite hills, caught sight of the party and approached. His greeting was that of a familiar friend; he addressed young Warricombe and his sister by their Christian names, and inquired after certain younger members of the household. Mr. Warricombe, regarding him with a look of repressed eagerness, laid a hand on his arm, and spoke in the subdued voice of one who has important news to communicate.

'If I am not much mistaken, I have chanced on a new species of *hamalonotus*!'

'Indeed!—not in your kitchen garden, I presume?'

'Hardly. Dr. Pollock sent me a box of specimens the other day'——

Buckland saw with annoyance the likelihood of prolonged discussion.

'I don't know whether you care to remain standing all the afternoon,' he said to his mother. 'At this rate we certainly shan't get seats.'

'We will walk on, Martin,' said the lady, glancing at her husband.

'We come! we come!' cried the Professor, with a wave of his arm.

The palæontological talk continued as far as the entrance of the assembly hall. The zest with which Mr. Warricombe spoke of his discovery never led him to raise his voice above the suave, mellow note, touched with humour, which expressed a modest assurance. Mr. Gale was distinguished by a blunter mode of speech; he discoursed with open-air vigour, making use now and then of a racy colloquialism which the other would hardly have permitted himself.

As young Warricombe had foreseen, the seats obtainable were none too advantageous; only on one of the highest rows of the amphitheatre could they at length establish themselves.

'Buckland will enjoy the more attention when he marches down to take his prizes,' observed the father. 'He must sit at the end here, that he mayn't have a struggle to get out.'

'Don't, Martin, don't!' urged his wife, considerately.

'Oh, it doesn't affect me,' said Buckland, with a laugh. 'I feel pretty sure I have got the Logic and the Chemistry, and those are what I care most about. I dare say Peak has beaten me in Geology.'

The appearance in the lower part of the hall of a dark-robed procession, headed by the tall figure of the Principal, imposed a moment's silence, broken by outbursts of welcoming applause. The Professors of Whitelaw College were highly popular, not alone with the members of their classes, but with all the educated inhabitants of Kingsmill; and deservedly, for several of them bore names of wide recognition, and as a body they did honour to the institution which had won their services. With becoming formality they seated themselves in face of the public. On tables before them were exposed a considerable number of well-bound books, shortly to be distributed among the collegians, who gazed in that direction with speculative eyes.

Among the general concourse might have been discovered two or three representatives of the wage-earning multitude which Kingsmill depended upon for its prosperity, but their presence was due to exceptional circumstances; the college provided for proletarian education by a system of evening classes, a curriculum necessarily quite apart from that followed by the regular students. Kingsmill, to be sure, was no nurse of Toryism; the robust employers of labour who sent their sons to Whitelaw—either to complete a training deemed sufficient for an active career, or by way of transition-stage between school and university—were for the most part avowed Radicals, in theory scornful of privilege, practically supporters of that mode of freedom which regards life as a remorseless conflict. Not a few of the young men (some of these the hardest and most successful workers) came from poor, middle-class homes, whence, but for Sir Job's foundation, they must have set forth into the world with no better equipment of knowledge than was supplied by some 'academy' of the old type: a glance distinguished such students from the well-dressed and well-fed offspring of Kingsmill plutocracy. The note of the assembly was something other than refinement; rather its high standard of health, spirits, and comfort—the characteristic of Capitalism. Decent reverence for learning, keen appreciation of scientific power, warm liberality of thought and sentiment within appreciable limits, enthusiasm for economic, civic, national ideals, —such attributes were abundantly discoverable in each serried row. From the expanse of countenances beamed a boundless self-satisfaction. To be connected in any way with Whitelaw formed a subject of pride, seeing that here was the sturdy outcome of the most modern educational endeavour, a noteworthy instance of what Englishmen can do for themselves, unaided by bureaucratic machinery. Every student who achieved distinction in to-day's class lists was felt to bestow a share of his honour upon each spectator who applauded him.

With occasional adjustment of his eye-glasses, and smiling his smile of modest tolerance, Mr. Warricombe surveyed the crowded hall. His connection with the town was not intimate, and he could discover few faces that were familiar to him. A native and, till of late, an inhabitant of Devon, he had come to reside on his property near Kingsmill because it seemed to him that the education of his children would be favoured by a removal thither. Two of his oldest friends held professorships at Whitelaw; here, accordingly, his eldest son was making preparation for Cambridge, whilst his daughter attended classes at the admirable High School, of which Kingsmill was only less proud than of its College.

Seated between his father and his sister, Buckland drew their attention to such persons or personages as interested his very selective mind.

'Admire the elegant languor of Wotherspoon,' he remarked, indicating the Professor of Greek. 'Watch him for a moment, and you'll see him glance contemptuously at old Plummer. He can't help it; they hate each other.'

'But why?' whispered the girl, with timid eagerness.

'Oh, it began, they say, when Plummer once had to take one of Wotherspoon's classes; some foolery about a second aorist. Thank goodness, I don't understand the profound dispute.—Oh, do look at that fatuous idiot Chilvers!'

The young gentleman of whom he spoke, a student of Buckland's own standing, had just attracted general notice. Risen from his seat in the lower part of the amphitheatre, at the moment when all were hushed in anticipation of the Principal's address, Mr. Chilvers was beckoning to someone whom his eye had descried at a great distance, and for whom, as he indicated by gesture, he had preserved a place.

'See how it delights him to make an exhibition of himself!' pursued the censorious youth. 'I'd bet a sovereign he's arranged it all. Look how he brandishes his arm to display his cuffs and gold links. Now he touches his hair, to point out how light and exquisite it is, and how beautifully he parts it!'

'What a graceful figure!' murmured Mrs. Warricombe, with genuine admiration.

'There, that's just what he hopes everyone is saying,' replied her son, in a tone of laughing disgust.

'But he certainly *is* graceful, Buckland,' persisted the lady.

'And in the meantime,' remarked Mr. Warricombe, drily, 'we are all awaiting the young gentleman's pleasure.'

'Of course; he enjoys it. Almost all the people on that row belong to him—father, mother, sisters, brothers, uncles, aunts, and cousins to the fourth degree. Look at their eyes fondly fixed upon him! Now he pretends to loosen his collar at the throat, just for a change of attitude—the puppy!'

'My dear!' remonstrated his mother, with apprehensive glance at her neighbours.

'But he is really clever, isn't he, Buckland?' asked the sister,—her name was Sidwell.

'After a fashion. I shouldn't wonder if he takes a dozen or two prizes. It's all a knack you know.'

'Where is your friend Peak?' Mr. Warricombe made inquiry.

But at this moment Mr. Chilvers abandoned his endeavour and became seated, allowing the Principal to rise, manuscript in hand. Buckland leaned back with an air of resignation to boredom; his father bent slightly forward, with lips close pressed and brows wrinkled; Mrs. Warricombe widened her eyes, as if hearing were performed with those organs, and assumed the smile she would have worn had the speaker been addressing her in particular. Sidwell's blue eyes imitated the movement of her mother's, with a look of profound gravity which showed that she had wholly forgotten herself in reverential listening; only when five minutes' strict attention induced a sense of weariness did she allow a glance to stray first along the professorial rank, then towards the place where the golden head of young Chilvers was easily distinguishable.

Nothing could be more satisfactory than the annual report summarised by Principal Nares, whose mellifluous voice and daintily pedantic utterance fell upon expectant hearing with the impressiveness of personal compliment. So delivered, statistics partook of the grace of culture; details of academic organisation acquired something more than secular significance. In this the ninth year of its existence, Whitelaw College was flourishing in every possible way. Private beneficence had endowed it with new scholarships and exhibitions; the scheme of lectures had been extended; the number of its students steadily increased, and their successes in the field of examination had been noteworthy beyond precedent. Truly, the heart of their founder, to whom honour had this day been rendered, must have gladdened if he could but have listened to the story of dignified progress! Applause, loud and long, greeted the close of the address. Buckland Warricombe was probably the only collegian who disdained to manifest approval in any way.

'Why don't you clap?' asked his sister, who, girl-like, was excited to warmth of cheek and brightness of eye by the enthusiasm about her.

'That kind of thing is out of date,' replied the young man, thrusting his hands deep into his pockets.

As Professor of Logic and Moral Philosophy, Dr. Nares began the distribution of prizes. Buckland, in spite of his resolve to exhibit no weakness, waited with unmistakable tremor for the announcement of the leading name, which might possibly be his own. A few words of comment prefaced the declaration:—never had it been the Professor's lot to review more admirable papers than those to which he had awarded the first prize. The name of the student called upon to come forward was—Godwin Peak.

'Beaten!' escaped from Buckland's lips.

Mrs. Warricombe glanced at her son with smiling sympathy; Sidwell, whose cheek had paled as her nerves quivered under the stress of expectancy, murmured a syllable of disappointment; Mr. Warricombe set his brows and did not venture to look aside. A moment, and all eyes were directed upon the successful student, who rose from a seat half-way down the hall and descended the middle passage towards the row of Professors. He was a young man of spare figure and unhealthy complexion, his age not easily conjectured. Embarrassment no doubt accounted for much of the awkwardness of his demeanour; but, under any circumstances, he must have appeared ungainly, for his long arms and legs had outgrown their garments, which were no fashionable specimens of tailoring. The nervous gravity of his countenance had a peculiar sternness; one might have imagined that he was fortifying his self-control with scorn of the elegantly clad people through whom he passed. Amid plaudits, he received from the hands of the Principal a couple of solid volumes, probably some standard work of philosophy, and, thus burdened, returned with hurried step to his place.

'No one expected that,' remarked Buckland to his father. 'He must have crammed furiously for the exam. It's outside his work for the First B.A.'

'What a shame!' Sidwell whispered to her mother; and the reply was a look which eloquently expressed Mrs. Warricombe's lack of sympathy with the victor.

But a second prize had been awarded. As soon as silence was restored, the Principal's gracious voice delivered a summons to 'Buckland Martin Warricombe.' A burst of acclamation, coming especially from that part of the amphitheatre where Whitelaw's nurslings had gathered in greatest numbers, seemed to declare the second prizeman distinctly more popular than the first. Preferences of this kind are always to be remarked on such occasions.

'Second prize be hanged!' growled the young man, as, with a flush of shame on his ruddy countenance, he set forth to receive the honour, leaving Mr. Warricombe convulsed with silent laughter.

'He would far rather have had nothing at all,' murmured Sidwell, who shared her brother's pique and humiliation.

'Oh, it'll do him good,' was her father's reply. 'Buckland has got into a way of swaggering.'

Undeniable was the swagger with which the good-looking, breezy lad went and returned.

'What is the book?' inquired Mr. Warricombe.

'I don't know.—Oh, Mill's Logic. Idiotic choice! They might have known I had it already.'

'They clap him far more than they did Mr. Peak,' Sidwell whispered to her mother, with satisfaction.

Buckland kept silence for a few minutes, then muttered:

'There's nothing I care about now till Chemistry and Geology. Here comes old Wotherspoon. Now we shall know who is strongest in second aorists. I shouldn't wonder if Peak takes both Senior Greek and Latin. I heartily hope he'll beat that ass Chilvers.'

But the name so offensive to young Warricombe was the first that issued from the Professor's lips. Beginning with the competition for a special classical prize, Professor Wotherspoon announced that the honours had fallen to 'Bruno Leathwaite Chilvers.'

'That young man is not badly supplied with brains, say what you will,' remarked Mr. Warricombe.

Upon Bruno Leathwaite Chilvers keen attention was directed; every pair of female eyes studied his graces, and female hands had a great part in the applause that greeted his arising. Applause different in kind from that hitherto bestowed; less noisy, but implying, one felt, a more delicate spirit of commendation. With perfect self-command, with singular facial decorum, with a walk which betokened elegant athleticism and safely skirted the bounds of foppery, Mr. Chilvers discharged the duty he was conscious of owing to a multitude of kinsfolk, friends, admirers. You would have detected something clerical in the young man's air. It became the son of a popular clergyman, and gave promise of notable aptitude for the sacred career to which Bruno Leathwaite, as was well understood, already had designed himself. In matters sartorial he presented a high ideal to his fellow-students; this seemly attention to externals, and the delicate glow of health discernible through the golden down of his cheeks, testified the compatibility of hard study and social observances. Bruno had been heard to say that the one thing it behoved Whitelaw to keep carefully in mind was the preservation of 'tone,' a quality far less easy to cultivate than mere academic excellence.

'How clever he must be!' purred Mrs. Warricombe. 'If he lives, he will some day be an archbishop.'

Buckland was leaning back with his eyes closed, disgusted at the spectacle. Nor did he move when Professor Wotherspoon's voice made the next announcement.

'In Senior Greek, the first prize is taken by—Bruno Leathwaite Chilvers.'

'Then I suppose Peak comes second,' muttered Buckland.

So it proved. Summoned to receive the inferior prize, Godwin Peak, his countenance harsher than before, his eyes cast down, moved ungracefully to the estrade. And during the next half-hour this twofold exhibition was several times repeated. In Senior Latin, in Modern and Ancient History, in English Language and Literature, in French, first sounded the name of Chilvers, whilst to the second award was invariably attached that of Peak. Mrs. Warricombe's delight expressed itself in every permissible way: on each occasion she exclaimed, 'How clever he is!' Sidwell cast frequent glances at her brother, in whom a shrewder eye could have divined conflict of feelings—disgust at the glorification of Chilvers and involuntary pleasure in the successive defeats of his own conqueror in Philosophy. Buckland's was by no means an ignoble face; venial malice did not ultimately prevail in him.

'It's Peak's own fault,' he declared at length, with vexation. 'Chilvers stuck to the subjects of his course. Peak has been taking up half-a-dozen extras, and they've done for him. I shouldn't wonder if he went in for the Poem and the Essay; I know he was thinking about both.'

Whether Godwin Peak had or had not endeavoured for these two prizes remained uncertain. When, presently, the results of the competition were made known, it was found that in each case the honour had fallen to a young man hitherto undistinguished. His name was John Edward Earwaker. Externally he bore a sort of generic resemblance to Peak, for his face was thin and the fashion of his clothing indicated narrow means.

'I never heard you mention him,' said Mr. Warricombe, turning to his son with an air of surprise.

'I scarcely know him at all; he's only in one or two of my classes. Peak is thick with him.'

The subject of the prize poem was 'Alaric'; that of the essay, 'Trades Unionism.' So it was probable that John Edward Earwaker did not lack versatility of intellect.

On the rising of the Professor of Chemistry, Buckland had once more to subdue signs of expectancy. He knew he had done good papers, but his confidence in the result was now clouded by a dread of the second prize. Which indeed fell to him, the first being taken by a student of no account save in this very special subject. Keen was his mortification; he growled, muttered, shrugged his shoulders nervously.

'If I had foreseen this, you'd never have caught me here,' was his reply, when Sidwell whispered consolation.

There still remained a chance for him, signalled by the familiar form of Professor Gale. Geology had been a lifelong study with Martin Warricombe, and his son pursued it with hereditary aptitude. Sidwell and her mother exchanged a look of courageous hope; each felt convinced that the genial Professor could not so far disregard private feeling as to place Buckland anywhere but at the head of the class.

'The results of the examination are fairly good; I'm afraid I can't say more than that,' thus rang out Mr. Gale's hearty voice.

'As for the first two names on my list, I haven't felt justified in placing either before the other. I have bracketed them, and there will be two prizes. The names are—Godwin Peak and Buckland Martin Warricombe.'

'He might have mentioned Buckland first,' murmured Mrs. Warricombe, resentfully.

'He of course gave them out in alphabetical order,' answered her husband.

'Still, it isn't right that Buckland should come second.'

'That's absurd,' was the good-natured reply.

The lady of course remained unconvinced, and for years she nourished a pique against Professor Gale, not so much owing to his having bracketed her son as because the letter P has alphabetical precedence of W.

In what remained of the proceedings the Warricombes had no personal interest. For a special reason, however, their attention was excited by the rising of Professor Walsh, who represented the science of Physics. Early in the present year had been published a speculative treatise which, owing to its supposed incompatibility with Christian dogmas, provoked much controversy and was largely discussed in all educated circles. The work was anonymous, but a rumour which gained general currency attributed it to Professor Walsh. In the year 1874 an imputation of religious heresy was not lightly to be incurred by a Professor—even Professor of Physics—at an English college. There were many people in Kingsmill who considered that Mr. Walsh's delay in repudiating so grave a charge rendered very doubtful the propriety of his retaining the chair at Whitelaw. Significant was the dispersed applause which followed slowly upon his stepping forward to-day; on the Professor's face was perchance legible something like a hint of amused defiance. Ladies had ceased to beam; they glanced meaningly at one another, and then from under their eyelids at the supposed heretic.

'A fine fellow, Walsh!' exclaimed Buckland, clapping vigorously.

His father smiled, but with some uneasiness. Mrs. Warricombe whispered to Sidwell:

'What a very disagreeable face! The only one of the Professors who doesn't seem a gentleman.'

The girl was aware of dark reports affecting Mr. Walsh's reputation. She hazarded only a brief examination of his features, and looked at the applauding Buckland with alarm.

'His lectures are splendid,' said her brother, emphatically. 'If I were going to be here next session, I should take them.'

For some minutes after the Professor's return to his seat a susurration was audible throughout the hall; bonnets bent together, and beards exchanged curt comments.

The ceremony, as is usual with all ceremonies, grew wearisome before its end. Buckland was deep in one of the chapters of his geologic prize when the last speaker closed the last report and left the assembly free to disperse. Then followed the season of congratulations: Professors, students, and the friendly public mingled in a conversazione. A nucleus of vivacious intercourse formed at the spot where young Mr. Chilvers stood amid trophies of examinational prowess. When his numerous relatives had all shaken hands with him, and laughed, smiled, or smirked their felicitations, they made way for the press of eager acquaintances. His prize library was reverently surveyed, and many were the sportive sallies elicited by the victor's obvious inability to carry away what he had won. Suavely exultant, ready with his reply to every flattering address, Bruno Chilvers exhibited a social tact in advance of his years: it was easy to imagine what he would become when Oxford terms and the seal of ordination had matured his youthful promise.

At no great distance stood his competitor, Godwin Peak—embarrassed, he also, with wealth of spoils; but about this young man was no concourse of admiring kinsfolk. No lady offered him her hand or shaped compliments for him with gracious lips. Half-a-dozen fellow-students, among them John Earwaker, talked in his vicinity of the day's results. Peak's part in the gossip was small, and when he smiled it was in a forced, anxious way, with brief raising of his eyes. For a moment only was the notice of a wider circle directed upon him when Dr. Nares, moving past with a train of colloquial attendants, turned aside to repeat his praise of the young man's achievements in Philosophy: he bestowed a kindly shake of the hand, and moved on.

The Warricombe group descended, in purposeless fashion, towards the spot where Chilvers held his court. Their personal acquaintance with Bruno and his family was slight, and though Mrs. Warricombe would gladly have pushed forward to claim recognition, natural diffidence restrained her. Sidwell kept in the rear, risking now and then a glance of vivid curiosity on either hand. Buckland, striving not to look petulant or sullen, allowed himself to be led on; but when he became aware of the tendency Bruno-wards, a protest broke from him.

'There's no need to swell that fellow's conceit. Here, father, come and have a word with Peak; he looks rather down in the mouth among his second prizes.'

Mr. Warricombe having beckoned his companions, they reluctantly followed to the more open part of the hall.

'It's very generous of Buckland,' fell from the lady's lips, and she at length resolved to show an equal magnanimity. Peak and Earwaker were conversing together when Buckland broke in upon them with genial outburst.

'Confound it, Peak! what do you mean by getting me stuck into a bracket?'

'I had the same question to ask *you*,' returned the other, with a grim smile.

Mr. Warricombe came up with extended hand.

'A species of bracket,' he remarked, smiling benevolently, 'which no algebraic process will remove. Let us hope it signifies that you and Buckland will work through life shoulder to shoulder in the field of geology. What did Professor Gale give you?'

Before he could reply, Peak had to exchange greetings with Mrs. Warricombe and her daughter. Only once hitherto had he met them. Six months ago he had gone out with Buckland to the country-house and passed an afternoon there, making at the time no very favourable impression on his hostess. He was not of the young men who easily insinuate themselves into ladies' affections: his exterior was against him, and he seemed too conscious of his disadvantages in that particular. Mrs. Warricombe found it difficult to shape a few civil phrases for the acceptance of the saturnine student. Sidwell, repelled and in a measure alarmed by his bilious countenance, could do no more than grant him her delicately gloved fingers. Peak, for his part, had nothing to say. He did not even affect an interest in these persons, and turned his eyes to follow the withdrawing Earwaker. Mr. Warricombe, however, had found topic for discourse in the prize volume; he began to comment on the excellence of certain sections of the book.

'Do you go home?' interrupted Buckland, addressing the question to his rival. 'Or do you stay in Kingsmill until the First B.A.?'

'I shall go home,' replied Peak, moving uneasily.

'Perhaps we may have the pleasure of seeing you at Thornhaw when you are up again for the examination?' said Mrs. Warricombe, with faltering tongue.

'I'm afraid I shan't be able to come, thank you,' was the awkward response.

Buckland's voice came to the relief.

'I daresay I may look in upon you at your torture. Good luck, old fellow! If we don't see each other again, write to me at Trinity before the end of the year.'

As soon as she was sufficiently remote, Mrs. Warricombe ejaculated in a subdued voice of irritation:

'Such a very unprepossessing young man I never met! He seems to have no breeding whatever.'

'Overweighted with brains,' replied her husband; adding to himself, 'and by no means so with money, I fear.'

Opportunity at length offering, Mrs. Warricombe stepped into the circle irradiated by Bruno Chilvers; her husband and Sidwell pressed after. Buckland, with an exclamation of disgust, went off to criticise the hero among a group of his particular friends.

Godwin Peak stood alone. On the bench where he had sat were heaped the prize volumes (eleven in all, some of them massive), and his wish was to make arrangements for their removal. Gazing about him, he became aware of the college librarian, with whom he was on friendly terms.

'Mr. Poppleton, who would pack and send these books away for me?'

'An *embarras de richesse!*' laughed the librarian. 'If you like to tell the porter to take care of them for the present, I shall be glad to see that they are sent wherever you like.'

Peak answered with a warmth of acknowledgment which seemed to imply that he did not often receive kindnesses. Before long he was free to leave the College, and at the exit he overtook Earwaker, who carried a brown paper parcel.

'Come and have some tea with me across the way, will you?' said the literary prizeman. 'I have a couple of hours to wait for my train.'

'All right. I envy you that five-volume Spenser.'

'I wish they had given me five authors I don't possess instead. I think I shall sell this.'

Earwaker laughed as he said it—a strange chuckle from deep down in his throat. A comparison of the young men, as they walked side by side, showed that Peak was of better physical type than his comrade. Earwaker had a slight, unshapely body and an ill-fitting head; he walked with excessive strides and swung his thin arm nervously. Probably he was the elder of the two, and he looked twenty. For Peak's disadvantages of person, his studious bashfulness and poverty of attire were mainly responsible. With improvement in general health even his features might have a tolerable comeliness, or at all events would not be disagreeable. Earwaker's visage was homely, and seemed the more so for his sprouting moustache and beard.

'Have you heard any talk about Walsh?' the latter inquired, as they walked on.

Peak shrugged his shoulders, with a laugh.

'No. Have you?'

'Some women in front of me just now were evidently discussing him. I heard "How shocking!" and "Disgraceful!"'

Peak's eyes flashed, and he exclaimed in a voice of wrath:

'Besotted idiots! How I wish I were in Walsh's position! How I should enjoy standing up before the crowd of fools and seeing their fear of me! But I couldn't keep it to myself; I should give in to the temptation to call them blockheads and jackasses.'

Earwaker was amused at his friend's vehemence. He sympathised with it, but had an unyouthful sobriety in the expression of his feelings.

'Most likely he despises them far too much to be disturbed by what they think of him. But, I say, isn't it desperately comical that one human being can hate and revile another because they think differently about the origin of the universe? Couldn't you roar with laughter when you've thought over it for a moment? "You be damned for your theory of irregular verbs!" is nothing to it.' And he uttered his croak of mirth, whilst Peak, with distorted features, laughed in rage and scorn.

They had crossed the open space in front of the College buildings, and were issuing into the highway, when a voice very unlike those that were wont to sound within the academic precincts (or indeed in the streets of Kingsmill) made sudden demand upon Peak's attention.

'Thet you, Godwin? Thoughts I, it must be 'im! 'Ow goes it, my bo-oy? You 'ardly reckonise me, I dessay, and I couldn't be sure as it was you till I'd 'ed a good squint at yer. I've jest called round at your lodgin's, and they towld me as you was at the Collige.'

He who thus accosted the student, with the most offensive purity of Cockney accent, was a man of five-and-forty, dressed in a new suit of ready-made tweeds, the folding crease strongly marked down the front of the trousers and the coat sleeves rather too long. His face bore a strong impress of vulgarity, but at the same time had a certain ingenuousness, a self-absorbed energy and simplicity, which saved it from being wholly repellent; the brow was narrow, the eyes small and bright, and the coarse lips half hid themselves under a struggling reddish growth. In these lineaments lurked a family resemblance to Godwin Peak, sufficient to support a claim of kindred which at this moment might have seemed improbable. At the summons of recognition Godwin stood transfixed; his arms fell straight, and his head drew back as if to avoid a blow. For an instant he was clay colour, then a hot flush broke upon his cheeks.

'I shan't be able to go with you,' he said, in a thick, abrupt voice, addressing Earwaker but not regarding him. 'Good-bye!'

The other offered his hand and, without speaking, walked away.

'Prize-dye at the Collige, they tell me,' pursued Godwin's relative, looking at a cluster of people that passed. 'What 'ave you took?'

'One or two class-prizes,' replied the student, his eyes on the ground. 'Shall we walk to my lodgings?'

'I thought you might like to walk me over the show. But pr'aps you're in a 'urry?'

'No, no. But there's nothing particular to see. I think the lecture-rooms are closed by now.'

'Oo's the gent as stands there?—the figger, I mean.'

'Sir Job Whitelaw, founder of the College.'

'Job, eh? And was you a-goin' 'ome to yer tea, Godwin?'

'Yes.'

'Well, then, look 'ere, 'spose we go to the little shop opposyte—nice little plyce it looks. I could do a cup o' tea myself, and we can 'ev a quiet confab. It's a long time since we 'ed a talk together. I come over from Twybridge this mornin'; slep' there last night, and saw yer mother an' Oliver. They couldn't give me a bed, but that didn't mike no matter; I put up at the Norfolk Harms—five-an'-six for bed an' breakfast. Come along, my bo-oy; I stand treat.'

Godwin glanced about him. From the College was approaching what seemed to be a formal procession; it consisted of Bruno Chilvers, supported on either hand by ladies and followed by an admiring train.

'You had better come to my lodgings with me, uncle,' said the young man hurriedly, moving forward.

'No, no; I won't be no expense to you, Godwin, bo-oy. And I 'ave a reason for wantin' to go to the little shop opposyte.'

Already several collegians had passed, giving Peak a nod and scanning his companion; a moment's delay and Chilvers would be upon him. Without another word, Godwin moved across the broad street to the place of refreshment which his uncle had indicated, and whither Earwaker had preceded them It was a pastrycook's, occasionally visited by the alumni of Whitelaw. In the rear of the shop a little room offered seats and tables, and here, Godwin knew, Earwaker would be found.

'Let us go up-stairs,' he said, leading to a side entrance. 'There's a quieter room.'

'Right you are!'

The uncle—his name was Andrew Peak—paused to make a survey of the premises. When he entered, his scrutiny of the establishment was close, and he seemed to reflect with interest upon all he saw. The upper room was empty; a long table exhibited knives and forks, but there were no signs of active business. Andrew pulled a bell-rope; the summons was answered by an asthmatic woman, who received an order for tea, toast, 'water-creases,' and sundry other constituents of a modest meal.

'Come 'ere often, Godwin?' inquired Andrew, as he stood by the window and mused.

'Now and then, for a bun.'

'Much custom from your show over the wye?'

'Not so much as a better place would have.'

'Young gents don't live at the Collige, they tell me?'

'No, there's no residence.'

'So naturally they want a plyce where they can 'ev a nibble, somewheres 'andy?'

'Yes. We have to go further into the town for a decent dinner.'

'Jest what I thought!' exclaimed Andrew, slapping his leg. 'With a establishment like that opposyte, there'd ought to be a medium-sized Spiers & Pond at this 'ere street corner for any man as knows 'is wye about. That's *my* idea, Godwin—see?'

Peak had as yet given but half an ear to his relative's discourse; he had answered mechanically, and only now was constrained to serious attention by a note of meaning in the last interrogative. He looked at the speaker; and Andrew, in the manner of one accustomed to regard life as a game of cunning, first winked with each eye, then extended one cheek with the pressure of his tongue. Sickened with disgust, Godwin turned suddenly away,—a movement entirely lost upon his uncle, who imagined the young man to be pondering a fruitful suggestion.

2

'I don't mind tellin' you, Godwin,' pursued Andrew presently, in a cautious voice, laying an open hand against his trousers-pocket, 'as I've been a-doin' pretty good business lytely. Been growin' a bit—see? I'm runnin' round an' keepin' my heyes open—understand? Thoughts I, now, if I could come acrosst a nicet little openin', somethink in the rest'rant line, *that's* what 'ud sewt me jest about down to the ground. I'm cut out for it—see? I've got the practical experience, and I've got the capital; and as soon as I got a squint of this little corner shop—understand what I mean?'

His eyes gleamed with eagerness which was too candid for the typically vulgar mind. In his self-satisfaction he exhibited a gross cordiality which might have made rather an agreeable impression on a person otherwise disinterested.

At this point the asthmatic woman reappeared, carrying a laden tray. Andrew at once entered into conversation with her, framing his remarks and queries so as to learn all he could concerning the state of the business and the disposition of its proprietors. His nephew, meanwhile, stung to the core with shame, kept apart, as if amusing himself with the prospect from the window, until summoned to partake of the meal. His uncle expressed contempt of everything laid before them.

'*This* ain't no wye of caterin' for young gents at Collige!' he exclaimed. 'If there ain't a openin' 'ere, then I never see one. Godwin, bo-oy, 'ow much longer 'll it be before you're out of you're time over there?'

'It's uncertain—I can't say.'

'But ain't it understood as you stay till you've passed the top standard, or whatever it's called?'

'I really haven't made up my mind what to do.'

'But you'll be studyin' 'ere for another twelve months, I dessay?'

'Why do you ask?'

'Why? cos s'posin' I got 'old o' this 'ere little shop, or another like it close by, me an' you might come to a understandin'—see? It might be worth your while to give a 'int to the young gents as you're in with—eh?'

Godwin was endeavouring to masticate a piece of toast, but it turned to sawdust upon his palate. Of a sudden, when the bilious gloom of his countenance foretold anything but mirth, he burst into hard laughter. Andrew smote him jovially on the back.

'Tickles you, eh, bo-oy? "Peak's Refreshment an' Dinin' Rooms!" Everything tip-top, mind; respectable business, Godwin; nothing for nobody to be ashamed of—*that* wouldn't do, of course.'

The young man's laughter ended as abruptly as it had begun, but his visage was no longer clouded with bitter misery. A strange indifference seemed to have come upon him, and whilst the speculative uncle talked away with increasing excitement, he ate and drank heedlessly.

'Mother expects you to-morrow, she tells me,' said Andrew, when his companion's taciturnity had suggested a change of topic. 'Shouldn't wonder if you see me over at Twybridge again before long. I was to remember your awnt and your cousin Jowey to you. You wouldn't know Jowey? the sharpest lad of his age as ever I knowed, is Jowey. Your father 'ud a' took a delight in 'im, if 'e'd lived, that 'e would.'

For a quarter of an hour or so the dialogue was concerned with domestic history. Godwin gave brief reply to many questions, but asked none, not even such as civility required. The elder man, however, was unaffected by this reticence, and when at length his nephew pleaded an engagement as excuse for leave-taking he shook hands with much warmth. The two parted close by the shop, and Godwin, casting a glance at the now silent College, walked hastily towards his lodgings.

II

IN THE PROSPEROUS year of 1856, incomes of between a hundred and a hundred and fifty pounds were chargeable with a tax of elevenpence halfpenny in the pound: persons who enjoyed a revenue of a hundred and fifty or more had the honour of paying one and fourpence. Abatements there were none, and families supporting life on two pounds a week might in some cases, perchance, be reconciled to the mulct by considering how equitably its incidence was graduated.

Some, on the other hand, were less philosophical; for instance, the household consisting of Nicholas Peak, his wife, their three-year-old daughter, their newly-born son, and a blind sister of Nicholas, dependent upon him for sustenance. Mr. Peak, aged thirty and now four years wedded, had a small cottage on the outskirts of Greenwich. He was employed as dispenser, at a salary of thirty-five shillings a week, by a medical man with a large practice. His income, therefore, fell considerably within the hundred pound limit; and, all things considered, it was not unreasonable that he should be allowed to expend the whole of this sum on domestic necessities. But it came to pass that Nicholas, in his greed of wealth, obtained supplementary employment, which benefited him to the extent of a yearly ten pounds. Called upon to render his statement to the surveyor of income-tax, he declared himself in possession of a hundred and one pounds per annum; consequently, he stood indebted to the Exchequer in the sum of four pounds, sixteen shillings, and ninepence. His countenance darkened, as also did that of Mrs. Peak.

'This is wrong and cruel—dreadfully cruel!' cried the latter, with tears in her eyes.

'It is; but that's no new thing,' was the bitter reply.

'I think it's wrong of *you*, Nicholas. What need is there to say anything about that ten pounds? It's taking the food out of our mouths.'

Knowing only the letter of the law, Mr. Peak answered sternly:

'My income is a hundred and one pounds. I can't sign my name to a lie.'

Picture the man. Tall, gaunt, with sharp intellectual features, and eyes of singular beauty, the face of an enthusiast—under given circumstances, of a hero. Poorly clad, of course, but with rigorous self-respect; his boots polished, *propria manu*, to the point of perfection; his linen washed and ironed by the indefatigable wife. Of simplest tastes, of most frugal habits, a few books the only luxury which he deemed indispensable; yet a most difficult man to live with, for to him applied precisely the description which Robert Burns gave of his own father; he was 'of stubborn, ungainly integrity and headlong irascibility.'

Ungainly, for his strong impulses towards culture were powerless to obliterate the traces of his rude origin. Born in a London alley, the son of a labourer burdened with a large family, he had made his way by sheer force of character to a position which would have seemed proud success but for the difficulty with which he kept himself alive. His parents were dead. Of his brothers, two had disappeared in the abyss, and one, Andrew, earned a hard livelihood as a journeyman baker; the elder of his sisters had married poorly, and the younger was his blind pensioner. Nicholas had found a wife of better birth than his own, a young woman with country kindred in decent circumstances, though she herself served as nursemaid in the house of the medical man who employed her future husband. He had taught himself the English language, so far as grammar went, but could not cast off the London accent; Mrs. Peak was fortunate enough to speak with nothing worse than the note of the Midlands.

His bent led him to the study of history, politics, economics, and in that time of military outbreak he was frenzied by the conflict of his ideals with the state of things about him. A book frequently in his hands was Godwin's *Political Justice*, and when a son had been born to him, he decided to name the child after that favourite author. In this way, at all events, he could find some expression for his hot defiance of iniquity.

He paid his income-tax, and felt a savage joy in the privation thus imposed upon his family. Mrs. Peak could not forgive her husband, and in this case, though she had but dim appreciation of the point of honour involved, her censures doubtless fell on Nicholas's vulnerable spot; it was the perversity of arrogance, at least as much as honesty, that impelled him to incur taxation. His wife's perseverance in complaint drove him to stern impatience, and for a long time the peace of the household suffered.

When the boy Godwin was five years old, the death of his blind aunt came as a relief to means which were in every sense overtaxed. Twelve months later, a piece of unprecedented good fortune seemed to place the Peaks beyond fear of want, and at the same time to supply Nicholas with a fulfilment of hopeless desires. By the death of Mrs. Peak's brother, they came into possession of a freehold house and about nine hundred pounds. The property was situated some twelve miles from the Midland town of Twybridge, and thither they at once removed. At Twybridge lived Mrs. Peak's elder sister, Miss Cadman; but between this lady and her nearest kinsfolk there had been but slight correspondence—the deceased Cadman left her only a couple of hundred pounds. With capital at command, Nicholas Peak took a lease of certain fields near his house, and turned farmer. The study of chemistry had given a special bent to his economic speculations; he fancied himself endowed with exceptional aptitude for agriculture, and the scent of the furrow brought all his energies into feverish activity—activity which soon impoverished him: that was in the order of things. 'Ungainly integrity' and 'headlong irascibility' wrought the same results for the ex-dispenser as for the Ayrshire husbandman. His farming came to a chaotic end; and when the struggling man died, worn out at forty-three, his wife and children (there was now a younger boy, Oliver, named after the Protector) had no very bright prospects.

Things went better with them than might have been anticipated. To Mrs. Peak her husband's death was not an occasion of unmingled mourning. For the last few years she had suffered severely from domestic discord, and when left at peace by bereavement she turned with a sense of liberation to the task of caring for her children's future. Godwin was just thirteen, Oliver was eleven; both had been well schooled, and with the help of friends they might soon be put in the way of self-support. The daughter, Charlotte, sixteen years of age, had accomplishments which would perhaps be profitable. The widow decided to make a home in Twybridge, where Miss Cadman kept a millinery shop. By means of this connection, Charlotte presently found employment for her skill in fine needlework. Mrs. Peak was incapable of earning money, but the experiences of her early married life enabled her to make more than the most of the pittance at her disposal.

Miss Cadman was a woman of active mind, something of a busy-body—dogmatic, punctilious in her claims to respect, proud of the acknowledgment by her acquaintances that she was not as other tradespeople; her chief weakness was a fanatical ecclesiasticism, the common blight of English womanhood. Circumstances had allowed her a better education than generally falls to women of that standing, and in spite of her shop she succeeded in retaining the friendship of certain ladies long ago her schoolfellows. Among these were the Misses Lumb—middle-aged sisters, who lived at Twybridge on a small independence, their time chiefly devoted to the support of the Anglican Church. An eldest Miss Lumb had been fortunate enough to marry that growing potentate of the Midlands, Mr. Job Whitelaw. Now Lady Whitelaw, she dwelt at Kingsmill, but her sisters frequently enjoyed the honour of entertaining her, and even Miss Cadman the milliner occasionally held converse with the baronet's wife. In this way it came to pass that the Widow Peak and her children were brought under the notice of persons who sooner or later might be of assistance to them.

Abounding in emphatic advice, Miss Cadman easily persuaded her sister that Godwin must go to school for at least two years longer. The boys had been at a boarding-school twenty miles away from their country home; it would be better for them now to be put under the care of some Twybridge teacher—such an one as Miss Cadman's acquaintances could recommend. For her own credit, the milliner was anxious that these nephews of hers should not be running about the town as errand-boys or the like, and with prudence there was no necessity for such degradation. An uncommon lad like Godwin (she imagined him named after the historic earl) must not be robbed of his fair chance in life; she would gladly spare a little money for his benefit; he was a boy to repay such expenditure.

Indeed it seemed probable. Godwin devoured books, and had a remarkable faculty for gaining solid information on any subject that took his fancy. What might be the special bent of his mind one could not yet discover. He read poetry with precocious gusto, but at the same time his aptitude for scientific pursuits was strongly marked. In botany, chemistry, physics, he made progress which the people about him, including his schoolmaster, were incapable of appreciating; and already the collection of books left by his father, most of them out of date, failed to satisfy his curiosity. It might be feared that tastes so discursive would be disadvantageous to a lad who must needs pursue some definite bread-study, and the strain of self-consciousness which grew strong in him was again a matter for concern. He cared nothing for boyish games and companionship; in the society of strangers—especially of females—he behaved with an excessive shyness which was easily mistaken for a surly temper. Reproof, correction, he could not endure, and it was fortunate that the decorum of his habits made remonstrance seldom needful.

Ludicrous as the project would have appeared to any unbiassed observer of character, Miss Cadman conceived a hope that Godwin might become a clergyman. From her point of view it was natural to assume that uncommon talents must be devoted to the service of the Church, and she would have gladly done her utmost for the practical furthering of such an end. Mrs. Peak, though well aware that her son had imbibed the paternal prejudices, was disposed to entertain the same hope, despite solid obstacles. For several years she had nourished a secret antagonism to her husband's spirit of political, social, and religious rebellion, and in her widowhood she speedily became a pattern of the conservative female. It would have gratified her to discern any possibility of Godwin's assuming the priestly garb. And not alone on the ground of conscience. Long ago she had repented the marriage which connected her with such a family as that of the Peaks, and she ardently desired that the children, now exclusively her own, might enter life on a plane superior to their father's.

'Godwin, how would you like to go to College and be a clergyman?' she asked one Sunday afternoon, when an hour or two of congenial reading seemed to have put the boy into a gentle humour.

'To go to College' was all very well (diplomacy had prompted this preface), but the words that followed fell so alarmingly on Godwin's ear that he looked up with a resentful expression, unable to reply otherwise.

'You never thought of it, I suppose?' his mother faltered; for she often stood in awe of her son, who, though yet but fourteen, had much of his father's commanding severity.

'I don't want to be a parson,' came at length, bluntly.

'Don't use that word, Godwin.'

'Why not? It's quite a proper word. It comes from the Latin *persona*.'

The mother had enough discretion to keep silence, and Godwin, after in vain trying to settle to his book again, left the room with disturbed countenance.

He had now been attending the day-school for about a year, and was distinctly ahead of his coevals. A Christmas examination was on the point of being held, and it happened that a singular test of the lad's moral character coincided with the proof of his intellectual progress. In a neighbouring house lived an old man named Rawmarsh, kindly but rather eccentric; he had once done a good business as a printer, and now supported himself by such chance typographic work of a small kind as friends might put in his way. He conceived an affection for Godwin; often had the boy to talk with him of an evening. On one such occasion, Mr. Rawmarsh opened a desk, took forth a packet of newly printed leaves, and with a mysterious air silently spread them before the boy's eyes. In an instant Godwin became aware that he was looking at the examination papers which a day or two hence would be set before him at school; he saw and recognised a passage from the book of Virgil which his class had been reading.

'That is *sub rosa*, you know,' whispered the old printer, with half averted face.

Godwin shrank away, and could not resume the conversation thus interrupted. On the following day he went about with a feeling of guilt. He avoided the sight of Mr. Rawmarsh, for whom he had suddenly lost all respect, and suffered torments in the thought that he enjoyed an unfair advantage over his class-mates. The Latin passage happened to be one which he knew thoroughly well; there was no need, even had he desired, to 'look it up'; but in sitting down to the examination, he experienced a sense of shame and self-rebuke. So strong were the effects of this, that he voluntarily omitted the answer to a certain important question which he could have 'done' better than any of the other boys, thus endeavouring to adjust in his conscience the terms of competition, though in fact no such sacrifice was called for. He came out at the head of the class, but the triumph had no savour for him, and for many a year he was subject to a flush of mortification whenever this incident came back to his mind.

Mr. Rawmarsh was not the only intelligent man who took an interest in Godwin. In a house which the boy sometimes visited with a school-fellow, lodged a notable couple named Gunnery—the husband about seventy, the wife five years older; they lived on a pension from a railway company. Mr. Gunnery was a dabbler in many sciences, but had a special enthusiasm for geology. Two cabinets of stones and fossils gave evidence of his zealous travels about the British Isles; he had even written a little hand-book of petrology which was for sale at certain booksellers' in Twybridge, and probably nowhere else. To him, about this time, Godwin began to resort, always sure of a welcome; and in the little uncarpeted room where Mr. Gunnery pursued his investigations many a fateful lesson was given and received. The teacher understood the intelligence he had to deal with, and was delighted to convey, by the mode of suggested inference, sundry results of knowledge which it perhaps would not have been prudent to declare in plain, popular words.

Their intercourse was not invariably placid. The geologist had an irritable temper, and in certain states of the atmosphere his rheumatic twinges made it advisable to shun argument with him. Godwin, moreover, was distinguished by an instability of mood peculiarly trying to an old man's testy humour. Of a sudden, to Mr. Gunnery's surprise and annoyance, he would lose all interest in this or that science. Thus, one day the lad declared himself unable to name two stones set before him, felspar and quartz, and when his instructor broke into angry impatience he turned sullenly away, exclaiming that he was tired of geology.

'Tired of geology?' cried Mr. Gunnery, with flaming eyes. 'Then *I* am tired of *you*, Master Peak! Be off, and don't come again till I send for you!'

Godwin retired without a word. On the second day he was summoned back again, but his resentment of the dismissal rankled in him for a long time; injury to his pride was the wrong he found it hardest to forgive.

His schoolmaster, aware of the unusual pursuits which he added to the routine of lessons, gave him as a prize the English translation of a book by Figuier—*The World before the Deluge*. Strongly interested by the illustrations of the volume (fanciful scenes from the successive geologic periods), Godwin at once carried it to his scientific friend. 'Deluge?' growled Mr. Gunnery. '*What* deluge? *Which* deluge?' But he restrained himself, handed the book coldly back, and began to talk of something else. All this was highly significant to Godwin, who of course began the perusal of his prize in a suspicious mood. Nor was he long before he sympathised with Mr. Gunnery's distaste. Though too young to grasp the arguments at issue, his prejudices were strongly excited by the conventional Theism which pervades Figuier's work. Already it was the habit of his mind to associate popular dogma with intellectual shallowness; herein, as at every other point which fell within his scope, he had begun to scorn average people, and to pride himself intensely on views which he found generally condemned. Day by day he grew into a clearer understanding of the memories bequeathed to him by his father; he began to interpret remarks, details of behaviour, instances of wrath, which, though they had stamped themselves on his recollection, conveyed at the time no precise significance. The issue was that he hardened himself against the influence of his mother and his aunt, regarding them as in league against the free progress of his education.

As women, again, he despised these relatives. It is almost impossible for a bright-witted lad born in the lower middle class to escape this stage of development. The brutally healthy boy contemns the female sex because he sees it incapable of his own athletic sports, but Godwin was one of those upon whose awaking intellect is forced a perception of the brain-defect so general in women when they are taught few of life's graces and none of its serious concerns,—their paltry prepossessions, their vulgar sequaciousness, their invincible ignorance, their absorption in a petty self. And especially is this phase of thought to be expected in a boy whose heart blindly nourishes the seeds of poetical passion. It was Godwin's sincere belief that he held girls, as girls, in abhorrence. This meant that he dreaded their personal criticism, and that the spectacle of female beauty sometimes overcame him with a despair which he could not analyse. Matrons and elderly unmarried women were truly the objects of his disdain; in them he saw nothing but their shortcomings. Towards his mother he was conscious of no tenderness; of as little towards his sister, who often censured him with trenchant tongue; as for his aunt, whose admiration of him was modified by reticences, he could never be at ease in her company, so strong a dislike had he for her look, her voice, her ways of speech.

He would soon be fifteen years old. Mrs. Peak was growing anxious, for she could no longer consent to draw upon her sister for a portion of the school fees, and no pertinent suggestion for the lad's future was made by any of the people who admired his cleverness. Miss Cadman still clung in a fitful way to the idea of making her nephew a cleric; she had often talked it over with the Misses Lumb, who of course held that 'any sacrifice' was justifiable with such a motive, and who suggested a hope that, by the instrumentality of Lady Whitelaw, a curacy might easily be obtained as soon as Godwin was old enough. But several years must pass before that Levitical stage could be reached; and then, after all, perhaps the younger boy, Oliver, placid of temper and notably pliant in mind, was better suited for the dignity of Orders. It was lamentable that Godwin should have become so intimate with that earth-burrowing Mr. Gunnery, who certainly never attended either church or chapel, and who seemed to have imbued his pupil with immoral theories concerning the date of creation. Godwin held more decidedly aloof from his aunt, and had been heard by Charlotte to speak very disrespectfully of the Misses Lumb. In short, there was no choice but to discover an opening for him in some secular pursuit. Could he, perhaps, become an assistant teacher? Or must he 'go into an office'?

No common lad. A youth whose brain glowed like a furnace, whose heart throbbed with tumult of high ambitions, of inchoate desires; endowed with knowledge altogether exceptional for his years; a nature essentially militant, displaying itself in innumerable forms of callow intolerance—apt, assuredly, for some vigorous part in life, but as likely as not to rush headlong on traverse roads if no judicious mind assumed control of him. What is to be done with the boy?

All very well, if the question signified, in what way to provide for the healthy development of his manhood. Of course it meant nothing of the sort, but merely: What work can be found for him whereby he may earn his daily bread? We—his kinsfolk even, not to think of the world at large—can have no concern with his growth as an intellectual being; we are hard pressed to supply our own mouths with food; and now that we have done our recognised duty by him, it is high time that he learnt to fight for his own share of provender. Happily, he is of the robust sex; he can hit out right and left, and make standing-room. We have armed him with serviceable weapons, and now he must use them against the enemy—that is to say, against all mankind, who will quickly enough deprive him of sustenance if he fail in the conflict. We neither know, nor in great measure care, for what employment he is naturally marked. Obviously he cannot heave coals or sell dogs' meat, but with negative certainty not much else can be resolved, seeing how desperate is the competition for minimum salaries. He has been born, and he must eat. By what licensed channel may he procure the necessary viands?

Paternal relatives Godwin had as good as none. In quitting London, Nicholas Peak had ceased to hold communication with any of his own stock save the younger brother Andrew. With him he occasionally exchanged a letter, but Andrew's share in the correspondence was limited to ungrammatical and often unintelligible hints of numerous projects for money-making. Just after the removal of the bereaved family to Twybridge, they were surprised by a visit from Andrew, in answer to one of whose letters Mrs. Peak had sent news of her husband's death. Though her dislike of the man amounted to loathing, the widow could not refuse him hospitality; she did her best, however, to prevent his coming in contact with anyone she knew. Andrew declared that he was at length prospering; he had started a coffee-shop at Dalston, in north-east London, and positively urged a proposal (well-meant, beyond doubt) that Godwin should be allowed to come to him and learn the business. Since then the Londoner had once again visited Twybridge, towards the end of Godwin's last school-year. This time he spoke of himself less hopefully, and declared a wish to transfer his business to some provincial town, where he thought his metropolitan experience might be of great value, in the absence of serious competition. It was not difficult to discover a family likeness between Andrew's instability and the idealism which had proved the ruin of Nicholas.

On this second occasion Godwin tried to escape a meeting with his uncle. Unable to do so, he sat mute, replying to questions monosyllabically. Mrs. Peak's shame and annoyance, in face of this London-branded vulgarian, were but feeble emotions compared with those of her son. Godwin hated the man, and was in dread lest any school-fellow should come to know of such a connection. Yet delicacy prevented his uttering a word on the subject to his mother. Mrs. Peak's silence after Andrew's departure made it uncertain how she regarded the obligation of kindred, and in any such matter as this the boy was far too sensitive to risk giving pain. But to his brother Oliver he spoke.

'What is the brute to us? When I'm a man, let him venture to come near me, and see what sort of a reception he'll get! I hate low, uneducated people! I hate them worse than the filthiest vermin!—don't you?'

Oliver, aged but thirteen, assented, as he habitually did to any question which seemed to await an affirmative.

'They ought to be swept off the face of the earth!' pursued Godwin, sitting up in bed—for the dialogue took place about eleven o'clock at night. 'All the grown-up creatures, who can't speak proper English and don't know how to behave themselves, I'd transport them to the Falkland Islands,'—this geographic precision was a note of the boy's mind,—'and let them die off as soon as possible. The children should be sent to school and purified, if possible; if not, they too should be got rid of.'

'You're an aristocrat, Godwin,' remarked Oliver, simply; for the elder brother had of late been telling him fearful stories from the French Revolution, with something of an anti-popular bias.

'I hope I am. I mean to be, that's certain. There's nothing I hate like vulgarity. That's why I can't stand Roper. When he beat me in mathematics last mid-summer, I felt so ashamed I could hardly bear myself. I'm working like a nigger at algebra and Euclid this half, just because I think it would almost kill me to be beaten again by a low cad.'

This was perhaps the first time that Godwin found expression for the prejudice which affected all his thoughts and feelings. It relieved him to have spoken thus; henceforth he had become clear as to his point of view. By dubbing him aristocrat, Oliver had flattered him in the subtlest way. If indeed the title were justly his, as he instantly felt it was, the inference was plain that he must be an aristocrat of nature's own making—one of the few highly favoured beings who, in despite of circumstance, are pinnacled above mankind. In his ignorance of life, the boy visioned a triumphant career; an aristocrat *de jure* might possibly become one even in the common sense did he but pursue that end with sufficient zeal. And in his power of persistent endeavour he had no lack of faith.

The next day he walked with exalted head. Encountering the

objectionable Roper, he smiled upon him contemptuously tolerant.

There being no hope of effective assistance from relatives, Mrs. Peak turned for counsel to a man of business, with whom her husband had made acquaintance in his farming days, and who held a position of influence at Twybridge. This was Mr. Moxey, manufacturing chemist, famous in the Midlands for his 'sheep and cattle dressings,' and sundry other products of agricultural enterprise. His ill-scented, but lucrative, works were situated a mile out of the town; and within sight of the reeking chimneys stood a large, plain house, uncomfortably like an 'institution' of some kind, in which he dwelt with his five daughters. Thither, one evening, Mrs. Peak betook herself, having learnt that Mr. Moxey dined at five o'clock, and that he was generally to be found digging in his garden until sunset. Her reception was civil. The manufacturer—sparing of words, but with no unkindly face—requested that Godwin should be sent to see him, and promised to do his best to be of use. A talk with the boy strengthened his interest. He was surprised at Godwin's knowledge of chemistry, pleased with his general intelligence, and in the end offered to make a place for him at the works, where, though for a year or two his earnings must be small, he would gain experience likely to be of substantial use to him. Godwin did not find the proposal distasteful; it brought a change into his life, and the excitement of novelty; it flattered him with the show of release from pupilage. To Mr. Moxey's he went.

The hours were not long, and it was understood that his theoretical studies should continue in the evening. Godwin's home was a very small house in a monotonous little street; a garret served as bedroom for the two boys, also as the elder one's laboratory. Servant Mrs. Peak had none. She managed everything herself, as in the old Greenwich days, leaving Charlotte free to work at her embroidery. Godwin took turns with Oliver at blacking the shoes.

As a matter of course the boys accompanied their mother each Sunday morning to the parish church, and this ceremony was becoming an insufferable tax on Godwin's patience. It was not only that he hated the name of religion, and scorned with much fierceness all who came in sympathetic contact therewith; the loss of time seemed to him an oppressive injury, especially now that he began to suffer from restricted leisure. He would not refuse to obey his mother's wish, but the sullenness of his Sabbatic demeanour made the whole family uncomfortable. As often as possible he feigned illness. He tried the effect of dolorous sighs and groans; but Mrs. Peak could not dream of conceding a point which would have seemed to her the condonation of deadly sin. 'When I am a man!' muttered Godwin. 'Ah! when I am a man!'

A year had gone by, and the routine to which he was bound began to have a servile flavour. His mind chafed at subjugation to commercial interests. Sick of 'sheep and cattle dressings,' he grew tired of chemistry altogether, and presently of physical science in general. His evenings were given to poetry and history; he took up the classical schoolbooks again, and found a charm in Latin syntax hitherto unperceived. It was plain to him now how he had been wronged by the necessity of leaving school when his education had but just begun.

Discontent becoming ripe for utterance, he unbosomed himself to Mr. Gunnery. It happened that the old man had just returned from a visit to Kingsmill, where he had spent a week in the museum, then newly enriched with geologic specimens. After listening in silence to the boy's complaints, and pondering for a long time, he began to talk of Whitelaw College.

'Does it cost much to study there?' Godwin asked, gloomily.

'No great sum, I think. There are scholarships to be had.'

Mr. Gunnery threw out the suggestion carelessly. Knowing the hazards of life, he could not quite justify himself in encouraging Godwin's restiveness.

'Scholarships? For free study?'

'Yes; but that wouldn't mean free living, you know. Students don't live at the College.'

'How do you go in for a scholarship?'

The old man replied, meditatively, 'If you were to pass the Cambridge Local Examination, and to get the first place in the

Kingsmill district, you would have three years of free study at Whitelaw.'

'Three years?' shouted Godwin, springing up from his chair. 'But how could you live, my boy?'

Godwin sat down again, and let his head fall forward.

How to keep oneself alive during a few years of intellectual growth?—a question often asked by men of mature age, but seldom by a lad of sixteen. No matter. He resolved that he would study for this Cambridge Local Examination, and have a try for the scholarship. His attainments were already up to the standard required for average success in such competitions. On obtaining a set of 'papers,' he found that they looked easy enough. Could he not come out first in the Kingsmill district?

He worked vigorously at special subjects; aid was needless, but he wished for more leisure. Not a word to any member of his household. When his mother discovered that he was reading in the bedroom till long past midnight, she made serious objection on the score of health and on that of gas bills. Godwin quietly asserted that work he must, and that if necessary he would buy candles out of his pocket-money. He had unexpectedly become more grave, more restrained; he even ceased to grumble about going to church, having found that service time could be utilised for committing to memory lists of dates and the like, jotted down on a slip of paper. When the time for the examination drew near, he at length told his mother to what end he had been labouring, and asked her to grant him the assistance necessary for his journey and the sojourn at Kingsmill; the small sum he had been able to save, after purchase of books, would not suffice. [illegible] Peak knew not whether to approve her son's ambition or [illegible] to repress it. She would welcome an improval in his pros[illegible], but, granting success, how was he to live whilst profiting [illegible] a scholarship? And again, what did he propose to make of himself when he had spent three years in study?

'In any case,' was Godwin's reply, 'I should be sure of a good place as a teacher. But I think I might try for something in the Civil Service; there are all sorts of positions to be got.'

It was idle to discuss the future whilst the first step was still speculative. Mrs. Peak consented to favour the attempt, and what was more to keep it a secret until the issue should be known. It was needful to obtain leave of absence from Mr. Moxey, and Godwin, when making the request, stated for what purpose he was going to Kingsmill, though without explaining the hope which had encouraged his studies. The project seemed laudable, and his employer made no difficulties.

Godwin just missed the scholarship; of candidates in the prescribed district, he came out second.

Grievous was the disappointment. To come so near success exasperated his impatient temper, and for a few days his bondage at the chemical works seemed intolerable; he was ready for almost any venture that promised release and new scope for his fretting energies. But at the moment when nervous irritation was most acute, a remarkable act of kindness suddenly restored to him all the hopes he had abandoned. One Saturday afternoon he was summoned from his surly retreat in the garret, to speak with a visitor. On entering the sitting-room, he found his mother in company with Miss Cadman and the Misses Lumb, and from the last-mentioned ladies, who spoke with amiable alternation, he learnt that they were commissioned by Sir Job Whitelaw to offer for his acceptance a three-years' studentship at Whitelaw College. Affected by her son's chagrin, Mrs. Peak had disclosed the story to her sister, who had repeated it to the Misses Lumb, who in turn had made it the subject of a letter to Lady Whitelaw. It was an annual practice with Sir Job to discover some promising lad whom he could benefit by the payment of his fees for a longer or shorter period of college study. The hint from Twybridge came to him just at the suitable time, and, on further inquiry, decided to make proffer of this advantage to Godwin Peak. The only condition was that arrangements should be made by the student's relatives for his support during the proposed period.

This generosity took away Godwin's breath. The expenditure it represented was trifling, but from a stranger in Sir Job's position it had something which recalled to so fervent a mind the poetry of Medicean patronage. For the moment no faintest doubt gave warning to his self-respect; he was eager to accept nobly a benefaction nobly intended.

Miss Cadman, flattered by Sir Job's attention to her nephew, now came forward with an offer to contribute towards Godwin's livelihood. Her supplement would eke into adequacy such slender allowance as the widow's purse could afford. Details were privately discussed, resolves were taken. Mr. Moxey, when it was made known to him, without explanation, that Godwin was to be sent to Whitelaw College, behaved with kindness; he at once released the lad, and added a present to the salary that was due. Proper acknowledgment of the Baronet's kindness was made by the beneficiary himself, who wrote a letter giving truer testimony of his mental calibre than would have been offered had he expressed himself by word of mouth. A genial reply summoned him to an interview as soon as he should have found an abode in Kingsmill. The lodging he had occupied during the examination was permanently secured, and a new period of Godwin's life began.

For two years, that is to say until his age drew towards nineteen, Peak pursued the Arts curriculum at Whitelaw. His mood on entering decided his choice, which was left free to him. Experience of utilitarian chemistry had for the present made his liberal tastes predominant, and neither the splendid laboratories of Whitelaw nor the repute of its scientific Professors tempted him to what had once seemed his natural direction. In the second year, however, he enlarged his course by the addition of one or two classes not included in Sir Job's design; these were paid for out of a present made to him by Mr. Gunnery.

It being customary for the regular students of Whitelaw to graduate at London University, Peak passed his matriculation, and worked on for the preliminary test then known as First B.A. In the meanwhile he rose steadily, achieving distinction in the College. The more observant of his teachers remarked him even where he fell short of academic triumph, and among his fellow-students he had the name of a stern 'sweater', one not easily beaten where he had set his mind on excelling. He was not generally liked, for his mood appeared unsocial, and a repelling arrogance was sometimes felt in his talk. No doubt—said the more fortunate young men—he came from a very poor home, and suffered from the narrowness of his means. They noticed that he did not subscribe to the College Union, and that he could never join in talk regarding the diversions of the town. His two or three intimates were chosen from among those contemporaries who read hard and dressed poorly.

The details of Godwin's private life were noteworthy. Accustomed hitherto to a domestic circle, at Kingsmill he found himself isolated, and it was not easy for him to surrender all at once the comforts of home. For a time he felt as though his ambition were a delinquency which entailed the punishment of loneliness. Nor did his relations with Sir Job Whitelaw tend to mitigate this feeling. In his first interview with the Baronet, Godwin showed to little advantage. A deadly bashfulness forbade him to be natural either in attitude or speech. He felt his dependence in a way he had not foreseen; the very clothes he wore, then fresh from the tailor's, seemed to be the gift of charity, and their stiffness shamed him. A man of the world, Sir Job could make allowance for these defects. He understood that the truest kindness would be to leave a youth such as this to the forming influences of the College. So Godwin barely had a glimpse of Lady Whitelaw in her husband's study, and thereafter for many months he saw nothing of his benefactors. Subsequently he was twice invited to interviews with Sir Job, who talked with kindness and commendation. Then came the Baronet's death. Godwin received an assurance that this event would be no check upon his career, but he neither saw nor heard directly from Lady Whitelaw.

Not a house in Kingsmill opened hospitable doors to the lonely student; nor was anyone to blame for this. With no family had he friendly acquaintance. When, towards the end of his second year, he grew sufficiently intimate with Buckland Warricombe to walk out with him to Thornhaw, it could be nothing more than a scarcely welcome exception to the rule of solitude. Impossible for him to cultivate the friendship of such people as the Warricombes, with their large and joyous scheme of life. Only at a hearth where homeliness and cordiality united to unthaw his proud reserve could Godwin perchance have found the companionship he needed. Many such homes existed in Kingsmill, but no kindly fortune led the young man within the sphere of their warmth.

His lodgings were in a very ugly street in the ugliest outskirts of the town; he had to take a long walk through desolate districts (brick-yard, sordid pasture, degenerate village) before he could refresh his eyes with the rural scenery which was so great a joy to him as almost to be a necessity. The immediate vicinage offered nothing but monotone of grimy, lower middle-class dwellings, occasionally relieved by a public-house. He occupied two rooms, not unreasonably clean, and was seldom disturbed by the attentions of his landlady.

An impartial observer might have wondered at the negligence which left him to arrange his life as best he could, notwithstanding youth and utter inexperience. It looked indeed as if there were no one in the world who cared what became of him. Yet this was merely the result of his mother's circumstances, and of his own character. Mrs. Peak could do no more than make her small remittances, and therewith send an occasional admonition regarding his health. She did not, in fact, conceive the state of things, imagining that the authority and supervisal of the College extended over her son's daily existence, whereas it was possible for Godwin to frequent lectures or not, to study or to waste his time, pretty much as he chose, subject only to official inquiry if his attendance became frequently irregular. His independent temper, and the seeming maturity of his mind, supplied another excuse for the imprudent confidence which left him to his own resources. Yet the perils of the situation were great indeed. A youth of less concentrated purpose, more at the mercy of casual allurement, would probably have gone to wreck amid trials so exceptional.

Trials not only of his moral nature. The sums of money with which he was furnished fell short of a reasonable total for bare necessities. In the calculation made by Mrs. Peak and her sister, outlay on books had practically been lost sight of; it was presumed that ten shillings a term would cover this item. But Godwin could not consent to be at a disadvantage in his armoury for academic contest. The first month saw him compelled to contract his diet, that he might purchase books; thenceforth he rarely had enough to eat. His landlady supplied him with breakfast, tea, and supper—each repast of the very simplest kind; for dinner it was understood that he repaired to some public table, where meat and vegetables, with perchance a supplementary sweet when nature demanded it, might be had for about a shilling. That shilling was not often at his disposal. Dinner as it is understood by the comfortably clad, the 'regular meal' which is a part of English respectability, came to be represented by a small pork-pie, or even a couple of buns, eaten at the little shop over against the College. After a long morning of mental application this was poor refreshment; the long afternoon which followed, again spent in rigorous study, could not but reduce a growing frame to ravenous hunger. Tea and buttered bread were the means of appeasing it, until another four hours' work called for reward in the shape of bread and cheese. Even yet the day's toil was not ended. Godwin sometimes read long after midnight, with the result that, when at length he tried to sleep, exhaustion of mind and body kept him for a long time feverishly wakeful.

These hardships he concealed from the people at Twybridge. Complaint, it seemed to him, would be ungrateful, for sacrifices were already made on his behalf. His father, as he well remembered, was wont to relate, with a kind of angry satisfaction, the miseries through which he had fought his way to education and the income-tax. Old enough now to reflect with compassionate understanding upon that life of conflict, Godwin resolved that he too would bear the burdens inseparable from poverty, and in some moods was even glad to suffer as his father had done. Fortunately he had a sound basis of health, and hunger and vigils would not easily affect his constitution. If, thus hampered, he could outstrip competitors who had every advantage of circumstance, the more glorious his triumph.

Sunday was an interval of leisure. Rejoicing in deliverance from Sabbatarianism, he generally spent the morning in a long walk, and the rest of the day was devoted to non-collegiate reading. He had subscribed to a circulating library, and thus obtained new publications recommended to him in the literary paper which again taxed his stomach. Mere class-work did not satisfy him. He was possessed with throes of spiritual desire, impelling him towards that world of unfettered speculation which he had long indistinctly imagined. It was a great thing to learn what the past could teach, to set himself on the common level of intellectual men; but he understood that college learning could not be an end in itself, that the Professors to whom he listened either did not speak out all that was in their minds, or, if they did, were far from representing the advanced guard of modern thought. With eagerness he at length betook himself to the teachers of philosophy and of geology. Having paid for these lectures out of his own pocket, he felt as if he had won a privilege beyond the conventional course of study, an initiation to a higher sphere of intellect. The result was disillusion. Not even in these class-rooms could he hear the word for which he waited, the bold annunciation of newly discovered law, the science which had completely broken with tradition. He came away unsatisfied, and brooded upon the possibilities which would open for him when he was no longer dependent.

His evening work at home was subject to a disturbance which would have led him to seek other lodgings, could he have hoped to find any so cheap as these. The landlady's son, a lank youth of the clerk species, was wont to amuse himself from eight to ten with practice on a piano. By dint of perseverance he had learned to strum two or three hymnal melodies popularised by American evangelists; occasionally he even added the charm of his voice, which had a pietistic nasality not easily endured by an ear of any refinement. Not only was Godwin harassed by the recurrence of these performances; the tunes worked themselves into his brain, and sometimes throughout a whole day their burden clanged and squalled incessantly on his mental hearing. He longed to entreat forbearance from the musician, but an excess of delicacy—which always ruled his behaviour—kept him silent. Certain passages in the classics, and many an elaborate mathematical formula, long retained for him an association with the cadences of revivalist hymnody.

Like all proud natures condemned to solitude, he tried to convince himself that he had no need of society, that he despised its attractions, and could be self-sufficing. So far was this from the truth that he often regarded with bitter envy those of his fellow-students who had the social air, who conversed freely among their equals, and showed that the pursuits of the College were only a part of their existence. These young man were either preparing for the University, or would pass from Whitelaw to business, profession, official training; in any case, a track was marked out for them by the zealous care of relatives and friends, and their efforts would always be aided, applauded, by a kindly circle. Some of them Godwin could not but admire, so healthful were they, so bright of intellect, and courteous in manner,—a type distinct from any he had formerly observed. Others were antipathetic to him. Their aggressive gentility conflicted with the wariness of his self-esteem; such a one, for instance, as Bruno Chilvers, the sound of whose mincing voice, as he read in the class, so irritated him that at times he had to cover his ears. Yet, did it chance that one of these offensive youths addressed a civil word to him, on the instant his prejudice was disarmed, and his emotions flowered forth in a response to which he would gladly have given free expression. When he was invited to meet the relatives of Buckland Warricombe, shyness prepossessed him against them; but the frank kindness of his reception moved him, and on going away he was ashamed to have replied so boorishly to attentions so amiably meant. The same note of character sounded in what personal intercourse he had with the Professors. Though his spirit of criticism was at times busy with these gentlemen, he had for most of them a profound regard; and to be elected by one or other for a word of commendation, a little private assistance, a well-phrased inquiry as to his progress, always made his heart beat high with gratitude. They were his first exemplars of finished courtesy, of delicate culture; and he could never sufficiently regret that no one of them was aware how thankfully he recognised his debt.

In longing for the intimacy of refined people, he began to modify his sentiments with regard to the female sex. His first prize-day at Whitelaw was the first occasion on which he sat in an assembly where ladies (as he understood the title) could be seen and heard. The impression he received was deep and lasting. On the seat behind him were two girls whose intermittent talk held him with irresistible charm throughout the whole ceremony. He had not imagined that girls could display such intelligence, and the sweet clearness of their intonation, the purity of their accent, the grace of their habitual phrases, were things altogether beyond his experience. This was not the English he had been wont to hear on female lips. His mother and his aunt spoke with propriety; their associates were soft-tongued; but here was something quite different from inoffensiveness of tone and diction. Godwin appreciated the differentiating cause. These young ladies behind him had been trained from the cradle to speak for the delight of fastidious ears; that they should be grammatical was not enough—they must excel in the art of conversational music. Of course there existed a world where only such speech was interchanged, and how inestimably happy those men to whom the sphere was native!

When the proceedings were over, he drew aside and watched the two girls as they mingled with acquaintances; he kept them in view until they left the College. An emotion such as this he had never known; for the first time in his life he was humiliated without embitterment.

The bitterness came when he had returned to his home in the back street of Twybridge, and was endeavouring to spend the holidays in a hard 'grind.' He loathed the penurious simplicity to which his life was condemned; all familiar circumstances were become petty, coarse, vulgar, in his eyes; the contrast with the idealised world of his ambition plunged him into despair. Even Mr. Gunnery seemed an ignoble figure when compared with the Professors of Whitelaw, and his authority in the sciences was now subjected to doubt. However much or little might result from the three years at college, it was clear to Godwin that his former existence had passed into infinite remoteness; he was no longer fit for Twybridge, no longer a companion for his kindred. Oliver, whose dullness as a schoolboy gave no promise of future achievements, was now learning the business of a seedsman; his brother felt ashamed when he saw him at work in the shop, and had small patience with the comrades to whom Oliver dedicated his leisure. Charlotte was estranged by religious differences. Only for his mother did the young man show increased consideration. To his aunt he endeavoured to be grateful, but his behaviour in her presence was elaborate hypocrisy. Hating the necessity for this, he laid the blame on fortune, which had decreed his birth in a social sphere where he must ever be an alien.

III

WITH THE GROWTH of his militant egoism, there had developed in Godwin Peak an excess of nervous sensibility which threatened to deprive his character of the initiative rightly belonging to it. Self-assertion is the practical complement of self-esteem. To be largely endowed with the latter quality, yet constrained by a coward delicacy to repress it, is to suffer martyrdom at the pleasure of every robust assailant, and in the end be driven to the refuge of a moody solitude. That encounter with his objectionable uncle after the prize distribution at Whitelaw showed how much Godwin had lost of the natural vigour which declared itself at Andrew Peak's second visit to Twybridge, when the boy certainly would not have endured his uncle's presence but for hospitable considerations and the respect due to his mother. The decision with which he then unbosomed himself to Oliver, still characterised his thoughts, but he had not courage to elude the dialogue forced upon him, still less to make known his resentment of the man's offensive vulgarity. He endured in silence, his heart afire with scornful wrath.

The affliction could not have befallen him at a time when he was less capable of supporting it resignedly. Notwithstanding his noteworthy success in two classes, it seemed to him that he had lost everything—that the day was one of signal and disgraceful defeat. In any case that sequence of second prizes must have filled him with chagrin, but to be beaten thus repeatedly by such a fellow as Bruno Chilvers was humiliation intolerable. A fopling, a mincer of effeminate English, a rote-repeater of academic catchwords—bah! The by-examinations of the year had whispered presage, but Peak always felt that he was not putting forth his strength; when the serious trial came he would show what was really in him. Too late he recognised his error, though he tried not to admit it. The extra subjects had exacted too much of him;

there was a limit to his powers. Within the College this would be well enough understood, but to explain a disagreeable fact is not to change it; his name was written in pitiful subordination. And as for the public assembly—he would have sacrificed some years of his life to have stepped forward in facile supremacy, beneath the eyes of those clustered ladies. Instead of that, they had looked upon his shame; they had interchanged glances of amusement at each repetition of his defeat; had murmured comments in their melodious speech; had ended by losing all interest in him—as intuition apprised him was the wont of women.

As soon as he had escaped from his uncle, he relapsed into musing upon the position to which he was condemned when the new session came round. Again Chilvers would be in the same classes with him, and, as likely as not, with the same result. In the meantime, they were both 'going in' for the First B.A.; he had no fear of failure, but it might easily happen that Chilvers would achieve higher distinction. With an eye to awards that might be won—substantial cash-annuities—he was reading for Honours; but it seemed doubtful whether he could present himself, as the second examination was held only in London. Chilvers would of course be an Honours candidate. He would smile—confound him!—at an objection on the score of the necessary journey to London. Better to refrain altogether than again to see Chilvers come out ahead. General surprise would naturally be excited, questions asked on all hands. How would it sound: 'I simply couldn't afford to go up'——?

At this point of the meditation he had reached his lodgings; he admitted himself with a latch-key, turned into his murky sitting-room, and sat down.

The table was laid for tea, as usual. Though he might have gone to Twybridge this evening, he had preferred to stay overnight, for an odd reason. At a theatre in Kingsmill a London company, headed by an actress of some distinction, was to perform 'Romeo and Juliet,' and he purposed granting himself this indulgence before leaving the town. The plan was made when his eye fell upon the advertisement, a few days ago. He then believed it probable that an evening at the theatre would appropriately follow upon a day of victory. His interest in the performance had collapsed, but he did not care to alter his arrangements.

The landlady came in bearing the tea-pot. He wanted nothing, yet could not exert himself to say so.

But he was losing sight of a menace more formidable than defeat by Chilvers. What was it his blackguard uncle had said? Had the fellow really threatened to start an eating-house opposite the College, and flare his name upon a placard? 'Peak's Dining and Refreshment Rooms'—merciful heavens!

Again the mood of laughter came upon him. Why, here was a solution of all difficulties, as simple as unanticipated. If indeed that awful thing came to pass, farewell to Whitelaw! What possibility of pursuing his studies when every class-companion, every Professor,—nay, the very porters,—had become aware that he was nephew to the man who supplied meals over the way? Moral philosophy had no prophylactic against an ordeal such as this. Could the most insignificant lad attending lectures afford to disregard such an occasion of ridicule and contempt?

But the scheme would not be realised; it sounded too unlikely. Andrew Peak was merely a loose-minded vagabond, who might talk of this and that project for making money, but would certainly never quit his dirty haunts in London. Godwin asked himself angrily why he had submitted to the fellow's companionship. This absurd delicacy must be corrected before it became his tyrant. The idea of scrupling to hurt the sensibilities of Andrew Peak! The man was coarse-hided enough to undergo kicking, and then take sixpence in compensation,—not a doubt of it. This detestable tie of kindred must no longer be recognised. He would speak gravely to his mother about it. If Andrew again presented himself at the house he should be given plainly to understand that his visits were something less than welcome,—if necessary, a downright blunt word must effect their liberation. Godwin felt strong enough for that, musing here alone. And, student-like, he passed on to debate the theory of the problem. Andrew was his father's brother, but what is a mere tie of blood if nature has alienated two persons by a subtler distinction? By the dead man, Andrew had never been loved or esteemed; memory supplied proof of this.

The widow shrank from him. No obligation of any kind lay upon them to tolerate the London ruffian.—Enough; he should be got rid of!

Alternating his causes of misery, which—he could not quite forget—might blend for the sudden transformation of his life, Godwin let the tea grow cold upon the table, until it was time, if he still meant to visit the theatre, for setting forth. He had no mind to go, but as little to sit here and indulge harassing reflection. With an effort, he made ready and left the house.

The cost of his seat at the theatre was two shillings. So nicely had he adjusted the expenses of these last days that, after paying the landlady's bill to-morrow morning, there would remain to him but a few pence more than the money needed for his journey home. Walking into the town, he debated with himself whether it were not better to save this florin. But as he approached the pit door, the spirit of pleasure revived in him; he had seen but one of Shakespeare's plays, and he believed (naturally at his age) that to see a drama acted was necessary for its full appreciation. Sidling with affected indifference, he added himself to the crowd.

To stand thus, expectant of the opening doors, troubled him with a sense of shame. To be sure he was in the spiritual company of Charles Lamb, and of many another man of brains who has waited under the lamp. But contact with the pittites of Kingsmill offended his instincts; he resented this appearance of inferiority to people who came at their leisure, and took seats in the better parts of the house. When a neighbour addressed him with a meaningless joke which defied grammar, he tried to grin a friendly answer, but inwardly shrank. The events of the day had increased his sensibility to such impressions. Had he triumphed over Bruno Chilvers, he could have behaved this evening with a larger humanity.

The fight for entrance—honest British stupidity, crushing ribs and rending garments in preference to seemly order of progress—enlivened him somewhat, and sent him laughing to his conquered place; but before the curtain rose he was again depressed by the sight of a familiar figure in the stalls, a fellow-student who sat there with mother and sister, black-uniformed, looking very much a gentleman. 'I, of course, am not a gentleman,' he said to himself, gloomily. Was there any chance that he might some day take his ease in that orthodox fashion? Inasmuch as it was conventionality, he scorned it; but the privileges which it represented had strong control of his imagination. That lady and her daughter would follow the play with intelligence. To exchange comments with them would be a keen delight. As for him—he had a shop-boy on one hand and a grocer's wife on the other.

By the end he had fallen into fatigue. Amid clamour of easily-won applause he made his way into the street, to find himself in a heavy downpour of rain. Having no umbrella, he looked about for a sheltered station, and the glare of a neighbouring public-house caught his eye; he was thirsty, and might as well refresh body and spirit with a glass of beer, an unwonted indulgence which had the pleasant semblance of dissipation. Arrived at the bar he came upon two acquaintances, who, to judge by their flushed cheeks and excited voices, had been celebrating jovially the close of their academic labours. They hailed him.

'Hollo, Peak! Come and help us to get sober before bedtime!'

They were not exactly studious youths, but neither did they belong to the class that Godwin despised, and he had a comrade-like feeling for them. In a few minutes his demeanour was wholly changed. A glass of hot whisky acted promptly upon his nervous system, enabled him to forget vexations, and attuned him to kindred sprightliness. He entered merrily into the talk of a time of life which is independent of morality—talk distinct from that of the blackguard, but equally so from that of the reflective man. His first glass had several successors. The trio rambled arm in arm from one place of refreshment to another, and presently sat down in hearty fellowship to a supper of such viands as recommend themselves at bibulous midnight. Peak was drawing recklessly upon the few coins that remained to him; he must leave his landlady's claim undischarged, and send the money from home. Prudence be hanged! If one cannot taste amusement once in a twelvemonth, why live at all?

He reached his lodgings, at something after one o'clock drenched with rain, gloriously indifferent to that and all other chances of life. Pooh! his system had been radically wrong. He should have allowed himself recreation once a week or so; he would have been all the better for it, body and mind. Books and that kind of thing are all very well in their way, but one must live; he had wasted too much of his youth in solitude. *O mihi præteritos referat si Jupiter annos!* Next session he would arrange things better. Success in examinations—what trivial fuss when one looked at it from the right point of view! And he had fretted himself into misery, because Chilvers had got more 'marks,'—ha, ha, ha!

The morrow's waking was lugubrious enough. Headache and nausea weighed upon him. Worse still, a scrutiny of his pockets showed that he had only the shamefaced change of half-a-crown wherewith to transport himself and his belongings to Twybridge. Now, the railway fare alone was three shillings; the needful cab demanded eighteenpence. O idiot!

And he hated the thought of leaving his bill unpaid; the more so because it was a trifling sum, a week's settlement. To put himself under however brief an obligation to a woman such as the landlady gnawed at his pride. Not that only. He had no business to make a demand upon his mother for this additional sum. But there was no way of raising the money; no one of whom he could borrow it; nothing he could afford to sell—even if courage had supported him through such a transaction. Triple idiot!

Bread turned to bran upon his hot palate; he could only swallow cups of coffee. With trembling hands he finished the packing of his box and portmanteau, then braced himself to the dreaded interview. Of course, it involved no difficulty, the words once uttered; but, when he was left alone again, he paced the room for a few minutes in flush of mortification. It had made his headache worse.

The mode of his homeward journey he had easily arranged. His baggage having been labelled for Twybridge, he himself would book as far as his money allowed, then proceed on foot for the remaining distance. With the elevenpence now in his pocket he could purchase a ticket to a little town called Dent, and by a calculation from the railway tariff he concluded that from

Dent to Twybridge was some five-and-twenty miles. Well and good. At the rate of four miles an hour it would take him from half-past eleven to about six o'clock. He could certainly reach home in time for supper.

At Dent station, ashamed to ask (like a tramp) the way to so remote a place as Twybridge, he jotted down a list of intervening railway stoppages, and thus was enabled to support the semblance of one who strolls on for his pleasure. A small hand-bag he was obliged to carry, and the clouded sky made his umbrella a requisite. On he trudged steadily, for the most part by muddy ways, now through a pleasant village, now in rural solitude. He had had the precaution, at breakfast time, to store some pieces of bread in his pocket, and after two or three hours this resource was welcome. Happily the air and exercise helped him to get rid of his headache. A burst of sunshine in the afternoon would have made him reasonably cheerful, but for the wretched meditations surviving from yesterday.

He pondered frequently on his spasmodic debauch, repeating, as well as memory permitted, all his absurdities of speech and action. Defiant self-justification was now far to seek. On the other hand, he perceived very clearly how easy it would be for him to lapse by degrees of weakened will into a ruinous dissoluteness. Anything of that kind would mean, of course, the abandonment of his ambitions. All he had to fight the world with was his brain; and only by incessant strenuousness in its exercise had he achieved the moderate prominence declared in yesterday's ceremony. By birth, by station, he was of no account; if he chose to sink, no influential voice would deplore his falling off or remind him of what he owed to himself. Chilvers, now—what a wide-spreading outcry, what calling upon gods and men, would be excited by any defection of that brilliant youth! Godwin Peak must make his own career, and that he would hardly do save by efforts greater than the ordinary man can put forth. The ordinary man?—Was he in any respect extraordinary? were his powers noteworthy? It was the first time that he had deliberately posed this question to himself, and for answer came a rush of confident blood, pulsing through all the mechanism of his being.

The train of thought which occupied him during this long trudge was to remain fixed in his memory; in any survey of the years of pupilage, this recollection would stand prominently forth, associated, moreover, with one slight incident which at the time seemed a mere interruption of his musing. From a point on the high-road he observed a small quarry, so excavated as to present an interesting section; though weary, he could not but turn aside to examine these strata. He knew enough of the geology of the county to recognise the rocks and reflect with understanding upon their position; a fragment in his hand, he sat down to rest for a moment. Then a strange fit of brooding came over him. Escaping from the influences of personality, his imagination wrought back through eras of geologic time, held him in a vision of the infinitely remote, shrivelled into insignificance all but the one fact of inconceivable duration. Often as he had lost himself in such reveries, never yet had he passed so wholly under the dominion of that awe which attends a sudden triumph of the pure intellect. When at length he rose, it was with wide, blank eyes, and limbs partly numbed. These needed half-an-hour's walking before he could recover his mood of practical self-search.

Until the last moment he could not decide whether to let his mother know how he had reached Twybridge. His arrival corresponded pretty well with that of a train by which he might have come. But when the door opened to him, and the familiar faces smiled their welcome, he felt that he must have nothing to do with paltry deceit; he told of his walk, explaining it by the simple fact that this morning he had found himself short of money. How that came to pass, no one inquired. Mrs. Peak, shocked at such martyrdom, tended him with all motherly care; for once, Godwin felt that it was good to have a home, however simple.

This amiable frame of mind was not likely to last beyond the first day. Matter of irritation soon enough offered itself, as was invariably the case at Twybridge. It was pleasant enough to be fêted as the hero of the family, to pull out a Kingsmill newspaper and exhibit the full report of prize-day at Whitelaw, with his own name, in very small type, demanding the world's attention, and finally to exhibit the volumes in tree-calf which his friend the librarian had forwarded to him. But domestic circumstances soon made assault upon his nerves, and trial of his brief patience.

First of all, there came an unexpected disclosure. His sister Charlotte had affianced herself to a young man of Twybridge, one Mr. Cusse, whose prospects were as slender as his present means. Mrs. Peak spoke of the affair in hushed privacy, with shaking of the head and frequent sighs, for to her mind Mr. Cusse had few even personal recommendations. He was a draper's assistant. Charlotte had made his acquaintance on occasions of church festivity, and urged the fact of his zeal in Sunday-school tuition as sufficient reply to all doubts. As he listened, Godwin bit his lips.

'Does he come here, then?' was his inquiry.

'Once or twice a week. I haven't felt able to say anything against it, Godwin. I suppose it will be a very long engagement.'

Charlotte was just twenty-two, and it seemed probable that she knew her own mind; in any case, she was of a character which would only be driven to obstinacy by adverse criticism. Godwin learnt that his aunt Emily (Miss Cadman) regarded this connection with serious disapproval. Herself a shopkeeper, she might have been expected to show indulgence to a draper's assistant, but, so far from this, her view of Mr. Cusse was severely scornful. She had nourished far other hopes for Charlotte, who surely at her age (Miss Cadman looked from the eminence of five-and-forty) should have been less precipitate. No undue harshness had been exhibited by her relatives, but Charlotte took a stand which sufficiently declared her kindred with Godwin. She held her head higher than formerly, spoke with habitual decision which bordered on snappishness, and at times displayed the absent-mindedness of one who in silence suffers wrong.

There passed but a day or two before Godwin was brought face to face with Mr. Cusse, who answered too well to the idea Charlotte's brother had formed of him. He had a very smooth and shiny forehead, crowned by sleek chestnut hair; his chin was deferential; the bend of his body signified a modest hope that he did his duty in the station to which Providence had summoned him. Godwin he sought to flatter with looks of admiring interest; also, by entering upon a conversation which was meant to prove that he did not altogether lack worldly knowledge, of however little moment that might be in comparison with spiritual concerns. Examining, volume by volume and with painful minuteness, the prizes Godwin had carried off, he remarked fervently, in each instance, 'I can see how very interesting that is! So thorough, so thorough!' Even Charlotte was at length annoyed, when Mr. Cusse had exclaimed upon the 'thoroughness' of Ben Jonson's works; she asked an abrupt question about some town affair, and so gave her brother an opportunity of taking the books away. There was no flagrant offence in the man. He spoke with passable accent, and manifested a high degree of amiability; but one could not dissociate him from the counter. At the thought that his sister might become Mrs. Cusse, Godwin ground his teeth. Now that he came to reflect on the subject he found in himself a sort of unreasoned supposition that Charlotte would always remain single; it seemed so unlikely that she would be sought by a man of liberal standing, and at the same time so impossible for her to accept any one less than a gentleman. Yet he remembered that to outsiders such fastidiousness must show in a ridiculous light. What claim to gentility had they, the Peaks? Was it not all a figment of his own self-conceit? Even in education Charlotte could barely assert a superiority to Mr. Cusse, for her formal schooling had ended when she was twelve, and she had never cared to read beyond the strait track of clerical inspiration.

There were other circumstances which helped to depress his estimate of the family dignity. His brother Oliver, now seventeen, was developing into a type of young man as objectionable as it is easily recognised. The slow, compliant boy had grown more flesh and muscle than once seemed likely, and his wits had begun to display that kind of vivaciousness which is only compatible with a nature moulded in common clay. He saw much company, and all of low intellectual order; he had purchased a bicycle, and regarded it as a source of distinction, a means of displaying himself before shopkeepers' daughters; he believed himself a modest tenor, and sang verses of sentimental imbecility;

he took in several weekly papers of unpromising title, for the chief purpose of deciphering cryptograms, in which pursuit he had singular success. Add to these characteristics a penchant for cheap jewellery, and Oliver Peak stands confessed.

It appeared to Godwin that his brother had leapt in a few months to these heights of vulgar accomplishment; each separate revelation struck unexpectedly upon his nerves and severely tried his temper. When at length Oliver, waiting for supper, began to dance grotesquely to an air which local talent had somehow caught from the London music-halls, Godwin's self-control gave way.

'Is it your ambition,' he asked, with fiery sarcasm, 'to join a troupe of nigger minstrels?'

Oliver was startled into the military posture of attention. He answered, with some embarrassment:

'I can't say it is.'

'Yet any one would suppose so,' went on Godwin, hotly. 'Though you are employed in a shop, I should have thought you might aim at behaving like a gentleman.'

Indisposed to quarrel, and possessed of small skill in verbal fence, Oliver drew aside with shadowed brow. As the brothers still had to share one bed-room, they were presently alone together, and their muteness, as they lay down to sleep, showed the estrangement that had at length come between them. When all had been dark and still for half-an-hour, Godwin spoke.

'Are you awake?'

'Yes.'

'There was something about Uncle Andrew I didn't mention. He talks of opening an eating-house just opposite Whitelaw.'

'Oh.'

The tone of this signified nothing more than curiosity.

'You don't see any reason why he shouldn't?'

Oliver delayed a little before replying.

'I suppose it wouldn't be very nice for you.'

'That's rather a mild way of putting it. It would mean that I should have to leave the College, and give up all my hopes.'

'I see,' returned the other, with slow apprehension.

There followed several minutes of silence. Then Godwin sat up in bed, as had always been his wont when he talked with earnestness at night.

'If you think I lost my temper without cause at supper-time, just remember that I had that blackguard before my mind, and that it isn't very pleasant to see you taking after that branch of our family.'

'Do you mean to say I am like uncle?'

'I mean to say that, if you are not careful, you won't be the kind of man I should like to see you. Do you know what is meant by inherited tendencies? Scientific men are giving a great deal of attention to such things nowadays. Children don't always take after their parents; very often they show a much stronger likeness to a grandfather, or an uncle, or even more distant relatives. Just think over this, and make up your mind to resist any danger of that sort. I tell you plainly that the habits you are getting into, and the people you make friends of, are detestable. For heaven's sake, spend more of your time in a rational way, and learn to despise the things that shopkeepers admire. Read! Force yourself to stick hard at solid books for two or three hours every day. If you don't, it's all up with you. I am speaking for your own good. Read, read, read!'

Quietness ensued. Then Oliver began to move uneasily in his bed, and at length his protest became audible.

'I can't see what harm I do.'

'No!' burst from his brother's lips, scornfully. 'And that's just your danger. Do you suppose *I* could sing nigger songs and run about the town with shopboys, and waste hours over idiotic puzzles?'

'We're not all alike, and it wouldn't do for us to be.'

'It would do very well for us all to have brains and to use them. The life you lead is a brainless life, brainless and vulgar.'

'Well, if I haven't got brains, I can't help it,' replied Oliver, with sullen resignation.

'You have enough to teach you to live respectably, if only you look to the right kind of example.'

There followed a vehement exhortation, now angry, now in

strain of natural kindliness. To this Oliver made only a few brief and muttered replies; when it was all over, he fell asleep. But Godwin was wakeful for hours.

The next morning he attempted to work for his approaching examination, but with small result. It had begun to be very doubtful to him whether he should 'go up' at all, and this uncertainty involved so great a change in all his prospects that he could not command the mental calm necessary for study. After dinner he went out with unsettled purpose. He would gladly have conversed with Mr. Gunnery, but the old people were just now on a stay with relatives in Bedfordshire, and their return might be delayed for another week. Perhaps it behoved him to go and see Mr. Moxey, but he was indisposed to visit the works, and if he went to the house this evening he would encounter the five daughters, who, like all women who did not inspire him with admiration, excited his bashful dislike. At length he struck off into the country and indulged restless thoughts in places where no one could observe him.

A result of the family's removal first from London to the farm, and then into Twybridge, was that Godwin had no friends of old standing. At Greenwich, Nicholas Peak formed no intimacies, nor did a single associate remain to him from the years of his growth and struggle; his wife, until the renewal of intercourse with her sister at Twybridge, had no society whatever beyond her home. A boy reaps advantage from the half parental kindness of men and women who have watched his growth from infancy; in general it affects him as a steadying influence, keeping before his mind the social bonds to which his behaviour owes allegiance. The only person whom Godwin regarded with feeling akin to this was Mr. Gunnery, but the geologist found no favour with Mrs. Peak, and thus he involuntarily helped to widen the gap between the young man and his relatives. Nor had the intimacies of school time supplied Godwin with friendships for the years to come; his Twybridge class-fellows no longer interested him, nor did they care to continue his acquaintance. One was articled to a solicitor; one was learning the drug-trade in his father's shop; another had begun to deal in corn; the rest were scattered about

England, as students or salary-earners. The dominion of the commonplace had absorbed them, all and sundry; they were the stuff which destiny uses for its every-day purposes, to keep the world a-rolling.

So that Godwin had no ties which bound him strongly to any district. He could not call himself a Londoner; for, though born in Westminster, he had grown to consciousness on the outskirts of Greenwich, and remembered but dimly some of the London streets, and a few places of public interest to which his father had taken him. Yet, as a matter of course, it was to London that his ambition pointed, when he forecast the future. Where else could he hope for opportunity of notable advancement? At Twybridge? Impossible to find more than means of subsistence; his soul loathed such a prospect. At Kingsmill? There was a slender hope that he might establish a connection with Whitelaw College, if he devoted himself to laboratory work; but what could come of that—at all events for many years? London, then? The only acceptable plan for supporting himself there was to succeed in a Civil Service competition. That, indeed, seemed the most hopeful direction for his efforts; a government office might afford him scope, and, he had heard, would allow him abundant leisure.

Or to go abroad? To enter for the Indian clerkships, and possibly cleave a wider way than could be hoped in England? There was allurement in the suggestion; travel had always tempted his fancy. In that case he would be safely severed from the humble origin which in his native country might long be an annoyance, or even an obstacle; no Uncle Andrew could spring up at inconvenient moments in the middle of his path. Yes; this indeed might be best of all. He must send for papers, and give attention to the matter.

Musing in this way, he had come within sight of the familiar chemical works. It was near the hour at which Mr. Moxey was about to go home for his afternoon dinner; why not interrupt his walk, and have a word with him? That duty would be over.

He pushed on, and, as he approached the buildings, was aware of Mr. Moxey stepping into the road, unaccompanied. Greetings speedily followed. The manufacturer, who was growing stout in his mellow years and looking more leisurely than when Godwin first knew him, beamed with smiles of approbation.

'Glad to see you; glad to see you! I have heard of your doings at College.'

'Nothing to boast of, Mr. Moxey.'

'Why, what would satisfy you? A nephew of mine was there last Friday, and tells me you carried off half a hundredweight of prizes. Here he comes, I see.'

There drew near a young man of about four-and-twenty, well-dressed, sauntering with a cane in his hand. His name was Christian Moxey.

'Much pleasure in meeting you, Mr. Peak,' he said, with a winning smile. 'I was at Whitelaw the other day, when you distinguished yourself, and if I had known then that you were an acquaintance of my uncle's I should have been tempted to offer a word of congratulation. Very glad indeed to meet you.'

Godwin, grateful as always for the show of kindness and flattered by such a reception, at once felt a liking for Christian Moxey. Most people would have admitted the young man's attractiveness. He had a thin and sallow face, and seemed to be of weak constitution. In talking he leant upon his cane, and his movements were languid; none the less, his person was distinguished by an air of graceful manhood. His features, separately considered, were ordinary enough; together they made a countenance of peculiar charm, vividly illumined, full of appeal to whosoever could appreciate emotional capabilities. The interest he excited in Peak appeared to be reciprocal, for his eyes dwelt as often and as long as possible on Godwin's features.

'Come along, and have something to eat with us,' said Mr. Moxey, in a tone of genial invitation. 'I daresay you had dinner long enough ago to have picked up a new appetite.'

Godwin had a perturbing vision of the five Miss Moxeys and of a dinner table, such as he was not used to sit at; he wished to decline, yet knew not how to do so with civility.

'Yes, yes; come along!' added his friend, heartily. 'Tell us something about your chemistry paper. Any posers this time?

My nephew won't be out of it; he belongs to the firm of Bates Brothers—the Rotherhithe people, you know.'

This information was a surprise to Godwin. He had imagined Christian Moxey either a gentleman at large, or at all events connected with some liberal profession. Glancing at the attractive face, he met a singular look, a smile which suggested vague doubts. But Christian made no remark, and Mr. Moxey renewed his inquiries about the examination in chemistry.

The five daughters—all assembled in a homely sitting-room—were nothing less than formidable. Plain, soft-spoken, not ill educated, they seemed to live in perfect harmony, and to derive satisfaction from pursuits independent of external society. In the town they were seldom seen; few families called upon them; and only the most inveterate gossips found matter for small-talk in their retired lives. It had never been heard that any one of them was sought in marriage. Godwin, superfluously troubled about his attire, met them with grim endeavour at politeness; their gravity, a result of shyness, he misinterpreted, supposing them to hold aloof from a young man who had been in their father's employ. But before he could suffer much from the necessity of formal conversation the door opened to admit yet another young lady, a perfect stranger to him. Her age was about seventeen, but she had nothing of the sprightly grace proverbially connected with that time of life in girls; her pale and freckled visage expressed a haughty reserve, intensified as soon as her eye fell upon the visitor. She had a slight but well-proportioned figure, and a mass of auburn hair carelessly arranged.

'My sister,' said Christian, glancing at Godwin. 'Marcella, you recognise Mr. Peak.'

'Oh yes,' the girl replied, as she came forward, and made a sudden offer of her hand.

She too had been present the other day at Whitelaw. Her 'Oh yes' sounded offensive to Godwin, yet in shaking hands with her he felt a warm pressure, and it flattered him when he became aware that Marcella regarded him from time to time with furtive interest. Presently he learnt that Christian and his sister were on a short visit at the house of their relatives; their home was in

London. Marcella had seated herself stiffly by a window, and seemed to pay more attention to the view without than to the talk which went on, until dinner was announced.

Speculating on all he saw, Godwin noticed that Christian Moxey showed a marked preference for the youngest of his cousins, a girl of eighteen, whose plain features were frequently brightened with a happy and very pleasant smile. When he addressed her (by the name of Janet) his voice had a playful kindness which must have been significant to everyone who heard it. At dinner, his place was by her side, and he attended to her with more than courtesy. This astonished Peak. He deemed it incredible that any man should conceive a tender feeling for a girl so far from beautiful. Constantly occupied with thought of sexual attachments, he had never imagined anything of the kind apart from loveliness of feature in the chosen object; his instincts were, in fact, revolted by the idea of love for such a person as Janet Moxey. Christian seemed to be degraded by such a suggestion. In his endeavour to solve the mystery, Godwin grew half unconscious of the other people about him.

Such play of the imaginative and speculative faculties accounts for the common awkwardness of intelligent young men in society that is strange to them. Only the cultivation of a double consciousness puts them finally at ease. Impossible to converse with suavity, and to heed the forms of ordinary good-breeding, when the brain is absorbed in all manner of new problems: one must learn to act a part, to control the facial mechanism, to observe and anticipate, even whilst the intellect is spending its sincere energy on subjects unavowed. The perfectly graceful man will always be he who has no strong apprehension either of his own personality or of that of others, who lives on the surface of things, who can be interested without emotion, and surprised without contemplative impulse. Never yet had Godwin Peak uttered a word that was worth listening to, or made a remark that declared his mental powers, save in most familiar colloquy. He was beginning to understand the various reasons of his seeming clownishness, but this very process of self-study opposed an obstacle to improvement.

When he found himself obliged to take part in conversation about Whitelaw College, Godwin was disturbed by an uncertainty which had never left his mind at rest during the past two years;—was it, or was it not, generally known to his Twybridge acquaintances that he studied as the pensioner of Sir Job Whitelaw? To outward seeming all delicacy had been exercised in the bestowal of Sir Job's benefaction. At the beginning of each academic session Mrs. Peak had privately received a cheque which represented the exact outlay in fees for the course her son was pursuing; payment was then made to the registrar as if from Peak himself. But Lady Whitelaw's sisters were in the secret, and was it likely that they maintained absolute discretion in talking with their Twybridge friends? There seemed, in the first instance, to be a tacit understanding that the whole affair should remain strictly private, and to Godwin himself, sensible enough of such refinements, it was by no means inconceivable that silence had been strictly preserved. He found no difficulty in imagining that Sir Job's right hand knew nothing of what the left performed, and it might be that the authorities of Whitelaw had no hint of his peculiar position. Still, he was perchance mistaken. The Professors perhaps regarded him as a sort of charity-boy, and Twybridge possibly saw him in the same light. The doubt flashed upon his mind while he was trying to eat and converse with becoming self-possession. He dug his heel into the carpet and silently cursed the burden of his servitude.

When the meal was over, Mr. Moxey led the way out into the garden. Christian walked apart with Janet; Godwin strolled about between his host and the eldest Miss Moxey, talking of he knew not what. In a short half-hour he screwed up his courage to the point of leave-taking. Marcella and three of her cousins had disappeared, so that the awkwardness of departure was reduced. Christian, who seemed to be in a very contented mood, accompanied the guest as far as the garden gate.

'What will be your special line of work when you leave Whitelaw?' he inquired. 'Your tastes seem about equally divided between science and literature.'

'I haven't the least idea what I shall do,' was Peak's reply.

'Very much my own state of mind when I came home from Zurich a year ago. But it had been taken for granted that I was preparing for business, so into business I went.' He laughed good-humouredly. 'Perhaps you will be drawn to London?'

'Yes—I think it likely,' Godwin answered, with an absent glance this way and that.

'In any case,' pursued the other, 'you'll be there presently for First B.A. Honours. Try to look in at my rooms, will you? I should be delighted to see you. Most of my day is spent in the romantic locality of Rotherhithe, but I get home about five o'clock, as a rule. Let me give you a card.'

'Thank you.'

'I daresay we shall meet somewhere about here before then. Of course you are reading hard, and haven't much leisure. I'm an idle dog, unfortunately. I should like to work, but I don't quite know what at. I suppose this is a transition time with me.'

Godwin tried to discover the implication of this remark. Had it any reference to Miss Janet Moxey? Whilst he stood in embarrassed silence, Christian looked about with a peculiar smile, and seemed on the point of indulging in further self-revelation; but Godwin of a sudden held out his hand for good-bye, and with friendly smiles they parted.

Peak was older than his years, and he saw in Christian one who might prove a very congenial associate, did but circumstances favour their intercourse. That was not very likely to happen, but the meeting at all events turned his thoughts to London once more.

His attempts to 'read' were still unfruitful. For one thing, the stress and excitement of the Whitelaw examinations had wearied him; it was characteristic of the educational system in which he had become involved that studious effort should be called for immediately after that frenzy of college competition. He ought now to have been 'sweating' at his London subjects. Instead of that, he procured works of general literature from a Twybridge library, and shut himself up with them in the garret bedroom.

A letter from Mr. Gunnery informed him that the writer

would be home in a day or two. This return took place late one evening, and on the morrow Godwin set forth to visit his friend. On reaching the house, he learnt that Mr. Gunnery had suffered an accident which threatened serious results. Walking barefoot in his bedroom the night before, he had stepped upon the point of a large nail, and was now prostrate, enduring much pain. Two days elapsed before Godwin could be admitted; he then found the old man a mere shadow of his familiar self—bloodless, hollow-eyed.

'This is the kind of practical joke that Fate likes to play upon us!' the sufferer growled in a harsh, quaking voice, his countenance divided between genial welcome and surly wrath. 'It'll be the end of me. Pooh! who doesn't know that such a thing is fatal at my age? Blood-poisoning has fairly begun. I'd a good deal rather have broken my neck among honest lumps of old red sandstone. A nail! A damned Brummagem nail!—So you collared the first prize in geology, eh? I take that as a kindness, Godwin. You've got a bit beyond Figuier and his *Deluge*, eh? His Deluge, bah!'

And he laughed discordantly. On the other side of the bed sat Mrs. Gunnery, grizzled and feeble dame. Shaken into the last stage of senility by this alarm, she wiped tears from her flaccid cheeks, and moaned a few unintelligible words.

The geologist's forecast of doom was speedily justified. Another day bereft him of consciousness, and when, for a short while, he had rambled among memories of his youth, the end came. It was found that he had made a will, bequeathing his collections and scientific instruments to Godwin Peak; his books were to be sold for the benefit of the widow, who would enjoy an annuity purchased out of her husband's savings. The poor old woman, as it proved, had little need of income; on the thirteenth day after Mr. Gunnery's funeral, she too was borne forth from the house, and the faithful couple slept together.

To inherit from the dead was an impressive experience to Godwin. At the present stage of his development, every circumstance affecting him started his mind upon the quest of reasons, symbolisms, principles; the 'natural supernatural' had hold upon him, and ruled his thought whenever it was free from the spur of arrogant instinct. This tendency had been strengthened by the influence of his friend Earwaker, a young man of singularly complex personality, positive and analytic in a far higher degree than Peak, yet with a vein of imaginative vigour which seemed to befit quite a different order of mind. Godwin was not distinguished by originality in thinking, but his strongly featured character converted to uses of his own the intellectual suggestions he so rapidly caught from others. Earwaker's habit of reflection had much to do with the strange feelings awakened in Godwin when he transferred to his mother's house the cabinets which had been Mr. Gunnery's pride for thirty or forty years. Joy of possession was subdued in him by the conflict of metaphysical questionings.

Days went on, and nothing was heard of Uncle Andrew. Godwin tried to assure himself that he had been needlessly terrified; the eating-house project would never be carried out. Practically dismissing that anxiety, he brooded over his defeat by Chilvers, and thought with extreme reluctance of the year still to be spent at Whitelaw, probably a year of humiliation. In the meantime, should he or should he not present himself for his First B.A.? The five pound fee would be a most serious demand upon his mother's resources, and did the profit warrant it, was it really of importance to him to take a degree?

He lived as much as possible alone, generally avoiding the society of his relatives, save at meal times. A careless remark (not intentionally offensive) with reference to Mr. Cusse had so affronted Charlotte that she never spoke to him save in reply to a question. Godwin regretted the pain he had given, but could not bring himself to express this feeling, for a discussion would inevitably have disclosed all his mind concerning the draper's assistant. Oliver seemed to have forgiven his brother's reproaches, but no longer behaved with freedom when Godwin was present. For all this, the elder's irritation was often aroused by things he saw and heard; and at length—on a memorable Saturday afternoon—debate revived between them. Oliver, as his custom was, had attired himself sprucely for a visit to acquaintances, and a silk hat of the very newest fashion lay together with his gloves upon the table.

'What is this thing?' inquired Godwin, with ominous calm, as he pointed to the piece of head-gear.

'A hat, I suppose,' replied his brother.

'You mean to say you are going to wear that in the street?'

'And why not?'

Oliver, not venturing to raise his eyes, stared at the table-cloth indignantly.

'Can't you feel,' burst from the other, 'that it's a disgrace to buy and wear such a thing?'

'Disgrace! what's the matter with the hat? It's the fashionable shape.'

Godwin mastered his wrath, and turned contemptuously away. But Oliver had been touched in a sensitive place; he was eager to defend himself.

'I can't see what you're finding fault with,' he exclaimed. 'Everybody wears this shape.'

'And isn't that quite sufficient reason why anyone who respects himself should choose something as different as possible? Everybody! That is to say, all the fools in the kingdom. It's bad enough to follow when you can't help it, but to imitate asses gratuitously is the lowest depth of degradation. Don't you know that that is the meaning of vulgarity? How you can offer such an excuse passes my comprehension. Have you no *self*? Are you made, like this hat, on a pattern with a hundred thousand others?'

'You and I are different,' said Oliver, impatiently. 'I am content to be like other people.'

'And I would poison myself with vermin-killer if I felt any risk of such contentment! Like other people? Heaven forbid and forfend! Like other people? Oh, what a noble ambition!'

The loud passionate voice summoned Mrs. Peak from an adjacent room.

'Godwin! Godwin!' she remonstrated. 'Whatever is it? Why should you put yourself out so?'

She was a short and slender woman, with an air of gentility, independent of her badly made and long worn widow's dress.

Self-possession marked her manner, and the even tones in which she spoke gave indication of a mild, perhaps an unemotional, temperament.

Oliver began to represent his grievance.

'What harm is there, if I choose to wear a hat that's in fashion? I pay for it out of my own'——

But he was interrupted by a loud visitor's knock at the front door, distant only a few paces. Mrs. Peak turned with a startled look. Godwin, dreading contact with friends of the family, strode upstairs. When the door was opened, there appeared the smiling countenance of Andrew Peak; he wore the costume of a traveller, and by his side stood a boy of ten, too plainly his son.

'Well, Grace!' was his familiar greeting, as the widow drew back. 'I told you you'd 'ev the pleasure of seein' me again before so very long. Godwin at 'ome with you, I s'pose? That you, Noll? 'Ow do, my bo-oy? 'Ere's yer cousin Jowey. Shike 'ands, Jowey bo-oy! Sorry I couldn't bring my old lady over this time, Grace; she sends her respects, as usual. 'Ow's Charlotte? Bloomin', I 'ope?'

He had made his way into the front parlour, dragging the youngster after him. Having deposited his handbag and umbrella on the sofa, he seated himself in the easy-chair, and began to blow his nose with vigour.

'Set down, Jowey; set down, bo-oy! Down't be afride of your awnt.'

'Oi ain't afride!' cried the youth, in a tone which supported his assertion.

Mrs. Peak trembled with annoyance and indecision. Andrew evidently meant to stay for some time, and she could not bring herself to treat him with plain discourtesy; but she saw that Oliver, after shaking hands in a very strained way, had abruptly left the room, and Godwin would be anything but willing to meet his uncle. When the name of her elder son was again mentioned she withdrew on the pretence of summoning him, and went up to his room. Godwin had heard the hateful voice, and was in profound disturbance.

'What does he say, mother?' he inquired anxiously. 'Anything about Kingsmill?'

'Not yet. Oh, I *do* so wish we could bring this connection to an end!'

It was the first time Mrs. Peak had uttered her sentiments so unreservedly.

'Then, shall I see him in private,' said Godwin, 'and simply let him know the truth?'

'I dread the thought of that, Godwin. He would very likely be coarse and violent. I must try to show him by my manner. Oliver has gone out, and when Charlotte comes home I'll tell her to keep out of sight. He has brought his boy. Suppose you don't come down at all? I might say you are too busy.'

'No, no; you shan't have to do it all alone. I'll come down with you. I must hear what he has to say.'

They descended. As soon as his nephew appeared, Andrew sprang up, and shouted joyfully:

'Well, Godwin, bo-oy! It's all settled! Got the bloomin' shop from next quarter dye! "Peak's Dinin' and Refreshment Rooms!" Jowey an' me was over there all yisterday—wasn't us, Jowey? Oh, it's immense!'

Godwin felt the blood buzz in his ears, and a hot choking clutch at his throat. He took his stand by the mantelpiece, and began to turn a little glass ornament round and round. Fate had spoken. On the instant, all his College life was far behind him, all his uneasiness regarding the next session was dispelled, and he had no more connection with Kingsmill.

Mrs. Peak had heard from Oliver of her brother-in-law's proposed undertaking. She had spoken of it with anxiety to Godwin, who merely shrugged his shoulders and avoided the topic, ashamed to dwell on the particulars of his shame. In hearing Andrew's announcement she had much ado to repress tears of vexation; silently she seated herself, and looked with pained countenance from uncle to nephew.

'Shall you make any changes in the place?' Godwin asked, carelessly.

'Shan't I, jest! It'll take a month to refit them eatin' rooms. I'm agoin' to do it proper—up to Dick! and I want your 'elp, my bo-oy. You an' me'll jest write a bit of a circular—see? to send round to the big pots of the Collige, an' all the parents of the young fellers as we can get the addresses of—see?'

Even amid his pangs of mortification Godwin found himself pondering an intellectual question. Was his uncle wholly unconscious of the misery he was causing? Had it never occurred to him that the public proximity of an uneducated shopkeeping relative must be unwelcome to a lad who was distinguishing himself at Whitelaw College? Were that truly the case, then it would be unjust to regard Andrew resentfully; destiny alone was to blame. And, after all, the man might be so absorbed in his own interest, so strictly confined to the views of his own class, as never to have dreamt of the sensibilities he wounded. In fact, the shame excited by this prospect was artificial. Godwin had already felt that it was unworthy alike of a philosopher and of a high-minded man of the world. The doubt as to Andrew's state of mind, and this moral problem, had a restraining effect upon the young man's temper. A practical person justifies himself in wrath as soon as his judgment is at one with that of the multitude. Godwin, though his passions were of exceptional force, must needs refine, debate with himself points of abstract justice.

'I've been tellin' Jowey, Grace, as I 'ope he may turn out such another as Godwin 'ere. 'E'll go to Collige, will Jowey. Godwin, jes arst the bo-oy a question or two, will you? 'E ain't been doin' bad at 'is school. Jest put 'im through 'is pyces, as yer may sye. Stend up, Jowey, bo-oy.'

Godwin looked askance at his cousin, who stood with pert face, ready for any test.

'What's the date of William the Conqueror?' he asked, mechanically.

'Ow!' shouted the youth. 'Down't mike me larff! Zif I didn't know that! Tensixsixtenightysivn, of course!'

The father turned round with an expression of such sincere pride that Godwin, for all his loathing, was obliged to smile.

'Jowey, jest sye a few verses of poitry; them as you learnt larst. 'E's good at poitry, is Jowey.'

The boy broke into fearsome recitation:

'The silly buckits *on* the deck
That 'ed so long rem'ined,
I dreamt as they was filled with jew,
End when I awowk, it r'ined.'

Half-a-dozen verses were thus massacred, and the reciter stopped with the sudden jerk of a machine.

'Goes str'ight on, don't 'e, Grace?' cried the father, exultantly. 'Jowey ain't no fool. Know what he towld me the other day? Somethin' as I never knew, and shouldn't never 'ave thought of s'long as I lived. We was talkin' about jewellery, an' Jowey, 'e pops up all at wunst. "It's called jewellery," says 'e, " 'cos it's mostly the Jews as sell it." Now, oo'd a thought o' that? But you see it's right as soon as you're towld, eh? Now ain't it right, Godwin?'

'No doubt,' was the dry answer.

'It never struck me,' murmured Mrs. Peak, who took her son's assent seriously, and felt that it was impossible to preserve an obstinate silence.

' 'E ain't no fool, ain't Jowey!' cried the parent. 'Wite till 'e gits to Collige. Godwin 'll put us up to all the ins and outs. Plenty o' time for that; 'e'll often run over an' 'ev a bit o' dinner, and no need to talk about p'yment.'

'Do you stay in Twybridge to-night?' inquired Godwin, who had changed in look and manner, so that he appeared all but cheerful.

'No, we're on our w'y 'ome, is Jowey an' me. Jest thought we'd break the journey 'ere. We shall ketch the six-fifty hup.'

'Then you will have a cup of tea with us,' said Mrs. Peak, surprised at Godwin's transformation, but seeing that hospitality was now unavoidable.

Charlotte presently entered the house, and, after a private conversation with her mother, went to greet Andrew. If only to signify her contempt for Godwin's prejudices, Charlotte would have behaved civilly to the London uncle. In the end, Andrew took his leave in the friendliest possible way, repeating often that he would soon have the pleasure of entertaining Mrs. Peak and all her family at his new dining-rooms over against Whitelaw College.

IV

IMMEDIATELY UPON HIS uncle's departure, Godwin disappeared; Mrs. Peak caught only a glimpse of him as he went by the parlour window. In a short time Oliver came home, and, having learned what had happened, joined his mother and sister in a dull, intermittent conversation on the subject of Godwin's future difficulties.

'He won't go back to Whitelaw,' declared the lad. 'He said he wouldn't.'

'People must be above such false shame,' was Charlotte's opinion. 'I can't see that it will make the slightest difference in his position or his prospects.'

Whereupon her mother's patience gave way.

'Don't talk such nonsense, Charlotte! You understand perfectly well how serious it will be. I never knew anything so cruel.'

'I was never taught,' persisted the girl, with calm obstinacy, 'that one ought to be ashamed of one's relatives just because they are in a humble position.'

Oliver brought the tedious discussion to an end by clamouring for supper. The table was laid, and all were about to sit down when Godwin presented himself. To the general astonishment, he seemed in excellent spirits, and ate more heartily than usual. Not a word was spoken of Uncle Andrew, until Mrs. Peak and her elder son were left alone together; then Godwin remarked in a tone of satisfied decision:

'Of course, this is the end of my work at Whitelaw. We must make new plans, mother.'

'But how can we, dear? What will Lady Whitelaw say?'

'I have to think it out yet. In a day or two I shall very likely write a letter to Lady Whitelaw. There's no need, you know, to go talking about this in Twybridge. Just leave it to me, will you?'

'It's not a subject I care to talk about, you may be sure. But I do hope you won't do anything rash, Godwin.'

'Not I. To tell you the truth, I'm not at all sorry to leave. It was a mistake that I went in for the Arts course—Greek, and Latin, and so on, you know; I ought to have stuck to science. I shall go back to it now. Don't be afraid. I'll make a position for myself before long. I'll repay all you have spent on me.'

To this conclusion had he come. The process of mind was favoured by his defeat in all the Arts subjects; in that direction he could see only the triumphant Chilvers, a figure which disgusted him with Greeks, Romans, and all the ways of literature. As to his future efforts he was by no means clear, but it eased him greatly to have cast off a burden of doubt; his theorising intellect loved the sensation of life thrown open to new, however vague, possibilities. At present he was convinced that Andrew Peak had done him a service. In this there was an indication of moral cowardice, such as commonly connects itself with intense pride of individuality. He desired to shirk the combat with Chilvers, and welcomed as an excuse for doing so the shame which another temper would have stubbornly defied.

Now he would abandon his B.A. examination,—a clear saving of money. Presently it might suit him to take the B.Sc. instead; time enough to think of that. Had he but pursued the Science course from the first, who at Whitelaw could have come out ahead of him? He had wasted a couple of years which might have been most profitably applied: by this time he might have been ready to obtain a position as demonstrator in some laboratory, on his way perhaps to a professorship. How had he thus been led astray? Not only had his boyish instincts moved strongly towards science, but was not the tendency of the age in the same direction? Buckland Warricombe, who habitually declaimed against classical study, was perfectly right; the world had learned all it could from those hoary teachers, and must now turn to Nature. On every hand, the future was with students of the laws of matter. Often, it was true, he had been tempted by the thought of a literary career; he had written in verse and prose, but with small success. An attempt to compose the Prize Poem was soon abandoned in discouragement; the essay he sent in had not been mentioned. These honours had fallen to Earwaker, with whom it was not easy to compete on such ground. No, he was not born a man of letters. But in science, granted fair opportunity, he might make a name. He might, and he would!

On the morrow, splendour of sunshine drew him forth to some distance from the town. He went along the lanes singing; now it was holiday with him, and for the first time he could enjoy the broad golden daylight, the genial warmth. In a hollow of grassy fields, where he least expected to encounter an acquaintance, it was his chance to come upon Christian Moxey, stretched at full length in the company of nibbling sheep. Since the dinner at Mr. Moxey's, he had neither seen nor heard of Christian, who, it seemed probable, was back at his work in Rotherhithe. As their looks met, both laughed.

'I won't get up,' said Christian; 'the effort would be too great. Sit down and let us have a talk.'

'I disturb your thoughts,' answered Godwin.

'A most welcome disturbance; they weren't very pleasant just then. In fact, I have come as far as this in the hope of escaping them. I'm not much of a walker, are you?'

'Well, yes, I enjoy a good walk.'

'You are of an energetic type,' said Christian, musingly. 'You will do something in life. When do you go up for Honours?'

'I have decided not to go in at all.'

'Indeed; I'm sorry to hear that.'

'I have half made up my mind not to return to Whitelaw.'

Observing his hearer's look of surprise, Godwin asked himself whether it signified a knowledge of his footing at Whitelaw. The possibility of this galled him; but it was such a great step to have declared, as it were in public, an intention of freeing himself, that he was able to talk on with something of aggressive confidence.

'I think I shall go in for some practical work of a scientific kind. It was a mistake for me to pursue the Arts course.'

Christian looked at him earnestly.

'Are you sure of that?'

'Yes, I feel sure of it.'

There was silence. Christian beat the ground with his stick.

'Your state of mind, then,' he said at length, 'is more like my own than I imagined. I, too, have wavered for a long time between literature and science, and now at last I have quite decided —quite—that scientific study is the only safe line for me. The fact is, a man must concentrate himself. Not only for the sake of practical success, but—well, for his own sake.'

He spoke lazily, dreamily, propped upon his elbow, seeming to watch the sheep which panted at a few yards from him.

'I have no right,' he pursued, with a shadow of kindly anxiety on his features, 'to offer you advice, but—well, if you will let me insist on what I have learned from my own experience. There's nothing like having a special line of work and sticking to it vigorously. I, unfortunately, shall never do anything of any account,—but I know so well the conflict between diverging tastes. It has played the deuce with me, in all sorts of ways. At Zurich I utterly wasted my time, and I've done no better since I came back to England. Don't think me presumptuous. I only mean—well, it is so important to—to go ahead in one line.'

His air of laughing apology was very pleasant. Godwin felt his heart open to the kind fellow.

'No one needs the advice more than I,' he replied. 'I am going back to the line I took naturally when I first began to study at all.'

'But why leave Whitelaw?' asked Christian, gently.

'Because I dislike it—I can't tell you why.'

With ready tact Moxey led away from a subject which he saw was painful.

'Of course there are many other places where one can study just as well.'

'Do you know anything of the School of Mines in London?' Godwin inquired, abruptly.

'I worked there myself for a short time.'

'Then you could tell me about the—the fees, and so on?'

Christian readily gave the desired information, and the listener mused over it.

'Have you any friends in London?' Moxey asked, at length.

'No. But I don't think that matters. I shall work all the harder.'

'Perhaps so,' said the other, with some hesitation. And he added thoughtfully, 'It depends on one's temperament. Doesn't answer to be too much alone—I speak for myself at all events. I know very few people in London—very few that I care anything about. That, in fact, is one reason why I am staying here longer than I intended.' He seemed to speak rather to himself than to Godwin; the half-smile on his lips expressed a wish to disclose circumstances and motives which were yet hardly a suitable topic in a dialogue such as this. 'I like the atmosphere of a—of a comfortable home. No doubt I should get on better—with things in general—if I had a home of my own. I live in lodgings, you know; my sister lives with friends. Of course one has a sense of freedom, but then'——

His voice murmured off into silence, and again he beat the ground with his cane. Godwin was strongly interested in this broken revelation; he found it difficult to understand Moxey's yearning for domesticity, all his own impulses leading towards quite a contrary ideal. To him, life in London lodgings made rich promise; that indeed would be freedom, and full of all manner of high possibilities!

Each communed with his thoughts. Happening to glance at Christian, Godwin was struck with the graceful attitude in which the young man reclined; he himself squatted awkwardly on the grass, unable to abandon himself in natural repose, even as he found it impossible to talk with the ease of unconsciousness. The contrast, too, between his garments, his boots, and those of the Londoner was painful enough to him. Without being a dandy, Christian, it was evident, gave a good deal of thought to costume. That kind of thing had always excited Godwin's contempt, but now he confessed himself envious; doubtless, to be well dressed was a great step towards the finished ease of what is called a gentlemanly demeanour, which he knew he was very far from having attained.

'Well,' exclaimed Christian, unexpectedly, 'if I can be of ever so little use to you, pray let me. I must get back to town in a few days, but you know my address. Write to me, I beg, if you wish for any more information.'

The talk turned to less difficult topics. Godwin made inquiries about Zurich, then about Switzerland in general.

'Did you see much of the Alps?'

'Not as a climber sees them. That sort of thing isn't in my way; I haven't the energy—more's the pity. Would you like to see a lot of good photographs I brought back? I have them here; brought them to show the girls.'

In spite of the five Miss Moxeys and Christian's sister, Peak accepted the invitation to walk back with his companion, and presently they began to stroll towards Twybridge.

'I have an absurd tendency to dream—to lose myself amid ideals—I don't quite know how to express it,' Christian resumed, when both had been silent for some minutes. 'That's why I mean to go in earnestly for science—as a corrective. Fortunately, I have to work for my living; otherwise, I should moon my life away—no doubt. My sister has ten times as much energy—she knows much more than I do already. What a splendid thing it is to be of an independent character! I had rather be a self-reliant coal-heaver than a millionaire of uncertain will. My uncle—there's a man who knows his own mind. I respect those strong practical natures. Don't be misled by ideals. Make the most of your circumstances. Don't aim at—but I beg your pardon; I don't know what right I have to lecture you in this way.' And he broke off with his pleasant, kind-hearted laugh, colouring a little.

They reached Mr. Moxey's house. In a garden chair on the lawn sat Miss Janet, occupied with a book. She rose to meet them, shook hands with Godwin, and said to her cousin:

'The postman has just left a letter for you—forwarded from London.'

'Indeed? I'm going to show Mr. Peak my Swiss photographs. You wouldn't care to come and help me in the toil of turning them over?'

'O lazy man!'

Her laugh was joyous. Any one less prejudiced than Peak

would have recognised the beauty which transformed her homely features as she met Christian's look.

On the hall table lay the letter of which Janet had spoken. Christian took it up, and Godwin, happening at that moment to observe him, caught the tremor of a sudden emotion on lip and eyelid. Instantly, prompted by he knew not what perception, he turned his gaze to Janet, and in time to see that she also was aware of her cousin's strong interest in the letter, which was at once put away in Christian's pocket.

They passed into the sitting-room, where a large portfolio stood against the back of a chair. The half-hour which ensued was to Godwin a time of uneasiness. His pleasure in the photographs suffered disturbance from a subtle stress on his nerves, due to something indeterminable in the situation, of which he formed a part. Janet's merry humour seemed to be subdued. Christian was obviously forcing himself to entertain the guest whilst his thoughts were elsewhere. As soon as possible, Godwin rose to depart. He was just saying good-bye to Janet, when Marcella entered the room. She stood still, and Christian said, hurriedly:

'It's possible, Marcella, that Mr. Peak will be coming to London before long. We may have the pleasure of seeing him there.'

'You will be glad, I'm sure,' answered his sister. Then, as if forcing herself to address Peak directly, she faced to him and added, 'It isn't easy to find sympathetic companions.'

'I, at all events, haven't found very many,' Godwin replied, meaning to speak in a tone only half-serious, but conscious at once that he had made what might seem an appeal for sympathy. Thereupon his pride revolted, and in a moment drove him from the room.

Christian followed, and at the front door shook hands with him. Nervous impatience was unmistakable in the young man's look and words. Again Godwin speculated on the meaning of this, and wondered, in connection therewith, what were the characteristics which Marcella Moxey looked for in a 'sympathetic companion.'

V

IN THE COURSE of the afternoon, Godwin sat down to pen the rough draft of a letter to Lady Whitelaw. When the first difficulties were surmounted, he wrote rapidly, and at considerable length. It was not easy, at his time of life, to compress into the limits of an ordinary epistle all he wished to say to the widow of his benefactor. His purpose was, with all possible respect yet as firmly as might be, to inform Lady Whitelaw that he could not spend the last of his proposed three years at the College in Kingsmill, and furthermore to request of her that she would permit his using the promised sum of money as a student at the Royal School of Mines. This had to be done without confession of the reasons for his change of plan; he could not even hint at them. Yet cause must be assigned, and the best form of words he could excogitate ran thus: 'Family circumstances render it desirable—almost necessary—that I should spend the next twelve months in London. In spite of sincere reluctance to leave Whitelaw College, I am compelled to take this step.' The lady must interpret that as best she might. Very hard indeed was the task of begging a continuance of her bounty under these changed conditions. Could he but have resigned the money, all had been well; his tone might then have been dignified without effort. But such disinterestedness he could not afford. His mother might grant him money enough barely to live upon until he discovered means of support—for his education she was unable to pay. After more than an hour's work he had moderately satisfied himself; indeed, several portions of the letter struck him as well composed, and he felt that they must heighten the reader's interest in him. With an author's pleasure (though at the same time with much uneasiness) he perused the appeal again and again.

Late in the evening, when he was alone with his mother, he

told her what he had done, and read the letter for her opinion. Mrs. Peak was gravely troubled.

'Lady Whitelaw will ask her sisters for an explanation,' she said.

'I have thought of that,' Godwin replied, with the confident, cheerful air he had assumed from the first. 'If the Miss Lumbs go to aunt, she must be prepared to put them off in some way. But look here, mother, when uncle has opened his shop, it's pretty certain that some one or other will hit on the true explanation of my disappearance. Let them. Then Lady Whitelaw will understand and forgive me.'

After much musing, the mother ventured a timid question, the result of her anxieties rather than of her judgment on the point at issue.

'Godwin, dear, are you quite sure that his shop would make so much difference?'

The young man gave a passionate start.

'What! To have the fellows going there to eat, and hearing his talk, and——? Not for a day could I bear it! Not for an hour!'

He was red with anticipated shame, and his voice shook with indignation at the suggested martyrdom. Mrs. Peak dried a tear.

'You would be so alone in London, Godwin.'

'Not a bit of it. Young Mr. Moxey will be a useful friend, I am convinced he will. To tell you the whole truth, I aim at getting a place at the works in Rotherhithe, where he no doubt has influence. You see, mother, I might manage it even before the end of the year. Our Mr. Moxey will be disposed to help me with his recommendation.'

'But, my dear, wouldn't it come to the same thing, then, if you went back to Mr. Moxey's?'

He made a gesture of impatience.

'No, no, no! I couldn't live at Twybridge. I have my way to make, mother, and the place for that is London. You know I am ambitious. Trust me for a year or two, and see the result. I depend upon your help in this whole affair. Don't refuse it me. I have done with Whitelaw, and I have done with Twybridge: now comes London. You can't regard me as a boy, you know.'

'No—but'——

'But me no buts!' he cried, laughing excitedly. 'The thing is settled. As soon as possible in the morning I post this letter. I feel it will be successful. See aunt to-morrow, and get her support. Mind that Charlotte and Oliver don't talk to people. If you all use discretion, there's no need for any curiosity to be excited.'

When Godwin had taken a resolve, there was no domestic influence strong enough to prevent his acting upon it. Mrs. Peak's ignorance of the world, her mild passivity, and the faith she had in her son's intellectual resources, made her useless as a counsellor, and from no one else—now that Mr. Gunnery was dead—would the young man have dreamt of seeking guidance. Whatever Lady Whitelaw's reply, he had made up his mind to go to London. Should his subsidy be refused, then he would live on what his mother could allow him until—probably with the aid of Christian Moxey—he might obtain a salaried position. The letter was dispatched, and with feverish impatience he awaited a reply.

Nine days passed, and he heard nothing. Half that delay sufficed to bring out all the self-tormenting capacities of a nature such as his. To his mother's conjectural explanations he could lend no ear. Doubtless Lady Whitelaw (against whom, for subtle reasons, he was already prejudiced) had taken offence; either she would not reply at all, or presently there would come a few lines of polite displeasure, intimating her disinclination to aid his project. He silently raged against 'the woman.' Her neglect was insolence. Had she not delicacy enough to divine the anxiety natural to one in his dependent position? Did she take him for an every-day writer of mendicant appeals? His pride fed upon the outrage and became fierce.

Then arrived a small glossy envelope, containing a tiny sheet of very thick note-paper, whereon it was written that Lady Whitelaw regretted her tardiness in replying to him (caused by her absence from home), and hoped he would be able to call upon her, at ten o'clock next morning, at the house of her sisters, the Misses Lumb, where she was stopping for a day—she remained his sincerely.

Having duly contorted this note into all manner of painful meanings, Godwin occupied an hour in making himself presentable (scornful that he should deem such trouble necessary), and with furiously beating heart set out to walk through Twybridge. Arrived at the house, he was led by a servant into the front room on the ground floor, where Lady Whitelaw, alone, sat reading a newspaper. Her features were of a very common order, and nothing distinguished her from middle-aged women of average refinement; she had chubby hands, rather broad shoulders, and no visible waist. The scrutiny she bestowed upon her visitor was close. To Godwin's feelings it too much resembled that with which she would have received an applicant for the post of footman. Yet her smile was friendly enough, and no lack of civility appeared in the repetition of her excuses for having replied so late.

'Let us talk about this,' she began, when Godwin was uneasily seated. (She spoke with an excess of precision, as though it had at one time been needful for her to premeditate polished phrases.) 'I am very sorry you should have to think of quitting the College; very sorry indeed. You are one of the students who do honour to the institution.'

This was pleasant, and Godwin felt a regret of the constraint that was upon him. In his endeavour not to display a purring smile, he looked grim, as if the compliment were beneath his notice.

'Pray don't think,' she pursued, 'that I wish you to speak more fully about the private circumstances you refer to in your letter. But do let me ask you: Is your decision final? Are you sure that when the vacations are over you will see things just as you do now?'

'I am quite sure of it,' he replied.

The emphasis was merely natural to him. He could not so govern his voice as to convey the respectful regret which at this moment he felt. A younger lady, one who had heightened the charm of her compliment with subtle harmony of tones and strongly feminine gaze, would perhaps have elicited from him a free confession. Gratitude and admiration would have made him capable of such frankness. But in the face of this newspaper-reading woman (yes, he had unaccountably felt it jar upon him that a lady should be reading a newspaper), under her matronly smile, he could do no more than plump out his 'quite sure.' To Lady Whitelaw it sounded altogether too curt; she was conscious of her position as patroness, and had in fact thought it likely that the young man would be disposed to gratify her curiosity in some measure.

'I can only say that I am sorry to hear it,' fell from her tightened lips, after a moment's pause.

Instantly Godwin's pride expelled the softer emotion. He pressed hard with his feet upon the floor, every nerve in his body tense with that distressing passion peculiar to the shyly arrogant. Regard him, and you had imagined he was submitting to rebuke for an offence he could not deny.

Lady Whitelaw waited. A minute, almost, and Peak gave no sign of opening his mouth.

'It is certainly much to be regretted,' she said at length, coolly. 'Of course, I don't know what prospects you may have in London, but, if you had remained at the College, something advantageous would no doubt have offered before long.'

There went small tact to the wording of this admonition. Impossible for Lady Whitelaw to understand the complexities of a character such as Godwin's, even had she enjoyed opportunities of studying it; but many a woman of the world would have directed herself more cautiously after reading that letter of his. Peak's impulse was to thank her for the past, and declare that henceforth he would dispense with aid; only the choking in his throat obstructed some such utterance. He resented profoundly her supposition (natural enough) that his chief aim was to establish himself in a self-supporting career. What? Am I to be grateful for a mere chance of earning my living? Have I not shown that I am capable of something more than the ordinary lot in life? From the heights of her assured independence, does she look down upon me as a young man seeking a 'place'? He was filled with wrath, and all because a good, commonplace woman could not divine that he dreamt of European fame.

'I am very sorry that I can't take that into account,' he managed to say. 'I wish to give this next year exclusively to scientific study, and after that I shall see what course is open to me.'

He was not of the men who can benefit by patronage and be simply grateful for it. His position was a false one: to be begging with awkward show of thankfulness for a benefaction which in his heart he detested. He knew himself for an undesigning hypocrite, and felt that he might as well have been a rascal complete. Gratitude! No man capable of it in fuller measure than he; but not to such persons as Lady Whitelaw. Before old Sir Job he could more easily have bowed himself. But this woman represented the superiority of mere brute wealth, against which his soul rebelled.

There was another disagreeable silence, during which Lady Whitelaw commented on her protégé very much as Mrs. Warricombe had done.

'Will you allow me to ask,' she said at length, with cold politeness, 'whether you have acquaintances in London?'

'Yes. I know some one who studied at the School of Mines.'

'Well, Mr. Peak, I see that your mind is made up. And no doubt you are the best judge of your private circumstances. I must ask you to let me think over the matter for a day or two. I will write to you.'

'And I to you,' thought Godwin; a resolve which enabled him to rise with something like a conventional smile, and thus put an end to a very brief and quite unsatisfactory interview.

He strode homewards in a state of feverish excitement. His own behaviour had been wretchedly clownish; he was only too well aware of that. He ought to have put aside all the grosser aspects of his case, and have exhibited the purely intellectual motives which made such a change as he purposed seem desirable to him. That would have been to act with dignity; that would have been the very best form of gratitude for the kindness he had received. But no, his accursed lack of self-possession had ruined all. 'The woman' was now offended in good earnest; he saw it in her face at parting. The fault was admittedly on his side, but what right had she to talk about 'something advantageous'? She would write to him, to be sure; that meant, she could not yet make up her mind whether to grant the money or not. Pluto take the money! Long before sitting down to her glossy note-paper she should have received a letter from *him*.

Composed already. Now he was up in the garret bedroom, scribbling as fast as pen could fly over paper. He had been guilty of a mistake—so ran the epistle; having decided to leave Whitelaw, he ought never to have requested a continuance of the pension. He begged Lady Whitelaw would forgive this thoughtless impropriety; she had made him understand the full extent of his error. Of course he could not accept anything more from her. As for the past, it would be idle for him to attempt an expression of his indebtedness. But for Sir Job's munificence, he must now have been struggling to complete a radically imperfect education,—'instead of going into the world to make a place for myself among the scientific investigators of our time.'

One's claims to respectful treatment must be put forward unmistakably, especially in dealing with such people as Lady Whitelaw. Now, perhaps, she would understand what his reserve concealed. The satisfaction of declining further assistance was enormous. He read his letter several times aloud. This was the great style; he could imagine this incident forming a landmark in the biography of a notable man. Now for a fair copy, and in a hand, mind you, that gave no hint of his care for caligraphic seemliness: bold, forthright.

The letter in his pocket, he went downstairs. His mother had been out all the morning; now she was just returned, and Godwin saw trouble on her forehead. Anxiously she inquired concerning the result of his interview.

Now that it was necessary to make an intelligible report of what had happened, Godwin found his tongue falter. How could he convey to another the intangible sense of wounded dignity which had impelled his pen? Instead of producing the letter with a flourish, he answered with affected carelessness:

'I am to hear in a day or two.'

'Did she seem to take it—in the right way?'

'She evidently thinks of me too much as a schoolboy.'

And he began to pace the room. Mrs. Peak sat still, with an air of anxious brooding.

'You don't think she will refuse, Godwin?' fell from her presently.

His hand closed on the letter.

'Why? Well, in that case I should go to London and find some occupation as soon as possible. You could still let me have the same money as before?'

'Yes.'

It was said absently, and did not satisfy Godwin. In the course of the conversation it appeared that Mrs. Peak had that morning been to see the legal friend who looked after her small concerns, and though she would not admit that she had any special cause for uneasiness, her son recalled similar occasions when an interview with Mr. Dutch had been followed by several days' gloom. The truth was that Mrs. Peak could not live strictly within the income at her disposal, and on being from time to time reminded of this, she was oppressed by passing worry. If Godwin and Oliver 'got on well,' things would come all right in the end, but in the meantime she could not face additional expenditure. Godwin did not like to be reminded of the razor's edge on which the affairs of the household were balanced. At present it brought about a very sudden change in his state of mind; he went upstairs again, and sat with the letter before him, sunk in misery. The reaction had given him a headache.

A fortnight, and no word from Lady Whitelaw. But neither was Godwin's letter posted.

Was he at liberty to indulge the self-respect which urged him to write? In a moment of heated confidence it was all very well to talk of 'getting some occupation' in London, but he knew that this might prove no easy matter. A year's work at the School of Mines would decidedly facilitate his endeavour; and, seeing that his mother's peace depended upon his being speedily self-supporting, was it not a form of selfishness to reject help from one who could well afford it? From a distance, he regarded Lady Whitelaw with more charity; a longer talk with her might have led to better mutual apprehension. And, after all, it was not she but her husband to whom he would stand indebted. Sir Job was a very kind-hearted old fellow; he had meant thoroughly well. Why, clearly, the bestower of this third year's allowance would not be Lady Whitelaw at all.

If it were granted. Godwin began to suffer a troublesome misgiving; perchance he had gone too far, and was now, in fact, abandoned to his own resources.

Three weeks. Then came the expected letter, and, as he opened it, his heart leaped at the sight of a cheque—talisman of unrivalled power over the emotions of the moneyless! Lady Whitelaw wrote briefly and formally. Having considered Godwin's request, she had no reason for doubting that he would make a good use of the proposed year at the School of Mines, and accordingly she sent him the sum which Sir Job had intended for his final session at Whitelaw College. She wished him all benefit from his studies, and prosperity henceforth.

Rejoicing, though shame-smitten, Godwin exhibited this remittance to his mother, from whom it drew a deep sigh of relief. And forthwith he sat down to write quite a different letter from that which still lay in his private drawer,—a letter which he strove to make the justification (to his own mind) of this descent to humility. At considerable length he dwelt upon the change of tastes of which he had been conscious lately, and did not fail to make obvious the superiority of his ambition to all thought of material advancement. He offered his thanks, and promised to give an account of himself (as in duty bound) at the close of the twelvemonths' study he was about to undertake: a letter in which the discerning would have read much sincerity, and some pathos; after all, not a letter to be ashamed of. Lady Whitelaw would not understand it; but then, how many people are capable of even faintly apprehending the phenomena of mental growth?

And now to plan seriously his mode of life in London. With Christian Moxey he was so slightly acquainted that it was impossible to seek his advice with regard to lodgings; besides, the lodgings must be of a character far too modest to come within Mr. Moxey's sphere of observation. Other acquaintance he had none in the capital, so it was clear that he must enter boldly upon the unknown world, and find a home for himself as best he might. Mrs. Peak could offer suggestions as to likely localities, and this was of course useful help. In the meantime (for it would be waste of money to go up till near the end of the holiday season) he made schemes of study and completed his information concerning the School of Mines. So far from lamenting the interruption of his promising career at Whitelaw, he persuaded himself that Uncle Andrew had in truth done him a very good turn: now at length he was fixed in the right course. The only thing he regretted was losing sight of his two or three student-friends, especially Earwaker and Buckland Warricombe. They, to be sure, would soon guess the reason of his disappearance. Would they join in the laughter certain to be excited by 'Peak's Dining and Refreshment Rooms'? Probably; how could they help it? Earwaker might be superior to a prejudice of that kind; his own connections were of humble standing. But Warricombe must wince and shrug his shoulders. Perhaps even some of the Professors would have their attention directed to the ludicrous mishap: they were gentlemen, and, even though they smiled, must certainly sympathise with him.

Wait a little. Whitelaw College should yet remember the student who seemed to have vanished amid the world's obscure tumult.

Resolved that he was about to turn his back on Twybridge for ever, he found the conditions of life there quite supportable through this last month or two; the family reaped benefit from his improved temper. Even to Mr. Cusse he behaved with modified contempt. Oliver was judicious enough to suppress his nigger minstrelsy and kindred demonstrations of spirit in his brother's presence, and Charlotte, though steadily resentful, did her best to avoid conflict.

Through the Misses Lumb, Godwin's change of purpose had of course become known to his aunt, who for a time took it ill that these debates had been concealed from her. When Mrs. Peak, in confidence, apprised her of the disturbing cause, Miss Cadman's indignation knew no bounds. What! That low fellow had been allowed to interfere with the progress of Godwin Peak's education, and not a protest uttered? He should have been *forbidden* to establish himself in Kingsmill! Why had they not taken *her* into council? She would have faced the man, and have overawed him; he should have been made to understand the gross selfishness of his behaviour. Never had she heard of such a monstrous case——

Godwin spent much time in quiet examination of the cabinets bequeathed to him by Mr. Gunnery. He used a pound or two of Lady Whitelaw's money for the purchase of scientific books, and set to work upon them with freshened zeal. The early morning and late evening were given to country walks, from which he always returned with brain excited by the forecast of great achievements.

When the time of his departure approached, he decided to pay a farewell visit to Mr. Moxey. He chose an hour when the family would probably be taking their ease in the garden. Three of the ladies were, in fact, amusing themselves with croquet, while their father, pipe in mouth, bent over a bed of calceolarias.

'What's this that I hear?' exclaimed Mr. Moxey, as he shook hands. 'You are not going back to Whitelaw?'

The story had of course spread among all Twybridge people who knew anything of the Peaks, and it was generally felt that some mystery was involved. Godwin had reasonably feared that his obligations to Sir Job Whitelaw must become known; impossible for such a matter to be kept secret; all who took any interest in the young man had long been privately acquainted with the facts of his position. Now that discussion was rife, it would have been prudent in the Misses Lumb to divulge as much of the truth as they knew, but (in accordance with the law of natural perversity) they maintained a provoking silence. Hence whispers and suspicious questions, all wide of the mark. No one had as yet heard of Andrew Peak, and it seemed but too likely that Lady Whitelaw, for some good reason, had declined to discharge the expenses of Godwin's last year at the College.

Mr. Moxey himself felt that an explanation was desirable, but he listened with his usual friendly air to Godwin's account of the matter—which of course included no mention of Lady Whitelaw.

'Have you friends in London?' he inquired—like everyone else.

'No. Except that your nephew was so kind as to ask me to call on him, if ever I happened to be there.'

There passed over Mr. Moxey's countenance a curious shadow. Godwin noticed it, and at once concluded that the manufacturer condemned Christian for undue advances to one below his own station. The result of this surmise was of course a sudden coldness on Godwin's part, increased when he found that Mr. Moxey turned to another subject, without a word about his nephew.

In less than ten minutes he offered to take leave, and no one urged him to stay longer. Mr. Moxey made sober expression of good wishes, and hoped he might hear that the removal to London had proved 'advantageous.' This word sufficed to convert Godwin's irritation into wrath; he said an abrupt 'good-evening,' raised his hat as awkwardly as usual, and stalked away.

A few paces from the garden gate, he encountered Miss Janet Moxey, just coming home from walk or visit. Another grab at his hat, and he would have passed without a word, but the girl stopped him.

'We hear that you are going to London, Mr. Peak.'

'Yes, I am, Miss Moxey.'

She examined his face, and seemed to hesitate.

'Perhaps you have just been to say good-bye to father?'

'Yes.'

Janet paused, looked away, again turned her eyes upon him.

'You have friends there, I hope?' she ventured.

'No, I have none.'

'My cousin—Christian, you remember—would, I am sure, be very glad to help you in any way.' Her voice sank, and at the same time she coloured just perceptibly under Godwin's gaze.

'So he assured me,' was the reply. 'But I must learn to be independent, Miss Moxey.'

Whereupon Godwin performed a salute, and marched forward.

His boxes were packed, and now he had but one more evening

in the old home. It was made less pleasant than it might have been by a piece of information upon which he by chance alighted in a newspaper. The result of the Honours examination for the First B.A. at London had just been made known, and in two subjects a high place was assigned to Bruno Leathwaite Chilvers—not the first place happily, but it was disagreeable enough.

Pooh! what matter? What are academic successes? Ten years hence, which name would have wider recognition—Bruno Chilvers or Godwin Peak? He laughed with scornful superiority.

No one was to accompany him to the station; on that he insisted. He had decided for as early a train as possible, that the dolours of leave-taking might be abridged. At a quarter to eight the cab drove up to the door. Out with the trunks labelled 'London'!

'Take care of the cabinets!' were his last words to his mother. 'I may want to have them sent before long.'

He implied, what he had not ventured to say plainly, that he was leaving Twybridge for good, and henceforth would not think of it as home. In these moments of parting, he resented the natural feeling which brought moisture to his eyes. He hardened himself against the ties of blood, and kept repeating to himself a phrase in which of late he had summed his miseries: 'I was born in exile—born in exile.' Now at length had he set forth on a voyage of discovery, to end perchance in some unknown land among his spiritual kith and kin.

PART THE SECOND

I

In the spring of 1882 Mr. Jarvis Runcorn, editor and co-proprietor of the London *Weekly Post*, was looking about for a young man of journalistic promise whom he might associate with himself in the conduct of that long established Radical paper. The tale of his years warned him that he could not hope to support much longer a burden which necessarily increased with the growing range and complexity of public affairs. Hitherto he had been the autocrat of the office, but competing Sunday papers exacted an alertness, a versatile vigour, such as only youth can supply; for there was felt to be a danger that the *Weekly Post* might lose its prestige in democratic journalism. Thus on the watch, Mr. Runcorn—a wary man of business, who had gone through many trades before he reached that of weekly literature—took counsel one day with a fellow-campaigner, Malkin by name, who owned two or three country newspapers, and had reaped from them a considerable fortune; in consequence, his attention was directed to one John Earwaker, then editing the *Wattleborough Courier*. Mr. Malkin's eldest son had recently stood as Liberal candidate for Wattleborough, and though defeated was loud in his praise of the *Courier*; with its editor he had come to be on terms of intimate friendship. Earwaker was well acquainted with journalistic life in the provinces. He sprang from a humble family living at Kingsmill, had studied at Whitelaw College, and was now but nine-and-twenty; the style of his 'leaders' seemed to mark him for a wider sphere of work. It was decided to invite him to London, and the young man readily accepted Mr. Runcorn's proposals. A few months later he exchanged temporary lodgings for chambers in Staple Inn, where he surrounded himself with plain furniture and many books.

In personal appearance he had changed a good deal since that prize-day at Whitelaw when his success as versifier and essayist foretold a literary career. His figure was no longer ungainly; the big head seemed to fit better upon the narrow shoulders. He neither walked with extravagant paces, nor waved his arms like a windmill. A sufficiency of good food, and the habit of intercourse with active men, had given him an every-day aspect; perhaps the sole peculiarity he retained from student times was his hollow chuckle of mirth, a laugh which struggled vainly for enlargement. He dressed with conventional decency, even submitting to the chimney-pot hat. His features betrayed connection with a physically coarse stock; but to converse with him was to discover the man of original vigour and wide intellectual scope. With ordinary companions, it was a rare thing for him to speak of his professional interests. But for his position on *The Weekly Post* it would not have been easy to surmise how he stood with regard to politics, and he appeared to lean as often towards the conservative as to the revolutionary view of abstract questions.

The newspaper left him time for other literary work, and it was known to a few people that he wrote with some regularity for reviews, but all the products of his pen were anonymous. A fact which remained his own secret was that he provided for the subsistence of his parents, old people domiciled in a quiet corner of their native Kingsmill. The strict sobriety of life which is indispensable to success in such a career as this cost him no effort. He smoked moderately, ate and drank as little as might be, could keep his health on six hours of sleep, and for an occasional holiday liked to walk his twenty or thirty miles. Earwaker was naturally marked for survival among the fittest.

On an evening of June in the year '84, he was interrupted whilst equipping himself for dinner abroad, by a thunderous rat-tat-tat.

'You must wait, my friend, whoever you are,' he murmured placidly, as he began to struggle with the stiff button-holes of his shirt.

The knock was repeated, and more violently.

'Now there's only one man of my acquaintance who knocks like that,' he mused, elaborating the bow of his white tie. 'He, I should imagine, is in Brazil; but there's no knowing. Perhaps our office is on fire.—Anon, anon!'

He made haste to don waistcoat and swallow-tail, then crossed his sitting-room and flung open the door of the chambers.

'Ha! Then it *is* you! I was reminded of your patient habits.'

A tall man, in a light overcoat and a straw hat of spacious brim, had seized both his hands, with shouts of excited greeting.

'Confound you! Why did you keep me waiting? I thought I had missed you for the evening. How the deuce are you! And why the devil have you left me without a line from you for more than six months?'

Earwaker drew aside, and allowed his tumultuous friend to rush into the nearest room.

'Why haven't you written?—confound you!' was again vociferated, amid bursts of boyish laughter. 'Why hasn't anybody written?'

'If everybody was as well informed of your movements as I, I don't wonder,' replied the journalist. 'Since you left Buenos Ayres, I have had two letters, each containing twenty words, which gave me to understand that no answer could by possibility reach you.'

'Humbug! You could have written to half-a-dozen likely places. Did I really say that? Ha, ha, ha!—Shake hands again, confound you! How do you do? Do I look well? Have I a tropical colour? I say, what a blessed thing it was that I got beaten down at Wattleborough! All this time I should have been sitting in the fog at Westminster. What a time I've had! What a time I've had!'

It was more than twelve months since Malkin's departure from England. Though sun and sea had doubtless contributed to his robustness, he must always have been a fair example of the vigorous Briton. His broad shoulders, upright bearing, open countenance, and frank resonant voice, declared a youth passed amid the wholesome conditions which wealth alone can command. The hearty extravagance of his friendliness was only possible in a man who has never been humiliated by circumstances, never restricted in his natural needs of body and mind. Yet he had more than the heartiness of a contented Englishman.

The vivacity which made a whirlwind about him probably indicated some ancestral mingling with the blood of a more ardent race. Earwaker examined him with a smile of pleasure.

'It's unfortunate,' he said, 'that I have to go out to dinner.'

'Dinner! Pooh! we can get dinner anywhere.'

'No doubt, but I am engaged.'

'The devil you are! Who is she? Why didn't you write to tell me?'

'The word has a less specific meaning, my dear fellow,' replied Earwaker, laughing. 'Only you of all men would have rushed at the wrong one. I mean to say—if your excitement can take in so common a fact—that I have promised to dine with some people at Notting Hill, and mustn't disappoint them.'

Malkin laughed at his mistake, then shouted:

'Notting Hill! Isn't that somewhere near Fulham? We'll take a cab, and I can drop you on my way.'

'It wouldn't be on the way at all.'

The journalist's quiet explanation was cut short by a petulant outcry.

'Oh, very well! Of course if you want to get rid of me! I should have thought after sixteen months'——

'Don't be idiotic,' broke in the other. 'There's a strong feminine element in you, Malkin; that's exactly the kind of talk with which women drive men to frenzy.'

'Feminine element!' shouted the traveller with hot face. 'What do you mean? I propose to take a cab with you, and you'——

Earwaker turned away laughing. 'Time and distance are nothing to you, and I shall be very glad of your company. Come by all means.'

His friend was instantly appeased.

'Don't let me make you late, Earwaker. Must we start this moment? Come along, then. Can I carry anything for you? Lord! if you could only see a tropical forest! How do you get on with old Runcorn? *Write?* What the devil was the use of my writing, when words are powerless to describe——? What a rum old place this seems, after experiences like mine; how the deuce can you live here? I say, I've brought you a ton of curiosities; will make your rooms look like a museum. Confound it! I've broken my shin against the turn in the staircase! Whew! Who are you going to dine with?—Moxey? Never heard the name.'

In Holborn a hansom was hailed, and the friends continued their dialogue as they drove westward. Having at length effervesced, Malkin began to exchange question and answer with something of the calm needful for mutual intelligibility.

'And how do you get on with old Runcorn?'

'As well as can be expected where there is not a single subject of agreement,' Earwaker replied. 'I have hopes of reducing our circulation.'

'What the deuce do you mean?'

'In other words, of improving the paper. Runcorn is strong on the side of blackguardism. We had a great fight the other day over a leader offered by Kenyon,—a true effusion of the political gutter-snipe. I refused point-blank to let it go in; Runcorn swore that, if I did not, *I* should go *out*. I offered to retire that moment. "We must write for our public," he bellowed. "True," said I, "but not necessarily for the basest among them. The standard at the best is low enough." "Do you call yourself a Radical?" "Not if this be Radicalism." "You ought to be on the *Morning* instead of the *Weekly Post*." I had my way, and probably shall end by sending Mr. Kenyon back to his tinker's work shop. If not, I must look out for cleaner occupation.'

'Go it, my boy! Go it!' cried Malkin, slapping his companion's knee violently. 'Raise the tone! To the devil with mercenary considerations! Help the proletariat out of its grovelling position.'

They approached the street where Earwaker had to alight. The other declared his intention of driving on to Fulham in the hope of finding a friend who lived there.

'But I must see you again. When shall you be home to-night?'

'About half-past eleven, I dare say.'

'Right! If I am free I'll come out to Staple Inn, and we'll talk till three or four.'

The house at which the journalist presented himself was such as might be inhabited by a small family of easy means. As he was taking off his overcoat, a door opened and Christian Moxey came forward to greet him. They shook hands like men who stood on friendly, but not exactly on intimate, terms.

'Will you come up to the laboratory for a moment?' said Moxey. 'I should like to show you something I have under the microscope.'

The room he spoke of was at the top of the house; two chambers had been made into one, and the fittings were those required by a student of physical science. Various odours distressed the air. A stranger to the pursuits represented might have thought that the general disorder and encumberment indicated great activity, but the experienced eye perceived at once that no methodical work was here in progress. Mineralogy, botany, biology, physics, and probably many other sciences, were suggested by the specimens and apparatus that lay confusedly on tables, shelves, or floor.

Moxey looked very slim and elegant in his evening costume. When he touched any object, his long, translucent fingers seemed soft and sensitive as a girl's. He stepped with peculiar lightness, and the harmonious notes of his voice were in keeping with these other characteristics. Ten years had developed in him that graceful languor which at four-and-twenty was only beginning to get mastery over the energies of a well-built frame.

'This stuff here,' he said, pointing to an open box full of mud, 'is silt from down the Thames. It's positively loaded with *diatomaceæ*,—you remember our talking about them when you were last here? I am working at the fabric of the valves. Now, just look!'

Earwaker, with attentive smile, followed the demonstration.

'Peak is busy with them as well,' said Christian, presently. 'Has he told you his theory of their locomotion? Nobody has found out yet how the little beggars move about. Peak has a bright idea.'

They spent ten minutes in the laboratory, then went downstairs. Two other guests had meanwhile arrived, and were conversing with the hostess, Miss Moxey. The shy, awkward, hard-featured girl was grown into a woman whose face made such declaration of intellect and character that, after the first moment, one became indifferent to its lack of feminine beauty. As if with the idea of compensating for personal disadvantages, she was ornately dressed; her abundant tawny hair had submitted to much manipulation, and showed the gleam of jewels; expense and finished craft were manifest in every detail of her garb. Though slightly round-shouldered, her form was well-proportioned and suggested natural vigour. Like Christian, she had delicate hands.

'Do you know a distinguished clergyman, named Chilvers?' she asked of Earwaker, with a laugh, when he had taken a place by her.

'Chilvers?—Is it Bruno Chilvers, I wonder?'

'That's the name!' exclaimed one of the guests, a young married lady of eager face and fidgety manners.

'Then I knew him at College, but I had no idea he had become distinguished.'

Miss Moxey again laughed.

'Isn't it amusing, the narrowness of a great clerical reputation? Mrs. Morton was astonished that I had never heard his name.'

'Please don't think,' appealed the lady, looking anxiously at Earwaker, 'that I consider it shameful not to know him. I only happened to mention a very ridiculous sermon of his, that was forced upon me by a distressingly orthodox friend of mine. They tell me, he is one of the newest lights of the Church.'

Earwaker listened with amusement, and then related anecdotes of Bruno Chilvers. Whilst he was talking, the door opened to admit another arrival, and a servant's voice announced 'Mr. Peak.' Miss Moxey rose, and moved a step or two forward; a change was visible on her countenance, which had softened and lightened.

'I am very sorry to be late,' said the new-comer, in a dull and rather husky voice, which made strong contrast with the humorous tones his entrance had interrupted.

He shook hands in silence with the rest of the company, giving merely a nod and a smile as reply to some gracious commonplace from Mrs. Morton.

'Has it come to your knowledge,' Earwaker asked of him,

'that Bruno Chilvers is exciting the orthodox world by his defence of Christianity against neo-heathenism?'

'Chilvers?—No.'

'Mrs. Morton tells us that all the Church newspapers ring with his name.'

'Please don't think,' cried Mrs. Morton, with the same anxious look as before, 'that I read such papers. We never have such a thing in our house, Mr. Peak. I have only been told about it.'

Peak smiled gravely, but made no other answer. Then he turned to Earwaker.

'Where is he?'

'I can't say. Perhaps Mrs. Morton'——

'They tell me he is somewhere in Norfolk,' replied the lady. 'I forget the town.'

A summons to dinner broke off the conversation. Moxey offered his arm to the one lady present as guest, and Earwaker did the same courtesy to the hostess. Mr. Morton, a meditative young man who had been listening with a smile of indifference, sauntered along in the rear with Godwin Peak.

At the dinner-table Peak was taciturn, and seemed to be musing on a disagreeable subject. To remarks, he answered briefly and absently. As Moxey, Earwaker, and Mrs. Morton kept up lively general talk, this muteness was not much noticed, but when the ladies had left the room, and Peak still frowned over his wine-glass, the journalist rebuked him.

'What's the matter with you? Don't depress us.'

The other laughed impatiently, and emptied his glass.

'Malkin has come back,' pursued Earwaker. 'He burst in upon me, just as I was leaving home—as mad as a March hare. You must come and meet him some evening.'

'As you please.'

Returned to the upper room, Peak seated himself in a shadowy corner, crossed his legs, thrust his hands into his pockets, and leaned back to regard a picture on the wall opposite. This attitude gave sufficient proof of the change that had been wrought in him by the years between nineteen and nine-and-twenty; even in a drawing-room, he could take his ease unconcernedly. His face would have led one to suppose him an older man; it was set in an expression of stern, if not morose, thoughtfulness.

He had small, hard lips, indifferent teeth (seldom exhibited), a prominent chin, a long neck; his body was of firm, not ungraceful build. Society's evening uniform does not allow a man much scope in the matter of adornments; it was plain, however, that Godwin no longer scorned the tailor and haberdasher. He wore a suit which confidently challenged the criticism of experts, and the silk socks visible above his shoes might have been selected by the most fastidious of worldlings.

When he had sat there for some minutes, his eyes happened to stray towards Miss Moxey, who was just then without a companion. Her glance answered to his, and a smile of invitation left him no choice but to rise and go to a seat beside her.

'You are meditative this evening,' she said, in a voice subdued below its ordinary note.

'Not very fit for society, to tell the truth,' Godwin answered, carelessly. 'One has such moods, you know. But how would you take it if, at the last moment, I sent a telegram, "Please excuse me. Don't feel able to talk"?'

'You don't suppose I should be offended?"

'Certainly you would.'

'Then you know less of me than I thought.'

Her eyes wandered about the room, their smile betokening an uneasy self-consciousness.

'Christian tells me,' she continued, 'that you are going to take your holiday in Cornwall.'

'I thought of it. But perhaps I shan't leave town at all. It wouldn't be worth while, if I go abroad at the end of the year.'

'Abroad?' Marcella glanced at him. 'What scheme is that?'

'Haven't I mentioned it? I want to go to South America and the Pacific islands. Earwaker has a friend, who has just come back from travel in the tropics; the talk about it has half decided me to leave England. I have been saving money for years to that end.'

'You never spoke of it—to me,' Marcella replied, turning a bracelet on her wrist. 'Should you go alone?'

'Of course. I couldn't travel in company. You know how impossible it would be for me to put up with the moods and idiosyncrasies of other men.'

There was a quiet arrogance in his tone. The listener still smiled, but her fingers worked nervously.

'You are not so unsocial as you pretend,' she remarked, without looking at him.

'Pretend! I make no pretences of any kind,' was his scornful answer.

'You are ungracious this evening.'

'Yes—and can't hide it.'

'Don't try to, I beg. But at least tell me what troubles you.'

'That's impossible,' Peak replied, drily.

'Then friendship goes for nothing,' said Marcella, with a little forced laugh.

'Yes—in all but a very few human concerns. How often could *you* tell *me* what it is that prevents your taking life cheerfully?'

He glanced at her, and Marcella's eyes fell; a moment after, there was a suspicion of colour in her cheek.

'What are you reading?' Peak asked abruptly, but in a voice of more conventional note.

'Still Hafiz.'

'I envy your power of abstraction.'

'Yet I hear that you are deeply concerned about the locomotive powers of the *diatomaceæ*?'

Their eyes met, and they laughed—not very mirthfully.

'It preserves me from worse follies,' said Peak. 'After all, there are ways more or less dignified of consuming time'——

As he spoke, his ear caught a familiar name, uttered by Christian Moxey, and he turned to listen. Moxey and Earwaker were again talking of the Rev. Bruno Chilvers. Straightway disregarding Marcella, Peak gave attention to the men's dialogue, and his forehead wrinkled into scornful amusement.

'It's very interesting,' he exclaimed, at a moment when there was silence throughout the company, 'to hear that Chilvers is really coming to the front. At Whitelaw it used to be prophesied that he would be a bishop, and now I suppose he's fairly on the way to that. Shall we write letters of congratulation to him, Earwaker?'

'A joint epistle, if you like.'

Mr. Morton, who had brightened since dinner, began to speak caustically of the form of intellect necessary nowadays in a popular clergyman.

'He must write a good deal,' put in Earwaker, 'and that in a style which would have scandalised the orthodox of the last century. Rationalised dogma is vastly in demand.'

Peak's voice drew attention.

'Two kinds of books dealing with religion are now greatly popular, and will be for a long time. On the one hand there is that growing body of people who, for whatever reason, tend to agnosticism, but desire to be convinced that agnosticism is respectable; they are eager for anti-dogmatic books, written by men of mark. They couldn't endure to be classed with Bradlaugh, but they rank themselves confidently with Darwin and Huxley. Arguments matter little or nothing to them. They take their rationalism as they do a fashion in dress, anxious only that it shall be "good form." Then there's the other lot of people—a much larger class—who won't give up dogma, but have learnt that bishops, priests, and deacons no longer hold it with the old rigour, and that one must be "broad"; these are clamorous for treatises which pretend to reconcile revolution and science. It's quite pathetic to watch the enthusiasm with which they hail any man who distinguishes himself by this kind of apologetic skill, this pious jugglery. Never mind how washy the book from a scientific point of view. Only let it obtain vogue, and it will be glorified as the new evangel. The day has gone by for downright assaults on science; to be marketable, you must prove that *The Origin of Species* was approvingly foreseen in the first chapter of Genesis, and that the Apostles' Creed conflicts in no single point with the latest results of biblical criticism. Both classes seek to avoid ridicule, and to adapt themselves to a standard of respectability. If Chilvers goes in for the newest apologetics, he is bound to be enormously successful. The man has brains, and really there are so few such men who still care to go into the Church.'

There was a murmur of laughing approval. The speaker had worked himself into eloquent nervousness; he leaned forward with his hands straining together, and the muscles of his face quivering.

'And isn't it surprising,' said Marcella, 'in how short a time this apologetic attitude has become necessary?'

Peak flashed a triumphant look at her.

'I often rejoice to think of it!' he cried. 'How magnificent it is that so many of the solemn jackasses who brayed against Darwin from ten to twenty years ago should live to be regarded as beneath contempt! I say it earnestly: this thought is one of the things that make life tolerable to me!'

'You have need of charity, friend Peak,' interposed Earwaker. 'This is the spirit of the persecutor.'

'Nothing of the kind! It is the spirit of justified reason. You may say that those people were honestly mistaken;—such honesty is the brand of a brainless obstructive. *They* would have persecuted, but too gladly! There were, and are, men who would have committed Darwin to penal servitude, if they had had the power. Men like Lyell, who were able to develop a new convolution in their brains, I respect heartily. I only speak of the squalling mass, the obscene herd of idiot mockers.'

'Who assuredly,' remarked Earwaker, 'feel no shame whatever in the retrospect of their idiocy. To convert a *mind* is a subject for high rejoicing; to confute a *temper* isn't worth the doing.'

'That is philosophy,' said Marcella, 'but I suspect you of often feeling as Mr. Peak does. I am sure *I* do.'

Peak, meeting an amused glance from the journalist, left his seat and took up a volume that lay on one of the tables. It was easy to see that his hands shook, and that there was perspiration on his forehead. With pleasant tact, Moxey struck into a new subject, and for the next quarter of an hour Peak sat apart in the same attitude as before his outburst of satire and invective. Then he advanced to Miss Moxey again, for the purpose of taking leave. This was the signal for Earwaker's rising, and in a few minutes both men had left the house.

'I'll go by train with you,' said Earwaker, as they walked away. 'Farringdon Street will suit me well enough.'

Peak vouchsafed no reply, but, when they had proceeded a little distance, he exclaimed harshly:

'I hate emancipated women!'

His companion stopped and laughed loudly.

'Yes, I hate emancipated women,' the other repeated, with deliberation. 'Women ought neither to be enlightened nor dogmatic. They ought to be sexual.'

'That's unusual brutality on your part.'

'Well, you know what I mean.'

'I know what you think you mean,' said Earwaker. 'But the woman who is neither enlightened nor dogmatic is only too common in society. They are fools, and troublesome fools.'

Peak again kept silence.

'The emancipated woman,' pursued his friend, 'needn't be a Miss Moxey, nor yet a Mrs. Morton.'

'Miss Moxey is intolerable,' said Peak. 'I can't quite say why I dislike her so, but she grows more antipathetic to me the better I know her. She has not a single feminine charm—not one. I often feel very sorry for her, but dislike her all the same.'

'Sorry for her,' mused Earwaker. 'Yes, so do I. I can't like her either. She is certainly an incomplete woman. But her mind is of no low order. I had rather talk with her than with one of the imbecile prettinesses. I half believe you have a sneaking sympathy with the men who can't stand education in a wife.'

'It's possible. In some moods.'

'In no mood can I conceive such a prejudice. I have no great attraction to women of any kind, but the uneducated woman I detest.'

'Well, so do I,' muttered Peak. 'Do you know what?' he added, abruptly. 'I shall be off to the Pacific. Yes, I shall go this next winter. My mind is made up.'

'I shan't try to dissuade you, old fellow, though I had rather have you in sight. Come and see Malkin. I'll drop you a note with an appointment.'

'Do.'

They soon reached the station, and exchanged but few more words before Earwaker's leaving the train at Farringdon Street. Peak pursued his journey towards the south-east of London.

On reaching home, the journalist flung aside his foolish coat of ceremony, indued a comfortable jacket, lit a pipe with long stem, and began to glance over an evening newspaper. He had not long reposed in his arm-chair when the familiar appeal thundered from without. Malkin once more shook his hand effusively.

'Had my journey to Fulham for nothing. Didn't matter; I ran over to Putney and looked up my old landlady. The rooms are occupied by a married couple, but I think we shall succeed in persuading them to make way for me. I promised to find them lodgings every bit as good in two days' time.'

'If that is so easy, why not take the new quarters yourself?'

'Why, to tell you the truth, I didn't think of it!—Oh, I had rather have the old crib; I can do as I like there, you know. Confound it! Now I shall have to spend all tomorrow lodging-hunting for other people. Couldn't I pay a man to do it? Some confidential agent—private police—you know what I mean?'

'A man of any delicacy,' replied Earwaker, with grave countenance, 'would feel bound by such a promise to personal exertion.'

'Right; quite right! I didn't mean it; of course I shall hunt conscientiously. Oh, I say; I have brought over a couple of armadilloes. Would you like one?'

'Stuffed, do you mean?'

'Pooh! Alive, man, alive! They only need a little care. I should think you might keep the creature in your kitchen; they become quite affectionate.'

The offer was unhesitatingly declined, and Malkin looked hurt. There needed a good deal of genial explanation before Earwaker could restore him to his sprightly mood.

'Where have you been dining?' cried the traveller. 'Moxey's—ah, I remember. But who *is* Moxey? A new acquaintance, eh?'

'Yes; I have known him about six months. Got to know him through Peak.'

'Peak? Peak? What, the fellow you once told me about—who

disappeared from Whitelaw because of his uncle, the cat's-meat man?'

'The man's-meat man, rather.'

'Yes, yes—the eating-house; I remember. You have met him again? Why on earth didn't you tell me in your letters? What became of him? Tell me the story.'

'Certainly, if you will cease to shake down plaster from the ceiling.—We met in a restaurant (appropriate scene), happening to sit at the same table. Whilst eating, we stared at each other fitfully. "I'll be hanged if that isn't Peak," I kept saying to myself. And at the same moment we opened our lips to question each other.'

'Just the same thing happened once to a friend of mine, and a friend of his. But it was on board ship, and both were devilish sea-sick. Walker—you remember my friend Walker?—tells the story in a side-splitting way. I wonder what has become of Walker? The last time I met him he was travelling agent for a menagerie—a most interesting fellow, Walker.—But I beg your pardon. Go on, old fellow!'

'Well, after that we at once saw a good deal of each other. He has been working for years at a chemical factory down on the river; Moxey used to be there, and got him the place.'

'Moxey?—Oh yes, the man you dined with. You must remember that these are new names to me. I must know all these new people, I say. You don't mind?'

'You shall be presented to the whole multitude, as soon as you like. Peak wants to see you. He thinks of an excursion like this last of yours.'

'He does? By Jove, we'll go together! I have always wanted a travelling companion. We'll start as soon as ever he likes!—well, in a month or two. I must just have time to look round. Oh, I haven't done with the tropics yet! I must tell him of a rattling good insect-powder I have invented; I think of patenting it. I say, how does one get a patent? Quite a simple matter, I suppose?'

'Oh, always has been. The simplest and least worrying of all business enterprises.'

'What? Eh? That smile of yours means mischief.'

In a quarter of an hour they had got back to the subject of Peak's history.

'And did he really run away because of the eating-house?' Malkin inquired.

'I shall never venture to ask, and it's not very likely he will admit it. It was some time before he cared to talk much of Whitelaw.'

'But what is he doing? You used to think he would come out strong, didn't you? Has he written anything?'

'A few things in *The Liberator*, five or six years ago.'

'What, the atheistic paper?'

'Yes. But he's ashamed of it now. That belongs to a bygone stage of development.'

'Turned orthodox?'

Earwaker laughed.

'I only mean that he is ashamed of the connection with street-corner rationalism.'

'Quite right. Devilish low, that kind of thing. But I went in for it myself once. Did I ever tell you that I debated with a parson on Mile-end Waste? Fact! That was in my hot-headed days. A crowd of costermongers applauded me in the most flattering way. —I say, Earwaker, you haven't any whisky?'

'Forgive me; your conversation makes me forget hospitality. Shall I make hot water? I have a spirit-kettle.'

'Cold for me. I get in such a deuced perspiration when I begin to talk.—Try this tobacco; the last of half a hundred-weight I took in at Bahia.'

The traveller refreshed himself with a full tumbler, and resumed the conversation cheerily.

'Has he just been wasting his time then, all these years?'

'He goes in for science—laboratory work, evolutionary speculations. Of course I can't judge his progress in such matters; but Moxey, a clever man in the same line, thinks very highly of him.'

'Just the fellow to travel with. I want to get hold of some solid scientific ideas, but I haven't the patience to work steadily. A confounded fault of mine, you know, Earwaker,—want of patience. You must have noticed it?'

'Oh—well, now and then, perhaps.'

'Yes, yes; but of course I know myself better. And now tell me about Moxey. A married man, of course?'

'No, lives with a sister.'

'Unmarried sister?—Brains?'

'Pretty well supplied with that commodity.'

'You must introduce me to her. I do like women with brains.—Orthodox or enlightened?'

'Bitterly enlightened.'

'Really? Magnificent! Oh, I must know her. Nothing like an emancipated woman! How any man can marry the ordinary female passes my understanding. What do *you* think?'

'My opinions are in suspense; not yet precipitated, as Peak might say.'

One o'clock sounded from neighbouring churches, but Malkin was wide awake as ever. He entered upon a detailed narrative of his travels, delightful to listen to, so oddly blended were the strains of conscious and unconscious humour which marked his personality. Two o'clock; three o'clock;—he would have talked till breakfast-time, but at last Earwaker declared that the hour had come for sleep. As Malkin had taken a room at the Inns of Court Hotel, it was easy for him to repair to his quarters. The last his friend heard of him was an unexplained laugh, echoing far down the staircase.

II

Peak's destination was Peckham Rye. On quitting the railway, he had a walk of some ten minutes along a road which smelt of new bricks and stucco heated by the summer sun; an obscure passage led him into a street partly of dwelling-houses, partly of shops, the latter closed. He paused at the side door of one over which the street lamp dimly revealed—'Button, Herbalist.'

His latch-key admitted him to total darkness, but he moved forward with the confidence of long use. He softly ascended two flights of stairs, opened a door, struck a match, and found himself in a comfortable sitting-room, soon illumined by a reading-lamp. The atmosphere, as throughout the house, was strongly redolent of dried simples. Anyone acquainted with the characteristics of furnished lodgings must have surmised that Peak dwelt here among his own moveables, and was indebted to the occupier of the premises for bare walls alone; the tables and chairs, though plain enough, were such as civilisation permits; and though there were no pictures, sundry ornaments here and there made strong denial of lodging-house affinity. It was at once laboratory, study, and dwelling-room. Two large cabinets, something the worse for transportation, alone formed a link between this abode and the old home at Twybridge. Books were not numerous, and a good microscope seemed to be the only scientific instrument of much importance. On door-pegs hung a knapsack, a botanist's vasculum, and a geologist's wallet.

A round table was spread with the materials of supper, and here again an experienced lodger must have bestowed contemplative scrutiny, for no hand of common landlady declared itself in the arrangement. The cloth was spotless, the utensils tasteful and carefully disposed. In a bowl lay an appetising salad, ready for mingling; a fragment of Camembert cheese was relieved upon a setting of green leafage; a bottle of ale, with adjacent corkscrew, stood beside the plate; the very loaf seemed to come from no ordinary baker's, or was made to look better than its kin by the fringed white cloth in which it nestled.

The custom of four years had accustomed Peak to take these things as a matter of course, yet he would readily have admitted that they were extraordinary enough. Indeed, he even now occasionally contrasted this state of comfort with the hateful experiences of his first six years in London. The subject of lodgings was one of those on which (often intemperate of speech) he spoke least temperately. For six years he had shifted from quarter to quarter, from house to house, driven away each time by the hateful contact of vulgarity in every form,—by foulness and dishonesty, by lying, slandering, quarrelling, by drunkenness, by brutal vice,—by all abominations that distinguish the lodging-letter of the metropolis. Obliged to practise extreme economy, he could not take refuge among self-respecting people, or at all events had no luck in endeavouring to find such among the poorer working class. To a man of Godwin's idiosyncrasy the London poor were of necessity abominable, and it anguished him to be forced to live among them.

Rescue came at last, and in a very unexpected way. Resident in the more open part of Bermondsey (winter mornings made a long journey to Rotherhithe intolerable), he happened to walk one day as far as Peckham Rye, and was there attracted by the shop window of a herbalist. He entered to make a purchase, and got into conversation with Mr. Button, a middle-aged man of bright intelligence and more reading than could be expected. The herbalist led his customer to an upper room, in which were stored sundry curiosities, and happened casually to say that he was desirous of finding a lodger for two superfluous chambers. Peak's inquiries led to his seeing Mrs. Button, whom he found to be a Frenchwoman of very pleasing appearance; she spoke fluent French-English, anything but disagreeable to an ear constantly tormented by the London vernacular. After short reflection he decided to take and furnish the rooms. It proved a most fortunate step, for he lived (after the outlay for furniture) at much less expense than theretofore, and in comparative luxury. Cleanliness, neatness, good taste by no means exhausted Mrs. Button's virtues; her cooking seemed to the lodger of incredible perfection, and the infinite goodwill with which he was tended made strange contrast with the base usage he had commonly experienced.

In these ten years he had paid but four visits to Twybridge, each of brief duration. Naturally there were changes among his kinsfolk: Charlotte, after an engagement which prolonged itself to the fifth twelvemonth, had become Mrs. Cusse, and her husband now had a draper's shop of his own, with two children already born into the world of draperdom. Oliver, twice fruitlessly affianced, had at length (when six-and-twenty) wedded a young person whom his mother and his aunt both regarded as a most undesirable connection, the daughter (aged thirty-two) of a man who was drinking himself to death on such money as he could earn by casual reporting for a Twybridge newspaper. Mrs. Peak the elder now abode with her sister at the millinery shop, and saw little of her two married children. With Oliver and Charlotte their brother had no sympathy and affected none; he never wrote to them, nor they to him; but years had strengthened his regard for his mother, and with her he had fairly regular correspondence. Gladly he would have seen her more often, but the air of shopkeeping he was compelled to breathe when he visited Twybridge nauseated and repelled him. He recognised the suitability both of Oliver and Charlotte for the positions to which life had consigned them—they suffered from no profitless aspiration; but it seemed to him a just cause of quarrel with fate that his kindred should thus have relapsed, instead of bettering the rank their father had bequeathed to them. He would not avow to such friends as Moxey and Earwaker the social standing of his only recognised relatives.

As for the unrecognised, he had long ago heard with some satisfaction that Andrew Peak, having ultimately failed in his Kingsmill venture, returned to London. Encounter with the fatal Andrew had been spared him ever since that decisive day when Master Jowey Peak recited from Coleridge and displayed his etymological genius.

For himself, he had earned daily bread, and something more; he had studied in desultory fashion; he had seen a good deal of the British Isles and had visited Paris. The result of it all was gnawing discontent, intervals of furious revolt, periods of black despair.

He had achieved nothing, and he was alone.

Young still, to be sure; at twenty-nine it is too early to abandon ambitions which are supported by force of brain and of will. But circumstances must needs help if the desires of his soul were to be attained. On first coming to London, received with all friendliness by Christian Moxey, he had imagined that it only depended upon himself to find admission before long to congenial society—by which he then understood the companionship of intelligent and aspiring young men. Christian, however, had himself no such circle, and knew that the awkward lad from Twybridge could not associate with the one or two wealthy families to which he could have presented him. The School of Mines was only technically useful; it helped Godwin to get his place with Bates & Sons, but supplied no friendships. In the third year, Moxey inherited means and left the chemical works for continental travel.

By tormenting attraction Godwin was often led to walk in the wealthy districts of London. Why was no one of these doors open to him? There were his equals; not in the mean streets where he dwelt. There were the men of culture and capacity, the women of exquisite person and exalted mind. Was he the inferior of such people? By heaven, no!

He chanced once to be in Hyde Park on the occasion of some public ceremony, and was brought to pause at the edge of a gaping plebeian crowd, drawn up to witness the passing of aristocratic vehicles. Close in front of him an open carriage came to a stop; in it sat, or rather reclined, two ladies, old and young. Upon this picture Godwin fixed his eyes with the intensity of fascination; his memory never lost the impress of these ladies' faces. Nothing very noteworthy about them; but to Godwin they conveyed a passionate perception of all that is implied in social superiority. Here he stood, one of the multitude, of the herd; shoulder to shoulder with boors and pickpockets; and within reach of his hand reposed those two ladies, in Olympian calm, seeming unaware even of the existence of the throng. Now they exchanged a word; now they smiled to each other. How delicate was the moving of their lips! How fine must be their enunciation! On the box sat an old coachman and a young footman; they too were splendidly impassive, scornful of the multitudinous gaze.—The block was relieved, and on the carriage rolled.

They were his equals, those ladies; merely his equals. With such as they he should by right of nature associate.

In his rebellion, he could not hate them. He hated the malodorous rabble who stared insolently at them and who envied their immeasurable remoteness. Of mere wealth he thought not; might he only be recognised by the gentle of birth and breeding for what he really was, and be rescued from the promiscuity of the vulgar!

Yet at this time he was drawn into connection with the movement of popular Radicalism which revolts against religious respectability. Inherited antipathy to all conventional forms of faith outweighed his other prejudices so far as to induce him to write savage papers for *The Liberator*. Personal contact with artisan freethinkers was disgusting to him. From the meeting of emancipated workmen he went away with scorn and detestation in his heart; but in the quiet of his lodgings he could sit down to aid their propaganda. One explanation of this inconsistency lay in the fact that no other channel was open to his literary impulses. Pure science could not serve him, for he had no original results to announce. Pure literature seemed beyond his scope, yet he was constantly endeavouring to express himself. He burned with the desire of fame, and saw no hope of achieving it save as an author. *The Liberator* would serve him as a first step. In time he might get foothold in the monthly reviews, and see his name side by side with those of the leaders of thought.

Occasions, of course, offered when he might have extended his acquaintance, but they were never of a kind that he cared to use; at best they would only have admitted him to the homes of decent, semi-educated families, and for such society he was altogether unfitted. The licence of the streets but seldom allured him. After his twenty-fourth year he was proof against the decoys of venal pleasure, and lived a life of asceticism exceedingly rare in young and lonely men. When Christian Moxey returned to London and took the house at Notting Hill, which he henceforth occupied together with his sister, a possibility of social intercourse at length appeared. Indeed it was a substantial gain to sit from time to time at a civilised table, and to converse amid graceful surroundings with people who at all events followed the intellectual current of the day. Careless hitherto of his personal appearance, he now cultivated an elegance of attire in conformity with his aristocratic instincts, and this habit became fixed. When next he visited Twybridge, the change in his appearance was generally remarked. Mrs. Peak naturally understood it as a significant result of his intercourse with Miss Moxey, of whom, as it seemed to her, he spoke with singular reticence.

But Marcella had no charm for Godwin's imagination, notwithstanding that he presently suspected a warmth of interest on her side which he was far from consciously encouraging. Nor did he find among his friends any man or woman for whose acquaintance he greatly cared. The Moxeys had a very small circle, consisting chiefly of intellectual inferiors. Christian was too indolent to make a figure in society, and his sister suffered from peculiarities of mind and temperament which made it as difficult for her as for Peak himself to form intimate friendships.

When chance encounter brought him into connection with Earwaker, the revival of bygone things was at first doubtfully pleasant. Earwaker himself, remarkably developed and become a very interesting man, was as welcome an associate as he could have found, but it cost him some effort to dismiss the thought of Andrew Peak's eating-house, and to accept the friendly tact with which the journalist avoided all hint of unpleasant memories. That Earwaker should refrain from a single question concerning that abrupt disappearance, nearly ten years ago, sufficiently declared his knowledge of the unspeakable cause, a reflection which often made Godwin writhe. However, this difficulty was overcome, and the two met very frequently. For several weeks Godwin enjoyed better spirits than he had known since the first excitement of his life in London faded away.

One result was easily foreseen. His mind grew busy with literary projects, many that he had long contemplated and some that were new. Once more he aimed at contributing to the 'advanced' reviews, and sketched out several papers of sociological tenor. None of these were written. As soon as he sat down to deliberate composition, a sense of his deficiencies embarrassed him. Godwin's self-confidence had nothing in common with the conceit which rests on imaginary strength. Power there was in him; of that he could not but be conscious: its true direction he had not yet learned. Defect of knowledge, lack of pen-practice, confusion and contradictoriness of aims, instability of conviction, —these faults he recognised in himself at every moment of inward scrutiny.

On his table this evening lay a library volume which he had of late been reading, a book which had sprung into enormous popularity. It was called *Spiritual Aspects of Evolution*, and undertook, with confidence characteristic of its kind, to reconcile the latest results of science with the dogmas of Oriental religion. This work was in his mind when he spoke so vehemently at Moxey's; already he had trembled with an impulse to write something on the subject, and during his journey home a possible essay had begun to shape itself. Late as was the hour he could not prepare for sleep. His brain throbbed with a congestion of thought; he struggled to make clear the lines on which his satire might direct itself. By two o'clock he had flung down on paper a conglomerate of burning ideas, and thus relieved he at length went to bed.

Two days later came a note from Staple Inn, inviting him to meet Malkin the next evening. By this time he had made a beginning of his critical essay, and the exordium so far satisfied him that he was tempted to take it for Earwaker's judgment. But no; better his friend should see the thing when it was complete.

About eight o'clock he reached the journalist's chambers. Malkin had not yet arrived. Peak amused himself with examining certain tropical products which the traveller had recently cast pell-mell into his friend's sitting-room. Then sounded a knock at the door, but it was not such as would have heralded the expected man.

'A telegram,' observed Earwaker, and went to take it in.

He returned with hoarse sounds of mirth.

'Our friend excuses himself. Read this characteristic despatch.'

Peak saw with surprise that the telegram far exceeded familiar dimensions. 'Unspeakably grieved,' it began. 'Cannot possibly with you. At moment's notice undertaken escort two poor girls Rouen. Not even time look in apologise. Go *viâ* Dieppe and leave Victoria few minutes. Hope be back Thursday. Express sincerest regret Mr. Peak. Lament appearance discourtesy. Will apologise personally. Common humanity constrains go Rouen. Will explain Thursday. No time add another word. Rush tickets train.'

'There you have the man!' cried Earwaker. 'How do you class such a mind as that? Ten to one this is some Quixotic obligation he has laid upon himself, and probably he has gone without even a handbag.'

'Vocally delivered,' said Peak, 'this would represent a certain stage of drunkenness. I suppose it isn't open to such an explanation?'

'Malkin never was intoxicated, save with his own vivacity.'

They discussed the singular being with good-natured mirth, then turned by degrees to other topics.

'I have just come across a passage that will delight you,' said Earwaker, taking up a book. 'Perhaps you know it.'

He read from Sir Thomas Brown's *Pseudodoxia Epidemica.* ' "Men's names should not only distinguish them. A man should be something that all men are not, and individual in somewhat beside his proper name. Thus, while it exceeds not the bound of reason and modesty, we cannot condemn singularity. *Nos numerus sumus* is the motto of the multitude, and for that reason are they fools." '

Peak laughed his approval.

'It astonishes me,' he said, lighting his pipe, 'that you can go on writing for this Sunday rag, when you have just as little sympathy with its aims as I have. Do get into some less offensive connection.'

'What paper would you recommend?' asked the other, with his significant smile.

'Why need you journalise at all?'

'On the whole, I like it. And remember, to admit that the multitude are fools is not the same thing as to deny the possibility of progress.'

'Do you really believe yourself a democrat, Earwaker?'

'M—m—m! Well, yes, I believe the democratic spirit is stronger in me than any other.'

Peak mused for a minute, then suddenly looked up.

'And what am I?'

'I am glad nothing much depends on my successfully defining you.'

They laughed together.

'I suppose,' said Godwin, 'you can't call a man a democrat who recognises in his heart and soul a true distinction of social classes. Social, mark. The division I instinctively support is by no means intellectual. The well-born fool is very often more sure of my respect than the working man who struggles to a fair measure of education.'

Earwaker would have liked to comment on this with remarks personal to the speaker, but he feared to do so. His silence, however, was eloquent to Peak, who resumed brusquely.

'I am not myself well-born,—though if my parents could have come into wealth early in their lives, perhaps I might reasonably have called myself so. All sorts of arguments can be brought against my prejudice, but the prejudice is ineradicable. I respect hereditary social standing, independently of the individual's qualities. There's nothing of the flunkey in this, or I greatly deceive myself. Birth in a sphere of refinement is desirable and respectable; it saves one, absolutely, from many forms of coarseness. The masses are not only fools, but very near the brutes. Yes, they can send forth fine individuals—but remain base. I don't deny the possibility of social advance; I only say that at present the lower classes are always disagreeable, often repulsive, sometimes hateful.'

'I could apply that to the classes above them.'

'Well, I can't. But I am quite ready to admit that there are all sorts of inconsistencies in me. Now, the other day I was reading

Burns, and I couldn't describe what exaltation all at once possessed me in the thought that a ploughman had so glorified a servant-girl that together they shine in the highest heaven, far above all the monarchs of earth. This came upon me with a rush —a very rare emotion. Wasn't that democratic?'

He inquired dubiously, and Earwaker for a moment had no reply but his familiar 'M—m—m!'

'No, it was not democratic,' the journalist decided at length; 'it was pride of intellect.'

'Think so? Then look here. If it happens that a whining wretch stops me in the street to beg, what do you suppose is my feeling? I am ashamed in the sense of my own prosperity. I can't look him in the face. If I yielded to my natural impulse, I should cry out, "Strike me! spit at me! show you hate me!—anything but that terrible humiliation of yourself before me!" That's how I feel. The abasement of which *he* isn't sensible affects *me* on his behalf. I give money with what delicacy I can. If I am obliged to refuse, I mutter apologies and hurry away with burning cheeks. What does that mean?'

Earwaker regarded him curiously.

'That is mere fineness of humanity.'

'Perhaps moral weakness?'

'I don't care for the scalpel of the pessimist. Let us give it the better name.'

Peak had never been so communicative. His progress in composition these last evenings seemed to have raised his spirits and spurred the activity of his mind. With a look of pleasure he pursued his self-analysis.

'Special antipathies—sometimes explicable enough—influence me very widely. Now, I by no means hate all orders of uneducated people. A hedger, a fisherman, a country mason,—people of that kind I rather like to talk with. I could live a good deal with them. But the London vulgar I abominate, root and branch. The mere sound of their voices nauseates me; their vilely grotesque accent and pronunciation—bah! I could write a paper to show that they are essentially the basest of English mortals. Unhappily, I know so much about them. If I saw the probability of my dying in a London lodging-house, I would go out into the sweet-scented fields and there kill myself.'

Earwaker understood much by this avowal, and wondered whether his friend desired him so to do.

'Well, I can't say that I have any affection for the race,' he replied. 'I certainly believe that, socially and politically, there is less hope of them than of the lower orders in any other part of England.'

'They are damned by the beastly conditions of their life!' cried Godwin, excitedly. 'I don't mean only the slum-denizens. All, all—Hammersmith as much as St. George's-in-the-East. I must write about this; I must indeed.'

'Do by all means. Nothing would benefit you more, than to get your soul into print.'

Peak delayed a little, then:

'Well, I am doing something at last.'

And he gave an account of his projected essay. By this time his hands trembled with nervous agitation, and occasionally a dryness of the palate half choked his voice.

'This may do very well,' opined Earwaker. 'I suppose you will try *The Critical*?'

'Yes. But have I any chance? Can a perfectly unknown man hope to get in?'

They debated this aspect of the matter. Seeing Peak had laid down his pipe, the journalist offered him tobacco.

'Thanks; I can't smoke just yet. It's my misfortune that I can't talk earnestly without throwing my body into disorder.'

'How stolid I am in comparison!' said Earwaker.

'That book of M'Naughten's,' resumed the other, going back to his subject. 'I suppose the clergy accept it?'

'Largely, I believe.'

Peak mused.

'Now, if I were a clergyman'——

But his eye met Earwaker's, and they broke into laughter.

'Why not?' pursued Godwin. 'Did I ever tell you that my people originally wished to make a parson of me? Of course I resisted tooth and nail, but it seems to me now that I was rather foolish in doing so. I wish I *had* been a parson. In many ways the position would have suited me very well.'

'M—m—m!'

'I am quite serious. Well, if I were so placed, I should preach Church dogma, pure and simple. I would have nothing to do with these reconciliations. I would stand firm as Jeremy Taylor; and in consequence I should have an immense and enthusiastic congregation.'

'I daresay.'

'Depend upon it, let the dogmas do what they still can. There's a vast police force in them, at all events. A man may very strongly defend himself for preaching them.'

The pursuit of this argument led Earwaker to ask:

'What proportion of the clergy can still take that standing in stolid conscientiousness?'

'What proportion are convinced that it is untenable?' returned Peak.

'Many wilfully shut their eyes to the truth.'

'No, they don't shut their eyes!' cried Godwin. 'They merely lower a nictitating membrane which permits them to gaze at light without feeling its full impact.'

'I recommend you to bring that into your paper,' said the journalist, with his deep chuckle.

An hour later they were conversing with no less animation, but the talk was not so critical. Christian Moxey had come up as a topic, and Earwaker was saying that he found it difficult to divine the man's personality.

'You won't easily do that,' replied Peak, 'until you know more of his story. I can't see that I am bound to secrecy—at all events with you. Poor Moxey imagines that he is in love, and the fancy has lasted about ten years.'

'Ten years?'

'When I first knew him he was paying obvious attentions to a rather plain cousin down at Twybridge. Why, I don't know, for he certainly was devoted to a girl here in London. All he has confessed to me is that he had given up hopes of her, but that a letter of some sort or other revived them, and he hastened back to town. He might as well have stayed away; the girl very soon married another man. Less than a year later she had bitterly repented this, and in some way or other she allowed Moxey to know it. Since then they have been Platonic lovers—nothing more, I am convinced. They see each other about once in six months, and presumably live on a hope that the obnoxious husband may decease. I only know the woman as "Constance"; never saw her.'

'So that's Moxey? I begin to understand better.'

'Admirable fellow, but deplorably weak. I have an affection for him, and have had from our first meeting.'

'Women!' mused Earwaker, and shook his head.

'You despise them?'

'On the whole, I'm afraid so.'

'Yes, but *what* women?' cried the other with impatience. 'It would be just as reasonable to say that you despise men. Can't you see that?'

'I doubt it.'

'Now look here; the stock objections to women are traditional. They take no account of the vast change that is coming about. Because women were once empty-headed, it is assumed they are all still so *en masse*. The defect of the female mind? It is my belief that this is nothing more nor less than the defect of the uneducated human mind. I believe most men among the brutally ignorant exhibit the very faults which are cried out upon as exclusively feminine. A woman has hitherto been an ignorant human being; that explains everything.'

'Not everything; something, perhaps. Remember your evolutionism. The preservation of the race demands in women many kinds of irrationality, of obstinate instinct, which enrage a reasoning man. Don't suppose I speak theoretically. Four or five years ago I had really made up my mind to marry; I wasted much valuable time among women and girls, of anything but low social standing. But my passions were choked by my logical faculty. I foresaw a terrible possibility—that I might beat my wife. One thing I learned with certainty was that the woman, *qua* woman, hates abstract thought—hates it. Moreover (and of consequence) she despises every ambition that has not a material end.'

He enlarged upon the subject, followed it into all its ramifications, elaborated the inconsistencies with which it is rife. Peak's reply was deliberate.

'Admitting that some of these faults are rooted in sex, I should only find them intolerable when their expression took a vulgar form. Between irrationality and coarseness of mind there is an enormous distinction.'

'With coarse minds I have nothing to do.'

'Forgive me if I ask you a blunt question,' said Peak, after hesitating. 'Have you ever associated with women of the highest refinement?'

Earwaker laughed.

'I don't know what that phrase means. It sounds rather odd on your lips.'

'Well, women of the highest class of commoners. With peeresses we needn't concern ourselves.'

'You imagine that social precedence makes all that difference in women?'

'Yes, I do. The daughter of a county family is a finer being than any girl who can spring from the nomad orders.'

'Even supposing your nomads produce a Rachel or a Charlotte Brontë?'

'We are not talking of genius,' Peak replied.

'It was irrelevant, I know.—Well, yes, I *have* conversed now and then with what you would call well-born women. They are delightful creatures, some of them, in given circumstances. But do you think I ever dreamt of taking a wife drenched with social prejudices?'

Peak's face expressed annoyance, and he said nothing.

'A man's wife,' pursued Earwaker, 'may be his superior in whatever you like, *except* social position. That is precisely the distinction that no woman can forget or forgive. On that account they are the obstructive element in social history. If I loved a woman of rank above my own she would make me a renegade; for her sake I should deny my faith. I should write for the *St. James's Gazette*, and at last poison myself in an agony of shame.'

A burst of laughter cleared the air for a moment, but for a moment only. Peak's countenance clouded over again, and at length he said in a lower tone:

'There are men whose character would defy that rule.'

'Yes—to their own disaster. But I ought to have made one exception. There *is* a case in which a woman will marry without much regard to her husband's origin. Let him be a parson, and he may aim as high as he chooses.'

Peak tried to smile. He made no answer, and fell into a fit of brooding.

'What's all this about?' asked the journalist, when he too had mused awhile. 'Whose acquaintance have you been making?'

'No one's.'

The suspicion was inevitable.

'If it were true, perhaps you would be justified in mistrusting my way of regarding these things. But it's the natural tendency of my mind. If I ever marry at all, it will be a woman of far higher birth than my own.'

'Don't malign your parents, old fellow. They gave you a brain inferior to that of few men. You will never meet a woman of higher birth.'

'That's a friendly sophism. I can't thank you for it, because it has a bitter side.'

But the compliment had excited Peak, and after a moment's delay he exclaimed:

'I have no other ambition in life—no other! Think the confession as ridiculous as you like; my one supreme desire is to marry a perfectly refined woman. Put it in the correct terms: I am a plebeian, and I aim at marrying a lady.'

The last words were flung out defiantly. He quivered as he spoke, and his face flushed.

'I can't wish you success,' returned his friend, with a grave smile.

'You couldn't help it sounding like a sneer, if you did. The desire is hopeless, of course. It's because I know that, that I have made up my mind to travel for a year or two; it'll help me on towards the age when I shall regard all women with indifference. We won't talk about it any more.'

'One question. You seriously believe that you could find satisfaction in the life to which such a marriage would condemn you?'

'What life?' asked Peak, impatiently.

'That of an average gentleman, let us say, with house in town and country, with friends whose ruling motive was social propriety.'

'I could enjoy the good and throw aside the distasteful.'

'What about the distastefulness of your wife's crass conventionalism, especially in religion?'

'It would not be *crass*, to begin with. If her religion were genuine, I could tolerate it well enough; if it were merely a form, I could train her to my own opinions. Society is growing liberal—the best of it. Please remember that I have in mind a woman of the highest type our civilisation can produce.'

'Then you mustn't look for her in society!' cried Earwaker.

'I don't care; where you will, so long as she had always lived among people of breeding and high education, and never had her thoughts soiled with the vile contact of poverty.'

Earwaker started up and reached a volume from a shelf. Quickly finding the desired page, he began to read aloud:

'Dear, had the world in its caprice
Deigned to proclaim—I know you both,
Have recognised your plighted troth,
Am sponsor for you; live in peace!'——

He read to the end of the poem, and then looked up with an admiring smile.

'An ideal!' exclaimed Peak. 'An ideal akin to Murger's and Musset's grisettes, who never existed.'

'An ideal, most decidedly. But pray what is this consummate lady you have in mind? An ideal every bit as much, and of the two I prefer Browning's. For my own part, I am a polygamist; my wives live in literature, and too far asunder to be able to quarrel. Impossible women, but exquisite. They shall suffice to me.'

Peak rose, sauntered about the room for a minute or two, then said:

'I have just got a title for my paper. I shall call it "The New Sophistry." '

'Do very well, I should think,' replied the other, smiling. 'Will you let me see it when it's done?'

'Who knows if I shall finish it? Nothing I ever undertook has been finished yet—nothing won that I ever aimed at. Good night. Let me hear about Malkin.'

In a week's time Godwin received another summons to Staple Inn, with promise of Malkin's assured presence. In reply he wrote:

'Owing to a new arrangement at Bates's, I start to-morrow for my holiday in Cornwall, so cannot see you for a few weeks. Please offer Malkin my apologies; make them (I mean it) as profuse as those he telegraphed. Herewith I send you my paper, "The New Sophistry," which I have written at a few vehement sittings, and have carelessly copied. If you think it worth while, will you have the kindness to send it for me to *The Critical?* I haven't signed it, as my unmeaning name would perhaps indispose the fellow to see much good in it. I should thank you if you would write in your own person, saying that you act for a friend; you are probably well known in those quarters. If it is accepted, time enough to claim my glory. If it seems to you to have no chance, keep it till I return, as I hate the humiliation of refusals.—Don't think I made an ass of myself the other night. We will never speak on that subject again. All I said was horribly sincere, but I'm afraid you can't understand that side of my nature. I should never have spoken so frankly to Moxey, though he has made no secret with me of his own weaknesses. If I perish before long in a South American swamp, you will be able to reflect on my personality with completer knowledge, so I don't regret the indiscretion.'

III

'*Pereunt et imputantur.*'

Godwin Peak read the motto beneath the clock in Exeter Cathedral, and believed it of Christian origin. Had he knew that the words were found in Martial, his rebellious spirit would have enjoyed the consecration of a phrase from such an unlikely author. Even as he must have laughed had he stood in the Vatican before the figures of those two Greek dramatists who, for ages, were revered as Christian saints.

His ignorance preserved him from a clash of sentiments. This afternoon he was not disposed to cynicism; rather he welcomed the softening influence of this noble interior, and let the golden sunlight form what shapes it would—heavenly beam, mystic aureole—before his mind's eye. Architecture had no special interest for him, and the history of church or faith could seldom touch his emotions; but the glorious handiwork of men long dead, the solemn stillness of an ancient sanctuary, made that appeal to him which is independent of names.

'*Pereunt et imputantur.*'

He sat down where the soft, slow, ticking of the clock could guide his thoughts. This morning he had left London by the earliest train, and after a night in Exeter would travel westward by leisurely stages, seeing as much as possible of the coast and of that inland scenery which had geological significance. His costume declared him bent on holiday, but, at the same time, distinguished him with delicate emphasis from the tourist of the season. Trustworthy sartorial skill had done its best for his person. Sitting thus, he had the air of a gentleman who enjoys no unwonted ease. He could forget himself in reverie, and be unaware of soft footfalls that drew near along the aisle.

But the sound of a young voice, subdued yet very clear, made claim upon his attention.

'Sidwell!—Sidwell!'

She who spoke was behind him; on looking up, he saw that a lady just in front had stopped and turned to the summons; smiling, she retraced her steps. He moved, so as to look discreetly in the backward direction, and observed a group of four persons, who were occupied with a tablet on the wall: a young man (not long out of boyhood), a girl who might be a year or two younger, and two ladies, of whom it could only be said that they were mature in the beauty of youth, probably of maidenhood—one of them, she who had been called back by the name of 'Sidwell.'

Surely an uncommon name. From a guide-book, with which he had amused himself in the train, he knew that one of the churches of Exeter was dedicated to St. Sidwell, but only now did his recollection apprise him of a long past acquaintance with the name of the saint. Had not Buckland Warricombe a sister called Sidwell? And—did he only surmise a connection between the Warricombes and Devon? No, no; on that remote day, when he went out with Buckland to the house near Kingsmill, Mr. Warricombe spoke to him of Exeter,—mentioning that the town of his birth was Axminster, where William Buckland, the geologist, also was born; whence the name of his eldest son. How suddenly it all came back!

He rose and moved apart to a spot whence he might quietly observe the strangers. 'Sidwell,' once remarked, could not be confused with the companion of her own age; she was slimmer, shorter (if but slightly), more sedate in movement, and perhaps better dressed—though both were admirable in that respect. Ladies, beyond a doubt. And the young man——

At this distance it was easy to deceive oneself, but did not that face bring something back? Now, as he smiled, it seemed to recall Buckland Warricombe—with a difference. This might well be a younger brother; there used to be one or two.

They were familiar with the Cathedral, and at present appeared to take exclusive interest in certain mural monuments. For perhaps ten minutes they lingered about the aisle, then, after a glance at the west window, went forth. With quick step, Godwin pursued them; he issued in time to see them entering an open carriage, which presently drove away towards High Street.

For half an hour he walked the Cathedral Close. Not long ago, on first coming into that quiet space, with its old houses, its smooth lawns, its majestic trees, he had felt the charm peculiar to such scenes—the natural delight in a form of beauty especially English. Now, the impression was irrecoverable; he could see nothing but those four persons, and their luxurious carriage, and the two beautiful horses which had borne them—whither? As likely as not the identity he had supposed for them was quite imaginary; yet it would be easy to ascertain whether a Warricombe family dwelt at Exeter. The forename of Buckland's father——? He never had known it. Still, it was worth while consulting a directory.

He walked to his hotel.

Yes, the name Warricombe stood there, but it occurred more than once. He sought counsel of the landlord. Which of these Warricombes was a gentleman of position, with grown-up sons and daughters? To such a description answered Martin Warricombe, Esquire, well known in the city. His house was in the Old Tiverton Road, out beyond St. Sidwell's, two miles away; anyone in that district would serve as guide to it.

With purpose indefinite, Godwin set forth in the direction suggested. At little more than a saunter, he passed out of High Street into its continuation, where he soon descried the Church of St. Sidwell, and thence, having made inquiry, walked towards the Old Tiverton Road. He was now quite beyond the town limits, and few pedestrians came in sight; if he really wished to find the abode of Martin Warricombe, he must stop the first questionable person. But to what end this inquiry? He could not even be certain that Martin was the man he had in mind, and even were he right in all his conjectures, what had he to do with the Warricombes?

Ten years ago the family had received him courteously as Buckland's fellow-student; he had spent an hour or two at their house, and subsequently a few words had passed when they saw him on prize-day at Whitelaw. To Buckland he had never written; he had never since heard of him; that name was involved in the miserable whirl of circumstances which brought his College life to a close, and it was always his hope that Buckland thought no more of him. Even had there been no disagreeable memories, it was surely impossible to renew after this interval so very slight an acquaintance. How could they receive him, save with civilly mild astonishment?

An errand-boy came along, whistling townwards, a big basket over his head. No harm in asking where Mr. Warricombe lived. The reply was prompt; second house on the right hand, rather a large one, not a quarter of a mile onward.

Here, then. The site was a good one. From this part of the climbing road one looked over the lower valley of the Exe, saw the whole estuary, and beyond that a horizon of blue sea. Fair, rich land, warm under the westering sun. The house itself seemed to be old, but after all was not very large; it stood amid laurels, and in the garden behind rose a great yew-tree. No person was visible; but for the wave-like murmur of neighbouring pines, scarce a sound would have disturbed the air.

Godwin walked past, and found that the road descended into a deep hollow, whence between high banks, covered with gorse and bracken and many a summer flower, it led again up a hill thick planted with firs; at the lowest point was a bridge over a streamlet, offering on either hand a view of soft green meadows. A spot of exquisite retirement: happy who lived here in security from the struggle of life!

It was folly to spoil his enjoyment of country such as this by dreaming impossible opportunities. The Warricombes could be nothing to him; to meet with Buckland would only revive the shame long ago outlived. After resting for a few minutes he turned back, passed the silent house again, delighted himself with the wide view, and so into the city once more, where he began to seek the remnants of its odd walls.

The next morning was Sunday, and he had planned to go by the Plymouth train to a station whence he could reach Start Point; but his mood was become so unsettled that ten o'clock, when already he should have been on his journey, found him straying about the Cathedral Close. A mere half-purpose, a vague wavering intention, which might at any moment be scattered by common sense, drew his steps to the door of the Cathedral, where people were entering for morning service; he moved idly within sight of the carriages which drew up. Several had discharged their freightage of tailoring and millinery, when two vehicles, which seemed companions, stopped at the edge of the pavement, and from the second alighted the young ladies whom Godwin had yesterday observed; their male companion, however, was different. The carriage in advance also contained four persons: a gentleman of sixty, his wife, a young girl, and the youth of yesterday. It needed but a glance to inform Godwin that the oldest of the party was Mr. Warricombe, Buckland's father; ten years had made no change in his aspect. Mrs. Warricombe was not less recognisable. They passed at once into the edifice, and he had scarcely time to bestow a keen look upon Sidwell.

That was a beautiful girl; he stood musing upon the picture registered by his brain. But why not follow, and from a neighbouring seat survey her and the others at his leisure? Pooh! But the impulse constrained him. After all, he could not get a place that allowed him to see Sidwell. Her companion, however, the one who seemed to be of much the same age, was well in view. Sisters they could not be; nothing of the Warricombe countenance revealed itself in those handsome but strongly-marked features. A beautiful girl, she also, yet of a type that made slight appeal to him. Sidwell was all he could imagine of sweet and dignified; more modest in bearing, more gracile, more——

Monday at noon, and he still walked the streets of Exeter. Early this morning he had been out to the Old Tiverton Road, and there, on the lawn amid the laurels, had caught brief glimpse of two female figures, in one of which he merely divined Sidwell. Why he tarried thus he did not pretend to explain to himself. Rain had just come on, and the lowering sky made him low-spirited; he mooned about the street under his umbrella.

And at this rate, might vapour away his holiday. Exeter was tedious, but he could not make up his mind to set forth for the sea-shore, where only his own thoughts awaited him. Packed away in his wallet lay geological hammer, azimuth compass, clinometer, miniature microscope,—why should he drag all that lumber about with him? What to him were the bygone millions of ages, the hoary records of unimaginable time? One touch of a girl's hand, one syllable of musical speech,—was it not that whereof his life had truly need?

As remote from him, however, as the age of the pterodactyl. How often was it necessary to repeat this? On a long voyage, such as he had all but resolved to take, one might perchance form acquaintances. He had heard of such things; not impossibly, a social circle might open to him at Buenos Ayres. But here in England his poor origin, his lack of means, would for ever bar him from the intimacy of people like the Warricombes.

He loitered towards the South-Western station, dimly conscious of a purpose to look for trains. Instead of seeking the time-tables he stood before the bookstall and ran his eye along the titles of new novels; he had half a mind to buy one of Hardy's and read himself into the temper which suited summer rambles. But just as his hand was stretched forth, a full voice, speaking beside him, made demand for a London weekly paper. Instantly he turned. The tones had carried him back to Whitelaw: the face disturbed that illusion, but substituted a reality which threw him into tremor.

His involuntary gaze was met with one of equal intensity. A man of his own years, but in splendid health and with bright eyes that looked enjoyment of life, suddenly addressed him.

'Godwin Peak—surely——?'

'Buckland Warricombe, no less surely.'

They shook hands with vigour, laughing in each other's faces; then, after a moment's pause, Warricombe drew aside from the bookstall, for sake of privacy.

'Why did we lose sight of each other?' he asked, flashing a glance at Godwin's costume. 'Why didn't you write to me at Cambridge? What have you been doing this half-century?'

'I have been in London all the time.'

'I am there most of the year. Well, I rejoice to have met you. On a holiday?'

'Loitering towards Cornwall.'

'In that case, you can come and have lunch with me at my father's house. It's only a mile or two off. I was going to walk, but we'll drive, if you like.'

There was no refusing, and no possibility of reflection. Buckland's hearty manner made the invitation in itself a thoroughly pleasant one, and before Peak could sufficiently command his thoughts to picture the scene towards which he was going they were walking side by side through the town. In appearance, Warricombe showed nothing of the revolutionary which, in old days, he aimed at making himself, and his speech had a suavity which no doubt resulted from much intercourse with the polished world; Godwin was filled with envious admiration of his perfect physique, and the mettle which kept it in such excellent vigour. Even for a sturdy walker, it was no common task to keep pace with Buckland's strides; Peak soon found himself conversing rather too breathlessly for comfort.

'What is your latest record for the mile?' he inquired.

Warricombe, understanding at once the reference to his old athletic pastime and its present application, laughed merrily, and checked his progress.

'A bad habit of mine; it gets me into trouble with everyone. By-the-bye, haven't you become a stronger man than used to seem likely? I'm quite glad to see how well you look.'

The sincerity of these expressions, often repeated, put Godwin far more at his ease than the first moment's sensation had promised. He too began to feel a genuine pleasure in the meeting, and soon bade defiance to all misgivings. Delicacy perhaps withheld Warricombe from further mention of Whitelaw, but on the other hand it was not impossible that he knew nothing of the circumstances which tormented Godwin's memory. On leaving the College perchance he had lost all connection with those common friends who might have informed him of subsequent jokes and rumours. Unlikely, to be sure; for doubtless some of his Whitelaw contemporaries encountered him at Cambridge; and again, was it not probable that the younger Warricombe had become a Whitelaw student? Then Professor Gale—no matter!

The Warricombes of course knew all about Andrew Peak and his dining-rooms, but they were liberal-minded, and could forgive a boy's weakness, as well as overlook an acquaintance's obscure origin. In the joy of finding himself exuberantly welcomed by a man of Buckland's world he overcame his ignoble self-consciousness.

'Did you know that we were in this part of the country?' Warricombe asked, once more speeding ahead.

'I always thought of you in connection with Kingsmill.'

'We gave up Thornhaw seven years ago. My father was never quite comfortable out of Devonshire. The house I am taking you to has been in our family for three generations. I have often tried to be proud of the fact, but, as you would guess, that kind of thing doesn't come very natural to me.'

In the effort to repudiate such sentiment, Buckland distinctly betrayed his hold upon him. He imagined he was meeting Godwin on equal ground, but the sensibility of the proletarian could not thus be deceived. There was a brief silence, during which each looked away from the other.

'Still keep up your geology?' was Warricombe's next question.

'I can just say that I haven't forgotten it all.'

'I'm afraid that's more than I can. During my Cambridge time it caused disagreeable debates with my father. You remember that his science is of the old school. I wouldn't say a word to disparage him. I believe the extent of his knowledge is magnificent; but he can't get rid of the old man of the sea, the Book of Genesis. A few years ago I wasn't too considerate in argument, and I talked as I oughtn't to have done, called names, and so on. The end of it was, I dropped science altogether, having got as much out of it as I needed. The good old pater has quite forgiven my rudeness. At present we agree to differ, and get on capitally. I'm sure he'll be delighted to see you. There are some visitors with us; a Miss Moorhouse and her brother. I think you'll like them. Couldn't you stay overnight?'

Godwin was unable to reply on the instant, and his companion proceeded with the same heartiness.

'Just as you like, you know. But do stay if you can. On Wednesday morning I must go back to town. I act as secretary to Godolphin, the member for Slacksea.'

Peak's acquaintance with current politics was slight, but Mr. Ellis Godolphin, the aristocratic Radical, necessarily stood before his imagination with some clearness of outline. So this was how life had dealt with Buckland. The announcement was made with a certain satisfaction, as if it implied more than the hearer would readily appreciate. Again there was a slight shrinking on Godwin's part; it would be natural for him to avow his own position, and so leave no room for misunderstandings, but before he could shape a phrase Buckland was again questioning.

'Do you ever see any of the old fellows?'

'I have met one or two of them, by chance.'

As if his tact informed him that this inquiry had been a mistake, Warricombe resumed the subject of his family.

'My brother Louis is at home—of course you can't remember him; he was a youngster when you were at Thornhaw. The younger boy died some years ago, a pony accident; cut up my father dreadfully. Then there's my sister Sidwell, and my sister Fanny—that's all of us. I can't quite answer for Louis, but the rest are of the old school. Liberal enough, don't be afraid. But—well, the old school.'

As Godwin kept silence, the speaker shot a glance at him, keenly scrutinising. Their eyes did not meet; Peak kept his on the ground.

'Care much about politics now-a-days?'

'Not very much.'

'Can't say that I do myself,' pursued Buckland. 'I rather drifted into it. Godolphin, I dare say, has as little humbug about him as most parliamentarians; we stick to the practical fairly well. I shall never go into the House on my own account. But there's a sort of pleasure in being in the thick of public movements. I'm not cut out for debate; should lose my temper, and tell disagreeable truths—which wouldn't do, you know. But behind the scenes—it isn't bad, in a way.'

A longer pause obliged Godwin to speak of himself.

'My life is less exciting. For years I have worked in a manufacturing laboratory at Rotherhithe.'

'So science has carried the day with you, after all. It used to be very doubtful.'

This was a kind and pleasant way of interpreting necessity. Godwin felt grateful, and added with a smile:

'I don't think I shall stick to it much longer. For one thing, I am sick of town. Perhaps I shall travel for a year or two; perhaps—I'm in a state of transition, to tell the truth.'

Buckland revolved this information; his face told that he found it slightly puzzling.

'You once had thoughts of literature.'

'Long given up.'

'Leisure would perhaps revive them?'

'Possibly; but I think not.'

They were now quitting the town, and Peak, unwilling to appear before strangers in a state of profuse perspiration, again moderated his friend's speed. They began to talk about the surrounding country, a theme which occupied them until the house was reached. With quick-beating heart, Godwin found himself at the gate by which he had already twice passed. Secure in the decency of his apparel, and no longer oppressed by bashfulness, he would have gone joyously forward but for the dread of a possible ridiculous association which his name might revive in the thoughts of Mr. and Mrs. Warricombe. Yet Buckland—who had no lack of kindly feeling—would hardly have brought him here had the reception which awaited him been at all dubious.

'If we don't come across anyone,' said Warricombe, 'we'll go straight up to my room.'

But the way was not clear. Within the beautiful old porch sat Sidwell Warricombe and her friend of the striking countenance, whom Godwin now knew as Miss Moorhouse. Buckland addressed his sister in a tone of lively pleasure.

'Whom do you think I have met and brought home with me? Here is my old friend, Godwin Peak.'

Under the two pairs of female eyes, Godwin kept a calm, if rather stern, face.

'I should have had no difficulty in recognising Mr. Peak,' said

Sidwell, holding out her hand. 'But was the meeting quite by chance?'

To Godwin himself the question was of course directed, with a look of smiling interest—such welcome as could not have been improved upon; she listened to his reply, then presented him to Miss Moorhouse. A slight languor in her movements and her voice, together with the beautiful coldness of her complexion, made it probable that she did not share the exuberant health manifest in her two brothers. She conversed with mature self-possession, yet showed a slight tendency to abstractedness. On being addressed, she regarded the speaker steadily for an instant before shaping her answer, which always, however trifling the subject, seemed carefully worded. In these few moments of dialogue, Godwin reached the conclusion that Sidwell had not much sense of humour, but that the delicacy of her mind was unsurpassable.

In Miss Moorhouse there was no defect of refinement, but her conversation struck a note of sprightliness at once more energetic and more subtle than is often found in English girls. Thus, though at times she looked so young that it might be doubted whether she had long been out of her teens, at others one suspected her older than Sidwell. The friends happened to be as nearly as possible of an age, which was verging to twenty-six.

When he spoke to Miss Moorhouse, Buckland's frank tone subdued itself. He watched her face with reverent attention, smiled when she smiled, and joined in her laughter with less than his usual volume of sound. In acuteness he was obviously inferior to her, and there were moments when he betrayed some nervousness under her rejoinders. All this was matter of observation for Peak, who had learnt to exercise his discernment even whilst attending to the proprieties.

The sounding of the first luncheon-bell left the young men free to go upstairs. When at length they presented themselves in the drawing-room, Mrs. Warricombe and her younger daughter sat there alone. The greeting of his hostess did not quite satisfy Godwin, though it was sufficiently courteous; he remembered that ten years ago Mrs. Warricombe had appeared to receive him with some restraint, and his sensation in renewing her acquaintance was one of dislike. But in a moment the master of the house joined them, and no visitor could have had a more kindly welcome than that he offered to his son's friend. With genial tact, Mr. Warricombe ignored the interval since his last conversation with Godwin, and spoke as if this visit were the most natural thing in the world.

'Do you already know the country about Exeter?'

'I have seen very little of it yet.'

'Oh, then, we must show you our points of view. Our own garden offers a glimpse of the river-mouth and a good prospect of Haldon—the ridge beyond the Exe; but there are many much better points within easy reach. You are in no hurry, I hope?'

Louis Warricombe and Miss Moorhouse's brother were away on a long walk; they did not return for lunch. Godwin was glad of this, for time had wrought the change in him that he felt more at ease in female society than under the eyes of young men whose social position inclined them to criticism. The meal proved as delightful as luncheon is wont to be in a luxurious country-house, when brilliant sunshine gleams on the foliage visible from windows, and the warmth of the season sanctions clear colours in costume. The talk was wholly of country pleasures. It afforded the visitor no little satisfaction to be able to make known his acquaintance with parts of England to which the Warricombes had not penetrated. Godwin learnt that the family were insular in their tastes; a mention by Miss Moorhouse of continental scenes led the host to avow a strong preference for his own country, under whatever aspect, and Sidwell murmured her sympathy.

No less introspective than in the old days, though he could better command his muscles, Peak after each of his short remarks, made comparison of his tone and phraseology with those of the other speakers. Had he still any marks of the ignoble world from which he sprang? Any defect of pronunciation, any native awkwardness of utterance? Impossible to judge himself infallibly, but he was conscious of no vulgar mannerism. Though it was so long since he left Whitelaw, the accent of certain of the Professors still remained with him as an example; when endeavouring to be graceful, he was wont to hear the voice of Dr. Nares, or of Professor Barber who lectured on English Literature. More recently he had been observant of Christian Moxey's speech, which had a languid elegance worth imitating in certain particulars. Buckland Warricombe was rather a careless talker, but it was the carelessness of a man who had never needed to reflect on such a matter, the refinement of whose enunciation was assured to him from the nursery. That now was a thing to be aimed at. Preciseness must be avoided, for in a young man it seemed to argue conscious effort: a loose sentence now and then, a colloqualism substituted for the more grammatical phrase.

Heaven be thanked that he was unconcerned on the point of garb! Inferiority in that respect would have been fatal to his ease. His clothes were not too new, and in quality were such as he had the habit of wearing. The Warricombes must have immediately detected any pretentiousness, were it but in a necktie; that would impress them more unfavourably than signs of poverty. But he defied inspection. Not Sidwell herself, doubtless sensitive in the highest degree, could conceive a prejudice against him on this account.

His misgivings were overcome. If these people were acquainted with the 'dining-rooms' joke, it certainly did not affect their behaviour to him, and he could hope, by the force of his personality, to obliterate from their minds such disagreeable thoughts as they might secretly entertain. Surely he could make good his claim to be deemed a gentleman. To Buckland he had declared his position, and no shame attached to it. A man of scientific tastes, like Mr. Warricombe, must consider it respectable enough. Grant him a little time, and why should he not become a recognised friend of this family?

If he were but resident in Exeter.

For the first time, he lost himself in abstraction, and only an inquiry from Sidwell recalled him.

'You have seen the Cathedral, Mr. Peak?'

'Oh yes! I attended service there yesterday morning.'

Had he reflected, perhaps he would not have added this circumstance; even in speaking he suffered a confused doubtfulness. But as soon as the words were uttered, he felt strangely glad. Sidwell bestowed upon him an unmistakable look of approval; her mother gazed with colder interest; Mr. Warricombe regarded him, and mused; Buckland, a smile of peculiar meaning on his close lips, glanced from him to Miss Moorehouse.

'Ah, then, you heard Canon Grayling,' remarked the father of the family, with something in his tone which answered to Sidwell's facial expression. 'How did you like his sermon?'

Godwin was trifling with a pair of nut-crackers, but the nervousness evident in his fingers did not prevent him from replying with a natural air of deliberation.

'I was especially struck with the passage about the barren fig-tree.'

The words might have expressed a truth, but in that case a tone of sarcasm must have winged them. As it was, they involved either hypocrisy or ungenerous irony at the expense of his questioner. Buckland could not but understand them in the latter sense; his face darkened. At that moment, Peak met his eye, and encountered its steady searching gaze with a perfectly calm smile. Half-a-dozen pulsings of his heart—violent, painful, and the fatal hour of his life had struck.

'What had he to say about it?' Buckland asked, carelessly.

Peak's reply was one of those remarkable efforts of mind—one might say, of character—which are sometimes called forth, without premeditation, almost without consciousness, by a profound moral crisis. A minute or two ago he would have believed it impossible to recall and state in lucid terms the arguments to which, as he sat in the Cathedral, he had barely given ear; he remembered vaguely that the preacher (whose name he knew not till now) had dwelt for a few moments on the topic indicated, but at the time he was indisposed to listen seriously, and what chance was there that the chain of thought had fixed itself in his memory? Now, under the marvelling regard of his conscious self, he poured forth an admirable rendering of the Canon's views, fuller than the original—more eloquent, more subtle. For five minutes he held his hearers in absorbed attention, even Buckland bending forward with an air of genuine interest; and when he stopped, rather suddenly, there followed a silence.

'Mr. Peak,' said the host, after a cough of apology, 'you have made that clearer to me than it was yesterday. I must thank you.'

Godwin felt that a slight bow of acknowledgment was perhaps called for, but not a muscle would obey his will. He was enervated; perspiration stood on his forehead. The most severe physical effort could not have reduced him to a feebler state.

Sidwell was speaking:

'Mr. Peak has developed what Canon Grayling only suggested.'

'A brilliant effort of exegesis,' exclaimed Buckland, with a good-natured laugh.

Again the young men exchanged looks. Godwin smiled as one might under a sentence of death. As for the other, his suspicion had vanished, and he now gave way to frank amusement. Luncheon was over, and by a general movement all went forth on to the lawn in front of the house. Mr. Warricombe, even more cordial than hitherto, named to Godwin the features of the extensive landscape.

'But you see that the view is in a measure spoilt by the growth of the city. A few years ago, none of those ugly little houses stood in the mid-distance. A few years hence, I fear there will be much more to complain of. I dare say you know all about the ship-canal: the story of the countess, and so forth?'

Buckland presently suggested that the afternoon might be used for a drive.

'I was about to propose it,' said his father. 'You might start by the Stoke Canon Road, so as to let Mr. Peak have the famous view from the gate; then go on towards Silverton, for the sake of the reversed prospect from the Exe. Who shall be of the party?'

It was decided that four only should occupy the vehicle. Miss Moorhouse and Fanny Warricombe to be the two ladies. Godwin regretted Sidwell's omission, but the friendly informality of the arrangement delighted him. When the carriage rolled softly from the gravelled drive, Buckland holding the reins, he felt an animation such as no event had ever produced in him. No longer did he calculate phrases. A spontaneous aptness marked his dialogue with Miss Moorhouse, and the laughing words he now and then addressed to Fanny. For a short time Buckland was laconic, but at length he entered into the joyous tone of the occasion. Earwaker would have stood in amazement, could he have seen and heard the saturnine denizen of Peckham Rye.

The weather was superb. A sea-breeze mitigated the warmth of the cloudless sun, and where a dark pine-tree rose against the sky it gave the azure depths a magnificence unfamiliar to northern eyes.

'On such a day as this,' remarked Miss Moorhouse, dividing her look between Buckland and his friend, 'one feels that there's a good deal to be said for England.'

'But for the vile weather,' was Warricombe's reply, 'you wouldn't know such enjoyment.'

'Oh, I can't agree with that for a moment! My capacity for enjoyment is unlimited. That philosophy is unworthy of you; it belongs to a paltry scheme called "making the best of things."'

'In which you excel, Miss Moorhouse.'

'That she does!' agreed Fanny—a laughing, rosy-cheeked maiden.

'I deny it! No one is more copious in railing against circumstances.'

'But you turn them all to a joke,' Fanny objected.

'That's my profound pessimism. I am misunderstood. No one expects irony from a woman.'

Peak found it difficult not to gaze too persistently at the subtle countenance. He was impelled to examine it, by a consciousness that he himself received a large share of Miss Moorhouses's attention, and a doubt as to the estimation in which she held him. Canon Grayling's sermon and Godwin's comment had elicited no remark from her. Did she belong to the ranks of emancipated women? With his experience of Marcella Moxey, he welcomed the possibility of this variation of the type, but at the same time, in obedience to a new spirit that had strange possession of him, recognised that such phenomena no longer aroused his personal interest. By the oddest of intellectual processes he had placed himself altogether outside the sphere of unorthodox spirits. Concerning Miss Moorhouse he cared only for the report she might make of him to the Warricombes.

Before long, the carriage was stopped that he might enjoy one of the pleasantest views in the neighbourhood of the city. A gate, interrupting a high bank with which the road was bordered, gave admission to the head of a great cultivated slope, which fell to the river Exe; hence was suddenly revealed a wide panorama. Three well-marked valleys—those of the Creedy, the Exe, and the Culm—spread their rural loveliness to remote points of the horizon; gentle undulations, with pasture and woodland, with long winding roads, and many a farm that gleamed white amid its orchard leafage, led the gaze into regions of evanescent hue and outline. Westward, a bolder swell pointed to the skirts of Dartmoor. No inappropriate detail disturbed the impression. Exeter was wholly hidden behind the hill on which the observers stood, and the line of railway leading thither could only be descried by special search. A foaming weir at the hill's foot blended its soft murmur with that of the fir branches hereabouts; else, no sound that the air could convey beyond the pulsing of a bird's note.

All had alighted, and for a minute or two there was silence. When Peak had received such geographical instruction as was needful, Warricombe pointed out to him a mansion conspicuous on the opposite slope of the Exe valley, the seat of Sir Stafford Northcote. The house had no architectural beauty, but its solitary lordship amid green pastures and tracts of thick wood declared the graces and privileges of ancestral wealth. Standing here alone, Godwin would have surveyed these possessions of an English aristocrat with more or less bitterness; envy would, for a moment at all events, have perturbed his pleasure in the natural scene. Accompanied as he was, his emotion took a form which indeed was allied to envy, but had nothing painful. He exulted in the prerogatives of birth and opulence, felt proud of hereditary pride, gloried that his mind was capable of appreciating to the full those distinctions which, by the vulgar, are not so much as suspected. Admitted to equal converse with men and women who represented the best in English society, he could cast away the evil grudge, the fierce spirit of self-assertion, and be what nature had proposed in endowing him with large brain, generous blood, delicate tissues. What room for malignancy? He was accepted by his peers, and could regard with tolerance even those ignoble orders of mankind, amid whom he had so long dwelt unrecognised.

A bee hummed past him, and this sound—of all the voices of nature that which most intenerates—filled his heart to overflowing. Moisture made his eyes dim, and at the impulse of a feeling of gratitude, such as only the subtlest care of psychology could fully have explained, he turned to Buckland, saying:

'But for my meeting with you I should have had a lonely and not very cheerful holiday. I owe you a great deal.'

Warricombe laughed, but as an Englishman does when he wishes to avoid show of emotion.

'I am very glad indeed that we did meet. Stay with us over tomorrow. I only wish I were not obliged to go to London on Wednesday.—Look, Fanny, isn't that a hawk, over Cowley Bridge?'

'Do you feel you would like to shoot it?' asked Miss Moorhouse—who a moment ago had very closely examined Peak's face.

'To shoot it—why do you ask that?'

'Confess that you felt the desire.'

'Every man does,' replied Buckland, 'until he has had a moment to recover himself. That's the human instinct.'

'The male human instinct. Thank you for your honesty.'

They drove on, and by a wide circuit, occasionally stopping for the view, returned to the Old Tiverton Road, and so home. By this time Louis Warricombe and Mr. Moorhouse were back from their walk. Reposing in the company of the ladies, they had partaken of such refreshments as are lawful at five o'clock, and now welcomed with vivacity the later arrivals. Moorehouse was something older than Buckland, a sallow-cheeked man with forehead and eyes expressive of much intelligence. Till of late he had been a Cambridge tutor, but was now privately occupied in mathematical pursuits. Louis Warricombe had not yet made up his mind what profession to follow, and to aid the process of resolve had for the present devoted himself to physical exercise.

Tea-cup in hand, Godwin seated himself by Sidwell, who began by inquiring how the drive had pleased him. The fervour of his reply caused her to smile with special graciousness, and their conversation was uninterrupted for some minutes. Then Fanny came forward with a book of mosses, her own collection, which she had mentioned to Peak as they were talking together in the carriage.

'Do you make special study of any science?' Sidwell asked, when certain remarks of Godwin's had proved his familiarity with the things he was inspecting.

'It is long since I worked seriously at anything of the kind,' he answered; adding in a moment, 'Except at chemistry—that only because it is my business.'

'Organic or inorganic chemistry?' inquired Fanny, with the promptness of a schoolgirl who wishes to have it known that her ideas are no longer vague.

'Organic for the most part,' Godwin replied, smiling at her. 'And of the most disagreeable kind.'

Sidwell reflected, then put another question, but with some diffidence.

'I think you were once fond of geology?'

It was the first allusion to that beginning of their acquaintance, ten years ago. Peak succeeded in meeting her look with steadiness.

'Yes, I still like it.'

'Father's collections have been much improved since you saw them at Thornhaw.'

'I hope Mr. Warricombe will let me see them.'

Buckland came up and made an apology for drawing his friend aside.

'Will you let us send for your traps? You may just as well have a room here for a night or two.'

Perpetually imagining some kind chance that might associate him with civilised people, Godwin could not even pack his portmanteau for a ramble to Land's End without stowing away a dress suit. He was thus saved what would have been an embarrassment of special annoyance. Without hesitation, he accepted Buckland's offer, and named the hotel at which the luggage was deposited.

'All right; the messenger shall explain. Our name's well enough known to them. If you would like to look up my father in his study, he'll be delighted to go over his collections with you. You still care for that kind of thing?'

'Most certainly. How can you doubt it?'

Buckland smiled, and gave no other reply.

'Ask Fanny to show you the way when you care to go.' And he left the room.

IV

SIDWELL HAD FALLEN into conversation with Mr. Moorhouse. Miss Moorhouse, Mrs. Warricombe, and Louis were grouped in animated talk. Observing that Fanny threw glances towards him from a lonely corner, Peak went over to her, and was pleased with the smile he met. Fanny had watchet eyes, much brighter than Sidwell's; her youthful vivacity blended with an odd little fashion of schoolgirl pedantry in a very piquant way. Godwin's attempts at conversation with her were rather awkward; he found it difficult to strike the suitable note, something not too formal yet not deficient in respect.

'Do you think,' he asked presently, 'that I should disturb your father if I went to him?'

'Oh, not at all! I often go and sit in the study at this time.'

'Will you show me the way?'

Fanny at once rose, and together they crossed the hall, passed through a sort of anteroom connecting with a fernery, and came to the study door. A tap was answered by cheerful summons, and Fanny looked in.

'Well, my ladybird? Ah, you are bringing Mr. Peak; come in, come in!'

It was a large and beautiful room, its wide windows, in a cushioned recess, looking upon the lawn where the yew tree cast solemn shade. One wall presented an unbroken array of volumes, their livery sober but handsome; detached bookcases occupied other portions of the irregular perimeter. Cabinets, closed and open, were arranged with due regard to convenience. Above the mantelpiece hung a few small photographs, but the wall-space at disposal was chiefly occupied with objects which illustrated Mr. Warricombe's scientific tastes. On a stand in the light of the window gleamed two elaborate microscopes, provocative of enthusiasm in a mind such as Godwin's.

In a few minutes, Fanny silently retired. Her father, by no means forward to speak of himself and his pursuits, was led in that direction by Peak's expressions of interest, and the two were soon busied with matters which had a charm for both. A collection of elvans formed the starting-point, and when they had entered upon the wide field of palæontology it was natural for Mr. Warricombe to invite his guest's attention to the species of hamalonotus which he had had the happiness of identifying some ten years ago—a discovery now recognised and chronicled. Though his sympathy was genuine enough, Godwin struggled against an uneasy sense of manifesting excessive appreciation. Never oblivious of himself, he could not utter the simplest phrase of admiration without criticising its justice, its tone. And at present it behoved him to bear in mind that he was conversing with no half-bred sciolist. Mr. Warricombe obviously had his share of human weakness, but he was at once a gentleman and a student of well-stored mind; insincerity must be very careful if it would not jar upon his refined ear. So Godwin often checked himself in the utterance of what might sound too much like flattery. A young man talking with one much older, a poor man in dialogue with a wealthy, must under any circumstances guard his speech; for one of Godwin's aggressive idiosyncrasy the task of discretion had peculiar difficulties, and the attitude he had assumed at luncheon still further complicated the operations of his mind. Only at moments could he speak in his true voice, and silence meant for the most part a studious repression of much he would naturally have uttered.

Resurgent envy gave him no little trouble. On entering the room, he could not but exclaim to himself, 'How easy for a man to do notable work amid such surroundings! If I were but thus equipped for investigation!' And as often as his eyes left a particular object to make a general survey, the same thought burned in him. He feared lest it should be legible on his countenance.

Taking a pamphlet from the table, Mr. Warricombe, with a humorous twinkle in his eyes, inquired whether Peak read German; the answer being affirmative:

'Naturally,' he enjoined, 'you could hardly have neglected so important a language. I, unfortunately, didn't learn it in my youth, and I have never had perseverance enough to struggle with it since. Something led me to take down this brochure the other day—an old attempt of mine to write about the weathering of rocks. It was printed in '76, and no sooner had it seen the light than friends of mine wanted to know what I meant by appropriating, without acknowledgment, certain facts quite recently pointed out by Professor Pfaff of Erlangen! Unhappily, Professor Pfaff's results were quite unknown to me, and I had to get them translated. The coincidences, sure enough, were very noticeable. Just before you came in, I was reviving that old discomfiture.'

Peak, in glancing over the pages, murmured with a smile:

'*Pereant qui ante nos nostra dixerunt!*'

'Even so!' exclaimed Mr. Warricombe, laughing with a subdued heartiness which was one of his pleasant characteristics. And, after a pause, he inquired, 'Do you find any time to keep up your classics?'

'By fits and starts. Sometimes I return to them for a month or two.'

'Why, it's pretty much the same with me. Here on my table, for instance, lies Tacitus. I found it mentioned not long ago that the first sentence of the *Annals* is a hexameter—did you know it?—and when I had once got hold of the book I thought it a shabby thing to return it to the dust of its shelf without reading at least a few pages. So I have gone on from day to day, with no little enjoyment. Buckland, as you probably know, regards these old fellows with scorn.'

'We always differed about that.'

'I can't quite decide whether he is still sincere in all he says about them. Time, I suspect, is mellowing his judgment.'

They moved to the shelves where Greek and Latin books stood in serried order, and only the warning dinner-bell put an end to their sympathetic discussion of the place such authors should hold in modern educational systems.

'Have they shown you your room?' Mr. Warricombe asked.

But, as he spoke, the face of his eldest son appeared at the door.

'Your traps have safely arrived, Peak.'

The bedroom to which Godwin was conducted had a delicious fragrance, of source indeterminable. When he had closed the door, he stood for a few moments looking about him; it was his first experience of the upper chambers of houses such as this. Merely to step upon the carpet fluttered his senses: merely to breathe the air was a purification. Luxury of the rational kind, dictated by regard for health of body and soul, appeared in every detail. On the walls were water-colours, scenery of Devon and Cornwall; a hanging book-case held about a score of volumes—poets, essayists, novelists. Elsewhere, not too prominent, lay a Bible and a Prayer-book.

He dressed, as never before, with leisurely enjoyment of the process. When the mirror declared him ready, his eyes returned frequently to an inspection of the figure he presented, and it seemed to him that he was not unworthy to take his place at the dinner-table. As for his visage, might he not console himself with the assurance that it was of no common stamp? 'If I met that man in a room, I should be curious about him; I should see at once that he didn't belong to the vulgar; I should desire to hear him speak.' And the Warricombes were not lacking in discernment. He would compare more than favourably with Mr. Moorhouse, whose aspect, bright and agreeable enough, made no promise of originality.—It must be time to go down. He left the room with an air of grave self-confidence.

At dinner he was careful to attempt no repetition of the display which had been done very well at luncheon; it must not be thought that he had the habit of talking for effect. Mrs. Warricombe, unless he mistook, had begun to view him more favourably; her remarks made less distinction between him and the other guests. But he could not like his hostess; he thought her unworthy to be the mother of Sidwell and Fanny, of Buckland and Louis; there was a marked strain of the commonplace in her. The girls, costumed for the evening, affected him with a return of the awe he had all but overcome. Sidwell was exquisite in dark colours, her sister in white. Miss Moorhouse (addressed by her friends as 'Sylvia') looked older than in the day time and had lost something of her animation; possibly the country routine had begun to weary her a little.

Peak was at a vast distance from the hour which saw him alight at Exeter and begin his ramble about the city. He no longer felt himself alone in the world; impossible to revive the mood in which he deliberately planned to consume his economies in a year or two of desert wandering; far other were the anticipations which warmed his mind when the after-dinner repose attuned him to unwonted hopefulness. This family were henceforth his friends, and it depended only upon himself to make the connection lasting, with all manner of benefits easily imagined. Established in the country, the Warricombes stood to him in quite a different relation from any that could have arisen had he met with them in London. There he would have been nothing more than a casual dinner-guest, welcomed for the hour and all but forgotten when he had said good-night. For years he had understood that London offered him no prospect of social advancement. But a night passed under this roof practically raised him to a level whence he surveyed a rich field of possible conquest. With the genial geologist he felt himself on excellent terms, and much of this was ascribable to a singular chance which had masked his real being, and represented him, with scarce an effort of his own, in a light peculiarly attractive to Mr. Warricombe. He was now playing the conscious hypocrite; not a pleasant thing to face and accept, but the fault was not his—fate had brought it about. At all events, he aimed at no vulgar profit; his one desire was for human fellowship; he sought nothing but that solace which every code of morals has deemed legitimate. Let the society which compelled to such an expedient bear the burden of its shame.

That must indeed have been a circle of great intellects amid which Godwin Peak felt himself subordinate. He had never known that impression, and in the Warricombe family was no one whom he could regard even as his equal. Buckland, doubtless, had some knowledge of the world, and could boast of a free mind; but he lacked subtlety: a psychological problem would easily puzzle him. Mr. Warricombe's attainments were respectable, but what could be said of a man who had devoted his life to geology, and still (in the year 1884) remained an orthodox member of the Church of England? Godwin, as he sat in the drawing-room and enjoyed its atmosphere of refinement, sincerely held himself of far more account as an intellectual being than all the persons about him.

But if his brain must dwell in solitude his heart might compass worthy alliances—the thing most needful to humanity. One may find the associates of his intellect in libraries— the friend of one's emotions must walk in flesh and blood. Earwaker, Moxey—these were in many respects admirable fellows, and he had no little love for them, but the world they represented was womanless, and so of flagrant imperfection. Of Marcella Moxey he could not think emotionally; indeed she emphasised by her personality the lack which caused his suffering. Sidwell Warricombe suggested, more completely than any woman he had yet observed, that companionship without which life must to the end taste bitter. His interest in her was not strictly personal; she moved and spoke before him as a typical woman, not as the daughter of Martin Warricombe and the sister of Buckland. Here at last opened to his view that sphere of female society which he had known as remotely existing, the desperate aim of ambition.

Conventional women—but was not the phrase tautological? In the few females who have liberated their souls, was not much of the woman inevitably sacrificed, and would it not be so for long years to come? On the other hand, such a one as Sidwell might be held a perfect creature, perfect in relation to a certain stage of human development. Look at her, as she sat conversing with Moorhouse, soft candle-light upon her face; compare her on the one hand with an average emancipated girl, on the other with a daughter of the people. How unsatisfying was the former; the latter, how repulsive! Here one had the exquisite mean, the lady as England has perfected her towards the close of this nineteenth century. A being of marvellous delicacy, of purest instincts, of unsurpassable sweetness. Who could not detail her limitations, obvious and, in certain moods, irritating enough? These were nothing to the point, unless one would roam the world a hungry idealist; and Godwin was weary of the famined pilgrimage.

The murmur of amiable voices softened him to the reception of all that was good in his present surroundings, and justified in the light of sentiment his own dishonour. This English home, was it not surely the best result of civilisation in an age devoted to material progress? Here was peace, here was scope for the kindliest emotions. Upon him—the born rebel, the scorner of average mankind, the consummate egoist—this atmosphere exercised an influence more tranquillising, more beneficent, than even the mood of disinterested study. In the world to which sincerity would condemn him, only the worst elements of his character found nourishment and range; here he was humanised, made receptive of all gentle sympathies. Heroism might point him to an unending struggle with adverse conditions. but how was heroism possible without faith? Absolute faith he had none; he was essentially a negativist, guided by the mere relations of phenomena. Nothing easier than to contemn the mode of life represented by this wealthy middle class; but compare it with other existences conceivable by a thinking man, and it was emphatically good. It aimed at placidity, at benevolence, at supreme cleanliness,—things which more than compensated for the absence of higher spirituality. We can be but what we are; these people accepted themselves, and in so doing became estimable mortals. No imbecile pretensions exposed them to the rebuke of a social satirist; no vulgarity tainted their familiar intercourse. Their allegiance to a worn-out creed was felt as an added grace; thus only could their souls aspire, and the imperfect poetry of their natures be developed.

He took an opportunity of seating himself by Mrs. Warricombe, with whom as yet he had held no continuous dialogue.

'Has there been anything of interest at the London theatres lately?' she asked.

'I know so little of them,' Godwin replied, truthfully. 'It must be several years since I saw a play.'

'Then in that respect you have hardly become a Londoner.'

'Nor in any other, I believe,' said Peak, with a smile. 'I have lived there ten years, but am far from regarding London as my home. I hope a few months more will release me from it altogether.'

'Indeed!—Perhaps you think of leaving England?'

'I should be very sorry to do that—for any length of time. My wish is to settle somewhere in the country, and spend a year or two in quiet study.'

Mrs. Warricombe looked amiable surprise, but corrected herself to approving interest.

'I have heard some of our friends say that their minds get unstrung, if they are long away from town, but I should have thought that country quietness would be much better than London noise. My husband certainly finds it so.'

'People are very differently constituted,' said Godwin. 'And then it depends much on the nature of one's work.'

Uttering these commonplaces with an air of reflection, he observed that they did not cost him the self-contempt which was wont to be his penalty for concession to the terms of polite gossip; rather, his mind accepted with gratitude this rare repose. He tasted something of the tranquil self-content which makes life so enjoyable when one has never seen a necessity for shaping original remarks. No one in this room would despise him for a platitude, were it but recommended with a pleasant smile. With the Moxeys, with Earwaker, he durst not thus have spoken.

When the hour of separation was at hand, Buckland invited his guest to retire with him to a part of the house where they could smoke and chat comfortably.

'Moorhouse and Louis are fagged after their twenty mile stretch this morning; I have caught both of them nodding during the last few minutes. We can send them to bed without apology.'

He led the way upstairs to a region of lumber-rooms, whence a narrow flight of steps brought them into a glass-house, octangular and with pointed tops, out upon the roof. This, he explained, had been built some twenty years ago, at a time when Mr. Warricombe amused himself with photography. A few indications of its original purposes were still noticeable; an easle and a box of oil-colours showed that someone—doubtless of the younger generation—had used it as a painting-room; a settee and deep cane chairs made it an inviting lounge on a warm evening like the present, when, by throwing open a hinged wall, one looked forth into the deep sky and tasted the air from the sea.

'Sidwell used to paint a little,' said Buckland, as his companion bent to examine a small canvas on which a landscape was roughed in. It lay on a side table, and was half concealed by an ordnance map, left unfolded. 'For the last year or two I think she has given it up. I'm afraid we are not strong in matters of art. Neither of the girls can play very well, though of course they both tinkle for their own amusement. Maurice—the poor lad who was killed—gave a good deal of artistic promise; father keeps some little water-colours of his, which men in that line have praised—perhaps sincerely.'

'I remember you used to speak slightly of art,' said Godwin, as he took an offered cigar.

'Did I? And of a good many other things, I daresay. It was my habit at one time, I believe, to grow heated in scorn of Euclid's definitions. What an interesting book Euclid is! Half a year ago, I was led by a talk with Moorhouse to go through some of the old 'props,' and you can't imagine how they delighted me. Moorhouse was so obliging as to tell me that I had an eminently deductive mind.'

He laughed, but not without betraying some pleasure in the remark.

'Surprising,' he went on, 'how very little such a mind as Moorhouse's suggests itself in common conversation. He is really profound in mathematics, a man of original powers, but I never heard him make a remark of the slightest value on any other subject. Now his sister—she has studied nothing in particular, yet she can't express an opinion that doesn't bear the stamp of originality.'

Godwin was contented to muse, his eyes fixed on a brilliant star in the western heaven.

'There's only one inconsistency in her that annoys and puzzles me,' Buckland pursued, speaking with the cigar in his mouth. 'In religion, she seems to be orthodox. True, we have never spoken on the subject but—well, she goes to church, and carries prayer-books. I don't know how to explain it. Hypocrisy is the last thing one could suspect her of. I'm sure she hates it in every form. And such a clear brain!—I can't understand it.'

The listener was still star-gazing. He had allowed his cigar, after the first few puffs, to smoulder untasted; his lips were drawn into an expression very unlike the laxity appropriate to pleasurable smoking. When the murmur of the pines had for a moment been audible, he said, with a forced smile:

'I notice you take for granted that a clear brain and religious orthodoxy are incompatible.'

The other gave him a keen look.

'Hardly,' was Buckland's reply, spoken with less ingenuousness of tone than usual. 'I say that Miss Moorhouse has undeniably a strong mind, and that it is impossible to suspect her of the slightest hypocrisy.'

'Whence the puzzle that keeps you occupied,' rejoined Peak, in a voice that sounded like assumption of superiority, though the accent had an agreeable softness.

Warricombe moved as if impatiently, struck a match to rekindle his weed, blew tumultuous clouds, and finally put a blunt question:

'What do you think about it yourself?'

'From my point of view, there is no puzzle at all,' Godwin replied, in a very clear voice, smiling as he met the other's look.

'How am I to understand that?' asked Buckland, good-naturedly, though with a knitting of his brows.

'Not as a doubt of Miss Moorhouse's sincerity. I can't see that a belief in the Christian religion is excluded by any degree of intellectual clearness.'

'No—your views have changed, Peak?'

'On many subjects, this among them.'

'I see.'

The words fell as if involuntarily from Warricombe's lips. He gazed at the floor awhile, then, suddenly looking up, exclaimed:

'It would be civil to accept this without surprise, but it is too much for me. How has it come about?'

'That would take me a long time to explain.'

'Then,' pursued his companion, watching him closely, 'you were quite in sympathy with that exposition you gave at lunch to-day?'

'Quite. I hope there was nothing in my way of speaking that made you think otherwise?'

'Nothing at all. I couldn't help wondering what it meant. You seemed perfectly in earnest, yet such talk had the oddest sound on your lips—to me, I mean. Of course I thought of you as I used to know you.'

'Naturally.' Peak was now in an attitude of repose, his legs crossed, thumb and forefinger stroking his chin. 'I couldn't very well turn aside to comment on my own mental history.'

Here again was the note of something like genial condescension. Buckland seemed sensible of it, and slightly raised his eyebrows.

'I am to understand that you have become strictly orthodox in matters of religious faith?'

'The proof is,' replied Godwin, 'that I hope before long to take Orders.'

Again there was silence, and again the sea-breath made its whispering in the pines. Warricombe, with a sudden gesture, pointed towards the sky.

'A shooting star—one of the brightest I ever saw!'

'I missed it,' said Peak, just glancing in that direction.

The interruption enabled Buckland to move his chair; in this new position he was somewhat further from Peak and had a better view of his face.

'I should never have imagined you a clergyman,' he said thoughtfully, 'but I can see that your mind has been developing powers in that direction.—Well, so be it! I can only hope you have found your true work in life.'

'But you doubt it?'

'I can't say that I doubt it, as I can't understand you. To be sure, we have been parted for many years. In some respects *I* must seem much changed'——

'Greatly changed,' Godwin put in, promptly.

'Yes,' pursued the other, correctively, 'but not in a way that would seem incredible to anyone whatever. I am conscious of growth in tolerance, but my attitude in essentials is unchanged. Thinking of you—as I have often enough done—I always kept the impression you made on me when we were both lads; you seemed most distinctly a modern mind—one of the most modern that ever came under my notice. Now, I don't find it impossible to understand my father, when he reconciles science with religion; he was born sixty years ago. But Godwin Peak as a—a'——

'Parson,' supplied Peak, drily.

'Yes, as a parson—I shall have to meditate much before I grasp the notion.'

'Perhaps you have dropped your philosophical studies?' said Godwin, with a smile of courteous interest.

'I don't know. Metaphysics have no great interest for me, but I philosophise in a way. I thought myself a student of human nature, at all events.'

'But you haven't kept up with philosophical speculation on the points involved in orthodox religion?'

'I confess my ignorance of everything of the kind—unless you include Bishop Blougram among the philosophers?'

Godwin bore the gaze which accompanied this significant inquiry. For a moment he smiled, but there followed an expression of gravity touched with pain.

'I hadn't thought of broaching this matter,' he said, with slow utterance, but still in a tone of perfect friendliness. 'Let us put it aside.'

Warricombe seemed to make an effort, and his next words had the accent of well-bred consideration which distinguished his ordinary talk.

'Pray forgive my bad joke. I merely meant that I have no right whatever to argue with anyone who has given serious attention to such things. They are altogether beyond my sphere. I was born an agnostic, and no subtlety of demonstration could incline me for a moment to theological views; my intellect refuses to admit a single preliminary of such arguments. You astonish me, and that's all I am justified in saying.'

'My dear Warricombe, you are justified in saying whatever your mind suggests. That is one of the principles which I hold unaltered— let me be quite frank with you. I should never have decided upon such a step as this, but for the fact that I have managed to put by a small sum of money which will make me independent for two or three years. Till quite lately I hadn't a thought of using my freedom in this way; it was clear to me that I must throw over the old drudgery at Rotherhithe, but this resolve which astonishes you had not yet ripened—I saw it only as one of the possibilities of my life. Well, now, it's only too true that there's something of speculation in my purpose; I look to the Church, not only as a congenial sphere of activity, but as a means of subsistence. In a man of no fortune this is inevitable; I hope there is nothing to be ashamed of. Even if the conditions of the case allowed it, I couldn't present myself for ordination forthwith; I must study and prepare myself in quietness. How the practical details will be arranged, I can't say; I have no family influence, and I must hope to make friends who will open a way for me. I have always lived apart from society; but that isn't natural to me, and it becomes more distasteful the older I grow. The probability is that I shall settle somewhere in the country, where I can live decently on a small income. After all, it's better I should have let you know this at once. I only realised a few minutes ago that to be silent about my projects was in a way to be guilty of false pretences.'

The adroitness of this last remark, which directed itself, with such show of candour, against a suspicion precisely the opposite of that likely to be entertained by the listener, succeeded in disarming Warricombe; he looked up with a smile of reassurance, and spoke encouragingly.

'About the practical details I don't think you need have any anxiety. It isn't every day that the Church of England gets such a recruit. Let me suggest that you have a talk with my father.'

Peak reflected on the proposal, and replied to it with grave thoughtfulness:

'That's very kind of you, but I should have a difficulty in asking Mr. Warricombe's advice. I'm afraid I must go on in my own way for a time. It will be a few months, I daresay, before I can release myself from my engagements in London.'

'But I am to understand that your mind is really made up?'

'Oh, quite!'

'Well, no doubt we shall have opportunities of talking. We must meet in town, if possible. You have excited my curiosity, and I can't help hoping you'll let me see a little further into your mind some day. When I first got hold of Newman's *Apologia*, I began to read it with the utmost eagerness, flattering myself that now at length I should understand how a man of brains could travel such a road. I was horribly disappointed, and not a little enraged, when I found that he began by assuming the very beliefs I thought he was going to justify. In you I shall hope for more logic.'

'Newman is incapable of understanding such an objection,' said Peak, with a look of amusement.

'But you are not.'

The dialogue grew chatty. When they exchanged good-night, Peak fancied that the pressure of Buckland's hand was less fervent than at their meeting, but his manner no longer seemed to indicate distrust. Probably the agnostic's mood was one of half-tolerant disdain.

Godwin turned the key in his bedroom door, and strayed aimlessly about. He was fatigued, but the white, fragrant bed did not yet invite him; a turbulence in his brain gave warning that it would be long before he slept. He wound up his watch; the hands pointed to twelve. Chancing to come before the mirror, he saw that he was unusually pale, and that his eyes had a swollen look.

The profound stillness was oppressive to him; he started nervously at an undefined object in a dim corner, and went nearer to examine it; he was irritable, vaguely discontented, and had even a moment of nausea, perhaps the result of tobacco stronger than he was accustomed to smoke. After leaning for five minutes at the open window, he felt a soothing effect from the air, and could think consecutively of the day's events. What had happened seemed to him incredible; it was as though he revived a mad dream, of ludicrous coherence. Since his display of rhetoric at luncheon all was downright somnambulism. What fatal power had subdued him? What extraordinary influence had guided his tongue, constrained his features? His conscious self had had no part in all this comedy; now for the first time was he taking count of the character he had played.

Had he been told this morning that—— Why, what monstrous folly was all this? Into what unspeakable baseness had he fallen? Happily, he had but to take leave of the Warricombe household, and rush into some region where he was unknown. Years hence, he would relate the story to Earwaker.

For a long time he suffered the torments of this awakening. Shame buffeted him on the right cheek and the left; he looked about like one who slinks from merited chastisement. Oh, thrice ignoble varlet! To pose with unctuous hypocrisy before people who had welcomed him under their roof, unquestioned, with all the grace and kindliness of English hospitality! To lie shamelessly in the face of his old fellow-student, who had been so genuinely glad to meet him again!

Yet such possibility had not been unforeseen. At the times of his profound gloom, when solitude and desire crushed his spirit, he had wished that fate would afford him such an opportunity of knavish success. His imagination had played with the idea that a man like himself might well be driven to this expedient, and might even use it with life-long result. Of a certainty, the Church numbered such men among her priests,—not mere lukewarm sceptics who made religion a source of income, nor yet those who had honestly entered the portal and by necessity were held from withdrawing, though their convictions had changed; but deliberate schemers from the first, ambitious but hungry natures, keen-sighted, unscrupulous. And they were at no loss to defend themselves against the attack of conscience. Life is a terrific struggle for all who begin it with no endowments save their brains. A hypocrite was not necessarily a harm-doer; easy to picture the unbelieving priest whose influence was vastly for good, in word and deed.

But he, he who had ever prided himself on his truth-fronting intellect, and had freely uttered his scorn of the credulous mob!

He who was his own criterion of moral right and wrong! No wonder he felt like a whipped cur. It was the ancestral vice in his blood, brought out by over-tempting circumstance. The long line of base-born predecessors, the grovelling hinds and mechanics of his genealogy, were responsible for this. Oh for a name wherewith honour was hereditary!

His eyes were blinded by a rush of hot tears. Down, down—into the depths of uttermost despondency, of self-pity and self-contempt! Had it been practicable, he would have fled from the house, leaving its occupants to think of him as they would; even as, ten years ago, he had fled from the shame impending over him at Kingsmill. A cowardly instinct, this; having once acted upon it gave to his whole life a taint of craven meanness. Mere bluster, all his talk of mental dignity and uncompromising scorn of superstitions. A weak and idle man, whose best years were already wasted!

He gazed deliberately at himself in the glass, at his red eyelids and unsightly lips. Darkness was best; perhaps he might forget his shame for an hour or two, ere the dawn renewed it. He threw off his garments heedlessly, extinguished the lamp, and crept into the ready hiding-place.

PART THE THIRD

I

'WHY ARE YOU obstinately silent?' wrote Earwaker, in a letter addressed to Godwin at his Peckham lodgings. 'I take it for granted that you must by this time be back from your holiday. Why haven't you replied to my letter of a fortnight ago? Nothing yet from *The Critical*. If you are really at work as usual, come and see me to-morrow evening, any time after eight. The posture of my affairs grows dubious; the shadow of Kenyon thickens about me. In all seriousness I think I shall be driven from *The Weekly Post* before long. My quarrels with Runcorn are too frequent, and his blackguardism keeps more than pace with the times. Come or write, for I want to know how things go with you.

Tuissimus, J. E. E.'

Peak read this at breakfast on a Saturday morning. It was early in September, and three weeks had elapsed since his return from the west of England. Upon the autumn had fallen a blight of cold and rainy weather, which did not enhance the cheerfulness of daily journeying between Peckham Rye and Rotherhithe. When it was necessary for him to set forth to the train, he muttered imprecations, for a mood of inactivity possessed him; he would gladly have stayed in his comfortable sitting-room, idling over books or only occupied with languid thought.

In the afternoon he was at liberty to follow his impulse, and this directed him to the British Museum, whither of late he had several times resorted as a reader. Among the half-dozen books for which he applied was one in German, Reusch's *Bibel und Natur*. After a little dallying, he became absorbed in this work, and two or three hours passed before its hold on his attention slackened. He seldom changed his position; the volume was propped against others, and he sat bending forward, his arms folded upon the desk. When he was thus deeply engaged, his face had a hard, stern aspect; if by chance his eye wandered for a moment, its look seemed to express resentment of interruption.

At length he threw himself back with a sudden yielding to weariness, crossed his legs, sank together in the chair, and for half-an-hour brooded darkly. A fit of yawning admonished him that it was time to quit the atmosphere of study. He betook himself to a restaurant in the Strand, and thence about eight o'clock made his way to Staple Inn, where the journalist gave him cheerful welcome.

'Day after day I have meant to write,' thus he excused himself. 'But I had really nothing to say.'

'You don't look any better for your holiday,' Earwaker remarked.

'Holiday? Oh, I had forgotten all about it. When do *you* go?'

'The situation is comical. I feel sure that if I leave town, my connection with the *Post* will come to an end. I shall have a note from Runcorn saying that we had better take this opportunity of terminating my engagement. On the whole I should be glad, yet I can't make up my mind to be ousted by Kenyon—that's what it means. They want to get me away, but I stick on, postponing holiday from week to week. Runcorn can't decide to send me about my business, yet every leader I write enrages him. But for Kenyon, I should gain my point; I feel sure of it. It's one of those cases in which homicide would be justified by public interest. If Kenyon gets my place, the paper becomes at once an organ of ruffiandom, the delight of the blackguardry.'

'How's the circulation?' inquired Peak.

'Pretty sound; that adds to the joke. This series of stories by Doubleday has helped us a good deal, and my contention is, if we can keep financially right by help of this kind, why not make a little sacrifice for the sake of raising our political tone? Runcorn won't see it; he listens eagerly to Kenyon's assurance that we might sell several thousand more by striking the true pot-house note.'

'Then pitch the thing over! Wash your hands, and go to cleaner work.'

'The work I am doing is clean enough,' replied Earwaker. 'Let me have my way, and I can make the paper a decent one and a useful one. I shan't easily find another such chance.'

'Your idealism has a strong root,' said Godwin, rather contemptuously. 'I half envy you. There must be a distinct pleasure in believing that any intellectual influence will exalt the English democracy.'

'I'm not sure that I do believe it, but I enjoy the experiment. The chief pleasure, I suppose, is in fighting Runcorn and Kenyon.'

'They are too strong for you, Earwaker. They have the spirit of the age to back them up.'

The journalist became silent; he smiled, but the harassment of conflict marked his features.

'I hear nothing about "The New Sophistry,"' he remarked, when Godwin had begun to examine some books that lay on the table. 'Dolby has the trick of keeping manuscripts a long time. Everything that seems at the first glance tolerable, he sends to the printer, then muses over it at his leisure. Probably your paper is in type.'

'I don't care a rap whether it is or not. What do you think of this book of Oldwinkle's?'

He was holding a volume of humorous stories, which had greatly taken the fancy of the public.

'It's uncommonly good,' replied the journalist, laughing. 'I had a prejudice against the fellow, but he has overcome me. It's more than good farce,—something like really strong humour here and there.'

'I quite believe it,' said Peak, 'yet I couldn't read a page. Whatever the mob enjoys is at once spoilt for me, however good I should otherwise think it. I am sick of seeing and hearing the man's name.'

Earwaker shook his head in deprecation.

'Narrow, my boy. One must be able to judge and enjoy impartially.'

'I know it, but I shall never improve. This book seems to me to have a bad smell; it looks mauled with dirty fingers. I despise Oldwinkle for his popularity. To make them laugh, and to laugh *with* them—pah!'

They debated this point for some time, Peak growing more violent, though his friend preserved a smiling equanimity. A tirade of virulent contempt, in which Godwin exhibited all his powers of savage eloquence, was broken by a visitor's summons at the door.

'Here's Malkin,' said the journalist; 'you'll see each other at last.'

Peak could not at once command himself to the look and tone desirable in meeting a stranger; leaning against the mantelpiece, he gazed with a scowl of curiosity at the man who presented himself, and when he shook hands, it was in silence. But Malkin made speech from the others unnecessary for several minutes. With animated voice and gesture, he poured forth apologies for his failure to keep the appointment of six or seven weeks ago.

'Only the gravest call of duty could have kept me away, I do assure you! No doubt Earwaker has informed you of the circumstances. I telegraphed—I think I telegraphed; didn't I, Earwaker?'

'I have some recollection of a word or two of scant excuse,' replied the journalist.

'But I implore you to consider the haste I was in,' cried Malkin; 'not five minutes, Mr. Peak, to book, to register luggage, to do everything; not five minutes, I protest! But here we are at last. Let us talk! Let us talk!'

He seated himself with an air of supreme enjoyment, and began to cram the bowl of a large pipe from a bulky pouch.

'How stands the fight with Kenyon and Co.?' he cried, as soon as the tobacco was glowing.

Earwaker briefly repeated what he had told Peak.

'Hold out! No surrender and no compromise! What's your opinion, Mr. Peak, on the abstract question? Is a popular paper likely, or not, to be damaged in its circulation by improvement of style and tone—within the limits of discretion?'

'I shouldn't be surprised if it were,' Peak answered, drily.

'I'm afraid you're right. There's no use in blinking truths, however disagreeable. But, for Earwaker, that isn't the main issue. What he has to do is to assert himself. Every man's first duty is to assert himself. At all events, this is how I regard the matter. I am all for individualism, for the development of one's personality at whatever cost. No compromise on points of faith! Earwaker has his ideal of journalistic duty, and in a fight with fellows like Runcorn and Kenyon he must stand firm as a rock.'

'I can't see that he's called upon to fight at all,' said Peak. 'He's in a false position; let him get out of it.'

'A false position? I can't see that. No man better fitted than Earwaker to raise the tone of Radical journalism. Here's a big Sunday newspaper practically in his hands; it seems to me that the circumstances give him a grand opportunity of making his force felt. What are we all seeking but an opportunity for striking out with effect?'

Godwin listened with a sceptical smile, and made answer in slow, careless tones.

'Earwaker happens to be employed and paid by certain capitalists to increase the sale of their paper.'

'My dear sir!' cried the other, bouncing upon his seat. 'How can you take such a view? A great newspaper surely cannot be regarded as a mere source of income. These capitalists declare that they have at heart the interests of the working classes; so has Earwaker, and he is far better able than they to promote those interests. His duty is to apply their money to the best use, morally speaking. If he were lukewarm in the matter, I should be the first to advise his retirement; but this fight is entirely congenial to him. I trust he will hold his own to the last possible moment.'

'You must remember,' put in the journalist, with a look of amusement, 'that Peak has no sympathy with Radicalism.'

'I lament it, but that does not affect my argument. If you were a high Tory, I should urge you just as strongly to assert yourself. Surely you agree with this point of mine, Mr. Peak? You admit that a man must develop whatever strength is in him.'

'I'm not at all sure of that.'

Malkin fixed himself sideways in the chair, and examined his collocutor's face earnestly. He endeavoured to subdue his excitement to the tone of courteous debate, but the words that at length escaped him were humorously blunt.

'Then of what *are* you sure?'

'Of nothing.'

'Now we touch bottom!' cried Malkin. 'Philosophically speaking, I agree with you. But we have to live our lives, and I suppose we must direct ourselves by some conscious principle.'

'I don't see the necessity,' Peak replied, still in an impassive tone. 'We may very well be guided by circumstances as they arise. To be sure, there's a principle in that, but I take it you mean something different.'

'Yes I do. I hold that the will must direct circumstances, not receive its impulse from them. How, then, are we to be guided? What do you set before yourself?'

'To get through life with as much satisfaction and as little pain as possible.'

'You are a hedonist, then. Well and good! Then that is your conscious principle'——

'No, it isn't.'

'How am I to understand you?'

'By recognising that a man's intellectual and moral principles as likely as not tend to anything but his happiness.'

'I can't admit it!' exclaimed Malkin, leaping from his chair. 'What *is* happiness?'

'I don't know.'

'Earwaker, *what* is happiness? What *is* happiness?'

'I really don't know,' answered the journalist, mirthfully.

'This is trifling with a grave question. We all know perfectly well that happiness is the conscious exertion of individual powers. Why is there so much suffering under our present social system? Because the majority of men are crushed to a dead level of mechanical toil, with no opportunity of developing their special faculties. Give a man scope, and happiness is put within his reach.'

'What do you mean by scope?' inquired Godwin.

'Scope? Scope? Why, room to expand. The vice of our society is hypocrisy; it comes of over-crowding. When a man isn't allowed to be himself, he takes refuge in a mean imitation of those other men who appear to be better off. That was what sent me off to South America. I got into politics, and found that I was in danger of growing dishonest, of compromising, and toadying. In the wilderness, I found myself again.—Do you seriously believe that happiness can be obtained by ignoring one's convictions?'

He addressed the question to both, snuffing the air with head thrown back.

'What if you have no convictions?' asked Peak.

'Then you are incapable of happiness in any worthy sense! You may graze, but you will never feast.'

The listeners joined in laughter, and Malkin, after a moment's hesitation, allowed his face to relax in good-humoured sympathy.

'Now look here!' he cried. 'You—Earwaker; suppose you sent conscience to the devil, and set yourself to please Runcorn by increasing the circulation of your paper by whatever means. You would flourish, undoubtedly. In a short time you would be chief editor, and your pockets would burst with money. But what about your peace of mind? What about happiness?'

'Why, I'm disposed to agree with Peak,' answered the journalist. 'If I *could* take that line, I should be a happier man than conscientiousness will ever make me.'

Malkin swelled with indignation.

'You don't mean it! You are turning a grave argument into jest!—Where's my hat? Where the devil is my hat? Send for me again when you are disposed to talk seriously.'

He strode towards the door, but Earwaker arrested him with a shout.

'You're leaving your pipe!'

'So I am. Where is it?—Did I tell you where I bought this pipe?'

'No. What's the wood?'

On the instant Malkin fell into a cheerful vein of reminiscence. In five minutes he was giving a rapturous description of tropical scenes, laughing joyously as he addressed now one now the other of his companions.

'I hear you have a mind to see those countries, Mr. Peak,' he said at length. 'If you care for a travelling-companion—rather short-tempered, but you'll pardon that—pray give me the preference. I should enjoy above all things to travel with a man of science.'

'It's very doubtful whether I shall ever get so far,' Godwin replied, musingly.

And, as he spoke, he rose to take leave. Earwaker's protest that it was not yet ten o'clock did not influence him.

'I want to reflect on the meaning of happiness,' he said, extending his hand to Malkin; and, in spite of the smile, his face had a sombre cast.

The two who were left of course discussed him.

'You won't care much for Peak,' said Earwaker. 'He and I suit each other, because there's a good deal of indifferentism in both of us. Moral earnestness always goes against the grain with him; I've noticed it frequently.'

'I'm sorry I spoke so dogmatically. It wasn't altogether good manners. Suppose I write him a short letter, just expressing my regret for having been led away'——

'Needless, needless,' laughed the journalist. 'He thinks all the better of you for your zeal. But happiness is a sore point with him; few men, I should think, have known less of it. I can't imagine any circumstances which would make him thoroughly at peace with himself and the world.'

'Poor fellow! You can see something of that in his face. Why doesn't he get married?'

'A remarkable suggestion!—By the way, why don't *you*?'

'My dear boy, there's nothing I wish more, but it's a business of such fearful precariousness. I'm one of those men whom marriage will either make or ruin. You know my characteristics; the slightest check upon my independence, and all's up with me. The woman I marry must be perfectly reasonable, perfectly good-tempered; she must have excellent education, and every delicacy of breeding. Where am I to find this paragon?'

'Society is open to you.'

'True, but I am not open to society. I don't take kindly to the people of my own class. No, I tell you what—my only chance of getting a suitable wife is to train some very young girl for the purpose. Don't misunderstand me, for heaven's sake! I mean that I must make a friendship with some schoolgirl in whose education I can have a voice, whose relatives will permit me to influence her mind and develop her character. What do you think of this idea?'

'Not bad, but it demands patience.'

'And who more patient than I? But let us talk of that poor Mrs. Jacox and her girls. You feel that you know them pretty well from my letters, don't you? Nothing more monstrous can be imagined than the treatment to which this poor woman has been subjected! I couldn't have believed that such dishonesty and brutality were possible in English families of decent position. Her husband deserted her, her brother robbed her, her sister-in-law libelled her,—the whole story is nauseating!'

'You're quite sure that she tells you the truth?'

Malkin glared with sudden resentment.

'The truth? What! you also desire to calumniate her? For shame, Earwaker! A poor widow toiling to support herself in a foreign country, with two children dependent on her.'

'Yes, yes, yes; but you seem to know very little of her.'

'I know her perfectly, and all her circumstances!'

Mrs. Jacox was the mother of the two girls whom Malkin had escorted to Rouen, after an hour or so of all but casual acquaintance. She and her history had come in a very slight degree under the notice of certain good-natured people with whom Malkin was on friendly terms, and hearing that the children, Bella and Lily, aged fourteen and twelve respectively, were about to undertake alone a journey to the Continent, the erratic hero felt it incumbent upon him to see them safe at their mother's side. Instead of returning forthwith, he lingered in Normandy for several weeks, striking off at length, on the summons of a friend, to Orleans, whence he was only to-day returned. Two or three letters had kept Earwaker informed of his movements. Of Mrs. Jacox he wrote as he now spoke, with compassionate respect, and the girls, according to him, were exquisite models of budding maidenhood.

'You haven't told me,' said Earwaker, calmly fronting the indignant outburst, 'what her circumstances are—at present.'

'She assists an English lady in the management of a boarding-house,' Malkin replied, with an air which forbade trivial comment.

'Bella and Lily will of course continue their studies. I dare say I shall run over now and then to see them.'

'May I, without offence, inquire if either of these young ladies seems suitable for the ideal training of which you spoke?'

Malkin smiled thoughtfully. He stood with his legs apart and stroked his blond beard.

'The surmise is not unnatural. Well, I confess that Bella has inspired me with no little interest. She is rather mature, unfortunately; I wish she had been Lily's age. We shall see; we shall see.'

Musing, he refilled his pipe, and gossip was prolonged till something after one o'clock. Malkin was never known to retire willingly from an evening's congenial talk until the small hours were in progress.

Peak, on reaching home about eleven, was surprised to see a light in his sitting-room window. As he entered, his landlady informed him that Mr. Moxey had been waiting upstairs for an hour or two. Christian was reading. He laid down the book and rose languidly. His face was flushed, and he spoke with a laugh which suggested that a fit of despondency (as occasionally happened) had tempted him to excess in cordials. Godwin understood these signs. He knew that his friend's intellect was rather brightened than impaired by such stimulus, and he affected not to be conscious of any peculiarity.

'As you wouldn't come to me,' Christian began, 'I had no choice but to come to you. My visit isn't unwelcome, I hope?'

'Certainly not. But how are you going to get home? You know the time?'

'Don't trouble. I shan't go to bed to-night. Let me sit here and read, will you? If I feel tired I can lie down on the sofa. What a delightful book this is! I must get it.'

It was a history of the Italian Renaissance, recently published.

'Where does this phrase come from?' he continued, pointing to a scrap of paper, used as a book-mark, on which Godwin had pencilled a note. The words were: '*Foris ut moris, intus ut libet.*'

'It's mentioned here,' Peak replied, 'as the motto of those humanists who outwardly conformed to the common faith.'

'I see. All very well when the Inquisition was flourishing, but sounds ignoble nowadays.'

'Do you think so? In a half-civilised age, whether the sixteenth or the nineteenth century, a wise man may do worse than adopt it.'

'Better be honest, surely?'

Peak stood for a moment as if in doubt, then exclaimed irritably:

'Honest? Honest? Who is or can be honest? Who truly declares himself? When a man has learnt that truth is indeterminable, how is it more moral to go about crying that you don't believe a certain dogma than to concede that the dogma may possibly be true? This new morality of the agnostics is here paltry conceit. Why must I make solemn declaration that I don't believe in absolute knowledge? I might as well be called upon to inform all my acquaintances how I stand with regard to the theories of chemical affinity. One's philosophy has nothing to do with the business of life. If I chose to become a Church of England clergyman, what moral objection could be made?'

This illustration was so amusing to Moxey, that his surprise at what preceded gave way to laughter.

'I wonder,' he exclaimed, 'that you never seriously thought of a profession for which you are so evidently cut out.'

Godwin kept silence; his face had darkened, and he seated himself with sullen weariness.

'Tell me what you've been doing,' resumed Moxey. 'Why haven't I heard from you?'

'I should have come in a day or two. I thought you were probably out of town.'

'Her husband is ill,' said the other, by way of reply. He leaned forward with his arms upon the table, and gazed at Godwin with eyes of peculiar brightness.

'Ill, is he?' returned Godwin with slow interest. 'In the same way as before?'

'Yes, but much worse.'

Christian paused; and when he again spoke it was hurriedly, confusedly.

'How can I help getting excited about it? How can I behave decently? You're the only man I ever speak to on the subject, and no doubt I both weary and disgust you; but I *must* speak to some one. My nerves are strung beyond endurance; it's only by speaking that I can ease myself from the intolerable strain.'

'Have you seen her lately?'

'Yesterday, for a moment, in the street. It's ten months since the last meeting.'

'Well,' remarked Godwin, abruptly, 'it's probable the man will die one of these days, then your trials will have a happy end. I see no harm in hoping that his life may be short—that's a conventional feeling. If two people can be benefited by the death of a single person, why shouldn't we be glad in the prospect of his dying? Not of his suffering—that's quite another thing. But die he must; and to curtail the life of a being who at length wholly ceases to exist is no injury. You can't injure a nonentity. Do you think I should take it ill if I knew that some persons were wishing my death? Why, look, if ever I crush a little green fly that crawls upon me in the fields, at once I am filled with envy of its fate—sincerest envy. To have passed so suddenly from being into nothingness—how blessed an extinction! To feel in that way, instinctively, in the very depths of your soul, is to be a true pessimist. If I had ever doubted my sincerity in pessimism, this experience, several times repeated, would have reassured me.'

Christian covered his face, and brooded for a long time, whilst Godwin sat with his eyes on vacancy.

'Come and see us to-morrow,' said the former, at length.

'Perhaps.'

'Why do you keep away?'

'I'm in no mood for society.'

'We'll have no one. Only Marcella and I.'

Again a long silence.

'Marcella is going in for comparative philology,' Christian resumed, with the gentle tone in which he invariably spoke of his sister. 'What a mind that girl has! I never knew any woman of half her powers.'

Godwin said nothing.

'No,' continued the other fervently, 'nor of half her goodness. I sometimes think that no mortal could come nearer to our ideal of moral justice and purity. If it were not for her, I should long ago have gone to perdition, in one way or another. It's her strength, not my own, that has saved me. I daresay you know this?'

'There's some truth in it, I believe,' Peak answered, his eye wandering.

'See how circumstances can affect one's judgment. If, just about the time I first knew you, I had abandoned myself to a life of sottish despair, of course I should have charged Constance with the blame of it. Now that I have struggled on, I can see that she has been a blessing to me instead of a curse. If Marcella has given me strength, I have to thank Constance for the spiritual joy which otherwise I should never have known.'

Peak uttered a short laugh.

'That is only saying that she *might* have been ruinous, but in the course of circumstances has proved helpful. I envy your power of deriving comfort from such reflections.'

'Well, we view things differently. I have the habit of looking to the consolatory facts of life, you to the depressing. There's an unfortunate lack in you, Peak; you seem insensible to female influence, and I believe that is closely connected with your desperate pessimism.'

Godwin laughed again, this time with mocking length of note.

'Come now, isn't it true?' urged the other. 'Sincerely, do you care for women at all?'

'Perhaps not.'

'A grave misfortune, depend upon it! It accounts for nearly everything that is unsatisfactory in your life. If you had ever been sincerely devoted to a woman, be assured your powers would have developed in a way of which you have no conception. It's no answer to tell me that *I* am still a mere trifler, never likely to do anything of account; I haven't it in me to be anything better, and I might easily have become much worse. But you might have made yourself a great position—I mean, you *might* do so; you are still very young. If only you knew the desire of a woman's help.'

'You really think so?' said Godwin, with grave irony.

'I am sure of it! There's no harm in repeating what you have often told me—your egoism oppresses you. A woman's influence takes one out of oneself. No man can be a better authority on this than I. For more than eleven years I have worshipped one woman with absolute faithfulness'——

'Absolute?' interrupted Godwin, bluntly.

'What exception occurs to you?'

'As you challenge inquiry, forgive me for asking what your interest was in one of your cousins at Twybridge?'

Christian started, and averted his face with a look of embarrassment.

'Do you mean to say that you knew anything about that?'

'I was always an observer,' Peak replied, smiling. 'You don't remember, perhaps, that I happened to be present when a letter had just arrived for you at your uncle's house—a letter which evidently disturbed you?'

'This is astonishing! Peak, you're a terrible fellow! Heaven forbid that I should ever be at your mercy! Yes, you are quite right,' he continued, despondently. 'But that was no real unfaithfulness. I don't quite know how to explain it. I *did* make love to poor Janet, and with the result that I have never since seen any of the family. My uncle, when he found I had drawn back, was very savage—naturally enough. Marcella and I never again went to Twybridge. I liked Janet; she was a good, kind girl. I believed just then that my love for Constance was hopeless; my mood impelled me to the conviction that the best thing I could do was to marry Janet and settle down to a peaceful domestic life. Then came that letter—it was from Constance herself. It meant nothing, yet it was enough to revive all my hopes. I rushed off——! How brutally I had behaved! Poor little Janet!'

He let his face fall upon his hands.

'Allow me an indiscreet question,' said Peak, after a silence. 'Have you any founded hope of marrying Constance if she becomes a widow?'

Christian started and looked up with wide eyes.

'Hope? Every hope! I have the absolute assurance of her love.'

'I see.'

'But I mustn't mislead you,' pursued the other, hurriedly. 'Our relations are absolutely pure. I have only allowed myself to see her at very long intervals. Why shouldn't I tell you? It was less than a year after her marriage; I found her alone in a room in a friend's house; her eyes were red with weeping. I couldn't help holding my hand to her. She took it, and held it for a moment, and looked at me steadily, and whispered my name—that was all. I knew then that she repented of her marriage—who can say what led her into it? I was poor, you know; perhaps—but in spite of all, she *did* love me. There has never since been anything like a scene of emotion between us—*that* her conscience couldn't allow. She is a noble-minded woman, and has done her duty. But if she is free'——

He quivered with passionate feeling.

'And you are content,' said Godwin, drily, 'to have wasted ten years of your life for such a possibility?'

'Wasted!' Christian exclaimed. 'Come, come, Peak; why *will* you affect this wretched cynicism? Is it waste of years to have lived with the highest and purest ideal perpetually before one's mind? What can a man do better than, having found an admirable woman, to worship her thenceforth, and defy every temptation that could lead him astray? I don't like to seem boastful, but I *have* lived purely and devotedly. And if the test endured to the end of my life, I could sustain it. Is the consciousness of my love nothing to Constance? Has it not helped her?'

Such profound sincerity was astonishing to Peak. He did not admire it, for it seemed to him, in this case at all events, the fatal weakness of a character it was impossible not to love. Though he could not declare his doubts, he thought it more than probable that this Laura of the voiceless Petrarch was unworthy of such constancy, and that she had no intention whatever of rewarding it, even if the opportunity arrived. But this was the mere speculation of a pessimist; he might be altogether wrong, for he had never denied the existence of high virtue, in man or woman.

'There goes midnight!' he remarked, turning from the subject. 'You can't sleep, neither can I. Why shouldn't we walk into town?'

'By all means; on condition that you will come home with me, and spend tomorrow there.'

'Very well.'

They set forth, and with varied talk, often broken by long silences, made their way through sleeping suburbs to the dark valley of Thames.

There passed another month, during which Peak was neither seen nor heard of by his friends. One evening in October, as he sat studying at the British Museum, a friendly voice claimed his attention. He rose nervously and met the searching eye of Buckland Warricombe.

'I had it in mind to write to you,' said the latter. 'Since we parted down yonder I have been running about a good deal, with few days in town. Do you often read here?'

'Generally on Saturday afternoon.'

Buckland glanced at the open volume and caught a heading, 'Apologetic Theology.'

'Still at the works?'

'Yes; I shall be there till Christmas—no longer.'

'Are you by chance disengaged tomorrow? Could you dine with me? I shall be alone; perhaps you don't mind that? We could exchange views on "fate, free-will, foreknowledge absolute."'

Godwin accepted the invitation, and Warricombe, unable to linger, took leave of him.

They met the next evening in Buckland's rooms, not far from the Houses of Parliament. Commonplace comfort was the note of these quarters. Peak wondered that a man who had it in his power to surround himself with evidences of taste should be content to dwell thus. His host seemed to detect this thought in the glances Godwin cast about him.

'Nothing but a *pied-à-terre*. I have been here three or four years, but I don't think of it as a home. I suppose I shall settle somewhere before long: yet, on the whole, what does it matter where one lives? There's something in the atmosphere of our time that makes one indisposed to strike roots in the old way. Who knows how long there'll be such a thing as real property? We are getting to think of ourselves as lodgers; it's as well to be indifferent about a notice to quit.'

'Many people would still make a good fight for the old homes,' replied Peak.

'Yes; I daresay I should myself, if I were a family man. A wife and children are strong persuasions to conservatism. In those who have anything, that's to say. Let the families who have nothing learn how they stand in point of numbers, and we shall see what we shall see.'

'And you are doing your best to teach them that.'

Buckland smiled.

'A few other things at the same time. One isn't necessarily an anarchist, you know.'

'What enormous faith you must have in the metaphysical powers of the multitude!'

'Trenchant! But say, rather, in the universal self-interest. That's the trait of human nature which we have in mind when we speak of enlightenment. The aim of practical Radicalism is to instruct men's selfishness. Astonishing how capable it is of being instructed! The mistake of the Socialist lies in his crediting men with far too much self-esteem, far too little perception of their own limits. The characteristic of mankind at large is humility.'

Peak began to understand his old acquaintance; he had imagined him less acute. Gratified by the smile of interest, Warricombe added:

'There are forces of madness; I have shown you that I make allowance for them. But they are only dangerous so long as privilege allies itself with hypocrisy. The task of the modern civiliser is to sweep away sham idealisms.'

'I agree with you,' Godwin replied.

With sudden change of mood, Buckland began to speak of an indifferent topic of the day, and in a few minutes they sat down to dinner.

Not till the welcome tobacco blended its aroma with that of coffee did a frankly personal note sound in their conversation.

'So at Christmas you are free,' said Warricombe. 'You still think of leaving London?'

'I have decided to go down into Devonshire.'

'The seaside?'

'I shall stay first of all in Exeter,' Godwin replied, with deliberation; 'one can get hold of books there.'

'Yes, especially of the ecclesiastical colour.'

'You are still unable to regard my position with anything but contempt?' Peak asked, looking steadily at the critical face.

'Come now; what does it all mean? Of course I quite understand how tolerant the Church is becoming: I know what latitude it permits in its servants. But what do you propose to yourself?'

'Precisely what you call the work of the civiliser—to attack sham ideals.'

'As for instance——?'

'The authority of the mob,' answered Peak, suavely.

'Your clericalism is political, then?'

'To a great extent.'

'I discern a vague sort of consistency in this. You regard the Church formulas as merely symbolical—useful for the purposes of the day?'

'Rather for the purposes of eternity.'

'In the human sense.'

'In every sense.'

Warricombe perceived that no directness of questioning would elicit literal response, and on the whole this relieved him. To hear Godwin Peak using the language of a fervent curate would have excited in him something more than disgust. It did not seem impossible that a nature like Peak's—intellectually arrogant, vehemently anti-popular—should have been attracted by the traditions, the social prestige, of the Anglican Church; nor at all unlikely that a mind so constituted should justify a seeming acceptance of dogmas, which in the strict sense it despised. But he was made uneasy by his ignorance of Peak's private life during the years since their parting at College. He did not like to think of the possible establishment of intimacy between this man of low origin, uncertain career, boundless ambition, and the household of Martin Warricombe. There could be no doubt that Peak had decided to go to Exeter because of the social prospects recently opened to him. In the vulgar phrase, he had probably 'taken stock' of Mr. Warricombe's idiosyncrasy, and saw therein a valuable opportunity for a theological student, who at the same time was a devotee of natural science. To be sure, the people at Exeter could be put on their guard. On the other hand, Peak had plainly avowed his desire to form social connections of the useful kind; in his position such an aim was essential, a mere matter of course.

Godwin's voice interrupted this train of thought.

'Let me ask you a plain question. You have twice been kind enough to introduce me to your home as a friend of yours. Am I guilty of presumption in hoping that your parents will continue to regard me as an acquaintance? I trust there's no need to assure you that I know the meaning of discretion.'

An appeal to Buckland's generosity seldom failed. Yes, it was true that he had more than once encouraged the hope now frankly expressed. Indulging a correspondent frankness, he might explain that Peak's position was so distasteful to him that it disturbed the future with many kinds of uncertainty. But this would be churlish. He must treat his guest as a gentleman, so long as nothing compelled him to take the less agreeable view.

'My dear Peak, let us have none of these formalities. My parents have distinctly invited you to go and see them whenever you are in the neighbourhood. I am quite sure they will help to make your stay in Exeter a pleasant one.'

Therewith closed the hazardous dialogue. Warricombe turned at once to a safe topic—that of contemporary fiction, and they chatted pleasantly enough for the rest of the evening.

Not many days after this, Godwin received by post an envelope which contained certain proof sheets, and therewith a note in which the editor of *The Critical Review* signified his acceptance of a paper entitled 'The New Sophistry.' The communication was originally addressed to Earwaker, who had scribbled at the foot, 'Correct, if you are alive, and send back to Dolby.'

The next morning he did not set out as usual for Rotherhithe. Through the night he had not closed his eyes; he was in a state of nervousness which bordered on fever. A dozen times he had read over the proofs, with throbbing pulse, with exultant self-admiration: but the printer's errors which had caught his eye, and a few faults of phrase, were still uncorrected. What a capital piece of writing it was! What a flagellation of M'Naughten and all his tribe! If this did not rouse echoes in the literary world——

Through the long day he sat in languor or paced his room like one made restless by pain. Only when the gloom of nightfall obliged him to light his lamp did he at length sit down to the table and carefully revise the proofs, pen in hand. When he had made up the packet for post, he wrote to Earwaker.

'I had forgotten all about this thing. Proofs have gone to Dolby. I have not signed; probably he would object to my doing so. As it is, the paper can be ascribed to anyone, and attention thus excited. We shall see paragraphs attributing it to men of mark—perhaps scandal will fix it on a bishop. In any case, don't let out the secret. I beg this seriously, and for a solid reason. Not a word to anyone, however intimate. If Dolby betrays *your* name, grin and bear it. I depend upon your friendship.'

II

IN A BY-WAY which declines from the main thoroughfare of Exeter, and bears the name of Longbrook Street, is a row of small houses placed above long strips of sloping garden. They are old and plain, with no architectural feature calling for mention, unless it be the latticed porch which gives the doors an awkward quaintness. Just beyond, the road crosses a hollow, and begins the ascent of a hill here interposed between the city and the island-winding valley of Exe. The little terrace may be regarded as urban or rural, according to the tastes and occasions of those who dwell there. In one direction, a walk of five minutes will conduct to the middle of High Street, and in the other it takes scarcely longer to reach the open country.

On the upper floor of one of these cottages, Godwin Peak had made his abode. Sitting-room and bedchamber, furnished with homely comfort, answered to his bachelor needs, and would allow of his receiving without embarrassment any visitor whom fortune might send him. Of quietness he was assured, for a widow and her son, alike remarkable for sobriety of demeanour, were the only persons who shared the house with him. Mrs. Roots could not compare in grace and skill with the little Frenchwoman who had sweetened his existence at Peckham Rye, but her zeal made amends for natural deficiency, and the timorous respect with which she waited upon him was by no means disagreeable to Godwin. Her reply to a request or suggestion was always, 'If you please, sir.' Throughout the day she went so tranquilly about her domestic duties, that Godwin seldom heard anything except the voice of the cuckoo-clock, a pleasant sound to him. Her son, employed at a nurseryman's, was a great sinewy fellow with a face of such ruddiness that it seemed to diffuse warmth; on Sunday afternoon, whatever the state of the sky, he sat behind the house in his shirt-sleeves, and smoked a pipe as he contemplated the hart's-tongue which grew there upon a rockery.

'The gentleman from London'—so Mrs. Roots was wont to style her lodger in speaking with neighbours—had brought his books with him; they found place on a few shelves. His microscope had its stand by the window, and one or two other scientific implements lay about the room. The cabinets bequeathed to him by Mr. Gunnery he had sent to Twybridge, to remain in his mother's care. In taking the lodgings, he described himself merely as a student, and gave his landlady to understand that he hoped to remain under her roof for at least a year. Of his extreme respectability, the widow could entertain no doubt, for he dressed with aristocratic finish, attended services at the Cathedral and elsewhere very frequently, and made the most punctual payments. Moreover, a casual remark had informed her that he was on friendly terms with Mr. Martin Warricombe, whom her son knew as a gentleman of distinction. He often sat up very late at night, but, doubtless, that was the practice of Londoners. No lodger could have given less trouble, or have acknowledged with more courtesy all that was done for his convenience.

No one ever called upon Mr. Peak, but he was often from home for many hours together, probably on visits to great people in city or country. It seemed rather strange, however, that the postman so seldom brought anything for him. Though he had now been more than two months in the house, he had received only three letters, and those at long intervals.

Noticeable was the improvement in his health since his arrival here. The pallor of his cheeks was giving place to a wholesome tinge; his eye was brighter; he showed more disposition to converse, and was readier with pleasant smiles. Mr. Roots even heard him singing in his bedroom—though, oddly enough, it was a secular song on Sunday morning. The weekly bills for food, which at first had been very modest, grew richer in items. Godwin had, in fact, never felt so well. He extended his walks in every direction, sometimes rambling up the valley to sleepy little towns where he could rest in the parlours of old inns, sometimes striking across country to this or that point of the sea-coast, or making his way to the nearer summits of Dartmoor, noble in their wintry desolation. He marked with delight every promise of returning spring. When he could only grant himself a walk of an hour or two in the sunny afternoon, there was many a deep lane within easy reach, where the gorse gleamed in masses of gold, and the little oak-trees in the hedges were ruddy with last year's clinging leafage, and catkins hung from the hazels, and the fresh green of sprouting ivy crept over bank and wall. Had he now been in London, the morning would have awakened him to fog and slush and misery. As it was, when he looked out upon the glow of sunrise, he felt the sweet air breathing health into his frame and vigour into his mind. There were moments when he could all but say of himself that he was at peace with the world.

As on a morning towards the end of March, when a wind from the Atlantic swept spaces of brightest blue amid the speeding clouds, and sang joyously as it rushed over hill and dale. It was the very day for an upland walk, for a putting forth of one's strength in conflict with boisterous gusts and sudden showers, that give a taste of earth's nourishment. But Godwin had something else in view. After breakfast, he sat down to finish a piece of work which had occupied him for two or three days, a translation from a German periodical. His mind wrought easily, and he often hummed an air as his pen moved over the paper. When the task was completed, he rolled his papers and the pamphlet together, put them into the pocket of his overcoat, and presently went forth.

Twenty minutes' walk brought him to the Warricombes' house. It was his second call within the present week, but such assiduity had not hitherto been his wont. Though already summoned twice or thrice by express invitation, he was sparing of voluntary visits. Having asked for Mr. Warricombe, he was forthwith conducted to the study. In the welcome which greeted his appearance, he could detect no suspicion of simulated warmth, though his ear had unsurpassable discrimination.

'Have you looked through it?' Martin exclaimed, as he saw the foreign periodical in his visitor's hand.

'I have written a rough translation'——

'Oh, how could you think of taking such trouble! These things are sent to me by the dozen—I might say, by the cartload. My curiosity would have been amply satisfied if you had just told me the drift of the thing.'

'It seemed to me,' said Peak, modestly, 'that the paper was worth a little careful thought. I read it rapidly at first, but found myself drawn to it again. It states the point of view of the average scientific mind with such remarkable clearness, that I wished to think it over, and the best way was to do so pen in hand.'

'Well, if you really did it on your own account'——

Mr. Warricombe took the offered sheets and glanced at the first of them.

'My only purpose,' said Godwin, 'in calling again so soon was to leave this with you.'

He made as though he would take his departure.

'You want to get home again? Wait at least till this shower is over. I enjoy that pelting of spring rain against the window. In a minute or two we shall have the laurels flashing in the sunshine, as if they were hung with diamonds.'

They stood together looking out on to the garden. Presently their talk returned to the German disquisition, which was directed against the class of quasi-scientific authors attacked by Peak himself in his *Critical* article. In the end Godwin sat down and began to read the translation he had made, Mr. Warricombe listening with a thoughtful smile. From time to time the reader paused and offered a comment, endeavouring to show that the arguments were merely plausible; his air was that of placid security, and he seemed to enjoy the irony which often fell from his lips. Martin frequently scrutinised him, and always with a look of interest which betokened grave reflection.

'Here,' said Godwin at one point, 'he has a note citing a passage from Reusch's book on *The Bible and Nature*. If I am not mistaken, he misrepresents his author, though perhaps not intentionally.'

'You know the book?'

'I have studied it carefully, but I don't possess it. I thought I remembered this particular passage very well.'

'Is it a work of authority?'

'Yes; it is very important. Unfortunately, it hasn't yet been translated. Rather bulky, but I shouldn't mind doing it myself if I were sure of finding a publisher.'

'*The Bible and Nature*,' said Martin, musingly. 'What is his scheme? How does he go to work?'

Godwin gave a brief but lucid description of the book, and Mr. Warricombe listened gravely. When there had been silence for some moments, the latter spoke in a tone he had never yet used when conversing with Peak. He allowed himself, for the first time, to betray a troubled doubt on the subject under discussion.

'So he makes a stand at Darwinism as it affects man?'

Peak had yet no means of knowing at what point Martin himself 'made a stand.' Modes of reconcilement between scientific discovery and religious tradition are so very numerous, and the geologist was only now beginning to touch upon these topics with his young acquaintance. That his mind was not perfectly at ease amid the conflicts of the day, Godwin soon perceived, and by this time he had clear assurance that Martin would willingly thrash out the whole debate with anyone who seemed capable of supporting orthodox tenets by reasoning not unacceptable to a man of broad views. The negativist of course assumed from the first that Martin, however respectable his knowledge, was far from possessing the scientific mind, and each conversation had supplied him with proofs of this defect; it was not at all in the modern spirit that the man of threescore years pursued his geological and kindred researches, but with the calm curiosity of a liberal intellect which has somehow taken this direction instead of devoting itself to literary study. At bottom, Godwin had no little sympathy with Mr. Warricombe; he too, in spite of his militant instincts, dwelt by preference amid purely human interests. He grasped with firm intelligence the modes of thought which distinguish scientific men, but his nature did not prompt him to a consistent application of them. Personal liking enabled him to subdue the impulses of disrespect which, under other circumstances, would have made it difficult for him to act with perfection his present part. None the less, his task was one of infinite delicacy. Martin Warricombe was not the man to unbosom himself on trivial instigation. It must be a powerful influence which would persuade him to reveal whatever self-questionings lay beneath his genial good breeding and long-established acquiescence in a practical philosophy. Godwin guarded himself against his eager emotions; one false note, one syllable of indiscretion, and his aims might be hopelessly defeated.

'Yes,' was his reply to the hesitating question. 'He argues strenuously against the descent of man. If I understand him, he regards the concession of this point as impossible.'

Martin was deep in thought. He held a paper-knife bent upon his knee, and his smooth, delicate features wore an unquiet smile.

'Do you know Hebrew, Mr. Peak?'

The question came unexpectedly, and Godwin could not help a momentary confusion, but he covered it with the tone of self-reproach.

'I am ashamed to say that I am only now taking it up seriously.'

'I don't think you need be ashamed,' said Martin, good-naturedly. 'Even a mind as active as yours must postpone some studies. Reusch, I suppose, is sound on that head?'

The inquiry struck Godwin as significant. So Mr. Warricombe attached importance to the verbal interpretation of the Old Testament.

'Distinctly an authority,' he replied. 'He devotes whole chapters to a minute examination of the text.'

'If you had more leisure,' Martin began, deliberately, when he had again reflected, 'I should be disposed to urge you to undertake that translation.'

Peak appeared to meditate.

'Has the book been used by English writers?' the other inquired.

'A good deal.—It was published in the sixties, but I read it in a new edition dated a few years ago. Reusch has kept pace with the men of science. It would be very interesting to compare the first form of the book with the latest.'

'It would, very.'

Raising his head from the contemplative posture, Godwin exclaimed, with a laugh of zeal:

'I think I must find time to translate him. At all events, I might address a proposal to some likely publisher. Yet I don't know how I should assure him of my competency.'

'Probably a specimen would be the surest testimony.'

'Yes. I might do a few chapters.'

Mr. Warricombe's lapse into silence and brevities intimated to Godwin that it was time to take leave. He always quitted this room with reluctance. Its air of luxurious culture affected his senses deliciously, and he hoped that he might some day be permitted to linger among the cabinets and the library shelves. There were so many books he would have liked to take down, some with titles familiar to him, others which kindled his curiosity when he chanced to observe them. The library abounded in such works as only a wealthy man can purchase, and Godwin, who had examined some of them at the British Museum, was filled with the humaner kind of envy on seeing them in Mr. Warricombe's possession. Those publications of the Palæontological Society, one volume of which (a part of Davidson's superb work on the *Brachiopoda*) even now lay open within sight—his hand trembled with a desire to touch them! And those maps of the Geological Surveys, British and foreign, how he would have enjoyed a day's poring over them!

He rose, but Martin seemed in no haste to bring the conversation to an end.

'Have you read M'Naughten's much-discussed book?'

'Yes.'

'Did you see the savage attack in the *Critical* not long ago?'

Godwin smiled, and made quiet answer:

'I should think it was the last word of scientific bitterness and intolerance.'

'Scientific?' repeated Martin, doubtfully. 'I don't think the writer was a man of science. I saw it somewhere attributed to Huxley, but that was preposterous. To begin with, Huxley would have signed his name; and, again, his English is better. The article seemed to me to be stamped with literary rancour; it was written by some man who envies M'Naughten's success.'

Peak kept silence. Martin's censure of the anonymous author's style stung him to the quick, and he had much ado to command his countenance.

'Still,' pursued the other, 'I felt that much of his satire was only too well pointed. M'Naughten is suggestive, very suggestive; but one comes across books of the same purpose which can have no result but to injure their cause with all thinking people.'

'I have seen many such,' remarked Godwin.

Mr. Warricombe stepped to a bookcase and took down a small volume.

'I wonder whether you know this book of Ampère's, *La Grèce, Rome, et Dante*? Delightful for odd moments!—There came into my mind a passage here at the beginning, apropos of what we were saying: "Il faut souvent un vrai courage pour persister dans un opinion juste en dépit de ses défenseurs."—Isn't that capital?'

Peak received it with genuine appreciation; for once he was able to laugh unfeignedly. The aphorism had so many applications from his own point of view.

'Excellent!—I don't remember to have seen the book.'

'Take it, if you care to.'

This offer seemed a distinct advance in Mr. Warricombe's friendliness. Godwin felt a thrill of encouragement.

'Then you will let me keep this translation for a day or two?' Martin added, indicating the sheets of manuscript. 'I am greatly obliged to you for enabling me to read the thing.'

They shook hands. Godwin had entertained a slight hope that he might be asked to stay to luncheon; but it could not be much past twelve o'clock, and on the whole there was every reason for feeling satisfied with the results of his visit. Before long he would probably receive another invitation to dine. So with light step he went out into the hall, where Martin again shook hands with him.

The sky had darkened over, and a shrilling of the wind sounded through the garden foliage—fir, and cypress, and laurel. Just as Godwin reached the gate, he was met by Miss Warricombe and Fanny, who were returning from a walk. They wore the costume appropriate to March weather in the country, close-fitting, defiant of gusts; and their cheeks glowed with health. As he exchanged greetings with them, Peak received a new impression of the sisters. He admired the physical vigour which enabled them to take delight in such a day as this, when girls of poorer blood and ignoble nurture would shrink from the sky's showery tumult, and protect their surface elegance by the fireside. Impossible for Sidwell and Fanny to be anything but graceful, for at all times they were perfectly unaffected.

'There'll be another storm in a minute,' said the younger of them, looking with interest to the quarter whence the wind came. 'How suddenly they burst! What a rush! and then in five minutes the sky is clear again.'

Her eyes shone as she turned laughingly to Peak.

'You're not afraid of getting wet? Hadn't you better come under cover?'

'Here it is!' exclaimed Sidwell, with quiet enjoyment. 'Take shelter for a minute or two, Mr. Peak.'

They led the way to the portico, where Godwin stood with them and watched the squall. A moment's downpour of furious rain was followed by heavy hailstones, which drove horizontally before the shrieking wind. The prospect had wrapped itself in grey gloom. At a hundred yards' distance, scarcely an object could be distinguished; the storm-cloud swooped so low that its skirts touched the branches of tall elms, a streaming, rushing raggedness.

'Don't you enjoy that?' Fanny asked of Godwin.

'Indeed I do.'

'You should be on Dartmoor in such weather,' said Sidwell. 'Father and I were once caught in storms far worse than this—far better, I ought to say, for I never knew anything so terrifically grand.'

Already it was over. The gusts diminished in frequency and force, the hail ceased, the core of blackness was passing over to the eastern sky. Fanny ran out into the garden, and pointed upward.

'Look where the sunlight is coming!'

An uncloaked patch of heaven shone with colour like that of the girl's eyes—faint, limpid blue. Reminding himself that to tarry longer in this company would be imprudent, Godwin bade the sisters good-morning. The frank heartiness with which Fanny pressed his hand, sent him on his way exultant. Not too strong a word; for, independently of his wider ambitions, he was moved and gratified by the thought that kindly feeling towards him had sprung up in such a heart as this. Nor did conscience so much as whisper a reproach. With unreflecting ingenuousness he tasted the joy as if it were his right. Thus long he had waited, through years of hungry manhood, for the look, the tone, which were in harmony with his native sensibilities. Fanny Warricombe was but an undeveloped girl, yet he valued her friendship above the passionate attachment of any woman bred on a lower social plane. Had it been possible, he would have kissed her fingers with purest reverence.

When out of sight of the house, he paused to regard the sky again. Its noontide splendour was dazzling; masses of rosy cloud sailed swiftly from horizon to horizon, the azure deepening about them. Yet before long the west would again send forth its turbulent spirits, and so the girls might perhaps be led to think of him.

By night the weather grew more tranquil. There was a full moon, and its radiance illumined the ever-changing face of heaven with rare grandeur. Godwin could not shut himself up over his books; he wandered far away into the country, and let his thoughts have freedom.

He was learning to review with calmness the course by which he had reached his now steadfast resolve. A revulsion such as he had experienced after his first day of simulated orthodoxy, half a year ago, could not be of lasting effect, for it was opposed to the whole tenor of his mature thought. It spoilt his holiday, but had no chance of persisting after his return to the atmosphere of Rotherhithe. That he should have been capable of such emotion was, he said to himself, in the just order of things; callousness in the first stages of an undertaking which demanded gross hypocrisy would signify an ignoble nature—a nature, indeed, which could never have been submitted to trial of so strange a kind. But he had overcome himself; that phase of difficulty was outlived, and henceforth he saw only the material obstacles to be defied by his vindicated will.

What he proposed to himself was a life of deliberate baseness.

Godwin Peak never tried to play the sophist with this fact. But he succeeded in justifying himself by a consideration of the circumstances which had compelled him to a vile expedience. Had his project involved conscious wrong to other persons, he would scarcely even have speculated on its possibilities. He was convinced that no mortal could suffer harm, even if he accomplished the uttermost of his desires. Whom was he in danger of wronging? The conventional moralist would cry: Everyone with whom he came in slightest contact! But a mind such as Peak's has very little to do with conventional morality. Injury to himself he foresaw and accepted; he could never be the man nature designed in him; and he must frequently submit to a self-contempt which would be very hard to bear. Those whom he consistently deceived, how would they suffer? Martin Warricombe to begin with. Martin was a man who had lived his life, and whose chief care would now be to keep his mind at rest in the faiths which had served him from youth onwards. In that very purpose, Godwin believed he could assist him. To see a young man, of strong and trained intellect, championing the old beliefs, must doubtless be a source of reassurance to one in Martin's position. Reassurance derived from a lie?—And what matter, if the outcome were genuine, if it lasted until the man himself was no more? Did not every form of content result from illusion? What was truth without the mind of the believer?

Society, then—at all events that part of it likely to be affected by his activity? Suppose him an ordained priest, performing all the functions implied in that office. Why, to think only of examples recognised by the public at large, how would he differ for the worse from this, that, and the other clergyman who taught Christianity, all but with blunt avowal, as a scheme of human ethics? No wolf in sheep's clothing he! He plotted against no man's pocket, no woman's honour; he had no sinister design of sapping the faith of congregations—a scheme, by-the-bye, which fanatic liberators might undertake with vast self-approval. If by a word he could have banished religious dogma from the minds of the multitude, he would not have cared to utter it. Wherein lay, indeed, a scruple to be surmounted. The Christian priest must be a man of humble temper; he must be willing, even eager, to sit down among the poor in spirit as well as in estate, and impart to them his unworldly solaces. Yes, but it had always been recognised that some men who could do the Church good service were personally unfitted for those meek ministrations. His place was in the hierarchy of intellect; if he were to be active at all, it must be with the brain. In his conversation with Buckland Warricombe, last October, he had spoken not altogether insincerely. Let him once be a member of the Church militant, and his heart would go with many a stroke against that democratic movement which desired, among other things, the Church's abolition. He had power of utterance. Roused to combat by the proletarian challenge, he could make his voice ring in the ears of men, even though he used a symbolism which he would not by choice have adopted.

For it was natural that he should anticipate distinction. Whatever his lot in life, he would not be able to rest among an inglorious brotherhood. If he allied himself with the Church, the Church must assign him leadership, whether titular or not was of small moment. In days to come, let people, if they would, debate his history, canvass his convictions. His scornful pride invited any degree of publicity, when once his position was secure.

But in the meantime he was leaving aside the most powerful of all his motives, and one which demanded closest scrutiny. Not ambition, in any ordinary sense; not desire of material luxury; no incentive recognised by unprincipled schemers first suggested his dishonour. This edifice of subtle untruth, had for its foundation a mere ideal of sexual love. For the winning of some chosen woman, men have wrought vehemently, have ruined themselves and others, have achieved triumphs noble or degrading. But Godwin Peak had for years contemplated the possibility of baseness at the impulse of a craving for love capable only of a social (one might say, of a political) definition. The woman throned in his imagination was no individual, but the type of an order. So strangely had circumstances moulded him, that he could not brood on a desire of spiritual affinities, could not, as is natural to most cultivated men, inflame himself with the ardour of soul reaching to soul; he was preoccupied with the contemplation of qualities which characterise a class. The sense of social distinctions was so burnt into him, that he could not be affected by any pictured charm of mind or person in a woman who had not the stamp of gentle birth and breeding. If once he were admitted to the intimacy of such women, then, indeed, the canons of selection would have weight with him; no man more capable of disinterested choice. Till then, the ideal which possessed him was merely such an assemblage of qualities as would excite the democrat to disdain or fury.

In Sidwell Warricombe this ideal found an embodiment; but Godwin did not thereupon come to the conclusion that Sidwell was the wife he desired. Her influence had the effect of deciding his career, but he neither imagined himself in love with her, nor tried to believe that he might win her love if he set himself to the endeavour. For the first time he was admitted to familiar intercourse with a woman whom he *could* make the object of his worship. He thought much of her; day and night her figure stood before him; and this had continued now for half a year. Still he neither was, nor dreamt himself, in love with her. Before long his acquaintance would include many of her like, and at any moment Sidwell might pale in the splendour of another's loveliness.

But what reasoning could defend the winning of a wife by false pretences? This, his final aim, could hardly be achieved without grave wrong to the person whose welfare must in the nature of things be a prime motive with him. The deception he had practised must sooner or later be discovered; lifelong hypocrisy was incompatible with perfect marriage; some day he must either involve his wife in a system of dishonour, or with her consent relinquish the false career, and find his happiness in the obscurity to which he would then be relegated. Admit the wrong. Grant that some woman whom he loved supremely must, on his account, pass through a harsh trial—would it not be in his power to compensate her amply? The wife whom he imagined (his idealism in this matter was of a crudity which made the strangest contrast with his habits of thought on every other subject) would be ruled by her emotions, and that part of her nature would be wholly under his governance. Religious fanaticism could not exist in her, for in that case she would never have attracted him. Little by little she would learn to think as he did, and her devotedness must lead her to pardon his deliberate insincerities. Godwin had absolute faith in his power of dominating the woman whom he should inspire with tenderness. This was a feature of his egoism, the explanation of those manifold inconsistencies inseparable from his tortuous design. He regarded his love as something so rare, so vehement, so exalting, that its bestowal must seem an abundant recompense for any pain of which he was the cause.

Thus, with perfect sincerity of argument, did Godwin Peak face the undertaking to which he was committed. Incidents might perturb him, but his position was no longer a cause of uneasiness —save, indeed, at those moments when he feared lest any of his old acquaintances might hear of him before time was ripe. This was a source of anxiety, but inevitable; one of the risks he dared.

Had it seemed possible, he would have kept even from his mother the secret of his residence at Exeter; but this would have necessitated the establishment of some indirect means of communication with her, a troublesome and uncertain expedience. He shrank from leaving her in ignorance of his whereabouts, and from passing a year or two without knowledge of her condition. And, on the whole, there could not be much danger in this correspondence. The Moxeys, who alone of his friends had ever been connected with Twybridge, were now absolutely without interests in that quarter. From them he had stolen away, only acquainting Christian at the last moment, in a short letter, with his departure from London. 'It will be a long time before we again see each other—at least, I think so. Don't trouble your head about me. I can't promise to write, and shall be sorry not to hear how things go with you; but may all happen as you wish!' In the same way he had dealt with Earwaker, except that his letter to Staple Inn was much longer, and contained hints which the philosophic journalist might perchance truly interpret. ' "He either fears his fate too much"—you know the old song. I have set out on my life's adventure. I have gone to seek that without which life is no longer worth having. Forgive my shabby treatment of you, old friend. You cannot help me, and your displeasure would be a hindrance in my path. A last piece of counsel: throw overboard the weekly rag, and write for people capable of understanding you.' Earwaker was not at all likely to institute a search; he would accept the situation, and wait with quiet curiosity for its upshot. No doubt he and Moxey would discuss the affair together, and any desire Christian might have to hunt for his vanished comrade would yield before the journalist's surmises. No one else had any serious reason for making inquiries. Probably he might dwell in Devonshire, as long as he chose, without fear of encountering anyone from his old world.

Occasionally—as to-night, under the full moon—he was able to cast off every form of trouble, and rejoice in his seeming liberty. Though every step in the life before him was an uncertainty, an appeal to fortune, his faith in himself grasped strongly at assurance of success. Once more he felt himself a young man, with unwearied energies; he had shaken off the burden of those ten frustrate years, and kept only their harvest of experience. Old in one sense, in another youthful, he had vast advantages over such men as would henceforth be his competitors—the complex brain, the fiery heart, passion to desire, and skill in attempting. If with such endowment he could not win the prize which most men claim as a mere matter of course, a wife of social instincts correspondent with his own, he must indeed be luckless. But he was not doomed to defeat! Foretaste of triumph urged the current of his blood and inflamed him with exquisite ardour. He sang aloud in the still lanes the hymns of youth and of love; and, when weariness brought him back to his lonely dwelling, he laid his head on the pillow, and slept in dreamless calm.

As for the details of his advance towards the clerical state, he had decided to resume his career at the point where it was interrupted by Andrew Peak. Twice had his education received a check from hostile circumstances: when domestic poverty compelled him to leave school for Mr. Moxey's service, and when shame drove him from Whitelaw College. In reflecting upon his own character and his lot he gave much weight to these irregularities, no doubt with justice. In both cases he was turned aside from the way of natural development and opportunity. He would now complete his academic course by taking the London degree at which he had long ago aimed; the preliminary examination might without difficulty be passed this summer, and next year he might write himself Bachelor of Arts. A return to the studies of boyhood probably accounted in some measure for the frequent gaiety which he attributed to improving health and revived hopes. Everything he undertook was easy to him, and by a pleasant self-deception he made the passing of a school task his augury of success in greater things.

During the spring he was indebted to the Warricombes' friendship for several new acquaintances. A clergyman named Lilywhite, often at the Warricombes' house, made friendly overtures to him; the connection might be a useful one, and Godwin made the most of it. Mr. Lilywhite was a man of forty—well-read, of scientific tastes, an active pedestrian. Peak had no difficulty in associating with him on amicable terms. With Mrs. Lilywhite, the mother of six children and possessed of many virtues, he presently became a favourite,—she saw in him 'a great deal of quiet moral force.' One or two families of good standing made him welcome at their houses; society is very kind to those who seek its benefits with recognised credentials. The more he saw of these wealthy and tranquil middle-class people, the more fervently did he admire the gracefulness of their existence. He had not set before himself an imaginary ideal; the girls and women were sweet, gentle, perfect in manner, and, within limits, of bright intelligence. He was conscious of benefiting greatly, and not alone in things extrinsic, by the atmosphere of such homes.

Nature's progress towards summer kept him in a mood of healthful enjoyment. From the window of his sitting-room he looked over the opposite houses to Northernhay, the hill where once stood Rougemont Castle, its wooded declivities now fashioned into a public garden. He watched the rooks at their building in the great elms, and was gladdened when the naked branches began to deck themselves, day by day the fresh verdure swelling into soft, graceful outline. In his walks he pried eagerly for the first violet, welcomed the earliest blackthorn blossom; every common flower of field and hedgerow gave him a new, keen pleasure. As was to be expected he found the same impulses strong in Sidwell Warricombe and her sister. Sidwell could tell him of secret spots where the wood-sorrel made haste to flower, or where the white violet breathed its fragrance in security from common pilferers. Here was the safest and pleasantest matter for conversation. He knew that on such topics he could talk agreeably enough, revealing without stress or importunity his tastes, his powers, his attainments. And it seemed to him that Sidwell listened with growing interest. Most certainly her father encouraged his visits to the house, and Mrs. Warricombe behaved to him with increase of suavity.

In the meantime he had purchased a copy of Reusch's *Bibel und Natur*, and had made a translation of some fifty pages. This experiment he submitted to a London publishing house, with proposals for the completion of the work; without much delay there came a civil letter of excuse, and with it the sample returned. Another attempt again met with rejection. This failure did not trouble him. What he really desired was to read through his version of Reusch with Martin Warricombe, and before long he had brought it to pass that Martin requested a perusal of the manuscript as it advanced, which it did but slowly. Godwin durst not endanger his success in the examination by encroaching upon hours of necessary study; his leisure was largely sacrificed to *Bibel und Natur*, and many an evening of calm golden loveliness, when he longed to be amid the fields, passed in vexatious imprisonment. The name of Reusch grew odious to him, and he revenged himself for the hypocrisy of other hours by fierce scorn, cast audibly at this laborious exegetist.

III

IT OCCASIONALLY HAPPENS that a woman whose early life has been directed by native silliness and social bias, will submit to a tardy education at the hands of her own children. Thus was it with Mrs. Warricombe.

She came of a race long established in squirearchic dignity amid heaths and woodlands. Her breeding was pure through many generations of the paternal and maternal lines, representative of a physical type, fortified in the males by much companionship with horse and hound, and by the corresponding country pursuits of dowered daughters. At the time of her marriage she had no charms of person more remarkable than rosy comeliness and the symmetry of supple limb. As for the nurture of her mind, it had been intrusted to home-governesses of respectable incapacity. Martin Warricombe married her because she was one of a little circle of girls, much alike as to birth and fortune, with whom he had grown up in familiar communication. Timidity imposed restraints upon him which made his choice almost a matter of accident. As befalls often enough, the bethrothal became an accomplished fact whilst he was still doubting whether he desired it or not. When the fervour of early wedlock was outlived, he had no difficulty in accepting as a matter of course that his life's companion should be hopelessly illogical and at heart indifferent to everything but the small graces and substantial comforts of provincial existence. One of the advantages of wealth is that it allows husband and wife to keep a great deal apart without any show of mutual unkindness, a condition essential to happiness in marriage. Time fostered in them a calm attachment, independent of spiritual sympathy, satisfied with a common regard for domestic honour.

Not that Mrs. Warricombe remained in complete ignorance of her husband's pursuits; social forms would scarcely have allowed this, seeing that she was in constant intercourse, as hostess or guest, with Martin's scientific friends. Of fossils she necessarily knew something. Up to a certain point they amused her; she could talk of ammonites, of brachiopods, and would point a friend's attention to the *Calceola sandalina* which Martin prized so much. The significance of palæontology she dimly apprehended, for in the early days of their union her husband had felt it desirable to explain to her what was meant by geologic time, and how he reconciled his views on that subject with the demands of religious faith. Among the books which he induced her to read were Buckland's Bridgewater Treatise and the works of Hugh Miller. The intellectual result was chaotic, and Mrs. Warricombe settled at last into a comfortable private opinion that though the record of geology might be trustworthy that of the Bible was more so. She would admit that there was no impiety in accepting the evidence of nature, but held to a secret conviction that it was safer to believe in Genesis. For anything beyond a quasi-permissible variance from Biblical authority as to the age of the world she was quite unprepared, and Martin, in his discretion, imparted to her nothing of the graver doubts which were wont to trouble him.

But as her children grew up, Mrs. Warricombe's mind and temper were insensibly modified by influences which operated through her maternal affections, influences no doubt aided by the progressive spirit of the time. The three boys—Buckland, Maurice, and Louis—were distinctly of a new generation. It needed some ingenuity to discover their points of kindred with paternal and maternal grandparents; nor even with father and mother had they much in common which observation could readily detect. Sidwell, up to at least her fifteenth year, seemed to present far less change of type. In her Mrs. Warricombe recognised a daughter, and not without solace. But Fanny again was a problematical nature, almost from the cradle. Latest born, she appeared to revive many characteristics of the youthful Buckland, so far as a girl could resemble her brother. It was a strange brood to cluster around Mrs. Warricombe. For many years the mother was kept in alternation between hopes and fears, pride and disapproval, the old hereditary habits of mind, and a new order of ideas which could only be admitted with the utmost slowness. Buckland's Radicalism deeply offended her; she marvelled how such depravity could display itself in a child of hers. Yet in the end her ancestral prejudices so far yielded as to allow of her smiling at sentiments which she once heard with horror. Maurice, whom she loved more tenderly, all but taught her to see the cogency of a syllogism—amiably set forth. And Louis, with his indolent good-nature, laughed her into a tolerance of many things which had moved her indignation. But it was to Sidwell that in the end she owed most. Beneath the surface of ordinary and rather backward girlhood, which discouraged her father's hopes, Sidwell was quietly developing a personality distinguished by the refinement of its ethical motives. Her orthodoxy seemed as unimpeachable as Mrs. Warricombe could desire, yet as she grew into womanhood, a curiosity, which in no way disturbed the tenor of her quietly contented life, led her to examine various forms of religion, ancient and modern, and even systems of philosophy which professed to establish a moral code, independent of supernatural faith. She was not of studious disposition—that is to say, she had never cared as a schoolgirl to do more mental work than was required of her, and even now it was seldom that she read for more than an hour or two in the day. Her habit was to dip into books, and meditate long on the first points which arrested her thoughts. Of continuous application she seemed incapable. She could read French, but did not attempt to pursue the other languages of which her teachers had given her a smattering. It pleased her best when she could learn from conversation. In this way she obtained some insight into her father's favourite sciences, occasionally making suggestions or inquiries which revealed a subtle if not an acute intelligence.

Little by little Mrs. Warricombe found herself changing places with the daughter whom she had regarded as wholly subject to her direction. Sidwell began to exercise an indeterminate control, the proofs of which were at length manifest in details of her mother's speech and demeanour. An exquisite social tact, an unfailing sincerity of moral judgment, a gentle force which operated as insensibly as the qualities of pure air: these were the points of character to which Mrs. Warricombe owed the humanisation observable when one compared her in 1885 with what she was, say, in 1874, when the sight of Professor Walsh moved her to acrimony, and when she conceived a pique against Professor Gale because the letter P has alphabetical precedence of W. Her limitations were of course the same as ever, and from her sons she had only learnt to be ashamed of announcing them too vehemently. Sidwell it was who had led her to that degree of genuine humility, which is not satisfied with hiding a fault but strives to amend it.

Martin Warricombe himself was not unaffected by the growth about him of young men and maidens who looked upon the world with new eyes, whose world, indeed, was another than that in which he had spent the better part of his life. In his case contact with the young generation tended to unsettlement, to a troublesome persistency of speculations which he would have preferred to dismiss altogether. At the time of his marriage, and for some years after, he was content to make a broad distinction between those intellectual pursuits which afforded him rather a liberal amusement than the pleasures of earnest study and the questions of metaphysical faith which concerned his heart and conscience. His native prejudices were almost as strong, and much the same, as those of his wife; but with the vagueness of emotional logic natural to his constitution, he satisfied himself that, by conceding a few inessential points, he left himself at liberty to follow the scientific movements of the day without damage to his religious convictions. The tolerant smile so frequently on his countenance was directed as often in the one quarter as in the other. Now it signified a gentle reproof of those men of science who, like Professor Walsh, 'went too far,' whose zeal for knowledge led them 'to forget the source of all true enlightenment;' now it expressed a forbearing sympathy with such as erred in the opposite direction, who were 'too literal in their interpretation of the sacred volume.' Amiable as the smile was, it betrayed weakness, and at moments Martin became unpleasantly conscious of indisposition to examine his own mind on certain points. His life, indeed, was one of debate postponed. As the realm of science extended, as his intercourse with men who frankly avowed their 'infidelity' grew more frequent, he ever and again said to himself that, one of these days, he must sit down and 'have it out' in a solemn self-searching. But for the most part he got on very well amid his inconsistencies. Religious faith has rarely any connection with reasoning. Martin believed because he believed, and avoided the impact of disagreeable arguments because he wished to do so.

The bent of his mind was anything but polemical; he cared not to spend time even over those authors whose attacks on the outposts of science, or whose elaborate reconcilements of old and new, might have afforded him some support. On the other hand, he altogether lacked that breadth of intellect which seeks to comprehend all the results of speculation, to discern their tendency, to derive from them a consistent theory of the nature of things. Though a man be well versed in a science such as palæontology it does not follow that he will view it in its philosophical relations. Martin had kept himself informed of all the facts appertaining to his study which the age brought forth, but without developing the new modes of mental life requisite for the recognition of all that such facts involved. The theories of evolution he did not venture openly to resist, but his acceptance of them was so half-hearted that practically he made no use of their teaching. He was no man of science, but an idler among the wonders which science uses for her own purposes.

He regarded with surprise and anxiety the tendencies early manifested in his son Buckland. Could he have had his way the lad would have grown up with an impossible combination of qualities, blending the enthusiasm of modern research with a spirit of expansive teleology. Whilst Buckland was still of boyish years, the father treated with bantering good-humour such outbreaks of irreverence as came immediately under his notice, weakly abstaining from any attempt at direct argument or influence. But, at a later time, there took place serious and painful discussions, and only when the young man had rubbed off his edges in the world's highways could Martin forget that stage of most unwelcome conflict.

At the death of his younger boy, Maurice, he suffered a blow which had results more abiding than the melancholy wherewith for a year or two his genial nature was overshadowed. From that day onwards he was never wholly at ease among the pursuits which had been wont to afford him an unfailing resource against whatever troubles. He could no longer accept and disregard, in a spirit of cheerful faith, those difficulties science was perpetually throwing in his way. The old smile of kindly tolerance had still its twofold meaning, but it was more evidently a disguise of indecision, and not seldom touched with sadness. Martin's life was still one of postponed debate, but he could not regard the day when conclusions would be demanded of him as indefinitely remote. Desiring to dwell in the familiar temporary abode, his structure of incongruities and facile reconcilements, he found it no longer weatherproof. The times were shaking his position with earthquake after earthquake. His sons (for he suspected that Louis was hardly less emancipated than Buckland) stood far aloof from him, and must in private feel contemptuous of his old-fashioned beliefs. In Sidwell, however, he had a companion more and more indispensable, and he could not imagine that *her* faith would ever give way before the invading spirit of agnosticism. Happily she was no mere pietist. Though he did not quite understand her attitude towards Christianity, he felt assured that Sidwell had thought deeply and earnestly of religion in all its aspects, and it was a solace to know that she found no difficulty in recognising the large claims of science. For all this, he could not deliberately seek her confidence, or invite her to a discussion of religious subjects. Some day, no doubt, a talk of that kind would begin naturally between them, and so strong was his instinctive faith in Sidwell that he looked forward to this future communing as to a certain hope of peace.

That a figure such as Godwin Peak, a young man of vigorous intellect, preparing to devote his life to the old religion, should excite Mr. Warricombe's interest was of course to be anticipated; and it seemed probable enough that Peak, exerting all the force of his character and aided by circumstances, might before long convert this advantage to a means of ascendency over the less self-reliant nature. But here was no instance of a dotard becoming the easy prey of a scientific Tartufe. Martin's intellect had suffered no decay. His hale features and dignified bearing expressed the mind which was ripened by sixty years of pleasurable activity, and which was learning to regard with steadier view the problems it had hitherto shirked. He could not change the direction nature had given to his thoughts, and prepossession would in some degree obscure his judgment where the merits and trustworthiness of a man in Peak's circumstances called for scrutiny; but self-respect guarded him against vulgar artifices, and a fine sensibility made it improbable that he would become the victim of any man in whom base motives predominated.

Left to his own impulses, he would still have proceeded with all caution in his offers of friendly services to Peak. A letter of carefully-worded admonition, which he received from his son, apprising him of Peak's resolve to transfer himself to Exeter, scarcely affected his behaviour when the young man appeared. It was but natural—he argued—that Buckland should look askance on a case of 'conversion'; for his own part, he understood that such a step might be prompted by interest, but he found it difficult to believe that to a man in Peak's position, the Church would offer temptation thus coercive. Nor could he discern in the candidate for a curacy any mark of dishonourable purpose. Faults, no doubt, were observable, among them a tendency to spiritual pride—which seemed (Martin could admit) an argument for, rather than against, his sincerity. The progress of acquaintance decidedly confirmed his favourable impressions; they were supported by the remarks of those among his friends to whom Peak presently became known.

It was not until Whitsuntide of the next year, when the student had been living nearly five months at Exeter, that Buckland again came down to visit his relatives. On the evening of his arrival, chancing to be alone with Sidwell, he asked her if Peak had been to the house lately.

'Not many days ago,' replied his sister, 'he lunched with us, and then sat with father for some time.'

'Does he come often?'

'Not very often. He is translating a German book which interests father very much.'

'Oh, what book?'

'I don't know. Father has only mentioned it in that way.'

They were in a little room sacred to the two girls, very daintily furnished and fragrant of sweet-brier, which Sidwell loved so much that, when the season allowed it, she often wore a little spray of it at her girdle. Buckland opened a book on the table, and, on seeing the title, exclaimed with a disparaging laugh:

'I can't get out of the way of this fellow M'Naughten! Wherever I go, there he lies about on the tables and chairs. I should have thought he was thoroughly smashed by an article that came out in the *Critical* last year.'

Sidwell smiled, evidently in no way offended.

'That article could "smash" nobody,' she made answer. 'It was too violent; it overshot the mark.'

'Not a bit of it!—So you read it, eh? You're beginning to read, are you?'

'In my humble way, Buckland.'

'M'Naughten, among other things. Humble enough, that, I admit.'

'I am not a great admirer of M'Naughten,' returned his sister, with a look of amusement.

'No? I congratulate you.—I wonder what Peak thinks of the book?'

'I really don't know.'

'Then let me ask another question. What do you think of Peak?'

Sidwell regarded him with quiet reflectiveness.

'I feel,' she said, 'that I don't know him very well yet. He is certainly interesting.'

'Yes, he is. Does he impress you as the kind of man likely to make a good clergyman?'

'I don't see any reason why he should not.'

Her brother mused, with wrinkles of dissatisfaction on his brow.

'Father gets to like him, you say?'

'Yes, I think father likes him.'

'Well, I suppose it's all right.'

'All right?'

'It's the most astounding thing that ever came under my observation,' exclaimed Buckland, walking away and then returning.

'That Mr. Peak should be studying for the Church?'

'Yes.'

'But do reflect more modestly!' urged Sidwell, with something that was not quite archness, though as near it as her habits of tone and features would allow. 'Why should you refuse to admit an error in your own way of looking at things? Wouldn't it be better to take this as a proof that intellect isn't necessarily at war with Christianity?'

'I never stated it so broadly as that,' returned her brother, with impatience. 'But I should certainly have maintained that *Peak's* intellect was necessarily in that position.'

'And you see how wrong you would have been,' remarked the girl, softly.

'Well—I don't know.'

'You don't know?'

'I mean that I can't acknowledge what I can't understand.'

'Then do try to understand, Buckland!—Have you ever put aside your prejudice for a moment to inquire what our religion really means? Not once, I think—at all events, not since you reached years of discretion.'

'Allow me to inform you that I studied the question thoroughly at Cambridge.'

'Yes, yes; but that was in your boyhood.'

'And when does manhood begin?'

'At different times in different persons. In your case it was late.'

Buckland laughed. He was considering a rejoinder, when they were interrupted by the appearance of Fanny, who asked at once:

'Shall you go to see Mr. Peak this evening, Buckland?'

'I'm in no hurry,' was the abrupt reply.

The girl hesitated.

'Let us all have a drive together—with Mr. Peak, I mean—like when you were here last.'

'We'll see about it.'

Buckland went slowly from the room.

Late the same evening he sat with his father in the study. Mr. Warricombe knew not the solace of tobacco, and his son, though never quite at ease without pipe or cigar, denied himself in this room, with the result that he shifted frequently upon his chair and fell into many awkward postures.

'And how does Peak impress you?' he inquired, when the subject he most wished to converse upon had been postponed to many others. It was clear that Martin would not himself broach it.

'Not disagreeably,' was the reply, with a look of frankness, perhaps over-emphasised.

'What is he doing? I have only heard from him once since he came down, and he had very little to say about himself.'

'I understand that he proposes to take the London B.A.'

'Oh, then, he never did that? Has he unbosomed himself to you about his affairs of old time?'

'No. Such confidences are hardly called for.'

'Speaking plainly, father, you don't feel any uneasiness?'

Martin deliberated, fingering the while an engraved stone which hung upon his watch-guard. He was at a disadvantage in this conversation. Aware that Buckland regarded the circumstances of Peak's sojourn in the neighbourhood with feelings allied to contempt, he could neither adopt the tone of easy confidence natural to him on other occasions of difference in opinion, nor express himself with the coldness which would have obliged his son to quit the subject.

'Perhaps you had better tell me,' he replied, 'whether *you* are really uneasy.'

It was impossible for Buckland to answer as his mind prompted. He could not without offence declare that no young man of brains now adopted a clerical career with pure intentions, yet such was his sincere belief. Made tolerant in many directions by the cultivation of his shrewdness, he was hopelessly biassed in judgment as soon as his anti-religious prejudice came into play—a point of strong resemblance between him and Peak. After fidgeting for a moment, he exclaimed:

'Yes, I am; but I can't be sure that there's any cause for it.'

'Let us come to matters of fact,' said Mr. Warricombe, showing that he was not sorry to discuss this side of the affair. 'I suppose there is no doubt that Peak had a position till lately at the place he speaks of?'

'No doubt, whatever. I have taken pains to ascertain that. His account of himself, so far, is strictly true.'

Martin smiled, with satisfaction he did not care to disguise.

'Have you met some acquaintance of his?'

'Well,' answered Buckland, changing his position, 'I went to work in rather an underhanded way, perhaps,—but the results are satisfactory. No, I haven't come across any of his friends, but I happened to hear not long ago that he was on intimate terms with some journalists.'

His father laughed.

'Anything compromising in that association, Buckland?'

'I don't say that—though the fellows I speak of are hot Radicals.'

'Though?'

'I mean,' replied the young man, with his shrewder smile, 'that they are not exactly the companions a theological student would select.'

'I understand. Possibly he has journalised a little himself?'

'That I can't say, though I should have thought it likely enough. I might, of course, find out much more about him, but it seemed to me that to have assurance of his truthfulness in that one respect was enough for the present.'

'Do you mean, Buckland,' asked his father, gravely, 'that you have been setting secret police at work?'

'Well, yes. I thought it the least objectionable way of getting information.'

Martin compressed his lips and looked disapproval.

'I really can't see that such extreme measures were demanded. Come, come; what is all this about? Do you suspect him of planning burglaries? That was an ill-judged step, Buckland; decidedly ill-judged. I said just now that Peak impressed me by no means disagreeably. Now I will add that I am convinced of his good faith—as sure of it as I am of his remarkable talents and aptitude for the profession he aims at. In spite of your extraordinary distrust, I can't feel a moment's doubt of his honour. Why, I could have told you myself that he has known Radical journalists. He mentioned it the other day, and explained how far his sympathy went with that kind of thing. No, no; that was hardly permissible, Buckland.'

The young man had no difficulty in bowing to his father's reproof when the point at issue was one of gentlemanly behaviour.

'I admit it,' he replied. 'I wish I had gone to Rotherhithe and made simple inquiries in my own name. That, all things considered, I might have allowed myself; at all events, I shouldn't have been at ease without getting that assurance. If Peak had heard, and had said to me, "What the deuce do you mean?" I should have told him plainly, what I have strongly hinted to him already, that I don't understand what he is doing in this galley.'

'And have placed yourself in a position not easy to define.'

'No doubt.'

'All this arises, my boy,' resumed Martin, in a tone of grave kindness, 'from your strange inability to grant that on certain matters you may be wholly misled.'

'It does.'

'Well, well; that is forbidden ground. But do try to be less narrow. Are you unable then to meet Peak in a friendly way?'

'Oh, by no means! It seems more than likely that I have wronged him.'

'Well said! Keep your mind open. I marvel at the dogmatism of men who are set on overthrowing dogma. Such a position is so strangely unphilosophic that I don't know how a fellow of your brains can hold it for a moment. If I were not afraid of angering you,' Martin added, in his pleasantest tone, 'I would quote the Master of Trinity.'

'A capital epigram, but it is repeated too often.'

Mr. Warricombe shook his head, and with a laugh rose to say good-night.

'It's a great pity,' he remarked next day to Sidwell, who had been saying that her brother seemed less vivacious than usual, 'that Buckland is defective on the side of humour. For a man who claims to be philosophical he takes things with a rather obtuse seriousness. I know nothing better than humour as a protection against the kind of mistake he is always committing.'

The application of this was not clear to Sidwell.

'Has something happened to depress him?' she asked.

'Not that I know of. I spoke only of his general tendency to intemperate zeal. That is enough to account for intervals of reaction. And how much sounder his judgment of men would be if he could only see through a medium of humour now and then! —You know he is going over to Budleigh Salterton this afternoon?'

Sidwell smiled, and said quietly:

'I thought it likely he would.'

At Budleigh Salterton, a nook on the coast some fifteen miles away, Sylvia Moorhouse was now dwelling. Her mother, a widow of substantial means, had recently established herself there, in the proximity of friends, and the mathematical brother made his home with them. That Buckland took every opportunity of enjoying Sylvia's conversation was no secret; whether the predilection was mutual, none of his relatives could say, for in a matter such as this Buckland was by nature disposed to reticence. Sidwell's intimacy with Miss Moorhouse put her in no better position than the others for forming an opinion; she could only suspect that the irony which flavoured Sylvia's talk with and concerning the Radical, intimated a lurking kindness. Buckland's preference was easily understood, and its growth for five or six years seemed to promise stability.

Immediately after luncheon the young man set forth, and did not reappear until the evening of the next day. His spirits had not benefited by the excursion; at dinner he was noticeably silent, and instead of going to the drawing-room afterwards he betook himself to the studio up on the roof, and smoked in solitude. There, towards ten o'clock, Sidwell sought him. Heavy rain was beating upon the glass, and a high wind blended its bluster with the cheerless sound.

'Don't you find it rather cold here?' she asked, after observing her brother's countenance of gloom.

'Yes; I'm coming down.—Why don't you keep up your painting?'

'I have lost interest in it, I'm afraid.'

'That's very weak, you know. It seems to me that nothing interests you permanently.'

Sidwell thought it better to make no reply.

'The characteristic of women,' Buckland pursued, with some asperity, throwing away the stump of his cigar. 'It comes, I suppose, of their ridiculous education—their minds are never trained to fixity of purpose. They never understand themselves, and scarcely ever make an effort to understand any one else. Their life is a succession of inconsistencies.'

'This generalising is so easy,' said Sidwell, with a laugh, 'and so worthless. I wonder you should be so far behind the times.'

'What light have the times thrown on the subject?'

'There's no longer such a thing as *woman* in the abstract. We are individuals.'

'Don't imagine it! That may come to pass three or four generations hence, but as yet the best of you can only vary the type in unimportant particulars. By the way, what is Peak's address?'

'Longbrook Street; but I don't know the number. Father can give it you, I think.'

'I shall have to drop him a note. I must get back to town early in the morning.'

'Really? We hoped to have you for a week.'

'Longer next time.'

They descended together. Now that Louis no longer abode here (he had decided at length for medicine, and was at work in London), the family as a rule spent very quiet evenings. By ten o'clock Mrs. Warricombe and Fanny had retired, and Sidwell was left either to talk with her father, or to pursue the calm meditations which seemed to make her independent of companionship as often as she chose.

'Are they all gone?' Buckland asked, finding a vacant room.

'Father is no doubt in the study.'

'It occurs to me——. Do you feel satisfied with this dead-alive existence?'

'Satisfied? No life could suit me better.'

'You really think of living here indefinitely?'

'As far as I am concerned, I hope nothing may ever disturb us.'

'And to the end of your life you will scent yourself with sweet-brier? Do try a bit of mint for a change.'

'Certainly, if it will please you.'

'Seriously, I think you might all come to town for next winter. You are rusting, all of you. Father was never so dull, and mother doesn't seem to know how to pass the days. It wouldn't be bad for Louis to be living with you instead of in lodgings. Do just think of it. It's ages since you heard a concert, or saw a picture.'

Sidwell mused, and her brother watched her askance.

'I don't know whether the others would care for it,' she said, 'but I am not tempted by a winter of fog.'

'Fog? Pooh! Well, there *is* an occasional fog, just now and then, but it's much exaggerated. Who ever thinks of the weather in England? Fanny might have a time at Bedford College or some such place—she learns nothing here. Think it over. Father would be delighted to get among the societies, and so on.'

He repeated his arguments in many forms, and Sidwell listened patiently, until they were joined by Mr. Warricombe, whereupon the subject dropped; to be resumed, however, in correspondence, with a persistency which Buckland seldom exhibited in anything which affected the interests of his relatives. As the summer drew on, Mrs. Warricombe began to lend serious ear to this suggestion of change, and Martin was at all events moved to discuss the pros and cons of half a year in London. Sidwell preserved neutrality, seldom making an allusion to the project; but Fanny supported her brother's proposal with sprightly zeal, declaring on one occasion that she began distinctly to feel the need of 'a higher culture,' such as London only could supply.

In the meantime there had been occasional interchange of visits between the family and their friends at Budleigh Salterton.

One evening, when Mrs. Moorhouse and Sylvia were at the Warricombes', three or four Exeter people came to dine, and among the guests was Godwin Peak—his invitation being due in this instance to Sylvia's express wish to meet him again.

'I am studying men,' she had said to Sidwell not long before, when the latter was at the seaside with her. 'In our day this is the proper study of womankind. Hitherto we have given serious attention only to one another. Mr. Peak remains in my memory as a type worth observing; let me have a chance of talking to him when I come next.'

She did not neglect her opportunity, and Mrs. Moorhouse, who also conversed with the theologian and found him interesting, was so good as to hope that he would call upon her if ever his steps turned towards Budleigh Salterton.

After breakfast next morning, Sidwell found her friend sitting with a book beneath one of the great trees of the garden. At that moment Sylvia was overcome with laughter, evidently occasioned by her reading.

'Oh,' she exclaimed, 'if this man isn't a great humorist! I don't think I ever read anything more irresistible.'

The book was Hugh Miller's *Testimony of the Rocks*, a richly bound copy belonging to Mrs. Warricombe.

'I daresay you know it very well; it's the chapter in which he discusses, with perfect gravity, whether it would have been possible for Noah to collect examples of all living creatures in the ark. He decides that it wouldn't—that the deluge *must* have spared a portion of the earth; but the details of his argument are delicious, especially this place where he says that all the insects could have been brought together only "at enormous expense of miracle"! I suspected a secret smile; but no—that's out of the question. "At enormous expense of miracle"!'

Sylvia's eyes winked as she laughed, a peculiarity which enhanced the charm of her frank mirth. Her dark, pure complexion, strongly-marked eyebrows, subtle lips, were shadowed beneath a great garden hat, and a loose white gown, with no oppressive moulding at the waist, made her a refreshing picture in the glare of mid-summer.

'The phrase is ridiculous enough,' assented Sidwell. 'Miracle can be but miracle, however great or small its extent.'

'Isn't it strange, reading a book of this kind nowadays? What a leap we have made! I should think there's hardly a country curate who would be capable of bringing this argument into a sermon.'

'I don't know,' returned Sidwell, smiling. 'One still hears remarkable sermons.'

'What will Mr. Peak's be like?'

They exchanged glances. Sylvia wore a look of reflective curiosity, and her friend answered with some hesitation, as if the thought were new to her:

'They won't deal with Noah, we may take that for granted.'

'Most likely not with miracles, however little expensive.'

'Perhaps not. I suppose he will deal chiefly with the moral teaching of Christianity.'

'Do you think him strong as a moralist?' inquired Sylvia.

'He has very decided opinions about the present state of our civilisation.'

'So I find. But is there any distinctly moral force in him?'

'Father thinks so,' Sidwell replied, 'and so do our friends the Lilywhites.'

Miss Moorhouse pondered awhile.

'He is a great problem to me,' she declared at length, knitting her brows with a hint of humorous exaggeration. 'I wonder whether he believes in the dogmas of Christianity.'

Sidwell was startled.

'Would he think of becoming a clergyman?'

'Oh, why not? Don't they recognise nowadays that the spirit is enough?'

There was silence. Sidwell let her eyes wander over the sunny grass to the red-flowering creeper on the nearest side of the house.

'That would involve a great deal of dissimulation,' she said at length. 'I can't reconcile it with what I know of Mr. Peak.'

'And I can't reconcile anything else,' rejoined the other.

'He impresses you as a rationalist?'

'You not?'

'I confess I have taken his belief for granted. Oh, think! He couldn't keep up such a pretence. However you justify it, it implies conscious deception. It would be dishonourable. I'm sure *he* would think it so.'

'How does your brother regard him?' Sylvia asked, smiling very slightly, but with direct eyes.

'Buckland can't credit any one with sincerity except an aggressive agnostic.'

'But I think he allows honest credulity.'

Sidwell had no answer to this. After musing a little, she put a question which indicated how her thoughts had travelled.

'Have you met many women who declared themselves agnostics?'

'Several.'

Sylvia removed her hat, and began to fan herself gently with the brim. Here, in the shade, bees were humming; from the house came faint notes of a piano—Fanny practising a mazurka of Chopin.

'But never, I suppose, one who found a pleasure in attacking Christianity?'

'A girl who was at school with me in London,' Sylvia replied, with an air of amused reminiscence. 'Marcella Moxey. Didn't I ever speak to you of her?'

'I think not.'

'She was bitter against religion of every kind.'

'Because her mother made her learn collects, I dare say?' suggested Sidwell, in a tone of gentle satire.

'No, no. Marcella was about eighteen then, and had neither father nor mother.—(How Fanny's touch improves!)—She was a born atheist, in the fullest sense of the word.'

'And detestable?'

'Not to me—I rather liked her. She was remarkably honest, and I have sometimes thought that in morals, on the whole, she stood far above most women. She hated falsehood—hated it with all her heart, and a story of injustice maddened her. When I think of Marcella it helps me to picture the Russian girls who propagate Nihilism.'

'You have lost sight of her?'

'She went abroad, I think. I should like to have known her fate. I rather think there will have to be many like her before women are civilised.'

'How I should like to ask her,' said Sidwell, 'on what she supported her morality?'

'Put the problem to Mr. Peak,' suggested the other, gaily. 'I fancy he wouldn't find it insoluble.'

Mrs. Warricombe and Mrs. Moorhouse appeared in the distance, walking hither under parasols. The girls rose to meet them, and were presently engaged in less interesting colloquy.

IV

THIS SUMMER PEAK became a semi-graduate of London University. To avoid the risk of a casual meeting with acquaintances, he did not go to London, but sat for his examination at the nearest provincial centre. The revival of boyish tremors at the successive stages of this business was anything but agreeable; it reminded him, with humiliating force, how far he had strayed from the path indicated to his self-respecting manhood. Defeat would have strengthened in overwhelming revolt all the impulses which from time to time urged him to abandon his servile course. But there was no chance of his failing to satisfy the examiners. With 'Honours' he had now nothing to do; enough for his purpose that in another year's time he would write himself Bachelor of Arts, and thus simplify the clerical preliminaries. In what quarter he was to look for a curacy remained uncertain. Meanwhile his enterprise seemed to prosper, and success emboldened his hopes.

Hopes which were no longer vague, but had defined themselves in a way which circumstances made inevitable. Though he had consistently guarded himself against the obvious suggestions arising out of his intercourse with the Warricombe family, though he still emphasised every discouraging fact, and strove to regard it as axiomatic that nothing could be more perilous to his future than a hint of presumption or self-interest in word or deed beneath that friendly roof, it was coming to pass that he thought of Sidwell not only as the type of woman pursued by his imagination, but as herself the object of his converging desires. Comparison of her with others had no result but the deepening of that impression she had at first made upon him. Sidwell exhibited all the qualities which most appealed to him in her class; in addition, she had the charms of a personality which he could not think of common occurrence. He was yet far from understanding her; she exercised his powers of observation, analysis, conjecture, as no other person had ever done; each time he saw her (were it but for a moment) he came away with some new perception of her excellence, some hitherto unmarked grace of person or mind whereon to meditate. He had never approached a woman who possessed this power at once of fascinating his senses and controlling his intellect to a glad reverence. Whether in her presence or musing upon her in solitude, he found that the unsparing naturalism of his scrutiny was powerless to degrade that sweet, pure being.

Rare, under any circumstances, is the passionate love which controls every motive of heart and mind; rarer still that form of it which, with no assurance of reciprocation, devotes exclusive ardour to an object only approachable through declared obstacles. Godwin Peak was not framed for romantic languishment. In general, the more complex a man's mechanism, and the more pronounced his habit of introspection, the less capable is he of loving with vehemence and constancy. Heroes of passion are for the most part primitive natures, nobly tempered; in our time they tend to extinction. Growing vulgarism on the one hand, and on the other a development of the psychological conscience, are unfavourable to any relation between the sexes, save those which originate in pure animalism, or in reasoning less or more generous. Never having experienced any feeling which he could dignify with the name of love, Godwin had no criterion in himself whereby to test the emotions now besetting him. In a man of his age this was an unusual state of things, for when the ardour which will bear analysis has at length declared itself, it is wont to be moderated by the regretful memory of that fugacious essence which gave to the first frenzy of youth its irrecoverable delight. He could not say in reply to his impulses: If that was love which overmastered me, this must be something either more or less exalted. What he *did* say was something of this kind: If desire and tenderness, if frequency of dreaming rapture, if the calmest approval of the mind and the heart's most exquisite, most painful throbbing, constitute love,—then assuredly I love Sidwell. But if to love is to be possessed with madness, to lose all taste of life when hope refuses itself, to meditate frantic follies, to deem it inconceivable that this woman should ever lose her dominion over me, or another reign in her stead,—then my passion falls short of the true œstrum, and I am only dallying with fancies which might spring up as often as I encountered a charming girl.

All things considered, to encourage this amorous preoccupation was probably the height of unwisdom. The lover is ready at deluding himself, but Peak never lost sight of the extreme unlikelihood that he should ever become Martin Warricombe's son-in-law, of the thousand respects which forbade his hoping that Sidwell would ever lay her hand in his. That deep-rooted sense of class which had so much influence on his speculative and practical life asserted itself, with rigid consistency, even against his own aspirations; he attributed to the Warricombes more prejudice on this subject than really existed in them. He, it was true, belonged to no class whatever, acknowledged no subordination save that of the hierarchy of intelligence; but this could not obscure the fact that his brother sold seeds across a counter, that his sister had married a haberdasher, that his uncle (notoriously) was somewhere or other supplying the public with cheap repasts. Girls of Sidwell's delicacy do not misally themselves, for they take into account the fact that such misalliance is fraught with elements of unhappiness, affecting husband as much as wife. No need to dwell upon the scruples suggested by his moral attitude; he would never be called upon to combat them with reference to Sidwell's future.

What, then, was he about? For what advantage was he playing the hypocrite? Would he, after all, be satisfied with some such wife as the average curate may hope to marry?

A hundred times he reviewed the broad question, by the light of his six months' experience. Was Sidwell Warricombe his ideal woman, absolutely speaking? Why, no; not with all his glow of feeling could he persuade himself to declare her that. Satisfied up to a certain point, admitted to the sphere of wealthy refinement, he now had leisure to think of yet higher grades, of the women who are not only exquisite creatures by social comparison but rank by divine right among the foremost of their race. Sidwell was far from intolerant, and held her faiths in a sincerely ethical spirit. She judged nobly, she often saw with clear vision. But must not something of kindly condescension always blend with his admiring devotedness? Were it but possible to win the love of a woman who looked forth with eyes thoroughly purged from all mist of tradition and conventionalism, who was at home among arts and sciences, who, like himself, acknowledged no class and bowed to no authority but that of the supreme human mind!

Such women are to be found in every age, but how many of them shine with the distinctive ray of womanhood? These are so rare that they have a place in the pages of history. The truly emancipated woman—it was Godwin's conviction—is almost always asexual; to him, therefore, utterly repugnant. If, then, he were not content to waste his life in a vain search for the priceless jewel, which is won and worn only by fortune's supreme favourites, he must acquiesce in the imperfect marriage commonly the lot of men whose intellect allows them but little companionship even among their own sex: for that matter, the lot of most men, and necessarily so until the new efforts in female education shall have overcome the vice of wedlock as hitherto sanctioned. Nature provides the hallucination which flings a lover at his mistress's feet. For the chill which follows upon attainment she cares nothing—let society and individuals make their account with that as best they may. Even with a wife such as Sidwell the process of disillusion would doubtless have to be faced, however liberal one's allowances in the forecast.

Reflections of this colour were useful; they helped to keep within limits the growth of agitating desire. But there were seasons when Godwin surrendered himself to luxurious reverie, hours of summer twilight which forbade analysis and listened only to the harmonies of passion. Then was Sidwell's image glorified, and all the delights promised by such love as hers fired his imagination to intolerable ecstasy. O heaven! to see the smile softened by rosy warmth which would confess that she had given her heart—to feel her supple fingers intertwined with his that clasped them—to hear the words in which a mind so admirable, instincts so delicate, would make expression of their tenderness! To live with Sidwell—to breathe the fragrance of that flower of womanhood in wedded intimacy—to prove the devotion of a nature so profoundly chaste! The visionary transport was too poignant; in the end it drove him to a fierce outbreak of despairing wrath. How could he dream that such bliss would be the reward of despicable artifice, of calculated dishonour? Born a rebel, how could his be the fate of those happy men who are at one with the order of things? The prophecy of a heart wrung with anguish foretold too surely that for him was no rapturous love, no joy of noble wedlock. Solitude, now and for ever, or perchance some base alliance of the flesh, which would involve his later days in sordid misery.

In moods of discouragement he thought with envy of his old self, his life in London lodgings, his freedom in obscurity. It belongs to the pathos of human nature that only in looking back can one appreciate the true value of those long tracts of monotonous ease which, when we are living through them, seem of no account save in relation to past or future; only at a distance do we perceive that the exemption from painful shock was in itself a happiness, to be rated highly in comparison with most of those disturbances known as moments of joy. A wise man would have entertained no wish but that he might grow old in that same succession of days and weeks and years. Without anxiety concerning his material needs (certainly the most substantial of earthly blessings), his leisure not inadequate to the gratification of a moderate studiousness, with friends who offered him an ever-ready welcome,—was it not much? If he were condemned to bachelorhood, his philosophy was surely capable of teaching him that the sorrows and anxieties he thus escaped made more than an offset against the satisfactions he must forego. Reason had no part in the fantastic change to which his life had submitted, nor was he ever supported by a hope which would bear his cooler investigation.

And yet hope had her periods of control, for there are times when the mind wearies of rationality, and, as it were in self-defence, in obedience to the instinct of progressive life, craves a specious comfort. It seemed undeniable that Mr. Warricombe regarded him with growth of interest, invited his conversation more unreservedly. He began to understand Martin's position with regard to religion and science, and thus could utter himself more securely. At length he ventured to discourse with some amplitude on his own convictions—the views, that is to say, which he thought fit to adopt in his character of a liberal Christian. It was on an afternoon of early August that this opportunity presented itself. They sat together in the study, and Martin was in a graver mood than usual, not much disposed to talk, but a willing listener. There had been mention of a sermon at the Cathedral, in which the preacher declared his faith that the maturity of science would dispel all antagonisms between it and revelation.

'The difficulties of the unbeliever,' said Peak, endeavouring to avoid a sermonising formality, though with indifferent success, 'are, of course, of two kinds; there's the theory of evolution, and there's modern biblical criticism. The more I study these objections, the less able I am to see how they come in conflict with belief in Christianity as a revealed religion.'

'Yet you probably had your time of doubt?' remarked the other, touching for the first time on this personal matter.

'Oh, yes; that was inevitable. It only means that one's development is imperfect. Most men who confirm themselves in agnosticism are kept at that point by arrested moral activity. They give up the intellectual question as wearisome, and accept the point of view which flatters their prejudices: thereupon follows a blunting of the sensibilities on the religious side.'

'There are men constitutionally unfitted for the reception of spiritual truth,' said Martin, in a troubled tone. He was playing with a piece of string, and did not raise his eyes.

'I quite believe that. There's our difficulty when we come to evidences. The evidences of science are wholly different in *kind* from those of religion. Faith cannot spring from any observation of phenomena, or scrutiny of authorities, but from the declaration made to us by the spiritual faculty. The man of science can only become a Christian by the way of humility—and that a kind of humility he finds it difficult even to conceive. One wishes to impress upon him the harmony of this faith with the spiritual voice that is in every man. He replies: I know nothing of that spiritual voice. And if that be true, one can't help him by argument.'

Peak had constructed for himself, out of his reading, a plausible system which on demand he could set forth with fluency. The tone of current apologetics taught him that, by men even of cultivated intellect, such a position as he was now sketching was deemed tenable; yet to himself it sounded so futile, so nugatory, that he had to harden his forehead as he spoke. Trial more severe to his conscience lay in the perceptible solicitude with which Mr. Warricombe weighed these disingenuous arguments. It was a hateful thing to practise such deception on one who probably yearned for spiritual support. But he had committed himself to this course, and must brave it out.

'Christianity,' he was saying presently—appropriating a passage of which he had once made careful note—'is an organism of such vital energy that it perforce assimilates whatever is good and true in the culture of each successive age. To understand this is to learn that we must depend rather on *constructive*, than on *defensive*, apology. That is to say, we must draw evidence of our faith from its latent capacities, its unsuspected affinities, its previsions, its adaptability, comprehensiveness, sympathy, adequacy to human needs.'

'That puts very well what I have always felt,' replied Mr. Warricombe. 'Yet there will remain the objection that such a faith may be of purely human origin. If evolution and biblical criticism seem to overthrow all the historic evidences of Christianity, how convince the objectors that the faith itself was divinely given?'

'But I cannot hold for a moment,' exclaimed Peak, in the words which he knew his interlocutor desired to hear, 'that all the historic evidences have been destroyed. That indeed would shake our position.'

He enlarged on the point, with display of learning, yet studiously avoiding the tone of pedantry.

'Evolution,' he remarked, when the dialogue had again

extended its scope, 'does not touch the evidence of design in the universe; at most it can correct our imperfect views (handed down from an age which had no scientific teaching because it was not ripe for it) of the mode in which that design was executed, or rather is still being executed. Evolutionists have not succeeded in explaining life; they have merely discovered a new law relating to life. If we must have an explanation, there is nothing for it but to accept the notion of a Deity. Indeed, how can there be religion without a divine author? Religion is based on the idea of a divine mind which reveals itself to us for moral ends. The Christian revelation, we hold, has been developed gradually, much of it in connection with secondary causes and human events. It has come down to us in anything but absolute purity—like a stream which has been made turbid by its earthly channel. The lower serves its purpose as a stage to the higher, then it falls away, the higher surviving. Hitherto, the final outcome of evolution is the soul in a bodily tenement. May it not be that the perfected soul alone survives in the last step of the struggle for existence?'——

Peak had been talking for more than a quarter of an hour. Under stress of shame and intellectual self-criticism (for he could not help confuting every position as he stated it) his mind often wandered. When he ceased speaking there came upon him an uncomfortable dreaminess which he had already once or twice experienced when in colloquy with Mr. Warricombe; a tormenting metaphysical doubt of his own identity strangely beset him. With involuntary attempt to recover the familiar self he grasped his own wrist, and then, before he was aware, a laugh escaped him, an all but mocking laugh, unsuitable enough to the spirit of the moment. Mr. Warricombe was startled, but looked up with a friendly smile.

'You fear,' he said, 'that this last speculation may seem rather fanciful to me?'

Godwin was biting his lip fiercely, and could not command himself to utterance of a word.

'By no means, I assure you,' added the other. 'It appeals to me very strongly.'

Peak rose from his chair.

'It struck me,' he said, 'that I had been preaching a sermon rather than taking part in a conversation. I'm afraid it is the habit of men who live a good deal alone to indulge in monologues.

On his return home, the sight of *Bibel und Natur* and his sheets of laborious manuscript filled him with disgust. It was two or three days before he could again apply himself to the translation. Yet this expedient had undoubtedly been of great service to him in the matter of his relations with Mr. Warricombe. Without the aid of Reusch he would have found it difficult to speak naturally on the theme which drew Martin into confidences and established an intimacy between them.

Already they had discussed in detail the first half of the book. How a man of Mr. Warricombe's intelligence could take grave interest in an arid exegesis of the first chapter of Genesis, Godwin strove in vain to comprehend. Often enough the debates were perilously suggestive of burlesque, and, when alone, he relieved himself of the laughter he had scarce restrained. For instance, there was that terrible *thohu wabohu* of the second verse, a phrase preserved from the original, and tossed into all the corners of controversy. Was *thohu wabohu* the first condition of the earth, or was it merely a period of division between a previous state of things and creation as established by the Hexæmeron? Did light exist or not, previous to the *thohu wabohu*? Then, again, what kind of 'days' were the three which passed before the birth of the sun? Special interest, of course, attached to the successive theories of theology on the origin of geologic strata. First came the 'theory of restitution,' which explained unbiblical antiquity by declaring that the strata belonged to a world before the Hexæmeron, a world which had been destroyed, and succeeded by the new creation. Less objectionable was the 'concordistic theory,' which interprets the 'six days' as so many vast periods of creative activity. But Reusch himself gave preference to the 'ideal theory,' the supporters whereof (diligently adapting themselves to the progress of science) hold that the six days are not to be understood as consecutive periods at all, but merely as six phases of the Creator's work.

By the exercise of watchfulness and dexterity, Peak managed for the most part to avoid expression of definite opinions. His attitude was that of a reverent (not yet reverend) student. Mr. Warricombe was less guarded, and sometimes allowed himself to profess that he saw nothing but vain ingenuity in Reusch's argument: as for example, where the theologian, convinced that the patriarchs did really live to an abnormal age, suggests that man's life was subsequently shortened in order that 'sin might not flourish with such exuberance.' This passage caused Martin to smile.

'It won't do, it won't do,' he said, quietly. 'Far better apply his rationalism here as elsewhere. These are wonderful old stories, not to be understood literally. Nothing depends upon them—nothing essential.'

Thereupon Peak mused anxiously. Not for the first time there occurred to him a thought which suited only too well with his ironic habits of mind. What if this hypocritic comedy were altogether superfluous? What if Mr. Warricombe would have received him no less cordially had he avowed his sincere position, and contented himself with guarding against offensiveness? Buckland, it was true, had suffered in his father's esteem on account of his unorthodoxy, but that young man had been too aggressive, too scornful. With prudence, would it not have been possible to win Martin's regard by fortifying the scientific rather than the dogmatic side of his intellect? If so, what a hopeless error had he committed!—But Sidwell? Was *she* liberal enough to take a personal interest in one who had renounced faith in revelation? He could not decide this question, for of Sidwell he knew much less than of her father. And it was idle to torment himself with such debate of the irreversible.

And, indeed, there seemed much reason for believing that Martin, whatever the extent of his secret doubts, was by temperament armed against agnosticism. Distinctly it comforted him to hear the unbelievers assailed—the friends of whom he spoke most heartily were all on the orthodox side; if ever a hint of gentle malice occurred in his conversation, it was when he spoke of a fallacy, a precipitate conclusion, detected in works of science. Probably he was too old to overcome this bias.

His view of the Bible appeared to harmonise with that which Peak put forth in one of their dialogues. 'The Scriptures were meant to be literally understood in primitive ages, and spiritually when the growth of science made it possible. Genesis was never intended to teach the facts of natural history; it takes phenomena as they appear to uninstructed people, and uses them only for the inculcation of moral lessons; it presents to the childhood of the world a few great elementary truths. And the way in which phenomena are spoken of in the Old Testament is never really incompatible with the facts as we know them nowadays. Take the miracle of the sun standing still, which is supposed to be a safe subject of ridicule. Why, it merely means that light was miraculously prolonged; the words used are those which common people would at all times understand.'

(Was it necessary to have admitted the miracle? Godwin asked himself. At all events Mr. Warricombe nodded approvingly.)

'Then the narrative of the creation of man; that's not at all incompatible with his slow development through ages. To teach the scientific fact—if we yet really know it—would have been worse than useless. The story is meant to express that spirit, and not matter, is the source of all existence. Indeed, our knowledge of the true meaning of the Bible has increased with the growth of science, and naturally that must have been intended from the first. Things which do not concern man's relation to the spiritual have no place in this book; they are not within its province. Such things were discoverable by human reason, and the knowledge which achieves has nothing to do with a divine revelation.'

To Godwin it was a grinding of the air, but the listener appeared to think it profitable.

With his clerical friend, Mr. Lilywhite, he rarely touched on matters of religion. The vicar of St. Ethelreda's was a man well suited to support the social dignity of his Church. A gentleman before everything, he seemed incapable of prying into the state of a parishioner's soul; you saw in him the official representative of a Divinity characterised by well-bred tolerance. He had written a pleasant little book on the by-ways of Devon and Cornwall, which brought about his intimacy with the Warricombe household. Peak liked him more the better he knew him, and in the course of the summer they had one or two long walks together, conversing exclusively of the things of earth. Mr. Lilywhite troubled himself little about evolution; he spoke of trees and plants, of birds and animals, in a loving spirit, like the old simple naturalists. Geology did not come within his sphere.

'I'm very sorry,' he said, 'that I could never care much for it. Don't think I'm afraid of it—not I! I feel the grandeur of its scope, just as I do in the case of astronomy; but I have never brought myself to study either science. A narrowness of mind, no doubt. I can't go into such remote times and regions. I love the sunlight and the green fields of this little corner of the world—too well, perhaps: yes, perhaps too well.'

After one of these walks, he remarked to Mrs. Lilywhite:

'It's my impression that Mr. Peak has somehow been misled in his choice of a vocation. I don't think he'll do as a churchman.'

'Why not, Henry?' asked his wife, with gentle concern, for she still spoke of Peak's 'quiet moral force.'

'There's something too restless about him. I doubt whether he has really made up his mind on any subject whatever. Well, it's not easy to explain what I feel, but I don't think he will take Orders.'

Calling at the vicarage one afternoon in September, Godwin found Mrs. Lilywhite alone. She startled him by saying at once:

'An old acquaintance of yours was with us yesterday, Mr. Peak.'

'Who could that be, I wonder?'

He smiled softly, controlling his impulse to show quite another expression.

'You remember Mr. Bruno Chilvers?'

'Oh, yes!'

There was a constriction in his throat. Struggling to overcome it, he added:

'But I should have thought he had no recollection of me.'

'Quite the contrary, I assure you. He is to succeed Mr. Bell of St. Margaret's, at Christmas; he was down here only for a day or two, and called upon my husband with a message from an old friend of ours. It appears he used to know the Warricombes, when they lived at Kingsmill, and he had been to see them before visiting us; it was there your name was mentioned to him.'

Godwin had seated himself, and leaned forward, his hands grasping the glove he had drawn off.

'We were contemporaries at Whitelaw College,' he observed.

'So we learnt from him. He spoke of you with the greatest interest; he was delighted to hear that you contemplated taking Orders. Of course we knew Mr. Chilvers by reputation, but my husband had no idea that he was coming to Exeter. What an energetic man he is! In a few hours he seemed to have met every-one, and to have learnt everything. My husband says he felt quite rebuked by such a display of vigour!'

Even in his discomposure, graver than any that had affected him since his talks with Buckland Warricombe, Peak was able to notice that the Rev. Bruno had not made a wholly favourable impression upon the Lilywhites. There was an amiable causticity in that mention of his 'display of vigour,' such as did not often characterise Mrs. Lilywhite's comments. Finding that the vicar would be away till evening, Godwin stayed for only a quarter of an hour, and when he had escaped it irritated and alarmed him to reflect how unusual his behaviour must have appeared to the good lady.

The blow was aimed at his self-possession from such an unlikely quarter. In Church papers he had frequently come across Chilvers' name, and the sight of it caused him a twofold disturbance: it was hateful to have memories of humiliation revived, and perhaps still more harassing to be forced upon acknowledgment of the fact that he stood as an obscure aspirant at the foot of the ladder which his old rival was triumphantly ascending. Bad enough to be classed in any way with such a man as Chilvers; but to be regarded as at one with him in religious faith, to be forbidden the utterance of scorn when Chilvers was extolled, stung him so keenly that he rushed into any distraction to elude the thought. When he was suffering shame under the gaze of Buckland Warricombe he remembered Chilvers, and shrank as before a merited scoff. But the sensation had not been abiding enough to affect his conduct. He had said to himself that he should never come in contact with the fellow, and that, after all, community of religious profession meant no more, under their respective circumstances, than if both were following law or physic.

But the unforeseen had happened. In a few months, the Rev. Bruno Chilvers would be a prominent figure about the streets of Exeter; would be frequently seen at the Warricombes', at the Lilywhites', at the houses of their friends. His sermons at St. Margaret's would doubtless attract, and form a staple topic of conversation. Worse than all, his expressions of 'interest' and 'delight,' made it probable that he would seek out his College competitor and offer the hand of brotherhood. These things were not to be avoided—save by abandonment of hopes, save by retreat, by yielding to a hostile destiny.

That Chilvers might talk here and there of Whitelaw stories was comparatively unimportant. The Warricombes must already know all that could be told, and what other people heard did not much matter. It was the man himself that Peak could not endure. Dissembling had hitherto been no light task. The burden had more than once pressed so gallingly that its permanent support seemed impossible; but to stand before Bruno Chilvers in the attitude of humble emulation, to give respectful ear whilst the popular cleric advised or encouraged, or bestowed pontifical praise, was comparable only to a searing of the flesh with red irons. Even with assured prospect of recompense in the shape of Sidwell Warricombe's heart and hand, he could hardly submit to such an ordeal. As it was, reason having so often convinced him that he clung to a visionary hope, the torture became gratuitous, and its mere suggestion inspired him with a fierce resentment destructive of all his purposes.

For several days he scarcely left the house. To wrath and dread had succeeded a wretched torpor, during which his mind kept revolving the thoughts prompted by his situation, turbidly and to no issue. He tasted all the bitterness of the solitude to which he had condemned himself; there was not a living soul with whom he could commune. At moments he was possessed with the desire of going straightway to London, and making Earwaker the confidant of all his folly. But that demanded an exertion of which he was physically incapable. He thought of the old home at Twybridge, and was tempted also in that direction. His mother would welcome him with human kindness; beneath her roof he could lie dormant until fate should again point his course. He even wrote a letter saying that in all probability he should pay a visit to Twybridge before long. But the impulse was only of an hour's duration, for he remembered that to talk with his mother would necessitate all manner of new falsehoods, a thickening of the atmosphere of lies which already oppressed him. No; if he quitted Exeter, it must be on a longer journey. He must resume his purpose of seeking some distant country, where new conditions of life would allow him to try his fortune at least as an honest adventurer. In many parts of colonial England his technical knowledge would have a value, and were there not women to be won beneath other skies—women perhaps of subtler charm than the old hidebound civilisation produced? Reminiscences of scenes and figures in novels he had read nourished the illusion. He pictured some thriving little town at the ends of the earth, where a young Englishman of good manners and unusual culture would easily be admitted to the intimacy of the richest families; he saw the ideal colonist (a man of good birth, but a sower of wild oats in his youth) with two or three daughters about him—beautiful girls, wondrously self-instructed—living amid romantic dreams of the old world, and of the lover who would some day carry them off (with a substantial share of papa's wealth) to Europe and the scenes of their imagination.

The mind has marvellous methods of self-defence against creeping lethargy of despair. At the point to which he had been reduced by several days of blank despondency, Peak was able to find genuine encouragement in visions such as this. He indulged his fancy until the vital force began to stir once more within him, and then, with one angry sweep, all his theological books and manuscripts were flung out of sight. Away with this detestable mummery! Now let Bruno Chilvers pour his eloquence from the pulpit of St. Margaret's, and rear to what heights he could the edifice of his social glory; men of that stamp were alone fitted to thrive in England. Was not *he* almost certainly a hypocrite, masking his brains (for brains he had) under a show of broadest Anglicanism? But his career was throughout consistent. He trod in the footsteps of his father, and with inherited aptitude moulded antique traditions into harmony with the taste of the times. Compared with such a man, Peak felt himself a bungler. The wonder was that his clumsy lying had escaped detection.

Another day, and he had done nothing whatever, but was still buoyed up by the reaction of visionary hope. His need now was of communicating his change of purpose to some friendly hearer. A week had passed since he had exchanged a word with anyone but Mrs. Roots, and converse he must. Why not with Mr. Warricombe? That was plainly the next step; to see Martin and make known to him that after all he could not become a clergyman. No need of hinting a conscientious reason. At all events, nothing more definite than a sense of personal unfitness, a growing perception of difficulties inherent in his character. It would be very interesting to hear Mr. Warricombe's replies.

A few minutes after this decision was taken, he set off towards the Old Tiverton Road, walking at great speed, flourishing his stick—symptoms of the nervous cramp (so to speak) which he was dispelling. He reached the house, and his hand was on the bell, when an unexpected opening of the door presented Louis Warricombe just coming forth for a walk. They exchanged amiabilities, and Louis made known that his father and mother were away on a visit to friends in Cornwall.

'But pray come in,' he added, offering to re-enter.

Peak excused himself, for it was evident that Louis made a sacrifice to courtesy. But at that moment there approached from the garden Fanny Warricombe and her friend Bertha Lilywhite, eldest daughter of the genial vicar; they shook hands with Godwin, Fanny exclaiming:

'Don't go away, Mr. Peak. Have a cup of tea with us—Sidwell is at home. I want to show you a strange sort of spleenwort that I gathered this morning.'

'In that case,' said her brother smiling, 'I may confess that I have an appointment. Pray forgive me for hurrying off, Mr. Peak.'

Godwin was embarrassed, but the sprightly girl repeated her summons, and he followed into the house.

V

Having led the way to the drawing-room, Fanny retired again for a few moments, to fetch the fern of which she had spoken, leaving Peak in conversation with little Miss Lilywhite. Bertha was a rather shy girl of fifteen, not easily induced, under circumstances such as these, to utter more than monosyllables, and Godwin, occupied with the unforeseen results of his call, talked about the weather. With half-conscious absurdity he had begun to sketch a theory of his own regarding rain-clouds and estuaries (Bertha listening with an air of the gravest attention) when Fanny reappeared, followed by Sidwell. Peak searched the latter's face for indications of her mood, but could discover nothing save a spirit of gracious welcome. Such aspect was a matter of course, and he knew it. None the less, his nervousness and the state of mind engendered by a week's miserable solitude, tempted him to believe that Sidwell did not always wear that smile in greeting a casual caller. This was the first time that she had received him without the countenance of Mrs. Warricombe. Observing her perfect manner, as she sat down and began to talk, he asked himself what her age really was. The question had never engaged his thoughts. Eleven years ago, when he saw her at the house near Kingsmill and again at Whitelaw College, she looked a very young girl, but whether of thirteen or sixteen he could not at the time have determined, and such a margin of possibility allowed her now to have reached—it might be—her twenty-seventh summer. But twenty-seven drew perilously near to thirty; no, no Sidwell could not be more than twenty-five. Her eyes still had the dewy freshness of flowering maidenhood; her cheek, her throat, were so exquisitely young——

In how divine a calm must this girl have lived to show, even at five-and-twenty, features as little marked by inward perturbation as those of an infant! Her position in the world considered, one could forgive her for having borne so lightly the inevitable sorrows of life, for having dismissed so readily the spiritual doubts which were the heritage of her time; but was she a total stranger to passion? Did not the fact of her still remaining unmarried make probable such a deficiency in her nature? Had she a place among the women whom coldness of temperament preserves in a bloom like that of youth, until fading hair and sinking cheek betray them——?

Whilst he thought thus, Godwin was in appearance busy with the fern Fanny had brought for his inspection. He talked about it, but in snatches, with intervals of abstractedness.

Yet might he not be altogether wrong? Last year, when he observed Sidwell in the Cathedral and subsequently at home, his impression had been that her face was of rather pallid and dreamy cast; he recollected that distinctly. Had she changed, or did familiarity make him less sensible of her finer traits? Possibly she enjoyed better health nowadays, and, if so, it might result from influences other than physical. Her air of quiet happiness seemed to him especially noticeable this afternoon, and, as he brooded there came upon him a dread which, under the circumstances, was quite irrational, but for all that troubled his views. Perhaps Sidwell was betrothed to some one? He knew of but one likely person—Miss Moorhouse's brother. About a month ago the Warricombes had been on a visit at Budleigh Salterton, and something might then have happened. Pangs of jealousy smote him, nor could he assuage them by reminding himself that he had no concern whatever in Sidwell's future.

'Will Mr. Warricombe be long away?' he asked, coldly.

'A day or two. I hope you didn't wish particularly to see him to-day?'

'Oh, no.'

'Do you know, Mr. Peak,' put in Fanny, 'that we are all going to London next month, to live there for half a year?'

Godwin exhibited surprise. He looked from the speaker to her sister, and Sidwell, as she smiled confirmation, bent very slightly towards him.

'We have made up our minds, after much uncertainty,' she

said. 'My brother Buckland seems to think that we are falling behind in civilisation.'

'So we are,' affirmed Fanny, 'as Mr. Peak would admit if only he could be sincere.'

'Am I never sincere then, Miss Fanny?' Godwin asked.

'I only meant to say that nobody can be when the rules of politeness interfere. Don't you think it's a pity? We might tell one another the truth in a pleasant way.'

'I agree with you. But then we must be civilised indeed. How do you think of London, Miss Warricombe? Which of its aspects most impresses you?'

Sidwell answered rather indefinitely, and ended by mentioning that in *Villette*, which she had just re-read, Charlotte Brontë makes a contrast between the City and the West End, and greatly prefers the former.

'Do you agree with her, Mr. Peak?'

'No, I can't. One understands the mood in which she wrote that; but a little more experience would have led her to see the contrast in a different light. That term, the West End, includes much that is despicable, but it means also the best results of civilisation. The City is hateful to me, and for a reason which I only understood after many an hour of depression in walking about its streets. It represents the ascendency of the average man.'

Sidwell waited for fuller explanation.

'A liberal mind,' Peak continued, 'is revolted by the triumphal procession that roars perpetually through the City highways. With myriad voices the City bellows its brutal scorn of everything but material advantage. There every humanising influence is contemptuously disregarded. I know, of course, that the trader may have his quiet home, where art and science and humanity are the first considerations; but the *mass* of traders, corporate and victorious, crush all such things beneath their heels. Take your stand (or try to do so) anywhere near the Exchange; the hustling and jolting to which you are exposed represents the very spirit of the life about you. Whatever is gentle and kindly and meditative must here go to the wall—trampled, spattered, ridiculed. Here the average man has it all his own way—a gross, utilitarian power.'

'Yes, I can see that,' Sidwell replied, thoughtfully. 'And perhaps it also represents the triumphant forces of our time.'

He looked keenly at her, with a smile of delight.

'That also! The power which centres in the world's money-markets—plutocracy.'

In conversing with Sidwell, he had never before found an opportunity of uttering his vehement prejudices. The gentler side of his character had sometimes expressed itself, but those impulses which were vastly more significant lay hidden beneath the dissumulation he consistently practised. For the first time he was able to look into Sidwell's face with honest directness, and what he saw there strengthened his determination to talk on with the same freedom.

'You don't believe, then,' said Sidwell, 'that democracy is the proper name for the state into which we are passing?'

'Only if one can understand democracy as the opening of social privileges to free competition amongst men of trade. And social privilege is everything; home politics refer to nothing else.'

Fanny, true to the ingenuous principle of her years, put a direct question:

'Do you approve of real democracy, Mr. Peak?'

He answered with another question:

'Have you read the "Life of Phokion" in Plutarch?'

'No, I'm sorry to say.'

'There's a story about him which I have enjoyed since I was your age. Phokion was once delivering a public speech, and at a certain point the majority of his hearers broke into applause; whereupon he turned to certain of his friends who stood near and asked, "What have I said amiss?"'

Fanny laughed.

'Then you despise public opinion?'

'With heart and soul!'

It was to Sidwell that he directed the reply. Though overcome by the joy of such an utterance, he felt that, considering the opinions and position of Buckland Warricombe, he was perhaps guilty of ill manners. But Sidwell manifested no disapproval.

'Did you know that story?' Fanny asked of her.

'It's quite new to me.'

'Then I'm sure you'll read the "Life of Phokion" as soon as possible. He will just suit you, Sidwell.'

Peak heard this with a shock of surprise which thrilled in him deliciously. He had the strongest desire to look again at Sidwell but refrained. As no one spoke, he turned to Bertha Lilywhite and put a commonplace question.

A servant entered with the tea-tray, and placed it on a small table near Fanny. Godwin looked at the younger girl; it seemed to him that there was an excess of colour in her cheeks. Had a glance from Sidwell rebuked her? With his usual rapidity of observation and inference he made much of this trifle.

Contrary to what he expected, Sidwell's next remark was in a tone of cheerfulness, almost of gaiety.

'One advantage of our stay in London will be that home will seem more delightful than ever when we return.'

'I suppose you won't be back till next summer?'

'I am afraid not.'

'Shall you be living here, then?' Fanny inquired.

'It's very doubtful.'

He wished to answer with a decided negative, but his tongue refused. Sidwell was regarding him with calm but earnest eyes, and he knew, without caring to reflect, that his latest projects were crumbling.

'Have you been to see our friends at Budleigh Salterton yet?' she asked.

'Not yet. I hope to in a few days.'

Pursuing the subject, he was able to examine her face as she spoke of Mr. Moorhouse. His conjecture was assuredly baseless.

Fanny and Bertha began to talk together of domestic affairs, and presently, when tea-cups were laid aside, the two girls went to another part of the room; then they withdrew altogether. Peak was monologising on English art as represented at the

Academy, but finding himself alone with Sidwell (it had never before happened) he became silent. Ought he to take his leave? He must already have been sitting here more than half-an-hour. But the temptation of *tête-à-tête* was irresistible.

'You had a visit from Mr. Chilvers the other day?' he remarked, abruptly.

'Yes; did he call to see you?'

Her tone gave evidence that she would not have introduced this topic.

'No; I heard from Mrs. Lilywhite. He had been to the vicarage. Has he changed much since he was at Whitelaw?'

'So many years must make a difference at that time of life,' Sidwell answered, smiling.

'But does he show the same peculiarities of manner?'

He tried to put the question without insistency, in a tone quite compatible with friendliness. Her answer, given with a look of amusement, satisfied him that there was no fear of her taking Mr. Chilvers too seriously.

'Yes. I think he speaks in much the same way.'

'Have you read any of his publications?'

'One or two. We have his lecture on *Altruism*.'

'I happen to know it. There are good things in it, I think. But I dislike his modern interpretation of old principles.'

'You think it dangerous?'

He no longer regarded her frankly, and in the consciousness of her look upon him he knit his brows.

'I think it both dangerous and offensive. Not a few clergymen nowadays, who imagine themselves free from the letter and wholly devoted to spirit, are doing their best in the cause of materialism. They surrender the very points at issue between religion and worldliness. They are so blinded by a vague humanitarian impulse as to make the New Testament an oracle of popular Radicalism.'

Sidwell looked up.

'I never quite understood, Mr. Peak, how you regard Radicalism. You think it opposed to all true progress?'

'Utterly, as concerns any reasonable limit of time.'

'Buckland, as you know, maintains that spiritual progress is only possible by this way.'

'I can't venture to contradict him,' said Godwin; 'for it may be that advance is destined only to come after long retrogression and anarchy. Perhaps the way *does* lie through such miseries. But we can't foresee that with certainty, and those of us who hate the present tendency of things must needs assert their hatred as strongly as possible, seeing that we *may* have a more hopeful part to play than seems likely.'

'I like that view,' replied Sidwell, in an undertone.

'My belief,' pursued Godwin, with an earnestness very agreeable to himself, for he had reached the subject on which he could speak honestly, 'is that an instructed man can only hold views such as your brother's—hopeful views of the immediate future—if he has never been brought into close contact with the lower classes. Buckland doesn't know the people for whom he pleads.'

'You think them so degraded?'

'It is impossible, without seeming inhumanly scornful, to give a just account of their ignorance and baseness. The two things, speaking generally, go together. Of the ignorant, there are very few indeed who can think purely or aspiringly. You, of course, object the teaching of Christianity; but the lowly and the humble of whom it speaks scarcely exist, scarcely can exist, in our day and country. A ludicrous pretence of education is banishing every form of native simplicity. In the large towns, the populace sink deeper and deeper into a vicious vulgarity, and every rural district is being affected by the spread of contagion. To flatter the proletariat is to fight against all the good that still characterises educated England—against reverence for the beautiful, against magnanimity, against enthusiasm of mind, heart, and soul.'

He quivered with vehemence of feeling, and the flush which rose to his hearer's cheek, the swimming brightness of her eye, proved that a strong sympathy stirred within her.

'I know nothing of the uneducated in towns,' she said, 'but the little I have seen of them in country places certainly supports your opinion. I could point to two or three families who have suffered distinct degradation owing to what most people call an improvement in their circumstances. Father often speaks of such instances, comparing the state of things now with what he can remember.'

'My own experience,' pursued Godwin, 'has been among the lower classes in London. I don't mean the very poorest, of whom one hears so much nowadays; I never went among them because I had no power of helping them, and the sight of their vileness would only have moved me to unjust hatred. But the people who earn enough for their needs, and whose spiritual guide is the Sunday newspaper—I know them, because for a long time I was obliged to lodge in their houses. Only a consuming fire could purify the places where they dwell. Don't misunderstand me; I am not charging them with what are commonly held vices and crimes, but with the consistent love of everything that is ignoble, with utter deadness to generous impulse, with the fatal habit of low mockery. And *these* are the people who really direct the democratic movement. They set the tone in politics; they are debasing art and literature; even the homes of wealthy people begin to show the effects of their influence. One hears men and women of gentle birth using phrases which originate with shop-boys; one sees them reading print which is addressed to the coarsest million. They crowd to entertainments which are deliberately adapted to the lowest order of mind. When commercial interest is supreme, how can the tastes of the majority fail to lead and control?'

Though he spoke from the depths of his conviction, and was so moved that his voice rose and fell in tones such as a drawing-room seldom hears, he yet kept anxious watch upon Sidwell's countenance. That hint afforded him by Fanny was invaluable; it had enabled him to appeal to Sidwell's nature by the ardent expression of what was sincerest in his own. She too, he at length understood, had the aristocratic temperament. This explained her to him, supplied the key of doubts and difficulties which had troubled him in her presence. It justified, moreover, the feelings with which she had inspired him—feelings which this hour of intimate converse had exalted to passion. His heart thrilled with hope. Where sympathies so profound existed, what did it matter that there was variance on a few points between his intellect and hers? He felt the power to win her, and to defy every passing humiliation that lay in his course.

Sidwell raised her eyes with a look which signified that she was shaping a question diffidently.

'Have you always thought so hopelessly of our times?'

'Oh, I had my stage of optimism,' he answered, smiling. 'Though I never put faith in the masses, I once believed that the conversion of the educated to a purely human religion would set things moving in the right way. It was ignorance of the world.'

He paused a moment, then added:

'In youth one marvels that men remain at so low a stage of civilisation. Later in life, one is astonished that they have advanced so far.'

Sidwell met his look with appreciative intelligence and murmured:

'In spite of myself, I believe that expresses a truth.'

Peak was about to reply, when Fanny and her friend reappeared. Bertha approached for the purpose of taking leave, and for a minute or two Sidwell talked with her. The young girls withdrew again together.

By the clock on the mantelpiece it was nearly six. Godwin did not resume his seat, though Sidwell had done so. He looked towards the window, and was all but lost in abstraction, when the soft voice again addressed him:

'But you have not chosen your life's work without some hope of doing good?'

'Do you think,' he asked gently, 'that I shall be out of place in the Christian Church?'

'No—no, I certainly don't think that. But will you tell me what you have set before yourself?'

He drew nearer and leaned upon the back of a chair.

'I hope for what I shall perhaps never attain. Whatever my first steps may be—I am not independent; I must take the work that offers—it is my ambition to become the teacher of some rural parish which is still unpolluted by the influences of which we have been speaking—or, at all events, is still capable of being rescued. For work in crowded centres, I am altogether unfit; my prejudices are too strong; I should do far more harm than good. But among a few simple people I think my efforts mightn't be useless. I can't pretend to care for anything but individuals. The few whom I know and love are of more importance to me than all the blind multitude rushing to destruction. I hate the word *majority*; it is the few, the very few, that have always kept alive whatever of effectual good we see in the human race. There are individuals who outweigh, in every kind of value, generations of ordinary people. To some remote little community I hope to give the best energies of my life. My teaching will avoid doctrine and controversy. I shall take the spirit of the Gospels, and labour to make it a practical guide. No doubt you find inconsistencies in me; but remember that I shall not declare myself to those I instruct as I have done to you. I have been laying stress on my antipathies. In the future it will be a duty and a pleasure to forget these and foster my sympathies, which also are strong when opportunity is given them.'

Sidwell listened, her face bent downwards but not hidden from the speaker.

'My nature is intolerant,' he went on, 'and I am easily roused to an antagonism which destroys my peace. It is only by living apart, amid friendly circumstances, that I can cultivate the qualities useful to myself and others. The sense that my life was being wasted determined me a year ago to escape the world's uproar and prepare myself in quietness for this task. The resolve was taken here, in your house.'

'Are you quite sure,' asked Sidwell, 'that such simple duties and satisfactions'——

The sentence remained incomplete, or rather was finished in the timid glance she gave him.

'Such a life wouldn't be possible to me,' he replied, with unsteady voice, 'if I were condemned to intellectual solitude. But I have dared to hope that I shall not always be alone.'

A parched throat would have stayed his utterance, even if words had offered themselves. But sudden confusion beset his mind—a sense of having been guilty of monstrous presumption—a panic which threw darkness about him and made him grasp the chair convulsively. When he recovered himself and looked at Sidwell there was a faint smile on her lips, inexpressibly gentle.

'That's the rough outline of my projects,' he said, in his ordinary voice, moving a few steps away. 'You see that I count much on fortune; at the best, it may be years before I can get my country living.'

With a laugh, he came towards her and offered his hand for good-bye. Sidwell rose.

'You have interested me very much. Whatever assistance it may be in my father's power to offer you, I am sure you may count upon.'

'I am already much indebted to Mr. Warricombe's kindness.'

They shook hands without further speech, and Peak went his way.

For an hour or two he was powerless to collect his thoughts. All he had said repeated itself again and again, mixed up with turbid comments, with deadly fears and frantic bursts of confidence, with tumult of passion and merciless logic of self-criticism. Did Sidwell understand that sentence: 'I have dared to hope that I shall not always be alone'? Was it not possible that she might interpret it as referring to some unknown woman whom he loved? If not, if his voice and features had betrayed him, what could her behaviour mean, except distinct encouragement? 'You have interested me very much.' But could she have used such words if his meaning had been plain to her? Far more likely that her frank kindness came of misconception. She imagined him the lover of some girl of his own 'station'—a toiling governess, or some such person; it could not enter into her mind that he 'dared' so recklessly as the truth implied.

But the glow of sympathy with which she heard his immeasurable scorn: there was the spirit that defies artificial distances. Why had he not been bolder? At this rate he must spend a lifetime in preparing for the decisive moment. When would another such occasion offer itself?

Women are won by audacity; the poets have repeated it from age to age, and some truth there must be in the saying. Suspicion of self-interest could not but attach to him; that was inherent in the circumstances. He must rely upon the sincerity of his passion, which indeed was beginning to rack and rend him. A woman is sensitive to that, especially a woman of Sidwell's refinement. In matters of the intellect she may be misled, but she cannot mistake quivering ardour for design simulating love. If it were impossible to see her again in private before she left Exeter, then he must write to her. Half a year of complete uncertainty, and of counterfeiting face to face with Bruno Chilvers, would overtax his resolution.

The evening went by he knew not how. Long after nightfall he was returning from an aimless ramble by way of the Old Tiverton Road. At least he would pass the house, and soothe or inflame his emotions by resting for a moment thus near to Sidwell.

What? He had believed himself incapable of erotic madness? And he pressed his forehead against the stones of the wall to relieve his sick dizziness.

It was Sidwell or death. Into what a void of hideous futility would his life be cast, if this desire proved vain, and he were left to combat alone with the memory of his dishonour! With Sidwell the reproach could be outlived. She would understand him, pardon him—and thereafter a glorified existence, rivalling that of whosoever has been most exultant among the sons of men!

PART THE FOURTH

I

Earwaker's struggle with the editor-in-chief of *The Weekly Post* and the journalist Kenyon came to its natural close about a month after Godwin Peak's disappearance. Only a vein of obstinacy in his character had kept him so long in a position he knew to be untenable. From the first his sympathy with Mr. Runcorn's politics had been doubtful, and experience of the working of a Sunday newspaper, which appealed to the ignobly restive, could not encourage his adhesion to this form of Radicalism. He anticipated dismissal by retirement, and Kenyon, a man of coarsely vigorous fibre, at once stepped into his place.

Now that he had leisure to review the conflict, Earwaker understood that circumstances had but hastened his transition from a moderate ardour in the parliamentary cause of the people, to a regretful neutrality regarding all political movements. Birth allied him with the proletarian class, and his sentiment in favour of democracy was unendangered by the disillusions which must come upon every intellectual man brought into close contact with public affairs. The course of an education essentially aristocratic (Greek and Latin can have no other tendency so long as they are the privilege of the few) had not affected his natural bent, nor was he the man to be driven into reaction because of obstacles to his faith inseparable from human weakness. He had learnt that the emancipation of the poor and untaught must proceed more slowly than he once hoped—that was all. Restored to generous calm, he could admit that such men as Runcorn and Kenyon—the one with his polyarchic commercialism, the other with his demagogic violence—had possibly a useful part to play at the present stage of things. He, however, could have no place in that camp. Too indiscreetly he had hoisted his standard of idealism, and by stubborn resistance of insuperable forces he had merely brought forward the least satisfactory elements of his own character. 'Hold on!' cried Malkin. 'Fight the grovellers to the end!' But Earwaker had begun to see himself in a light of ridicule. There was just time to save his self-respect.

He was in no concern for his daily bread. With narrower resources in the world of print, he might have been compelled, like many another journalist, to swallow his objections and write as Runcorn dictated; for the humble folks at home could not starve to allow him the luxury of conscientiousness, whatever he might have been disposed to do on his own account. Happily, his pen had a scope beyond politics, and by working steadily for reviews, with which he was already connected, he would be able to keep his finances in reasonable order until, perchance, some hopeful appointment offered itself. In a mood of much cheerfulness he turned for ever from party uproar, and focussed his mind upon those interests of humanity which so rarely coincide with the aims of any league among men.

Half a year went by, and at length he granted himself a short holiday, the first in a twelvemonth. It took the form of a voyage to Marseilles, and thence of a leisurely ramble up the Rhone. Before returning, he spent a day or two in Paris, for the most part beneath café awnings, or on garden seats—an indulgence of contented laziness.

On the day of his departure, he climbed the towers of Notre Dame, and lingered for half-an-hour in pleasant solitude among the stone monsters. His reverie was broken by an English voice, loud and animated:

'Come and look at this old demon of a bird; he has always been a favourite of mine.—Sure you're not tired, Miss Bella? When you want to rest, Miss Lily, mind you say so at once. What a day!—What a sky!—When I was last up here I had my hat blown away. I watched it as far as Montmartre. A fact! Never knew such a wind in my life—unless it was that tornado I told you about——Hollo! By the powers, if that isn't Earwaker! Confound you, old fellow! How the deuce do you do? What a glorious meeting! Hadn't the least idea where you were!—Let me have the pleasure of introducing you to Mrs. Jacox—and to Miss Jacox—and to Miss Lily. They all know you thoroughly well. Now who would have thought of our meeting up here! Glorious!'

It was with some curiosity that Earwaker regarded the companions of his friend Malkin—whose proximity was the last thing he could have imagined, as only a few weeks ago he had heard of the restless fellow's departing, on business unknown, for Boston, U.S. Mrs. Jacox, the widow whose wrongs had made such an impression on Malkin, announced herself, in a thin, mealy face and rag-doll figure, as not less than forty, though her irresponsible look made it evident that years profited her nothing, and suggested an explanation of the success with which she had been victimised. She was stylishly dressed, and had the air of enjoying an unusual treat. Her children were of more promising type, though Earwaker would hardly have supposed them so old as he knew them to be. Bella, just beyond her fourteenth year, had an intelligent prettiness, but was excessively shy; in giving her hand to the stranger she flushed over face and neck, and her bosom palpitated visibly. Her sister, two years younger, was a mere child, rather self-conscious, but of laughing temper. Their toilet suited ill with that of their mother; its plainness and negligence might have passed muster in London, but here, under the lucent sky, it seemed a wrong to their budding maidenhood.

'Mrs. Jacox is on the point of returning to England,' Malkin explained. 'I happened to meet her, by chance—I'm always meeting my friends by chance; you, for instance, Earwaker. She is so good as to allow me to guide her and the young ladies to a few of the sights of Paris.'

'O Mr. Malkin!' exclaimed the widow, with a stress on the exclamation peculiar to herself—two notes of deprecating falsetto. 'How can you say it is good of me, when I'm sure there are no words for your kindness to us all! If only you knew our debt to your friend, Mr. Earwaker! To our dying day we must all remember it. It is entirely through Mr. Malkin that we are able to leave that most disagreeable Rouen—a place I shall never cease to think of with horror. O Mr. Earwaker! you have only to think of that wretched railway station, stuck between two black tunnels! O Mr. Malkin!'

'What are you doing?' Malkin inquired of the journalist. 'How long shall you be here? Why haven't I heard from you?'

'I go to London to-night.'

'And we to-morrow. On Friday I'll look you up. Stay, can't you dine with me this evening? Anywhere you like. These ladies will be glad to be rid of me, and to dine in peace at their hotel.'

'O Mr. Malkin!' piped the widow, 'you know how very far that is from the truth. But we shall be very glad indeed to know that you are enjoying yourself with Mr. Earwaker.'

The friends made an appointment to meet near the Madeleine, and Earwaker hastened to escape the sound of Mrs. Jacox's voice.

Punctual at the rendezvous, Malkin talked with his wonted effusiveness as he led towards the Café Anglais.

'I've managed it, my boy! The most complete success! I had to run over to Boston to get hold of a scoundrelly relative of that poor woman. You should have seen how I came over him—partly dignified sternness, partly justifiable cajolery. The affair only wanted some one to take it up in earnest. I have secured her about a couple of hundred a year—withheld on the most paltry and transparent pretences. They're going to live at Wrotham, in Kent, where Mrs. Jacox has friends. I never thought myself so much of a man of business. Of course old Haliburton, the lawyer, had a hand in it, but without my personal energy it would have taken him a year longer. What do you think of the girls? How do you like Bella?'

'A pretty child.'

'Child? Well, yes, yes—immature of course; but I'm rather in the habit of thinking of her as a young lady. In three years she'll be seventeen, you know. Of course you couldn't form a judgment of her character. She's quite remarkably mature for her age and, what delights me most of all, a sturdy Radical! She takes the most intelligent interest in all political and social movements, I assure you! There's a great deal of democratic fire in her.'

'You're sure it isn't reflected from your own fervour?'

'Not a bit of it! You should have seen her excitement when we were at the Bastille Column yesterday. She'll make a splendid woman, I assure you. Lily's very interesting, too—profoundly interesting. But then she is certainly very young, so I can't feel so sure of her on the great questions. She hasn't her sister's earnestness, I fancy.'

In the after-glow of dinner, Malkin became still more confidential.

'You remember what I said to you long since? My mind is made up—practically made up. I shall devote myself to Bella's education, in the hope—you understand me? Impossible to have found a girl who suited better with my aspirations. She has known the hardships of poverty, poor thing, and that will keep her for ever in sympathy with the downtrodden classes. She has a splendid intelligence, and it shall be cultivated to the utmost.'

'One word,' said Earwaker, soberly. 'We have heard before of men who waited for girls to grow up. Be cautious, my dear fellow, both on your own account and hers.'

'My dear Earwaker! Don't imagine for a moment that I take it for granted she will get to be fond of me. My attitude is one of the most absolute discretion. You must have observed how I behaved to them all—scrupulous courtesy, I trust; no more familiarity than any friend might be permitted. I should never dream of addressing the girls without ceremonious prefix—never! I talk of Bella's education, but be assured that I regard my own as a matter of quite as much importance. I mean, that I shall strive incessantly to make myself worthy of her. No laxity! For these next three years I shall live as becomes a man who has his eyes constantly on a high ideal—the pure and beautiful girl whom he humbly hopes to win for a wife.'

The listener was moved. He raised his wine-glass to conceal the smile which might have been misunderstood. In his heart he felt more admiration than had yet mingled with his liking for this strange fellow.

'And Mrs. Jacox herself,' pursued Malkin; 'she has her weaknesses, as we all have. I don't think her a very strong-minded woman, to tell the truth. But there's a great deal of goodness in her. If there's one thing I desire in people, it is the virtue of gratitude, and Mrs. Jacox is grateful almost to excess for the paltry exertions I have made on her behalf. You know that kind of thing costs me nothing; you know I like running about and getting things done. But the poor woman imagines that I have laid her under an eternal obligation. Of course I shall show her in time that it was nothing at all; that she might have done just as much for herself, if she had known how to go about it.'

Earwaker was musing, a wrinkle of uneasiness at the corner of his eye.

'She isn't the kind of woman, you know, one can regard as a mother. But we are the best possible friends. She *may*, perhaps, think of me as a possible son-in-law. Poor thing; I hope she does. Perhaps it will help to put her mind at rest about the girls.'

'Then shall you often be down at Wrotham?' inquired the journalist, abstractedly.

'Oh, not often—that is to say, only once a month or so, just to look in. I wanted to ask you: do you think I might venture to begin a correspondence with Bella?'

'M—m—m! I can't say.'

'It would be so valuable, you know. I could suggest books for her reading; I could help her in her study of politics, and so on.'

'Well, think about it. But be cautious, I beg of you. Now I must be off. Only just time enough to get my traps to the station.'

'I'll come with you. Gare du Nord? Oh, plenty of time, plenty of time! Nothing so abominable as waiting for trains. I make a point of never getting to the station more than three minutes before time. Astonishing what one can do in three minutes! I want to tell you about an adventure I had in Boston. Met a fellow so devilish like Peak that I *couldn't* believe it wasn't he himself. I spoke to him, but he swore that he knew not the man. Never saw such a likeness!'

'Curious. It may have been Peak.'

'By all that's suspicious, I can't help thinking the same! He had an English accent, too.'

'Queer business, this of Peak's. I hope I may live to hear the end of the story.'

They left the restaurant, and in a few hours Earwaker was again on English soil.

At Staple Inn a pile of letters awaited him, among them a note from Christian Moxey, asking for an appointment as soon as possible after the journalist's return. Earwaker at once sent an invitation, and on the next evening Moxey came. An intimacy had grown up between the two, since the mysterious retreat of their common friend. Christian was at first lost without the companionship of Godwin Peak; he forsook his studies, and fell into a state of complete idleness which naturally fostered his tendency to find solace in the decanter. With Earwaker, he could not talk as unreservedly as with Peak, but on the other hand there was a tonic influence in the journalist's personality which he recognised as beneficial. Earwaker was steadily making his way in the world, lived a life of dignified independence. What was the secret of these strong, calm natures? Might it not be learnt by studious inspection?

'How well you look!' Christian exclaimed, on entering. 'We enjoyed your Provençal letter enormously. That's a ramble I have always meant to do. Next year perhaps.'

'Why not this? Haven't you got into a dangerous habit of postponement?'

'Yes, I'm afraid I have. But by-the-bye, no news of Peak, I suppose?'

Earwaker related the story he had heard from Malkin, adding:

'You must remember that they met only once in London; Malkin might very well mistake another man for Peak.'

'Yes,' replied the other musingly. 'Yet it isn't impossible that Peak has gone over there. If so, what on earth can he be up to? Why *should* he hide from his friends?'

'*Cherchez la femme*,' said the journalist, with a smile. 'I can devise no other explanation.'

'But I can't see that it would be an explanation at all. Grant even—something unavowable, you know—are we Puritans? How could it harm him, at all events, to let us know his whereabouts? No such mystery ever came into my experience. It is too bad of Peak; it's confoundedly unkind.'

'Suppose he has found it necessary to assume a character wholly fictitious—or, let us say, quite inconsistent with his life and opinions as known to us?'

This was a fruitful suggestion, long in Earwaker's mind, but not hitherto communicated. Christian did not at once grasp its significance.

'How could that be necessary? Peak is no swindler. You don't imply that he is engaged in some fraud?'

'Not in the ordinary sense, decidedly. But picture some girl or woman of conventional opinions and surroundings. What if he resolved to win such a wife, at the expense of disguising his true self?'

'But what an extraordinary idea!' cried Moxey. 'Why Peak is all but a woman-hater!'

The journalist uttered croaking laughter.

'Have I totally misunderstood him?' asked Christian, confused and abashed.

'I think it not impossible.'

'You amaze me!—But no, no; you are wrong, Earwaker. Wrong in your suggestion, I mean. Peak could never sink to that. He is too uncompromising'——

'Well, it will be explained some day, I suppose.'

And with a shrug of impatience, the journalist turned to another subject. He, too, regretted his old friend's disappearance, and in a measure resented it. Godwin Peak was not a man to slip out of one's life and leave no appreciable vacancy. Neither of these men admired him, in the true sense of the word, yet had his voice sounded at the door both would have sprung up with eager welcome. He was a force—and how many such beings does one encounter in a lifetime?

II

In different ways, Christian and Marcella Moxey had both been lonely since their childhood. As a schoolgirl, Marcella seemed to her companions conceited and repellent; only as the result of reflection in after years did Sylvia Moorhouse express so favourable an opinion of her. In all things she affected singularity; especially it was her delight to utter democratic and revolutionary sentiments among hearers who, belonging to a rigidly conservative order, held such opinions impious. Arrived at womanhood, she affected scorn of the beliefs and habits cherished by her own sex, and shrank from association with the other. Godwin Peak was the first man with whom she conversed in the tone of friendship, and it took a year or more before that point was reached. As her intimacy with him established itself, she was observed to undergo changes which seemed very significant in the eyes of her few acquaintances. Disregard of costume had been one of her characteristics, but now she moved gradually towards the opposite extreme, till her dresses were occasionally more noticeable for richness than for good taste.

Christian, for kindred reasons, was equally debarred from the pleasures and profits of society. At school, his teachers considered him clever, his fellows for the most part looked down upon him as a sentimental weakling. The death of his parents, when he was still a lad, left him to the indifferent care of a guardian nothing akin to him. He began life in an uncongenial position, and had not courage to oppose the drift of circumstances. The romantic attachment which absorbed his best years naturally had a debilitating effect, for love was never yet a supporter of the strenuous virtues, save when it has survived fruition and been blessed by reason. In most men a fit of amorous mooning works its own cure; energetic rebound is soon inevitable. But Christian was so constituted that a decade of years could not exhaust his capacity for sentimental languishment. He made it a point of honour to seek no female companionship which could imperil his faith. Unfortunately, this avoidance of the society which would soon have made him a happy renegade, was but too easy. Marcella and he practically encouraged each other in a life of isolation, though to both of them such an existence was anything but congenial. Their difficulties were of the same nature as those which had always beset Godwin Peak; they had no relatives with whom they cared to associate, and none of the domestic friends who, in the progress of time, establish and extend a sphere of genuine intimacy.

Most people who are capable of independent thought rapidly outgrow the stage when compromise is abhorred; they accept, at first reluctantly but ere long with satisfaction, that code of polite intercourse which, as Steele says, is 'an expedient to make fools and wise men equal.' It was Marcella's ill-fate that she could neither learn tolerance nor persuade herself to affect it. The emancipated woman has fewer opportunities of relieving her mind than a man in corresponding position; if her temper be aggressive she must renounce general society, and, if not content to live alone, ally herself with some group of declared militants. By correspondence, or otherwise, Marcella might have brought herself into connection with women of a sympathetic type, but this effort she had never made. And chiefly because of her acquaintance with Godwin Peak. In him she concentrated her interests; he was the man to whom her heart went forth with every kind of fervour. So long as there remained a hope of moving him to reciprocal feeling she did not care to go in search of female companions. Year after year she sustained herself in solitude by this faint hope. She had lost sight of the two or three school-fellows who, though not so zealous as herself, would have welcomed her as an interesting acquaintance; and the only woman who assiduously sought her was Mrs. Morton, the wife of one of Christian's friends, a good-natured but silly person bent on making known that she followed the 'higher law.'

Godwin's disappearance sank her in profound melancholy. Through the black weeks of January and February she scarcely left the house, and on the plea of illness refused to see any one but her brother. Between Christian and her there was no avowed confidence, but each knew the other's secret; their mutual affection never spoke itself in words, yet none the less it was indispensable to their lives. Deprived of his sister's company, Christian must have yielded to the vice which had already too strong a hold upon him, and have become a maudlin drunkard. Left to herself, Marcella had but slender support against a grim temptation already beckoning her in nights of sleeplessness. Of the two, her nature was the more tragic. Circumstances aiding, Christian might still forget his melancholy, abandon the whisky bottle, and pass a lifetime of amiable uxuriousness, varied with scientific enthusiasm. But for Marcella, frustrate in the desire with which every impulse of her being had identified itself, what future could be imagined?

When a day or two of sunlight (the rays through a semi-opaque atmosphere which London has to accept with gratitude) had announced that the seven-months' winter was overcome, and when the newspapers began to speak, after their fashion, of pictures awaiting scrutiny, Christian exerted himself to rouse his sister from her growing indolence. He succeeded in taking her to the Academy. Among the works of sculpture, set apart for the indifference of the public, was a female head, catalogued as 'A Nihilist'—in itself interesting, and specially so to Marcella, because it was executed by an artist whose name she recognised as that of a schoolmate, Agatha Walworth. She spoke of the circumstance to Christian, and added:

'I should like to have that. Let us go and see the price.'

The work was already sold. Christian, happy that his sister could be aroused to this interest, suggested that a cast might be obtainable.

'Write to Miss Walworth,' he urged. 'Bring yourself to her recollection.—I should think she must be the right kind of woman.'

Though at the time she shook her head, Marcella was presently tempted to address a letter to the artist, who responded with friendly invitation. In this way a new house was opened to her; but, simultaneously, one more illusion was destroyed. Knowing little of life, and much of literature, she pictured Miss Walworth as inhabiting a delightful Bohemian world, where the rules of conventionalism had no existence, and everything was judged by the brain-standard. Modern French biographies supplied all her ideas of studio society. She prepared herself for the first visit with a joyous tremor, wondering whether she would be deemed worthy to associate with the men and women who lived for art. The reality was a shock. In a large house at Chiswick she found a gathering of most respectable English people, chatting over the regulation tea-cup; not one of them inclined to disregard the dictates of Mrs. Grundy in dress, demeanour, or dialogue. Agatha Walworth lived with her parents and her sisters like any other irreproachable young woman. She had a nice little studio, and worked at modelling with a good deal of aptitude; but of Bohemia she knew nothing whatever, save by hearsay. Her 'Nihilist' was no indication of a rebellious spirit; some friend had happened to suggest that a certain female model, a Russian, would do very well for such a character, and the hint was tolerably well carried out—nothing more. Marcella returned in a mood of contemptuous disappointment. The cast she had desired to have was shortly sent to her as a gift, but she could take no pleasure in it.

Still, she saw more of the Walworths and found them not illiberal. Agatha was intelligent, and fairly well read in modern authors; no need to conceal one's opinions in conversation with her. Marcella happened to be spending the evening with these acquaintances whilst her brother was having his chat at Staple Inn; on her return, she mentioned to Christian that she had been invited to visit the Walworths in Devonshire a few weeks hence.

'Go by all means,' urged her brother.

'I don't think I shall. They are too respectable.'

'Nonsense! They seem very open-minded; you really can't expect absolute unconventionality. Is it desirable? Really is it, now?—Suppose I were to marry some day, Marcella; do you think my household would be unconventional?'

His voice shook a little, and he kept his eyes averted. Marcella, to whom her brother's romance was anything but an agreeable subject,—the slight acquaintance she had with the modern Laura did not encourage her to hope for that lady's widowhood,—gave no heed to the question.

'They are going to have a house at Budleigh Salterton; do you know of the place? Somewhere near the mouth of the Exe. Miss Walworth tells me that one of our old school friends is living there—Sylvia Moorhouse. Did I ever mention Sylvia? She had gleams of sense, I remember; but no doubt society has drilled all that out of her.'

Christian sighed.

'Why?' he urged. 'Society is getting more tolerant than you are disposed to think. Very few well-educated people would nowadays object to an acquaintance on speculative grounds. Someone —who was it?—was telling me of a recent marriage between the daughter of some well-known Church people and a man who made no secret of his agnosticism; the parents acquiescing cheerfully. The one thing still insisted on is decency of behaviour.'

Marcella's eyes flashed.

'How can you say that? You know quite well that most kinds of immorality are far more readily forgiven by people of the world than sincere heterodoxy on moral subjects.'

'Well, well, I meant decency from *their* point of view. And there really must be such restrictions, you know. How very few people are capable of what you call sincere heterodoxy, in morals or religion! Your position is unphilosophical; indeed it is. Take the world as you find it, and make friends with kind, worthy people. You have suffered from a needless isolation. Do accept this opportunity of adding to your acquaintances!—Do, Marcella! I shall take it as a great kindness, dear girl.'

His sister let her head lie back against the chair, her face averted. A stranger seated in Christian's place, regarding Marcella whilst her features were thus hidden, would have thought it probable that she was a woman of no little beauty. Her masses of tawny hair, her arms and hands, the pose and outline of her figure, certainly suggested a countenance of corresponding charm, and the ornate richness of her attire aided such an impression. This thought came to Christian as he gazed at her; his eyes, always so gentle, softened to a tender compassion. As the silence continued, he looked uneasily about him; when at length he spoke, it was as though a matter of trifling moment had occurred to him.

'By-the-bye, I am told that Malkin (Earwaker's friend, you know) saw Peak not long ago—in America.'

Marcella did not change her position, but at the sound of Peak's name she stirred, as if with an intention, at once checked, of bending eagerly forward.

'In America?' she asked, incredulously.

'At Boston. He met him in the street—or thinks he did. There's a doubt. When Malkin spoke to the man, he declared that he was not Peak at all—said there was a mistake.'

Marcella moved so as to show her face; endeavouring to express an unemotional interest she looked coldly scornful.

'That ridiculous man can't be depended upon,' she said.

There had been one meeting between Marcella and Mr. Malkin, with the result that each thoroughly disliked the other—an antipathy which could have been foreseen.

'Well, there's no saying,' replied Christian. 'But of one thing I feel pretty sure: we have seen the last of Peak. He'll never come back to us.'

'Why not?'

'I can only say that I feel convinced he has broken finally with all his old friends.—We must think no more of him, Marcella.'

His sister rose slowly, affected to glance at a book, and in a few moments said good-night. For another hour Christian sat by himself in gloomy thought.

At breakfast next morning Marcella announced that she would be from home the whole day; she might return in time for dinner, but it was uncertain. Her brother asked no questions, but said that he would lunch in town. About ten o'clock a cab was summoned, and Marcella, without leave-taking, drove away.

Christian lingered as long as possible over the morning paper, unable to determine how he should waste the weary hours that lay before him. There was no reason for his remaining in London through this brief season of summer glow. Means and leisure were his, he could go whither he would. But the effort of decision and departure seemed too much for him. Worst of all, this lassitude (not for the first time) was affecting his imagination; he thought with a full discontent of the ideal love to which he had bound himself. Could he but escape from it, and begin a new life! But he was the slave of his airy obligation; for very shame's sake his ten year's consistency must be that of a lifetime.

There was but one place away from London to which he felt himself drawn, and that was the one place he might not visit. This morning's sunshine carried him back to that day when he had lain in the meadow near Twybridge and talked with Godwin Peak. How distinctly he remembered his mood! 'Be practical—don't be led astray after ideals—concentrate yourself';—yes, it was he who had given that advice to Peak: and had he but recked his own rede——! Poor little Janet! was she married? If so, her husband must be a happy man.

Why should he not go down to Twybridge? His uncle, undoubtedly still living, must by this time have forgotten the old resentment, perhaps would be glad to see him. In any case he might stroll about the town and somehow obtain news of the Moxey family.

With vague half-purpose he left the house and walked westward. The stream of traffic in Edgware Road brought him to a pause; he stood for five minutes in miserable indecision, all but resolving to go on as far as Euston and look for the next northward train. But the vice in his will prevailed; automaton-like he turned in another direction, and presently came out into Sussex Square. Here was the house to which his thoughts had perpetually gone forth ever since that day when Constance gave her hand to a thriving City man, and became Mrs. Palmer. At present, he knew, it was inhabited only by domestics: Mr. Palmer, recovering from illness that threatened to be fatal, had gone to Bournemouth, where Constance of course tended him. But he would walk past and look up at the windows.

All the blinds were down—naturally. Thrice he went by and retraced his steps. Then, still automaton-like, he approached the door, rang the bell. The appearance of the servant choked his voice for an instant, but he succeeded in shaping an inquiry after Mr. Palmer's health.

'I'm sorry to say, sir,' was the reply, 'that Mr. Palmer died last night. We received the news only an hour or two ago.'

Christian tottered on his feet and turned so pale that the servant regarded him with anxiety. For a minute or two he stared vacantly into the gloomy hall; then, without a word, he turned abruptly and walked away.

Unconscious of the intervening distance, he found himself at home, in his library. The parlour-maid was asking him whether he would have luncheon. Scarcely understanding the question, he muttered a refusal and sat down.

So, it had come at last. Constance was a widow. In a year or so she might think of marrying again.

He remained in the library for three or four hours. At first incapable of rejoicing, then ashamed to do so, he at length suffered from such a throbbing of the heart that apprehension of illness recalled him to a normal state of mind. The favourite decanter was within reach, and it gave him the wonted support. Then at length did heart and brain glow with exulting fervour.

Poor Constance! Noble woman! Most patient of martyrs! The hour of her redemption had struck. The fetters had fallen from her tender, suffering body. Of *him* she could not yet think. He did not wish it. Her womanhood must pay its debt to nature before she could gladden in the prospect of a new life. Months must go by before he could approach her, or even remind her of his existence. But at last his reward was sure.

And he had thought of Twybridge, of his cousin Janet! O unworthy lapse!

He shed tears of tenderness. Dear, noble Constance! It was now nearly twelve years since he first looked upon her face. In those days he mingled freely with all the society within his reach. It was not very select, and Constance Markham shone to him like a divinity among creatures of indifferent clay. They said she was coquettish, that she played at the game of love with every presentable young man—envious calumny! No, she was single-hearted, inexperienced, a lovely and joyous girl of not yet twenty. It is so difficult for such a girl to understand her own emotions. Her parents persuaded her into wedding Palmer. That was all gone into the past, and now his concern—their concern—was only with the blessed future.

At three o'clock he began to feel a healthy appetite. He sent for a cab and drove towards the region of restaurants.

Had he yielded to the impulse which this morning directed him to Twybridge, he would have arrived in that town not very long after his sister.

For that was the aim of Marcella's journey. On reaching the station, she dropped a light veil over her face and set forth on foot to discover the abode of Mrs. Peak. No inhabitant of Twybridge save her uncle and his daughters could possibly recognise her, but she shrank from walking through the streets with exposed countenance. Whether she would succeed in her quest was uncertain. Godwin Peak's mother still dwelt here, she knew, for less than a year ago she had asked the question of Godwin himself; but a woman in humble circumstances might not have a house of her own, and her name was probably unknown save to a few friends.

However, the first natural step was to inquire for a directory. A stationer supplied her with one, informing her, with pride, that he himself was the author of it—that this was only the second year of its issue, and that its success was 'very encouraging.' Retiring to a quiet street, Marcella examined her purchase, and came upon 'Peak, Oliver; seedsman'—the sole entry of the name. This was probably a relative of Godwin's. Without difficulty she found Mr. Peak's shop; behind the counter stood Oliver himself, rubbing his hands. Was there indeed a family likeness between this fresh-looking young shopkeeper and the stern, ambitious, intellectual man whose lineaments were ever before her mind? Though with fear and repulsion, Marcella was constrained to recognise something in the commonplace visage. With an uncertain voice, she made known her business.

'I wish to find Mrs. Peak—a widow—an elderly lady'——

'Oh yes, madam! My mother, no doubt. She lives with her

sister, Miss Cadman—the milliner's shop in the first street to the left. Let me point it out.'

With a sinking of the heart Marcella murmured thanks and walked away. She found the milliner's shop—and went past it.

Why should discoveries such as these be so distasteful to her? Her own origin was not so exalted that she must needs look down on trades-folk. Still, for the moment she all but abandoned her undertaking. Was Godwin Peak in truth of so much account to her? Would not the shock of meeting his mother be final? Having come thus far, she must go through with it. If the experience cured her of a hopeless passion, why, what more desirable?

She entered the shop. A young female assistant came forward with respectful smile, and waited her commands.

'I wish, if you please, to see Mrs. Peak.

'Oh yes, madam! Will you have the goodness to walk this way?'

Too late Marcella remembered that she ought to have gone to the house-entrance. The girl led her out of the shop into a dark passage, and thence into a sitting-room which smelt of lavender. Here she waited for a few moments; then the door opened softly, and Mrs. Peak presented herself.

There was no shock. The widow had the air of a gentlewoman—walked with elderly grace—and spoke with propriety. She resembled Godwin, and this time it was not painful to remark the likeness.

'I have come to Twybridge,' began Marcella, gently and respectfully, 'that is to say, I have stopped in passing—to ask for the address of Mr. Godwin Peak. A letter has failed to reach him.'

It was her wish to manage without either disclosing the truth about herself or elaborating fictions, but after the first words she felt it impossible not to offer some explanation. Mrs. Peak showed a slight surprise. With the courage of cowardice, Marcella continued more rapidly:

'My name is Mrs. Ward. My husband used to know Mr. Peak, in London, a few years ago, but we have been abroad, and unfortunately have lost sight of him. We remembered that Mr.

Peak's relatives lived at Twybridge, and, as we wish very much to renew the old acquaintance, I took the opportunity—passing by rail. I made inquiries in the town, and was directed to you—I hope rightly'——

The widow's face changed to satisfaction. Evidently her straightforward mind accepted the story as perfectly credible. Marcella, with bitterness, knew herself far from comely enough to suggest perils. She looked old enough for the part she was playing, and the glove upon her hand might conceal a wedding-ring.

'Yes, you were directed rightly,' Mrs. Peak made quiet answer. 'I shall be very glad to give you my son's address. He left London about last Christmas, and went to live at Exeter.'

'Exeter? We thought he might be out of England.'

'No; he has lived all the time at Exeter. The address is Longbrook Street'—she added the number. 'He is studying, and finds that part of the country pleasant. I am hoping to see him here before very long.'

Marcella did not extend the conversation. She spoke of having to catch a train, and veiled as well as she could beneath ordinary courtesies her perplexity at the information she had received.

When she again reached the house at Notting Hill, Christian was absent. He came home about nine in the evening. It was impossible not to remark his strange mood of repressed excitement; but Marcella did not question him, and Christian had resolved to conceal the day's event until he could speak of it without agitation. Before they parted for the night, Marcella said carelessly:

'I have decided to go down to Budleigh Salterton when the time comes.'

'That's right!' exclaimed her brother, with satisfaction. 'You couldn't do better—couldn't possibly. It will be a very good thing for you in several ways.'

And each withdrew to brood over a perturbing secret.

III

THREE OR FOUR years ago, when already he had conceived the idea of trying his fortune in some provincial town, Peak persuaded himself that it would not be difficult to make acquaintances among educated people, even though he had no credentials to offer. He indulged his fancy and pictured all manner of pleasant accidents which surely, sooner or later, must bring him into contact with families of the better sort. One does hear of such occurrences, no doubt. In every town there is someone or other whom a stranger may approach: a medical man—a local antiquary—a librarian—a philanthropist; and with moderate advantages of mind and address, such casual connections may at times be the preface to intimacy, with all resulting benefits. But experience of Exeter had taught him how slight would have been his chance of getting on friendly terms with any mortal if he had depended solely on his personal qualities. After a nine months' residence, and with the friendship of such people as the Warricombes, he was daily oppressed by his isolation amid this community of English folk. He had done his utmost to adopt the tone of average polished life. He had sat at the tables of worthy men, and conversed freely with their sons and daughters; he exchanged greetings in the highways: but this availed him nothing. Now, as on the day of his arrival, he was an alien—a lodger. What else had he ever been, since boyhood? A lodger in Kingsmill, a lodger in London, a lodger in Exeter. Nay, even as a boy he could scarcely have been said to 'live at home,' for from the dawn of conscious intelligence he felt himself out of place among familiar things and people, at issue with prevalent opinions. Was he never to win a right of citizenship, never to have a recognised place among men associated in the duties and pleasures of life?

Sunday was always a day of weariness and despondency, and at present he suffered from the excitement of his conversation with Sidwell, followed as it had been by a night of fever. Extravagant hope had given place to a depression which could see nothing beyond the immediate gloom. Until mid-day he lay in bed. After dinner, finding the solitude of his little room intolerable, he went out to walk in the streets.

Not far from his door some children had gathered in a quiet corner, and were playing at a game on the pavement with pieces of chalk. As he drew near, a policeman, observing the little group, called out to them in a stern voice:

'Now then! what are you doing there? Don't you know *what day* it is?'

The youngsters fled, conscious of shameful delinquency.

There it was! There spoke the civic voice, the social rule, the public sentiment! Godwin felt that the policeman had rebuked *him*, and in doing so had severely indicated the cause of that isolation which he was condemned to suffer. Yes, all his life he had desired to play games on Sunday; he had never been able to understand why games on Sunday should be forbidden. And the angry laugh which escaped him as he went by the guardian of public morals, declared the impossibility of his ever being at one with communities which made this point the prime test of worthiness.

He walked on at a great speed, chafing, talking to himself. His way took him through Heavitree (when Hooker saw the light here, how easy to believe that the Anglican Church was the noblest outcome of human progress!) and on and on, until by a lane with red banks of sandstone, thick with ferns, shadowed with noble boughs, he came to a hamlet which had always been one of his favourite resorts, so peacefully it lay amid the exquisite rural landscape. The cottages were all closed and silent; hark for the reason! From the old church sounded an organ prelude, then the voice of the congregation, joining in one of the familiar hymns.

A significant feature of Godwin's idiosyncrasy. Notwithstanding his profound hatred and contempt of multitudes, he could never hear the union of many voices in song but his breast heaved and a choking warmth rose in his throat. Even where prejudice wrought most strongly with him, it had to give way before this rush of emotion; he often hurried out of earshot when a group of Salvationists were singing, lest the involuntary sympathy of his senses should agitate and enrage him. At present he had no wish to draw away. He entered the churchyard, and found the leafy nook with a tombstone where he had often rested. And as he listened to the rude chanting of verse after verse, tears fell upon his cheeks.

This sensibility was quite distinct from religious feeling. If the note of devotion sounding in that simple strain had any effect upon him at all, it merely intensified his consciousness of pathos as he thought of the many generations that had worshipped here, living and dying in a faith which was at best a helpful delusion. He could appreciate the beautiful aspects of Christianity as a legend, its nobility as a humanising power, its rich results in literature, its grandeur in historic retrospect. But at no moment in his life had he felt it as a spiritual influence. So far from tending in that direction, as he sat and brooded here in the churchyard, he owed to his fit of tearfulness a courage which determined him to abandon all religious pretences, and henceforth trust only to what was sincere in him—his human passion. The future he had sketched to Sidwell was impossible; the rural pastorate, the life of moral endeavour which in his excitement had seemed so nearly a genuine aspiration that it might perchance become reality—dreams, dreams! He must woo as a man, and trust to fortune for his escape from a false position. Sidwell should hear nothing more of clerical projects. He was by this time convinced that she held far less tenaciously than he had supposed to the special doctrines of the Church; and, if he had not deceived himself in interpreting her behaviour, a mutual avowal of love would involve ready consent on her part to his abandoning a career which—as he would represent it—had been adopted under a mistaken impulse. He returned to the point which he had reached when he set forth with the intention of bidding goodbye to the Warricombes—except that in flinging away hypocrisy he no longer needed to trample his desires. The change need not be declared till after a lapse of time. For the present his task was to obtain one more private interview with Sidwell ere she went to London, or, if that could not be, somehow to address her in unmistakable language.

The fumes were dispelled from his brain, and as he walked homeward he plotted and planned with hopeful energy. Sylvia Moorhouse came into his mind; could he not in some way make use of her? He had never yet been to see her at Budleigh Salterton. That he would do forthwith, and perchance the visit might supply him with suggestions.

On the morrow he set forth, going by train to Exmouth, and thence by the coach which runs twice a day to the little seaside town. The delightful drive, up hill and down dale, with its magnificent views over the estuary, and its ever-changing wayside beauties, put him into the best of spirits. About noon, he alighted at the Rolle Arms, the hotel to which the coach conducts its passengers, and entered to take a meal. He would call upon the Moorhouses at the conventional hour. The intervening time was spent pleasantly enough in loitering about the pebbled beach. A south-west breeze which had begun to gather clouds drove on the rising tide. By four o'clock there was an end of sunshine, and spurts of rain mingled with flying foam. Peak turned inland, pursued the leafy street up the close-sheltered valley, and came to the house where his friends dwelt.

In crossing the garden he caught sight of a lady who sat in a room on the ground floor; her back was turned to the window, and before he could draw near enough to see her better she had moved away, but the glimpse he had obtained of her head and shoulders affected him with so distinct an alarm that his steps were checked. It seemed to him that he had recognised the figure, and if he were right—But the supposition was ridiculous; at all events so vastly improbable, that he would not entertain it. And now he descried another face, that of Miss Moorhouse herself, and it gave him a reassuring smile. He rang the door bell.

How happy—he said to himself—those men who go to call upon their friends without a tremor! Even if he had not received that shock a moment ago, he would still have needed to struggle against the treacherous beating of his heart as he waited for admission. It was always so when he visited the Warricombes, or any other family in Exeter. Not merely in consequence of the dishonest part he was playing, but because he had not quite overcome the nervousness which so anguished him in earlier days. The first moment after his entering a drawing-room cost him pangs of complex origin.

His eyes fell first of all upon Mrs. Moorhouse, who advanced to welcome him. He was aware of three other persons in the room. The nearest, he could perceive without regarding her, was Sidwell's friend; the other two, on whom he did not yet venture to cast a glance, sat—or rather had just risen—in a dim background. As he shook hands with Sylvia, they drew nearer; one of them was a man, and, as his voice at once declared, no other than Buckland Warricombe. Peak returned his greeting, and, in the same moment, gazed at the last of the party. Mrs. Moorhouse was speaking.

'Mr. Peak—Miss Moxey.'

A compression of the lips was the only sign of disturbance that anyone could have perceived on Godwin's countenance. Already he had strung himself against his wonted agitation, and the added trial did not sensibly enhance what he suffered. In discovering that he had rightly identified the figure at the window, he experienced no renewal of the dread which brought him to a standstill. Already half prepared for this stroke of fate, he felt a satisfaction in being able to meet it so steadily. Tumult of thought was his only trouble; it seemed as if his brain must burst with the stress of its lightning operations. In three seconds, he relived the past, made several distinct anticipations of the future, and still discussed with himself how he should behave this moment. He noted that Marcella's face was bloodless; that her attempt to smile resulted in a very painful distortion of brow and lips. And he had leisure to pity her. This emotion prevailed. With a sense of magnanimity, which afterwards excited his wonder, he pressed the cold hand and said in a cheerful tone:

'Our introduction took place long ago, if I'm not mistaken. I had no idea, Miss Moxey, that you were among Mrs. Moorhouse's friends.'

'Nor I that you were, Mr. Peak,' came the answer, in a steadier voice than Godwin had expected.

Mrs. Moorhouse and her daughter made the pleasant exclamations that were called for. Buckland Warricombe, with a doubtful smile on his lips, kept glancing from Miss Moxey to her acquaintance and back again. Peak at length faced him.

'I hoped we should meet down here this autumn.'

'I should have looked you up in a day or two,' Buckland replied, seating himself. 'Do you propose to stay in Exeter through the winter?'

'I'm not quite sure—but I think it likely.'

Godwin turned to the neighbour of whose presence he was most conscious.

'I hope your brother is well, Miss Moxey?'

Their eyes encountered steadily.

'Yes, he is quite well, thank you. He often says that it seems very long since he heard from you.'

'I'm a bad correspondent.—Is he also in Devonshire?'

'No. In London.'

'What a storm we are going to have!' exclaimed Sylvia, looking to the window. 'They predicted it yesterday. I should like to be on the top of Westdown Beacon—wouldn't you, Miss Moxey?'

'I am quite willing to go with you.'

'And what pleasure do you look for up there?' asked Warricombe, in a blunt, matter-of-fact tone.

'Now, there's a question!' cried Sylvia, appealing to the rest of the company.

'I agree with Mr. Warricombe,' remarked her mother. 'It's better to be in a comfortable room.'

'Oh, you Radicals! What a world you will make of it in time!'

Sylvia affected to turn away in disgust, and happening to glance through the window she saw two young ladies approaching from the road.

'The Walworths—struggling desperately with their umbrellas.'

'I shouldn't wonder if you think it unworthy of an artist to carry an umbrella,' said Buckland.

'Now you suggest it, I certainly do. They should get nobly drenched.'

She went out into the hall, and soon returned with her friends—Miss Walworth the artist, Miss Muriel Walworth, and a youth, their brother. In the course of conversation Peak learnt that Miss Moxey was the guest of this family, and that she had been at Budleigh Salterton with them only a day or two. For a time he listened and observed, endeavouring to postpone consideration of the dangers into which he had suddenly fallen. Marcella had made herself his accomplice, thus far, in disguising the real significance of their meeting, and whether she would betray him in her subsequent talk with the Moorhouses remained a matter of doubt. Of course he must have assurance of her disposition—but the issues involved were too desperate for instant scrutiny. He felt the gambler's excitement, an irrational pleasure in the consciousness that his whole future was at stake. Buckland Warricombe had a keen eye upon him, and doubtless was eager to strike a train of suspicious circumstances. His face, at all events, should give no sign of discomposure. Indeed, he found so much enjoyment in the bright gossip of this assembly of ladies that the smile he wore was perfectly natural.

The Walworths, he gathered, were to return to London in a week's time. This meant, in all probability, that Marcella's stay here would not be prolonged beyond that date. Perhaps he could find an opportunity of seeing her apart from her friends. In reply to a question from Mrs. Moorhouse, he made known that he proposed staying at the Rolle Arms for several days, and when he had spoken he glanced at Marcella. She understood him, he felt sure. An invitation to lunch here on the morrow was of course accepted.

Before leaving, he exchanged a few words with Buckland.

'Your relatives will be going to town very soon, I understand.'

Warricombe nodded.

'Shall I see you at Exeter?' Godwin continued.

'I'm not sure. I shall go over tomorrow, but it's uncertain whether I shall still be there when you return.'

The Radical was distinctly less amicable than even on the last occasion of their meeting. They shook hands in rather a perfunctory way.

Early in the evening there was a temporary lull in the storm; rain no longer fell, and in spaces of the rushing sky a few stars showed themselves. Unable to rest at the hotel, Peak set out for a walk towards the cliff summit called Westdown Beacon; he could see little more than black vacancies, but a struggle with the wind suited his temper, and he enjoyed the incessant roar of surf in the darkness. After an hour of this buffeting he returned to the beach, and stood as close as possible to the fierce breakers. No person was in sight. But when he began to move towards the upper shore, three female figures detached themselves from the gloom and advanced in his direction. They came so near that their voices were audible, and thereupon he stepped up to them.

'Are you going to the Beacon after all, Miss Moorhouse?'

Sylvia was accompanied by Agatha Walworth and Miss Moxey. She explained laughingly that they had stolen out, by agreement, whilst the males of their respective households still lingered at the dinner-table.

'But Mr. Warricombe was right after all. We shall be blown to pieces. A very little of the romantic goes a long way, nowadays.'

Godwin was determined to draw Marcella aside. Seemingly she met his wish, for as all turned to regain the shelter of houses she fell behind her female companions, and stood close by him.

'I want to see you before you go back to London,' he said, bending his head near to hers.

'I wrote a letter to you, this morning,' was her reply.

'A letter? To what address?'

'Your address at Exeter.'

'But how did you know it?'

'I'll explain afterwards.'

'When can I see you?'

'Not here. It's impossible. I shall go to Exeter, and there write to you again.'

'Very well. You promise to do this?'

'Yes, I promise.'

There was danger even in the exchange of these hurried sentences. Miss Walworth had glanced back, and might possibly have caught a phrase that aroused curiosity. Having accompanied the girls to within view of their destination, Peak said good-night, and went home to spend the rest of the evening in thought which was sufficiently absorbing.

The next day he had no sight of Marcella. At luncheon the Moorhouses were alone. Afterwards Godwin accepted a proposal of the mathematician (who was generally invisible amid his formulæ) for a walk up the Otter valley. Naturally they talked of Coleridge, whose metaphysical side appealed to Moorhouse. Peak dwelt on the human and poetical, and was led by that peculiar recklessness of mood, which at times relieved his nervous tension, to defend opium eating, as a source of pleasurable experience.

'You will hardly venture on that paradox in the pulpit,' remarked his companion, with laughter.

'Perhaps not. But I have heard arguments from that place decidedly more immoral.'

'No doubt.'

Godwin corrected the impression he perhaps had made by turning with sudden seriousness to another subject. The ironic temptation was terribly strong in him just now. One is occasionally possessed by a desire to shout in the midst of a silent assembly; an impulse of the same kind kept urging him to utter words which would irretrievably ruin his prospects. The sense that life is an intolerable mummery can with difficulty be controlled by certain minds, even when circumstances offer no keen incitement to rebellion. But Peak's position to-day demanded an incessant effort to refrain from self-betrayal. What a joy to declare himself a hypocrite, and snap mocking fingers in the world's face! As a safeguard, he fixed his mind upon Sidwell, recalled her features and her voice as clearly as possible, stamped into his heart the conviction that she half loved him.

When he was alone again, he of a sudden determined to go to Exeter. He could no longer endure uncertainty as to the contents of Marcella's letter. As it was too late for the coach, he set off and walked five miles to Exmouth, where he caught a train.

The letter lay on his table, and with it one on which he recognised his mother's handwriting.

Marcella wrote in the simplest way, quite as if their intercourse had never been disturbed. As she happened to be staying with friends at Budleigh Salterton, it seemed possible for her to meet him. Might she hope that he would call at the hotel in Exeter, if she wrote again to make an appointment?

Well, that needed no reply. But how had she discovered the address? Was his story known in London? In a paroxysm of fury, he crushed the letter into a ball and flung it away. The veins of his forehead swelled; he walked about the room with senseless violence, striking his fist against furniture and walls. It would have relieved him to sob and cry like a thwarted child, but only a harsh sound, half-groan, half-laughter, burst from his throat.

The fit passed, and he was able to open the letter from Twybridge, the first he had received from his mother for more than a month. He expected to find nothing of interest, but his attention was soon caught by a passage, which ran thus:

'Have you heard from some friends of yours, called Ward? Some time ago a lady called here to ask for your address. She said her name was Mrs. Ward, and that her husband, who had been abroad for a long time, very much wished to find you again. Of course I told her where you were to be found. It was just after I had written, or I should have let you know about it before.'

Ward? He knew no one of that name. Could it be Marcella who had done this? It looked more than likely; he believed her capable of strange proceedings.

In the morning he returned to the seaside. Prospect of pleasure there was none, but by moving about he made the time pass more quickly. Wandering in the lanes (which would have delighted him with their autumnal beauties had his mind been at rest), he came upon Miss Walworth, busy with a water-colour sketch. Though their acquaintance was so slight, he stopped for conversation, and the artist's manner appeared to testify that

Marcella had as yet made no unfavourable report of him. By mentioning that he would return home on the morrow, he made sure that Marcella would be apprised of this. Perhaps she might shorten her stay, and his suspense.

Back in Longbrook Street once more, he found another letter. It was from Mrs. Warricombe, who wrote to tell him of their coming removal to London, and added an invitation to dine four days hence. Then at all events he would speak again with Sidwell. But to what purpose? Could he let her go away for months, and perhaps all but forget him among the many new faces that would surround her. He saw no feasible way of being with her in private. To write was to run the gravest risk; things were not ripe for that. To take Martin into his confidence? That asked too much courage. Deliberate avowals of this kind seemed to him ludicrous and humiliating, and under the circumstances—no, no; what force of sincerity could make him appear other than a scheming adventurer?

He lived in tumult of mind and senses. When at length, on the day before his engagement with the Warricombes, there came a note from Marcella, summoning him to the interview agreed upon, he could scarcely endure the hour or two until it was time to set forth; every minute cost him a throb of pain. The torment must have told upon his visage, for on entering the room where Marcella waited he saw that she looked at him with a changing expression, as if something surprised her.

They shook hands, but without a word. Marcella pointed to a chair, yet remained standing. She was endeavouring to smile; her eyes fell, and she coloured.

'Don't let us make each other uncomfortable,' Peak exclaimed suddenly, in the off-hand tone of friendly intimacy. 'There's nothing tragic in this affair, after all. Let us talk quietly.'

Marcella seated herself,

'I had reasons,' he went on, 'for going away from my old acquaintances for a time. Why not, if I chose? You have found me out. Very well; let us talk it over as we have discussed many another moral or psychological question.'

He did not meditate these sentences. Something must of necessity be said, and words shaped themselves for him. His impulse was to avoid the emotional, to talk with this problematic woman as with an intellectual friend of his own sex.

'Forgive me,' were the first sounds that came from Marcella's lips. She spoke with bent head, and almost in a whisper.

'What have I to forgive?' He sat down and leaned sideways in the easy chair. 'You were curious about my doings? What more natural?'

'Do you know how I learnt where you were?'

She looked up for an instant.

'I have a suspicion. You went to Twybridge?'

'Yes.'

'But not in your own name?'

'I can hardly tell why not.'

Peak laughed. He was physically and mentally at rest in comparison with his state for the past few days. Things had a simpler aspect all at once. After all, who would wish to interfere maliciously with him? Women like to be in secrets, and probably Marcella would preserve his.

'What conjectures had you made about me?' he asked, with an air of amusement.

'Many, of course. But I heard something not long ago which seemed so unlikely, yet was told so confidently, that at last I couldn't overcome my wish to make inquiries.'

'And what was that?'

'Mr. Malkin has been to America, and he declared that he had met you in the streets of Boston—and that you refused to admit you were yourself.'

Peak laughed still more buoyantly. His mood was eager to seize on any point that afforded subject for jest.

'Malkin seems to have come across my *Doppelgänger*. One mustn't pretend to certainty in anything, but I am disposed to think I never was in Boston.'

'He was of course mistaken.'

Marcella's voice had an indistinctness very unlike her ordinary tone. As a rule she spoke with that clearness and decision which corresponds to qualities of mind not commonly found in women.

But confidence seemed to have utterly deserted her; she had lost her individuality, and was weakly feminine.

'I have been here since last Christmas,' said Godwin, after a pause.

'Yes. I know.'

Their eyes met.

'No doubt your friends have told you as much as they know of me?'

'Yes—they have spoken of you.'

'And what does it amount to?'

He regarded her steadily, with a smile of indifference.

'They say'—she gazed at him as if constrained to do so—'that you are going into the Church.' And as soon as she uttered the last word, a painful laugh escaped her.

'Nothing else? No comments?'

'I think Miss Moorhouse finds it difficult to understand.'

'Miss Moorhouse?' He reflected, still smiling. 'I shouldn't wonder. She has a sceptical mind, and she doesn't know me well enough to understand me.'

'Doesn't know you well enough?'

She repeated the words mechanically. Peak gave her a keen glance.

'Has she led you to suppose,' he asked, 'that we are on intimate terms?'

'No.' The word fell from her, absently, despondently.

'Miss Moxey, would anything be gained by our discussing my position? If you think it a mystery, hadn't we better leave it so?'

She made no answer.

'But perhaps,' he went on, 'you have told them—the Walworths and the Moorhouses—that I owe my friends an explanation? When I see them again, perhaps I shall be confronted with cold, questioning faces?'

'I haven't said a word that could injure you,' Marcella replied, with something of her usual self-possession, passing her eyes distantly over his face as she spoke.

'I knew the suggestion was unjust, when I made it.'

'Then why should you refuse me your confidence?'

She bent forward slightly, but with her eyes cast down. Tone and features intimated a sense of shame, due partly to the feeling that she offered complicity in deceit.

'What can I tell you more than you know?' said Godwin, coldly. 'I propose to become a clergyman, and I have acknowledged to you that my motive is ambition. As the matter concerns my conscience, that must rest with myself; I have spoken of it to no one. But you may depend upon it that I am prepared for every difficulty that may spring up. I knew, of course, that sooner or later some one would discover me here. Well, I have changed my opinions, that's all; who can demand more than that?'

Marcella answered in a tone of forced composure.

'You owe me no explanation at all. Yet we have known each other for a long time, and it pains me that—to be suddenly told that we are no more to each other than strangers.'

'Are we talking like strangers, Marcella?'

She flushed, and her eyes gleamed as they fixed themselves upon him for an instant. He had never before dreamt of addressing her so familiarly, and least of all in this moment was she prepared for it. Godwin despised himself for the impulse to which he had yielded, but its policy was justified. He had taken one more step in disingenuousness—a small matter.

'Let it be one of those things on which even friends don't open their minds to each other,' he pursued. 'I am living in solitude, and perhaps must do so for several years yet. If I succeed in my purposes, you will see me again on the old terms; if I fail, then too we shall be friends—if you are willing.'

'You won't tell me what those purposes are?'

'Surely you can imagine them.'

'Will you let me ask you—do you look for help to anyone that I have seen here?' She spoke with effort and with shame.

'To no one that you have met,' he answered, shortly.

'Then to some one in Exeter? I have been told that you have friends.'

He was irritated by her persistency, and his own inability to decide upon the most prudent way of answering.

'You mean the Warricombe family, I suppose?'

'Yes.'

'I think it very likely that Mr. Warricombe may be able to help me substantially.'

Marcella kept silence. Then, without raising her eyes, she murmured:

'You will tell me no more?'

'There is nothing more to tell.'

She bit her lips, as if to compel them to muteness. Her breath came quickly; she glanced this way and that, like one who sought an escape. After eyeing her askance for a moment, Peak rose.

'You are going?' she said.

'Yes; but surely there is no reason why we shouldn't say good-bye in a natural and friendly way?'

'Can you forgive me for that deceit I practised?'

Peak laughed.

'What does it matter? We should in any case have met at Budleigh Salterton.'

'No. I had no serious thought of accepting their invitation.'

She stood looking away from him, endeavouring to speak as though the denial had but slight significance, Godwin stirred impatiently.

'I should never have gone to Twybridge,' Marcella continued, 'but for Mr. Malkin's story.'

He turned to her.

'You mean that his story had a disagreeable sound?'

Marcella kept silence, her fingers working together.

'And is your mind relieved?' he added.

'I wish you were back in London. I wish this change had never come to pass.'

'I wish that several things in my life had never come to pass. But I am here, and my resolve is unalterable. One thing I must ask you—how shall you represent my position to your brother?'

For a moment Marcella hesitated. Then, meeting his look, she answered with nervous haste:

'I shall not mention you to him.'

Ashamed to give any sign of satisfaction, and oppressed by the feeling that he owed her gratitude, Peak stood gazing towards the windows with an air of half-indifferent abstractedness. It was better to let the interview end thus, without comment or further question; so he turned abruptly, and offered his hand.

'Good-bye. You will hear of me, or from me.'

'Good-bye!'

He tried to smile; but Marcella had a cold face, expressive of more dignity than she had hitherto shown. As he closed the door she was still looking towards him.

He knew what the look meant. In his position, a man of ordinary fibre would long ago have nursed the flattering conviction that Marcella loved him. Godwin had suspected it, but in a vague, unemotional way, never attaching importance to the matter. What he *had* clearly understood was, that Christian wished to inspire him with interest in Marcella, and on that account, when in her company, he sometimes set himself to display a deliberate negligence. No difficult undertaking, for he was distinctly repelled by the thought of any relations with her more intimate than had been brought about by his cold intellectual sympathy. Her person was still as disagreeable to him as when he first met her in her uncle's house at Twybridge. If a man sincerely hopes that a woman does not love him (which can seldom be the case where a suggestion of such feeling ever arises), he will find it easy to believe that she does not. Peak not only had the benefit of this principle; the constitution of his mind made it the opposite of natural for him to credit himself with having inspired affection. That his male friends held him in any warm esteem always appeared to him improbable, and as regards women his modesty was profound. The simplest explanation, that he was himself incapable of pure devotedness, perhaps hits the truth. Unsympathetic, however, he could with no justice be called, and now that the reality of Marcella's love was forced upon his consciousness he thought of her with sincere pity,—the emotion which had already possessed him (though he did not then analyse it) when he unsuspectingly looked into her troubled face a few days ago.

It was so hard to believe, that, on reaching home, he sat for a long time occupied with the thought of it, to the exclusion of his own anxieties. What! this woman had made of *him* an ideal such as he himself sought among the most exquisite of her sex? How was that possible? What quality of his, personal, psychical, had such magnetic force? What sort of being was he in Marcella's eyes? Reflective men must often enough marvel at the success of whiskered and trousered mortals in wooing the women of their desire, for only by a specific imagination can a person of one sex assume the emotions of the other. Godwin had neither that endowment nor the peculiar self-esteem which makes love-winning a matter of course to some intelligent males. His native arrogance signified a low estimate of mankind at large, rather than an over-weening appreciation of his own qualities, and in his most presumptuous moments he had never claimed the sexual prefulgence which many a commonplace fellow so gloriously exhibits. At most, he had hoped that some woman might find him *interesting*, and so be led on to like him well enough for the venture of matrimony. Passion at length constrained him to believe that his ardour might be genuinely reciprocated, but even now it was only in paroxysms that he held this assurance; the hours of ordinary life still exposed him to the familar self-criticism, sometimes more scathing than ever. He dreaded the looking-glass, consciously avoided it; and a like disparagement of his inner being tortured him through the endless labyrinths of erotic reverie.

Yet here was a woman who so loved him that not even a proud temper and his candid indifference could impose restraint upon her emotions. As he listened to the most significant of her words he was distressed with shame, and now, in recalling them, he felt that he should have said something, done something, to disillusion her. Could he not easily show himself in a contemptible light? But reflection taught him that the shame he had experienced on Marcella's behalf was blended with a gratification which forbade him at the moment to be altogether unamiable. It was not self-interest alone that prompted his use of her familiar name. In the secret places of his heart he was thankful to her for a most effective encouragement. She had confirmed him in the hope that he was loved by Sidwell.

And now that he no longer feared her, Marcella was gradually dismissed from mind. For a day or two he avoided the main streets of the town, lest a chance meeting with her should revive disquietude; but, by the time that Mrs. Warricombe's invitation permitted him once more to follow his desire, he felt assured that Marcella was back in London, and the sense of distance helped to banish her among unrealities.

The hours had never pressed upon him with such demand for resolution. In the look with which Sidwell greeted him when he met her in the drawing-room, he seemed to read much more than wonted friendliness; it was as though a half secret already existed between them. But no occasion offered for a word other than trivial. The dinner-party consisted of about a score of people, and throughout the evening Peak found himself hopelessly severed from the one person whose presence was anything but an importunity to him. He maddened with jealousy, with fear, with ceaseless mental manœuvring. More than one young man of agreeable aspect appeared to be on dangerous terms with Sidwell, approaching her with that air of easy, well-bred intimacy which Godwin knew too well he would never be able to assume in perfection. Again he was humiliated by self-comparison with social superiors, and again reminded that in this circle he had a place merely on sufferance. Mrs. Warricombe, when he chanced to speak with her, betrayed the slight regard in which she really held him, and Martin devoted himself to more important people. The evening was worse than lost.

Yet in two more days Sidwell would be beyond reach. He writhed upon his bed as the image of her loveliness returned again and again,—her face as she conversed at table, her dignity as she rose with the other ladies, her smile when he said good-night. A smile that meant more than civility; he was convinced of it. But memory would not support him through half-a-year of solitude and ill-divining passion.

He would write to her, and risk all. Two o'clock in the morning saw him sitting half-dressed at the table, raging over the difficulties of a composition which should express his highest self. Four o'clock saw the blotched letter torn into fragments. He could not write as he wished, could not hit the tone of manly appeal. At five o'clock he turned wretchedly into bed again.

A day of racking headache; then the long restful sleep which brings good counsel. It was well that he had not sent a letter, nor in any other way committed himself. If Sidwell were ever to be his wife, the end could only be won by heroic caution and patience. Thus far he had achieved notable results; to rush upon his aim would be the most absurd departure from a hopeful scheme gravely devised and pursued. To wait, to establish himself in the confidence of this family, to make sure his progress step by step,—that was the course indicated from the first by his calm reason. Other men might triumph by sudden audacity; for him was no hope save in slow, persevering energy of will. Passion had all but ruined him; now he had recovered self-control.

Sidwell's six months in London might banish him from her mind, might substitute some rival against whom it would be hopeless to contend. Yes; but a thousand possibilities stood with menace in the front of every great enterprise. Before next spring he might be dead.

Defiance, then, of every foreboding, of every shame; and a life that moulded itself in the ardour of unchangeable resolve.

IV

Martin Warricombe was reconciled to the prospect of a metropolitan winter by the fact that his old friend Thomas Gale, formerly Geological Professor at Whitelaw College, had of late returned from a three years' sojourn in North America, and now dwelt in London. The breezy man of science was welcomed back among his brethren with two-fold felicitation; his book on the Appalachians would have given no insufficient proof of activity abroad, but evidence more generally interesting accompanied him in the shape of a young and beautiful wife. Not every geologist whose years have entered the fifties can go forth and capture in second marriage a charming New England girl, thirty years his junior. Yet those who knew Mr. Gale—his splendid physique, his bluff cordiality, the vigour of his various talk—were scarcely surprised. The young lady was no heiress; she had, in fact, been a school teacher, and might have wearied through her best years in that uncongenial pursuit. Transplanted to the richest English soil, she developed remarkable aptitudes. A month or two of London exhibited her as a type of all that is most attractive in American womanhood.

Between Mrs. Gale and the Warricombes intimacy was soon established. Sidwell saw much of her, and liked her. To this meditative English girl the young American offered an engrossing problem, for she avowed her indifference to all religious dogmas, yet was singularly tolerant and displayed a moral fervour which Sidwell had believed inseparable from Christian faith. At the Gales' house assembled a great variety of intellectual people, and with her father's express approval (Martin had his reasons) Sidwell made the most of this opportunity of studying the modern world. Only a few days after her arrival in London, she became acquainted with a Mr. Walsh, a brother of that heresiarch, the Whitelaw Professor, whose name was still obnoxious to her mother. He was a well-favoured man of something between thirty and forty, brilliant in conversation, personally engaging, and known by his literary productions, which found small favour with conservative readers. With surprise, Sidwell in a short time became aware that Mr. Walsh had a frank liking for her society. He was often to be seen in Mrs. Warricombe's drawing-room, and at Mrs. Gale's he yet more frequently obtained occasions of talking with her. The candour with which he expressed himself on most subjects enabled her to observe a type of mind which at present had peculiar interest for her. Discretion often put restraint upon her curiosity, but none the less Mr. Walsh had plausible grounds for believing that his advances were not unwelcome. He saw that Sidwell's gaze occasionally rested upon him with a pleasant gravity, and noted the mood of meditation which sometimes came upon her when he had drawn apart. The frequency of these dialogues was observed by Mrs. Warricombe, and one evening she broached the subject to her daughter rather abruptly.

'I am surprised that you have taken such a liking to Mr. Walsh.'

Sidwell coloured, and made answer in the quiet tone which her mother had come to understand as a reproof, a hint of defective delicacy:

'I don't think I have behaved in a way that should cause you surprise.'

'It seemed to me that you were really very—friendly with him.'

'Yes, I am always friendly. But nothing more.'

'Don't you think there's a danger of his misunderstanding you, Sidwell?'

'I don't, mother. Mr. Walsh understands that we differ irreconcilably on subjects of the first importance. I have never allowed him to lose sight of that.'

Intellectual differences were of much less account to Mrs. Warricombe than to her daughter, and her judgment in a matter such as this was consequently far more practical.

'If I may advise you, dear, you oughtn't to depend much on

that. I am not the only one who has noticed something—I only mention it, you know.'

Sidwell mused gravely. In a minute or two she looked up and said in her gentlest voice:

'Thank you, mother, I will be more careful.'

Perhaps she had lost sight of prudence, forgetting that Mr. Walsh could not divine her thoughts. Her interest in him was impersonal; when he spoke she was profoundly attentive, only because her mind would have been affected in the same way had she been reading his words instead of listening to them. She could not let him know that another face was often more distinct to her imagination than his to her actual sight, and that her thoughts were frequently more busy with a remembered dialogue than with this in which she was engaged. She had abundantly safeguarded herself against serious misconstruction, but if gossip were making her its subject, it would be inconsiderate not to regard the warning.

It came, indeed, at a moment when she was very willing to rest from social activity. At the time of her last stay in London, three years ago, she had not been ripe for reflection on what she saw. Now her mind was kept so incessantly at strain, and her emotions answered so intensely to every appeal, that at length she felt the need of repose. It was not with her as with the young women who seek only to make the most of their time in agreeable ways. Sidwell's vital forces were concentrated in an effort of profound spiritual significance. The critical hour of her life was at hand, and she exerted every faculty in the endeavour to direct herself aright.

Having heard from his brother that Sidwell had not been out for several days, Buckland took an opportunity of calling at the house early one morning. He found her alone in a small drawing-room, and sat down with an expression of weary discontent. This mood had been frequent in the young man of late. Sidwell remarked a change that was coming over him, a gloominess unnatural to his character.

'Seen the Walworths lately?' he asked, when his sister had assured him that she was not seriously ailing.

'We called a few days ago.'

'Meet anyone there?'

'Two or three people. No one that interested me.'

'You haven't come across some friends of theirs called Moxey?'

'Oh, yes! Miss Moxey was there one afternoon about a fortnight ago.'

'Did you talk to her at all?' Buckland asked.

'Yes; we hadn't much to say to each other, though. How do you know of her? Through Sylvia, I daresay.'

'Met her when I was last down yonder.'

Sidwell had long since heard from her friend of Miss Moxey's visit to Budleigh Salterton, but she was not aware that Buckland had been there at the same time. Sylvia had told her, however, of the acquaintance existing between Miss Moxey and Peak, a point of much interest to her, though it remained a mere unconnected fact. In her short conversation with Marcella, she had not ventured to refer to it.

'Do you know anything of the family?'

'I was going to ask you the same,' returned Buckland. 'I thought you might have heard something from the Walworths.'

Sidwell had in fact sought information, but, as her relations with the Walworths were formal, such inquiry as she could make from them elicited nothing more than she already knew from Sylvia.

'Are you anxious to discover who they are?' she asked.

'Oh, not particularly.'

Buckland moved uneasily, and became silent.

'I dined with Walsh yesterday,' he said, at length, struggling to shake off the obvious dreariness that oppressed him. 'He suits me; we can get on together.'

'No doubt.'

'But you don't dislike him, I think?'

'Implying that I dislike *you*,' said Sidwell, lightsomely.

'You have no affection for my opinions.—Walsh is an honest man.'

'I hope so.'

'He says what he thinks. No compromise with fashionable hypocrisy.'

'I despise that kind of thing quite as much as you do.'

They looked at each other. Buckland had a sullen air.

'Yes, in your own way,' he replied, 'you are sincere enough, I have no doubt. I wish all women were so.'

'What exception have you in mind?'

He did not seem inclined to answer.

'Perhaps it is your understanding of them that's at fault,' added Sidwell, gently.

'Not in one case, at all events,' he exclaimed. 'Suppose you were asked to define Miss Moorhouse's religious opinions, how would you do it?'

'I am not well enough acquainted with them.'

'Do you imagine for a moment that she has any more faith in the supernatural than I have?'

'I think there is a great difference between her position and yours.'

'Because she is hypocritical!' cried Buckland, angrily. 'She deceives you. She hasn't the courage to be honest.'

Sidwell wore a pained expression.

'You judge her,' she replied, 'far too coarsely. No one is called upon to make an elaborate declaration of faith as often as such subjects are spoken of. Sylvia thinks so differently from you about almost everything that, when she happens to agree with you, you are misled and misinterpret her whole position.'

'I understand her perfectly,' Buckland went on, in the same irritated voice. 'There are plenty of women like her—with brains enough, but utter and contemptible cowards. Cowards even to themselves, perhaps. What can you expect, when society is based on rotten shams?'

For several minutes he pursued this vein of invective, then took an abrupt leave. Sidwell had a piece of grave counsel ready to offer him, but he was clearly in no mood to listen, so she postponed it.

A day or two after this, she received a letter from Sylvia. Miss Moorhouse was anything but a good correspondent; she often confessed her inability to compose anything but the briefest and driest statement of facts. With no little surprise, therefore, Sidwell found that the envelope contained two sheets all but covered with her friend's cramped handwriting. The letter began with apology for long delay in acknowledging two communications.

'But you know well enough my dilatory disposition. I have written to you mentally at least once a day, and I hope you have mentally received the results—that is to say, have assured yourself of my goodwill to you, and I had nothing else to send.'

At this point Sylvia had carefully obliterated two lines, blackening the page into unsightliness. In vain Sidwell pored over the effaced passage, led to do so by a fancy that she could discern a capital P, which looked like the first letter of a name. The writer continued:

'Don't trouble yourself so much about insoluble questions. Try to be more positive—I don't say become a Positivist. Keep a receptive mind, and wait for time to shape your views of things. I see that London has agitated and confused you; you have lost your bearings amid the maze of contradictory finger-posts. If you were here I could soothe you with Sylvian (much the same as sylvan) philosophy, but I can't write.'

Here the letter was to have ended, for on the line beneath was legible 'Give my love to Fanny,' but this again had been crossed out, and there followed a long paragraph:

'I have been reading a book about ants. Perhaps you know all the wonderful things about them, but I had neglected that branch of natural history. Their doings are astonishingly like that of an animal called man, and it seems to me that I have discovered one point of resemblance which perhaps has never been noted. Are you aware that at an early stage of their existence ants have wings? They fly—how shall I express it?—only for the brief time of their courtship and marriage, and when these important affairs are satisfactorily done with their wings wither away, and thenceforth they have to content themselves with running about on the earth. Now isn't this a remarkable parallel to one stage of human life? Do not men and women also soar and flutter—at a certain time? And don't their wings manifestly drop off as soon as the end of that skyward movement has been achieved? If the gods had made me poetical, I would sonnetise on this idea. Do you know any poet with a fondness for the ant-philosophy? If so, offer him this suggestion with liberty to "make any use of it he likes."

'But the fact of the matter is that some human beings are never winged at all. I am decidedly coming to the conclusion that I am one of those. Think of me henceforth as an apteryx—you have a dictionary at hand? Like the tailless fox, I might naturally maintain that my state is the more gracious, but honestly I am not assured of that. It may be (I half believe it is) a good thing to soar and flutter, and at times I regret that nature has forbidden me that experience. Decidedly I would never try *to persuade anyone else* to forego the use of wings. Bear this in mind, my dear girl. But I suspect that in time to come there will be an increasing number of female human creatures who from their birth are content with *walking*. Not long ago, I had occasion to hint that—though under another figure—to your brother Buckland. I hope he understood me—I think he did—and that he wasn't offended.

'I had something to tell you. I have forgotten it—never mind.'

And therewith the odd epistle was concluded. Sidwell perused the latter part several times. Of course she was at no loss to interpret it. Buckland's demeanour for the past two months had led her to surmise that his latest visit to Budleigh Salterton had finally extinguished the hopes which drew him in that direction. His recent censure of Sylvia might be thus explained. She grieved that her brother's suit should be discouraged, but could not persuade herself that Sylvia's decision was final. The idea of a match between those two was very pleasant to her. For Buckland she imagined it would be fraught with good results, and for Sylvia, on the whole, it might be the best thing.

Before she replied to her friend nearly a month passed, and Christmas was at hand. Again she had been much in society. Mr. Walsh had renewed his unmistakable attentions, and, when her manner of meeting them began to trouble him with doubts, had cleared the air by making a formal offer of marriage. Sidwell's negative was absolute, much to her mother's relief. On the day of that event, she wrote rather a long letter to Sylvia, but Mr. Walsh's name was not mentioned in it.

'Mother tells me,' it began, 'that *your* mother has written to her from Salisbury, and that you yourself are going there for a stay of some weeks. I am sorry, for on the Monday after Christmas Day I shall be in Exeter, and hoped somehow to have seen you. We—mother and I—are going to run down together, to see after certain domestic affairs; only for three days at most.

'Your ant-letter was very amusing, but it saddened me, dear Sylvia. I can't make any answer. On these subjects it is very difficult even for the closest friends to open their minds to each other. I don't—and don't wish to—believe in the *apteryx* profession; that's all I must say.

'My health has been indifferent since I last wrote. We live in all but continuous darkness, and very seldom indeed breathe anything that can be called air. No doubt this state of things has its effect on me. I look forwards, not to the coming of spring, for here we shall see nothing of its beauties, but to the month which will release us from London. I want to smell the pines again, and to see the golden gorse in *our* road.

'By way of being more "positive," I have read much in the newspapers, supplementing from them my own experience of London society. The result is that I am more and more confirmed in the fears with which I have already worried you. Two movements are plainly going on in the life of our day. The decay of religious belief is undermining morality, and the progress of Radicalism in politics is working to the same end by overthrowing social distinctions. Evidence stares one in the face from every column of the papers. Of course you have read more or less about the recent "scandal"—I mean the *most* recent.—It isn't the kind of thing one cares to discuss, but we can't help knowing about it, and does it not strongly support what I say? Here is materialism sinking into brutal immorality, and high social rank degrading itself by intimacy with the corrupt vulgar. There are newspapers that make political capital out of these "revelations." I have read some of them, and they make me so *fiercely* aristocratic that I find it hard to care anything at all even for the humanitarian efforts of people I respect. You will tell me, I know, that this is quite the wrong way of looking at it. But the evils are so monstrous that it is hard to fix one's mind on the good that may long hence result from them.

'I cling to the essential (that is the *spiritual*) truths of Christianity as the only absolute good left in our time. I would say that I care nothing for forms, but some form there must be, else one's faith evaporates. It has become very easy for me to understand how men and women who know the world refuse to believe any longer in a directing Providence. A week ago I again met Miss Moxey at the Walworths', and talked with her more freely than before. This conversation showed me that I have become much more tolerant towards individuals. But though this or that person may be supported by moral sense alone, the world cannot dispense with religion. If it tries to—and it *will*—there are dreadful times before us.

'I wish I were a man! I would do something, however ineffectual. I would stand on the side of those who are fighting against mob-rule and mob-morals. How would you like to see Exeter Cathedral converted into a "coffee music-hall"? And that will come.'

Reading this, Sylvia had the sense of listening to an echo. Some of the phrases recalled to her quite a different voice from Sidwell's. She smiled and mused.

On the morning appointed for her journey to Exeter Sidwell rose early, and in unusually good spirits. Mrs. Warricombe was less animated by the prospect of five hours in a railway carriage, for London had a covering of black snow, and it seemed likely that more would fall. Martin suggested postponement, but circumstances made this undesirable.

'Let Fanny go with me,' proposed Sidwell, just after breakfast. 'I can see to everything perfectly well, mother.'

But Fanny hastened to decline. She was engaged for a dance on the morrow.

'Then I'll run down with you myself, Sidwell,' said her father.

Mrs. Warricombe looked at the weather and hesitated. There were strong reasons why she should go, and they determined her to brave discomforts.

It chanced that the morning post had brought Mr. Warricombe a letter from Godwin Peak. It was a reply to one that he had written with Christmas greetings; a kindness natural in him, for he had remembered that the young man was probably hard at work in his lonely lodgings. He spoke of it privately to his wife.

'A very good letter—thoughtful and cheerful. You're not likely to see him, but if you happen to, say a pleasant word.'

'I shouldn't have written, if I were you,' remarked Mrs. Warricombe.

'Why not? I was only thinking the other day that he contrasted very favourably with the younger generation as we observe it here. Yes, I have faith in Peak. There's the right stuff in him.'

'Oh, I dare say. But still'——

And Mrs. Warricombe went away with an air of misgiving.

V

In volunteering a promise not to inform her brother of Peak's singular position, Marcella spoke with sincerity. She was prompted by incongruous feelings—a desire to compel Godwin's gratitude, and disdain of the circumstances in which she had discovered him. There seemed to be little likelihood of Christian's learning from any other person that she had met with Peak at Budleigh Salterton; he had, indeed, dined with her at the Walworths', and might improve his acquaintance with that family, but it was improbable that they would ever mention in his hearing the stranger who had casually been presented to them, or indeed ever again think of him. If she held her peace, the secret of Godwin's retirement must still remain impenetrable. He would pursue his ends as hitherto, thinking of *her*, if at all, as a weak woman who had immodestly betrayed a hopeless passion, and who could be trusted never to wish him harm.

That was Marcella's way of reading a man's thoughts. She did not attribute to Peak the penetration which would make him uneasy. In spite of masculine proverbs, it is the habit of women to suppose that the other sex regards them confidingly, ingenuously. Marcella was unusually endowed with analytic intelligence, but in this case she believed what she hoped. She knew that Peak's confidence in her must be coloured with contempt, but this mattered little so long as he paid her the compliment of feeling sure that she was superior to ignoble temptations. Many a woman would behave with treacherous malice. It was in her power to expose him, to confound all his schemes, for she knew the authorship of that remarkable paper in *The Critical Review*. Before receiving Peak's injunction of secrecy, Earwaker had talked of 'The New Sophistry' with Moxey and with Malkin; the request came too late. In her interview with Godwin at the Exeter hotel, she had not even hinted at this knowledge, partly because she was unconscious that Peak imagined the affair a secret between himself and Earwaker, partly because she thought it unworthy of her even to seem to threaten. It gratified her, however, to feel that he was at her mercy, and the thought preoccupied her for many days.

Passion which has the intellect on its side is more easily endured than that which offers sensual defiance to all reasoning, but on the other hand it lasts much longer. Marcella was not consumed by her emotions; she often thought calmly, coldly, of the man she loved. Yet he was seldom long out of her mind, and the instigation of circumstances at times made her suffering intense. Such an occasion was her first meeting with Sidwell Warricombe, which took place at the Walworths', in London. Down in Devonshire she had learnt that a family named Warricombe were Peak's intimate friends; nothing more than this, for indeed no one was in a position to tell her more. Wakeful jealousy caused her to fix upon the fact as one of significance; Godwin's evasive manner when she questioned him confirmed her suspicions; and as soon as she was brought face to face with Sidwell, suspicion became certainty. She knew at once that Miss Warricombe was the very person who would be supremely attractive to Godwin Peak.

An interval of weeks, and again she saw the face that in the meantime had been as present to her imagination as Godwin's own features. This time she conversed at some length with Miss Warricombe. Was it merely a fancy that the beautiful woman looked at her, spoke to her, with some exceptional interest? By now she had learnt that the Moorhouses and the Warricombes were connected in close friendship; it was all but certain, then, that Miss Moorhouse had told Miss Warricombe of Peak's visit to Budleigh Salterton, and its incidents. Could this in any way be explanatory of the steady, searching look in those soft eyes?

Marcella had always regarded the emotion of jealousy as characteristic of a vulgar nature. Now that it possessed her, she endeavoured to call it by other names; to persuade herself that she was indignant on abstract grounds, or anxious only with reference to Peak's true interests. She could not affect surprise.

So intensely sympathetic was her reading of Godwin's character that she understood—or at all events recognised—the power Sidwell would possess over him. He did not care for enlightenment in a woman; he was sensual—though in a subtle way; the aristocratic vein in his temper made him subject to strong impressions from trivialities of personal demeanour, of social tone.

Yet all was mere conjecture. She had not dared to utter Peak's name, lest in doing so she should betray herself. Constantly planning to make further discoveries, she as constantly tried to dismiss all thought of the matter—to learn indifference. Already she had debased herself, and her nature must be contemptible indeed if anything could lure her forward on such a path.

None the less, she was assiduous in maintaining friendly relations with the Walworths. Christian, too, had got into the habit of calling there; it was significant of the noticeable change which was come upon him—a change his sister was at no loss to understand from the moment that he informed her (gravely, but without expressiveness) of Mr. Palmer's death. Instead of shunning ordinary society, he seemed bent on extending the circle of his acquaintance. He urged Marcella to invite friendly calls, to have guests at dinner. There seemed to be a general revival of his energies, exhibited in the sphere of study as well as of amusement. Not a day went by without his purchasing books or scientific apparatus, and the house was brightened with works of art chosen in the studios which Miss Walworth advised him to visit. All the amiabilities of his character came into free play; with Marcella he was mirthful, affectionate, even caressing. He grew scrupulous about his neckties, his gloves, and was careful to guard his fingers against corroding acids when he worked in the laboratory. Such indications of hopefulness caused Marcella more misgiving than pleasure; she made no remark, but waited with anxiety for some light on the course of events.

Just before dinner, one evening, as she sat alone in the drawing-room, Christian entered with a look which portended some strange announcement. He spoke abruptly:

'I have heard something astonishing.'

'What is that?'

'This afternoon I went to the matinée at the Vaudeville, and found myself among a lot of our friends—the Walworths and the Hunters and the Mortons. Between the acts I was talking to Hunter, when a man came up to us, spoke to Hunter, and was introduced to me—a Mr. Warricombe. What do you think he said? "I believe you know my friend Peak, Mr. Moxey?" "Peak? To be sure! Can you tell me what has become of him?" He gave me an odd look. "Why, I met him last, some two months ago, in Devonshire." At that moment we were obliged to go to our places, and I couldn't get hold of the fellow again. Hunter told me something about him; he knows the Walworths, it seems—belongs to a good Devonshire family. What on earth can Peak be doing over there?'

Marcella kept silence. The event she had judged improbable had come to pass. The chance of its doing so had of course increased since Christian began to associate freely with the Walworths and their circle. Yet, considering the slightness of the connection between that group of people and the Warricombe family, there had seemed no great likelihood of Christian's getting acquainted with the latter. She debated rapidly in her troubled mind how to meet this disclosure. Curiosity would, of course, impel her brother to follow up the clue; he would again encounter Warricombe, and must then learn all the facts of Peak's position. To what purpose should she dissemble her own knowledge?

Did she desire that Godwin should remain in security? A tremor more akin to gladness than its opposite impeded her utterance. If Warricombe became aware of all that was involved in Godwin Peak's withdrawal from among his friends—if (as must follow) he imparted the discovery to his sister——

The necessity of speaking enabled her to ignore these turbulent speculations, which yet were anything but new to her.

'They met at Budleigh Salterton,' she said, quietly.

'Who did? Warricombe and Peak?'

'Yes, At the Moorhouses'. It was when I was there.'

Christian stared at her.

'When you were there? But *you* met Peak?'

His sister smiled, turning from the astonished gaze.

'Yes, I met him.'

'But, why the deuce——? Why didn't you tell me, Marcella?'

'He asked me not to speak of it. He didn't wish you to know that—that he has decided to become a clergyman.'

Christian was stricken dumb. In spite of his sister's obvious agitation, he could not believe what she told him; her smile gave him an excuse for supposing that she jested.

'Peak a clergyman?' He burst out laughing. 'What's the meaning of all this?—Do speak intelligibly! What's the fellow up to?'

'I am quite serious. He is studying for Orders—has been for this last year.'

In desperation, Christian turned to another phase of the subject.

'Then Malkin *was* mistaken?'

'Plainly.'

'And you mean to tell me that Peak——? Give me more details. Where's he living? How has he got to know people like these Warricombes?'

Marcella told all that she knew, and without injunction of secrecy. The affair had passed out of her hands; destiny must fulfil itself. And again the tremor that resembled an uneasy joy went through her frame.

'But how,' asked Christian, 'did this fellow Warricombe come to know that *I* was a friend of Peak's?'

'That's a puzzle to me. I shouldn't have thought he would have remembered my name; and, even if he had, how could he conclude——?'

She broke off, pondering. Warricombe must have made inquiries, possibly suggested by suspicions.

'I scarcely spoke of Mr. Peak to anyone,' she added. 'People saw, of course, that we were acquaintances, but it couldn't have seemed a thing of any importance.'

'You spoke with him in private, it seems?'

'Yes, I saw him for a few minutes—in Exeter.'

'And you hadn't said anything to the Walworths that—that would surprise them?'

'Purposely not.—Why should I injure him?'

Christian knit his brows. He understood too well why his sister should refrain from such injury.

'You would have behaved in the same way,' Marcella added.

'Why really—yes, perhaps so. Yet I don't know.—In plain English, Peak is a wolf in sheep's clothing!'

'I don't know anything about that,' she replied, with gloomy evasion.

'Nonsense, my dear girl!—Had he the impudence to pretend to you that he was sincere?'

'He made no declaration.'

'But you are convinced he is acting the hypocrite, Marcella. You spoke of the risk of injuring him.—What are his motives? What does he aim at?'

'Scarcely a bishopric, I should think,' she replied, bitterly.

'Then, by Jove! Earwaker may be right!'

Marcella darted an inquiring look at him.

'What has he thought?'

'I'm ashamed to speak of it. He suggested once that Peak might disguise himself for the sake of—of making a good marriage.'

The reply was a nervous laugh.

'Look here, Marcella.' He caught her hand. 'This is a very awkward business. Peak is disgracing himself; he will be unmasked; there'll be a scandal. It was kind of you to keep silence—when don't you behave kindly, dear girl?—but think of the possible results to *us*. We shall be something very like accomplices.'

'How?' Marcella exclaimed, impatiently. 'Who need know that we were so intimate with him?'

'Warricombe seems to know it.'

'Who can prove that he isn't sincere?'

'No one, perhaps. But it will seem a very odd thing that he hid away from all his old friends. You remember, I betrayed that to Warricombe, before I knew that it mattered.'

Yes, and Mr. Warricombe could hardly forget the circumstance. He would press his investigation—knowing already, perhaps, of Peak's approaches to his sister Sidwell.

'Marcella, a man plays games like that at his own peril. I don't like this kind of thing. Perhaps he has audacity enough to face out any disclosure. But it's out of the question for you and me to nurse his secret. We have no right to do so.'

'You propose to denounce him?'

Marcella gazed at her brother with an agitated look.

'Not denounce. I am fond of Peak; I wish him well. But I can't join him in a dishonourable plot.—Then, we mustn't endanger our place in society.'

'I have no place in society,' Marcella answered, coldly.

'Don't say that, and don't think it. We are both going to make more of our lives; we are going to think very little of the past, and a great deal of the future. We are still young; we have happiness before us.'

'We?' she asked, with shaken voice.

'Yes—both of us! Who can say'——

Again he took her hand and pressed it warmly in both his own. Just then the door opened, and dinner was announced. Christian talked on, in low hurried tones, for several minutes, affectionately, encouragingly. After dinner, he wished to resume the subject, but Marcella declared that there was no more to be said; he must act as honour and discretion bade him; for herself, she should simply keep silence as hitherto. And she left him to his reflections.

Though with so little of ascertained fact to guide her, Marcella interpreted the hints afforded by her slight knowledge of the Warricombes with singular accuracy. Precisely as she had imagined, Buckland Warricombe was going about on Peak's track, learning all he could concerning the theological student, forming acquaintance with anyone likely to supplement his discoveries. And less than a fortnight after the meeting at the theatre, Christian made known to his sister that Warricombe and he had had a second conversation, this time uninterrupted.

'He inquired after you, Marcella, and—really I had no choice but to ask him to call here. I hardly think he'll come. He's not the kind of man I care for—though liberal enough, and all that.'

'Wasn't it rather rash to give that invitation?'

'The fact was, I so dreaded the appearance of—of seeming to avoid him,' Christian pleaded, awkwardly. 'You know, that affair—we won't talk any more of it; but, if there *should* be a row about it, you are sure to be compromised unless we have managed to guard ourselves. If Warricombe calls, we must talk about Peak without the least show of restraint. Let it appear that we thought his choice of a profession unlikely, but not impossible. Happily, we needn't know anything about that anonymous *Critical* article.—Indeed, I think I have acted wisely.'

Marcella murmured:

'Yes, I suppose you have.'

'And, by the way, I have spoken of it to Earwaker. Not of your part in the story, of course. I told him that I had met a man who knew all about Peak.—Impossible, you see, for me to keep silence with so intimate a friend.'

'Then Mr. Earwaker will write to him?' said Marcella, reflectively.

'I couldn't give him any address.'

'How does Mr. Warricombe seem to regard Mr. Peak?'

'With a good deal of interest, and of the friendliest kind. Naturally enough; they were College friends, as you know, before I had heard of Peak's existence.'

'He has no suspicions?'

Christian thought not, but her brother's judgment had not much weight with Marcella.

She at once dreaded and desired Warricombe's appearance. If he thought it worth while to cultivate her acquaintance, she would henceforth have the opportunity of studying Peak's relations with the Warricombes; on the other hand, this was to expose herself to suffering and temptation from which the better part of her nature shrank with disdain. That she might seem to have broken the promise voluntarily made to Godwin was a small matter; not so the risk of being overcome by an ignoble jealousy. She had no overweening confidence in the steadfastness of her self-respect, if circumstances were all on the side of sensual impulse. And the longer she brooded on this peril, the more it allured her. For therewith was connected the one satisfaction which still remained to her; however little he desired to keep her constantly in mind, Godwin Peak must of necessity do so after what had passed between them. Had but her discovery remained her own secret, then the pleasure of commanding her less pure emotions, of proving to Godwin that she was above the weakness of common women, might easily have prevailed. Now that her knowledge was shared by others, she had lost that safeguard against lower motive. The argument that to unmask hypocrisy was in itself laudable she dismissed with contempt; let that be the resource of a woman who would indulge her rancour whilst keeping up the inward pretence of sanctity. If *she* erred in the ways characteristic of her sex, it should at all events be a conscious degradation.

'Have you seen that odd creature Malkin lately?' she asked of Christian, a day or two after.

'No, I haven't; I thought of him to make up our dinner on Sunday; but you had rather not have him here, I daresay?'

'Oh, he is amusing. Ask him by all means,' said Marcella, carelessly.

'He may have heard about Peak from Earwaker, you know. If he begins to talk before people'——

'Things have gone too far for such considerations,' replied his sister, with a petulance strange to her habits of speech.

'Well, yes,' admitted Christian, glancing at her. 'We can't be responsible.'

He reproached himself for this attitude towards Peak, but was heartily glad that Marcella seemed to have learnt to regard the intriguer with a wholesome indifference.

On the second day after Christmas, as they sat talking idly in the dusking twilight, the door of the drawing-room was thrown open, and a visitor announced. The name answered with such startling suddenness to the thought with which Marcella had been occupied that, for an instant, she could not believe that she had heard aright. Yet it was undoubtedly Mr. Warricombe who presented himself. He came forward with a slightly hesitating air, but Christian made haste to smooth the situation. With the help of those commonplaces by which even intellectual people are at times compelled to prove their familiarity with social usages, conversation was set in movement.

Buckland could not be quite himself. The consciousness that he had sought these people not at all for their own sake made him formal and dry; his glances, his half-smile, indicated a doubt whether the Moxeys belonged entirely to the sphere in which he was at home. Hence a rather excessive politeness, such as the man who sets much store on breeding exhibits to those who may at any moment, even in a fraction of a syllable, prove themselves his inferiors. With men and women of the unmistakably lower orders, Buckland could converse in a genial tone that recommended him to their esteem; on the borderland of refinement, his sympathies were repressed, and he held the distinctive part of his mind in reserve.

Marcella desired to talk agreeably, but a weight lay upon her tongue; she was struck with the resemblance in Warricome's features to those of his sister, and this held her in a troubled preoccupation, occasionally evident when she made a reply, or tried to diversify the talk by leading to a new topic. It was rather early in the afternoon, and she had slight hope that any other caller would appear; a female face would have been welcome to her, even that of foolish Mrs. Morton, who might possibly look in before six o'clock. To her relief, the door did presently open, but the sharp, creaking footstep which followed was no lady's; the servant announced Mr. Malkin.

Marcella's eyes gleamed strangely. Not with the light of friendly welcome, though for that it could be mistaken. She rose quietly, and stepped forward with a movement which again seemed to betoken eagerness of greeting. In presenting the newcomer to Mr. Warricombe, she spoke with an uncertain voice. Buckland was more than formal. The stranger's aspect impressed him far from favourably, and he resented as an impudence the hearty hand-grip to which he perforce submitted.

'I come to plead with you,' exclaimed Malkin, turning to Marcella, in his abrupt, excited way. 'After accepting your invitation to dine, I find that the thing is utterly and absolutely impossible. I had entirely forgotten an engagement of the very gravest nature. I am conscious of behaving in quite an unpardonable way.'

Marcella laughed down his excuses. She had suddenly become so mirthful that Christian looked at her in surprise, imagining that she was unable to restrain her sense of the ridiculous in Malkin's demeanour.

'I have hurried up from Wrotham,' pursued the apologist. 'Did I tell you, Moxey, that I had taken rooms down there, to be able to spend a day or two near my friends the Jacoxes occasionally? On the way here, I looked in at Staple Inn, but Earwaker is away somewhere. What an odd thing that people will go off without letting one know! It's such common ill-luck of mine to find people gone away—I'm really astonished to find you at home, Miss Moxey.'

Marcella looked at Warricombe and laughed.

'You must understand that subjectively,' she said, with nervous gaiety which again excited her brother's surprise. 'Please don't be discouraged by it from coming to see us again; I am very rarely out in the afternoon.'

'But,' persisted Malkin, 'it's precisely my ill fortune to hit on those rare moments when people *are* out!—Now, I never meet acquaintances in the streets of London; but, if I happen to be abroad, as likely as not I encounter the last person I should expect to find. Why, you remember, I rush over to America for scarcely a week's stay, and there I come across a man who has disappeared astonishingly from the ken of all his friends!'

Christian looked at Marcella. She was leaning forward, her lips slightly parted, her eyes wide as if in gaze at something that fascinated her. He saw that she spoke, but her voice was hardly to be recognised.

'Are you quite sure of that instance, Mr. Malkin?'

'Yes, I feel quite sure, Miss Moxey. Undoubtedly it was Peak!'

Buckland Warricombe, who had been waiting for a chance of escape, suddenly wore a look of interest. He rapidly surveyed the trio. Christian, somewhat out of countenance, tried to answer Malkin in a tone of light banter.

'It happens, my dear fellow that Peak has not left England since we lost sight of him.'

'What? He has been heard of? Where is he then?'

'Mr. Warricombe can assure you that he has been living for a year at Exeter.'

Buckland, perceiving that he had at length come upon something important to his purposes, smiled genially.

'Yes, I have had the pleasure of seeing Peak down in Devon from time to time.'

'Then it was really an illusion!' cried Malkin. 'I was too hasty. Yet that isn't a charge that can be often brought against me, I think. Does Earwaker know of this?'

'He has lately heard,' replied Christian, who in vain sought for a means of checking Malkin's loquacity. 'I thought he might have told you.'

'Certainly not. The thing is quite new to me. And what is Peak doing down there, pray? Why did he conceal himself?'

Christian gazed appealing at his sister. She returned the look steadily, but neither stirred not spoke. It was Warricombe's voice that next sounded:

'Peak's behaviour seems mysterious,' he began, with ironic gravity. 'I don't pretend to understand him. What's *your* view of his character, Mr. Malkin?'

'I know him very slightly indeed, Mr. Warricombe. But I have a high opinion of his powers. I wonder he does so little. After that article of his in *The Critical*'——

Malkin became aware of something like agonised entreaty on Christian's countenance, but this had merely the effect of heightening his curiosity.

'In *The Critical*?' said Warricombe, eagerly. 'I didn't know of that. What was the subject?'

'To be sure, it was anonymous,' went on Malkin, without a suspicion of the part he was playing before these three excited people. 'A paper called "The New Sophistry," a tremendous bit of satire.'

Marcella's eyes closed as if a light had flashed before them; she drew a short sigh, and at once seemed to become quite at ease, the smile with which she regarded Warricombe expressing a calm interest.

'That article was Peak's?' Buckland asked, in a very quiet voice.

Christian at last found his opportunity.

'He never mentioned it to you? Perhaps he thought he had gone rather too far in his Broad Churchism, and might be misunderstood.'

'Broad Churchism?' cried Malkin. 'Uncommonly broad, I must say!'

And he laughed heartily; Marcella seemed to join in his mirth.

'Then it would surprise you,' said Buckland, in the same quiet tone as before, 'to hear that Peak is about to take Orders?'

'Orders?—For what?'

Christian laughed. The worst was over; after all, it came as a relief.

'Not for wines,' he replied. 'Mr. Warricombe means that Peak is going to be ordained.'

Malkin's amazement rendered him speechless. He stared from one person to another, his features strangely distorted.

'You can hardly believe it?' pressed Buckland.

The reply was anticipated by Christian saying:

'Remember, Malkin, that you had no opportunity of studying Peak. It's not so easy to understand him.'

'But I don't see,' burst out the other, 'how I could possibly so *mis*understand him! What has Earwaker to say?'

Buckland rose from his seat, advanced to Marcella, and offered his hand. She said mechanically 'Must you go?' but was incapable of another word. Christian came to her relief, performed the needful civilities, and accompanied his acquaintance to the foot of the stairs. Buckland had become grave, stiff, monosyllabic; Christian made no allusion to the scene thus suddenly interrupted, and they parted with a formal air.

Malkin remained for another quarter of an hour, when the muteness of his companions made it plain to him that he had better withdraw. He went off with a sense of having been mystified, half resentful, and vastly impatient to see Earwaker.

PART THE FIFTH

I

THE CUCKOO CLOCK in Mrs. Roots's kitchen had just struck three. A wind roared from the north-east, and light thickened beneath a sky which made threat of snow. Peak was in a mood to enjoy the crackling fire; he settled himself with a book in his easy-chair, and thought with pleasure of two hours' reading, before the appearance of the homely teapot.

Christmas was just over—one cause of the feeling of relief and quietness which possessed him. No one had invited him for Christmas Eve or the day that followed, and he did not regret it. The letter he had received from Martin Warricombe was assurance enough that those he desired to remember him still did so. He had thought of using this season for his long postponed visit to Twybridge, but reluctance prevailed. All popular holidays irritated and depressed him; he loathed the spectacle of multitudes in Sunday garb. It was all over, and the sense of that afforded him a brief content.

This book, which he had just brought from the circulating library, was altogether to his taste. The author, Justin Walsh, he knew to be a brother of Professor Walsh, long ago the object of his rebellious admiration. Matter and treatment rejoiced him. No intellectual delight, though he was capable of it in many forms, so stirred his spirit as that afforded him by a vigorous modern writer joyously assailing the old moralities. Justin Walsh was a modern of the moderns; at once man of science and man of letters; defiant without a hint of popular cynicism, scornful of English reticences yet never gross. '*Oui, répondit Pococurante, il est beau d'écrire ce qu'on pense; c'est le privilége de l'homme.*' This stood by way of motto on the title-page, and Godwin felt his nerves thrill in sympathetic response.

What a fine fellow he must be to have for a friend! Now a man like this surely had companionship enough and of the kind he wished? He wrote like one who assocates freely with the educated classes both at home and abroad. Was he married? Where would *he* seek his wife? The fitting mate for him would doubtless be found among those women, cosmopolitan and emancipated, whose acquaintance falls only to men in easy circumstances and of good social standing, men who travel much, who are at home in all the great centres of civilisation.

As Peak meditated, the volume fell upon his knee. Had it not lain in his own power to win a reputation like that which Justin Walsh was achieving? His paper in *The Critical Review*, itself a decided success, might have been followed up by others of the same tenor. Instead of mouldering in a dull cathedral town, he might now be living and working in France or Germany. His money would have served one purpose as well as the other, and two or three years of determined effort——

Mrs. Roots showed her face at the door.

'A gentleman is asking for you, sir,—Mr. Chilvers.'

'Mr. Chilvers? Please ask him to come up.'

He threw his book on to the table, and stood in expectancy. Someone ascended the stairs with rapid stride and creaking boots. The door was flung open, and a cordial but affected voice burst forth in greeting.

'Ha, Mr. Peak! I hope you haven't altogether forgotten me? Delighted to see you again!'

Godwin gave his hand, and felt it strongly pressed, whilst Chilvers gazed into his face with a smiling wistfulness which could only be answered with a grin of discomfort. The Rev. Bruno had grown very tall, and seemed to be in perfect health; but the effeminacy of his brilliant youth still declared itself in his attitudes, gestures, and attire. He was dressed with marked avoidance of the professional pattern. A hat of soft felt but not clerical, fashionable collar and tie, a sweeping ulster, and beneath it a frock-coat, which was doubtless the pride of some West End tailor. His patent-leather boots were dandiacally diminutive; his glove fitted like that of a lady who lives but to be *bien gantée*. The feathery hair, which at Whitelaw he was wont to pat and smooth, still had its golden shimmer, and on his face no growth was permitted.

'I had heard of your arrival here, of course,' said Peak, trying to appear civil, though anything more than that was beyond his power. 'Will you sit down?'

'This is the "breathing time o' the day" with you, I hope? I don't disturb your work?'

'I was only reading this book of Walsh's. Do you know it?'

But for some such relief of his feelings, Godwin could not have sat still. There was a pleasure in uttering Walsh's name. Moreover, it would serve as a test of Chilver's disposition.

'Walsh?' He took up the volume. 'Ha! Justin Walsh. I know him. A wonderful book! Admirable dialectic! Delicious style!'

'Not quite orthodox, I fancy,' replied Godwin, with a curling of the lips.

'Orthodox? Oh, of course not, of course not! But a rich vein of humanity. Don't you find that?—Pray allow me to throw off my overcoat. Ha, thanks!—A rich vein of humanity. Walsh is by no means to be confused with the nullifidians. A very broad-hearted, large-souled man; at bottom the truest of Christians. Now and then he effervesces rather too exuberantly. Yes, I admit it. In a review of his last book, which I was privileged to write for one of our papers, I ventured to urge upon him the necessity of *restraint*; it seems to me that in this new work he exhibits more self-control, an approach to the serene fortitude which I trust he may attain. A man of the broadest brotherliness. A most valuable ally of renascent Christianity.'

Peak was hardly prepared for this strain. He knew that Chilvers prided himself on 'breadth,' but as yet he had enjoyed no intercourse with the broadest school of Anglicans, and was uncertain as to the limits of modern latitudinarianism. The discovery of such fantastic liberality in a man whom he could not but dislike and contemn gave him no pleasure, but at least it disposed him to amusement rather than antagonism. Chilvers' pronunciation and phraseology were distinguished by such original affectation that it was impossible not to find entertainment in listening to him. Though his voice was naturally thin and piping, he managed to speak in head notes which had a ring of robust utterance. The sound of his words was intended to correspond with their virile warmth of meaning. In the same way he had cultivated a habit of the muscles which conveyed an impression that he was devoted to athletic sports. His arms occasionally swung as if brandishing dumb-bells, his chest now and then spread itself to the uttermost, and his head was often thrown back in an attitude suggesting self-defence.

'So you are about to join us,' he exclaimed, with a look of touching interest, much like that of a ladies' doctor speaking delicately of favourable symptoms. Then, as if consciously returning to the virile note, 'I think we shall understand each other. I am always eager to study the opinions of those among us who have scientific minds. I hear of you on all hands; already you have strongly impressed some of the thinking people in Exeter.'

Peak crossed his legs and made no reply.

'There is distinct need of an infusion of the scientific spirit into the work of the Church. The churchman hitherto has been, as a matter of course, of the literary stamp; hence much of our trouble during the last half-century. It behoves us to go in for science—physical, economic—science of every kind. Only thus can we resist the morbific influences which inevitably beset an Established Church in times such as these. I say it boldly. Let us throw aside our Hebrew and our Greek, our commentators ancient and modern! Let us have done with polemics and with compromises! What we have to do is to construct a spiritual edifice on the basis of scientific revelation. I use the word revelation advisedly. The results of science are the divine message to our age; to neglect them, to fear them, is to remain under the old law whilst the new is demanding our adherence, to repeat the Jewish error of bygone time. Less of St. Paul, and more of Darwin! Less of Luther, and more of Herbert Spencer!'

'Shall I have the pleasure of hearing this doctrine at St. Margaret's?' Peak inquired.

'In a form suitable to the intelligence of my parishioners, taken in the mass. Were my hands perfectly free, I should begin by preaching a series of sermons on *The Origin of Species*. Sermons! An obnoxious word! One ought never to use it. It signifies everything inept, inert.'

'Is it your serious belief, then, that the mass of parishioners—here or elsewhere—are ready for this form of spiritual instruction?'

'Most distinctly—given the true capacity in the teacher. Mark me; I don't say that they are capable of receiving much absolute knowledge. What I desire is that their minds shall be relieved from a state of harassing conflict—put at the right point of view. They are not to think that Jesus of Nazareth teaches faith and conduct incompatible with the doctrines of Evolutionism. They are not to spend their lives in kicking against the pricks, and regard as meritorious the punctures which result to them. The establishment in their minds of a few cardinal facts—that is the first step. Then let the interpretation follow—the solace, the encouragement, the hope for eternity!'

'You imagine,' said Godwin, with a calm air, 'that the mind of the average church-goer is seriously disturbed on questions of faith?'

'How can you ignore it, my dear Peak?—Permit me this familiarity; we are old fellow-collegians.—The average church-goer is the average citizen of our English commonwealth,—a man necessarily aware of the great Radical movement, and all that it involves. Forgive me. There has been far too much blinking of actualities by zealous Christians whose faith is rooted in knowledge. We gain nothing by it; we lose immensely. Let us recognise that our churches are filled with sceptics, endeavouring to believe in spite of themselves.'

'Your experience is much larger than mine,' remarked the listener, submissively.

'Indeed I have widely studied the subject.'

Chilvers smiled with ineffable self-content, his head twisted like that of a sagacious parrot.

'Granting your average citizen,' said the other, 'what about the average citizeness? The female church-goers are not insignificant in number.'

'Ha! There we reach the core of the matter! Woman! woman!

Precisely *there* is the most hopeful outlook. I trust you are strong for female emancipation?'

'Oh, perfectly sound on that question!'

'To be sure! Then it must be obvious to you that women are destined to play the leading part in our Christian renascence, precisely as they did in the original spreading of the faith. What else is the meaning of the vast activity in female education? Let them be taught, and forthwith they will rally to our Broad Church. A man may be content to remain a nullifidian; women cannot rest at that stage. They demand the spiritual significance of everything—I grieve to tell you, Peak, that for three years I have been a widower. My wife died with shocking suddenness, leaving me her two little children. Ah, but leaving me also the memory of a singularly pure and noble being. I may say, with all humility, that I have studied the female mind in its noblest modern type. I *know* what can be expected of woman, in our day and in the future.'

'Mrs. Chilvers was in full sympathy with your views?'

'Three years ago I had not yet reached my present standpoint. In several directions I was still narrow. But her prime characteristic was the tendency to spiritual growth. She would have accompanied me step by step. In very many respects, I must regard myself as a man favoured by fortune,—I know it, and I trust I am grateful for it,—but that loss, my dear Peak, counterbalances much happiness. In moments of repose, when I look back on work joyously achieved, I often murmur to myself, with a sudden sigh, *Excepto quod non simul esses, cætera lætus!*'

He pronounced his Latin in the new-old way, with Continental vowels. The effect of this on an Englishman's lips is always more or less pedantic, and in his case it was intolerable.

'And when,' he exclaimed, dismissing the melancholy thought, 'do you present yourself for ordination?'

It was his habit to pay slight attention to the words of anyone but himself, and Peak's careless answer merely led him to talk on wide subjects with renewal of energy. One might have suspected that he had made a list of uncommon words wherewith to adorn his discourse, for certain of these frequently recurred. 'Nullifidian,' 'morbific,' 'renascent,' were among his favourites. Once or twice he spoke of 'psychogenesis,' with an emphatic enunciation which seemed to invite respectful wonder. In using Latin words which have become fixed in the English language, he generally corrected the common errors of quantity: '*minnus* the spiritual fervour,' 'acting as his *loccum tennens*.' When he referred to Christian teachers with whom he was acquainted, they were seldom or ever members of the Church of England. Methodists, Romanists, Presbyterians, appeared to stand high in his favour, and Peak readily discerned that this was a way of displaying 'large-souled tolerance.' It was his foible to quote foreign languages, especially passages which came from heretical authors. Thus he began to talk of Feuerbach for the sole purpose of delivering a German sentence.

'He has been of infinite value to me—quite infinite value. You remember his definition of God? It is constantly in my mind. "*Gott ist eine Thräne der Liebe, in tiefster Verborgenheit vergossen über das menschliche Elend.*" Profoundly touching! I know nothing to approach it.'

Suddenly he inquired:

'Do you see much of the Exeter clergy?'

'I know only the Vicar of St. Ethelreda's, Mr. Lilywhite.'

'Ha! Admirable fellow! Large-minded, broad of sympathies. Has distinctly the scientific turn of thought.'

Peak smiled, knowing the truth. But he had hit upon a way of meeting the Rev. Bruno which promised greatly to diminish the suffering inherent in the situation. He would use the large-souled man deliberately for his mirth. Chilvers' self-absorption lent itself to persiflage, and by indulging in that mood Godwin tasted some compensation for the part he had to play.

'And I believe you know the Warricombes very well?' pursued Chilvers.

'Yes.'

'Ha! I hope to see much of them. They are people after my own heart. Long ago I had a slight acquaintance with them. I hear we shan't see them till the summer.'

'I believe not.'

'Mr. Warricombe is a great geologist, I think?—Probably he frequents public worship as a mere tribute to social opinion?'

He asked the question in the airiest possible way, as if it mattered nothing to him what the reply might be.

'Mr. Warricombe is a man of sincere piety,' Godwin answered, with grave countenance.

'That by no means necessitates church-going, my dear Peak,' rejoined the other, waving his hand.

'You think not? I am still only a student, you must remember. My mind is in suspense on not a few points.'

'Of course! Of course! Pray let me give you the results of my own thought on this subject.'

He proceeded to do so, at some length. When he had rounded his last period, he unexpectedly started up, swung on his toes, spread his chest, drew a deep breath, and with the sweetest of smiles announced that he must postpone the delight of further conversation.

'You must come and dine with me as soon as my house is in reasonable order. As yet, everything is *sens dessus-dessous*. Delightful old city, Exeter! Charming! Charming!'

And on the moment he was gone.

What were this man's real opinions? He had brains and literature; his pose before the world was not that of an ignorant charlatan. Vanity, no doubt, was his prime motive, but did it operate to make a cleric of a secret materialist, or to invite a display of excessive liberalism in one whose convictions were orthodox? Godwin could not answer to his satisfaction, but he preferred the latter surmise.

One thing, however, became clear to him. All his conscientious scruples about entering the Church were superfluous. Chilvers would have smiled pityingly at anyone who disputed his right to live by the Establishment, and to stand up as an authorised preacher of the national faith. And beyond a doubt he regulated his degree of 'breadth' by standards familiar to him in professional intercourse. To him it seemed all-sufficient to preach a gospel of moral progress, of intellectual growth, of universal fraternity. If this were the tendency of Anglicanism, then almost any man who desired to live a cleanly life, and to see others do the same, might without hesitation become a clergyman. The old formulæ of subscription were so symbolised, so volatilised, that they could not stand in the way of anyone but a combative nihilist. Peak was conscious of positive ideals by no means inconsistent with Christian teaching, and in his official capacity these alone would direct him.

He spent his evening pleasantly, often laughing as he recalled a phrase or gesture of the Rev. Bruno's.

In the night fell a sprinkling of snow, and when the sun rose it gleamed from a sky of pale, frosty blue. At ten o'clock Godwin set out for his usual walk, choosing the direction of the Old Tiverton Road. It was a fortnight since he had passed the Warricombes' house. At present he was disposed to indulge the thoughts which a sight of it would make active.

He had begun the ascent of the hill when the sound of an approaching vehicle caused him to raise his eyes—they were generally fixed on the ground when he walked alone. It was only a hired fly. But, as it passed him, he recognised the face he had least expected to see,—Sidwell Warricombe sat in the carriage, and unaccompanied. She noticed him—smiled—and bent forward. He clutched at his hat, but it happened that the driver had turned to look at him, and, instead of the salute he had intended, his hand waved to the man to stop. The gesture was scarcely voluntary; when he saw the carriage pull up, his heart sank; he felt guilty of monstrous impudence. But Sidwell's face appeared at the window, and its expression was anything but resentful; she offered her hand, too. Without preface of formal phrase he exclaimed:

'How delightful to see you so unexpectedly! Are you all here?'

'Only mother and I. We have come for a day or two.'

'Will you allow me to call? If only for a few minutes'——

'We shall be at home this afternoon.'

'Thank you! Don't you enjoy the sunshine after London?'

'Indeed I do!'

He stepped back and signed to the driver. Sidwell bent her head and was out of sight.

But the carriage was visible for some distance, and even when he could no longer see it he heard the horse's hoofs on the hard road. Long after the last sound had died away his heart continued to beat painfully, and he breathed as if recovering from a hard run.

How beautiful were these lanes and hills, even in mid-winter! Once more he sang aloud in his joyous solitude. The hope he had nourished was not unreasonable; his boldness justified itself. Yes, he was one of the men who succeed, and the life before him would be richer for all the mistakes and miseries through which he had passed. Thirty, forty, fifty—why, twenty years hence he would be in the prime of manhood, with perhaps yet another twenty years of mental and bodily vigour. One of the men who succeed!

II

ON THE MORNING after her journey down from London, Mrs. Warricombe awoke with the conviction that she had caught a cold. Her health was in general excellent, and she had no disposition to nurse imaginary ailments, but when some slight disorder broke the routine of her life she made the most of it, enjoying—much as children do—the importance with which for the time it invested her. At such seasons she was wont to regard herself with a mildly despondent compassion, to feel that her family and her friends held her of slight account; she spoke in a tone of conscious resignation, often with a forgiving smile. When the girls redoubled their attentions, and soothed her with gentle words, she would close her eyes and sigh, seeming to remind them that they would know her value when she was no more.

'You are hoarse, mother,' Sidwell said to her, when they met at breakfast.

'Am I, dear? You know I felt rather afraid of the journey. I hope I shan't be laid up.'

Sidwell advised her not to leave the house today. Having seen the invalid comfortably established in an upper room, she went into the city on business which could not be delayed. On her way occurred the meeting with Peak, but of this, on her return, she made no mention. Mother and daughter had luncheon upstairs, and Sidwell was full of affectionate solicitude.

'This afternoon you had better lie down for an hour or two,' she said.

'Do you think so? Just drop a line to father and warn him that we may be kept here for some time.'

'Shall I send for Dr. Endacott?'

'Just as you like, dear.'

But Mrs. Warricombe had eaten such an excellent lunch, that Sidwell could not feel uneasy.

'We'll see how you are this evening. At all events, it will be safer for you not to go downstairs. If you lie quiet for an hour or two, I can look for those pamphlets that father wants.'

'Just as you like, dear.'

By three o'clock the invalid was calmly slumbering. Having entered the bedroom on tiptoe and heard regular breathing, Sidwell went down and for a few minutes lingered about the hall. A servant came to her for instructions on some domestic matter; when this was dismissed she mentioned that, if anyone called, she would be found in the library.

The pamphlets of which her father had spoken were soon discovered. She laid them aside, and seated herself by the fire, but without leaning back. At any sound within or outside the house she moved her head to listen. Her look was anxious, but the gleam of her eyes expressed pleasurable agitation.

At half-past three she went into the drawing-room, where all the furniture was draped, and the floor bare. Standing where she could look from a distance through one of the windows, at which the blind had been raised, she waited for a quarter of an hour. Then the chill atmosphere drove her back to the fireside. In the study, evidences of temporary desertion were less oppressive, but the windows looked only upon a sequestered part of the garden. Sidwell desired to watch the approach from the high-road, and in a few minutes she was again in the drawing-room. But scarcely had she closed the door behind her when a ringing of the visitors' bell sounded with unfamiliar distinctness. She started, hastened from the room, fled into the library, and had time to seat herself before she heard the footsteps of a servant moving in answer to the summons.

The door opened, and Peak was announced.

Sidwell had never known what it was to be thus overcome with emotion. Shame at her inability to command the calm features with which she would naturally receive a caller flushed her cheeks and neck; she stepped forward with downcast eyes, and only in offering her hand could at length look at him who stood before her. She saw at once that Peak was unlike himself; he too had unusual warmth in his countenance, and his eyes seemed strangely large, luminous. On his forehead were drops of moisture.

This sight restored her self-control, or such measure of it as permitted her to speak in the conventional way.

'I am sorry that mother can't leave her room. She had a slight cold this morning, but I didn't think it would give her any trouble.'

Peak was delighted, and betrayed the feeling even whilst he constrained his face into a look of exaggerated anxiety.

'It won't be anything serious, I hope? The railway journey, I'm afraid.'

'Yes, the journey. She has a slight hoarseness, but I think we shall prevent it from'——

Their eyes kept meeting, and with more steadfastness. They were conscious of mutual scrutiny, and, on both sides, of changes since they last met. When two people have devoted intense study to each other's features, a three months' absence not only revives the old impressions but subjects them to sudden modification which engrosses thought and feeling. Sidwell continued to utter commonplaces, simply as a means of disguising the thoughts that occupied her; she was saying to herself that Peak's face had a purer outline than she had believed, and that his eyes had gained in expressiveness. In the same way Godwin said and replied he knew not what, just to give himself time to observe and enjoy the something new—the increased animation or subtler facial movements—which struck him as often as he looked at his companion. Each wondered what the other had been doing, whether the time had seemed long or short.

'I hope you have kept well?' Sidwell asked.

Godwin hastened to respond with civil inquiries.

'I was very glad to hear from Mr. Warricombe a few days ago,' he continued. Sidwell was not aware that her father had written, but her pleased smile seemed to signify the contrary.

'She looks younger,' Peak said in his mind. 'Perhaps that London dress and the new way of arranging her hair have something to do with it. But no, she looks younger in herself. She must have been enjoying the pleasures of town.'

'You have been constantly occupied, no doubt,' he added aloud, feeling at the same time that this was a clumsy expression of what he meant. Though he had unbuttoned his overcoat, and seated himself as easily as he could, the absurd tall hat which he held embarrassed him; to deposit it on the floor demanded an effort of which he was yet incapable.

'I have seen many things and heard much talk,' Sidwell was replying, in a gay tone. It irritated him; he would have preferred her to speak with more of the old pensiveness. Yet perhaps she was glad simply because she found herself again talking with him?

'And you?' she went on. 'It has not been all work, I hope?'

'Oh no! I have had many pleasant intervals.'

This was in imitation of her vivacity. He felt the words and the manner to be ridiculous, but could not restrain himself. Every moment increased his uneasiness; the hat weighed in his hands like a lump of lead, and he was convinced that he had never looked so clownish. Did her smile signify criticism of his attitude?

With a decision which came he knew not how, he let his hat drop to the floor and pushed it aside. There, that was better; he felt less of a bumpkin.

Sidwell glanced at the glossy grotesque, but instantly averted her eyes, and asked rather more gravely:

'Have you been in Exeter all the time?'

'Yes.'

'But you didn't spend your Christmas alone, I hope?'

'Oh, I had my books.'

Was there not a touch of natural pathos in this? He hoped so; then mocked at himself for calculating such effects.

'I think you don't care much for ordinary social pleasures, Mr. Peak?'

He smiled bitterly.

'I have never known much of them,—and you remember that I look forward to a life in which they will have little part. Such a life,' he continued, after a pause, 'seems to you unendurably dull? I noticed that, when I spoke of it before.'

'You misunderstood me.' She said it so undecidedly that he gazed at her with puzzled look. Her eyes fell.

'But you like society?'

'If you use the word in its narrowest meaning,' she answered, 'then I not only dislike society, but despise it.'

She had raised her eyebrows, and was looking coldly at him. Did she mean to rebuke him for the tone he had adopted? Indeed, he seemed to himself presumptuous. But if they were still on terms such as these, was it not better to know it, even at the cost of humiliation? One moment he believed that he could read Sidwell's thoughts, and that they were wholly favourable to him; at another he felt absolutely ignorant of all that was passing in her, and disposed to interpret her face as that of a conventional woman who had never regarded him as on her own social plane. These uncertainties, these frequent reversions to a state of mind which at other times he seemed to have long outgrown, were a singular feature of his relations with Sidwell. Could such experiences consist with genuine love? Never had he felt more willing to answer the question with a negative. He felt that he was come here to act a part, and that the end of the interview, be it what it might, would only affect him superficially.

'No,' he replied, with deliberation; 'I never supposed that you had any interest in the most foolish class of wealthy people. I meant that you recognise your place in a certain social rank, and regard intercourse with your equals as an essential of happiness.'

'If I understood why you ask'—— she began abruptly, but ceased as she met his glance. Again he thought she was asserting a distant dignity.

'The question arose naturally out of a train of thought which always occupies me when I talk with you. I myself belong to no class whatever, and I can't help wondering how—if the subject ever occurred to you—you would place me.'

He saw his way now, and, having said thus much, could talk on defiantly. This hour must decide his fortune with Sidwell, yet his tongue utterly refused any of the modes of speech which the situation would have suggested to an ordinary mind. He could not 'make love.' Instead of humility, he was prompted to display a rough arrogance; instead of tender phrases, he uttered what sounded like deliberate rudeness. His voice was less gently tuned than Sidwell had been wont to hear it. It all meant that he despaired of wooing successfully, and more than half wished to force some word from Sidwell which would spare him the necessity of a plain avowal.

But before he had finished speaking, her face changed. A light of sudden understanding shone in her eyes; her lips softened to a smile of exquisite gentleness.

'The subject never *did* occur to me,' she answered. 'How should it? A friend is a friend.'

It was not strictly true, but in the strength of her emotion she could forget all that contradicted it.

'A friend—yes.'

Godwin began with the same note of bluntness. But of a sudden he felt the influence of Sidwell's smile. His voice sank into a murmur, his heart leapt, a thrill went through his veins.

'I wish to be something more than a friend.'

He felt that it was bald, inadequate. Yet the words had come of their own accord, on an impulse of unimpaired sincerity. Sidwell's head was bent.

'That is why I can't take simple things for granted,' he continued, his gaze fixed upon her. 'If I thought of nothing but friendship, it would seem rational enough that you should accept me for what I am—a man of education, talking your own language. Because I have dared to hope something more, I suffer from the thought that I was not born into your world, and that you must be always remembering this difference.'

'Do you think me so far behind the age?' asked Sidwell, trying to laugh.

'Classes are getting mixed, confused. Yes, but we are so conscious of the process that we talk of class distinctions more than of anything else,—talk and think of them incessantly. You have never heard me make a profession of Radicalism; *I* am decidedly behind the age. Be what I may—and I have spiritual pride more than enough—the fact that I have relatives in the lower, even the lowest, social class must necessarily affect the whole course of my life. A certain kind of man declares himself proud of such an origin—and most often lies. Or one may be driven by it into rebellion against social privilege. To me, my origin is simply a grave misfortune, to be accepted and, if possible, overcome. Does that sound mean-spirited? I can't help it; I want you to know me.'

'I believe I know you very well,' Sidwell replied.

The consciousness that she was deceived checked the words which were rising to his lips. Again he saw himself in a pitiful light, and this self-contempt reflected upon Sidwell. He could not doubt that she was yielding to him; her attitude and her voice declared it; but what was the value of love won by imposture? Why had she not intelligence enough to see through his hypocrisy, which at times was so thin a veil? How defective must her sympathy be!

'Yet you have seen very little of me,' he said, smiling.

There was a short silence; then he exclaimed in a voice of emotion:

'How I wish we had known each other ever since that day when your brother brought me to your house near Kingsmill! If we had met and talked through all those years! But that was impossible for the very reason which makes me inarticulate now that I wish to say so much. When you first saw me I was a gawky schoolboy, learning to use my brains, and knowing already that life had nothing to offer me but a false position. Whether I remained with my kith and kin, or turned my back upon them in the hope of finding my equals, I was condemned to a life of miserable incompleteness. I was born in exile. It took a long time before I had taught myself how to move and speak like one of the class to which I belonged by right of intellect. I was living alone in London, in mean lodging-houses. But the day came when I felt more confidence in myself. I had saved money, and foresaw that in a year or two I should be able to carry out a plan, make one serious attempt to win a position among educated people.'

He stopped. Had he intended a full confession, it was thus he might have begun it. Sidwell was regarding him, but with a gentle look, utterly unsuspecting. She was unable to realise his character and his temptations.

'And have you not succeeded?' she asked, in a low voice.

'Have I? Let me put it to the test. I will set aside every thought of presumption; forget that I am a penniless student looking forward to a country curacy; and say what I wished to when we had our last conversation. Never mind how it sounds. I have dared to hope that some day I shall ask you to be my wife, and that you won't refuse.'

The word 'wife' reverberated on his ears. A whirl of emotion broke the defiant calm he had supported for the last few minutes. The silence seemed to be endless; when he looked at Sidwell, her head was bent, the eyes concealed by their drooping lids. Her expression was very grave.

'Such a piece of recklessness,' he said at length, 'deserves no answer.'

Sidwell raised her eyes and spoke gently, with voice a little shaken.

'Why should you call it recklessness? I have never thought of the things that seem to trouble you so much. You were a friend of ours. Wasn't that enough?'

It seemed to him an evasive reply. Doubtless it was much that she showed neither annoyance nor prudish reserve. He had won the right of addressing her on equal terms, but she was not inclined to anticipate that future day to which he pointed.

'You have never thought of such things, because you have never thought of me as I of you. Every day of your absence in London has caused me torments which were due most often to the difference between your social position and mine. You have been among people of leisure and refinement and culture. Each evening you have talked with men whom it cost no effort to make themselves liked and respected. I think of that with bitterness.'

'But why? I have made many acquaintances; have met very interesting people. I am glad of it; it enables me to understand you better than I could before.'

'You are glad on that account?'

'Yes; indeed I am.'

'Dare I think you mean more than a civil phrase?'

'I mean quite simply all that my words imply. I have thought of you, though certainly without bitterness. No one's conversation in London interested me so much as yours.'

Soothed with an exquisite joy, Godwin felt his eyes moisten. For a moment he was reconciled to all the world, and forgot the hostilities of a lifetime.

'And will it still be so, now, when you go back?' he asked, in a soft tone.

'I am sure it will.'

'Then it will be strange if I ever feel bitterly again.'

Sidwell smiled.

'You could have said nothing that could please me more. Why should your life be troubled by these dark moods? I could understand it if you were still struggling with—with doubts, with all manner of uncertainties about your course'——

She hesitated, watching his face.

'You think I have chosen well?' said Godwin, meeting her look.

Sidwell's eyes were at once averted.

'I hope,' she said, 'we may talk of that again very soon. You have told me much of yourself, but I have said little or nothing of my own—difficulties. It won't be long before we come back from London, and then'——

Once more their eyes met steadily.

'You think,' Godwin asked, 'that I am right in aiming at a life of retirement?'

'It is one of my doubts. Your influence would be useful anywhere; but most useful, surely, among people of active mind.'

'Perhaps I shan't be able to choose. Remember that I am seeking for a livelihood as well as for a sphere of usefulness.'

His eyes fell as he spoke. Hitherto he had had no means of learning whether Sidwell would bring her husband a dowry substantial enough to be considered. Though he could not feel that she had betrothed herself to him, their talk was so nearly that of avowed lovers that perchance she would disclose whatever might help to put his mind at rest. The thought revived his painful self-consciousness; it was that of a schemer, yet would not the curse of poverty have suggested it to any man?

'Perhaps you won't be able to choose—at first,' Sidwell assented, thereby seeming to answer his unspoken question. 'But I am sure my father will use whatever influence he has.'

Had he been seated near enough, he would have been tempted to the boldness of taking her hand. What more encouragement did he await? But the distance between them was enough to check his embarrassed impulses. He could not even call her 'Sidwell'; it would have been easier a few minutes ago, before she had begun to speak with such calm friendliness. Now, in spite of everything, he felt that to dare such a familiarity must needs call upon him the reproof of astonished eyes.

'You return tomorrow?' he asked, suddenly.

'I think so. You have promised me to be cheerful until we are home again.'

'A promise to be cheerful wouldn't mean much. But it *does* mean much that I can think of what you have said to-day.'

Sidwell did not speak, and her silence seemed to compel him to rise. It was strange how remote he still felt from her pure, grave face, and the flowing outlines of her figure. Why could he not say to her, 'I love you; give me your hands; give me your lips'? Such words seemed impossible. Yet passion thrilled in him as he watched the grace of her movements, the light and shadow upon her features. She had risen and come a step or two forward.

'I think you look taller—in that dress.'

The words rather escaped him than were spoken. His need was to talk of common things, of trifles, that so he might come to feel humanly.

Sidwell smiled with unmistakable pleasure.

'Do I? Do you like the dress?'

'Yes. It becomes you.'

'Are you critical in such things?'

'Not with understanding. But I should like to see you every day in a new and beautiful dress.'

'Oh, I couldn't afford it!' was the laughing reply.

He offered his hand; the touch of her warm, soft fingers fired his blood.

'Sidwell!'

It was spoken at last, involuntarily, and he stood with his eyes on hers, her hand crushed in his.

'Some day!' she whispered.

If their lips met, the contact was so slight as to seem accidental; it was the mere timorous promise of a future kiss. And both were glad of the something that had imposed restraint.

When Sidwell went up to her mother's sitting-room a servant had just brought tea.

'I hear that Mr. Peak has been,' said Mrs. Warricombe, who looked puffy and uncomfortable after her sleep. 'Emma was going to take tea to the study, but I thought it unnecessary. How could he knew that we were here?'

'I met him this morning on my way into the town.'

'Surely it was rather inconsiderate of him to call.'

'He asked if he might.'

Mrs. Warricombe turned her head and examined Sidwell.

'Oh! And did he stay long?'

'Not very long,' replied Sidwell, who was in quiet good-humour.

'I think it would have been better if you had told him by the servant that I was not well enough to see callers. You didn't mention that he might be coming.'

Mrs. Warricombe's mind worked slowly at all times, and at present she was suffering from a cold.

'Why didn't you speak of it, Sidwell?'

'Really—I forgot,' replied the daughter, lightly.

'And what had he to say?'

'Nothing new, mother. Is your head better, dear?'

There was no answer. Mrs. Warricombe had conceived a vague suspicion which was so alarming that she would not press inquiries alluding to it. The encouragement given by her husband to Godwin Peak in the latter's social progress had always annoyed her, though she could not frame solid objections. To be sure, to say of a man that he is about to be ordained meets every possible question that society can put; but Mrs. Warricombe's uneasiness was in part due to personal dislike. Oftener than not, she still thought of Peak as he appeared some eleven years ago—an evident plebeian, without manners, without a redeeming grace. She knew the story of his relative who had opened a shop in Kingsmill; thinking of that now, she shuddered.

Sidwell began to talk of indifferent matters, and Peak was not again mentioned.

Her throat being still troublesome, Mrs. Warricombe retired very soon after dinner. About nine o'clock Sidwell went to the library, and sat down at her father's writing-table, purposing a letter to Sylvia. She penned a line or two, but soon lapsed into reverie, her head on her hands. Of a sudden the door was thrown open, and there stood Buckland, fresh from travel.

'What has brought you?' exclaimed his sister, starting up anxiously, for something in the young man's look seemed ominous.

'Oh, nothing to trouble about. I had to come down—on business. Mother gone to bed?'

Sidwell explained.

'All right; doesn't matter. I suppose I can sleep here? Let them get me a mouthful of something; cold meat, anything will do.'

His needs were quickly supplied, and before long he was smoking by the library fire.

'I was writing to Sylvia,' said his sister, glancing at her fragmentary letter.

'Oh!'

'You know she is at Salisbury?'

'Salisbury? No, I didn't.'

His carelessness proved to Sidwell that she was wrong in conjecturing that his journey had something to do with Miss Moorhouse. Buckland was in no mood for conversation; he smoked for a quarter of an hour whilst Sidwell resumed her writing.

'Of course you haven't seen Peak?' fell from him at length.

His sister looked at him before replying.

'Yes. He called this afternoon.'

'But who told him you were here?'

His brows were knitting, and he spoke very abruptly. Sidwell gave the same explanation as to her mother, and had further to reply that she alone received the caller.

'I see,' was Buckland's comment.

Its tone troubled Sidwell.

'Has your coming anything to do with Mr. Peak?'

'Yes, it has. I want to see him the first thing tomorrow.'

'Can you tell me what about?'

He searched her face, frowning.

'Not now. I'll tell you in the morning.'

Sidwell saw herself doomed to a night of suspense. She could not confess how nearly the mystery concerned her. Had Buckland made some discovery that irritated him against Peak? She knew he was disposed to catch at anything that seemed to tell against Godwin's claims to respectful treatment, and it surely must be a grave affair to hurry him on so long a journey. Though she could imagine no ground of fear, the situation was seriously disturbing.

She tried to go on with her letter, but failed. As Buckland smoked in silence, she at length rose and said she would go upstairs.

'All right! Shall see you at breakfast. Good-night!'

At nine next morning, Mrs. Warricombe sent a message to Buckland that she wished to see him in her bedroom. He entered hurriedly.

'Cold better, mother? I have only just time to drink a cup of coffee. I want to catch Peak before he can have left home.'

'Mr. Peak? Why? I was going to speak about him.'

'What were you going to say?' Buckland asked, anxiously.

His mother began in a roundabout way which threatened long detention. In a minute or two Buckland had gathered enough to interrupt her with the direct inquiry:

'You don't mean that there's anything between him and Sidwell?'

'I do hope not; but I can't imagine why she should—really, almost make a private appointment. I am very uneasy, Buckland. I have hardly slept. Sidwell is rather—you know'——

'The deuce! I can't stop now. Wait an hour or two, and I shall have seen the fellow. You needn't alarm yourself. He will probably have disappeared in a few days.'

'What do you mean?' Mrs. Warricombe asked with nervous eagerness.

'I'll explain afterwards.'

He hurried away. Sidwell was at the breakfast-table. Her eyes seemed to declare that she had not slept well. With an insignificant word or two, the young man swallowed his cup of coffee, and had soon left the house.

III

THE WRATH WHICH illumined Buckland's countenance as he strode rapidly towards Longbrook Street was not unmingled with joy. In the deep pocket of his ulster lay something heavy which kept striking against his leg, and every such contact spurred him with a sense of satisfaction. All his suspicions were abundantly justified. Not only would his father and Sidwell be obliged to confess that his insight had been profounder than theirs, but he had the pleasure of standing justified before his own conscience. The philosophy by which he lived was strikingly illustrated and confirmed.

He sniffed the morning air, enjoyed the firmness of the frozen ground, on which his boots made a pleasant thud. To be sure, the interview before him would have its disagreeableness, but Buckland was not one of those over-civilised men who shrink from every scene of painful explanation. The detection of a harmful lie was decidedly congenial to him—especially when he and his had been made its victims. He was now at liberty to indulge that antipathetic feeling towards Godwin Peak which sundry considerations had hitherto urged him to repress. Whatever might have passed between Peak and Sidwell, he could not doubt that his sister's peace was gravely endangered; the adventurer (with however much or little sincerity) had been making subtle love to her. Such a thought was intolerable. Buckland's class-prejudice asserted itself with brutal vigour now that it had moral indignation for an ally.

He had never been at Peak's lodgings, but the address was long since noted. Something of disdain came into his eyes as he approached the row of insignificant houses. Having pulled the bell, he stood at his full height, looking severely at the number painted on the door.

Mrs. Roots opened to him, and said that her lodger was at

home. He gave his name, and after waiting for a moment was led to the upper floor. Godwin, who had breakfasted later than usual, still sat by the table. On Warricombe's entrance, he pushed back his chair and rose, but with deliberate movement, scarcely smiling. That Buckland made no offer of a friendly hand did not surprise him. The name of his visitor had alarmed him with a sudden presentiment. Hardening his features, he stood in expectancy.

'I want to have a talk with you,' Buckland began. 'You are at leisure, I hope?'

'Pray sit down.'

Godwin pointed to a chair near the fire, but Warricombe, having thrown his hat on to a side table, seated himself by one of the windows. His motions proved that he found it difficult to support a semblance of courtesy.

'I have come down from London on purpose to see you. Unless I am strangely misinformed you have been guilty of conduct which I shouldn't like to call by its proper name.'

Remembering that he was in a little house, with thin partitions, he kept his voice low, but the effort this cost him was obvious. He looked straight at Peak, who did not return the gaze.

'Indeed?' said Godwin, coldly. 'What is my crime?'

'I am told that you have won the confidence of my relatives by what looks like a scheme of gross dishonesty.'

'Indeed? Who has told you so?'

'No one in so many words. But I happened to come across certain acquaintances of yours in London—people who know you very well indeed; and I find that they regard your position here as altogether incredible. You will remember I had much the same feeling myself. In support of their view it was mentioned to me that you had published an article in *The Critical*—the date less than a year ago, observe. The article was anonymous, but I remember it very well. I have re-read it, and I want you to tell me how the views it expresses can be reconciled with those you have maintained in conversation with my father.'

He drew from his pocket the incriminating periodical, turned it back at the article headed 'The New Sophistry,' and held it out for inspection.

'Perhaps you would like to refresh your memory.'

'Needless, thank you,' returned Godwin, with a smile—in which the vanity of an author had its part.

Had Marcella betrayed him? He had supposed she knew nothing of this article, but Earwaker had perhaps spoken of it to Moxey before receiving the injunction of secrecy. On the other hand, it might be Earwaker himself from whom Warricombe had derived his information. Not impossible for the men to meet, and Earwaker's indignation might have led him to disregard a friend's confidence.

The details mattered little. He was face to face with the most serious danger that could befall him, and already he had strung himself to encounter it. Yet even in the same moment he asked, 'Is it worth while?'

'Did you write this?' Buckland inquired.

'Yes, I wrote it.'

'Then I wait for your explanation.'

'You mustn't expect me to enter upon an elaborate defence,' Godwin replied, taking his pipe from the mantelpiece and beginning to fill it. 'A man charged with rascality can hardly help getting excited—and that excitement, to one in your mood, seems evidence against him. Please to bear in mind that I have never declared myself an orthodox theologian. Mr. Warricombe is well acquainted with my views; to you I have never explained them.'

'You mean to say that my father knew of this article?'

'No, I have not spoken of it.'

'And why not?'

'Because, for one thing, I shouldn't write in that way now; and, for another, the essay seems to imply more than I meant when I did write it.'

' "Seems to imply"——? I understand. You wish to represent that this attack on M'Naughten involves no attack on Christianity?'

'Not on Christianity as I understand it.'

Buckland's face expressed profound disgust, but he controlled his speech.

'Well, I foresaw this. You attacked a new sophistry, but there is a newer sophistry still, and uncommonly difficult it is to deal with. Mr. Peak, I have a plain word to say to you. More than a year ago you asked me for my goodwill, to aid you in getting a social position. Say what you like, I see now that you dealt with me dishonestly. I can no longer be your friend in any sense, and I shall do my best to have you excluded from my parents' house. My father will re-read this essay—I have marked the significant passages throughout—and will form his own judgment; I know what it will be.'

'You are within your rights.'

'Undoubtedly,' replied Buckland, with polished insolence, as he rose from his seat. 'I can't forbid you to go to the house again, but—I hope we mayn't meet there. It would be very unpleasant.'

Godwin was still pressing down the tobacco in the bowl of his pipe. He smiled, and glanced about the room. Did Warricombe know how far things had gone between him and Sidwell? Whether or no, it was certain now that Sidwell would be informed of this disastrous piece of authorship—and the result?

What did it matter? There is no struggling against destiny. If he and Sidwell were ever fated to come together, why, these difficulties would all be surmounted. If, as seemed more than likely, he was again to be foiled on the point of success—he could bear it, perhaps even enjoy the comedy.

'There is no possibility of arguing against determined anger,' he said, quietly. 'I am not all inclined to plead for justice; one only does that with a friend who desires to be just. My opinions are utterly distasteful to you, and personal motives have made you regard me as—a scoundrel to be got rid of. Well, there's an end of it. I don't see what is to be gained by further talk.'

This was a dismissal. Godwin felt the necessity of asserting himself thus far.

'One question,' said Warricombe, as he put the periodical

back into his pocket. 'What do you mean by my "personal motives"?'

Their eyes met for an instant.

'I mean the motives which you have spoken of.'

It was Buckland's hope that Peak might reveal his relations with Sidwell, but he shrank from seeming to know anything of the matter. Clearly, no light was to be had from this source.

'I am afraid,' he said, moving to the door, 'that you will find my motives shared by all the people whose acquaintance you have made in Exeter.'

And without further leave-taking he departed.

There was a doubt in his mind. Peak's coolness might be the audacity of rascaldom; he preferred to understand it so; but it *might* have nothing to do with baseness.

'Confound it!' he muttered to himself, irritably. 'In our times life is so deucedly complicated. It used to be the easiest thing to convict a man of religious hypocrisy; nowadays, one has to bear in mind such a multiplicity of fine considerations. There's that fellow Bruno Chilvers: mightn't any one who had personal reasons treat him precisely as I have treated Peak? Both of them may be honest. Yet in Peak's case all appearances are against him—just because he is of low birth, has no means, and wants desperately to get into society. The fellow is a scoundrel; I am convinced of it. Yet his designs may be innocent. How, then, a scoundrel?——

'Poor devil! Has he really fallen in love with Sidwell?——

'Humbug! He wants position, and the comfort it brings. And if he hadn't acted like a blackguard—if he had come among us telling the truth, who knows? Sidwell wouldn't then have thought of him, but for my own part I would willingly have given him a hand. There are plenty of girls who have learned to think for themselves.'

This was an unhappy line of reflection. It led to Sylvia Moorhouse—and to grinding of the teeth. By the time he reached the house, Buckland was again in remorseless mood.

He would have it out with Sidwell. The desire of proving to her that he had been right from the first overrode all thought of the pain he might inflict.

She was in the library. At breakfast he had noticed her heavy eyes, and that she made only a pretence of eating. She was now less unlike herself, but her position at the window showed that she had been waiting impatiently.

'Isn't mother coming down to-day?' he asked.

'Yes; after luncheon she will go out for an hour, if it keeps fine.'

'And tomorrow you return?'

'If mother feels able to travel.'

He had *The Critical* in his hand, and stood rustling the pages with his fingers.

'I have been to see Peak.'

'Have you?'

She moved a few steps and seated herself sideways on a small chair.

'My business with him was confoundedly unpleasant. I'm glad it's over. I wish I had known what I now do half a year ago.'

'Let me hear what it is.'

'You remember that I told you to be on your guard against Peak?'

Sidwell smiled faintly, and glanced at him, but made no answer.

'I knew he wasn't to be trusted,' pursued her brother, with gloomy satisfaction. 'And I had far better means of judging than father or you; but, of course, my suspicions were ungenerous and cynical.'

'Will you come to the point?' said Sidwell, in an irritated tone.

'I think you read this article in *The Critical*?' He approached and showed it to her. 'We spoke of it once, *à propos* of M'Naughten's book.'

She raised her eyes, and met his with a look of concern she could not disguise.

'What of that?'

'Peak is the author of it. It seems to have been written just about the time when I met him and brought him here as a visitor, and it was published after he had begun to edify you with his zeal for Christianity.'

She held out her hand.

'You remember the tone of the thing?' Buckland added. 'I'll leave it with you; but just glance at one or two of the passages I have marked. The Anglicanism of their writer is decidedly "broad," it seems to me.'

He moved apart and watched his sister as she bent over the pages. There was silence for five minutes. Seeing that Sidwell had ceased to read, he ejaculated, 'Well?'

'Has Mr. Peak admitted the authorship?' she asked, slowly and distinctly.

'Yes, and with a cool impudence I hardly expected.'

'Do you mean that he has made no attempt to justify himself?'

'None worth listening to. Practically, he refused an explanation.'

Sidwell rested her forehead lightly upon the tips of her fingers; the periodical slipped from her lap and lay open on the floor.

'How did you find this out?'

'In the simplest way. Knowing perfectly well that I had only to get familiar with some of his old friends to obtain proof that he was an impostor, I followed up my acquaintance with Miss Moxey—got hold of her brother—called upon them. Whilst I was there, a man named Malkin came in, and somehow or other he began talking of Peak. I learned at once precisely what I expected, that Peak was known to all these people as a violent anti-Christian. Malkin refused to believe the story of his going in for the Church—it sounded to him a mere joke. Then came out the fact that he had written this article. They all knew about it.'

He saw a flush of shame upon Sidwell's half-hidden face. It gratified him. He was resolved to let her taste all the bitterness of her folly.

'It seems pretty clear that the Moxeys—at all events Miss Moxey—knew the rascally part he was playing. Whether they wished to unmask him, or not, I can't say. Perhaps not. Yet I caught an odd look on Miss Moxey's face when that man Malkin began to talk of Peak's characteristics and achievements. It came out, by-the-bye, that he had given all his acquaintances the slip; they had completely lost sight of him—I suppose until Miss

Moxey met him by chance at Budleigh Salterton. There's some mystery still. She evidently kept Peak's secret from the Moorhouses and the Walworths. A nice business, altogether!'

Again there was a long silence. Then Sidwell raised her face and said, abruptly:

'You may be quite mistaken.'

'How?'

'You went to Mr. Peak in a spirit of enmity and anger. It is not likely he would explain himself. You may have quite misunderstood what he said.'

'Ridiculous! You mean that he was perhaps "converted" after writing this article?—Then why did he allow it to be published?'

'He did not sign it. He may have been unable to withdraw it from the editor's hands.'

'Bosh! He didn't sign it, because the idea of this Exeter campaign came between the reception and the appearance of his paper. In the ordinary course of things, he would have been only too glad to see his name in *The Critical*. The scoundrelly project was conceived perhaps the very day that I brought him here—perhaps in that moment—at lunch, do you remember?—when he began to talk of the sermon at the Cathedral?'

'Why did he go to the Cathedral and hear that sermon?'

'To amuse a Sunday morning, I suppose.'

'That is not very likely in a man who hates and ridicules religion.'

'It is decidedly more probable than the idea of his conversion.'

Sidwell fell back again into her brooding attitude.

'The reason of your mistake in judging him' resumed Buckland, with emphasis, 'is that you have undervalued his intellect. I told you long ago that a man of Peak's calibre could not possibly be a supporter of dogmas and churches. No amount of plausible evidence would have made me believe in his sincerity. Let me beg you to appreciate the simple fact, that *no* young man of brains and education is nowadays an honest defender of mediæval Christianity—the Christianity of your churches. Such fellows may transact with their conscience, and make a more or less decent business of the clerical career; or, in rare cases, they may believe that society is served by the maintenance of a national faith, and accordingly preach with all manner of mental reserves and symbolical interpretations. These are in reality politicians, not priests. But Peak belongs to neither class. He is an acute cynic, bent on making the best of this world, since he believes in no other. How he must have chuckled after every visit to this house! He despises you, one and all. Believe me, he regards you with profound contempt.'

Buckland's obtuseness on the imaginative side spared him the understanding of his sister's state of mind. Though in theory he recognised that women were little amenable to reasoning, he took it for granted that a clear demonstration of Peak's duplicity must at once banish all thought of him from Sidwell's mind. Therefore he was unsparing in his assaults upon her delusion. It surprised him when at length Sidwell looked up with flashing, tear-dewed eyes and addressed him indignantly:

'In all this there is not one word of truth! You know that in representing the clergy as a body of ignorant and shallow men you speak out of prejudice. If you believed what you say, you would be yourself both ignorant and shallow. I can't trust your judgment of anyone whatever.'

She paused, but in a moment added the remark which would have come first had she spoken in the order of her thoughts.

'It is because the spirit of contempt is so familar to you that you are so ready to perceive it in others. I consider that habit of mind worse than hypocrisy—yes, worse, far worse!'

Buckland was sorry for the pain he had given. The retort did not affect him, but he hung his head and looked uncomfortable. His next speech was in a milder strain:

'I feel it a duty, Sidwell, to represent this man to you in what I verily believe to be the true light. To be despised by one who is immeasurably contemptible surely can't distress you. If a butler gets into your house by means of a forged character, and then lays his plans for a great burglary, no doubt he scorns you for being so easily taken in,—and that is an exact parallel to Peak's proceedings. He has somehow got the exterior of a gentleman; you could not believe that one who behaved so agreeably and talked so well was concealing an essentially base nature. But I must remind you that Peak belongs by origin to the lower classes, which is as much as to say that he lacks the sense of honour generally inherited by men of our world. A powerful intellect by no means implies a corresponding development of the moral sense.'

Sidwell could not close her ears against the argument. But her features were still set in an expression of resentment, and she kept silence lest her voice should sound tearful.

'And don't be tempted by personal feeling,' pursued her brother, 'to make light of hypocrisy—especially this kind. The man who can act such a part as Peak's has been for the last twelve months must be capable of any depravity. It is difficult for you to estimate his baseness, because you are only half convinced that any one can really be an enemy of religious faith. You suspect a lurking belief even in the minds of avowed atheists. But take the assurance from me that a man like Peak (and I am at one with him in this matter) regards with absolute repugnance every form of supernaturalism. For him to affect belief in *your* religion, is a crime against conscience. Peak has committed this crime with a mercenary motive,—what viler charge could be brought against him?'

Without looking at him, his sister replied:

'Whether he is guilty or not, I can't yet determine. But the motive of his life here was not mercenary.'

'Then how would you describe it?' Buckland asked, in astonishment.

'I only know that it can't be called mercenary.'

'Then the distinction you draw must be a very fine one.—He has abandoned the employment by which he lived, and by his own admission he looks to the Church for means of support. It was necessary for him to make interest with people of social position; the closer his relations with them the better. From month to month he has worked skilfully to establish his footing in this house, and among your friends. What do you call this?'

She had no verbal answer to make, but her look declared that she held to another interpretation.

'Well,' Buckland added, impatiently, 'we will hear father's opinion. He, remember, has been deceived in a very gross and cruel way. Possibly he may help you to see the thing in all its hatefulness.'

Sidwell turned to him.

'You go to London this afternoon?'

'In an hour or two,' he replied, consulting his watch.

'Is it any use my asking you to keep silence about everything until I am back in town?'

Buckland frowned and hesitated.

'To mother as well as father, you mean?'

'Yes. Will you do me this kindness?'

'Answer me a question, Sidwell. Have you any thought of seeing Peak?'

'I can't say,' she replied, in agitation. 'I must leave myself free. I have a right to use my own judgment.'

'Don't see him! I beg you not to see him!'

He was so earnest that Sidwell suspected some other reason in his request than regard for her dignity.

'I must leave myself free,' she repeated, with shaking voice. 'In any case I shall be back in London tomorrow evening—that is, if—but I am sure mother will wish to go. Grant me this one kindness; say nothing here or there till I am back and have seen you again.'

He turned a deaf ear, for the persistency with which she resisted proof of Peak's dishonour had begun to alarm him. Who could say what miserable folly she might commit in the next four-and-twenty hours? The unavoidable necessity of his own return exasperated him; he wished to see her safe back in London, and under her father's care.

'No,' he exclaimed, with a gesture of determination, 'I can't keep such a thing as this secret for another hour. Mother must know at once—especially as you mean to invite that fellow into the house again.—I have half a mind to telegraph to Godolphin that I can't possibly be with him to-night.'

Sidwell regarded him and spoke with forced composure.

'Do as seems right to you, Buckland. But don't think that by remaining here you would prevent me from seeing Mr. Peak, if I wish to do so. That is treating me too much like a child. You have done your part—doubtless your duty; now I must reflect and judge for myself. Neither you nor anyone else has authority over me in such circumstances.'

'Very well. I have no authority, as you say, but common sense bids me let mother know how the case stands.'

And angrily he left the room.

The Critical still lay where it had fallen. When Sidwell had stood a while in confused thought, her eye turned to it, and she went hurriedly to take it up. Yes, that was the first thing to be done, to read those pages with close care. For this she must have privacy. She ran up-stairs and shut herself in her bedroom.

But she did not at once begin to read. It concerned her deeply to know whether Peak had so expressed himself in this paper, that no room was left for doubt as to his convictions; but another question pressed upon her with even more urgency—could it be true that he did not love her? If Buckland were wholly right, then it mattered little in what degree she had been misled by intellectual hypocrisy.

It was impossible to believe that Peak had made love to her in cold blood, with none but sordid impulses. The thought was so humiliating that her mind resolutely rejected it; and she had no difficulty in recalling numberless minutiæ of behaviour——nuances of look and tone such as abide in a woman's memory—any one of which would have sufficed to persuade her that he felt genuine emotion. How had it come to pass that a feeling of friendly interest, which did not for a moment threaten her peace, changed all at once to an agitation only the more persistent the more she tried to subdue it,—how, if it were not that her heart responded to a passionate appeal, effectual as only the sincerest love can prove. Prior to that long talk with Godwin, on the eve of her departure for London, she had not imagined that he loved her; when they said good-bye to each other, she knew by her own sensations all that the parting meant to him. She felt glad, instead of sorry, that they were not to meet again for several months; for she wished to think of him calmly and prudently, now that he presented himself to her imagination in so new an aspect. The hand-clasp was a mutual assurance of fidelity.

'I should never have loved him, if he had not first loved me. Of that I am as firmly convinced as of my own existence. It is not in my nature to dream romances. I never did so even as a young girl, and at this age I am not likely to fall into a foolish self-deception. I had often thought about him. He seemed to me a man of higher and more complex type than those with whom I was familiar; but most surely I never attributed to him even a corresponding interest in me. I am neither vain, nor very anxious to please; I never suffered because men did not woo me; I have only moderate good looks, and certainly no uncommon mental endowments.—If he had been attracted by Sylvia, I should have thought it natural; and I more than once suspected that Sylvia was disposed to like him. It seemed strange at first that his choice should have fallen upon me; yet when I was far away from him, and longed so to sit once more by him and hear him talk, I understood that it might be in my power to afford him the companionship he needed.—Mercenary? If I had been merely a governess in the house, he would have loved me just the same!'

Only by a painful effort could she remind herself that the ideal which had grown so slowly was now defaced. He loved her, but it was not the love of an honest man. After all, she had no need to peruse this writing of his; she remembered so well how it had impressed her when she read it on its first appearance, how her father had spoken of it. Buckland's manifold evidence was irresistible. Why should Peak have concealed his authorship? Why had he disappeared from among the people who thoroughly knew him?

She had loved a dream. What a task would it be to distinguish between those parts of Peak's conversation which represented his real thoughts, and those which were mockery of his listeners! The plan of a retired life which he had sketched to her—was it all falsehood? Impossible, for his love was inextricably blended with the details. Did he imagine that the secret of his unbelief could be preserved for a lifetime, and that it would have no effect whatever upon his happiness as a man? This seemed a likely reading of the problem. But what a multitude of moral and intellectual obscurities remained! The character which had seemed to her nobly simple was become a dark and dread enigma.

She knew so little of his life. If only it could all be laid bare to her, the secret of his position would be revealed. Buckland's violence altogether missed its mark; the dishonour of such a man as Godwin Peak was due to no gross incentive.

It was probable that, in talk with her father, he had been guilty of more deliberate misrepresentation than had marked his intercourse with the rest of the family. Her father, she felt sure, had come to regard him as a valuable source of argument in the battle against materialism. Doubtless the German book, which Peak was translating, bore upon that debate, and consequently was used as an aid to dissimulation. Thinking of this, she all but shared her brother's vehement feeling. It pained her to the inmost heart that her father's generous and candid nature should thus have been played upon. The deceit, as it concerned herself alone, she could forgive; at least she could suspend judgment until the accused had offered his defence—feeling that the psychology of the case must till then be beyond her powers of analysis. But the wrong done to her father revolted her.

A tap at the door caused her to rise, trembling. She remembered that by this time her mother must be aware of the extraordinary disclosure, and that a new scene of wretched agitation had to be gone through.

'Sidwell!'

It was Mrs. Warricombe's voice, and the door opened.

'Sidwell!—What *does* all this mean? I don't understand half that Buckland has been telling me.'

The speaker's face was mottled, and she stood panting, a hand pressed against her side.

'How very, very imprudent we have been! How wrong of father not to have made inquiries! To think that such a man should have sat at our table!'

'Sit down, mother; don't be so distressed,' said Sidwell, calmly. 'It will all very soon be settled.'

'Of course not a word must be said to anyone. How very fortunate that we shall be in London till the summer! Of course he must leave Exeter.'

'I have no doubt he will. Let us talk as little of it as possible, mother. We shall go back to-morrow'——

'This afternoon! We will go back with Buckland. That is decided. I couldn't sleep here another night.'

'We must remain till tomorrow,' Sidwell replied, with quiet determination.

'Why? What reason can there be?'

Mrs. Warricombe's voice was suspended by a horrible surmise. 'Of course we shall go to-day, Sidwell,' she continued, in nervous haste. 'To think of that man having the impudence to call and sit talking with you! If I could have dreamt'——

'Mother,' said Sidwell, gravely, 'I am obliged to see Mr. Peak, either this evening or tomorrow morning.'

'To—to *see* him——? Sidwell! What can you mean?'

'I have a reason for wishing to hear from his own lips the whole truth.'

'But we *know* the whole truth!—What can you be thinking of, dear? Who is this Mr. Peak that you should ask him to come and see you, under *any* circumstances?'

It would never have occurred to Sidwell to debate with her mother on subtle questions of character and motive, but the agitation of her nerves made it difficult for her to keep silence under these vapid outcries. She desired to be alone; commonplace discussion of the misery that had come upon her was impossible. A little more strain, and she would be on the point of tears, a weakness she was resolute to avoid.

'Let me think quietly for an hour or two,' she said, moving away. 'It's quite certain that I must stay here till tomorrow. When Buckland has gone, we can talk again.'

'But, Sidwell'——

'If you insist, I must leave the house, and find a refuge somewhere else.'

Mrs. Warricombe tossed her head.

'Oh, if I am not permitted to speak to you! I only hope you

won't have occasion to remember my warning! Such extraordinary behaviour was surely never known! I should have thought'——

Sidwell was by this time out of the room. Safe in privacy she sat down as if to pen a letter. From an hour's agitated thought, the following lines resulted:

'My brother has told me of a conversation he held with you this morning. He says you admit the authorship of an article which seems quite inconsistent with what you have professed in our talks. How am I to understand this contradiction? I beg that you will write to me at once. I shall anxiously await your reply.'

This, with her signature, was all. Having enclosed the note in an envelope, she left it on her table and went down to the library, where Buckland was sitting alone in gloomy reverie. Mrs. Warricombe had told him of Sidwell's incredible purpose. Recognising his sister's independence, and feeling sure that if she saw Peak it could only be to take final leave of him, he had decided to say no more. To London he must perforce return this afternoon, but he had done his duty satisfactorily, and just in time. It was plain that things had gone far between Peak and Sidwell; the latter's behaviour avowed it. But danger there could be none, with 'The New Sophistry' staring her in the eyes. Let her see the fellow, by all means. His evasions and hair-splittings would complete her deliverance.

'There's a train at 1.53,' Buckland remarked, rising, 'and I shall catch it if I start now. I can't stay for the discomfort of luncheon. You remain here till tomorrow, I understand?'

'Yes.'

'It's a pity you are angry with me. It seems to me I have done you a kindness.'

'I am not angry with you, Buckland,' she replied, gently. 'You have done what you were plainly obliged to do.'

'That's a sensible way of putting it. Let us say good-bye with friendliness then.'

Sidwell gave her hand, and tried to smile. With a look of pained affection, Buckland went silently away.

Shortly after, Sidwell fetched her note from upstairs, and gave it to the housekeeper to be delivered by hand as soon as possible. Mrs. Warricombe remained invisible, and Sidwell went back to the library, where she sat with *The Critical* open before her at Godwin's essay.

Hours went by; she still waited for an answer from Longbrook Street.

At six o'clock she went upstairs and spoke to her mother.

'Shall you come down to dinner?'

'No, Sidwell,' was the cold reply. 'Be so good as to excuse me.'

Towards eight, a letter was brought to her; it could only be from Godwin Peak. With eyes which endeavoured to take in all at once, and therefore could at first distinguish nothing, she scanned what seemed to be hurriedly written lines.

'I have tried to answer you in a long letter, but after all I can't send it. I fear you wouldn't understand. Better to repeat simply that I wrote the article you speak of. I should have told you about it some day, but now my intentions and hopes matter nothing. Whatever I said now would seem dishonest pleading. Good-bye.'

She read this so many times that at length she had but to close her eyes to see every word clearly traced on the darkness. The meanings she extracted from each sentence were scarcely less numerous than her perusals. In spite of reason, this enigmatic answer brought her some solace. He *could* defend himself; that was the assurance she had longed for. Impossible (she again and again declared to herself with emphasis) for their intimacy to be resumed. But in secret she could hold him, if not innocent, at all events not base. She had not bestowed her love upon a mere impostor.

But now a mournful, regretful passion began to weigh upon her heart. She shed tears, and presently stole away to her room for a night of sorrow.

What must be her practical course? If she went back to London without addressing another word to him, he must understand her silence as a final farewell. In that case his departure from Exeter would, no doubt, speedily follow, and there was little likelihood that she would ever again see him. Were Godwin a vulgar schemer, he would not so readily relinquish the advantage he had gained; he would calculate upon the weakness of a living woman, and make at least one effort to redeem his position. As it was, she could neither hope nor fear that he would try to see her again. Yet she wished to see him, desired it ardently.

And yet—for each impulse of ardour was followed by a cold fit of reasoning—might not his abandonment of the position bear a meaning such as Buckland would of course attribute to it? If he were hopeless of the goodwill of her parents, what profit would it be to him to retain her love? She was no heiress; supposing him actuated by base motive, her value in his eyes came merely of his regarding her as a means to an end.

But this was to reopen the question of whether or not he truly loved her. No; he was forsaking her because he thought it impossible for her to pardon the deceit he had undeniably practised—with whatever palliating circumstances. He was overcome with shame. He imagined her indignant, scornful.

Why had she written such a short, cold note, the very thing to produce in his mind a conviction of her resentment?

Hereupon came another paroxysm of tearful misery. It was intensified by a thought she had half consciously been repressing ever since the conversation with her brother. Was it true that Miss Moxey had had it in her power to strip Godwin of a disguise? What, then, were the relations existing between him and that strangely impressive woman? How long had they known each other? It was now all but certain that a strong intellectual sympathy united their minds—and perhaps there had been something more.

She turned her face upon the pillow and moaned.

IV

AND FROM THE Moxeys Buckland had derived his information. What was it he said—something about 'an odd look' on Miss Moxey's face when that friend of theirs talked of Peak? Might not such a look signify a conflict between the temptation to injure and the desire to screen?

Sidwell constructed a complete romance. Ignorance of the past of both persons concerned allowed her imagination free play. There was no limit to the possibilities of self-torment.

The desire to see Godwin took such hold upon her, that she had already begun to think over the wording of another note to be sent to him the first thing in the morning. His reply had been insufficient: simple justice required that she should hear him in his own defence before parting with him for ever. If she kept silence, he would always remember her with bitterness, and this would make her life-long sorrow harder to bear. Sidwell was one of those few women whose love, never demonstrative, never exigent, only declares itself in all its profound significance when it is called upon to pardon. What was likely to be the issue of a meeting with Godwin she could not foresee. It seemed all but impossible for their intercourse to continue, and their coming face to face might result in nothing but distress to both, better avoided; yet judgment yielded to emotion. Yesterday—only yesterday—she had yielded herself to the joy of loving, and before her consciousness had had time to make itself familiar with its new realm, before her eyes had grown accustomed to the light suddenly shed about her, she was bidden to think of what had happened as only a dream. Her heart refused to make surrender of its hope. Though it could be held only by an encouragement of recognised illusion, she preferred to dream yet a little longer. Above all, she must taste the luxury of forgiving her lover, of making sure that her image would not dwell in his mind as that of a self-righteous woman who had turned coldly from his error, perhaps from his repentance.

A little after midnight, she rose from bed, slipped on her dressing-gown, and sat down by the still burning lamp to write what her passion dictated:

'Why should you distrust my ability, or my willingness to understand you? It would have been so much better if you had sent what you first wrote. These few lines do not even let me know whether you think yourself to blame. Why do you leave me to form a judgment of things as they appear on the surface? If you *wish* to explain, if you sincerely feel that I am in danger of wronging you by misconstruction, come to me as soon as you have received this note. If you will not come, then at least write to me—the letter you at first thought of sending. This afternoon (Friday) I return to London, but you know my address there. Don't think because I wrote so briefly that I have judged you. S.W.'

To have committed this to paper was a relief. In the morning she would read it over and consider again whether she wished to send it.

On the table lay *The Critical*. She opened it once more at the page that concerned her, and glanced over the first few lines. Then, having put the lamp nearer to the bed, she again lay down, not to sleep but to read.

This essay was not so repugnant to her mind or her feelings as when she first became acquainted with it. Its bitterness no longer seemed to be directed against herself. There was much in it with which she could have agreed at any time during the last six months, and many strokes of satire, which till the other day would have offended her, she now felt to be legitimate. As she read on, a kind of anger such as she had never experienced trembled along her nerves. Was it not flagrantly true that English society at large made profession of a faith which in no sense whatever it could be said sincerely to hold? Was there not every reason to believe that thousands of people keep up an ignoble formalism, because they feared the social results of declaring their severance from the religion of the churches? This was a monstrous evil; she had never till this moment understood the scope of its baneful effects. But for the prevalence of such a spirit of hypocrisy, Godwin Peak would never have sinned against his honour. Why was it not declared in trumpet-tones of authority, from end to end of the Christian world, that Christianity, as it has been understood through the ages, can no longer be accepted? For that was the truth, the truth, the *truth!*

She lay back, quivering as if with terror. For an instant her soul had been filled with hatred of the religion for which she could once have died. It had stood before her as a power of darkness and ignorance, to be assailed, crushed, driven from the memory of man.

Last night she had hardly slept, and now, though her body was numb with weariness, her mind kept up a feverish activity. She was bent on excusing Godwin, and the only way in which she could do so was by arraigning the world for its huge dishonesty. In a condition between slumber and waking, she seemed to plead for him before a circle of Pharisaic accusers. Streams of silent eloquence rushed through her brain, and the spirit which prompted her was closely akin to that of 'The New Sophistry.' Now and then, for a few seconds, she was smitten with a consciousness of extraordinary change in her habits of thought. She looked about her with wide, fearful eyes, and endeavoured to see things in the familiar aspect. As if with physical constraint her angry imagination again overcame her, until at length from the penumbra of sleep she passed into its profoundest gloom.

To wake when dawn was pale at the window. A choking odour reminded her that she had not extinguished the lamp, which must have gone out for lack of oil. She opened the window, took a draught of water, and addressed herself to sleep again. But in recollecting what the new day meant for her, she had spoilt the chances of longer rest. Her head ached; all worldly thoughts were repulsive, yet she could not dismiss them. She tried to repeat the prayers she had known since childhood, but they were meaningless, and a sense of shame attached to their utterance.

When the first gleam of sun told her that it was past eight o'clock, she made an effort and rose.

At breakfast Mrs. Warricombe talked of the departure for London. She mentioned an early train; by getting ready as soon as the meal was over, they could easily reach the station in time. Sidwell made no direct reply and seemed to assent; but when they rose from the table, she said, nervously:

'I couldn't speak before the servants. I wish to stay here till the afternoon.'

'Why, Sidwell?'

'I have asked Mr. Peak to come and see me this morning.'

Her mother knew that expostulation was useless, but could not refrain from a long harangue made up of warning and reproof.

'You have very little consideration for me,' was her final remark. 'Now we shan't get home till after dark, and of course my throat will be bad again.'

Glad of the anti-climax, Sidwell replied that the day was much warmer, and that with care no harm need come of the journey.

'It's easy to say that, Sidwell. I never knew you to behave so selfishly, never!'

'Don't be angry with me, mother. You don't know how grieved I am to distress you so. I can't help it, dear; indeed, I can't. Won't you sacrifice a few hours to put my mind at rest?'

Mrs. Warricombe once more gave expression to her outraged feelings. Sidwell could only listen silently with bent head.

If Godwin were coming at all, he would be here by eleven o'clock. Sidwell had learnt that her letter was put into his hands. She asked him to come at once, and nothing but a resolve not to meet her could delay him more than an hour or two.

At half-past ten the bell sounded. She was sitting in the library with her back turned to the door. When a voice announced 'Mr. Peak,' she did not at once rise, and with a feeling akin to terror she heard the footstep slowly approaching. It stopped at some distance from her; then, overcoming a weakness which threatened to clog her as in a nightmare, she stood up and looked round.

Peak wore neither overcoat nor gloves, but otherwise was dressed in the usual way. As Sidwell fixed her eyes upon him, he threw his hat into a chair and came a step or two nearer. Whether he had passed the night in sleep or vigil could not be determined; but his look was one of shame, and he did not hold himself so upright as was his wont.

'Will you come and sit down?' said Sidwell, pointing to a chair not far from that on which one of her hands rested.

He moved forward, and was about to pass near her, when Sidwell involuntarily held her hand to him. He took it and gazed into her face with a melancholy smile.

'What does it mean?' she asked, in a low voice.

He relinquished her fingers, which he had scarcely pressed, and stood with his arms behind his back.

'Oh, it's all quite true,' was his reply, wearily spoken.

'What is true?'

'All that you have heard from your brother.'

'All?—But how can you know what he has said?'

They looked at each other, Peak's lips were set as if in resistance of emotion, and a frown wrinkled his brows. Sidwell's gaze was one of fear and appeal.

'He said, of course, that I had deceived you.'

'But in what?—Was there no truth in anything you said to me?'

'To you I have spoken far more truth than falsehood.'

A light shone in her eyes, and her lips quivered.

'Then,' she murmured, 'Buckland was not right in everything.'

'I understand. He wished you to believe that my love was as much a pretence as my religion?'

'He said that.'

'It was natural enough.—And you were disposed to believe it?'

'I thought it impossible. But I should have thought the same of the other things.'

Peak nodded, and moved away. Watching him, Sidwell was

beset with conflicting impulses. His assurance had allayed her worst misgiving, and she approved the self-restraint with which he bore himself, but at the same time she longed for a passionate declaration. As a reasoning woman, she did her utmost to remember that Peak was on his defence before her, and that nothing could pass between them but grave discussion of the motives which had impelled him to dishonourable behaviour. As a woman in love, she would fain have obscured the moral issue by indulgence of her heart's desire. She was glad that he held aloof, but if he had taken her in his arms, she would have forgotten everything in the moment's happiness.

'Let us sit down, and tell me—tell me all you can.'

He delayed a moment, then seated himself opposite to her. She saw now that his movements were those of physical fatigue; and the full light from the window, enabling her to read his face more distinctly, revealed the impress of suffering. Instead of calling upon him to atone in such measure as was possible for the wrong he had done her, she felt ready to reproach herself for speaking coldly when his need of solace was so great.

'What can I tell you,' he said, 'that you don't know, or that you can't conjecture?'

'But you wrote that there was so much I could not be expected to understand. And I can't, can't understand you. It still seems impossible. Why did you hide the truth from me?'

'Because if I had begun by telling it, I should never have won a kind look or a kind thought from you.'

Sidwell reflected.

'But what did you care for me then—when it began?'

'Not so much as I do now, but enough to overthrow all the results of my life up to that time. Before I met you in this house I had seen you twice, and had learned who you were. I was sitting in the Cathedral when you came there with your sister and Miss Moorhouse—do you remember? I heard Fanny call you by your name, and that brought to my mind a young girl whom I had known in a slight way years before. And the next day I again saw you there, at the service; I waited about the entrance only to see you. I cared enough for you then to conceive a design which for a long time seemed too hateful really to be carried out, but—at last it was, you see.'

Sidwell breathed quickly. Nothing he could have urged for himself would have affected her more deeply than this. To date back and extend the period of his love for her was a flattery more subtle than Peak imagined.

'Why didn't you tell me that the day before yesterday?' she asked, with tremulous bosom.

'I had no wish to remind myself of baseness in the midst of a pure joy.'

She was silent, then exclaimed, in accents of pain:

'Why should you have thought it necessary to be other than yourself? Couldn't you see, at first meeting with us, that we were not bigoted people? Didn't you know that Buckland had accustomed us to understand how common it is nowadays for people to throw off the old religion? Would father have looked coldly on you if he had known that you followed where so many good and thoughtful men were leading?'

He regarded her anxiously.

'I had heard from Buckland that your father was strongly prejudiced; that you also were quite out of sympathy with the new thought.'

'He exaggerated—even then.'

'Exaggerated? But on what plea could I have come to live in this neighbourhood? How could I have kept you in sight—tried to win your interest? I had no means, no position. The very thought of encouraging my love for you demanded some extraordinary step. What course was open to me?'

Sidwell let her head droop.

'I don't know. You might perhaps have discovered a way.'

'But what was the use, when the mere face of my heresy would have forbidden hope from the outset?'

'Why should it have done so?'

'Why? You know very well that you could never even have been friendly with the man who wrote that thing in the review.'

'But here is the proof how much better it is to behave truthfully! In this last year I have changed so much that I find it difficult to understand the strength of my former prejudices. What is it to me now that you speak scornfully of attempts to reconcile things that can't be reconciled? I understand the new thought, and how natural it is for you to accept it. If only I could have come to know you well, your opinions would not have stood between us.'

Peak made a slight gesture, and smiled incredulously.

'You think so now.'

'And I have such good reason for my thought,' rejoined Sidwell, earnestly, 'that when you said you loved me, my only regret in looking to the future was—that you had resolved to be a clergyman.'

He leaned back in the chair, and let a hand fall on his knee. The gesture seemed to signify a weary relinquishment of concern in what they were discussing.

'How could I foresee that?' he uttered, in a corresponding tone.

Sidwell was made uneasy by the course upon which she had entered. To what did her words tend? If only to a demonstration that fate had used him as the plaything of its irony—if, after all, she had nothing to say to him but 'See how your own folly has ruined you,' then she had better have kept silence. She not only appeared to be offering him encouragement, but was in truth doing so. She wished him to understand that his way of thinking was no obstacle to her love, and with that purpose she was even guilty of a slight misrepresentation. For it was only since the shock of this disaster that she had clearly recognised the change in her own mind. True, the regret of which she spoke had for an instant visited her, but it represented a mundane solicitude rather than an intellectual scruple. It had occurred to her how much brighter would be their prospect if Peak were but an active man of the world, with a career before him distinctly suited to his powers.

His contention was undeniably just. The influence to which she had from the first submitted was the same that her father felt so strongly. Godwin interested her as a self-reliant champion of the old faiths, and his personal characteristics would never have awakened such sympathy in her but for that initial recommendation. Natural prejudice would have prevented her from perceiving the points of kindred between his temperament and her own. His low origin, the ridiculous stories connected with his youth—why had she, in spite of likelihood, been able to disregard these things? Only because of what she then deemed his spiritual value.

But for the dishonourable part he had played, this bond of love would never have been formed between them. The thought was a new apology for his transgression; she could not but defy her conscience, and look indulgently on the evil which had borne such fruit.

Godwin had begun to speak again.

'This is quite in keeping with the tenor of my whole life. Whatever I undertake ends in frustration at a point where success seems to have just come within my reach. Great things and trifles —it's all the same. My course at College was broken off at the moment when I might have assured my future. Later, I made many an effort to succeed in literature, and when at length something of mine was printed in a leading review, I could not even sign it, and had no profit from the attention it excited. Now —well, you see. Laughable, isn't it?'

Sidwell scarcely witheld herself from bending forward and giving him her hand.

'What shall you do?' she asked.

'Oh, I am not afraid. I have still enough money left to support me until I can find some occupation of the old kind. Fortunately, I am not one of those men whose brains have no marketable value.'

'If you knew how it pains me to hear you!'

'If I didn't believe that, I couldn't speak to you like this. I never thought you would let me see you again, and if you hadn't asked me to come, I could never have brought myself to face you. But it would have been a miserable thing to go off without even knowing what you thought of me.'

'Should you never have written to me?'

'I think not. You find it hard to imagine that I have any pride, no doubt; but it is there, explain it how one may.'

'It would have been wrong to leave me in such uncertainty.'

'Uncertainty?'

'About you—about your future.'

'Did you quite mean that? Hadn't your brother made you doubt whether I loved you at all?'

'Yes. But no, I didn't doubt. Indeed, indeed, I didn't doubt! But I felt such a need of hearing from your own lips that—— Oh, I can't explain myself!'

Godwin smiled sadly.

'I think I understand. But there was every reason for my believing that *your* love could not bear such a test. You must regard me as quite a different man—one utterly unknown to you.'

He had resolved to speak not a word that could sound like an appeal to her emotions. When he entered the room he felt a sincere indifference as to what would result from the interview, for to his mind the story was ended, and he had only to retire with the dignity still possible to a dishonoured man. To touch the note of pathos would be unworthy; to exert what influence might be left to him, a wanton cruelty. But he had heard such unexpected things, that it was not easy for him to remember how complete had seemed the severance between him and Sidwell. The charm of her presence was reasserting itself, and when avowal of continued love appeared so unmistakably in her troubled countenance, her broken words, he could not control the answering fervour. He spoke in a changed voice, and allowed his eyes to dwell longingly upon hers.

'I felt so at first,' she answered. 'And it would be wrong to pretend that I can still regard you as I did before.'

It cost her a great effort to add these words. When they were spoken, she was at once glad and fearful.'

'I am not so foolish, as to think it possible,' said Peak, half turning away.

'But that is no reason,' she pursued, 'why we should become strangers. You are still so young a man; life must be so full of possibilities for you. This year has been wasted, but when you leave Exeter'——

An impatient movement of Godwin's checked her.

'You are going to encourage me to begin the struggle once more,' he said, bitterly. 'Where? How? It is so easy to talk of "possibilities." '

'You are not without friends—I mean friends whose sympathy is of real value to you.'

Saying this, she looked keenly at him.

'Friends,' he replied, 'who perhaps at this moment are laughing over my disgrace.'

'How do they know of—what has happened?'

'How did your brother get his information? I didn't care to ask him.—No, I don't even wish you to say anything about that.'

'But surely there is no reason for keeping it secret. Why may I not speak freely? Buckland told me that he had heard you spoken of at the house of people named Moxey.'

She endeavoured to understand the smile which rose to his lips.

'Now it is clear to me,' he said. 'Yes, I suppose that was inevitable, sooner or later.'

'You knew that he had become acquainted with the Moxeys?'

Her tone was more reserved than hitherto.

'Yes, I knew he had. He met Miss Moxey by chance at Budleigh Salterton, and I happened to be there—at the Moorhouses'—on the same day.'

Sidwell glanced at him inquiringly, and waited for something more.

'I saw Miss Moxey in private,' he added, speaking more quickly, 'and asked her to keep my secret. I ought to be ashamed to tell you this, but it is better you should know how far my humiliation has gone.'

He saw that she was moved with strong feeling. The low tone in which she answered had peculiar significance.

'Did you speak of me to Miss Moxey?'

'I must forgive you for asking that,' Peak replied, coldly. 'It may well seem to you that I have neither honour nor delicacy left.'

There had come a flush on her cheeks. For some moments she was absorbed in thought.

'It seems strange to you,' he continued at length, 'that I could ask Miss Moxey to share such a secret. But you must understand on what terms we were—she and I. We have known each other for several years. She has a man's mind, and I have always thought of her in much the same way as of my male companions.—Your brother has told you about her, perhaps?'

'I have met her in London.'

'Then that will make my explanation easier,' said Godwin, disregarding the anxious questions that at once suggested themselves to him. 'Well, I misled her, or tried to do so. I allowed her to suppose that I was sincere in my new undertakings, and that I didn't wish—— Oh!' he exclaimed, suddenly breaking off, 'Why need I go any further in confession? It must be as miserable for you to hear as for me to speak. Let us make an end of it. I can't understand how I have escaped detection so long.'

Remembering every detail of Buckland's story, Sidwell felt that she had possibly been unjust in representing the Moxeys as her brother's authority; in strictness, she ought to mention that a friend of theirs was the actual source of information. But she could not pursue the subject; like Godwin, she wished to put it out of her mind. What question could there be of honour or dishonour in the case of a person such as Miss Moxey, who had consented to be party to a shameful deceit? Strangely, it was a relief to her to have heard this. The moral repugnance which threatened to estrange her from Godwin, was now directed in another quarter; unduly restrained by love, it found scope under the guidance of jealousy.

'You have been trying to adapt yourself,' she said, 'to a world for which you are by nature unfitted. Your place is in the new order; by turning back to the old, you condemned yourself to a wasted life. Since we have been in London, I have come to understand better the great difference between modern intellectual life and that which we lead in these far-away corners. You must go out among your equals, go and take your part with men who are working for the future.'

Peak rose with a gesture of passionate impatience.

'What is it to me, new world or old? My world is where *you* are. I have no life of my own; I think only of you, live only by you.'

'If I could help you!' she replied, with emotion. 'What can I do—but be your friend at a distance? Everything else has become impossible.'

'Impossible for the present—for a long time to come. But is there no hope for me?'

She pressed her hands together, and stood before him unable to answer.

'Remember,' he continued, 'that you are almost as much changed in my eyes as I in yours. I did not imagine that you had moved so far towards freedom of mind. If my love for you was profound and absorbing, think what it must now have become! Yours has suffered by my disgrace, but is there no hope of its reviving—if I live worthily—if I——?'

His voice failed.

'I have said that we can't be strangers,' Sidwell murmured brokenly. 'Wherever you go, I must hear of you.'

'Everyone about you will detest my name. You will soon wish to forget my existence.'

'If I know myself, never!—Oh, try to find your true work! You have such abilities, powers so much greater than those of ordinary men. You will always be the same to me, and if ever circumstances'——

'You would have to give up so much, Sidwell. And there is little chance of my ever being well-to-do; poverty will always stand between us, if nothing else.'

'It must be so long before we can think of that.'

'But can I ever see you?—No, I won't ask that. Who knows? I may have to go too far away. But I *may* write to you, after a time?'

'I shall live in the hope of good news from you,' she replied, trying to smile and to speak cheerfully. 'This will always be my home. Nothing will be changed.'

'Then you don't think of me as irredeemably base?'

'If I thought you base,' Sidwell answered, in a low voice, 'I should not now be speaking with you. It is because I feel and know that you have erred only—that is what makes it impossible for me to think of your fault as outweighing the good in your nature.'

'The good? I wonder how you understand that. What is there *good* in me? You don't mean mere intellect?'

He waited anxiously for what she would say. A necessity for speaking out his inmost thoughts had arisen with the emotion, scarcely to be called hope, excited by Sidwell's magnanimity. Now, or never, he must stand before this woman as his very self, and be convinced that she loved him for his own sake.

'No, I don't mean intellect,' she replied, with hesitation.

'What then? Tell me of one quality in me strong enough to justify a woman's love.'

Sidwell dropped her eyes in confusion.

'I can't analyse your character—I only know'——

She became silent.

'To myself,' pursued Godwin, with the modulated, moving voice which always expressed his genuine feeling, 'I seem anything but lovable. I don't underrate my powers—rather the opposite, no doubt; but what I always seem to lack is the gift of pleasing—moral grace. My strongest emotions seem to be absorbed in revolt; for once that I feel tenderly, I have a hundred fierce, resentful, tempestuous moods. To be suave and smiling in common intercourse costs me an effort. I have to act the part, and this habit makes me sceptical, whenever I am really prompted to gentleness. I criticise myself ceaselessly; expose without mercy all those characteristics which another man would keep out of sight. Yes, and for this very reason, just because I think myself unlovable—the gift of love means far more to me than to other men. If you could conceive the passion of gratitude which possessed me for hours after I left you the other day! You cannot!'

Sidwell regarded him fixedly.

'In comparison with this sincerity, what becomes of the pretence you blame in me? If you knew how paltry it seems—

that accusation of dishonesty! I believe the world round, and pretended to believe it flat: that's what it amounts to! Are you, on such an account as that, to consider worthless the devotion which has grown in me month by month? You—I was persuaded—thought the world flat, and couldn't think kindly of any man who held the other hypothesis. Very well; why not concede the trifle, and so at least give myself a chance? I did so—that was all.'

In vain her conscience strove to assert itself. She was under the spell of a nature infinitely stronger than hers; she saw and felt as Godwin did.

'You think, Sidwell, that I stand in need of forgiveness. Then be great enough to forgive me, wholly—once and for all. Let your love be strengthened by the trial it has passed through. That will mean that my whole life is yours, directed by the ever-present thought of your beauty, face and soul. Then there *will* be good in me, thanks to you. I shall no longer live a life of hypocrisy, of suppressed rage and scorn. I know how much I am asking; perhaps it means that for my sake you give up everything else that is dear to you'——

The thought checked him. He looked at her despondently.

'You can trust me,' Sidwell answered, moving nearer to him, tears on her cheeks. 'I must hear from you, and I will write.'

'I can ask no more than that.'

He took her hands, held them for a moment, and turned away. At the door he looked round. Sidwell's head was bowed, and, on her raising it, he saw that she was blinded with tears.

So he went forth.

PART THE SIXTH

I

FOR SEVERAL DAYS after the scene in which Mr. Malkin unconsciously played an important part, Marcella seemed to be ill. She appeared at meals, but neither ate nor conversed. Christian had never known her so sullen and nervously irritable; he did not venture to utter Peak's name. Upon seclusion followed restless activity. Marcella was rarely at home between breakfast and dinner-time, and her brother learnt with satisfaction that she went much among her acquaintances. Late one evening, when he had just returned from he knew not where, Christian tried to put an end to the unnatural constraint between them. After talking cheerfully for a few minutes, he risked the question:

'Have you seen anything of the Warricombes?'

She replied with a cold negative.

'Nor heard anything?'

'No. Have you?'

'Nothing at all. I have seen Earwaker. Malkin had told him about what happened here the other day.'

'Of course.'

'But he had no news.—Of Peak, I mean.'

Marcella smiled, as if the situation amused her; but she would not discuss it. Christian began to hope that she was training herself to a wholesome indifference.

A month of the new year went by, and Peak seemed to be forgotten. Marcella had returned to her studious habits, was fenced around with books, seldom left the house. Another month and the brother and sister were living very much in the old way, seeing few people, conversing only of intellectual things. But Christian concealed an expectation which enable him to pass hours of retirement in the completest idleness. Since the death of her husband, Mrs. Palmer had been living abroad. Before the end of March, as he had been careful to discover, she would be back in

13*

London, at the house in Sussex Square. By that time he might venture, without indelicacy, to call upon her. And after the first interview——

The day came, when, ill with agitation, he set forth to pay this call. For two or three nights he had scarcely closed his eyes; he looked ghastly. The weather was execrable, and on that very account he made choice of this afternoon, hoping that he might find his widowed Laura alone. Between ringing the bell and the opening of the door, he could hardly support himself. He asked for Mrs. Palmer in a gasping voice which caused the servant to look at him with surprise.

The lady was at home. At the drawing-room door, before his name could be announced, he caught the unwelcome sound of voices in lively conversation. It seemed to him that a score of persons were assembled. In reality there were six, three of them callers.

Mrs. Palmer met him with the friendliest welcome. A stranger would have thought her pretty, but by no means impressive. She was short, anything but meagre, fair-haired, brisk of movement, idly vivacious in look and tone. The mourning she wore imposed no restraint upon her humour, which at present was not far from gay.

'Is it really Mr. Moxey?' she exclaimed. 'Why, I had all but forgotten you, and positively it is your own fault! It must be a year or more since you came to see me. No? Eight months?—But I have been through so much trouble, you know.' She sighed mechanically. 'I thought of you one day at Bordighera, when we were looking at some funny little sea-creatures—the kind of thing you used to know all about. How is your sister?'

A chill struck upon his heart. Assuredly he had no wish to find Constance sunk in the semblance of dolour; such hypocrisy would have pained him. But her sprightliness was a shock. Though months had passed since Mr. Palmer's decease, a decent gravity would more have become her condition. He could reply only in broken phrases, and it was a relief to him when the widow, as if tiring of his awkwardness, turned her attention elsewhere.

He was at length able to survey the company. Two ladies in

mourning he faintly recognised, the one a sister of Mr. Palmer's, comely but of dull aspect; the other a niece, whose laugh was too frequent even had it been more musical, and who talked of athletic sports with a young man evidently better fitted to excel in that kind of thing than in any pursuit demanding intelligence. This gentleman Christian had never met. The two other callers, a grey-headed, military-looking person, and a lady, possibly his wife, were equally strangers to him.

The drawing-room was much changed in appearance since Christian's last visit. There was more display, a richer profusion of ornaments not in the best taste. The old pictures had given place to showily-framed daubs of the most popular school. On a little table at his elbow, he remarked the photograph of a jockey who was just then engrossing public affection. What did all this mean? Formerly, he had attributed every graceful feature of the room to Constance's choice. He had imagined that to her Mr. Palmer was indebted for guidance on points of æsthetic propriety. Could it be that——?

He caught a glance which she cast in his direction, and instantly forgot the troublesome problem. How dull of him to misunderstand her! Her sportiveness had a double significance. It was the expression of a hope which would not be subdued, and at the same time a means of disguising the tender interest with which she regarded *him*. If she had been blithe before his appearance, how could she suddenly change her demeanour as soon as he entered? It would have challenged suspicion and remark. For the same reason she affected to have all but forgotten him. Of course! how could he have failed to see that? 'I thought of you one day at Bordighera'—was not that the possible way of making known to him that he had never been out of her mind?

Sweet, noble, long-suffering Constance!

He took a place by her sister, and began to talk of he knew not what, for all his attention was given to the sound of Constance's voice.

'Yes,' she was saying to the man of military appearance, 'it's very early to come back to London, but I did get so tired of those foreign places.'

(In other words, of being far from her Christian—thus he interpreted.)

'No, we didn't make a single pleasant acquaintance. A shockingly tiresome lot of people wherever we went.'

(In comparison with the faithful lover, who waited, waited.)

'Foreigners are so stupid—don't you think so? Why should they always expect you to speak *their* language?—Oh, of course I speak French; but it is such a disagreeable language—don't you think so?'

(Compared with the accents of English devotion, of course.)

'Do you go in for cycling, Mr. Moxey?' inquired Mrs. Palmer's laughing niece, from a little distance.

'For cycling?' With a great effort he recovered himself and grasped the meaning of the words. 'No, I—I'm sorry to say I don't. Capital exercise!'

'Mr. Dwight has just been telling me such an awfully good story about a friend of his. Do tell it again, Mr. Dwight! It'll make you laugh no end, Mr. Moxey.'

The young man appealed to was ready enough to repeat his anecdote, which had to do with a bold cyclist, who, after dining more than well, rode his machine down a steep hill and escaped destruction only by miracle. Christian laughed desperately, and declared that he had never heard anything so good.

But the tension of his nerves was unendurable. Five minutes more of anguish, and he sprang up like an automaton.

'Must you really go, Mr. Moxey?' said Constance, with a manner which of course was intended to veil her emotion. 'Please don't be another year before you let us see you again.'

Blessings on her tender heart! What more could she have said, in the presence of all those people? He walked all the way to Notting Hill through a pelting rain, his passion aglow.

Impossible to be silent longer concerning the brilliant future. Arrived at home, he flung off hat and coat, and went straight to the drawing-room, hoping to find Marcella alone. To his annoyance, a stranger was sitting there in conversation, a very simply dressed lady, who, as he entered, looked at him with a grave smile and stood up. He thought he had never seen her before.

Marcella wore a singular expression; there was a moment of silence, for Christian decidedly embarrassing, since it seemed to be expected that he should greet the stranger.

'Don't you remember Janet?' said his sister.

'Janet?' He felt his face flush. 'You don't meant to say——? But how you have altered! And yet, no; really, you haven't. It's only my stupidity.' He grasped her hand, and with a feeling of genuine pleasure, despite awkward reminiscences.

'One does alter in eleven years,' said Janet Moxey, in a very pleasant, natural voice—a voice of habitual self-command, conveying the idea of a highly cultivated mind, and many other agreeable things.

'Eleven years? Yes, yes! How very glad I am to see you! And I'm sure Marcella was. How very kind of you to call on us!'

Janet was as far as ever from looking handsome or pretty, but it must have been a dullard who proclaimed her face unpleasing. She had eyes of remarkable intelligence, something like Marcella's, but milder, more benevolent. Her lips were softly firm; they would not readily part in laughter; their frequent smile meant more than that of the woman who sets herself to be engaging.

'I am on my way home,' she said, 'from a holiday in the South,—an enforced holiday, I'm sorry to say.'

'You have been ill?'

'Overworked a little. I am practising medicine in Kingsmill.'

Christian did not disguise his astonishment.

'Medicine?'

'You don't remember that I always had scientific tastes?'

If it was a reproach, none could have been more gently administered.

'Of course—of course I do! Your botany, your skeletons of birds and cats and mice—of course! But where did you study?'

'In London. The Women's Medical School. I have been in practice for nearly four years.'

'And have overworked yourself.—But why are we standing? Let us sit down and talk. How is your father?'

Marcella was watching her brother closely, and with a curious smile.

Janet remained for another hour. No reference was made to the long rupture of intercourse between her family and these relatives. Christian learnt that his uncle was still hale, and that Janet's four sisters all lived, obviously unmarried. To-day he was disposed to be almost affectionate with any one who showed him a friendly face: he expressed grief that his cousin must leave for Twybridge early in the morning.

'Whenever you pass through the Midlands,' was Janet's indirect reply, addressed to Marcella, 'try to stop at Kingsmill.'

And a few minutes after that she took her leave. There lingered behind her that peculiar fragrance of modern womanhood, refreshing, inspiriting, which is so entirely different from the merely feminine perfume, however exquisite.

'What a surprising visit!' was Christian's exclamation, when he and his sister were alone. 'How did she find us?'

'Directory, I suppose.'

'A lady doctor!' he mused.

'And a very capable one, I fancy,' said Marcella. 'We had nearly an hour's talk before you came. But she won't be able to stand the work. There'll be another breakdown before long.'

'Has she a large practice, then?'

'Not very large, perhaps; but she studies as well. I never dreamt of Janet becoming so interesting a person.'

Christian had to postpone till after dinner the talk he purposed about Mrs. Palmer. When that time came, he was no longer disposed for sentimental confessions; it would be better to wait until he could announce a settled project of marriage. Through the evening, his sister recurred to the subject of Janet with curious frequency, and on the following day her interest had suffered no diminution. Christian had always taken for granted that she understood the grounds of the breach between him and his uncle; without ever unbosoming himself, he had occasionally, in his softer moments, alluded to the awkward subject in language which he thought easy enough to interpret. Now at length, in reply to some remark of Marcella's, he said with significant accent:

'Janet was very friendly to me.'

'She has studied science for ten years,' was his sister's comment.

'Yes, and can forgive a boy's absurdities.'

'Easier to forgive, certainly, than those of a man,' said Marcella, with a curl of the lip.

Christian became silent, and went thoughtfully away.

A week later, he was again in Mrs. Palmer's drawing-room, where again he met an assemblage of people such as seemed to profane this sanctuary. To be sure—he said to himself—Constance could not at once get rid of the acquaintances forced upon her by her husband; little by little she would free herself. It was a pity that her sister and her niece—persons anything but intelligent and refined—should be permanent members of her household; for their sake, no doubt, she felt constrained to welcome men and women for whose society she herself had little taste. But when the year of her widowhood was past——

Petrarch's Laura was the mother of eleven children; Constance had had only three, and one of these was dead. The remaining two, Christian now learnt, lived with a governess in a little house at Bournemouth, which Mrs. Palmer had taken for that purpose.

'I'm going down to see them tomorrow,' she informed Christian, 'and I shall stay there over the next day. It's so quiet and restful.'

These words kept repeating themselves to Christian's ear, as he went home, and all through the evening. Were they not an invitation? Down there at Bournemouth, Constance would be alone the day after tomorrow. 'It is so quiet and restful'; that was to say, no idle callers would break upon her retirement; she would be able to welcome a friend, and talk reposefully with him. Surely she must have meant that; for she spoke with a peculiar intonation—a look——

By the second morning he had worked himself up to a persuasion that yonder by the seaside Constance was expecting him. To miss the opportunity would be to prove himself dull of apprehension, a laggard in love. With trembling hands, he hurried through his toilet and made haste downstairs to examine a railway time-table. He found it was possible to reach Bournemouth by about two o'clock, a very convenient hour; it would allow him to take refreshment, and walk to the house shortly after three.

His conviction strong as ever, he came to the journey's end, and in due course discovered the pleasant little house of which Constance had spoken. At the door, his heart failed him; but retreat could not now be thought of. Yes, Mrs. Palmer was at home. The servant led him into a sitting-room on the ground floor, took his name, and left him.

It was nearly ten minutes before Constance appeared. On her face he read a frank surprise.

'I happened to—to be down here; couldn't resist the temptation'——

'Delighted to see you, Mr. Moxey. But how did you know I was here?'

He gazed at her.

'You—don't you remember? The day before yesterday—in Sussex Square—you mentioned'——

'Oh, did I?' She laughed. 'I had quite forgotten.'

Christian sank upon his chair. He tried to convince himself that she was playing a part; perhaps she thought that she had been premature in revealing her wish to talk with him.

Mrs. Palmer was good-natured. This call evidently puzzled her, but she did not stint her hospitality. When Christian asked after the children, they were summoned; two little girls daintily dressed, pretty, affectionate with their mother. The sight of them tortured Christian, and he sighed deeply with relief when they left the room. Constance appeared rather absent; her quick glance at him signified something, but he could not determine what. In agony of constraint, he rose as if to go.

'Oh, you will have a cup of tea with me,' said Mrs. Palmer. 'It will be brought in a few minutes.'

Then she really wished him to stop. Was he not behaving like an obtuse creature? Why, everything was planned to encourage him.

He talked recklessly of this and that, and got round to the years long gone by. When the tea came, he was reviving memories of occasions on which he and she had met as young people.

Constance laughed merrily, declared she could hardly remember.

'Oh, what a time ago!—But I was quite a child.'

'No—indeed, no! You were a young lady, and a brilliant one.'

The tea seemed to intoxicate him. He noticed again that Constance glanced at him significantly. How good of her to allow him this delicious afternoon!

'Mr. Moxey,' she said, after meditating a little, 'why haven't you married? I should have thought you would have married long ago.'

He was stricken dumb. Her jerky laugh came as a shock upon his hearing.

'Married——?'

'What is there astonishing in the idea?'

'But—I— How can I answer you?'

The pretty, characterless face betrayed some unusual feeling. She looked at him furtively; seemed to suppress a tendency to laugh.

'I mustn't pry into secrets,' she simpered.

'But there is no secret!' Christian panted, laying down his teacup for fear he should drop it. 'Whom should I—could I have married?'

Constance also put aside her cup. She was bewildered, and just a little abashed. With courage which came he knew not whence, Christian bent forward and continued speaking:

'Whom should I marry after that day when I met you in the little drawing-room at the Robinsons'?'

She stared in genuine astonishment, then was embarrassed.

'You cannot—cannot have forgotten——?'

'You surely don't mean to say, Mr. Moxey, that *you* have remembered? Oh, I'm afraid I was a shocking flirt in those days!'

'But I mean *after* your marriage—when I found you in tears'——

'Please, please don't remind me!' she exclaimed, giggling nervously. 'Oh how silly!—of me, I mean. To think that—but you are making fun of me, Mr. Moxey?'

Christian rose and went to the window. He was not only

shaken by his tender emotions—something very like repugnance had begun to affect him. If Constance were feigning, it was in very bad taste; if she spoke with sincerity—what a woman had he worshipped! It did not occur to him to lay the fault upon his own absurd romanticism. After eleven years' persistence in one point of view, he could not suddenly see the affair with the eyes of common sense.

He turned and approached her again.

'Do you not know, then,' he asked, with quiet dignity, 'that ever since the day I speak of, I have devoted my life to the love I then felt? All these years, have you not understood me?'

Mrs. Palmer was quite unable to grasp ideas such as these. Neither her reading nor her experience prepared her to understand what Christian meant. Courtship of a married woman was intelligible enough to her; but a love that feared to soil itself, a devotion from afar, encouraged by only the faintest hope of reward other than the most insubstantial—of that she had as little conception as any woman among the wealthy vulgar.

'Do you really mean, Mr. Moxey, that you—have kept unmarried for *my* sake?'

'You don't know that?' he asked, hoarsely.

'How could I? How was I to imagine such a thing? Really, was it proper? How could you expect me, Mr. Moxey——?'

For a moment she looked offended. But her real feelings were astonishment and amusement, not unmingled with an idle gratification.

'I must ask you to pardon me,' said Christian, whose forehead gleamed with moisture.

'No, don't say that. I am really so sorry! What an odd mistake!'

'And I have hoped in vain—since you were free——?'

'Oh, you mustn't say such things! I shall never dream of marrying again—never!'

There was a matter-of-fact vigour in the assertion which proved that Mrs. Palmer spoke her genuine thought. The tone could not be interpreted as devotion to her husband's memory; it meant, plainly and simply, that she had had enough of marriage, and delighted in her freedom.

Christian could not say another word. Disillusion was complete. The voice, the face, were those of as unspiritual a woman as he could easily have met with, and his life's story was that of a fool.

He took his hat, held out his hand, with 'Good-bye, Mrs, Palmer.' The cold politeness left her no choice but again to look offended, and with merely a motion of the head she replied, 'Good-bye, Mr. Moxey.'

And therewith permitted him to leave the house.

II

On calling at Earwaker's chambers one February evening, Malkin became aware, from the very threshold of the outer door, that the domicile was not as he had known it. With the familiar fragrance of Earwaker's special 'mixture' blended a suggestion of new upholstery. The little vestibule had somehow put off its dinginess, and an unwontedly brilliant light from the sitting-room revealed changes of the interior which the visitor remarked with frank astonishment.

'What the deuce! Has it happened at last? Are you going to be married?' he cried, staring about him at unrecognised chairs, tables, and bookcases, at whitened ceiling and pleasantly papered walls, at pictures and ornaments which he knew not.

The journalist shook his head, and smiled contentedly.

'An idea that came to me all at once. My editorship seemed to inspire it.'

After a year of waiting upon Providence, Earwaker had received the offer of a substantial appointment much more to his taste than those he had previously held. He was now literary editor of a weekly review which made no kind of appeal to the untaught multitude.

'I have decided to dwell here for the rest of my life,' he added, looking round the walls. 'One must have a homestead, and this shall be mine; here I have set up my penates. It's a portion of space, you know; and what more can be said of Longleat or Chatsworth? A house I shall never want, because I shall never have a wife. And on the whole I prefer this situation to any other. I am well within reach of everything urban that I care about, and as for the country, that is too good to be put to common use; let it be kept for holiday. There's an atmosphere in the old Inns that pleases me. The new flats are insufferable. How can one live sandwiched between a music-hall singer and a female politician? For lodgings of any kind no sane man had ever a word of approval. Reflecting on all these things, I have established myself in perpetuity.'

'Just what I can't do,' exclaimed Malkin, flinging himself into a broad, deep, leather-covered chair. 'Yet I have leanings that way. Only a few days ago I sat for a whole evening with the map of England open before me, wondering where would be the best place to settle down—a few years hence, I mean, you know; when Bella is old enough.—That reminds me. Next Sunday is her birthday, and do you know what? I wish you'd go down to Wrotham with me.'

'Many thanks, but I think I had better not.'

'Oh, but do! I want you to see how Bella is getting on. She's grown wonderfully since you saw her in Paris—an inch taller, I should think. I don't go down there very often, you know, so I notice these changes. Really, I think no one could be more discreet than I am, under the circumstances. A friend of the family; that's all. Just dropping in for a casual cup of tea now and then. Sunday will be a special occasion, of course. I say, what are your views about early marriage? Do you think seventeen too young?'

'I should think seven-and-twenty much better.'

Malkin broke into fretfulness.

'Let me tell you, Earwaker, I don't like the way you habitually speak of this project of mine. Plainly, I don't like it. It's a very serious matter indeed—eh? What? Why are you smiling?'

'I agree with you as to its seriousness.'

'Yes, yes; but in a very cynical and offensive way. It makes me confoundedly uncomfortable, let me tell you. I don't think that's very friendly on your part. And the fact is, if it goes on I'm very much afraid we shan't see so much of each other as we have done. I like you, Earwaker, and I respect you; I think you know that. But occasionally you seem to have too little regard for one's feelings. No, I don't feel able to pass it over with a joke.—There! The deuce take it! I've bitten off the end of my pipe.'

He spat out a piece of amber, and looked ruefully at the broken stem.

'Take a cigar,' said Earwaker, fetching a box from a cupboard.

'I don't mind.—Well—what was I saying? Oh yes; I was quarrelling with you. Now, look here, what fault have you to find with Bella Jacox?'

'None whatever. She seemed to me a very amiable child.'

'Child! Pooh! pshaw! And fifteen next Sunday, I tell you. She's a young lady, and to tell you the confounded plain truth, I'm in love with her. I am, and there's nothing to be ashamed of. If you smile, we shall quarrel. I warn you, Earwaker, we shall quarrel.'

The journalist, instead of smiling, gave forth his deepest laugh. Malkin turned very red, scowled, and threw his cigar aside.

'You really wish me to go on Sunday?' Earwaker asked, in a pleasant voice.

The other's countenance immediately cleared.

'I shall take it as a great kindness. Mrs. Jacox will be delighted. Meet me at Holborn Viaduct at one-twenty-five. No, to make sure I'll come here at one o'clock.'

In a few minutes he was chatting as unconcernedly as ever.

'Talking of settling down, my brother Tom and his wife are on the point of going to New Zealand. Necessity of business; may be out there for the rest of their lives. Do you know that I shall think very seriously of following them some day? With Bella, you know. The fact of the matter is, I don't believe I could ever make a solid home in England. Why, I can't quite say; partly, I suppose, because I have nothing to do. Now there's a good deal to be said for going out to the colonies. A man feels that he is helping the spread of civilisation; and that's something, you know. I should compare myself with the Greek and Roman colonists—something inspiriting in that thought—what? Why shouldn't I found a respectable newspaper, for instance? Yes, I shall think very seriously of this.'

'You wouldn't care to run over with your relatives, just to have a look?'

'It occurred to me,' Malkin replied, thoughtfully. 'But they sail in ten days, and—well, I'm afraid I couldn't get ready in time. And then I've promised to look after some little affairs for Mrs. Jacox—some trifling money matters. But later in the year —who knows?'

Earwaker half repented of his promise to visit the Jacox household, but there was no possibility of excusing himself. So on Sunday he journeyed with his friend down to Wrotham. Mrs. Jacox and her children were very comfortably established in a small new house. When the companions entered they found the mother alone in her sitting-room, and she received them with an effusiveness very distasteful to Earwaker.

'Now you shouldn't!' was her first exclamation to Malkin. 'Indeed you shouldn't! It's really very naughty of you. O Mr. Earwaker! Who ever took so much pleasure in doing kindnesses? Do look at this *beautiful* book that Mr. Malkin has sent as a present to my little Bella. O Mr. Earwaker!'

The journalist was at once struck with her tone and manner as she addressed Malkin. He remarked that phrase, 'my little Bella,' and it occurred to him that Mrs. Jacox had been growing younger since he made her acquaintance on the towers of Notre Dame. When the girls presented themselves, they also appeared to him more juvenile; Bella, in particular, was dressed with an exaggeration of childishness decidedly not becoming. One had but to look into her face to see that she answered perfectly to Malkin's description; she was a young lady, and no child. A very pretty young lady, moreover; given to colouring, but with no silly simper; intelligent about the eyes and lips; modest, in a natural and sweet way. He conversed with her, and in doing so was disagreeably affected by certain glances she occasionally cast towards her mother. One would have said that she feared censure, though it was hard to see why.

On the return journey Earwaker made known some of his impressions, though not all.

'I like the girls,' he said, 'Bella especially. But I can't say much good of their mother.'

They were opposite each other in the railway carriage. Malkin leaned forward with earnest, anxious face.

'That's my own trouble,' he whispered. 'I'm confoundedly uneasy about it. I don't think she's bringing them up at all in a proper way. Earwaker, I would pay down five thousand pounds for the possibility of taking Bella away altogether.'

The other mused.

'But, mind you,' pursued Malkin, 'she's not a *bad* woman. By no means! Thoroughly good-hearted I'm convinced; only a little weak here.' He tapped his forehead. 'I respect her, for all she has suffered, and her way of going through it. But she isn't the ideal mother, you know.'

On his way home, Malkin turned into his friend's chambers 'for five minutes.' At two in the morning he was still there, and his talk in the meanwhile had been of nothing but schemes for protecting Bella against her mother's more objectionable influences. On taking leave, he asked:

'Any news of Peak yet?'

'None, I haven't seen Moxey for a long time.'

'Do you think Peak will look you up again, if he's in London?'

'No, I think he'll keep away. And I half hope he will; I shouldn't quite know how to behave. Ten to one he's in London now. I suppose he couldn't stay at Exeter. But he may have left England.'

They parted, and for a week did not see each other. Then, on Monday evening, when Earwaker was very busy with a mass of manuscript, the well-known knock sounded from the passage, and Malkin received admission. The look he wore was appalling, a look such as only some fearful catastrophe could warrant.

'Are you busy?' he asked in a voice very unlike his own.

Earwaker could not doubt that the trouble was this time serious. He abandoned his work, and gave himself wholly to his friend's service.

'An awful thing has happened,' Malkin began. 'How the deuce shall I tell you? Oh, the ass I have made of myself! But I couldn't help it; there seemed no way out of it.'

'Well? What?'

'It was last night, but I couldn't come to you till now. By Jove! I veritably thought of sending you a note, and then killing myself. Early this morning I was within an ace of suicide. Believe me, old friend. This is no farce.'

'I'm waiting.'

'Yes, yes; but I can't tell you all at once. Sure you're not busy? I know I pester you. I was down at Wrotham yesterday. I hadn't meant to go, but the temptation was too strong. I got there at five o'clock, and found that the girls were gone to have tea with some young friends. Well, I wasn't altogether sorry; it was a good opportunity for a little talk with their mother. And I *had* the talk. But, oh, ass that I was!'

He smote the side of his head savagely.

'Can you guess, Earwaker? Can you give a shot at what happened?'

'Perhaps I might,' replied the other gravely.

'Well?'

'That woman asked you to marry her.'

Malkin leapt from his chair, and sank back again.

'It came to that. Yes, upon my word, it came to that. She said she had fallen in love with me—that was the long and short of it. And I had never said a word that could suggest—— Oh, confound it! What a frightful scene it was!'

'You took a final leave of her?'

Malkin stared with eyes of anguish into his friend's face, and at length whispered thickly:

'I said I would!'

'What? Take leave?'

'Marry her!'

Earwaker had much ado to check an impatiently remonstrant laugh. He paused awhile, then began his expostulation, at first treating the affair as too absurd for grave argument.

'My boy,' he concluded, 'you have got into a preposterous scrape, and I see only one way out of it. You must flee. When does your brother start for the Antipodes?'

'Thursday morning.'

'Then you go with him; there's an end of it.'

Malkin listened with the blank, despairing look of a man condemned to death.

'Do you hear me?' urged the other. 'Go home and pack. On Thursday I'll see you off.'

'I can't bring myself to that,' came in a groan from Malkin. 'I've never yet done anything to be seriously ashamed of, and I can't run away after promising marriage. It would weigh upon me for the rest of my life.'

'Humbug! Would it weigh upon you less to marry the mother, and all the time be in love with the daughter? To my mind, there's something peculiarly loathsome in the suggestion.'

'But, look here; Bella is very young, really very young indeed. It's possible that I have deluded myself. Perhaps I don't really care for her in the way I imagined. It's more than likely that I might be content to regard her with fatherly affection.'

'Even supposing that, with what sort of affection do you regard Mrs. Jacox?'

Malkin writhed on his chair before replying.

'You mustn't misjudge her!' he exclaimed. 'She is no heartless schemer. The poor thing almost cried her eyes out. It was a frightful scene. She reproached herself bitterly. What *could* I do? I have a tenderness for her, there's no denying that. She has been so vilely used, and has borne it all so patiently. How abominable it would be if I dealt her another blow!'

The journalist raised his eyebrows, and uttered inarticulate sounds.

'Was anything said about Bella?' he asked, abruptly.

'Not a word. I'm convinced she doesn't suspect that I thought of Bella like that. The fact is, I have misled her. She thought all along that my chief interest was in *her*.'

'Indeed? Then what was the ground of her self-reproach that you speak of?'

'How defective you are in the appreciation of delicate feeling!' cried Malkin frantically, starting up and rushing about the room. 'She reproached herself for having permitted me to get entangled with a widow older than myself, and the mother of two children. What could be simpler?'

Earwaker began to appreciate the dangers of the situation. If he insisted upon his view of Mrs. Jacox's behaviour (though it was not the harshest that the circumstances suggested, for he was disposed to believe that the widow had really lost her heart to her kind, eccentric champion), the result would probably be to confirm Malkin in his resolution of self-sacrifice. The man must be saved, if possible, from such calamity, and this would not be affected by merely demonstrating that he was on the highroad to ruin. It was necessary to try another tack.

'It seems to me, Malkin,' he resumed gravely, 'that it is you who are deficient in right feeling. In offering to marry this poor woman, you did her the gravest wrong.'

'What? How?'

'You know that it is impossible for you to love her. You know that you will repent, and that she will be aware of it. You are not the kind of man to conceal your emotions. Bella will grow up, and—well, the state of things won't tend to domestic felicity. For Mrs. Jacox's own sake, it is your duty to put an end to this folly before it has gone too far.'

The other gave earnest ear, but with no sign of shaken conviction.

'Yes,' he said. 'I know this is one way of looking at it. But it assumes that a man can't control himself, that his sense of honour isn't strong enough to keep him in the right way. I don't think you quite understand me. I am not a passionate man; the proof is that I have never fallen in love since I was sixteen. I think a great deal of domestic peace, a good deal more than of romantic enthusiasm. If I marry Mrs. Jacox, I shall make her a good and faithful husband,—so much I can safely say of myself.'

He waited, but Earwaker was not ready with a rejoinder.

'And there's another point. I have always admitted the defect of my character—an inability to settle down. Now, if I run away to New Zealand, with the sense of having dishonoured myself, I shall be a mere Wandering Jew for the rest of my life. All hope of redemption will be over. Of the two courses now open to me, that of marriage with Mrs. Jacox is decidedly the less disadvantageous. Granting that I have made a fool of myself, I must abide by the result, and make the best of it. And the plain fact is, I *can't* treat her so disgracefully; I *can't* burden my conscience in this way. I believe it would end in suicide; I do, indeed.'

'This sounds all very well, but it is weakness and selfishness.'

'How can you say so?'

'There's no proving to so short-sighted a man the result of his mistaken course. I've a good mind to let you have your way just for the satisfaction of saying afterwards, "Didn't I tell you so?" You propose to behave with abominable injustice to two people, putting yourself aside. Doesn't it occur to you that Bella may already look upon you as her future husband? Haven't you done your best to plant that idea in her mind?'

Malkin started, but quickly recovered himself.

'No, I haven't! I have behaved with the utmost discretion. Bella thinks of me only as of a friend much older than herself.

'I don't believe it!'

'Nonsense, Earwaker! A child of fifteen!'

'The other day you had quite a different view, and after seeing her again I agreed with you. She is a young girl, and if not already in love with you, is on the way to be so.'

'That will come to nothing when she hears that I am going to be her step-father.'

'Far more likely to develop into a grief that will waste the best part of her lifetime. She will be shocked and made miserable. But do as you like. I am tired of arguing.'

Earwaker affected to abandon the matter in disgust. For several minutes there was silence, then a low voice sounded from the corner where Malkin stood leaning.

'So it is your honest belief that Bella has begun to think of me in that way?'

'I am convinced of it.'

'But if I run away, I shall never see her again.'

'Why not? *She* won't run away. Come back when things have squared themselves. Write to Mrs. Jacox from the ends of the earth, and let her understand that there is no possibility of your marrying her.'

'Tell her about Bella, you mean?'

'No, that's just what I don't mean. Avoid any mention of the girl. Come back when she is seventeen, and, if she is willing, carry her off to be happy ever after.'

'But she may have fallen in love with someone else.'

'I think not. You must risk it, at all events.'

'Look here!' Malkin came forward eagerly. 'I'll write to Mrs. Jacox tonight, and make a full confession. I'll tell her exactly how the case stands. She's a good woman; she'll gladly sacrifice herself for the sake of her daughter.'

Earwaker was firm in resistance. He had no faith whatever in the widow's capacity for self-immolation, and foresaw that his friend would be drawn into another 'frightful scene,' resulting probably in a marriage as soon as the licence could be obtained.

'When are you to see her again?' he inquired.

'On Wednesday.'

'Will you undertake to do nothing whatever till Wednesday morning, and then to have another talk with me? I'll come and see you about ten o'clock.'

In the end Malkin was constrained into making this engagement, and not long after midnight the journalist managed to get rid of him.

On Tuesday afternoon arrived a distracted note. 'I shall keep my promise, and I won't try to see you till you come here to-morrow. But I am sore beset. I have received *three* letters from Mrs. Jacox, all long and horribly pathetic. She seems to have a presentiment that I shall forsake her. What a beast I shall be if I do! Tom comes here to-night, and I think I shall tell him all.'

The last sentence was a relief to the reader; he knew nothing of Mr. Thomas Malkin, but there was a fair presumption that this gentleman would not see his brother bent on making such a notable fool of himself without vigorous protest.

At the appointed hour next morning, Earwaker reached his friend's lodgings, which were now at Kilburn. On entering the room he saw, not the familiar figure, but a solid, dark-faced, black-whiskered man, whom a faint resemblance enabled him to identify as Malkin the younger.

'I was expecting you,' said Thomas, as they shook hands. 'My brother is completely floored. When I got here an hour ago, I insisted on his lying down, and now I think he's asleep. If you don't mind, we'll let him rest for a little. I believe he has hardly closed his eyes since this unfortunate affair happened.'

'It rejoiced me to hear that he was going to ask your advice. How do matters stand?'

'You know Mrs. Jacox?'

Thomas was obviously a man of discretion, but less intellectual than his brother; he spoke like one who is accustomed to the management of affairs. At first he was inclined to a polite reserve, but Earwaker's conversation speedily put him more at ease.

'I have quite made up my mind,' he said presently, 'that we must take him away with us tomorrow. The voyage will bring him to his senses.'

'Of course he resists?'

'Yes, but if you will give me your help, I think we can manage him. He is not very strong-willed. In a spasmodic way he can defy everyone, but the steady pressure of common sense will prevail with him, I think.'

They had talked for half-an-hour, when the door opened and the object of their benevolent cares stood before them. He was clad in a dressing-gown, and his disordered hair heightened the look of illness which his features presented.

'Why didn't you call me?' he asked his brother, irritably. 'Earwaker, I beg a thousand pardons! I'm not very well; I've overslept myself.'

'Yes, yes; come and sit down.'

Thomas made an offer to leave them.

'Don't go,' said Malkin. 'No need whatever. You know why Earwaker has been so kind as to come here. We may as well talk it over together.'

He sat on the table, swinging a tassel of his dressing-gown round and round.

'Now, what do you really think of doing?' asked the journalist, in a kind voice.

'I don't know. I absolutely do not know. I'm unutterably wretched.'

'In that case, will you let your brother and me decide for you?

We have no desire but for your good, and we are perfectly at one in our judgment.'

'Of course I know what you will propose!' cried the other, excitedly. 'From the prudential point of view, you are right, I have no doubt. But how can you protect me against remorse? If you had received letters such as these three,' he pulled them out of a pocket, 'you would be as miserable as I am. If I don't keep my promise, I shall never know another moment of peace.'

'You certainly won't if you *do* keep it,' remarked Thomas.

'No,' added Earwaker, 'and one if not two other persons will be put into the same case. Whereas by boldly facing these reproaches of conscience, you do a great kindness to the others.'

'If only you could assure me of that!'

'I *can* assure you. That is to say, I can give it as my unassailable conviction.'

And Earwaker once more enlarged upon the theme, stating it from every point of view that served his purpose.

'You're making a mountain out of a mole-heap,' was the confirmatory remark that came from Thomas. 'This respectable lady will get over her sorrows quickly enough, and some day she'll be only too glad to have you for a son-in-law, if Miss Bella still pleases you.'

'It's only right,' urged Earwaker, in pursuance of his subtler intention, 'that you should bear the worst of the suffering, for the trouble has come out of your own thoughtlessness. You are fond of saying that you have behaved with the utmost discretion; so far from that you have been outrageously indiscreet. I foresaw that something of this kind might come to pass'——

'Then why the devil didn't you warn me?' shouted Malkin, in an agony of nervous strain.

'It would have been useless. In fact, I foresaw it too late.'

The discussion continued for an hour. By careful insistence on the idea of self-sacrifice, Earwaker by degrees demolished the arguments his friend kept putting forward. Thomas, who had gone impatiently to the window, turned round with words that were meant to be final.

'It's quite decided. You begin your preparations at once, and tomorrow morning you go on board with us.'

'But if I don't go to Wrotham this afternoon, she'll be here either tonight or the first thing tomorrow. I'm sure of it!'

'By four or five o'clock,' said Earwaker, 'you can have broken up the camp. You've often done it at shorter notice. Go to an hotel for the night.'

'I must write to the poor woman.'

'Do as you like about that.'

'Who is to help her, if she gets into difficulties—as she's always doing? Who is to advise her about Bella's education? Who is to pay——I mean, who will see to——? Oh, confound it!'

The listeners glanced at each other.

'Are her affairs in order?' asked Earwaker. 'Has she a sufficient income?'

'For ordinary needs, quite sufficient. But'——

'Then you needn't be in the least uneasy. Let her know where you are, when the equator is between you. Watch over her interests from a distance, if you like. I can as good as promise you that Bella will wait hopefully to see her friend again.'

Malkin succumbed to argument and exhaustion. Facing Earwaker with a look of pathetic appeal, he asked hoarsely:

'Will you stand by me till it's over? Have you time?'

'I can give you till five o'clock.'

'Then I'll go and dress. Ring the bell, Tom, and ask them to bring up some beer.'

Before three had struck, the arrangements for flight were completed. A heavily-laden cab bore away Malkin's personal property; within sat the unhappy man and his faithful friend.

The next morning Earwaker went down to Tilbury, and said farewell to the travellers on board the steamship *Orient*. Mrs. Thomas had already taken her brother-in-law under her special care.

'It's only three children to look after, instead of two,' she remarked, in a laughing aside to the journalist. 'How grateful he will be to you in a few days! And I'm sure *we* are already.'

Malkin's eyes were no longer quite lustreless. At the last moment he talked with animation of 'two years hence,' and there was vigour in the waving of his hand as the vessel started seaward.

III

Peak lost no time in leaving Exeter. To lighten his baggage, and to get rid of possessions to which hateful memories attached, he sold all his books that had any bearing on theology. The incomplete translation of *Bibel und Natur* he committed to the flames in Mrs. Roots's kitchen, scattering its black remnants with savage thrusts of the poker. Whilst engaged in packing, he debated with himself whether or not he should take leave of the few acquaintances to whom he was indebted for hospitality, and other kindness. The question was: Had Buckland Warricombe already warned these people against him? Probably it had seemed to Buckland the wiser course to be content with driving the hyprocrite away; and, if this were so, regard for the future dictated a retirement from Exeter which should in no way resemble secret flight. Sidwell's influence with her parents would perhaps withhold them from making his disgrace known, and in a few years he might be glad that he had behaved with all possible prudence. In the end, he decided to write to Mr. Lilywhite, saying that he was obliged to go away at a moment's notice, and that he feared it would be necessary altogether to change the scheme of life which he had had in view. This was the best way. From the Lilywhites, other people would hear of him, and perchance their conjectures would be charitable.

Without much hesitation he had settled his immediate plans. To London he would not return, for he dreaded the temptations to which the proximity of Sidwell would expose him, and he had no mind to meet with Moxey or Earwaker. As it was now imperative that he should find work of the old kind, he could not do better than go to Bristol, where, from the safe ground of a cheap and obscure lodging, he might make inquiries, watch advertisements, and so on. He already knew of establishments in Bristol where he might possibly obtain employment. Living with the utmost economy, he need not fall into difficulties for more than a year, and before then his good repute with the Rotherhithe firm would ensure him some position or other; if not in Bristol, then at Newcastle, St. Helen's—any great centre of fuming and malodorous industry. He was ready to work, would delight in work. Idleness was now the intolerable thing.

So to Bristol he betook himself, and there made his temporary abode. After spending a few weeks in fruitless search for an engagement, he at length paid his oft-postponed visit to Twybridge. In the old home he felt completely a stranger, and his relatives strengthened the feeling by declaring him so changed in appearance that they hardly knew his face. With his mother only could he talk in anything like an intimate way, and the falsehoods with which he was obliged to answer her questions all but destroyed the pleasure he would otherwise have found in being affectionately tended. His sister, Mrs. Cusse, was happy in her husband, her children, and a flourishing business. Oliver was making money, and enjoyed distinction among the shopkeeping community. His aunt still dealt in millinery, and kept up her acquaintance with respectable families. To Godwin all was like a dream dreamt for the second time. He could not acknowledge any actual connection between these people and himself. But their characteristics no longer gravely offended him, and he willingly recognised the homespun worth which their lives displayed. It was clear to him that by no possible agency of circumstances could he have been held in normal relations with his kinsfolk. However smooth his career, it must have wafted him to an immeasurable distance from Twybridge. Nature had decreed that he was to resemble the animals which, once reared, go forth in complete independence of birthplace and the ties of blood. It was a harsh fate, but in what had not fate been harsh to him? The one consolation was that he alone suffered. His mother was no doubt occasionally troubled by solicitude on his account, but she could not divine his inward miseries, and an assurance that he had no material cares sufficed to set her mind at ease.

'You are very like your father, Godwin,' she said, with a sigh. 'He couldn't rest, however well he seemed to be getting on.

There was always something he wanted, and yet he didn't know what it was.'

'Yes, I must be like him,' Godwin replied, smiling.

He stayed five days, then returned to Bristol. A week after that, his mother forwarded to him a letter which had come to Twybridge. He at once recognised the writing, and broke the envelope with curiosity.

'If you should be in London,' the note began, 'I beg you to let me see you. There is something I have to say. To speak to you for a few minutes I would come any distance. Don't accuse me of behaving treacherously; it was not my fault. I know you would rather avoid me, but do consent to hear what I have to say. If you have no intention of coming to London, will you write and let me know where you are living? M. M.'

What could Marcella have to say to him? Nothing surely that he at all cared to hear. No doubt she imagined that he might be in ignorance of the circumstances which had led to Buckland Warricombe's discovery; she wished to defend herself against the suspicion of 'treachery.' He laughed carelessly, and threw her note aside.

Two months passed, and his efforts to find employment were still vain, though he had received conditional promises. The solitude of his life grew burdensome. Several times he began a letter to Sidwell, but his difficulty in writing was so great that he destroyed the attempt. In truth, he knew not how to address her. The words he penned were tumid, meaningless. He could not send professions of love, for his heart seemed to be suffering a paralysis, and the laborious artificiality of his style must have been evident. The only excuse for breaking silence would be to let her know that he had resumed honest work; he must wait till the opportunity offered. It did not distress him to be without news of her. If she wished to write, and was only withheld by ignorance of his whereabouts, it was well; if she had no thought of sending him a word, it did not matter. He loved her, and consciously nourished hope, but for the present there was nothing intolerable in separation. His state of mind resulted partly from nervous reaction, and in part from a sense that only by silent suffering could his dignity in Sidwell's eyes be ultimately restored. Between the evil past and the hopeful future must be a complete break.

His thoughts kept turning to London, though not because Sidwell might still be there. He felt urgent need of speaking with a friend. Moxey was perhaps no longer to be considered one; but Earwaker would be tolerant of human weaknesses. To have a long talk with Earwaker would help him to recover his mental balance, to understand himself and his position better. So one morning in March, on the spur of the moment, he took train and was once more in the metropolis. On his way he had determined to send a note to Earwaker before calling at Staple Inn. He wrote it at a small hotel in Paddington, where he took a room for the night, and then spent the evening at a theatre, as the best way of killing time.

By the first post next morning came a card, whereon Earwaker had written:—'Be here, if you can, at two o'clock. Shall be glad to see you.'

'So you have been new-furnishing!' Godwin remarked, as he was admitted to the chambers. 'You look much more comfortable.'

'I'm glad you think so. It is the general opinion.'

They had shaken hands as though this were one of the ordinary meetings of old time, and their voices scarcely belied the appearance. Peak moved about the study, glancing at pictures and books, Earwaker eyeing him the while with not unfriendly expression. They were sincerely glad to see each other, and when Peak seated himself it was with an audible sigh of contentment.

'And what are you doing?' he inquired.

The journalist gave a brief account of his affairs, and Peak brightened with pleasure.

'This is good news. I knew you would shake off the ragamuffins before long. Give me some of your back numbers, will you? I shall be curious to examine your new style.'

'And you?—Come to live in London?'

'No; I am at Bristol, but only waiting. There's a chance of an analyst's place in Lancashire; but I may give the preference to an opening I have heard of in Belgium. Better to go abroad, I think.'

'Perhaps so.'

'I have a question to ask you. I suppose you talked about that *Critical* article of mine *before* you received my request for silence?'

'That's how it was,' Earwaker replied, calmly.

'Yes; I understood. It doesn't matter.'

The other puffed at his pipe, and moved uneasily.

'I am taking for granted,' Peak continued, 'that you know how I have spent my time down in Devonshire.'

'In outline. Need we trouble about the details?'

'No. But don't suppose that I should feel any shame in talking to you about them. That would be a confession of base motive. You and I have studied each other, and we can exchange thoughts on most subjects with mutual understanding. You know that I have only followed my convictions to their logical issue. An opportunity offered of achieving the supreme end to which my life is directed, and what scruple could stand in my way? We have nothing to do with names and epithets. *Here* are the facts of life as I had known it; *there* is the existence promised as the reward of successful artifice. To live was to pursue the object of my being. I could not feel otherwise; therefore, could not act otherwise. You imagine me defeated, flung back into the gutter.' His words came more quickly, and the muscles of his face worked under emotion. 'It isn't so. I have a great and reasonable hope. Perhaps I have gained everything I really desired. I could tell you the strangest story, but there scruple *does* interpose. If we live another twenty years—but now I can only talk about myself.'

'And this hope of which you speak,' said Earwaker, with a grave smile, 'points you at present to sober work among your retorts and test-tubes?'

'Yes, it does.'

'Good. Then I can put faith in the result.'

'Yet the hope began in a lie,' rejoined Peak, bitterly. 'It will always be pleasant to look back upon that, won't it? You see: by no conceivable honest effort could I have gained this point. Life utterly denied to me the satisfaction of my strongest instincts, so long as I plodded on without cause of shame; the moment I denied my faith, and put on a visage of brass, great possibilities opened before me. Of course I understand the moralist's position. It behoved me, though I knew that a barren and solitary track would be my only treading to the end, to keep courageously onward. If I can't *believe* that any such duty is imposed upon me, where is the obligation to persevere, the morality of doing so? That is the worst hypocrisy. I have been honest, inasmuch as I have acted in accordance with my actual belief.'

'M—m—m,' muttered Earwaker, slowly. 'Then you have never been troubled with a twinge of conscience?'

'With a thousand! I have been racked, martyred. What has that to do with it? Do you suppose I attach any final significance to those torments? Conscience is the same in my view as an inherited disease which may possibly break out on any most innocent physical indulgence.—What end have I been pursuing? Is it criminal? Is it mean? I wanted to win the love of a woman—nothing more. To do that, I have had to behave like the grovelling villain who has no desire but to fill his pockets. And with success!—You understand that, Earwaker? I have succeeded! What respect can I have for the common morality, after this?'

'You have succeeded?' the other asked thoughtfully. 'I could have imagined that you had been in appearance successful'——

He paused, and Peak resumed with vehemence:

'No, not in appearance only. I can't tell you the story'——

'I don't wish you to'——

'But what I have won is won for ever. The triumph no longer rests on deceit. What I insist upon is that by deceit only was it rendered possible. If a starving man succeeds in stealing a loaf of bread, the food will benefit him no less than if he had purchased it; it is good, true sustenance, no mattter how he got it. To be sure, the man may prefer starvation; he may have so strong a metaphysical faith that death is welcome in comparison with what he calls dishonour. I—I have no such faith; and millions of other men in this country would tell the blunt truth if they said the same. I have *used means*, that's all. The old way of candour led me to bitterness and cursing; by dissimulation I have won something more glorious than tongue can tell.'

It was in the endeavour to expel the subtlest enemy of his peace that Godwin dwelt so defiantly upon this view of the temptation to which he had yielded. Since his farewell interview with Sidwell, he knew no rest from the torment of a mocking voice which bade him bear in mind that all his dishonour had been superfluous, seeing that whilst he played the part of a zealous Christian, Sidwell herself was drifting further and further from the old religion. This voice mingled with his dreams, and left not a waking hour untroubled. He refused to believe it, strove against the suggestion as a half-despairing man does against the persistent thought of suicide. If only he could obtain Earwaker's assent to the plan he put forward, it would support him in disregard of idle regrets.

'It is impossible,' said the journalist, 'for anyone to determine whether that is true or not—for you, as much as for anyone else. Be glad that you have shaken off the evil and retained the good,—no use in saying more than that.'

'Yes,' declared the other, stubbornly, 'there is good in exposing false views of life. I ought to have come utterly to grief and shame, and instead'——

'Instead——? Well?'

'What I have told you.'

'Which I interpret thus: that you have permission to redeem your character, if possible, in the eyes of a woman you have grievously misled.'

Godwin frowned.

'Who suggested this to you, Earwaker?'

'You; no one else. I don't even know who the woman is, of whom you speak.'

'Grant you are right. As an honest man, I should never have won her faintest interest.'

'It is absurd for us to talk about it. Think in the way that is most helpful to you,—that, no doubt, is a reasonable rule. Let us have done with all these obscurities, and come to a practical question. Can I be of any use to you? Would you care, for instance, to write an article now and then on some scientific matter that has a popular interest? I think I could promise to get that kind of thing printed for you. Or would you review an occasional book that happened to be in your line?'

Godwin reflected.

'Thank you,' he replied, at length. 'I should be glad of such work—if I can get into the mood for doing it properly. That won't be just yet; but perhaps when I have found a place'——

'Think it over. Write to me about it.'

Peak glanced round the room.

'You don't know how glad I am,' he said, 'that your prosperity shows itself in this region of bachelordom. If I had seen you in a comfortable house, married to a woman worthy of you—I couldn't have been sincere in my congratulations: I should have envied you so fiercely.'

'You're a strange fellow. Twenty years hence—as you said just now—you will one way or another have got rid of your astounding illusions. At fifty—well, let us say at sixty—you will have a chance of seeing things without these preposterous sexual spectacles.'

'I hope so. Every stage of life has its powers and enjoyments. When I am old, I hope to perceive and judge without passion of any kind. But is that any reason why my youth should be frustrated? We have only one life, and I want to live mine throughout.'

Soon after this Peak rose. He remembered that the journalist's time was valuable, and that he no longer had the right to demand more of it than could be granted to any casual caller. Earwaker behaved with all friendliness, but their relations had necessarily suffered a change. More than a year of separation, spent by the one in accumulating memories of dishonour, had given the other an enviable position among men; Earwaker had his place in the social system, his growing circle of friends, his congenial labour; perhaps—notwithstanding the tone in which he spoke of marriage—his hopes of domestic happiness. All this was no sacrifice of principle. He was fortunate in his temper, moral and intellectual; partly directing circumstances, partly guided by their pressure, he advanced on the way of harmonious development. Nothing great would come of his endeavours, but what he aimed at he steadily perfected. And this in spite of the adverse conditions under which he began his course. Nature had been kind to him; what more could one say?

When he went forth into the street again, Godwin felt his heart sink. His solitude was the more complete for this hour of friendly dialogue. No other companionship offered itself; if he lingered here, it must be as one of the drifting crowd, as an idle and envious spectator of the business and pleasure rife about him. He durst not approach that quarter of the town where Sidwell was living—if indeed she still remained here. Happily, the vastness of London enabled him to think of her as at a great distance; by keeping to the district in which he now wandered he was practically as remote from her as when he walked the streets of Bristol.

Yet there was one person who would welcome him eagerly if he chose to visit her. And, after all, might it not be as well if he heard what Marcella had to say to him? He could not go to the house, for it would be disagreeable to encounter Moxey; but, if he wrote, Marcella would speedily make an appointment. After an hour or two of purposeless rambling, he decided to ask for an interview. He might learn something that really concerned him; in any case, it was a final meeting with Marcella, to whom he perhaps owed this much courtesy.

The reply was as prompt as that from Earwaker. By the morning post came a letter inviting him to call upon Miss Moxey as soon as possible before noon. She added, 'My brother is away in the country; you will meet no one here.'

By eleven o'clock he was at Notting Hill; in the drawing-room, he sat alone for two or three minutes. Marcella entered silently, and came towards him without a smile; he saw that she read his face eagerly, if not with a light of triumph in her eyes. The expression might signify that she rejoiced at having been an instrument of his discomfiture; perhaps it was nothing more than gladness at seeing him again.

'Have you come to live in London?' she asked, when they had shaken hands without a word.

'I am only here for a day or two.'

'My letter reached you without delay?'

'Yes. It was sent from Twybridge to Bristol. I didn't reply then, as I had no prospect of being in London.'

'Will you sit down? You can stay for a few minutes?'

He seated himself awkwardly. Now that he was in Marcella's presence, he felt that he had acted unaccountably in giving occasion for another scene between them which could only end as painfully as that at Exeter. Her emotion grew evident; he could not bear to meet the look she had fixed upon him.

'I want to speak of what happened in this house about Christmas time,' she resumed. 'But I must know first what you have been told.'

'What have *you* been told?' he replied, with an uneasy smile. 'How do you know that anything which happened here had any importance for me?'

'I don't know that it had. But I felt sure that Mr. Warricombe meant to speak to you about it.'

'Yes, he did.'

'But did he tell you the exact truth? Or were you led to suppose that I had broken my promise to you?'

Unwilling to introduce any mention of Sidwell, Peak preferred to simplify the story by attributing to Buckland all the information he had gathered.

'I understood,' he replied, 'that Warricombe had come here in the hope of learning more about me, and that certain facts came out in general conversation. What does it matter how he learned what he did? From the day when he met you down in Devonshire, it was of course inevitable that the truth should sooner or later come out. He always suspected me.'

'But I want you to know,' said Marcella, 'that I had no willing part in it. I promised you not to speak even to my brother, and I should never have done so but that Christian somehow met Mr. Warricombe, and heard him talk of you. Of course he came to me in astonishment, and for your own interest I thought it best to tell Christian what I knew. When Mr. Warricombe came here, neither Christian nor I would have enlightened him about

—about your past. It happened most unfortunately that Mr. Malkin was present, and he it was who began to speak of the *Critical* article—and other things. I was powerless to prevent it.'

'Why trouble about it? I quite believe your account.'

'You *do* believe it? You know I would not have injured you?'

'I am sure you had no wish to,' Godwin replied, in as unsentimental a tone as possible. And, he added after a moment's pause, 'Was this what you were so anxious to tell me?'

'Yes. Chiefly that.'

'Let me put your mind at rest,' pursued the other, with quiet friendliness. 'I am disposed to turn optimist; everything has happened just as it should have done. Warricombe relieved me from a false position. If *he* hadn't done so, I must very soon have done it for myself. Let us rejoice that things work together for such obvious good. A few more lessons of this kind, and we shall acknowledge that the world is the best possible.'

He laughed, but the tense expression of Marcella's features did not relax.

'You say you are living in Bristol?'

'For a time.'

'Have you abandoned Exeter?'

The word implied something that Marcella could not utter more plainly. Her face completed the question.

'And the clerical career as well,' he answered.

But he knew that she sought more than this, and his voice again broke the silence.

'Perhaps you have heard that already? Are you in communication with Miss Moorhouse?'

She shook her head.

'But probably Warricombe has told your brother——?'

'What?'

'Oh, of his success in ridding Exeter of my objectionable presence.'

'Christian hasn't seen him again, nor have I.'

'I only wish to assure you that I have suffered no injury. My experiment was doomed to failure. What led me to it, how I regarded it, we won't discuss; I am as little prepared to do so now as when we talked at Exeter. That chapter in my life is happily over. As soon as I am established again in a place like that I had at Rotherhithe, I shall be quite contented.'

'Contented?' She smiled incredulously. 'For how long?'

'Who can say? I have lost the habit of looking far forward.'

Marcella kept silence so long that he concluded she had nothing more to say to him. It was an opportunity for taking leave without emotional stress, and he rose from his chair.

'Don't go yet,' she said at once. 'It wasn't only this that I'——

Her voice was checked.

'Can I be of any use to you in Bristol?' Peak asked, determined to avoid the trial he saw approaching.

'There is something more I wanted to say,' she pursued, seeming not to hear him. 'You pretend to be contented, but I know that is impossible. You talk of going back to a dull routine of toil, when what you most desire is freedom. I want—if I can—to help you.'

Again she failed to command her voice. Godwin raised his eyes, and was astonished at the transformation she had suddenly undergone. Her face, instead of being colourless and darkly vehement, had changed to a bright warmth, a smiling radiance such as would have become a happy girl. His look seemed to give her courage.

'Only hear me patiently. We are such old friends—are we not? We have so often proclaimed our scorn of conventionality, and why should a conventional fear hinder what I want to say? You know—don't you?—that I have far more money than I need or am ever likely to. I want only a few hundreds a year, and I have more than a thousand.' She spoke more and more quickly, fearful of being interrupted. 'Why shouldn't I give you some of my superfluity? Let me help you in this way. Money can do so much. Take some from me, and use it as you will—just as you will. It is useless to *me*. Why shouldn't someone whom I wish well benefit by it?'

Godwin was not so much surprised as disconcerted. He knew that Marcella's nature was of large mould, and that whether she acted for good or evil its promptings would be anything but commonplace. The ardour with which she pleaded, and the magnitude of the benefaction she desired to bestow upon him, so affected his imagination that for the moment he stood as if doubting what reply to make. The doubt really in his mind was whether Marcella had calculated upon his weakness, and hoped to draw him within her power by the force of such an obligation, or if in truth she sought only to appease her heart with the exercise of generosity.

'You will let me?' she panted forth, watching him with brilliant eyes. 'This shall be a secret for ever between you and me. It imposes no debt of gratitude—how I despise the thought! I give you what is worthless to me,—except that it can do *you* good. But you can thank me if you will. I am not above being thanked.' She laughed unnaturally. 'Go and travel at first, as you wished to. Write me a short letter every month—every two months, just that I may know you are enjoying your life. It is agreed, isn't it?'

She held her hand to him, but Peak drew away, his face averted.

'How can you give me the pain of refusing such an offer?' he exclaimed, with remonstrance which was all but anger. 'You know the thing is utterly impossible. I should be ridiculous if I argued about it for a moment.'

'I can't see that it is impossible.'

'Then you must take my word for it. But I have no right to speak to you in that way,' he added, more kindly, seeing the profound humiliation which fell upon her. 'You meant to come to my aid at a time when I seemed to you lonely and miserable. It was a generous impulse, and I do indeed thank you. I shall always remember it and be grateful to you.'

Marcella's face was again in shadow. Its lineaments hardened to an expression of cold, stern dignity.

'I have made a mistake,' she said. 'I thought you above common ways of thinking.'

'Yes, you put me on too high a pedestal,' Peak answered, trying to speak humorously. 'One of my faults is that I am apt to mistake my own position in the same way.'

'You think yourself ambitious. Oh, if you knew really great

ambition! Go back to your laboratory, and work for wages. I would have saved you from that.'

The tone was not vehement, but the words bit all the deeper for their unimpassioned accent. Godwin could make no reply.

'I hope,' she continued, 'we may meet a few years hence. By that time you will have learnt that what I offered was not impossible. You will wish you had dared to accept it. I know what your *ambition* is. Wait till you are old enough to see it in its true light. How you will scorn yourself! Surely there was never a man who united such capacity for great things with so mean an ideal. You will never win even the paltry satisfaction on which you have set your mind—never! But you can't be made to understand that. You will throw away all the best part of your life. Meet me in a few years, and tell me the story of the interval.'

'I will engage to do that, Marcella.'

'You will? But not to tell me the truth. You will not dare to tell the truth.'

'Why not?' he asked, indifferently. 'Decidedly I shall owe it you in return for your frankness to-day. Till then—good-bye.'

She did not refuse her hand, and as he moved away she watched him with a smile of slighting good-nature.

On the morrow Godwin was back in Bristol, and there he dwelt for another six months, a period of mental and physical lassitude. Earwaker corresponded with him, and urged him to attempt the work that had been proposed, but such effort was beyond his power.

He saw one day in a literary paper an announcement that Reusch's *Bibel und Natur* was about to be published in an English translation. So someone else had successfully finished the work he undertook nearly two years ago. He amused himself with the thought that he could ever have persevered so long in such profitless labour, and with a contemptuous laugh he muttered '*Thohu wabohu*.'

Just when the winter had set in, he received an offer of a post in chemical works at St. Helen's, and without delay travelled northwards. The appointment was a poor one, and seemed unlikely to be a step to anything better, but his resources would not last more than another half year, and employment of whatever kind came as welcome relief to the tedium of his existence. Established in his new abode, he at length wrote to Sidwell. She answered him at once in a short letter which he might have shown to anyone, so calm were its expressions of interest, so uncompromising its words of congratulation. It began 'Dear Mr. Peak,' and ended with 'Yours sincerely.' Well, he had used the same formalities, and had uttered his feelings with scarcely more of warmth. Disappointment troubled him for a moment, and for a moment only. He was so far from Exeter, and further still from the life that he had led there. It seemed to him all but certain that Sidwell wrote coldly, with the intention of discouraging his hopes. What hope was he so foolish as to entertain? His position poorer than ever, what could justify him in writing love-letters to a girl who, even if willing to marry him, must not do so until he had a suitable home to offer her?

Since his maturity, he had never known so long a freedom from passion. One day he wrote to Earwaker: 'I begin to understand your independence with regard to women. It would be a strange thing if I became a convert to that way of thinking, but once or twice of late I have imagined that it was happening. My mind has all but recovered its tone, and I am able to read, to think—I mean really to *think*, not to muse. I get through big and solid books. Presently, if your offer still hold good, I shall send you a scrap of writing on something or other. The pestilent atmosphere of this place seems to invigorate me. Last Saturday evening I took train, got away into the hills, and spent the Sunday geologising. And a curious experience befell me,—one I had long, long ago, in the Whitelaw days. Sitting down before some interesting strata, I lost myself in something like nirvana, grew so subject to the idea of vastness in geological time that all human desires and purposes shrivelled to ridiculous unimportance. Awaking for a minute, I tried to realise the passion which not long ago rent and racked me, but I was flatly incapable of understanding it. Will this philosophic state endure? Perhaps I have used up all my emotional energy? I hardly know whether to hope or fear it.'

About midsummer, when his short holiday (he would only be released for a fortnight) drew near, he was surprised by another letter from Sidwell. 'I am anxious,' she wrote, 'to hear that you are well. It is more than half a year since your last letter, and of late I have been constantly expecting a few lines. The spring has been a time of trouble with us. A distant relative, an old and feeble lady who has passed her life in a little Dorsetshire village, came to see us in April, and in less than a fortnight she was seized with illness and died. Then Fanny had an attack of bronchitis, from which even now she is not altogether recovered. On her account we are all going to Royat, and I think we shall be away until the end of September. Will you let me hear from you before I leave England, which will be in a week's time? Don't refrain from writing because you think you have no news to send. Anything that interests you is of interest to me. If it is only to tell me what you have been reading, I shall be glad of a letter.'

It was still 'Yours sincerely'; but Godwin felt that the letter meant more. In re-reading it he was pleasantly thrilled with a stirring of the old emotions. But his first impulse, to write an ardent reply, did not carry him away; he reflected and took counsel of the experience gained in his studious solitude. It was evident that by keeping silence he had caused Sidwell to throw off something of her reserve. The course dictated by prudence was to maintain an attitude of dignity, to hold himself in check. In this way he would regain what he had so disastrously lost, Sidwell's respect. There was a distinct pleasure in this exercise of self-command; it was something new to him; it flattered his pride. 'Let her learn that, after all, I am her superior. Let her fear to lose me. Then, if her love is still to be depended upon, she will before long find a way to our union. It is in her power, if only she wills it.'

So he sat down and wrote a short letter which seemed to him a model of dignified expression.

IV

SIDWELL TOOK NO one into her confidence. The case was not one for counsel; whatever her future action, it must result from the maturing of self-knowledge, from the effect of circumstance upon her mind and heart. For the present she could live in silence. 'We hear,' she wrote from London to Sylvia Moorhouse, 'that Mr. Peak has left Exeter, and that he is not likely to carry out his intention of being ordained. You, I dare say, will feel no surprise.' Nothing more than that; and Sylvia's comments in reply were equally brief.

Martin Warricombe, after conversations with his wife and with Buckland, felt it impossible not to seek for an understanding of Sidwell's share in the catastrophe. He was gravely perturbed, feeling that with himself lay the chief responsibility for what had happened. Buckland's attitude was that of the man who can only keep repeating 'I told you so'; Mrs. Warricombe could only lament and upbraid in the worse than profitless fashion natural to women of her stamp. But in his daughter Martin had every kind of faith, and he longed to speak to her without reserve. Two days after her return from Exeter, he took Sidwell apart, and, with a distressing sense of the delicacy of the situation, tried to persuade her to frank utterance.

'I have been hearing strange reports,' he began, gravely, but without show of displeasure. 'Can you help me to understand the real facts of the case, Sidwell?—What is your view of Peak's behaviour?'

'He has deceived you, father,' was the quiet reply.

'You are convinced of that?—It allows of no——?'

'It can't be explained away. He pretended to believe what he did not and could not believe.'

'With interested motives, then?'

'Yes.—But not motives in themselves dishonourable.'

There was a pause. Sidwell had spoken in a steady voice, though with eyes cast down. Whether her father could understand a position such as Godwin's, she felt uncertain. That he would honestly endeavour to do so, there could be no doubt, especially since he must suspect that her own desire was to distinguish between the man and his fault. But a revelation of all that had passed between her and Peak was not possible; she had the support neither of intellect nor of passion; it would be asking for guidance, the very thing she had determined not to do. Already she found it difficult to recover the impulses which had directed her in that scene of parting; to talk of it would be to see her action in such a doubtful light that she might be led to some premature and irretrievable resolve. The only trustworthy counsellor was time; on what time brought forth must depend her future.

'Do you mean, Sidwell,' resumed her father, 'that you think it possible for us to overlook this deception?'

She delayed a moment, then said:

'I don't think it possible for you to regard him as a friend.'

Martin's face expressed relief.

'But will he remain in Exeter?'

'I shouldn't think he can.'

Again a pause. Martin was of course puzzled exceedingly, but he began to feel some assurance that Peak need not be regarded as a danger.

'I am grieved beyond expression,' he said at length. 'So deliberate a fraud—it seems to me inconsistent with any of the qualities I thought I saw in him.'

'Yes—it must.'

'Not—perhaps—to you?' Martin ventured, anxiously.

'His nature is not base.'

'Forgive me, dear.—I understand that you spoke with him after Buckland's call at his lodgings——?'

'Yes, I saw him.'

'And—he strove to persuade you that he had some motive which justified his conduct?'

'Excused, rather than justified.'

'Not—it seems—to your satisfaction?'

'I can't answer that question, father. My experience of life is too slight. I can only say that untruthfulness in itself is abhorrent to me, and that I could never try to make it seem a light thing.'

'That, surely, is a sound view, think as we may on speculative points. But allow me one more question, Sidwell. Does it seem to you that I have no choice but to break off all communication with Mr. Peak?'

It was the course dictated by his own wish, she knew. And what could be gained by any middle way between hearty good-will and complete repudiation? Time—time alone must work out the problem.

'Yes, I think you have no choice,' she answered.

'Then I must make inquiries—see if he leaves the town.'

'Mr. Lilywhite will know, probably.'

'I will write before long.'

So the dialogue ended, and neither sought to renew it.

Martin enjoined upon his wife a discreet avoidance of the subject. The younger members of the family were to know nothing of what had happened, and, if possible, the secret must be kept from friends at Exeter. When a fortnight had elapsed, he wrote to Mr. Lilywhite, asking whether it was true that Peak had gone away. 'It seems that private circumstances have obliged him to give up his project of taking Orders. Possibly he has had a talk with you?' The clergyman replied that Peak had left Exeter. 'I have had a letter from him, explaining in general terms his change of views. It hardly surprises me that he has reconsidered the matter. I don't think he was cut out for clerical work. He is far more likely to distinguish himself in the world of science. I suspect that conscientious scruples may have something to do with it; if so, all honour to him!'

The Warricombes prolonged their stay in London until the end of June. On their return home, Martin was relieved to find that scarcely an inquiry was made of him concerning Peak. The young man's disappearance excited no curiosity in the good people who had come in contact with him, and who were so far from suspecting what a notable figure had passed across their placid vision. One person only was urgent in his questioning. On an afternoon when Mrs. Warricombe and her daughters were alone, the Rev. Bruno Chilvers made a call.

'Oh!' he exclaimed, after a few minutes' conversation. 'I am so anxious to ask you what has become of Mr. Peak. Soon after my arrival in Exeter, I went to see him, and we had a long talk—a most interesting talk. Then I heard all at once that he was gone, and that we should see no more of him. Where is he? What is he doing?'

There was a barely appreciable delay before Mrs. Warricombe made answer.

'We have quite lost sight of him,' she said, with an artificial smile. 'We know only that he was called away on some urgent business—family affairs, I suppose.'

Chilvers, in the most natural way, glanced from the speaker to Sidwell, and instantly, without the slightest change of expression, brought his eyes back again.

'I hope most earnestly,' he went on, in his fluty tone, 'that he will return. A most interesting man! A man of *large* intellectual scope, and really *broad* sympathies. I looked forward to many a chat with him. Has he, I wonder, been led to change his views? Possibly he would find a secular sphere more adapted to his special powers.'

Mrs. Warricombe had nothing to say. Sidwell, finding that Mr. Chilvers' smile now beamed in her direction, replied to him with steady utterance:

'It isn't uncommon, I think, nowadays, for doubts to interfere with the course of study for ordination?'

'Far from uncommon!' exlaimed the Rector of St. Margaret's, with almost joyous admission of the fact. 'Very far from uncommon. Such students have my profound sympathy. I know from experience exactly what it means to be overcome in a struggle with the modern spirit. Happily for myself, I was enabled to recover what for a time I lost. But charity forbid that I should judge those who think they must needs voyage for ever in "sunless gulfs of doubt," or even absolutely deny that the human intellect can be enlightened from above.'

At a loss even to follow this rhetoric, Mrs. Warricombe, who was delighted to welcome the Rev. Bruno, and regarded him as a gleaming pillar of the Church, made haste to introduce a safer topic. After that, Mr. Chilvers was seen at the house with some frequency. Not that he paid more attention to the Warricombes than to his other acquaintances. Relieved by his curate from the uncongenial burden of mere parish affairs, he seemed to regard himself as an apostle at large, whose mission directed him to the households of well-to-do people throughout the city. His brother clergymen held him in slight esteem. In private talk with Martin Warricombe, Mr. Lilywhite did not hesitate to call him 'a mountebank,' and to add other depreciatory remarks.

'My wife tells me—and I can trust her judgment in such things—that his sole object just now is to make a good marriage. Rather disagreeable stories seem to have followed him from the other side of England. He makes love to all unmarried women—never going beyond what is thought permissible, but doing a good deal of mischief, I fancy. One lady in Exeter—I won't mention names—has already pulled him up with a direct inquiry as to his intentions; at her house, I imagine, he will no more be seen.'

The genial parson chuckled over his narrative, and Martin, by no means predisposed in the Rev. Bruno's favour, took care to report these matters to his wife.

'I don't believe a word of it!' exclaimed Mrs. Warricombe. 'All the clergy are jealous of Mr. Chilvers.'

'What? Of his success with ladies?'

'Martin! It is something new for you to be profane!—They are jealous of his high reputation.'

'Rather a serious charge against our respectable friends.'

'And the stories are all nonsense,' pursued Mrs. Warricombe. 'It's very wrong of Mr. Lilywhite to report such things. I don't believe any other clergyman would have done so.'

Martin smiled—as he had been accustomed to do all through his married life—and let the discussion rest there. On the next occasion of Mr. Chilvers being at the house, he observed the reverend man's behaviour with Sidwell, and was not at all pleased. Bruno had a way of addressing women which certainly went beyond the ordinary limits of courtesy. At a little distance, anyone would have concluded that he was doing his best to excite Sidwell's affectionate interest. The matter of his discourse might be unobjectionable, but the manner of it was not in good taste.

Mrs. Warricombe was likewise observant, but with other emotions. To her it seemed a subject for pleasurable reflection, that Mr. Chilvers should show interest in Sidwell. The Rev. Bruno had bright prospects. With the colour of his orthodoxy she did not concern herself. He was ticketed 'broad,' a term which carried with it no disparagement; and Sidwell's sympathies were altogether with the men of 'breadth.' The time drew near when Sidwell must marry, if she ever meant to do so, and in comparison with such candidates as Mr. Walsh and Godwin Peak, the Rector of St. Margaret's would be an ideal husband for her. Sidwell's attitude towards Mr. Chilvers was not encouraging, but Mrs. Warricombe suspected that a lingering regard for the impostor, so lately unmasked, still troubled her daughter's mind: a new suitor, even if rejected, would help the poor girl to dismiss that shocking infatuation.

Sidwell and her father nowadays spent much time together, and in the autumn days it became usual for them to have an afternoon ramble about the lanes. Their talk was of science and literature, occasionally skirting very close upon those questions which both feared to discuss plainly—for a twofold reason. Sidwell read much more than had been her wont, and her choice of authors would alone have indicated a change in her ways of thinking, even if she had not allowed it to appear in the tenor of her talk. The questions she put with reference to Martin's favourite studies were sometimes embarrassing.

One day they happened to meet Mr. Chilvers, who was driving with his eldest child, a boy of four. The narrowness of the road made it impossible—as Martin would have wished—to greet and pass on. Chilvers stopped the carriage and jumped out. Sidwell could not but pay some attention to the youthful Chilvers.

'Till he is ten years old,' cried Bruno, 'I shall think much more of his body than of his mind. In fact, at this age the body *is* the mind. Books, books—oh, we attach far too much importance to them. Over-study is one of the morbific tendencies of our time. Some one or other has been trying to frown down what he calls the excessive athleticism of our public schools. No, no! Let us rejoice that our lads have such an opportunity of vigorous physical development. The culture of the body is a great part of religion.' He always uttered remarks of this kind as if suggesting that his hearers should note them in a collection of aphorisms. 'If to labour is to pray, so also is the practice of open-air recreation.'

When they had succeeded in getting away, father and daughter walked for some minutes without speaking. At length Sidwell asked, with a smile:

'How does this form of Christianity strike you?'

'Why, very much like a box on the ear with a perfumed glove,' replied Martin.

'That describes it very well.'

They walked a little further, and Sidwell spoke in a more serious tone.

'If Mr. Chilvers were brought before the ecclesiastical authorities and compelled to make a clear statement of his faith, what sect, in all the history of heresies, would he really seem to belong to?'

'I know too little of him, and too little of heresies.'

'Do you suppose for a moment that he sincerely believes the dogmas of his Church?'

Martin bit his lips and looked uneasy.

'We can't judge him, Sidwell.'

'I don't know,' she persisted. 'It seems to me that he does his best to give us the means of judging him. I half believe that he often laughs in himself at the success of his audacity.'

'No, no. I think the man is sincere.'

This was very uncomfortable ground, but Sidwell would not avoid it. Her eyes flashed, and she spoke with a vehemence such as Martin had never seen in her.

'Undoubtedly sincere in his determination to make a figure in the world. But a Christian, in any intelligible sense of that much-abused word,—no! He is one type of the successful man of our day. Where thousands of better and stronger men struggle vainly for fair recognition, he and his kind are glorified. In comparison with a really energetic man, he is an acrobat. The crowd stares at him and applauds, and there is nothing he cares for so much as that kind of admiration.'

Martin kept silence, and in a few minutes succeeded in broaching a wholly different subject.

Not long after this, Mr. Chilvers paid a call at the conventional hour. Sidwell, hoping to escape, invited two girls to step out with her on to the lawn. The sun was sinking, and, as she stood with eyes fixed upon it, the Rev. Bruno's voice disagreeably broke her reverie. She was perforce involved in a dialogue, her companions moving aside.

'What a magnificent sky!' murmured Chilvers. ' "There sinks the nebulous star." Forgive me, I have fallen into a tiresome trick of quoting. How differently a sunset is viewed nowadays from what it was in old times! Our impersonal emotions are on a higher plane—don't you think so? Yes, scientific discovery has done more for religion that all the ages of pious imagination. A theory of Galileo or Newton is more to the soul than a psalm of David.'

'You think so?' Sidwell asked, coldly.

In everyday conversation she was less suave than formerly. This summer she had never worn her spray of sweet-brier, and the omission might have been deemed significant of a change in herself. When the occasion offered, she no longer hesitated to express a difference of opinion; at times she uttered her dissent with a bluntness which recalled Buckland's manner in private.

'Does the comparison seem to you unbecoming?' said Chilvers, with genial condescension. 'Or untrue?'

'What do you mean by "the soul"?' she inquired, still gazing away from him.

'The principle of conscious life in man—that which understands and worships.'

'The two faculties seem to me so different that'—— She broke off. 'But I mustn't talk foolishly about such things.'

'I feel sure you have thought of them to some purpose. I wonder whether you ever read Francis Newman's book on *The Soul*?'

'No, I never saw it.'

'Allow me to recommend it to you. I believe you would find it deeply interesting.'

'Does the Church approve it?'

'The Church?' He smiled. 'Ah! what Church? Churchmen there are, unfortunately, who detest the name of its author, but I hope you have never classed me among them. The Church, rightly understood, comprehends every mind and heart that is striving upwards. The age of intolerance will soon be as remote from us as that of persecution. Can I be mistaken in thinking that this broader view has your sympathy, Miss Warricombe?'

'I can't sympathise with what I don't understand, Mr. Chilvers.'

He looked at her with tender solicitude, bending slightly from his usual square-shouldered attitude.

'Do let me find an opportunity of talking over the whole matter with you—by no means as an instructor. In my view, a clergyman may seek instruction from the humblest of those who are called his flock. The thoughtful and high-minded among them will often assist him materially in his endeavour at self-development. To my "flock," ' he continued, playfully, 'you don't belong; but may I not count you one of that circle of friends to whom I look for the higher kind of sympathy?'

Sidwell glanced about her in the hope that some one might be approaching. Her two friends were at a distance, talking and laughing together.

'You shall tell me some day,' she replied, with more attention to courtesy, 'what the doctrines of the Broad Church really are. But the air grows too cool to be pleasant; hadn't we better return to the drawing-room?'

The greater part of the winter went by before she had again to submit to a *tête-à-tête* with the Rev. Bruno. It was seldom that she thought of him save when compelled to do so by his exacting presence, but in the meantime he exercised no small influence on her mental life. Insensibly she was confirmed in her alienation from all accepted forms of religious faith. Whether she wished it or not, it was inevitable that such a process should keep her constantly in mind of Godwin Peak. Her desire to talk with him at times became so like passion that she appeared to herself to love him more truly than ever. Yet such a mood was always followed by doubt, and she could not say whether the reaction distressed or soothed her. These months that had gone by brought one result, not to be disguised. Whatever the true nature of her feeling for Godwin, the thought of marrying him was so difficult to face that it seemed to involve impossibilities. He himself had warned her that marriage would mean severance from all her kindred. It was practically true, and time would only increase the difficulty of such a determination.

The very fact that her love (again, if love it were) must be indulged in defiance of universal opinion tended to keep emotion alive. A woman is disposed to cling to a lover who has disgraced himself, especially if she can believe that the disgrace was incurred as a result of devotion to her. Could love be separated from thought of marriage, Sidwell would have encouraged herself in fidelity, happy in the prospect of a life-long spiritual communion—for she would not doubt of Godwin's upward progress, of his eventual purification. But this was a mere dream. If Godwin's passion were steadfast, the day would come when she must decide either to cast in her lot with his, or to bid him be free. And could she imagine herself going forth into exile?

There came a letter from him, and she was fortunate enough to receive it without the knowledge of her relatives. He wrote that he had obtained employment. The news gave her a troubled joy, lasting for several days. That no emotion appeared in her reply was due to a fear lest she might be guilty of misleading him. Perhaps already she had done so. Her last whisper—'Some day!' —was it not a promise and an appeal? Now she had not the excuse of profound agitation, there must be no word her conscience could not justify. But in writing those formal lines she felt herself a coward. She was drawing back—preparing her escape.

Often she had the letter beneath her pillow. It was the first she had ever received from a man who professed to love her. So long without romance in her life, she could not but entertain this semblance of it, and feel that she was still young.

It told much in Godwin's favour that he had not ventured to write before there was this news to send her. It testified to the force of his character, the purity of his purpose. A weaker man, she knew, would have tried to excite her compassion by letters of mournful strain, might even have distressed her with attempts at clandestine meeting. She had said rightly—his nature was not base. And she loved him! She was passionately grateful to him for proving that her love had not been unworthily bestowed.

When he wrote again, her answer should not be cowardly.

The life of the household went on as it had been wont to do for years, but with the spring came events. An old lady died whilst on a visit to the house (she was a half-sister of Mrs. Warricombe), and by a will executed a few years previously she left a thousand pounds, to be equally divided between the children of this family. Sidwell smiled sadly on finding herself in possession of this bequest, the first sum of any importance that she had ever held in her own right. If she married a man of whom all her kith and kin so strongly disapproved that they would not give her even a wedding present, two hundred and fifty pounds would be better than no dowry at all. One could furnish a house with it.

Then Fanny had an attack of bronchitis, and whilst she was recovering Buckland came down for a few days, bringing with him a piece of news for which no one was prepared. As if to make reparation to his elder sister for the harshness with which he had behaved in the affair of Godwin Peak, he chose her for his first confidante.

'Sidwell, I am going to be married. Do you care to hear about it?'

'Certainly I do.'

Long ago she had been assured of Sylvia Moorhouse's sincerity in rejecting Buckland's suit. That was still a grief to her, but she acknowledged her friend's wisdom, and was now very curious to learn who it was that the Radical had honoured with his transferred affections.

'The lady's name,' Buckland began, 'is Miss Matilda Renshaw. She is the second daughter of a dealer in hides, tallow, and that kind of thing. Both her parents are dead; she has lived of late with her married sister at Blackheath.'

Sidwell listened with no slight astonishment, and her countenance looked what she felt.

'That's the bald statement of the cause,' pursued her brother, seeming to enjoy the consternation he had excited. 'Now, let me fill up the outline. Miss Renshaw is something more than good-looking, has had an admirable education, is five-and-twenty, and for a couple of years has been actively engaged in humanitarian work in the East End. She has published a book on social questions, and is a very good public speaker. Finally, she owns property representing between three and four thousand a year.'

'The picture has become more attractive,' said Sidwell.

'You imagined a rather different person? If I persuade mother to invite her down here presently, do you think you could be friendly with her?'

'I see no reason why I should not be.'

'But I must warn you. She has nothing to do with creeds and dogmas.'

He tried to read her face. Sidwell's mind was a mystery to him.

'I shall make no inquiry about her religious views,' his sister replied, in a dispassionate tone, which conveyed no certain meaning.

'Then I feel sure you will like her, and equally sure that she will like you.'

His parents had no distinct fault to find with this choice though they would both greatly have preferred a daughter-in-law whose genealogy could be more freely spoken of. Miss Renshaw was invited to Exeter, and the first week of June saw her arrival. Buckland had in no way exaggerated her qualities. She was a dark-eyed beauty, perfect from the social point of view, a very interesting talker,—in short, no ordinary woman. That Buckland should have fallen in love with her, even after

Sylvia, was easily understood; it seemed likely that she would make him as good a wife as he could ever hope to win.

Sidwell was expecting another letter from the north of England. The silence which during those first months had been justifiable was now a source of anxiety. But whether fear or hope predominated in her expectancy, she still could not decide. She had said to herself that her next reply should not be cowardly, yet she was as far as ever from a courageous resolve.

Mental harassment told upon her health. Martin, watching her with solicitude, declared that for her sake as much as for Fanny's they must have a thorough holiday abroad.

Urged by the approaching departure, Sidwell overcame her reluctance to write to Godwin before she had a letter to answer. It was done in a mood of intolerable despondency, when life looked barren before her, and the desire of love all but triumphed over every other consideration. The letter written and posted, she would gladly have recovered it—reserved, formal as it was. Cowardly still; but then Godwin had not written.

She kept a watch upon the postman, and again, when Godwin's reply was delivered, escaped detection.

Hardly did she dare to open the envelope. Her letter had perchance been more significant than she supposed; and did not the mere fact of her writing invite a lover's frankness?

But the reply was hardly more moving than if it had come from a total stranger. For a moment she felt relieved; in an hour's time she suffered indescribable distress. Godwin wrote—so she convinced herself after repeated perusals—as if discharging a task; not a word suggested tenderness. Had the letter been unsolicited, she could have used it like the former one; but it was the answer to an appeal. The phrases she had used were still present in her mind. 'I am anxious . . . it is more than half a year since you wrote . . . I have been expecting . . . anything that is of interest to you will interest me . . .' How could she imagine that this was reserved and formal? Shame fell upon her; she locked herself from all companionship, and wept in rebellion against the laws of life.

A fortnight later, she wrote from Royat to Sylvia Moorhouse. It was a long epistle, full of sunny descriptions, breathing renewed vigour of body and mind. The last paragraph ran thus:

'Yesterday was my birthday; I was twenty-eight. At this age, it is wisdom in a woman to remind herself that youth is over. I don't regret it; let it go with all its follies! But I am sorry that I have no serious work in life; it is not cheerful to look forward to perhaps another eight-and-twenty years of elegant leisure—that is to say, of wearisome idleness. What can I do? Try and think of some task for me, something that will last a lifetime.'

PART THE SEVENTH

I

AT THE CLOSE of a sultry day in September, when factory fumes hung low over the town of St. Helen's, and twilight thickened luridly, and the air tasted of sulphur, and the noises of the streets, muffled in their joint effect, had individually an ominous distinctness, Godwin Peak walked with languid steps to his lodgings and the meal that there awaited him. His vitality was at low ebb. The routine of his life disgusted him; the hope of release was a mockery. What was to be the limit of this effort to redeem his character? How many years before the past could be forgotten, and his claim to the style of honourable be deemed secure? Rubbish! It was an idea out of old-fashioned romances. What he was, he was, and no extent of dogged duration at St. Helen's or elsewhere, could affect his personality. What, practically, was to be the end? If Sidwell had no money of her own, and no expectations from her father, how could she ever become his wife? Women liked this kind of thing, this indefinite engagement to marry when something should happen, which in all likelihood never would happen—this fantastic mutual fidelity with only the airiest reward. Especially women of a certain age.

A heavy cart seemed to be rumbling in the next street. No, it was thunder. If only a good rattling storm would sweep the bituminous atmosphere, and allow a breath of pure air before midnight.

She could not be far from thirty. Of course there prevails much conventional nonsense about women's age; there are plenty of women who reckon four decades, and yet retain all the essential charm of their sex. And as a man gets older, as he begins to persuade himself that at forty one has scarce reached the prime of life —

The storm was coming on in earnest. Big drops began to fall. He quickened his pace, reached home, and rang the bell for a light.

His landlady came in with the announcement that a gentleman had called to see him, about an hour ago; he would come again at seven o'clock.

'What name?'

None had been given. A youngish gentleman, speaking like a Londoner.

It might be Earwaker, but that was not likely. Godwin sat down to his plain meal, and after it lit a pipe. Thunder was still rolling, but now in the distance. He waited impatiently for seven o'clock.

To the minute, sounded a knock at the house-door. A little delay, and there appeared Christian Moxey.

Godwin was surprised and embarrassed. His visitor had a very grave face, and was thinner, paler, than three years ago; he appeared to hesitate, but at length offered his hand.

'I got your address from Earwaker. I was obliged to see you—on business.'

'Business?'

'May I take my coat off? We shall have to talk.'

They sat down, and Godwin, unable to strike the note of friendship lest he should be met with repulse, broke silence by regretting that Moxey should have had to make a second call.

'Oh, that's nothing! I went and had dinner.—Peak, my sister is dead.'

Their eyes met; something of the old kindness rose to either face.

'That must be a heavy blow to you,' murmured Godwin, possessed with a strange anticipation which he would not allow to take clear form.

'It is. She was ill for three months. Whilst staying in the country last June she met with an accident. She went for a long walk alone one day, and in a steep lane she came up with a carter who was trying to make a wretched horse drag a load beyond its strength. The fellow was perhaps half drunk; he stood there beating the horse unmercifully. Marcella couldn't endure that kind of thing—impossible for her to pass on and say nothing. She interfered, and tried to persuade the man to lighten his cart.

He was insolent, attacked the horse more furiously than ever, and kicked it so violently in the stomach that it fell. Even then he wouldn't stop his brutality. Marcella tried to get between him and the animal—just as it lashed out with its heels. The poor girl was so badly injured that she lay by the roadside until another carter took her up and brought her back to the village. Three months of accursed suffering, and then happily came the end.'

A far, faint echoing of thunder filled the silence of their voices. Heavy rain splashed upon the pavement.

'She said to me just before her death,' resumed Christian, '"I have ill luck when I try to do a kindness—but perhaps there is one more chance." I didn't know what she meant till afterwards. Peak, she has left nearly all her money to you.'

Godwin knew it before the words were spoken. His heart leaped, and only the dread of being observed enabled him to control his features. When his tongue was released he said harshly:

'Of course I can't accept it.'

The words were uttered independently of his will. He had no such thought, and the sound of his voice shook him with alarm.

'Why can't you?' returned Christian.

'I have no right—it belongs to you, or to some other relative—it would be'——

His stammering broke off. Flushes and chills ran through him; he could not raise his eyes from the ground.

'It belongs to no one but you,' said Moxey, with cold persistence. 'Her last wish was to do you a kindness, and I, at all events, shall never consent to frustrate her intention. The legacy represents something more than eight hundred a year, as the investments now stand. This will make you independent—of everything and everybody.' He looked meaningly at the listener. 'Her own life was not a very happy one; she did what she could to save yours from a like doom.'

Godwin at last looked up.

'Did she speak of me during her illness?'

'She asked me once, soon after the accident, what had become of you. As I knew from Earwaker, I was able to tell her.'

A long silence followed. Christian's voice was softer when he resumed.

'You never knew her. She was the one women in ten thousand—at once strong and gentle; a fine intellect, and a heart of rare tenderness. But because she had not the kind of face that'——

He checked himself.

'To the end her mind kept its clearness and courage. One day she reminded me of Heine—how we had talked of that "conversion" on the mattress-grave, and had pitied the noble intellect subdued by disease. "I shan't live long enough," she said, "to incur that danger. What I have thought ever since I could study, I think now, and shall to the last moment." I buried her without forms of any kind, in the cemetery at Kingsmill. That was what she wished. I should have despised myself if I had lacked that courage.'

'It was right,' muttered Godwin.

'And I wear no mourning, you see. All that kind of thing is ignoble. I am robbed of a priceless companionship, but I don't care to go about inviting people's pity. If only I could forget those months of suffering! Some day I shall, perhaps, and think of her only as she lived.'

'Were you alone with her all the time?'

'No. Our cousin Janet was often with us.' Christian spoke with averted face. 'You don't know, of course, that she has gone in for medical work—practises at Kingsmill. The accident was at a village called Lowton, ten miles or more from Kingsmill. Janet came over very often.'

Godwin mused on this development of the girl whom he remembered so well. He could not direct his thoughts; a languor had crept over him.

'Do you recollect, Peak,' said Christian presently, 'the talk we had in the fields by Twybridge, when we first met?'

The old friendliness was reappearing in his manner. He was yielding to the impulse to be communicative, confidential, which had always characterised him.

'I remember,' Godwin murmured.

'If only my words then had had any weight with you! And if

only I had acted upon my own advice! Just for those few weeks I was sane; I understood something of life; I saw my true way before me. You and I have both gone after ruinous ideals, instead of taking the solid good held out to us. Of course, I know your story in outline. I don't ask you to talk about it. You are independent now, and I hope you can use your freedom.—Well, and I too am free.'

The last words were in a lower tone. Godwin glanced at the speaker, whose sadness was not banished, but illumined with a ray of calm hope.

'Have you ever thought of me and my infatuation?' Christian asked.

'Yes.'

'I have outlived that mawkish folly. I used to drink too much; the two things went well together. It would shame me to tell you all about it. But, happily, I have been able to go back about thirteen years—recover my old sane self—and with it what I then threw away.'

'I understand.'

'Do you? Marcella knew of it, just before her death, and it made her glad. But the waste of years, the best part of a lifetime! It's incredible to me as I look back. Janet called on us one day in London. Heaven be thanked that she was forgiving enough to do so! What would have become of me now?'

'How are you going to live, then?' Godwin asked, absently.

'How? My income is sufficient'——

'No, no; I mean, where and how will you live in your married life?'

'That's still uncertain. Janet mustn't go on with professional work. In any case, I don't think she could for long; her strength isn't equal to it. But I shouldn't wonder if we settle in Kingsmill. To you it would seem intolerable? But why should we live in London? At Kingsmill Janet has a large circle of friends; in London we know scarcely half-a-dozen people—of the kind it would give us any pleasure to live with. We shall have no lack of intellectual society; Janet knows some of the Whitelaw professors. The atmosphere of Kingsmill isn't illiberal, you know;

we shan't be fought shy of because we object to pass Sundays in a state of coma. But the years that I have lost! The irrecoverable years!'

'There's nothing so idle as regretting the past,' said Godwin, with some impatience. 'Why groan over what couldn't be otherwise? The probability is, Janet and you are far better suited to each other now than you ever would have been if you had married long ago.'

'You think that?' exclaimed the other eagerly. 'I have tried to see it in that light. If I didn't feel so despicable!'

'She, I take it, doesn't think you so,' Godwin muttered.

'But how can she understand? I have tried to tell her everything, but she refused to listen. Perhaps Marcella told her all she cared to know.'

'No doubt.'

Each brooded for a while over his own affairs, then Christian reverted to the subject which concerned them both.

'Let us speak frankly. You will take this gift of Marcella's as it was meant?'

How *was* it meant? Critic and analyst as ever, Godwin could not be content to see in it the simple benefaction of a woman who died loving him. Was it not rather the last subtle device of jealousy? Marcella knew that the legacy would be a temptation he could scarcely resist—and knew at the same time that, if he accepted it, he practically renounced his hope of marrying Sidwell Warricombe. Doubtless she had learned as much as she needed to know of Sidwell's position. Refusing this bequest, he was as far as ever from the possibility of asking Sidwell to marry him. Profiting by it, he stood for ever indebted to Marcella, must needs be grateful to her, and some day, assuredly, would reveal the truth to whatever woman became his wife. Conflict of reasonings and emotions made it difficult to answer Moxey's question.

'I must take time to think of it,' he said, at length.

'Well, I suppose that is right. But—well, I know so little of your circumstances'——

'Is that strictly true?' Peak asked.

'Yes. I have only the vaguest idea of what you have been doing since you left us. Of course I have tried to find out.'

Godwin smiled, rather gloomily.

'We won't talk of it. I suppose you stay in St. Helen's for the night?'

'There's a train at 10.20. I had better go by it.'

'Then let us forget everything but your own cheerful outlook. At ten, I'll walk with you to the station.'

Reluctantly at first, but before long with a quiet abandonment to the joy that would not be suppressed. Christian talked of his future wife. In Janet he found every perfection. Her mind was something more than the companion of his own. Already she had begun to inspire him with a hopeful activity, and to foster the elements of true manliness which he was conscious of possessing, though they had never yet had free play. With a sense of luxurious safety, he submitted to her influence, knowing none the less that it was in his power to complete her imperfect life. Studiously he avoided the word 'ideal'; from such vaporous illusions he had turned to the world's actualities; his language dealt with concretes, with homely satisfactions, with prospects near enough to be soberly examined.

A hurry to catch the train facilitated parting. Godwin promised to write in a few days.

He took a roundabout way back to his lodgings. The rain was over, the sky had become placid. He was conscious of an effect from Christian's conversation which half counteracted the mood he would otherwise have indulged,—the joy of liberty and of an outlook wholly new. Sidwell might perchance be to him all that Janct was to Christian. Was it not the luring of 'ideals' that prompted him to turn away from his long hope?

There must be no more untruthfulness. Sidwell must have all the facts laid before her, and make her choice.

Without a clear understanding of what he was going to write, he sat down at eleven o'clock, and began, 'Dear Miss Warricombe.' Why not 'Dear Sidwell'? He took another sheet of paper.

'Dear Sidwell,—Tonight I can remember only your last word to me when we parted. I cannot address you coldly, as though half a stranger. Thus long I have kept silence about everything but the outward events of my life; now, in telling you of something that has happened, I must speak as I think.

'Early this evening I was surprised by a visit from Christian Moxey—a name you know. He came to tell me that his sister (she of whom I once spoke to you) was dead, and had bequeathed to me a large sum of money. He said that it represented an income of eight hundred pounds.

'I knew nothing of Miss Moxey's illness, and the news of her will came to me as a surprise. In word or deed, I never sought more than her simple friendship—and even *that* I believed myself to have forfeited.

'If I were to refuse this money, it would be in consequence of a scruple which I do not in truth respect. Christian Moxey tells me that his sister's desire was to enable me to live the life of a free man, and if I have any duty at all in the matter, surely it does not constrain me to defeat her kindness. No condition whatever is attached. The gift releases me from the necessity of leading a hopeless existence—leaves me at liberty to direct my life how I will.

'I wish, then, to put aside all thoughts of how this opportunity came to me, and to ask you if you are willing to be my wife.

'Though I have never written a word of love, my love is unchanged. The passionate hope of three years ago still rules my life. Is *your* love strong enough to enable you to disregard all hindrances? I cannot of course know whether, in your sight, dishonour still clings to me, or whether you understand me well enough to have forgiven and forgotten those hateful things in the past. Is it yet too soon? Do you wish me still to wait, still to prove myself? Is your interest in the free man less than in the slave? For my life has been one of slavery and exile—exile, if you know what I mean by it, from the day of my birth.

'Dearest, grant me this great happiness! We can live where we will. I am not rich enough to promise all the comforts and refinements to which you are accustomed, but we should be safe from sordid anxieties. We can travel; we can make a home in any European city. It would be idle to speak of the projects and ambitions that fill my mind—but surely I may do something worth doing, win some position among intellectual men of which you would not be ashamed. You yourself urged me to hope that. With you at my side—Sidwell, grant me this chance, that I may know the joy of satisfied love! I am past the age which is misled by vain fancies. I have suffered unspeakably, longed for the calm strength, the pure, steady purpose which would result to me from a happy marriage. There is no fatal divergence between our minds; did you not tell me that? You said that if I had been truthful from the first, you might have loved me with no misgiving. Forget the madness into which I was betrayed. There is no soil upon my spirit. I offer you love as noble as many man is capable of. Think—think well—before replying to me; let your true self prevail. You *did* love me, dearest.—Yours ever,

'GODWIN PEAK.'

At first he wrote slowly, as though engaged on a literary composition, with erasions, insertions. Facts once stated, he allowed himself to forget how Sidwell would most likely view them, and thereafter his pen hastened: fervour inspired the last paragraph. Sidwell's image had become present to him, and exercised all—or near all—its old influence.

The letter must be copied, because of that laboured beginning. Copying one's own words is at all times a disenchanting drudgery, and when the end was reached Godwin signed his name with hasty contempt. What answer could he expect to such an appeal? How vast an improbability that Sidwell would consent to profit by the gift of Marcella Moxey!

Yet how otherwise could he write? With what show of sincerity could he offer to refuse the bequest? Nay, in that case he must not *offer* to do so, but simply state the fact that his refusal was beyond recall. Logically, he had chosen the only course open to him,—for to refuse independence was impossible.

A wheezy clock in his landlady's kitchen was striking two. For very fear of having to revise his letter in the morning, he put it into its envelope, and went out to the nearest pillar-post.

That was done. Whether Sidwell answered with 'Yes' or with 'No,' he was a free man.

On the morrow he went to his work as usual, and on the day after that. The third morning might bring a reply—but did not. On the evening of the fifth day, when he came home, there lay the expected letter. He felt it; it was light and thin. That hideous choking of suspense—— Well, it ran thus:

'I cannot. It is not that I am troubled by your accepting the legacy. You have every right to do so, and I know that your life will justify the hopes of her who thus befriended you. But I am too weak to take this step. To ask you to wait yet longer, would only be a fresh cowardice. You cannot know how it shames me to write this. In my very heart I believe I love you, but what is such love worth? You must despise me, and you will forget me. I live in a little world; in the greater world where your place is, you will win a love very different. S. W.'

Godwin laughed aloud as the paper dropped from his hand.

Well, she was not the heroine of a romance. Had he expected her to leave home and kindred—the 'little world' so infinitely dear to her—and go forth with a man deeply dishonoured? Very young girls have been known to do such a thing; but a thoughtful mature woman——! Present, his passion had dominated her; and perhaps her nerves only. But she had had time to recover from that weakness.

A woman, like most women, of cool blood, temperate fancies. A domestic woman; the ornament of a typical English home.

Most likely it was true that the matter of the legacy did not trouble her. In any case she would not have consented to marry him, and *therefore* she knew no jealousy. Her love! why, truly, what was it worth?

(Much, much! of no less than infinite value. He knew it, but this was not the moment for such a truth.)

A cup of tea to steady the nerves. Then thoughts, planning, world-building.

He was awake all night, and Sidwell's letter lay within reach.—

Did *she* sleep calmly? Had she never stretched out her hand for *his* letter, when all was silent? There were men who would not take such a refusal. A scheme to meet her once more—the appeal of passion, face to face, heart to heart—the means of escape ready—and then the 'greater world'——

But neither was he cast in heroic mould. He had not the self-confidence, he had not the hot, youthful blood. A critic of life, an analyst of moods and motives; not the man who dares and acts. The only important resolve he had ever carried through was a scheme of ignoble trickery—to end in frustration.

'The greater world.' It was a phrase that had been in his own mind once or twice since Moxey's visit. To point him thither was doubtless the one service Sidwell could render him. And in a day or two, that phrase was all that remained to him of her letter.

On a Sunday afternoon at the end of October, Godwin once more climbed the familiar stairs at Staple Inn, and was welcomed by his friend Earwaker. The visit was by appointment. Earwaker knew all about the legacy; that it was accepted; and that Peak had only a few days to spend in London, on his way to the Continent.

'You are regenerated,' was his remark as Godwin entered.

'Do I look it? Just what I feel. I have shaken off a good (or a bad) ten years.'

The speaker's face, at all events in this moment, was no longer that of a man at hungry issue with the world. He spoke cheerily.

'It isn't often that fortune does a man such a kind turn. One often hears it said: If only I could begin life again with all the experience I have gained! That is what I *can* do. I can break utterly with the past, and I have learnt how to live in the future.'

'Break utterly with the past?'

'In the practical sense. And even morally to a great extent.'

Earwaker pushed a box of cigars across the table. Godwin accepted the offer, and began to smoke. During these moments of silence, the man of letters had been turning over a weekly paper, as if in search of some paragraph; a smile announced his discovery.

'Here is something that will interest you—possibly you have seen it.'

He began to read aloud:

'"On the 23rd inst. was celebrated at St. Bragg's, Torquay, the marriage of the Rev. Bruno Leathwaite Chilvers, late Rector of St. Margaret's, Exeter, and the Hon. Bertha Harriet Cecilia Jute, eldest daughter of the late Baron Jute. The ceremony was conducted by the Hon. and Rev. J. C. Jute, uncle of the bride, assisted by the Rev. F. Miller, the Very Rev. Dean Pinnock, the Rev. H. S. Crook, and the Rev. William Tomkinson. The bride was given away by Lord Jute. Mr. Horatio Dukinfield was best man. The bridal dress was of white brocade, draped with Brussels lace, the corsage being trimmed with lace and adorned with orange blossoms. The tulle veil, fastened with three diamond stars, the gifts of"—— Well, shall I go on?'

'The triumph of Chilvers!' murmured Godwin. 'I wonder whether the Hon. Bertha is past her fortieth year?'

'A blooming beauty, I dare say. But Lord! how many people it takes to marry a man like Chilvers! How sacred the union must be!—Pray take a paragraph more: "The four bridesmaids—Miss —etc., etc.—wore cream crépon dresses trimmed with turquoise blue velvet, and hats to match. The bridegroom's presents to them were diamond and ruby brooches."'

'Chilvers *in excelsis!*—So he is no longer at Exeter; has no living, it seems. What does he aim at next, I wonder?'

Earwaker cast meaning glances at his friend.

'I understand you,' said Godwin, at length. 'You mean that this merely illustrates my own ambition. Well, you are right, I confess my shame—and there's an end of it.'

He puffed at his cigar, resuming presently:

'But it would be untrue if I said that I regretted anything. Constituted as I am, there was no other way of learning my real needs and capabilities. Much in the past is hateful to me, but it all had its use. There are men—why, take your own case. You look back on life, no doubt, with calm and satisfaction.'

'Rather, with resignation.'

Godwin let his cigar fall, and laughed bitterly.

'Your resignation has kept pace with life. I was always a rebel. My good qualities—I mean what I say—have always wrecked me. Now that I haven't to fight with circumstances, they may possibly be made subservient to my happiness.'

'But what form is your happiness to take?'

'Well, I am leaving England. On the Continent I shall make no fixed abode, but live in the places where cosmopolitan people are to be met. I shall make friends; with money at command, one may hope to succeed in that. Hotels, boarding-houses, and so on, offer the opportunities. It sounds oddly like the project of a swindler, doesn't it? There's the curse I can't escape from! Though my desires are as pure as those of any man living, I am compelled to express myself as if I were about to do something base and underhand. Simply because I have never had a social place. I am an individual merely; I belong to no class, town, family, club'——

'Cosmopolitan people,' mused Earwaker. 'Your ideal is transformed.'

'As you know. Experience only could bring that about. I seek now only the free, intellectual people—men who have done with the old conceptions—women who'——

His voice grew husky, and he did not complete the sentence.

'I shall find them in Paris, Rome.—Earwaker, think of my being able to speak like this! No day-dreams, but actual sober plans, their execution to begin in a day or two. Paris, Rome! And a month ago I was a hopeless slave in a vile manufacturing town.—I wish it were possible for me to pray for the soul of that poor dead woman. I don't speak to you of her; but do you imagine I am brutally forgetful of her to whom I owe all this?'

'I do you justice,' returned the other, quietly.

'I believe you can and do.'

'How grand it is to go forth as I am now going!' Godwin resumed, after a long pause. 'Nothing to hide, no shams, no pretences. Let who will inquire about me. I am an independent Englishman, with so and so much a year. In England I have one friend only—that is you. The result, you see, of all these years' savage striving to knit myself into the social fabric.'

'Well, you will invite me some day to your villa at Sorrento,' said Earwaker, encouragingly.

'That I shall!' Godwin's eyes flashed with imaginative delight. 'And before very long. Never to a home in England!'

'By-the-bye, a request. I have never had your portrait. Sit before you leave London.'

'No. I'll send you one from Paris—it will be better done.'

'But I am serious. You promise?'

'You shall have the thing in less than a fortnight.'

The promise was kept. Earwaker received an admirable photograph, which he inserted in his album with a curious sense of satisfaction. A face by which every intelligent eye must be arrested; which no two observers would interpret in the same way.

'His mate must be somewhere,' thought the man of letters, 'but he will never find her.'

II

In his acceptance of Sidwell's reply, Peak did not care to ask himself whether the delay of its arrival had any meaning one way or another. Decency would hardly have permitted her to answer such a letter by return of post; of course she waited a day or so.

But the interval meant more than this.

Sylvia Moorhouse was staying with her friend. The death of Mrs. Moorhouse, and the marriage of the mathematical brother, had left Sylvia homeless, though not in any distressing sense; her inclination was to wander for a year or two, and she remained in England only until the needful arrangements could be concluded.

'You had better come with me,' she said to Sidwell, as they walked together on the lawn after luncheon.

The other shook her head.

'Indeed, you had better.—What are you doing here? What are you going to make of your life?'

'I don't know.'

'Precisely. Yet one ought to live on some kind of plan. I think it is time you got away from Exeter; it seems to me you are finding its atmosphere *morbific*.'

Sidwell laughed at the allusion.

'You know,' she said, 'that the reverend gentleman is shortly to be married?'

'Oh, yes, I have heard all about it. But is he forsaking the Church?'

'Retiring only for a time, they say.'

'Forgive the question, Sidwell—did he honour you with a proposal?'

'Indeed, no!'

'Some one told me it was imminent, not long ago.'

'Quite a mistake,' Sidwell answered, with her grave smile.

'Mr. Chilvers had a singular manner with women in general. It was meant, perhaps, for subtle flattery; he may have thought it the most suitable return for the female worship he was accustomed to receive.'

Mr. Warricombe was coming towards them. He brought a new subject of conversation, and as they talked the trio drew near to the gate which led into the road. The afternoon postman was just entering; Mr. Warricombe took from him two letters.

'One for you, Sylvia, and—one for you, Sidwell.'

A slight change in his voice caused Sidwell to look at her father as he handed her the letter. In the same moment she recognised the writing of the address. It was Godwin Peak's, and undoubtedly her father knew it.

With a momentary hesitation Mr. Warricombe continued his talk from the point at which he had broken off, but he avoided his daughter's look, and Sidwell was too well aware of an uneasiness which had fallen upon him. In a few minutes he brought the chat to an end, and walked away towards the house.

Sidwell held her letter tightly. Conversation was no longer possible for her; she had a painful throbbing of the heart, and felt that her face must be playing traitor. Fortunately, Sylvia found it necessary to write a reply to the missive she had received, and her companion was soon at liberty to seek solitude.

For more than a hour she remained alone. However unemotional the contents of the letter, its arrival would have perturbed her seriously, as in the two previous instances; what she found on opening the envelope threw her into so extreme an agitation that it was long before she could subdue the anguish of disorder in all her senses. She had tried to believe that Godwin Peak was henceforth powerless to affect her in this way, write what he would. The romance of her life was over; time had brought the solution of difficulties to which she looked forward; she recognised the inevitable, as doubtless did Godwin also. But all this was self-deception. The passionate letter delighted as much as it tortured her; in secret her heart had desired this, though reason suppressed and denied the hope. No longer need she remember with pangs of shame the last letter she had written, and the cold response; once again things were as they should be—the lover pleading before her—she with the control of his fate. The injury to her pride was healed, and in the thought that perforce she must answer with a final 'No,' she found at first more of solace than of distress.

Subsidence of physical suffering allowed her to forget this emotion, in its nature unavowable. She could think of the news Godwin sent, could torment herself with interpretations of Marcella Moxey's behaviour, and view in detail the circumstances which enabled Godwin to urge a formal suit. Among her various thoughts there recurred frequently a regret that this letter had not reached her, like the other two, unobserved. Her father had now learnt that she was in correspondence with the disgraced man; to keep silence would be to cause him grave trouble; yet how much better if fortune had only once more favoured her, so that the story might have remained her secret, from beginning to end.

For was not this the end?——

At the usual time she went to the drawing-room, and somehow succeeded in conversing as though nothing had disturbed her. Mr. Warricombe was not seen till dinner. When he came forth, Sidwell noticed his air of preoccupation, and that he avoided addressing her. The evening asked too much of her self-command; she again withdrew, and only came back when the household was ready for retiring. In bidding her father good-night, she forced herself to meet his gaze; he looked at her with troubled inquiry, and she felt her cheek redden.

'Do you want to get rid of me?' asked Sylvia, with wonted frankness, when her friend drew near.

'No. Let us go to the glass-house.'

Up there on the roof Sidwell often found a retreat when her thoughts were troublesome. Fitfully, she had resumed her water-colour drawing, but as a rule her withdrawal to the glass-house was for reading or reverie. Carrying a small lamp, she led the way before Sylvia, and they sat down in the chairs which on one occasion had been occupied by Buckland Warricombe and Peak.

The wind, rarely silent in this part of Devon, blew boisterously from the south-west. A far-off whistle, that of a train speeding up the valley on its way from Plymouth, heightened the sense of retirement and quietude always to be enjoyed at night here under the stars.

'Have you been thinking over my suggestion?' asked Sylvia, when there had been silence awhile.

'No,' was the murmured reply.

'Something has happened, I think.'

'Yes. I should like to tell you, Sylvia, but'——

'But'——

'I *must* tell you! I can't keep it in my own mind, and you are the only one'——

Sylvia was surprised at the agitation which suddenly revealed itself in her companion's look and voice. She became serious, her eyes brightening with intellectual curiosity. Feminine expressions of sympathy were not to be expected from Miss Moorhouse; far more reassuring to Sidwell was the kind attentiveness with which her friend bent forward.

'That letter father handed me to-day was from Mr. Peak.'

'You hear from him?'

'This is the third time—since he went away. At our last meeting'—her voice dropped—'I pledged my faith to him.—Not absolutely. The future was too uncertain'——

The gleam in Sylvia's eyes grew more vivid. She was profoundly interested, and did not speak when Sidwell's voice failed.

'You never suspected this?' asked the latter, in a few moments.

'Not exactly that. What I did suspect was that Mr. Peak's departure resulted from—your rejection of him.'

'There is more to be told,' pursued Sidwell, in tremulous accents. 'You must know it all—because I need your help. No one here has learnt what took place between us. Mr. Peak did not go away on that account. But—you remember being puzzled to explain his orthodoxy in religion?'

She paused. Sylvia gave a nod, signifying much.

'He never believed as he professed,' went on Sidwell, hurriedly. 'You were justified in doubting him. He concealed the truth—pretended to champion the old faiths'——

For an instant she broke off, then hastened through a description of the circumstances which had brought about Peak's discovery. Sylvia could not restrain a smile, but it was softened by the sincere kindliness of her feeling.

'And it was after this,' she inquired impartially, 'that the decisive conversation between you took place?'

'No; just before Buckland's announcement. We met again, after that.—Does it seem incredible to you that I should have let the second meeting end as it did?'

'I think I understand. Yes, I know you well enough to follow it. I can even guess at the defence he was able to urge.'

'You can?' asked Sidwell eagerly. 'You see a possibility of his defending himself?'

'I should conjecture that it amounted to the old proverb, "All's fair in love and war." And, putting aside a few moral prejudices, one can easily enough absolve him.—The fact is, I had long ago surmised that his motives in taking to such a career had more reference to this world than the next. You know, I had several long talks with him; I told you how he interested me. Now I can piece together my conclusions.'

'Still,' urged Sidwell, 'you must inevitably regard him as ignoble—as guilty of base deceit. I must hide nothing from you, having told so much. Have you heard from anyone about his early life?'

'Your mother told me some old stories.'

Sidwell made an impatient gesture. In words of force and ardour, such as never before had been at her command, she related all she knew of Godwin's history prior to his settling at Exeter, and depicted the mood, the impulses, which, by his own confession, had led to that strange enterprise. Only by long exercise of an impassioned imagination could she thus thoroughly have identified herself with a life so remote from her own. Peak's pleading for himself was scarcely more impressive. In listening, Sylvia understood how completely Sidwell had cast off the beliefs for which her ordinary conversation seemed still to betray a tenderness.

'I know,' the speaker concluded, 'that he cannot in that first hour have come to regard me with a feeling strong enough to determine what he then undertook. It was not I as an individual, but all of us here, and the world we represented. Afterwards, he persuaded himself that he had felt love for me from the beginning. And I, I tried to believe it—because I wished it true; for his sake, and for my own. However it was, I could not harden my heart against him. A thousand considerations forbade me to allow him further hope; but I refused to listen—no, I *could* not listen. I said I would remain true to him. He went away to take up his old pursuits, and if possible to make a position for himself. It was to be our secret. And in spite of everything, I hoped for the future.'

Silence followed, and Sidwell seemed to lose herself in distressful thought.

'And now,' asked her friend, 'what has come to pass?'

'Do you know that Miss Moxey is dead?'

'I haven't heard of it.'

'She is dead, and has left Mr. Peak a fortune.—His letter of today tells me this. And at the same time he claims my promise.'

Their eyes met. Sylvia still had the air of meditating a most interesting problem. Impossible to decide from her countenance how she regarded Sidwell's position.

'But why in the world,' she asked, 'should Marcella Moxey have left her money to Mr. Peak?'

'They were friends,' was the quick reply. 'She knew all that had befallen him, and wished to smooth his path.'

Sylvia put several more questions, and to all of them Sidwell replied with a peculiar decision, as though bent on making it clear that there was nothing remarkable in this fact of the bequest. The motive which impelled her was obscure even to her own mind, for ever since receiving the letter she had suffered harassing doubts where now she affected to have none.

'She knew, then,' was Sylvia's last inquiry, 'of the relations between you and Mr. Peak?'

'I am not sure—but I think so. Yes, I think she must have known.'

'From Mr. Peak himself, then?'

Sidwell was agitated.

'Yes—I think so. But what does that matter?'

The other allowed her face to betray perplexity.

'So much for the past,' she said at length. 'And now?'—

'I have not the courage to do what I wish.'

There was a long silence.

'About your wish,' asked Sylvia at length, 'you are not at all doubtful?'

'Not for one moment.—Whether I err in my judgment of him could be proved only by time; but I know that if I were free, if I stood alone'——

She broke off and sighed.

'It would mean, I suppose,' said the other, 'a rupture with your family?'

'Father would not abandon me, but I should darken the close of his life. Buckland would utterly cast me off; mother would wish to do so.—You see, I cannot think and act simply as a woman, as a human being. I am bound to a certain sphere of life. The fact that I have outgrown it, counts for nothing. I cannot free myself without injury to people whom I love. To act as I wish would be to outrage every rule and prejudice of the society to which I belong. You yourself—you know how you would regard me.'

Sylvia replied deliberately.

'I am seeing you in a new light, Sidwell. It takes a little time to reconstruct my conception of you.'

'You think worse of me than you did.'

'Neither better nor worse, but differently. There has been too much reserve between us. After so long a friendship, I ought to have known you more thoroughly. To tell the truth, I have thought now and then of you and Mr. Peak; that was inevitable. But I went astray; it seemed to me the most unlikely thing that you should regard him with more than a doubtful interest. I knew, of course, that he had made you his ideal, and I felt sorry for him.'

'I seemed to you unworthy?'——

'Too placid, too calmly prudent.—In plain words, Sidwell, I do think better of you.'

Sidwell smiled.

'Only to know me henceforth as the woman who did not dare to act upon her best impulses.'

'As for "best"—I can't say. I don't glorify passion, as you know; and on the other hand I have little sympathy with the people who are always crying out for self-sacrifice. I don't know whether it would be "best" to throw over your family, or to direct yourself solely with regard to their comfort.'

Sidwell broke in.

'Yes, that is the true phrase—"their comfort." No higher word should be used. That is the ideal of the life to which I have been brought up. Comfort, respectability.—And has *he* no right? If I sacrifice myself to father and mother, do I not sacrifice *him* as well? He has forfeited all claim to consideration—that is what people say. With my whole soul, I deny it! If he sinned against anyone, it was against me, and the sin ended as soon as I understood him. That episode in his life is blotted out; by what law must it condemn to imperfection the whole of his life and of my own? Yet because people will not, cannot, look at a thing in a spirit of justice, I must wrong myself and him.'

'Let us think of it more quietly,' said Sylvia, in her clear, dispassionate tones. 'You speak as though a decision must be taken at once. Where is the necessity for that? Mr. Peak is now independent. Suppose a year or two be allowed to pass, may not things look differently?'

'A year or two!' exclaimed Sidwell, with impatience. 'Nothing will be changed. What I have to contend against is unchangeable. If I guide myself by such a hope as that, the only reasonable thing would be for me to write to Mr. Peak, and ask him to wait until my father and mother are dead.'

'Very well. On that point we are at rest, then. The step must be taken at once, or never.'

The wind roared, and for some minutes no other sound was audible. By this, all the inmates of the house save the two friends were in bed, and most likely sleeping.

'You must think it strange,' said Sidwell, 'that I have chosen to tell you all this, just when the confession is most humiliating to me. I want to feel the humiliation, as one only can when another is witness of it. I wish to leave myself no excuse for the future.'

'I'm not sure that I quite understand you. You have made up your mind to break with him?'

'Because I am a coward.'

'If my feeling in any matter were as strong as that, I should allow it to guide me.'

'Because your will is stronger. You, Sylvia, would never (in my position) have granted him that second interview. You would have known that all was at an end, and have acted upon the knowledge. I knew it, but yielded to temptation—at *his* expense. I could not let him leave me, though that would have been kindest. I held him by a promise, basely conscious that retreat was always open to me. And now I shall have earned his contempt'——

Her voice failed. Sylvia, affected by the outbreak of emotion in one whom she had always known so strong in self-command, spoke with a deeper earnestness.

'Dear, do you wish me to help you against what you call your cowardice? I cannot take it upon me to encourage you until your own will has spoken. The decision must come from yourself. Choose what course you may, I am still your friend. I have no idle prejudices and no social bonds. You know how I wish you to come away with me; now I see only more clearly how needful it is for you to breathe new air. Yes, you have outgrown these conditions, just as your brothers have, just as Fanny will—indeed has. Take tonight to think of it. If you can decide to travel with me for a year, be frank with Mr. Peak, and ask him to wait so long—till you have made up your mind. He cannot reasonably find fault with you, for he knows all you have to consider. Won't this be best?'

Sidwell was long silent.

'I will go with you,' she said at last, in a low voice. 'I will ask him to grant me perfect liberty for a year.'

When she came down next morning it was Sidwell's intention to seek a private interview with her father, and make known her resolve to go abroad with Sylvia; but Mr. Warricombe anticipated her.

'Will you come to the library after breakfast, Sidwell?' he said, on meeting her in the hall.

She interpreted his tone, and her heart misgave her. An hour later she obeyed the summons. Martin greeted her with a smile, but hardly tried to appear at ease.

'I am obliged to speak to you,' were his first words. 'The letter you had yesterday was from Mr. Peak?'

'Yes, father.'

'Is he'—Mr. Warricombe hesitated—'in these parts again?'

'No; in Lancashire.'

'Sidwell, I claim no right whatever to control your correspondence; but it was a shock to me to find that you are in communication with him.'

'He wrote,' Sidwell replied with difficulty, 'to let me know of a change that has come upon his prospects. By the death of a friend, he is made independent.'

'For his own sake, I am glad to hear that. But how could it concern *you*, dear?'

She struggled to command herself.

'It was at my invitation that he wrote, father.'

Martin's face expressed grave concern.

'Sidwell! Is this right?'

She was very pale, and kept her eyes unmovingly directed just aside from her father.

'What can it mean?' Mr. Warricombe pursued, with sad remonstrance. 'Will you not take me into your confidence, Sidwell?'

'I can't speak of it,' she replied, with sudden determination. 'Least of all with you, father.'

'Least of all?—I thought we were very near to each other.'

'For that very reason, I can't speak to you of this. I *must* be left free! I am going away with Sylvia, for a year, and for so long I must be absolutely independent. Father, I entreat you not to'——

A sob checked her. She turned away, and fought against the hysterical tendency; but it was too strong to be controlled. Her father approached, beseeching her to be more like herself. He held her in his arms, until tears had their free course, and a measure of calmness returned.

'I can't speak to you about it,' she repeated, her face hidden from him. 'I must write you a long letter, when I have gone. You shall know everything in that way.'

'But, my dearest, I can't let you leave us under these circumstances. This is a terrible trial to me. You cannot possibly go until we understand each other!'

'Then I will write to you here—today or tomorrow.'

With this promise Martin was obliged to be contented, Sidwell left him, and was not seen, except by Sylvia, during the whole day.

Nor did she appear at breakfast on the morning that followed. But when this meal was over, Sylvia received a message, summoning her to the retreat on the top of the house. Here Sidwell sat in the light and warmth, a glass door wide open to the west, the rays of a brilliant sun softened by curtains which fluttered lightly in the breeze from the sea.

'Will you read this?' she said, holding out a sheet of notepaper on which were a few lines in her own handwriting.

It was a letter, beginning—'I cannot.'

Sylvia perused it carefully, and stood in thought.

'After all?' were the words with which she broke silence. They were neither reproachful nor regretful, but expressed grave interest.

'In the night,' said Sidwell, 'I wrote to father, but I shall not give him the letter. Before it was finished, I knew that I must write *this*. There's no more to be said, dear. You will go abroad without me—at all events for the present.'

'If that is your resolve,' answered the other, quietly, 'I shall keep my word, and only do what I can to aid it.' She sat down shielding her eyes from the sunlight with a Japanese fan. 'After all, Sidwell, there's much to be said for a purpose formed on such a morning as this; one can't help distrusting the midnight.'

Sidwell was lying back in a low chair, her eyes turned to the woody hills on the far side of the Exe.

'There's one thing I should like to say,' her friend pursued. 'It struck me as curious that you were not at all affected, by what to me would have been the one insuperable difficulty.'

'I know what you mean—the legacy.'

'Yes. It still seems to you of no significance?'

'Of very little,' Sidwell answered wearily, letting her eyelids droop.

'Then we won't talk about it. From the higher point of view, I believe you are right; but—still let it rest.'

In the afternoon, Sidwell penned the following lines which she enclosed in an envelope and placed on the study table, when her father was absent.

'The long letter which I promised you, dear father, is needless. I have today sent Mr. Peak a reply which closes our correspondence. I am sure he will not write again; if he were to do so, I should not answer.

'I have given up my intention of going away with Sylvia. Later, perhaps, I shall wish to join her somewhere on the Continent, but by that time you will be in no concern about me.'

To this Mr. Warricombe replied only with the joyous smile which greeted his daughter at their next meeting. Mrs. Warricombe remained in ignorance of the ominous shadow which had passed over her house. At present, she was greatly interested in the coming marriage of the Rev. Bruno Chilvers, whom she tried *not* to forgive for having disappointed her secret hope.

Martin had finally driven into the background those uneasy questionings, which at one time it seemed likely that Godwin Peak would rather accentuate than silence. With Sidwell, he could never again touch on such topics. If he were still conscious of a postponed debate, the adjournment was *sine die*. Martin rested in the faith that, without effort of his own, the mysteries of life and time would ere long be revealed to him.

III

EARWAKER SPENT CHRISTMAS with his relatives at Kingsmill. His father and mother both lived; the latter very infirm, unable to leave the house; the former a man of seventy, twisted with rheumatism, his face rugged as a countenance picked out by fancy on the trunk of a big old oak, his hands scarred and deformed with labour. Their old age was restful. The son who had made himself a 'gentleman,' and who in London sat at the tables of the high-born, the wealthy, the famous, saw to it that they lacked no comfort.

A bright, dry morning invited the old man and the young to go forth together. They walked from the suburb countrywards, and their conversation was of the time when a struggle was being made to bear the expense of those three years at Whitelaw—no bad investment, as it proved. The father spoke with a strong Midland accent, using words of dialect by no means disagreeable to the son's ear—for dialect is a very different thing from the bestial jargon which on the lips of the London vulgar passes for English. They were laughing over some half grim reminiscence, when Earwaker became aware of two people who were approaching along the pavement, they also in merry talk. One of them he knew; it was Christian Moxey.

Too much interested in his companion to gaze about him, Christian came quite near before his eyes fell on Earwaker. Then he started with a pleasant surprise, changed instantly to something like embarrassment when he observed the aged man. Earwaker was willing to smile and go by, had the other consented; but a better impulse prevailed in both. They stopped and struck hands together.

'My father,' said the man of letters, quite at his ease.

Christian was equal to the occasion; he shook hands heartily with the battered toiler, then turned to the lady at his side.

'Janet, you guess who this is.—My cousin, Earwaker, Miss Janet Moxey.'

Doubtless Janet was aware that her praises had suffered no diminution when sung by Christian to his friends. Her eyes just fell, but in a moment were ready with their frank, intelligent smile. Earwaker experienced a pang—ever so slight—suggesting a revision of his philosophy.

They talked genially, and parted with good wishes for the New Year.

Two days later, on reaching home, Earwaker found in his letter-box a scrap of paper on which were scribbled a few barely legible lines. 'Here I am!' he at length deciphered. 'Got into Tilbury at eleven this morning. Where the devil are you? Write to Charing Cross Hotel.' No signature, but none was needed. Malkin's return from New Zealand had been signalled in advance.

That evening the erratic gentleman burst in like a whirlwind. He was the picture of health, though as far as ever from enduing the comfortable flesh which accompanies robustness in men of calmer temperament. After violent greetings, he sat down with abrupt gravity, and began to talk as if in continuance of a dialogue just interrupted.

'Now, don't let us have any misunderstanding. You will please remember that my journey to England is quite independent of what took place two years and a half ago. It has *nothing whatever* to do with those circumstances.'

Earwaker smiled.

'I tell you,' pursued the other, hotly, 'that I am here to see *you*—and one or two other old friends; and to look after some business matters. You will oblige me by giving credit to my assertion!'

'Don't get angry. I am convinced of the truth of what you say.'

'Very well! It's as likely as not that, on returning to Auckland, I shall marry Miss Maccabe—of whom I have written to you. I needn't repeat the substance of my letters. I am not in love with her, you understand, and I needn't say that my intercourse with that family has been guided by extreme discretion. But she is a very sensible young lady. My only regret is that I didn't know her half-a-dozen years ago, so that I could have directed her education. She might have been even more interesting than she is. But—you are at leisure, I hope, Earwaker?'

'For an hour or two.'

'Oh, confound it! When a friend comes back from the ends of the earth!—Yes, yes; I understand. You are a busy man; forgive my hastiness. Well now, I was going to say that I shall probably call upon Mrs. Jacox.' He paused, and gave the listener a stern look, forbidding misconstruction. 'Yes, I shall probably go down to Wrotham. I wish to put my relations with that family on a proper footing. Our correspondence has been very satisfactory, especially of late. The poor woman laments more sincerely her—well, let us say, her folly of two years and a half ago. She has outlived it; she regards me as a friend. Bella and Lily seem to be getting on very well indeed. That governess of theirs—we won't have any more mystery; it was I who undertook the trifling expense. A really excellent teacher, I have every reason to believe. I am told that Bella promises to be a remarkable pianist, and Lily is uncommonly strong in languages. But my interest in them is merely that of a friend; let it be understood.'

'Precisely. You didn't say whether the girls have been writing to you?'

'No, no, no! Not a line. I have exchanged letters only with their mother. Anything else would have been indiscreet. I shall be glad to see them, but my old schemes are things of the past. There is not the faintest probability that Bella has retained any recollection of me at all.'

'I daresay not,' assented Earwaker.

'You think so? Very well; I have acted wisely. Bella is still a child, you know—compared with a man of my age. She is seventeen and a few months; quite a child! Miss Maccabe is just one-and-twenty; the proper age. When we are married, I think I shall bring her to Europe for a year or two. Her education needs that; she will be delighted to see the old countries.'

'Have you her portrait?'

'Oh no! Things haven't got so far as that. What a hasty fellow you are, Earwaker! I told you distinctly'——

He talked till after midnight, and at leave-taking apologised profusely for wasting his friend's valuable time.

Earwaker awaited with some apprehension the result of Malkin's visit to Wrotham. But the report of what took place on that occasion was surprisingly commonplace. Weeks passed, and Malkin seldom showed himself at Staple Inn; when he did so, his talk was exclusively of Miss Maccabe; all he could be got to say of the young ladies at Wrotham was, 'Nice girls; very nice girls. I hope they'll marry well.' Two months had gone by, and already the journalist had heard by letter of his friend's intention to return to New Zealand, when, on coming home late one night, he found Malkin sitting on the steps.

'Earwaker, I have something very serious to tell you. Give me just a quarter of an hour.'

What calamity did this tone portend? The eccentric man seated himself with slow movement. Seen by a good light, his face was not gloomy, but very grave.

'Listen to me, old friend,' he began, sliding forward to the edge of his chair. 'You remember I told you that my relations with the Maccabe family had been marked throughout with extreme discretion.'

'You impressed that upon me.'

'Good! I have never made love to Miss Maccabe, and I doubt whether she has ever thought of me as a possible husband.'

'Well?'

'Don't be impatient. I want you to grasp the fact. It is important, because—I am going to marry Bella Jacox.'

'You don't say so?'

'Why not?' cried Malkin, suddenly passing to a state of excitement. 'What objection can you make? I tell you that I am absolutely free to choose'——

The journalist calmed him, and thereupon had to hear a glowing account of Bella's perfections. All the feeling that Malkin had suppressed during these two months rushed forth in a flood of turbid eloquence.

'And now,' he concluded, 'you will come down with me to Wrotham. I don't mean tonight; let us say the day after tomorrow, Sunday. You remember our last joint visit! Ha, ha!'

'Mrs. Jacox is reconciled?'

'My dear fellow, she rejoices! A wonderful nobility in that poor little woman! She wept upon my shoulder! But you must see Bella! I shan't take her to New Zealand, at all events not just yet. We shall travel about Europe, completing her education. Don't you approve of that?'

On Sunday, the two travelled down into Kent. This time they were received by Lily, now a pretty, pale, half-developed girl of fifteen. In a few minutes her sister entered. Bella was charming; nervousness made her words few, and it could be seen that she was naturally thoughtful, earnest, prone to reverie; her beauty had still to ripen, and gave much promise for the years between twenty and thirty. Last of all appeared Mrs. Jacox, who blushed as she shook hands with Earwaker, and for a time was ill at ease; but her vocatives were not long restrained, and when all sat down to the tea-table she chattered away with astonishing vivacity. After tea the company was joined by a lady of middle age, who, for about two years, had acted as governess to the girls. Earwaker formed his conclusions as to the 'trifling expense' which her services represented; but it was probably a real interest in her pupils which had induced a person of so much refinement to bear so long with the proximity of Mrs. Jacox.

'A natural question occurs to me,' remarked Earwaker, as they were returning. 'Who and what was *Mr.* Jacox?'

'Ah! Bella was talking to me about him the other day. He must have been distinctly an interesting man. Bella had a very clear recollection of him, and she showed me two or three photographs. Engaged in some kind of commerce. I didn't seek particulars. But a remarkable man, one can't doubt.'

He resumed presently.

'Now don't suppose that this marriage entirely satisfies me. Bella has been fairly well taught, but not, you see, under my supervision. I ought to have been able to watch and direct her month by month. As it is, I shall have to begin by assailing her views on all manner of things. Religion, for example. Well, I have no religion, that's plain. I might call myself this or that for the sake of seeming respectable, but it all comes to the same thing. I don't mind Bella going to church if she wishes, but I must teach her that there's no merit whatever in doing so. It isn't an ideal marriage, but perhaps as good as this imperfect world allows. If I have children, I can then put my educational theories to the test.'

By way of novel experience, Earwaker, not long after this, converted his study into a drawing-room, and invited the Jacox family to taste his tea and cake. With Malkin's assistance, the risky enterprise was made a great success. When Mrs. Jacox would allow her to be heard, Bella talked intelligently, and showed eager interest in the details of literary manufacture.

'O Mr. Earwaker!' cried her mother, when it was time to go. 'What a delightful afternoon you have given us! We must think of you from now as one of our very best friends. Mustn't we, Lily?'

But troubles were yet in store. Malkin was strongly opposed to a religious marriage; he wished the wedding to be at a registrar's office, and had obtained Bella's consent to this, but Mrs. Jacox would not hear of such a thing. She wept and bewailed herself. 'How *can* you think of being married like a costermonger? O Mr. Malkin, you will break my heart, indeed you will!' And she wrote an ejaculatory letter to Earwaker, imploring his intercession. The journalist took his friend in hand.

'My good fellow, don't make a fool of yourself. Women are born for one thing only, the Church of England marriage service. How can you seek to defeat the end of their existence? Give in to the inevitable. Grin and bear it.'

'I can't! I won't! It shall be a runaway match! I had rather suffer the rack than go through an ordinary wedding!'

Dire was the conflict. Down at Wrotham there were floods of tears. In the end, Bella effected a compromise; the marriage was to be at a church, but in the greatest possible privacy. No carriages, no gala dresses, no invitations, no wedding feast; the bare indispensable formalities. And so it came to pass. Earwaker and the girls' governess were the only strangers present, when, on a morning of June, Malkin and Bella were declared by the Church to be henceforth one and indivisible. The bride wore a graceful travelling costume; the bridegroom was in corresponding attire.

'Heaven be thanked, that's over!' exclaimed Malkin, as he issued from the portal. 'Bella, we have twenty-three minutes to get to the railway station. Don't cry!' he whispered to her. 'I can't stand that!'

'No, no; don't be afraid,' she whispered back. 'We have said good-bye already.'

'Capital! That was very thoughtful of you.—Good-bye, all! Shall write from Paris, Earwaker. Nineteen minutes; we shall just manage it!'

He sprang into the cab, and away it clattered.

A letter from Paris, a letter from Strasburg, from Berlin, Munich—letters about once a fortnight. From Bella also came an occasional note, a pretty contrast to the incoherent enthusiasm of her husband's compositions. Midway in September she announced their departure from a retreat in Switzerland.

'We are in the utmost excitement, for it is now decided that in three days we start for Italy! The heat has been terrific, and we have waited on what seems to me the threshold of Paradise until we could hope to enjoy the delights beyond. We go first to Milan. My husband, of course, knows Italy, but he shares my impatience. I am to entreat you to write to Milan, with as much news as possible. Especially have you heard anything more of Mr. Peak?'

November the pair spent in Rome, and thence was dispatched the following in Malkin's hand:

'This time I am *not* mistaken! I have seen Peak. He didn't see me; perhaps wouldn't have known me. It was in Piale's reading-room. I had sat down to *The Times*, when a voice behind me sounded in such a curiously reminding way that I couldn't help looking round. It was Peak; not a doubt of it. I might have been uncertain about his face, but the voice brought back that conversation at your rooms too unmistakably—long ago as it was. He was talking to an American, whom evidently he had met somewhere else, and had now recognised. "I've had a fever," he said, "and can't quite shake off the results. Been in Ischia for the last month. I'm going north to Vienna." Then the two walked away together. He looked ill, sallow, worn out. Let me know if you hear.'

On that same day, Earwaker received another letter, with the Roman post-mark. It was from Peak.

'I have had nothing particular to tell you. A month ago I thought I should never write to you again; I got malarial fever, and lay desperately ill at the *Ospedale Internazionale* at Naples. It came of some monstrous follies there's no need to speak of. A new and valuable experience. I know what it is to look steadily into the eyes of Death.

'Even now, I am far from well. This keeps me in low spirits. The other day I was half decided to start for London. I am miserably alone, want to see a friend. What a glorious place Staple Inn seemed to me as I lay in the hospital! Proof how low I had sunk: I thought longingly of Exeter, of a certain house there—never mind!

'I write hastily. An invitation from some musical people has decided me to strike for Vienna. Up there, I shall get my health back. The people are of no account—boarding-house acquaintances—but they may lead to better. I never in my life suffered so from loneliness.'

This was the eighteenth of November. On the twenty-eighth the postman delivered a letter of an appearance which puzzled Earwaker. The stamp was Austrian, the mark 'Wien.' From Peak, therefore. But the writing was unknown, plainly that of a foreigner.

The envelope contained two sheets of paper. The one was covered with a long communication in German; on the other stood a few words of English, written, or rather scrawled, in a hand there was no recognising:

'Ill again, and alone. If I die, act for me. Write to Mrs. Peak, Twybridge.'

Beneath was added, 'J. E. Earwaker, Staple Inn, London.'

He turned hurriedly to the foreign writing. Earwaker read a German book as easily as an English, but German manuscript was a terror to him. And the present correspondent wrote so execrably that beyond *Geehrter Herr*, scarcely a word yielded sense to his anxious eyes. Ha! One he had made out—*gestorben*.

Crumpling the papers into his pocket, he hastened out, and knocked at the door of an acquaintance in another part of the Inn. This was a man who had probably more skill in German cursive. Between them, they extracted the essence of the letter.

He who wrote was the landlord of an hotel in Vienna. He reported that an English gentleman, named Peak, just arrived from Italy, had taken a bedroom at that house. In the night, the stranger became very ill, sent for a doctor, and wrote the lines enclosed, the purport whereof he at the same time explained to his attendants. On the second day Mr. Peak died. Among his effects were found circular notes, and a sum of loose money. The body was about to be interred. Probably Mr. Earwaker would receive official communications, as the British consul had been informed of the matter. To whom should *bills* be sent?

The man of letters walked slowly back to his own abode.

'Dead, too, in exile!' was his thought. 'Poor old fellow!'

SELECT BIBLIOGRAPHY

Of Gissing's important novels, only *New Grub Street* and *The Town Traveller* are currently available at standard prices. All his works are available in facsimile reproductions of the first editions, from AMS, Inc., but the reader should be warned that the prices range from $30. The fullest bibliography is to be found in *George Gissing*, by Mabel Collins Donnelly, Harvard, 1954. Gissing's most important out-of-print novels, which are unfortunately hard to find on the second-hand market, are:

Demos, 3 vols., London, 1886.

Thyrza, 3 vols., London, 1887.

The Odd Woman, 3 vols., London, 1893.

In the Year of Jubilee, 3 vols., London, 1894.

Our Friend the Charlatan, London, 1901.

His two famous non-fiction works, *By the Ionian Sea* and *The Private Papers of Henry Ryecroft* are currently available.

The best book about Gissing remains the novel:

The Private Life of Henry Maitland, by Morley Roberts. It is essential to read the new edition, with Morchard Bishop's introduction, London, 1958.

The best critical book is:

George Gissing, by Jacob Korg, Seattle, 1963.

An excellent introduction is:

Gissing, by A. C. Ward, London, 1959 (Writers and Their Work, No. 111).